THE DARK
FOREST

Prologue

The brown ant had already forgotten its home. To the twilight Earth and the stars that were just coming out, the span of time may have been negligible, but, for the ant, it was eons. In days now forgotten, its world had been overturned. Soil had taken flight, leaving a broad and deep chasm, and then soil had come crashing down to fill it back in. At one end of the disturbed earth stood a lone black formation. Such things happened frequently throughout this vast domain, the soil flying away and returning, chasms opening up and being filled, and rock formations appearing like visible markers of each catastrophic change. Under the setting sun, the ant and hundreds of its brethren had carried off the surviving queen to establish a new empire. Its return visit was only a chance passing while searching for food.

The ant arrived at the foot of the formation, sensing its indomitable presence with its feelers. Noting that the surface was hard and slippery, yet still climbable, up it went, with no purpose in mind but the random turbulence of its simple neural network. Turbulence was everywhere, within every blade of grass, every drop of dew on a leaf, every cloud in the sky, and every star beyond. The turbulence was purposeless, but in huge quantities of purposeless turbulence, purpose took shape.

The ant sensed vibrations in the ground and knew from how they intensified that another giant presence was approaching from somewhere on the ground. Paying it no mind, the ant continued its climb up the formation. At the right angle where the foot of

the formation met the ground, there was a spider web. This, the ant knew. It carefully detoured around the sticky hanging strands, passing by the spider lying in wait, its legs extended to feel for vibrations in the threads. Each knew of the other's presence but— as it had been for eons—there was no communication.

The vibrations crescendoed and then stopped. The giant being had reached the formation. It was far taller than the ant and blotted out most of the sky. The ant was not unfamiliar with beings of this sort. It knew that they were alive, that they frequently appeared in this region, and that their appearances were closely related to the swiftly disappearing chasms and multiplying formations.

The ant continued its climb, knowing that the beings were not a threat, with a few exceptions. Down below, the spider encountered one such exception when the being, which had evidently noticed its web reaching between the formation and the ground, whisked away the spider and web with the stems of a bundle of flowers it held in one limb, causing them to land broken in a pile of weeds. Then the being gently placed the flowers in front of the formation.

Then another vibration, weak but intensifying, told the ant that a second living being of the same sort was moving toward the formation. At the same time, the ant encountered a long trough, a depression in the surface of the formation with a rougher texture and different color: off-white. It followed the trough, for its rough-ness made for a far easier climb. At each end was a short, thinner trough: a horizontal base from which the main trough rose, and an upper trough that extended at an angle. By the time the ant climbed back out onto the slick black surface, it had gained an overall impression of the shape of the troughs: "1."

Then the height of the being in front of the formation was cut in half, so it was roughly even with the formation. Evidently it had dropped to its knees, revealing a patch of dim blue sky where the stars had begun to come out behind it. The being's eyes gazed at the top of the formation, causing the ant to hesitate momentarily while deciding whether it ought to intrude into his line of sight. Instead, it changed direction and started crawling parallel with the

ground, quickly reaching another trough and lingering in its rough depression as it savored the pleasant sensation of the crawl. The color was reminiscent of the eggs that surrounded its queen. With no hesitation, the ant followed the trough downward, and after a while, the layout become more complicated, a curve extended beneath a complete circle. It reminded the ant of the process of searching out scent information and eventually stumbling across the way home. A pattern was established in its neural network: "9."

Then the being kneeling before the formation made a sound, a series of sounds that far exceeded the ant's capacity to comprehend: "It's a wonder to be alive. If you don't understand that, how can you search for anything deeper?"

The being made a sound like a gust of wind blowing across the grass—a sigh—and then stood up.

The ant continued to crawl parallel to the ground and entered a third trough, one that was nearly vertical until it turned, like this: "7." The ant didn't like this shape. A sharp, sudden turn usually meant danger or battle.

The first being's voice had obscured the vibrations, so it was only now that the ant realized that the second being had reached the formation. Shorter and frailer, the second being had white hair that stood out against the dark blue background of the sky, bobbing silver in the wind, connected somehow to the increasing number of stars.

The first being stood up to welcome her. "Dr. Ye, is it?"

"You're . . . Xiao Luo?"[1]

"Luo Ji. I went to high school with Yang Dong. Why are you . . . here?"

"It's a nice place, and easy to get to by bus. Lately, I've been coming here to take walks fairly often."

"My condolences, Dr. Ye."

"That's all in the past. . . ."

1 *Translator's Note: Xiǎo* is a diminutive meaning "little" or "young" and is used before a surname when addressing children or to show affection.

Down on the formation, the ant wanted to turn toward the sky, but then discovered another trough ahead of it, identical to the "9"-shaped trough it had crawled through before the "7." So it continued horizontally through the "9," which it found better than both the "7" and the "1," although it could not say exactly why. Its aesthetic sense was primitive and single-celled. The indistinct pleasure it had felt upon crawling through the "9" intensified. A primitive, single-celled state of happiness. These two spiritual monocells, aesthetics and pleasure had never evolved. They had been the same a billion years ago, and would be the same a billion years hence.

"Xiao Luo, Dong Dong often spoke of you. She said you're in . . . astronomy?"

"I used to be. I teach college sociology now. At your school, actually, although you had already retired when I got there."

"Sociology? That's a pretty big leap."

"Yeah. Yang Dong always said my mind wasn't focused."

"She wasn't kidding when she said you're smart."

"Just clever. Nothing like your daughter's level. I just felt astronomy was an undrillable chunk of iron. Sociology is a plank of wood, and there's bound to be someplace thin enough to punch through. It's easier to get by."

In the hope of reaching another "9," the ant continued its horizontal advance, but the next thing it encountered was a perfectly straight horizontal like the first trough, except longer than the "1" and turned on its side. And no smaller troughs at the ends. A "–" shape.

"You shouldn't put it like that. It's a normal person's life. Not everyone can be Dong Dong."

"I really don't have that kind of ambition. I drift."

"I've got a suggestion. Why don't you study cosmic sociology?"

"Cosmic sociology?"

"A name chosen at random. Suppose a vast number of civilizations are distributed throughout the universe, on the order of the number of detectable stars. Lots and lots of them. Those

4

civilizations make up the body of a cosmic society. Cosmic sociology is the study of the nature of this supersociety."

The ant had not crawled very much farther along the formation. It had hoped, after crawling out of the "–" depression, to find a pleasurable "9," but instead it encountered a "2," with a comfortable initial curve but a sharp turn at the end that was as fearsome as that of the "7." The premonition of an uncertain future. The ant continued onward to the next trough, a closed shape: "0." The path seemed like part of a "9," but it was a trap. Life needed smoothness, but it also needed direction. One could not always be returning to the point of origin. This, the ant understood. Although there were still two more troughs up ahead, it had lost interest. It turned vertically again.

"But . . . ours is the only civilization we know of right now."

"Which is why no one's done it before. The opportunity is left to you."

"Fascinating, Dr. Ye. Please go on."

"My thinking is that this can link your two disciplines together. The mathematical structure of cosmic sociology is far clearer than that of human sociology."

"Why do you say that?"

Ye Wenjie pointed at the sky. Twilight still illuminated the west, and they could still count the stars that had come out, making it easy to remember how the firmament had looked a few moments ago: a vast expanse and a blue void, or a face without pupils, like a marble statue. Now, though the stars were few in number, the giant eyes had pupils. The void was filled. The universe had sight. The stars were tiny, just single twinkling points of silver that hinted at some unease on the part of its creator. The cosmic sculptor had felt compelled to dot pupils onto the universe, yet had a tremendous terror of granting it sight. This balance of fear and desire resulted in the tininess of the stars against the hugeness of space, a declaration of caution above all.

"See how the stars are points? The factors of chaos and randomness in the complex makeups of every civilized society in

the universe get filtered out by the distance, so those civilizations can act as reference points that are relatively easy to manipulate mathematically."

"But there's nothing concrete to study in your cosmic sociology, Dr. Ye. Surveys and experiments aren't really possible."

"That means your ultimate result will be purely theoretical. Like Euclidean geometry, you'll set up a few simple axioms at first, then derive an overall theoretic system using those axioms as a foundation."

"It's all fascinating, but what would the axioms of cosmic sociology be?"

"First: Survival is the primary need of civilization. Second: Civilization continuously grows and expands, but the total matter in the universe remains constant."

The ant had not gone far before it realized that there were other troughs above it, many of them, in a complicated maze structure. The ant was sensitive to shapes and was confident of being able to work it out, but the limited storage capacity of its tiny neural network meant it had to forget the shapes it had previously crawled through. It did not feel any regret at forgetting the "9," for constant forgetting was part of life. There were few things that it needed to remember forever, and those were etched by its genes into the storage area known as instinct.

Having cleared its memory, the ant entered the maze. After navigating its twists and turns, it established another pattern in its simple consciousness: the Chinese character 墓—*mu,* meaning "grave," although the character and its meaning were not known to the ant. Farther up was another combination of troughs—far simpler this time, but to continue its exploration the ant had no choice but to clear its memory and forget the *mu.* Then it entered a wonderful line-trough, a shape that reminded it of the abdomen of a recently deceased cricket it had discovered not long ago. It quickly made out the new structure: 之, *zhi,* the Chinese possessive modifier. Then, as it continued upward, it encountered two more trough combinations, the first of which consisted of two droplet-shaped

depressions and a cricket stomach: the character 冬—*dong,* meaning "winter." The top one was split into two parts, which together formed the character 杨—*yang,* meaning "poplar." This was the last shape the ant remembered, and the only one it retained from its entire journey. The interesting shapes it previously encountered had all been forgotten.

"Those two axioms are solid enough from a sociological perspective . . . but you rattled them off so quickly, like you'd already worked them out," Luo Ji said, a little surprised.

"I've been thinking about this for most of my life, but I've never spoken about it with anyone before. I don't know why, really. . . . One more thing: To derive a basic picture of cosmic sociology from these two axioms, you need two other important concepts: chains of suspicion, and the technological explosion."

"Interesting terms. Can you explain them?"

Ye Wenjie glanced at her watch. "There's no time. But you're clever enough to figure them out. Use those two axioms as a starting point for your discipline, and you might end up becoming the Euclid of cosmic sociology."

"I'm no Euclid. But I'll remember what you said and give it a whirl. I might come to you for guidance, though."

"I'm afraid there won't be that opportunity. . . . In that case, you might as well just forget I said anything. Either way, I've fulfilled my duty. Well, Xiao Luo, I've got to go."

"Take care, Professor."

Ye Wenjie went off through the twilight to her final meetup.

The ant continued its climb and reached a round basin on the rock face, whose slick surface bore an extremely complicated image. It knew that its tiny neural net had no way to store such a thing, but after determining the overall shape of the image, its primitive one-cell aesthetic was as sparked as it had been by the sense of the "9." And somehow it seemed to recognize part of the image, a pair of eyes. The ant was sensitive to eyes, because their gaze meant danger. Yet it felt no anxiety now, for it knew the eyes were lifeless. It had already forgotten that when the giant being

7

named Luo Ji knelt down in silence before the formation, he had been looking at those eyes. The ant climbed out of the basin and up onto the formation's peak. It felt no sense of towering above its surroundings, because it had no fear of falling. It had been blown off of places higher than this many times without any injury. Without the fear of heights, there can be no appreciation for the beauty of high places.

At the foot of the formation, the spider that Luo Ji had swept aside with the flowers was beginning to reconstruct its web. It drew a glistening strand from the rock face and swung itself like a pendulum to the ground. Three more swings and the skeleton of the web was complete. Ten thousand times the web could be destroyed, and ten thousand times the spider would rebuild it. There was neither annoyance nor despair, nor any delight, just as it had been for a billion years.

Luo Ji stood in silence for a while and then departed. When the vibrations in the ground had dissipated, the ant crawled a different way down the formation to hurry back to the nest and report on the location of a dead beetle. The stars had grown dense in the sky. When the ant passed the spider down at the foot of the formation, they felt each other's presence, but did not communicate.

As that distant world held its breath to listen, neither ant nor spider was aware that they, out of all life on Earth, were the sole witnesses to the birth of the axioms of cosmic civilization.

Somewhat earlier, in the dead of night, Mike Evans was standing on the bow of *Judgment Day* as the Pacific Ocean slipped past like a swath of satin beneath the heavens. Evans enjoyed talking with the distant world at times like these because the text the sophon displayed on his retinas stood out wonderfully against the night sea and sky.

This is our twenty-second real-time conversation. We have come across some difficulties in our communication.

"Yes, Lord. I've learned that you can't actually understand a significant amount of the reference materials on humanity we've given you."

Yes. You've explained the parts very clearly, but we are unable to understand the whole. Something is different.

"Just one thing?"

Yes. But it sometimes seems as if your world is missing something, other times that it has something extra, and we don't know which.

"What is the area of confusion?"

We've carefully studied your documents and have discovered that the key to understanding the problem lies in a pair of synonyms.

"Synonyms?"

There are many synonyms and near-synonyms in your languages. In the first language we received from you, Chinese, there were words that expressed the same meaning, like "cold" and "chill," "heavy" and "weighty," "long" and "far."

"What pair of synonyms created the obstacle to understanding you've just mentioned?"

"Think" and "say." We've just learned, to our surprise, that they are not, in fact, synonyms.

"They are not synonyms at all."

In our understanding, they ought to be. "Think" means using thought organs to conduct mental activity. "Say" means communicating the content of thoughts to a counterpart. The latter, in your world,

9

is accomplished through the modulation of vibrations in the air produced by the vocal cords. Are these definitions correct?

"They are. But doesn't this demonstrate that 'think' and 'say' aren't synonyms?"

In our understanding, this shows that they are synonyms.

"May I think about this for a moment?"

Very well. We both need to think about it.

For two minutes, Evans gazed in thought at the waves undulating beneath the starlight.
"My Lord, what are your organs of communication?"

We do not have organs of communication. Our brains can display our thoughts to the outside world, thereby achieving communication.

"Display thoughts? How is that done?"

The thoughts in our brains emit electromagnetic waves on all frequencies, including what is visible light to us. They can be displayed at a significant distance.

"So that means that to you, thinking is speaking?"

Hence they are synonyms.

"Oh . . . That is not the case for us, but even so, that shouldn't present an obstacle to understanding those documents."

True. In the areas of thought and communication, the differences between us are not large. We both have brains, and our brains produce intelligence through huge numbers of neural connections.

The only difference is that our brain waves are stronger and can be directly received by our counterparts, eliminating the need for communication organs. That's the only difference.

"No. I suspect a major difference might be getting lost. My Lord, let me think about it again."

Very well.

Evans left the bow and strolled along the deck. Over the gunwale, the Pacific rose and fell silently in the night. He imagined it as a thinking brain.

"My Lord, let me tell you a story. To prepare for it, you need to understand the following elements: wolf, child, grandmother, and a house in the forest."

These elements are all easy to understand, except for "grandmother." I know that this is a blood relation among humans, and usually means a woman of advanced age. But her actual kinship status requires more explanation.

"Lord, that is not important. All you need to know is that she and the children have a close relationship. She is one of the only people the children trust."

Understood.

"I'll make it simple. Grandmother had to go out, so she left the children in the house, telling them they must make sure the door is shut and not to open it to anyone but her. On the road, Grandmother met a wolf, which ate her, and then put on her clothing and assumed her appearance. Then it went to the house and came up to the door, and said to the children, 'I'm your grandmother. I've come back. Open the door for me.' The children looked through the crack in the door and saw what looked like

their grandmother, and so they opened the door, and the wolf came in the house and ate them. Do you understand this story, my Lord?"

Not the slightest bit.

"Then maybe I've guessed right."

First of all, the wolf wanted all along to enter the house and eat the children, correct?

"Correct."

It engaged in communication with the children, correct?

"Correct."

This is what's incomprehensible. In order to achieve its own aims, it shouldn't have communicated with the children.

"Why?"

Isn't it obvious? If there was communication between them, the children would have known that the wolf wanted to come in and eat them, and they wouldn't have opened the door.

Evans stayed silent for a while. "I understand, my Lord. I understand."

What do you understand? Isn't what I said obvious?

"Your thoughts are completely exposed to the outside world. You can't hide."

How can thoughts hide? Your ideas are confusing.

"I mean, your thoughts and memories are transparent to the outside world, like a book placed out in public, or a film projected in a plaza, or a fish in a clear fishbowl. Totally exposed. Readable at a glance. Er, maybe some of the elements I just mentioned are . . ."

I understand them all. But isn't all that perfectly natural?

Evans was silent again. "So that's it. . . . My Lord, when you communicate face-to-face, everything you communicate is true. It's impossible for you to cheat or lie, so you can't pursue complicated strategic thinking."

We can communicate over significant distances, not just face-to-face. The words "cheating" and "lying" are another two that we have had a hard time understanding.

"What sort of a society is it when thought is completely transparent? What sort of culture does it produce? What sort of politics? No scheming, no pretending."

What are "scheming" and "pretending"?

Evans said nothing.

Human communication organs are but an evolutionary deficiency, a necessary compensation for the fact that your brains can't emit strong thought waves. This is one of your biological weaknesses. Direct display of thought is a superior, more efficient form of communication.

"A deficiency? A weakness? No, my Lord, you are wrong. This time you are totally wrong."

Is that so? Let me think about it. It's a shame you can't see my thoughts.

This time the interruption was longer. When twenty minutes had passed and no more text had appeared, Evans strolled from bow to stern, watching a school of fish leaping out of the ocean, tracing an arc on the surface that glittered silver under the starlight. Several years ago, he had spent some time on a fishing boat in the South China Sea investigating the effect of overfishing on coastal life. The fishermen called this phenomenon "the passing of dragon soldiers." To Evans, they looked like text projected on the eye of the ocean. Then text appeared before his own eyes.

You are correct. Looking back at those documents, I understand them a little better.

"My Lord, there's a long road to travel before you arrive at a true understanding of human matters. I'm almost afraid that you'll never be able to."

Indeed, they are complicated. All I know now is why I didn't understand them before. You are right.

"My Lord, you need us."

I am afraid of you.

The conversation stopped. This was the last time that Evans received a message from Trisolaris. He stood at the stern watching the snow-white body of *Judgment Day* stretch off into the hazy night, like time slipping away.

PART I

THE WALLFACERS

Year 3, Crisis Era

Distance of the Trisolaran Fleet from the Solar System:
4.21 light-years

It looks so old. . . .

This was Wu Yue's first thought as he faced *Tang,* the massive ship under construction in front of him, bathed in the flickering of electric arcs. Of course, this impression was simply the result of countless inconsequential smudges on the manganese steel plates of the ship's nearly completed body, left behind by the advanced gas-shield welding used on the hull. He tried unsuccessfully to imagine how sturdy and new *Tang* would look with a fresh coat of gray paint.

Tang's fourth offshore fleet training session had just concluded. During that two-month session, *Tang*'s commanders, Wu Yue and Zhang Beihai, who was standing just beside Wu Yue, had occupied an uncomfortable role. Formations of destroyers, submarines, and supply ships were directed by battle group commanders, but *Tang* was still under construction in the dock, so the carrier's position was either occupied by the training ship *Zheng He* or simply left empty. During the sessions, Wu Yue often stared vacantly at an empty patch of sea where the surface of the water, disturbed by crisscrossing trails left by passing ships, undulated uneasily, much like his mood. *Would the empty spot ever be filled?* he asked himself more than once.

Looking now at the unfinished *Tang,* what he saw was not just age but the passage of time itself. It seemed like an ancient, giant,

17

discarded fortress, its mottled body a stone wall, the shower of welding sparks falling from the scaffolding like plants covering the stones . . . like it was less construction than archeology.

Afraid of pursuing these thoughts, Wu Yue turned his attention to Zhang Beihai next to him. "Is your father any better?" he asked.

Zhang Beihai gently shook his head. "No. He's just holding on."

"Ask for leave."

"I did when he first went to the hospital. Given the situation, I'll deal with it when the time comes."

Then they went silent. Every social interaction between the two of them was like this. Where work was concerned they had more to say, of course, but something always lay between them.

"Beihai, work isn't going to be like it was. Since we're sharing this position now, I think we ought to communicate more."

"We've communicated just fine in the past. Our superiors put us together on *Tang,* no doubt thanks to our successful cooperation aboard *Chang'an.*" Zhang Beihai laughed as he said this, but it was the sort of laugh that Wu Yue couldn't read. Zhang Beihai's eyes could easily read deep into the heart of everyone aboard the ship, be they captain or sailor. Wu Yue was entirely transparent to him. But Wu Yue could not read what was inside Zhang. He was certain that the man's smile came from within him, but had no hope of understanding him. Successful cooperation does not equate to successful understanding. There was no question that Zhang Beihai was the most capable political commissar on the ship, and he was forthright in his work, exploring every last issue with complete precision. But his internal world was a bottomless gray to Wu Yue, who always felt like Zhang Beihai was saying: *Just do it this way. This way's best, or most correct. But it's not what I really want.* It began as an indistinct feeling that grew increasingly obvious. Of course, whatever Zhang Beihai did was always the best or most correct, but Wu Yue had no idea what he actually wanted.

Wu Yue adhered to one article of faith: Command of a warship was a dangerous position, so the two commanders must understand each other's minds. This presented Wu Yue with a knotty

problem. At first, he thought that Zhang Beihai was somehow on guard, which offended Wu. In the tough post of captain of a destroyer, was anyone more forthright and guileless than he was? *What do I have worth guarding against?*

When Zhang Beihai's father had briefly been their superior officer, Wu Yue had spoken with him about his difficulties talking to his commissar. "Isn't it enough for the work to be done well? Why do you need to know how he thinks?" the general had said, gently, then added, perhaps involuntarily, "Actually, I don't know either."

"Let's get a closer look," Zhang Beihai said, pointing to *Tang* through the sparks. Then both their phones chirped at the same time: a text message recalling them back to their car. This usually meant an emergency, since secured communications equipment was only available in the vehicle. Wu Yue opened the car door and picked up the receiver. It was a call from an advisor at battle group HQ.

"Captain Wu, Fleet Command have issued you and Commissar Zhang emergency orders. The two of you are to report to General Staff immediately."

"General Staff? What about the fifth fleet training exercise? Half the battle group is at sea, and the rest of the ships will join them tomorrow."

"I'm not aware of that. The order is simple. Just that one command. You can look at the specifics when you get back."

The captain and commissar of the still-unlaunched *Tang* glanced at each other, then had one of the rare moments throughout the years where their thoughts aligned: *Looks like that patch of water will remain empty.*

Fort Greely, Alaska. Several fallow deer ambling along the snowy plain grew alert, sensing vibrations in the earth beneath the snow. Ahead of them, a white hemisphere opened. It had been placed there long ago, a giant egg half-buried beneath the ground, but the deer always felt it didn't belong to this frozen world. The egg split open and issued forth thick smoke and flames, then, with a roar,

it hatched a cylinder that accelerated upward, spurting flames from its bottom. The surrounding snowdrifts were thrown by the fire into the air, where they fell again as rain. When the cylinder gained enough height, the explosions that had terrified the deer were again replaced by peace. The cylinder vanished into the sky trailing a long white tail behind it, as if the snowscape was a giant ball of yarn from which a giant invisible hand had pulled a strand skyward.

"Damn it! Just a few more seconds and I'd have confirmed a launch interrupt!" said Target Screening Officer Raeder as he tossed aside his mouse. Raeder was thousands of kilometers away in the Nuclear Missile Defense Control Room at the NORAD Command Center, three hundred meters beneath Cheyenne Mountain near Colorado Springs.

"I figured it was nothing as soon as the system warning came up," Orbital Monitor Jones said, shaking his head.

"Then what's the system attacking?" asked General Fitzroy. Nuclear Missile Defense was just one of the duties of his new position, and he wasn't entirely familiar with it yet. Looking at the monitor-covered wall, the general attempted to locate the intuitive graphical displays they'd had at the NASA control center: a red line snaking across the world map, forming a sine wave atop the map's planar transformation. Novices found this inexplicable, but at least it let you know that something was shooting into space. But there was nothing so simple here. The lines on the screens were a complicated abstract jumble that was meaningless to him. Not to mention all the screens with swiftly scrolling numbers that had meaning only to the NMD duty officers.

"General, do you remember when they replaced the reflective film on the ISS multipurpose module last year? They lost the old film. That's what this was. It balls up and then unfurls in the solar wind."

"But . . . it ought to be included in the target screening database."

"It is. Here." Raeder brought up a page with his mouse. Below piles of complicated text, data, and forms, there was an inconspicuous photograph, probably taken with an Earth telescope,

of an irregular white patch against a black background. The strong reflection made it difficult to make out details.

"Major, since you've got this, why didn't you terminate the launch program?"

"The system ought to have searched the target database automatically. Human reaction times aren't quick enough. But data from the old system hasn't been reformatted for the new one, so it wasn't linked in with the recognition module," Raeder said. His tone was a little aggrieved, as if to say, *I've demonstrated my proficiency by managing to pull this up so quickly in a manual search when the NMD supercomputer couldn't, but I still have to put up with your clueless questions.*

"General, the order came to switch over to actual operational state after the NMD moved its intercept headings into space, but before software recalibration was completed," a duty officer said.

Fitzroy said nothing. The chatter of the control room annoyed him. Here in front of him was humanity's first planetary defense system, but it was nothing more than an existing NMD system whose intercepts had been redirected from various terrestrial continents and into space.

"I say we should take a photo for a memento!" Jones said. "This has got to be Earth's first strike at a common enemy."

"Cameras are prohibited," Raeder said coldly.

"Captain, what are you talking about?" Fitzroy said, angry all of a sudden. "The system didn't detect an enemy target at all. It's not a first strike."

After an uncomfortable silence, someone said, "The interceptors carry nuclear warheads."

"Yeah, one point five megatons. So what?"

"It's nearly dark outside. Given the target location, we ought to be able to see the flash!"

"You can see it on the monitor."

"It's more fun from outside," Raeder said.

Jones stood up nervously. "General, I . . . my shift's over."

"Mine too, General," Raeder said. This was just a courtesy.

Fitzroy was a high-level coordinator with the Planetary Defense Council and had no command over NORAD and the NMDs.

Fitzroy waved his hand: "I'm not your commanding officer. Do as you please. But let me remind all of you that in the future, we may be spending a lot of time working together."

Raeder and Jones headed topside at a run. After passing through the multi-ton antiradiation door, they were out on the peak of Cheyenne Mountain. It was dusk and the sky was clear, but they didn't see the flash of a nuclear blast in outer space.

"It should be right there," Jones said, gesturing skyward.

"Maybe we've missed it," Raeder said. He didn't look upward. Then, with an ironic smile, he said, "Do they really believe the sophon will unfold in lower dimensions?"

"Unlikely. It's intelligent. It won't give us that chance," Jones said.

"NMD's eyes are pointed upward. Is there really nothing to defend against on Earth? Even if the terrorist countries have all turned into saints, there's still the ETO, right?" He snorted. "And the PDC. Those military guys clearly want to chalk up a quick accomplishment. Fitzroy's one of them. Now they can declare that the first stage of the Planetary Defense System is complete, even though they've done practically nothing to the hardware. The system's sole purpose is to stop her from unfolding in lower dimensions near to Earth's orbit. The technology's even simpler than what's needed for intercepting guided missiles, because if the target really does appear, it'll cover an immense area. . . . Captain, that's why I've asked you up here. Why were you acting like a child, what with that first-strike photograph business? You've upset the general, you know. Can't you see he's a petty man?"

"But . . . wasn't that a compliment?"

"He's one of the best hype artists in the military. He's not going to announce at the press conference that this was a system error. Like the rest of them, he'll say it was a successful maneuver. Wait and see. That's how it's gonna be." As he was speaking, Raeder sat down and leaned back on the ground, looking up with a face full of yearning at the sky, where the stars had already emerged.

"You know, Jones, if the sophon really does unfold again, she'll give us a chance to destroy her. Wouldn't that be something!"

"What's the use? The fact is that they're streaming toward the Solar System right now. Who knows how many of them. . . . Hey, why did you say 'she' rather than 'it' or 'he'?"

The expression on Raeder's upturned face turned dreamy: "Yesterday, a Chinese colonel who just arrived at the center told me that in his language, she has the name of a Japanese woman, Tomoko."[2]

The day before, Zhang Yuanchao filed his retirement papers and left the chemical plant where he had worked for more than four decades. In the words of his neighbor Lao Yang,[3] today was the start of his second childhood. Lao Yang told him that sixty, like sixteen, was the best time in life, an age where the burdens of one's forties and fifties had been laid down, but the slowdown and illness of the seventies and eighties had not yet arrived. An age to enjoy life. Zhang Yuanchao's son and daughter-in-law had steady jobs, and although his son had married late, he would be holding a grandson before long. He and his wife wouldn't have been able to afford their current house except that they had been bought out when their old place had been demolished. They had been living in the new place for a year now. . . .

When Zhang Yuanchao thought about it, everything was completely satisfactory. He had to admit that as far as affairs of state were concerned, Lao Yang was right. Still, as he looked out from his eighth-story window at the clear sky over the city, he felt like there was no sunlight in his heart, much less a second childhood.

Lao Yang, first name Jinwen, was a retired middle school

2 *Translator's Note: Zhìzi* (智子), literally "knowledge particle." The character for "particle" frequently appears in female given names in Japanese, where it is pronounced "ko."

3 *Translator's Note: Lǎo*, meaning "old," is often used before a surname of those older than the speaker to show respect or familiarity.

teacher who frequently advised Zhang Yuanchao that if he wanted to enjoy his waning years, he ought to be learning new things. For example: "The Internet. Even babies can learn it, so why don't you?" He even pointed out that Zhang Yuanchao's biggest failing was that he had absolutely no interest in the outside world: "Your old lady can at least brush aside her tears while sitting in front of the TV watching those trashy soaps. But you, you don't even watch TV. You should pay attention to national and world affairs. That's part of a full life." Zhang Yuanchao may have been an old Beijinger, but he didn't seem like one. A taxi driver could hold forth with cogent analyses of domestic and world situations, but even if Zhang Yuanchao knew the current president's name, he certainly didn't know the premier's. This was actually a point of pride for him. He lived the steady-going life of a commoner, he said, and couldn't be bothered to care about such irrelevant things. They had nothing to do with him, and ignoring them rid him of a significant number of headaches in life. Yang Jinwen paid attention to affairs of state and made a point of watching the evening news every day, arguing with online commenters till he was red in the face over national economic policy and the tide of international nuclear proliferation, but what had it gotten him? The government hadn't increased his pension by even a cent. He said, "You're being ridiculous. You think it's irrelevant? That it's got nothing to do with you? Listen, Lao Zhang. Every major national and international issue, every major national policy, and every UN resolution is connected to your life, through both direct and indirect channels. You think the US invasion of Venezuela is none of your concern? I say it's got more than a penny's worth of lasting implications for your pension." At the time, Zhang had merely laughed at Lao Yang's wonkish outburst. But now he knew that his neighbor was right.

Zhang Yuanchao rang Yang Jinwen's doorbell, and Yang answered, looking like he had just gotten back home. He seemed particularly relaxed. Zhang Yuanchao looked at him like a man in the desert who has encountered a fellow traveler and won't let him go.

"I was just looking for you. Where did you go off to?"

"I took a trip to the market. I saw your old lady shopping for food."

"Why is our building so empty? It's like a . . . mausoleum."

"It's not a holiday today. That's all." He laughed. "Your first day of retirement. That feeling is totally normal. At least you weren't a leader. They've got it worse when they retire. You'll soon get used to it. Come on, let's check out the neighborhood activity center and see what we can do for fun."

"No, no. It's not because I've retired. It's because . . . how should I put it? Because of the country, or rather, the world situation."

Yang Jinwen pointed at him and laughed. "The world situation? I never thought I'd hear those words come out of your mouth. . . ."

"That's right, I didn't use to care about the big issues, but they've gotten too huge. I never thought anything could get so big!"

"Lao Zhang, it's actually really funny, but I've started to come around to your way of thinking. I don't care about those irrelevant issues anymore. Believe it or not, I haven't watched the news in two weeks. I used to care about the big issues because people matter. We could have an effect on the outcome of current events. But no one has the power to overcome this. What's the point of troubling yourself about it?"

"But you can't simply not care. Humanity will be gone in four hundred years!"

"Hmph. You and I will be gone in forty-odd years."

"What about our descendants? They'll be wiped out."

"That doesn't concern me as much as it does you. My son in America is married but doesn't want children, so I don't really care. But the Zhang family will last another dozen generations, right? Isn't that enough?"

Zhang Yuanchao stared at Yang Jinwen for a few seconds, then looked at his watch. He turned on the television, where the news channel was airing the day's major stories:

The AP reports that at 6:30 p.m. EST on the twenty-ninth, the US National Missile Defense System successfully completed

the test destruction of a lower-dimensional unfolded sophon in near-Earth orbit. This is the third test of an NMD intercept since targets were shifted to outer space. The latest target was the reflective film discarded from the International Space Station last October. A Planetary Defense Council spokesman said that the warhead-equipped interceptor successfully destroyed the three-thousand-square-meter target. This means that well before the sophon's three-dimensional unfolding reaches sufficient area, and before it presents a reflective surface that is a threat to human targets on the ground, the NMD system will be able to destroy it. . . .

"What pointlessness. A sophon's not going to unfold," Yang said as he reached for the remote in Zhang's hand. "Change the station. There might be a repeat of the European Cup semifinals. I fell asleep on the sofa last night. . . ."

"Watch it at home." Zhang Yuanchao gripped the remote and didn't let him have it. The news continued:

The physician at 301 Military Hospital in charge of the treatment of academician Jia Weilin confirmed that Jia's death was due to a hematological malignancy, also known as leukemia, the proximate cause of death being organ failure and loss of blood in the advanced stage of the disease. No abnormalities were present. Jia Weilin, a noted expert in superconductivity who made major contributions in the field of room-temperature superconductors, died on the tenth. Stories claiming that Jia died in a sophon strike are pure rumor. In a separate report, a spokesman for the Ministry of Health confirmed that several other deaths supposedly due to sophon strikes were in fact due to ordinary illnesses or accidents. The station spoke with noted physicist Ding Yi about the matter.

Reporter: What's your take on the emerging panic over the sophons?

Ding Yi: It's due to a lack of common knowledge about physics. Representatives of the government and the scientific community have explained this on numerous occasions: A sophon is just a microscopic particle which, despite possessing a high intelligence, has the potential for only a limited effect on the macroscopic world due to its microscopic scale. The primary threats they pose to humanity lie in their erroneous and random interference to high-energy physics experiments, and in the quantum entanglement network that monitors Earth. In its microscopic state, a sophon cannot kill, and it cannot engage in any other offensive attack. If a sophon wants to produce a larger effect on the macroscopic world, it can only do so in a lower-dimensional unfolded state. And even in that situation, its effects are highly limited, because a sophon unfolded in lower dimensions on a macroscopic scale is very weak. Now that humanity has established a defense system, sophons cannot do this without providing us with an excellent opportunity to destroy them. I believe that the mainstream media ought to do a better job of disseminating this scientific information to the public to rid it of a panic that has no basis in science.

Zhang Yuanchao heard someone enter the living room without knocking, calling "Lao Zhang" and "Master Zhang." He knew who it was from the footsteps he'd heard hammering up the staircase just before. Miao Fuquan, another neighbor on their floor, came in. A Shanxi coal boss who ran a fair number of mines in that province, Miao Fuquan was a few years younger than Zhang Yuanchao. He owned a larger home in another part of Beijing and used this apartment as a place to keep a mistress from Sichuan who was about the same age as his daughter. When he had first moved in, the Zhang and Yang families had basically ignored him save for an argument over the stuff he left strewn about the hallway, but they eventually discovered that although he was a little vulgar, he was

27

a decent, friendly man. Once building management had smoothed over a dispute or two, harmony was gradually established among the three families. Although Miao Fuquan said he had turned over his business affairs to his son, he was still a busy man and rarely spent any time at this "home," so the three-bedroom place was usually only occupied by the Sichuan woman.

"Lao Miao, you haven't been around for months. Where have you struck it rich this time?" asked Yang Jinwen.

Miao Fuquan casually picked up a glass, filled it halfway from the water dispenser, and gulped down the water. Then he wiped his mouth and said, "No one's getting rich. . . . There's trouble at the mine, and I've got to go clean it up. It's practically war time. The government really means it this time. The laws on wildcat mining never used to work, but the mines aren't going to be running for much longer now."

"Bad days are here," Yang Jinwen said, without taking his eyes from the game on television.

The man had been lying on the bed for several hours. The light shining through the basement window, the room's only source of illumination, was moonlight now, and the cool rays cast bright spots on the floor. In the shadows, everything looked like it was carved from gray stone, as if the entire room was a tomb.

No one ever knew the man's true name, but eventually, they called him the Second Wallbreaker.

The Second Wallbreaker had spent several hours looking back on his life. After confirming that there had been no omissions, he twisted the muscles of his numb body, reached under the pillow, and drew out a gun, which he slowly aimed at his temple. Just then, a sophon text appeared before his eyes.

Don't do that. We need you.

"Lord? Every night for a year I dreamt that you called, but the

28

dreams went away recently. I figured I'd stopped dreaming, but that doesn't seem to be the case now."

This is not a dream. I am in real-time communication with you.

The Wallbreaker gave a chilly laugh. "Good. It's over, then. There definitely aren't any dreams on the other side."

You require proof?

"Proof that there aren't dreams on that side?"

Proof that it's really me.

"Fine. Tell me something I don't know."

Your goldfish are dead.

"Hah! That doesn't matter. I'm about to meet them in a place where there's no darkness."

You should really take a look. This morning when you were distracted, you flicked away a half-smoked cigarette and it landed in the fishbowl. The nicotine that leached into the water was fatal to your fish.

The Second Wallbreaker opened his eyes, put down his gun, and rolled out of bed, his lethargy completely wiped away. He groped for the light and then went over to look at the fishbowl on the small table. Five dragon eye goldfish were floating in the water, their white bellies at the surface, and in their midst was a half-smoked cigarette.

I'll perform an additional confirmation. Evans once gave you an encrypted letter, but the encryption has changed. He died before he

was able to notify you of the new password, and you've never been able to read the letter. I'll tell you the password: CAMEL, the brand of cigarette you poisoned your fish with.

The Second Wallbreaker scrambled to retrieve his laptop, and as he waited for it to start up, tears streamed down his face. "Lord, my Lord, is it really you? Is it really you?" he choked out through his sobs. After the computer booted up, he opened the e-mail attachment in the Earth-Trisolaris Organization's proprietary dedicated reader. He entered the password into the popup box, and when the text was displayed he no longer had any mind to read it carefully. Throwing himself to his knees, he cried out, "Lord! It really is you, my Lord!" When he had calmed down, he raised his head and said, his eyes still wet, "We were never notified of the attack on the gathering the commander attended, or of the ambush at the Panama Canal. Why did you cast us aside?"

We were afraid of you.

"Is it because our thoughts aren't transparent? That doesn't matter, you know. All of the skills that you lack—deceit, trickery, disguise, and misdirection—we use in your service."

We don't know if that's true. Even supposing it is true, the fear remains. Your Bible mentions an animal called the snake. If a snake crawled up to you and said it would serve you, would your fear and disgust cease?

"If it told the truth, then I would overcome my disgust and fear and accept it."

That would be difficult.

"Of course. I know that you've already been bitten once by the snake. Once real-time notification became possible and you gave detailed answers to our questions, there was no reason for you to

tell us quite a bit of that information, such as how you received the first signal from humanity, and how the sophons are constructed. It was hard for us to understand: We were not communicating via transparent display of thoughts, so why not be more selective in the information you sent?"

That option did exist, but it doesn't cover up as much as you imagine it might. In fact, forms of communication do exist in our world that don't require displays of thought, particularly in the age of technology. But transparent thought has become a cultural and social custom. This might be hard for you to understand, just like it's hard for us to understand you.

"I can't imagine that deceit and scheming are totally absent in your world."

They exist, but they are far simpler than in yours. For example, in the wars on our world, opposing sides will adopt disguises, but an enemy who becomes suspicious about the disguise and inquires about it directly will usually obtain the truth.

"That's unbelievable."

You are equally unbelievable to us. You have a book on your bookshelf called A Story of Three Kingdoms.

"*Romance of the Three Kingdoms*.[4] You won't understand that."

I understand a small part, like how an ordinary person who has a hard time understanding a mathematics monograph can make out some

4 *Translator's Note:* A historical novel attributed to Luo Guanzhong (c. 1330–1400), *Romance of the Three Kingdoms* describes the contest between three regional powers from the waning days of the Eastern Han Dyansty (184) to the reunification of the empire under the Jin Dynasty (280). It is known for its iconic characters, battle scenes, and political intrigue.

of it through enormous mental effort, and by giving full play to the imagination.

"Indeed, that book lays out the highest levels of human schemes and strategy."

But our sophons can make everything in the human world transparent.

"Except for people's own minds."

Yes. The sophon can't read thoughts.

"You must know about the Wallfacer Project."

More than you do. It is about to be put into action. This is why we have come to you.

"What do you think of the project?"

The same feeling you get when you look at the snake.

"But the snake in the Bible helped humans gain knowledge. The Wallfacer Project will set up one or several mazes that will seem to you to be particularly tricky and treacherous. We can help you find your way out."

This difference in mental transparency gives us all the more resolve to wipe out humanity. Please help us wipe out humanity, and then we will wipe you out.

"My Lord, the way you express yourself is problematic. Clearly, it's determined by how you communicate through the display of transparent thoughts, but in our world, even if you express your true thoughts, you must do so in an appropriately euphemistic way. For example, although what you just said is in accord with the ideals

32

of ETO, its overly direct formulation might repel some of our members and cause unanticipated consequences. Of course, it may be that you'll never be able to learn to express yourself appropriately."

It is precisely the expression of deformed thoughts that makes the exchange of information in human society, particularly in human literature, so much like a twisted maze. As far as I am aware, ETO is on the brink of collapse.

"That's because you abandoned us. Those two strikes were fatal, and now, the Redemptionists have disintegrated and only the Adventists have maintained an organized existence. You're certainly aware of this, but the most fatal blow was a psychological one. Your abandonment means that the devotion of our members to our Lord is being tested. To maintain that devotion, ETO desperately needs our Lord's support."

We can't give you technology.

"That won't be necessary, so long as you go back to transmitting information to us through the sophons."

Naturally. But what ETO must do first is execute the critical order you just read. We issued it to Evans before his death, and he ordered you to execute it, but you never solved the encryption.

The Wallbreaker remembered the letter he had just decrypted on his computer and read it over carefully.

Simple enough to carry out, is it not?

"It's not too difficult. But is it truly that important?"

It used to be important. Now, because of humanity's Wallfacer Project, it is incredibly important.

"Why?"

The text did not show for a while.

Evans knew why, but evidently he didn't tell anyone. He was right. This is fortunate. Now, we don't need to tell you why.

The Wallbreaker was overjoyed. "My Lord, you have learned how to conceal! This is progress!"

Evans taught us much, but we are still at the very beginning, or in his words, only at the level of one of your five-year-old children. The order he gave you contains one of the strategies we can't learn.

"Do you mean this stipulation: 'To avoid attention, you must not reveal that it was done by ETO'? This . . . well, if the target is important, then this requirement is only natural."

To us it is a complicated plan.

"Fine. I will take care of it in accordance with Evans's wishes. My Lord, we will prove our devotion to you."

In one remote corner of the vast sea of information on the Internet, there was a remote corner, and in a remote corner of that remote corner, and then in a remote corner of a remote corner of a remote corner of that remote corner—that is, in the very depths of the most remote corner of all—a virtual world came back to life.

Under the strange, chilly dawn was no pyramid, UN building, or pendulum, just a broad and hard expanse of emptiness, like a giant slab of frozen metal.

King Wen of Zhou came over the horizon. Wearing tattered robes, he carried a tarnished bronze sword, and his face was as filthy and wrinkled as the pelt he was wrapped in. But there was energy in his eyes, and his pupils reflected the rising sun.

"Is anybody here?" he shouted. "Anyone?"

King Wen's voice was swallowed up immediately by the wilderness. He shouted for a while, and then sat wearily on the ground and accelerated the passage of time, watching the suns turn into shooting stars, and the shooting stars turn back into suns, and the suns of the Stable Eras sweep across the sky like clock pendulums, and the days and nights of the Chaotic Eras turn the world into a vast stage where the lighting was out of control. Time sped by, but nothing changed. It remained the eternal, metallic wasteland. The three stars danced in the heavens, and King Wen turned into a pillar of ice in the cold. Then a shooting star turned into a sun, and when that fiery giant disc passed overhead, the ice on his body melted and his body became a pillar of fire. Just before turning entirely to ash, he let out a long sigh, and then exited.

Thirty army, navy, and air force officers fixed their eyes on the insignia on the deep-red screen, a silver star shooting rays in four directions. The rays, in the shape of sharp swords, were flanked by the Chinese characters for eight and one.[5] It was the insignia of the Chinese Space Force.

General Chang Weisi motioned for everyone to be seated. Then, placing his cap squarely down upon the conference table, he said, "The ceremony formally establishing the space force will be held tomorrow morning, at which time you will be issued uniforms and pins. However, comrades, as of this moment we belong to the same branch of the military."

They looked at each other, noting that among the thirty people there were fifteen dressed in navy uniforms, nine in air force uniforms, and six in army uniforms. When they turned their attention back to General Chang, they had a hard time disguising their confusion.

5 *Translator's Note:* The insignia of the People's Liberation Army is a star inscribed with the characters eight and one.

With a smile, Chang Weisi said, "It's an odd ratio, isn't it? You can't use the scale of today's aerospace program to assess space forces of the future. Spaceships, when their day comes, will probably be even bigger and carry a larger crew than today's aircraft carriers. Future space warfare will be based on large-tonnage, high-endurance combat platforms, and engagements will resemble naval battles more than air combat, with a battlefield in three dimensions instead of two. So the military's space branch must be based upon the navy. I know, we all assumed that the foundation would be the air force, which means our naval comrades might be ill prepared. You've got to adapt as quickly as possible."

"Sir, we had no idea," Zhang Beihai said. Wu Yue sat ramrod straight and motionless beside him, but Zhang Beihai acutely sensed that something in his level eyes had been extinguished.

Chang Weisi nodded. "In fact, the navy's not all that far removed from space. Don't they call them 'space ships' rather than 'space planes'? That's because space and the ocean have long been linked together in the popular mind."

The mood of the room relaxed somewhat. He continued, "Comrades, at this moment, the thirty-one of us are all that makes up this new branch of the military. As for the future space fleet, basic research is being conducted in all scientific disciplines, with a particular focus on the space elevator, and on fusion engines for large-scale space ships. . . . But this isn't the work of the space force. Our duty is to establish a theoretical framework for space warfare. It's a daunting task, since we have zero knowledge of this type of warfare, but the future space fleet will be built atop this foundation. In its preliminary stage, then, the space force will be more like a military academy. The primary task of those of us seated here is to organize that academy, and then invite a sizeable group of scholars and researchers to join up."

Chang stood up and walked over to the insignia, where he addressed the assembled officers with words they would remember for the rest of their lives: "Comrades, the space force has a tough road ahead of it. Initial predictions see basic research taking at

least fifty years across all disciplines, with at least another hundred years before practical use of the technology required for large-scale space travel becomes possible. Then, after its initial construction, the space fleet will require another century and a half to achieve its planned scale. That means that full combat capacity will take the space force three centuries from its establishment. Comrades, I'm sure you all understand what that means. None of us sitting here will make it to space, much less have the chance to see our space fleet, and we may not even see a credible model of a space warship. The first generation of officers and crew won't be born until two centuries from now, and two and a half centuries from that, Earth's fleet will meet the alien invaders. Aboard those ships will be the fifteenth generation of our grandchildren."

The assembly fell into a prolonged silence. Ahead of them stretched the leaden road of time, terminating somewhere in the mists of the future, where all they could see were flickering flames and luster of blood. The brevity of a human lifespan tormented them as never before, and their hearts soared above the vault of time to join with their descendants and plunge into blood and fire in the icy cold of space, the eventual meeting place for the souls of all soldiers.

As usual, when Miao Fuquan returned, he asked Zhang Yuanchao and Yang Jinwen to have a drink at his place, where the Sichuan woman had laid out a sumptuous feast on the table. As they were drinking, Zhang Yuanchao brought up Miao Fuquan's visit to the Construction Bank that morning to withdraw some money.

"Haven't you heard?" Miao Fuquan said. "People were being trampled to death at the banks! There were people three deep on the floor at the counter."

"And your money?" asked Zhang Yuanchao.

"I was able to get some of it. The rest was frozen. It's criminal!"

"The hair you shed is worth more than the rest of us have altogether," said Zhang Yuanchao.

Yang Jinwen said, "The news said that when the social panic

eases a little, the government will gradually unfreeze accounts. Perhaps just a certain percentage at first, but the situation will eventually return to normal."

Zhang Yuanchao said, "I hope so. The government made a mistake in calling it a state of war so early on, putting people in a panic. Now people are only thinking of themselves. How many people are thinking about the defense of Earth four hundred years in the future?"

"That's not the biggest problem," Yang Jinwen said. "I said it before and I'll say it again, China's savings rate is an enormous land mine. Am I right? High savings, low social security. People's life savings are in the bank, and then everyone goes into mass hysteria at the slightest gust of wind."

Zhang Yuanchao asked, "So this wartime economy, what do you think it'll be like?"

"It's too sudden. I don't think anyone has a full mental picture of it yet, and the new economic policies are still being drafted. But one thing's certain: Tough days are ahead."

"Tough days, my ass. It's nothing people our age haven't seen before. It'll be like the sixties all over again, I expect," said Miao Fuquan.

"I just feel for the kids," said Zhang Yuanchao, and drained his glass.

Just then a news fanfare drew their attention to the television. A familiar sound these days, the music had the ability to make everyone drop what they were doing and pay attention. It was the bumper fanfare for a breaking news announcement, which were being broadcast more often than ever these days. The three old men remembered how this sort of news was frequently broadcast over radio and television prior to the 1980s, but during the long period of prosperity and tranquility that came afterward, it disappeared.

The broadcast began:

According to this station's correspondent at the UN Secretariat, a UN spokesperson at a just-concluded press conference announced that

a special session of the General Assembly will be convened in the near future to discuss the problem of Escapism. The special session will be co-facilitated by the permanent members of the Planetary Defense Council and will be aimed at pushing the international community to reach a consensus on Escapist attitudes and develop corresponding international laws.

Let's take a brief look back at the emergence and development of Escapism.

The doctrine of Escapism arose alongside the Trisolar Crisis. Its primary argument holds that given the locked state of humanity's advanced sciences, it does not make any sense to plan for a defense of Earth and the Solar System in four and a half centuries. Considering the extent to which human technology can develop over the next four centuries, a more realistic goal would be to construct starships to enable a small portion of the human race to flee to outer space, thereby avoiding the total extinction of human civilization.

Escapism has three possible destinations. Option one: a New World—that is, searching among the stars for a world where humanity can survive. Without question, this is the ideal, but it requires extremely high navigation speeds and the voyage will be long. Given the level that human technology can attain during the Crisis period, this option is unlikely to be realized. Option two: a Starship Civilization—that is, humanity will use their escape ships as a permanent abode, and human civilization will endure on an eternal voyage. This option faces the same difficulties as the New World, although it places a greater emphasis on the establishment of closed ecosystem technologies. A generation ship running a fully enclosed biosphere is far beyond humanity's current technical capabilities. Option three: Temporary Refuge. Once Trisolaris has completed settlement of the Solar System, there can be active exchanges between Trisolaran society and the humans that have fled to outer space. By pushing for a relaxation of policies toward residual humans in outer space, they will eventually be able to return to the Solar System and coexist on a smaller scale with the Trisolarans. Although Temporary Refuge is considered the most realistic plan, there are still too many variables.

Not long after the emergence of Escapism, news outlets worldwide reported that the United States and Russia, two leaders in space technology, had secretly started work on plans for fleeing into outer space. Although the governments of the two countries denied the existence of any plans, an uproar in the international community sparked a "socialized technology" movement. At the third special session, a host of developing countries demanded that the United States, Russia, Japan, China, and the European Union release their technology and provide all advanced technology, including aerospace technology, free of charge to the international community so that all nations of humanity would have an equal opportunity to face the Trisolar Crisis. The supporters of the socialized technology movement brought up a precedent: At the beginning of the century, several major European pharmaceutical companies exacted high license fees from African countries for the manufacture of state-of-the-art AIDS treatments, prompting high-profile litigation. Under pressure from public opinion and the rapid spread of the disease in Africa, the companies renounced their patent rights prior to trial. The ultimate crisis that Earth is now facing means that open technology is the unavoidable responsibility that advanced countries have to all humanity. The socialized technology movement found a unanimous response from developing countries and even won the support of some members of the EU, but all related initiatives were rejected at meetings of the UN-PDC. At the fifth special session of the UN General Assembly, a proposal by China and Russia of a "limited socialized technology" plan that advocated making technology open to all permanent members of the PDC was vetoed by the US and Britain. The US government said that no form of socialized technology was realistic, that it was a naïve idea, and that under the present circumstances US national security was a priority "second only to planetary defense." The failure of the limited socialized technology proposal caused a split among technological powers and led to the bankruptcy of the plan to establish a United Earth Space Force.

The implications of the frustrated socialized technology movement are far-reaching, and people have been made aware that even in the

face of the devastating Trisolar Crisis, the unity of the human race is still a distant dream.

The socialized technology movement was launched by the Escapists. Only when the international community reaches a consensus on Escapism will it be able to bridge the gap that has opened up between developed and developing nations, and between the developed countries themselves. This is the environment in which the UN special session is set to open.

"Oh, that reminds me," Miao Fuquan said. "The information I told you over the phone a few days ago is reliable."

"What's that?"

"The escape fund."

"Lao Miao, how can you believe that? You don't seem like an easy mark," Yang Jinwen said disapprovingly.

"No, no," Miao Fuquan said, lowering his voice and looking back and forth between the other two. "The young guy's name is Shi Xiaoming. I checked out his background through various channels, and his father Shi Qiang works for the PDC's security department! He used to be chief of a municipal antiterrorism squad, and now he's a key person in the PDC in charge of combatting the ETO. I've got a number here for his department. You can check it out for yourselves."

The other two looked at each other, and Yang Jinwen laughed as he picked up the bottle and poured himself another glass. "So what if it's true? Who cares if there's an escape fund? How can I afford it?"

"That's right. It's for you rich folks," Zhang Yuanchao slurred out.

Yang Jinwen suddenly grew excited: "And if it's really true, then the state's a pack of morons! If anyone's going to flee, it should be the cream of our descendants. Why the hell would you give it to anyone who can pay? What's the point of that?"

Miao Fuquan pointed at him and laughed. "Fine, Yang. Let's get to your real point. What you really want is for your descendants

to be the ones to go, right? Look at your son and daughter-in-law: Ph.D. scientists. Elites. So your grandsons and great-grandsons will most likely be elites too." He lifted his glass and nodded. "But if you think about it, everyone should be equal, right? There's no reason elites should get a, you know, free lunch, right?"

"What do you mean?"

"Everything has a cost. It's a law of nature. I'll spend to ensure a future for the Miaos. That's a law of nature, too!"

"Why is this something that can be bought? The duty of escaping is to extend human civilization. They'll naturally want the cream of civilization. Sending a bunch of rich dudes across the cosmos," he snorted. "What'll that do? Hmph."

The awkward smile on Miao Fuquan's face vanished, and he pointed a thick finger at Yang Jinwen. "I've always known you look down on me. No matter how rich I get, I'll just be a vulgar money-bags to you. Isn't that right?"

"Who do you think you are?" asked Yang Jinwen, fueled by the alcohol.

Miao Fuquan slapped the table and stood up. "Yang Jinwen, I'm not going to stand for your bile. I'm gonna—"

Then Zhang Yuanchao slammed the table with a noise three times louder, knocking over two of the cups and startling a yelp from the Sichuan woman. He pointed his finger at the other two in turn. "Fine. You're an elite, and you've got money. That leaves me. What the hell do I have? I'm just a poor man, so it serves me right that my line will be wiped out?" With obvious effort he restrained himself from kicking over the table, then turned and stormed out. Yang Jinwen followed him.

The Second Wallbreaker carefully put new goldfish into the bowl. Like Evans, he enjoyed isolation, but he needed the companionship of beings other than humans. He often spoke to the goldfish like he spoke to the Trisolarans, two forms of life whose long-term presence on Earth he was looking forward to.

Just then the sophon's text appeared on his retina.

I've recently been studying A Story of Three Kingdoms, and like you said, deceit and trickery are an art, just like the markings on a snake.

"My Lord, once again you bring up the snake."

The more beautiful the markings on a snake, the more fearsome it looks. We didn't use to care about humanity escaping, so long as they stopped existing in the Solar System, but now we have adjusted our plans and have decided to prevent humanity from fleeing. Letting an enemy whose thoughts are totally opaque flee into the cosmos is very dangerous.

"Do you have a specific plan in mind?"

The fleet has made adjustments to its Solar System deployment. It will detour in four directions at the Kuiper Belt[6] and encircle the Solar System.

"If humanity really flees, your fleet will be too late to do anything by the time they do."

That is true, so we require your assistance. The next mission of the ETO is to halt or delay humanity's escape plans.

The Wallbreaker smiled. "My Lord, you really don't have to worry about that at all. No large-scale flight of humanity will ever happen."

Even given the present, limited space for technological development, humanity might be able to build generation ships.

6 *Translator's Note:* The Kuiper Belt is a region extending from the orbit of Neptune, at roughly 30 AU, to roughly 50 AU, and is home to Pluto and two other dwarf planets, among other objects.

"The greatest obstacle to flight is not technology."

Then is it disputes among countries? This UN special session may resolve that problem, and if it can't, then developed countries are entirely capable of brushing aside the opposition of developing countries and forcing a plan through.

"The greatest obstacle to flight is not disputes among countries, either."

Then what is it?

"Disputes among people. The question of who goes and who stays behind."

That doesn't seem like a problem to us.

"We thought so at first, but it turns out to be an insurmountable obstacle."

Can you explain?

"You may be familiar with human history, but you will probably find this hard to comprehend: Who goes and who remains involves basic human values, values which in the past promoted progress in human society, but which, in the face of ultimate disaster, are a trap. Right now, the majority of humanity has not realized how deep this trap is. Lord, please believe my words. No human can escape this trap."

"Uncle Zhang, you don't have to decide now. You've asked all the necessary questions, and it's not a small amount of money, after all," Shi Xiaoming said to Zhang Yuanchao, his face a picture of serenity.

"It's not that. Is the plan for real? The TV says—"

"Don't you mind what the TV says. Two weeks ago the government spokesperson said that freezing accounts was impossible, but now look what's happened. . . . Think reasonably. You're an ordinary man, and you're thinking about the continuation of your family line. What about the president and the premier? Won't they be thinking about the continuation of the Chinese people? And the UN about the continuation of the human race? This UN special session is actually an international cooperative plan that will formally launch the Human Escape Plan. This is a pressing matter."

Lao Zhang slowly nodded. "It does seem that way when you think about it. But I still feel like escape is a long way off. Should I really be worrying about it?"

"Uncle Zhang, you misunderstand. Escape can't be all that far off. Do you think the escape ships will only take off three or four hundred years from now? If that were true, then the Trisolaran Fleet could catch them easily."

"Then when will the ships head out?"

"You're about to have a grandson, right?"

"Yes."

"Your grandson will see those ships take off."

"He'll be aboard one?"

"No, that's impossible. But his grandson could be."

"That's . . ." Zhang worked it out. "About seventy or eighty years."

"It'll be longer than that. The wartime government will tighten population controls and build delays into the birth restrictions, so it'll be forty years to a generation. The ships will take off in about one hundred twenty years."

"That's pretty quick. Can they be built in time?"

"Uncle Zhang, think back to what things were like one hundred twenty years ago. It was still the Qing Dynasty! It took over a month to go from Hangzhou to Beijing, and the emperor had to spend days cooped up in a sedan chair to get to his summer retreat. Now it's less than three days from Earth to the moon. Technology develops

45

fast, which means that the pace of development is always on the increase. If you add to that the fact that the whole world is pouring all its energy into space technology, then there's no question at all that spaceships can be created in about one hundred twenty years."

"Isn't space travel pretty dangerous?"

"That's true, but won't Earth be dangerous then, too? Look at how things are changing now. The country's main economic force is being used to establish a space fleet, which is not a commercial good and will not bring in one cent in profit. People's lives will only get worse. Add to that the sheer size of our base population, and simply having enough to eat becomes a problem. And then take a look at the international situation. Developing countries don't have the ability to escape, and developed countries have refused to socialize their technology. But the poorer and smaller countries won't give up. Aren't they threatening to pull out of the Non-Proliferation Treaty? And they may take more extreme actions in the future. Who knows—in a hundred and twenty years, before the alien fleet even arrives, the world might be engulfed in the flames of war! Who knows what sort of life your great-grandson's generation will lead. Besides, the escape ships aren't what you imagine. Comparing them to the Shenzhou spaceship and the ISS is ridiculous. The ships will be big, each of them a small city, and a complete ecosystem to boot. Just like a tiny Earth. Humanity can live on them forever without any outside supplies. And most importantly, there will be hibernation. We can do that now, even. The passengers on board will spend most of their time in hibernation, where a century feels like no more than a day, until they reach the new world or they reach an accord with the Trisolarans to return to the Solar System. Then they'll wake up. Isn't that a much better life than suffering back on Earth?"

Zhang Yuanchao thought this over in silence.

Shi Xiaoming went on. "Of course, to be completely honest with you, space travel is indeed a dangerous thing. No one knows what sort of hazards they might encounter in space. I know you're mostly doing this for the continuation of your Zhang lineage, but don't let it worry you . . ."

Zhang stared at him as if he had been pricked. "How can you young people say things like that? Why wouldn't I worry?"

"Let me finish, Uncle Zhang. I don't mean it like that. I just mean that even if you don't plan on sending your descendants to flee in spaceships, this fund is worth buying, guaranteed. Once it's available for the general public to buy, the price will soar. There are lots of rich people, you know, and there aren't many other avenues for investment, and hoarding is illegal. Besides, the more money you have, the more you think about preserving your line, wouldn't you say?"

"Right. I know that."

"Uncle Zhang, I'm being totally honest here. The escape fund is currently in a preliminary phase and has only a small number of special internal salespeople. It wasn't easy for me to get in on the quota. At any rate, when you've thought it over, give me a call, and I'll help you fill out the paperwork."

When Shi Xiaoming had gone, Lao Zhang stood on the balcony looking out at the sky, which hung a little hazily over the halo of the city, and said to himself, *My children, will your grandpa really send you someplace where night lasts forever?*

When King Wen of Zhou next set foot onto the desolation of *Three Body* world, a small sun was rising. Although it did not give much heat, it lit the wasteland quite clearly. The wasteland was completely empty.

"Is there anyone here? Anyone?"

Then his eyes lit up as he saw someone riding a galloping horse from the horizon. Recognizing him at a distance as Newton, he ran toward him, waving wildly. Newton soon reached his side, reined in his horse, and, after dismounting, hurriedly adjusted his wig.

"What are you shouting for? Who restarted this damned place?"

King Wen didn't answer his question, but took his hand and said urgently, "Comrade, my comrade, listen to me. The Lord has not abandoned us. Or, rather, Its abandonment was for a reason, and It will need us in the future. It . . ."

"I know that," Newton said, impatiently brushing aside King Wen's hand. "The sophons sent me a message too."

"So that means that the Lord sent a message to lots of us at the same time. Excellent. The organization's contact with the Lord won't ever be monopolized again."

"Does the organization still exist?" Newton wiped away sweat with a handkerchief.

"Of course it exists. The Redemptionists totally collapsed after the global strike, and the Survivors split off and developed into an independent force. Only the Adventists are left in the org now."

"The strike purified the org. This is a good thing."

"Since you're here, you must be an Adventist. But you seem to be out of the loop. Are you on your own?"

"My only contact is with one other comrade, and he didn't tell me anything but this Web address. I barely escaped the awful global strike with my life."

"Your escape instincts were ably demonstrated during the Qin Shi Huang era."

Newton looked around. "Is it safe?"

"Of course. We're at the bottom of a multilevel maze, and it's practically impossible to discover. Anyone who managed to storm their way in here wouldn't be able to trace user locations. For security reasons, after the strike, the org put every branch into isolation with mutual contact kept to a minimum. We need a place to meet, and a buffer area for new members. This is more secure than the real world."

"Have you noticed that attacks on the organization in the real world have slackened considerably?"

"They're clever. They know the org is the only means of obtaining intelligence on the Lord, as well as the only opportunity of getting their hands on the technology that the Lord passes to us, even though there's only a minute chance of that happening. That's the reason they'll let the org continue to exist to a certain extent, but I think they'll come to regret it."

"The Lord isn't so clever. It doesn't even comprehend the ability to be clever."

"So It needs us. The existence of the org is valuable, and all comrades should know of this as soon as possible."

Newton mounted his horse. "Very well. I've got to go. I'll stay longer once I've verified that it's really secure here."

"I guarantee to you that it's absolutely safe."

"If that's true, then there'll be more comrades gathering here next time. Good-bye." Saying this, Newton urged his horse off into the distance. By the time its hoofbeats had dissipated, the small sun had become a shooting star, and a cloak of darkness descended upon the world.

Luo Ji lay limp on the bed, watching the woman put on clothes after a shower through eyes still hazy from sleep. The sun, already high in the sky, shone through the curtains and turned her into a graceful projected silhouette, like a scene from a black-and-white movie he had forgotten the name of. But what he needed to remember now was her name. What was she called? Keep calm. First, her last name: If it was Zhang, then she would be Zhang Shan. Or was it Chen? Then, Chen Jingjing . . . no, those were previous women. He thought about looking at his phone, but it was still in his pocket and he had tossed his clothes on the carpet. Besides, they had only known each other for a little while and he hadn't entered her number into his phone yet. The important thing now was not to have it be like that one time he'd asked outright—the consequences had been disastrous. So he turned to the television, which she had turned on and muted. On the screen, seated around a large round table, the UN Security Council was in session—wait, it wasn't the Security Council anymore, but he couldn't remember its new name. He was really out of it.

"Turn it up," he said. His words sounded distant without a term of endearment, but he didn't care about that now.

"You really seem to be interested." She sat combing her hair but didn't adjust the sound.

Luo Ji reached over to the bedside table and picked up a lighter

and a cigarette and lit it as he stretched his bare feet out of his towel and wiggled his big toes in satisfaction.

"Look at you. You call yourself a scholar?" She watched his wriggling toes in the mirror.

"A young scholar," he added, "with few accomplishments. But that's because I don't put in the effort. I'm actually full of inspiration. Sometimes, what other people might spend a lifetime working on, I can figure out with a moment's thought. . . . Believe it or not, I was almost famous once."

"Because of that subculture stuff?"

"No, not that. It was another thing I was working on at the same time. I established cosmic sociology."

"What?"

"It's the sociology of aliens."

She snickered, then tossed her comb aside and began putting on her makeup.

"Don't you know about the celebrity tendency in academia? I could've been a star."

"Alien researchers are a dime a dozen these days."

"That's only after all this new crap came out," Luo Ji said as he pointed at the mute television, which was still showing the large table and the people seated round it. The segment was awfully long. Was it live? "Academics didn't use to study aliens. They sifted through piles of old paper and become celebrities that way. But later the public got tired of the cultural necrophilia of that old crew, and that's when I came along." He stretched his bare arms toward the ceiling. "Cosmic sociology, aliens, and lots of alien races. More of them than there are people on Earth, tens of billions! The producer of that *Lecture Room* television program talked about doing a series with me, but then it all actually happened, and then . . ." He swept a circle with a finger, and sighed.

She wasn't listening too closely to him, reading the subtitles on the television instead: "'We reserve all options in regard to Escapism . . .' What does that mean?"

"Who's talking?"

"It looks like Karnoff."

"He's saying that Escapism needs to be treated as harshly as the ETO, and that a guided missile needs to be dropped on anyone making a Noah's Ark."

"That's kind of harsh."

"No," he said forcefully. "It's the wisest strategy. I came up with it long ago. And even if it doesn't come to that, no one's going to fly away, anyway. You ever read a book by Liang Xiaosheng called *Floating City*?"

"I haven't. It's pretty old, isn't it?"

"Right. I read it when I was a kid. Shanghai's about to fall into the ocean, and a group of people go house to house seizing life preservers and then destroying them en masse, for the sole purpose of making sure that no one would live if everyone couldn't. I remember in particular there was one little girl who took the group to the door of one house and cried out, 'They still have one!'"

"You're just the sort of asshole that always sees society as trash."

"Bullshit. The fundamental axiom of economics is the human mercenary instinct. Without that assumption, the entire field would collapse. There isn't any fundamental axiom for sociology yet, but it might be even darker than economics. The truth always picks up dust. A small number of people could fly off into space, but if we knew it would come to that, why would we have bothered in the first place?"

"Bothered with what?"

"Why would we have had the Renaissance? Why the Magna Carta? Why the French Revolution? If humanity had stayed divided into classes, kept in place by the law's iron rule, then when the time came, the ones who needed to leave would leave, and the ones who had to stay behind would stay. If this took place in the Ming or Qing Dynasties, then I'd leave, of course, and you'd stay behind. But that's not possible now."

"I wouldn't mind if you took off right now," she said.

Which was, in fact, the truth. They had reached a mutual parting of ways. He had been able to reach this point with all of his

previous lovers, never early or late. He was especially pleased with his control over the pace this time. He had known her for just one week, and the breakup proceeded smoothly, as elegantly as a rocket discarding its booster.

He backtracked to an earlier topic: "Hey, it wasn't my idea to establish cosmic sociology, you know. Do you want to know whose it was? You're the only one I'm going to tell, so don't get scared."

"Whatever. I can't believe most of what you say anyway, apart from one thing."

"Uh . . . forget it. What one thing?"

"Come on and get up. I'm hungry." She picked up his clothes from the carpet and threw them on the bed.

They ate breakfast in the main restaurant of the hotel. Most of the occupants of the tables around them looked serious, and at times they could catch snatches of conversation. Luo Ji didn't want to listen, but he was like a candle on a summer night. The words, like insects crowding around the flame, kept working their way into his head: Escapism, socialized technology, ETO, transformation to a wartime economy, equatorial base, charter amendment, PDC, near-Earth primary warning and defensive perimeter, independent integrated mode . . .

"Our age has gotten really dull, hasn't it?" Luo Ji said. He stopped cutting his egg and set down his fork.

She nodded. "I agree. I saw a game show question on TV yesterday that was really moronic. Hands on buzzers." She pointed a fork at Luo Ji in imitation of the host. "One hundred and twenty years before the doomsday, your thirteenth generation will be alive. True or false?"

Luo Ji picked up his fork again and shook his head. "It's not going to be any generation of mine." He folded his hands as if in prayer. "My grand family line will die out with me."

She gave a dismissive snort. "You asked me which of your lines I believe. That's the one. You've said it before. That's the sort of person you are."

So that's why she was leaving him? He didn't want to ask about

it for fear of complicating the issue, but she seemed to read his thoughts, and said, "I'm that sort of person too. It's really annoying to see certain things about yourself in other people."

"Particularly in a member of the opposite sex," Luo Ji said, nodding.

"But if you need to justify it, it's perfectly responsible behavior."

"What behavior? Not having kids? Of course it is." Luo Ji pointed his fork at the people around them discussing economic transformation. "You know what sort of lives their descendants will be living? They'll be spending their days slaving away in the shipyards—the spaceship yards—and then they'll line up at the canteen, bellies rumbling as they hold out their lunch pails waiting for that ladle of porridge . . . and when they're older, it'll be Uncle Sam Wants . . . no, Earth Wants You, and it's off to find glory in the army."

"It'll be better for the doomsday generation."

"Retiring to face doomsday. How miserable. And besides, that last generation's grandparents might not get enough to eat. Still, even *that* future's not going to come to pass. Just look at how stubborn the people of Earth are. I bet they resist till the end, at which point the real mystery is how they'll eventually die."

They left the hotel after their meal and emerged into the warm embrace of the morning sun. The air had a sweetness that was intoxicating.

"I've got to learn how to live. If I can't swing that, it'll be a damn shame," Luo Ji said as he watched the passing traffic.

"Neither of us is gonna learn," she said, her eyes searching for a taxi.

"Then . . ." Luo Ji looked inquiringly at her. Evidently there would be no need to remember her name.

"Good-bye." She nodded in his direction, and then they shook hands and shared a quick kiss.

"Maybe we'll meet again." He regretted this as soon as he said it. Everything had been fine up till this point, so why risk causing trouble? But his concern was unnecessary.

"I doubt it." She turned quickly as she spoke, sending the bag on her shoulder flying into the air, a detail that Luo Ji repeatedly called to mind afterward in an attempt to determine whether or not it had been deliberate. It was a distinctive LV bag, and he had seen her send it swinging while turning around many times before. But this time the bag swung straight at his face, and when he took a step backward to dodge it, he stumbled over the fire hydrant behind him and fell flat on his back.

That fall saved his life.

Meanwhile, the following was taking place on the street in front of them: Two cars collided head on, but before the noise of the impact had subsided, a Polo swerved to avoid the crash and came hurtling toward where the two of them were standing. Luo Ji's fall turned into a successful dodge. Only the front bumper of the Polo brushed one of his feet, the one that was still elevated, nudging his body into a ninety-degree turn on the ground so that he faced the back end of the car. He didn't hear the heavy thud of the other impact, but then he saw the woman's body soar over the top of the car and fall behind it on the road like a boneless rag doll. As it tumbled, the trail of blood it left behind on the ground seemed like it ought to mean something. As he stared at the bloody symbol, Luo Ji finally remembered her name.

Zhang Yuanchao's daughter-in-law was about to give birth. She had been moved into the delivery room while the rest of the family gathered in the waiting room outside, where a television was playing a video of mother and baby wellness information. It all gave him a feeling of warmth and humanity that he had never felt before, a lingering coziness of a past Golden Age being eroded by the ever worsening era of crisis.

Yang Jinwen came in. Zhang Yuanchao's first thought was that he was taking this opportunity to patch up their relationship, but Yang Jinwen's expression told him that wasn't the case. Without so much as a greeting, Yang Jinwen dragged him from the waiting

room into the hallway. "Did you really buy into the escape fund?" he asked.

Zhang Yuanchao ignored him and turned to go, as if to say, *That's none of your business.*

"Look at this," Yang Jinwen said, handing him a newspaper. "It's today's." The top headline stood out in black before his eyes:

Special UN Session Passes Resolution 117, Declares Escapism Illegal

Zhang Yuanchao carefully read through the start of the article underneath:

By an overwhelming majority, a special session of the United Nations General Assembly passed a resolution declaring Escapism a violation of international law. In strong language, the resolution condemned the division and turmoil that Escapism has created within human society, and described Escapism as a crime against humanity in the eyes of international law. The resolution called on member states to enact legislation as soon as possible to put a stop to Escapism.

In a statement, the Chinese delegate reiterated the stance of the Chinese government regarding Escapism and said that it firmly supports UN Resolution 117. He conveyed the Chinese government's pledge to take immediate action to establish and improve legislation, and to adopt effective measures to stop the spread of Escapism. He concluded by saying, "We must cherish the unity and solidarity of the international community in this time of crisis and uphold the principle, recognized by the international community, that all humanity has an equal right to survival. The Earth is the common home of its people, and we must not abandon her."

"Why . . . why are they doing this?" he stammered.

"Isn't it obvious? Put a little thought into it, and you'll realize that escape into the cosmos was never going to work. The critical question is who gets to leave, and who has to stay. This isn't

ordinary inequality. It's a question of survival, and no matter who gets to leave—elites, the rich, or ordinary people—so long as some people get left behind, it means the collapse of humanity's fundamental value system and ethical bottom line. Human rights and equality have deep roots. Inequality of survival is the worst sort of inequality, and the people and countries left behind will never just sit and wait for death while others have a way out. There will be increasingly extreme confrontations between the two sides until there's world chaos, and then no one goes! The UN resolution is quite wise. How much did you spend, Lao Zhang?"

Zhang Yuanchao scrambled for his phone. He called Shi Xiaoming's number, but it was unreachable. His legs threatened to give out, and he slid down the wall to sit on the ground. He had spent 400,000 yuan[7].

"Call the police! There's one thing that that Shi kid doesn't know: Lao Miao looked up his daddy's work unit. The scammer won't get away."

Zhang Yuanchao just sat there shaking his head. He said with a sigh, "Sure, we can find him, but the money's long gone. What'll I say to my family?"

There was the sound of crying, and then a nurse shouted, "Number nineteen. It's a boy!" Zhang Yuanchao bounded off into the waiting room as everything else suddenly became insignificant.

In the thirty minutes that he had been waiting, ten thousand new babies had come into the world, babies whose combined cries formed a tremendous chorus. Behind them was the Golden Age, the good times that began in the 1980s and ended with the Crisis. Ahead of them, humanity's arduous years were about to unfold.

All Luo Ji knew was that he was locked in a tiny basement room. The basement was deep, and he had felt the descent of the elevator (one of those rare old-style elevators with a manually operated

7 *Translator's Note:* Roughly equivalent to $65,000 in early 2015.

lever) even as the mechanism confirmed his sensations, counting backward to negative ten. Ten levels below ground! Once again he took stock of his small room. The twin bed, simple furnishings, and an ancient wooden writing desk gave the place the look of a guard room, not a prison cell. Clearly no one had been here for quite some time, and although the bedclothes were new, the rest of the furniture was covered in dust and gave off a dank, musty smell.

The door opened and a stocky middle-aged man entered. He nodded wearily at Luo Ji. "Dr. Luo, I'm here to keep you company, but since you've just come over I don't expect you're climbing the walls just yet."

Just come over. The phrase grated—surely "sent down" would have been more accurate. Luo Ji's heart sank. His guess had been confirmed, it seemed: Although the men who had brought him here had been polite, it was clear he had been arrested.

"Are you a policeman?"

The man nodded. "Used to be. Name's Shi Qiang." He sat down on the bed and pulled out a pack of cigarettes. *The smoke wouldn't have any place to dissipate in this sealed room,* Luo Ji thought, but he didn't dare say anything. As if reading his mind, Shi Qiang looked around and said, "There ought to be a ventilation fan." Then he pulled a cord next to the door, and a fan started humming. It was pretty rare to see a pull-cord switch. Luo Ji also noticed an obsolete red rotary phone lying in a corner, covered in dust. Shi Qiang handed him a cigarette, which he accepted after a moment's hesitation.

When they had lit their cigarettes, Shi Qiang said, "It's early yet. Shall we chat?"

"Ask away," Luo Ji said, head down as he exhaled a cloud of smoke.

"Ask what?" Shi Qiang said, looking at Luo Ji in surprise.

Luo Ji jumped up from the bed and tossed the cigarette aside. "How can you suspect me? You've got to know it was just a traffic accident! The two cars collided, and then she was hit by the one behind them as it tried to avoid the crash. It's plain as day." He held out his hands, at a loss for words.

Shi Qiang raised his head and looked at him, his tired eyes suddenly alert, as if an invisible malice, honed with practice, were hidden behind the smile he usually wore. "You said that, not me. My superiors don't want me to say anything more, and I don't know anything more. To think I was worried we wouldn't have anything to talk about. Come, sit down."

Luo Ji didn't sit down. He got in Shi Qiang's face and continued: "I'd only known her for a week. We met at a bar next to the university, and when the accident happened I couldn't even remember her name. Tell me, what could there possibly have been between us to lead your thoughts in that direction?"

"You couldn't even remember her name? No wonder you didn't care at all when she died. You're pretty much the same as another genius I know." He chuckled. "The wonderful life of Dr. Luo, meeting a new woman every time you turn around. And what women they are!"

"Is that a crime?"

"Of course not. I'm just jealous. I've got one rule in my work: Never make moral judgments. The guys I've got to deal with, they're the real deal. If I go and nag them, 'Look at what you've done! Think about your parents, and about society . . .' and so on, I might as well be slapping them across the face."

"I'd rather talk about her, Officer Shi. Do you really believe I killed her?"

"Look at you, bringing up the issue on your own. Saying you may have killed her, even. We're just having a casual chat. What's your hurry? You're new at this, that much is clear."

Luo Ji stared at Shi Qiang, and for a moment the hum of the fan was the only audible sound. Then he cackled and picked up his cigarette. "Luo, my man," Shi Qiang said. "Luo, my boy. Destiny's brought us together. You know, I've been involved in sixteen cases that ended in the death penalty. I personally escorted nine of them."

Luo Ji handed a cigarette to Shi Qiang. "I'm not going to let you escort me. So, if you'll be so good as to notify my lawyer."

"Excellent, my boy," Shi Qiang said, clapping Luo Ji on the

shoulder. "Decisiveness is a trait I admire." Then he drew up close to him and said, through a cloud of smoke, "You can come across all sorts of things, but what's happened to you is really . . ." He trailed off. "Actually, I'm here to help. You know how the joke goes: On the way to the execution ground, a condemned criminal complained that it was going to rain, and the executioner said, 'What have you got to worry about? We're the ones who've got to go back through it!' That's the attitude you and I ought to have for what comes next. Well, then. There's still some time before we get going. Might as well get some sleep."

"Get going?" Again, Luo Ji stared at Shi Qiang.

There was a knock at the door, and then a keen-eyed young man entered and dropped a suitcase on the ground. "Captain Shi, it's been moved ahead. We're leaving now."

Zhang Beihai gently pushed open the door to his father's hospital room. Half-reclining against a pillow on the bed, his father looked better than he had imagined. The golden rays of the setting sun that shone in through the window gave his face some color and made him look less like a man at death's door. Zhang Beihai set his hat on the coatrack by the door and took a seat beside his father's bed. He didn't ask about his condition, because the old soldier would give him a straight answer, and he didn't want a straight answer.

"Dad, I've joined the space force."

His father nodded but said nothing. For father and son, the silence conveyed more information than words. Growing up, his father had used silence rather than speech to educate him, and words were merely the punctuation between the silences. It was his silent father who had made him into the man he was today.

"Just like you thought, they're building the space fleet on a naval foundation. They believe space warfare will be closest in form and theory to naval warfare."

His father nodded. "Very good."

"So what should I do?"

I've finally asked it, Dad. The question I spent a sleepless night gathering the resolve to ask. I hesitated just now when I saw you, because I know it's the question that will disappoint you the most. I remember when I finished grad school and joined the fleet as a cadet lieutenant, you told me, "Beihai, you've got a long way to go. I say that because I can still easily understand you, and being understandable to me means that your mind is still too simple, not subtle enough. On the day I can no longer read you or figure you out, but you can easily understand me, that's when you'll finally have grown up." And then I grew up like you said, and you could no longer so easily understand your son. I know you must have felt at least some sorrow at that. But your son is indeed becoming the kind of person you'd hoped for, someone not particularly likeable, but capable of succeeding in the complicated and dangerous realm of the navy. For me to ask this question surely means that the training you've given me for three decades has failed at the crucial juncture. But Dad, tell me anyway. Your son is not as great as you imagine. Tell me, just this once.

"Think some more," his father said.

Fine, Dad. You've given me an answer. They've told me quite a lot, those three words, more than could be said in thirty thousand. Believe me, I'm listening to them with my whole heart, but I still need you to be clearer, because this is far too important.

"And after I've thought?" Zhang Beihai asked, gripping the bedsheet with both hands. His palms and forehead were laced with sweat.

Dad, forgive me. If I disappointed you the last time, then let me go further, go back to being a kid once more.

"Beihai, all I can say is to think long and hard first," his father replied.

Thank you, Dad. You've made it very clear, and I understand.

Zhang Beihai let go of the sheet and grasped his father's bony hand. "Dad, I'm not going to sea anymore. I'll come and see you all the time."

His father smiled but shook his head: "This isn't anything serious. Concentrate on your work."

They spoke for a while longer, first of family matters, and then about the establishment of the space force, with his father contributing lots of ideas of his own, including advice for Zhang Beihai's future work. They imagined the shape and size of space battleships, debated the weaponry of space warfare, and even whether Mahan's theory of sea power applied to space battles. . . .

But there was little significance in their conversation, just father and son taking a verbal stroll together. The significance was in the three lines their hearts exchanged:

"Think some more."

"And after I've thought?"

"Beihai, all I can say is to think long and hard first."

Zhang Beihai said good-bye to his father. As he was leaving the room, he turned back at the door to look at him, shrouded in shadow now that the light of the setting sun had departed. His eyes pierced the shadows and noticed one last scrap of illumination on the wall opposite. Although it was about to fade, this was the time when the setting sun was at its most beautiful. The last rays of sunlight shone, too, on the waves that rolled endlessly on the angry ocean and in shafts of light that pierced the jumbled clouds in the west and cast enormous golden bands on the water's surface like petals fallen from heaven. Beyond the petals, dark clouds loomed over a world black as night as a thunderstorm hung between heaven and earth like the curtain of the gods, and only periodic lightning lit the snowlike spray thrown up by the waves. In one golden band, a destroyer struggled to lift its prow from the trough, and then broke through the wall of the wave with a thunderous crash, the spray greedily absorbing the light like a giant roc stretching enormous glittering wings to the sky.

Zhang Beihai put on his cap, which bore the insignia of the Chinese Space Force. He said to himself, *Dad, we think alike. This is my good fortune. I won't bring you glory, but I'll give you rest.*

"Mr. Luo, please change into this," said the young man, who knelt down to open a suitcase upon entering the room. Though the man seemed entirely polite, Luo Ji couldn't shake a certain discomfort, like he had swallowed a fly. But when he saw the clothing the man took out, he realized that he wouldn't be wearing a convict's uniform: It looked like an ordinary brown jacket. He took it and inspected the thick material. Shi Qiang and the young man put on similar jackets in different colors.

"Put it on. It's comfortable and it breathes. Not like the old stuff we used to wear, which was sticky as hell," Shi Qiang said.

"Bulletproof," the young man said.

Who would want to kill me? Luo Ji thought as he changed jackets.

The three of them left the room and followed the corridor to the elevator. The ceiling was lined with rectangular metal ductwork and they passed several heavy, sealed doorways. Luo Ji noticed a faint slogan on one of the mottled walls. Only part of it was visible, but he knew the whole slogan: "Dig deep tunnels, keep vast stores of grain, don't seek hegemony."[8]

"Civil Air Defense?" he asked.

"Not the ordinary kind. Defense against the atom bomb, but it's obsolete now. Back in the day, you had to be someone special to get in here."

"So we're at . . . the Western Hills?" Luo Ji asked, but Shi Qiang and the young man did not reply. Luo Ji had heard stories about the secret command center. They entered the old-style elevator and began to ascend immediately, accompanied by a tremendous scraping. The operator was a People's Armed Police soldier armed with a submachine gun. This seemed to be his first time at this job, and he had to fiddle with the controls a bit before the elevator finally stopped at floor 1.

8 *Translator's Note:* Vast networks of tunnels were built in cities across China beginning in the late 1960s as defensive measures against enemy attack. This slogan, adapted from advice given to the founder of the Ming Dynasty, was promulgated as a directive from Mao Zedong in the *People's Daily*'s annual New Year's Editoral in January 1973.

Exiting the elevator, Luo Ji saw that they were in a large hall with a low ceiling, like an underground parking garage. A number of different cars were parked here, some of them with engines on, filling the air with noxious exhaust. People were standing beside the lines of cars or walking among them. With only one light in a distant corner turned on, the place was dim and the people dark shadows. Only when they passed the lamplight did Luo Ji see that they were fully armed soldiers. Some were shouting into radios, trying to be heard over the engine noise. Their voices sounded tense.

Shi Qiang led Luo Ji through the two lines of cars, with the young man close behind. The lamplight and red taillights shining though the gaps in the cars cast an ever-changing pattern of color on Shi Qiang's body and reminded Luo Ji of the dim bar where he had met the woman.

Shi Qiang led Luo Ji to one car, opened the door, and had him get in. The car was roomy, but the edges of its abnormally tiny windows revealed the thickness of the car's body. A reinforced vehicle with tinted glass in its small windows, probably as an antibomb measure. The car door was ajar, and Luo Ji could hear Shi Qiang and the young man talking.

"Captain Shi, they called just now to say they've been over the route. All guard positions have been set up."

"The route is too complicated. We've only been able to do a couple of quick runs through the whole thing. Not enough for comfort. And about the guard positions—it's like I said, you've got to think like them. If you were on their side, where would you be hiding? Consult with the experts from the People's Armed Police again. Hey, what's the plan for the handoff?"

"They didn't say."

Shi Qiang raised his voice. "Morons. They can't leave such an important part up in the air."

"Captain Shi, it looks like the brass want us to follow along the entire way."

"I can follow along my entire life, but since there's got to be a handoff once we're there, there needs to be a clear demarcation of

responsibilities. There's got to be a line. Anything that happens before it is on us, and afterward on them."

"They didn't say . . ." The young man sounded uncomfortable.

"Zheng, I know you've been feeling sorry for yourself since Chang Weisi got promoted. Hell, it's like we don't even exist to his former subordinates. But we should have some self-respect. Who the fuck are they? Have they been under fire, or have they ever fired at anyone? That crew used so many high-tech tricks in the last operation it was like a circus. They even brought out the airborne early warning system. But in the end, who did they use to find the meeting place? Us. That won us some cred. Zheng, it took a lot of convincing to get the lot of you over here, but I wonder if that might not end up causing you harm."

"Captain Shi, don't say that."

"It's a troubled world. Do you get that? Morality isn't what it used to be. Everyone foists their bad luck off onto other people, so you've got to be on your guard. . . . I'm going on like this because I'm worried about how long I'm going to last. I'm afraid that all of it's going to land in your lap."

"Captain Shi, you've really got to think about your illness. Didn't the higher-ups schedule you for hibernation?"

"I've got to get lots of things taken care of first. Family, work. And do you think I'm not worried about the lot of you here?"

"Don't worry about us. With your condition, you can't put it off. Your teeth were bleeding out again this morning."

"That's nothing. I've got good luck. You should know. Three of the guns I've been shot at with were duds."

The cars at one end of the hall were beginning to pull out. Shi Qiang got in and closed the door, and when the neighboring car started to move, their car followed. Shi Qiang pulled the curtains closed on either side, and the opaque divider between the back and front seats totally obscured Luo Ji's view of the outside. As they rode, Shi Qiang's radio chirped endlessly, but Luo Ji couldn't make out the comments Shi Qiang was replying to in clipped sentences.

When they had ridden a short way, Luo Ji said to Shi Qiang, "Things are more complicated than you said."

"That's right. Everything's complicated now," Shi Qiang said perfunctorily, his attention still focused on the radio. They spoke no more for the rest of the trip.

The ride was smooth and unbroken, and after about an hour they came to a stop.

When Shi Qiang got out of the car, he motioned to Luo Ji to wait inside, and then closed the door. Luo Ji heard a rumbling that seemed to come from above the vehicle. After a few minutes, Shi Qiang opened the door again and had Luo Ji get out, at which point he realized they were at an airport. The rumbling had turned thunderous. He looked up to see two helicopters hovering overhead, oriented in opposite directions like they were monitoring the open area. In front of him was a large aircraft that looked like a passenger plane, except that there was no insignia on any part he could see. An airstair stood in front of the car door, and Shi Qiang and Luo Ji took it up to the aircraft. When Luo Ji glanced back out the door after they entered, the first thing that caught his eye were the fighter jets lined up on a distant apron, which informed him that this wasn't a civilian airport. Closer in, he saw the cars from their convoy and the soldiers that had exited their vehicles in a ring around the plane. The sun was setting, casting a long shadow down the runway ahead of the plane, like a giant exclamation point.

Luo Ji and Shi Qiang entered the cabin. Three men in black suits welcomed them and took them past the forward cabin, which was totally empty but resembled a passenger plane with four rows of seats. In the middle cabin, Luo Ji saw a fairly spacious office, and another suite through whose half-open door he glimpsed a bedroom. The furnishings were unremarkable but neat and orderly, and apart from the green safety belts on the sofa and chairs you wouldn't have known you were on a plane. Luo Ji knew that there were very few charter planes of this kind in the country.

Two of the three men who led them in vanished through a door to the rear cabin, leaving behind the youngest one, who said,

"You can sit anywhere you like, but you need to buckle up, not just on takeoff and landing but throughout the entire flight. If you sleep, then buckle the sleep-belt too. Nothing that's not fixed in place can be left out in the open. Stay in your seat or bunk at all times, and if you must move about, please inform the captain first. This is an intercom button. There's one at every seat and every bunk. Hold it down to talk. If there's anything you need, please use it to call us at any time."

Luo Ji looked in confusion at Shi Qiang, who said, "The plane may execute some special maneuvers."

The man nodded. "Correct. Please let me know if you have any problems. Call me Xiao Zhang. I'll bring you dinner when we're in the air."

After Xiao Zhang left, Luo Ji and Shi Qiang sat on the sofa and fastened their seatbelts. Luo Ji looked about him. Apart from the round windows and the slightly curved walls they were set into, the room seemed so conventional and familiar that it felt a little strange to be wearing seatbelts in an ordinary office. But soon the noise and vibration of the engine reminded him he was aboard a plane taxiing down the runway, and a few minutes later the engine noise changed and the two of them were pressed back into the sofa. Then the ground vibrations disappeared and the office floor took on a slant. As the plane climbed, the sun, which had already dipped below the ground, returned through the window, just as the same sun had sent the day's final rays of sunlight into the hospital room of Zhang Beihai's father just ten minutes before.

By the time Luo Ji's plane reached the coast, Wu Yue and Zhang Beihai were once again looking over the unfinished *Tang*, ten thousand meters below. This was the closest he would ever get to the two soldiers.

As on their previous visit, *Tang*'s enormous frame was shrouded in the dim light of dusk. The showers of sparks on the hull didn't seem quite as plentiful, and the lamps illuminating the ship had

dimmed substantially. And this time, Wu Yue and Zhang Beihai no longer belonged to the navy.

"I heard the General Armaments Department has decided to terminate the *Tang* project," Zhang Beihai said.

"What's that got to do with us?" Wu Yue said coldly, his eyes sweeping from *Tang* to the last bits of sunset in the west.

"You've been in a bad mood since joining the space force."

"You should know the reason. You can always read my thoughts, sometimes more clearly than I can, and then you remind me what it is I'm really thinking about."

Zhang Beihai turned to Wu Yue. "You're depressed about joining what's inevitably a losing war. You're jealous of that final generation that will be young enough to fight in the space force at the end and be buried in the cosmos together with their fleet. Devoting a lifetime of effort to a hopeless endeavor is hard for you to accept."

"Do you have any advice?"

"No. Technofetishism and technological triumphalism are deeply rooted in your mind, and I learned long ago that I can't change you. I can only try to minimize the harm that sort of thinking can cause. Besides, I don't think it's impossible for humanity to win this war."

Wu Yue dropped his cold mask and met Zhang Beihai's gaze. "Beihai, you used to be a practical person. You opposed building *Tang,* and on multiple occasions, on the record, voiced doubts about building a blue-water navy, arguing that it was incompatible with our national strength. You believe that our naval forces ought to remain in coastal waters under the support and protection of shore-based firepower, an idea ridiculed as a turtle-shell strategy by the young hotheads, but you've persisted in it. . . . So where do you get your confidence in a space victory from now? Do you really believe that wooden boats can sink an aircraft carrier?"

"After independence, the newly founded navy used wooden boats to sink Nationalist destroyers. And even earlier, there were times when our army used cavalry to defeat tanks."

"You can't seriously think those miracles count as ordinary military theory."

"On this battlefield, terrestrial civilization won't need to follow commonplace, ordinary military theory." Zhang Beihai held up a finger. "One exception is sufficient."

Wu Yue shot him a mocking smile. "I'd like to hear how you'll achieve this exception."

"I don't know anything about space warfare, of course, but if you want to compare it to a wooden boat versus a carrier, then I think it's just a matter of having the courage to act and the confidence in a victory. A wooden boat could carry a small squad of divers who'll wait in the carrier's path. When the enemy draws near, they'll dive in and the boat will leave. Then when the carrier comes close, they'll attach a bomb to the bottom of the hull and sink the carrier. . . . Of course this would be exceedingly difficult, but it's not impossible."

Wu Yue nodded. "Not bad. People have tried it before. In the Second World War, the British did that as part of the effort to sink the *Tirpitz,* only they used a minisub. In the 1980s, during the Malvinas War, a few Argentine special forces soldiers took Italian limpet mines into Spain and attempted to blow up a British warship docked in the harbor at Gibraltar. You know what happened to them."

"But what we have is not just a small wooden boat. A one- or two-thousand-ton nuclear bomb can be made small enough for one or two divers to take underwater, and when it's attached to the underside of a carrier, it won't just sink it, it'll blow the whole carrier to smithereens."

"Sometimes you've got a fantastic imagination," Wu Yue said with a smile.

"I've got confidence in our victory." Zhang Beihai looked out at *Tang,* the distant shower of welding sparks reflected in his pupils like two small flames.

Wu Yue too looked out at *Tang,* and a new vision took hold of him: The ship was no longer a ruined ancient fortress but a

prehistoric cliff with a multitude of deep caves carved into it, and the scattered sparks were flickering firelight in those caves.

After takeoff and all through dinner, Luo Ji refrained from asking Shi Qiang anything about where they were headed, or what exactly had happened, reasoning that if Shi Qiang was going to tell him anything, he would already have come out with it. Once, he unbuckled his seatbelt and got up to look out the cabin window, even though he knew he would see nothing through the darkness, but Shi Qiang followed him and pulled down the window shade, saying that there was nothing to see out there.

"Why don't we chat for a while longer, and then go to sleep. What do you say?" asked Shi Qiang as he drew out a cigarette, then quickly put it back, remembering he was on a plane.

"Sleep? So this is a long flight?"

"Who cares? It's a plane with beds. I say we take advantage of them."

"You're only responsible for taking me to my destination, right?"

"What are you complaining for? We've still got to make the return trip!" Shi Qiang grinned broadly, as if immensely pleased with himself. Cutting humor seemed to give him pleasure. But then he turned more serious: "I don't know much more about your trip than you do. Besides, it's not yet time for me to tell you anything. Take it easy. There'll be someone at the handoff to explain things to you."

"I've been guessing for hours, but I've only come up with one possible explanation."

"Let me hear it, and let's see if it's the same as what I'm thinking."

"The woman who died was an ordinary person, so that means her social or family connections had to be something special." Luo Ji didn't know anything about her family, just like his previous lovers. He wasn't interested, and forgot whatever they told him.

"Who? Oh, that lover of yours? Put her out of your mind, since you don't care anyway. Or, if you want, why not compare her name and face to some famous figures?"

Luo Ji's mind flipped through comparisons, but nothing matched.

"Luo, my man, can you bluff?" Shi Qiang asked. Luo had noticed a pattern in how he addressed him. When he was joking, he called him "my boy," but when he was a little more serious, it was "my man."

"Do I need to bluff against someone?"

"Of course you do. . . . So how about I teach you how to bluff? Of course, I'm not a master of it either. My work is more along the lines of breaking scams. Here, I'll tell you a few tricks for the interrogation room. You might find it useful later to figure out what's going on. Naturally, these are just the most basic, common ones. It's hard to explain anything more complicated. We'll start with the gentlest one, which happens to be the simplest: The List. That means drawing up a whole list of questions connected to the case, and then asking them one by one and recording the subject's answers, and then starting over again from the top and recording those answers too. Questions can be asked repeatedly if necessary, and then you can compare the transcripts of the answers and find out if the subject is lying about something, since the answers will be different every time. The technique is simple, but don't look down your nose at it. No one who hasn't undergone training in counter-interrogation techniques will be able to pass it, so the most effective way of dealing with The List is simply to remain silent." Shi Qiang fiddled unconsciously with his cigarette as he spoke, but then put it away again.

"Ask them. It's a charter flight, so they ought to allow smoking," Luo Ji said.

Shi Qiang had grown excited while speaking and seemed a little put out at Luo Ji's interruption. It occurred to Luo Ji that he might be serious, or else he had an odd sense of humor. Shi Qiang pressed the red intercom button beside the sofa, and Xiao Zhang told him he could do what he liked. So the two of them lit up.

"The next technique is only half-gentle. You can reach the ashtray—it's fixed in place, you've just got to pull it up. Right. This technique is called Black and White. It requires the cooperation

of lots of people and is a little more complicated. First, the bad cops come out, at least two of them on most occasions, and they're really nasty to you. Some of them verbally and others physically, but they're all mean. There's a strategy to it: not just to make you afraid, but more importantly to make you feel alone, to make you feel like the whole world wants to consume you. Then the good cop comes out, just one, and he's got a kind face, and he stops the bad cops and tells them that you're a human being, that you've got rights, so how can they treat you that way? The bad cops tell him to beat it, that he's affecting their work. The good cop persists, and says, 'You can't do this!' The bad cops say, 'I always knew you didn't have the stones for this work. If you can't handle it, then get lost.' The good cop shields you with his body, and says, 'I'm going to protect his rights, and protect justice under the law!' The bad cops say, 'Tomorrow you're out of here, just you wait!' Then they leave in a huff. So it's just the two of you left, and the good cop wipes off your blood and sweat and tells you not to be afraid, and that you have the right to be silent! Then, as you can imagine, he becomes your one friend in the world, so when he draws you out, you aren't silent anymore. . . . This technique is most effective against intellectuals, but it differs from The List in that it loses its effect when you're aware of it."

He spoke animatedly and seemed about to take off his seatbelt and stand up. Luo Ji was seized by dread and despair and felt as if he had fallen into an ice pit. Noticing his discomfort, Shi Qiang stopped. "Well, then, let's not talk about interrogation, even if it might be useful to you. You can't take it in all at once. Besides, I was going to tell you how to trick people, so just remember this: Real shrewdness means not letting any shrewdness show. It's not like in the movies. The truly astute don't sit in the shadows all day striking a pose. They don't show off that they're using their brains. They look all carefree and innocent. Some of them are tacky and mawkish, others careless and unserious. What's critical is not to let others think you're a person of interest. Let them look down on you or dismiss you and they won't feel you're an obstacle. You're

just a broom in the corner. The pinnacle of this is to make them not notice you at all, as if you don't exist until the moment right before they die at your hands."

"Will I ever have the need or opportunity to become that sort of person?" Luo Ji broke in to ask.

"Like I said, I know no more about this than you do. But I've got a premonition that you need to become such a person. Luo, my man, you've got to!" Shi Qiang grew excited again and clapped him on the shoulder with enough force to make him wince.

Then they sat in silence watching the clouds of smoke curl upward to the ceiling, where they were sucked away into a crack.

"Screw it. Let's hit the sack," Shi Qiang said as he ground out his cigarette in the ashtray. He shook his head with a smile. "I've been going on like an idiot. When you think back on this, don't laugh at me."

In the bedroom, Luo Ji took off his bulletproof jacket and wrapped himself in the safety sleeping bag. Shi Qiang helped him tighten the straps holding it to the bed, and then set down a small vial on the bedside cabinet.

"Sleeping pills. Take them if you can't sleep. I asked for alcohol, but they said there isn't any."

Shi Qiang reminded Luo Ji that he should notify the captain before getting out of bed, then turned to leave.

"Officer Shi," Luo Ji called after him.

At the door, Shi Qiang half-turned back to look at him. "I'm not any sort of cop. The police aren't involved in this thing. Everyone calls me Da Shi."

"Well then, Da Shi, when we were talking just now, I noticed the first thing you said. Or, I guess, the first thing you said in reply to me. I said, 'the woman,' and you didn't realize for a moment who I was talking about. That means that she's not a major part of this case."

"You're one of the calmest people I've ever met."

"The calmness comes from cynicism. There's not much in the world that can make me care."

"Whatever it is, I've never seen someone who could stay calm

in a situation like this. Forget all that stuff I said before. I just like to kid around about things."

"You're just looking for something to hold my attention so that you can smoothly complete your mission."

"If I've set your imagination going, I apologize."

"What do you think I should think about now?"

"In my experience, any thinking is liable to go off the rails. You should just go to sleep."

Shi Qiang left. After he closed the door, the room was dark except for a small red lamp at the head of the bed. The ever-present background rumble of the engine was particularly conspicuous, as if the infinite night sky on the other side of the wall was emitting a deep hum.

Then Luo Ji felt that it wasn't an illusion, that the sound really was coming from some far-off place outside. He unbuckled the sleeping bag and crawled out, then pushed up the shade over the window by the bed. Outside, the moon was shining on a sea of clouds, a vast ocean of silver. Luo Ji realized that above the clouds were other things shining with a silver light, four ramrod-straight lines that caught the eye against the backdrop of the night sky. They were extending at the same speed as the plane, and their trailing ends faded out and blended into the night like four silver swords flying over the clouds. Luo Ji looked back at the tips and noticed that the silver lines were being drawn out by four objects with a metallic glint. Four fighter jets. It wasn't hard to guess that another four were on the other side of the plane.

Luo Ji pulled down the shade and burrowed back into the sleeping bag. He closed his eyes and willed his mind to relax. He didn't want to sleep, but to wake up from his dream.

In the dead of night, the space force work meeting was still in progress. Zhang Beihai pushed aside the notebook and documents that lay on the desk in front of him and stood up, scanning the tired faces of the officers before turning toward Chang Weisi.

"Commander, before we report on our work, I'd first like to share some of my own views. I believe that the military leadership has not paid sufficient attention to political and ideological work among the forces. For example, the political department is the last of the six established departments to present its report at this meeting."

Chang Weisi nodded. "I concur. The political commissars have not yet reported for duty, so it's fallen to me to oversee political work. Now that we've finally begun work in all areas, it's difficult to give it enough attention. For the bulk of the work, we'll have to rely on you and the others who are in charge of specifics."

"Commander, in my opinion, the present situation is dangerous." This remark drew the attention of several officers, and Zhang Beihai continued. "Please forgive me for speaking pointedly. For one thing, we've been in meetings all day and we're all tired, so no one will listen if I'm not blunt." A few people laughed, but the rest were still mired in their fatigue. "More importantly, I'm truly worried. The battle we are facing has a force disparity unprecedented in the history of human warfare, so I believe that for the indefinite future the greatest danger facing the space force is defeatism. Its threat can't be overstated. The spread of defeatism will not only result in an erosion of morale, but may lead to the total collapse of space-based military power."

Chang Weisi nodded again. "I agree. Defeatism is our greatest enemy at present. The military commission is acutely aware of this. It's why political and ideological work in the services will be critical. Once the basic units of the space force are in place, the work will become more complex."

Zhang Beihai flipped open his notebook. "The work report follows," he said, and began to read: "Since the establishment of the space force, our primary focus in political and ideological work among the troops has been to conduct a survey of the overall ideological status of officers and soldiers. Since the organization of this new branch is simple at the present time, with few members and few administrative levels, the survey was conducted through informal meetings and personal interaction, and a corresponding

forum was set up on the intranet. The results of the survey are worrying. Defeatist thinking is prevalent and spreading swiftly among the troops. The mentality of a sizeable proportion of our comrades consists of terror toward the enemy and a lack of confidence in the future of war.

"The source of this defeatism stems primarily from the worship of technology, and the underestimation or complete dismissal of the role of human initiative and the human spirit in war. It is a development and extension of techno-triumphalism and the 'weapons decide everything' theory that has cropped up in the armed forces in recent years. The trend is particularly pronounced among highly educated officers. Defeatism among the troops takes the following forms:

"One. Treating one's duty in the space force as an ordinary job: despite working with dedication and responsibility, lacking enthusiasm and sense of mission and doubting the ultimate significance of one's work.

"Two. Passive waiting: believing that the outcome of the war depends on scientists and engineers; believing that prior to breakthroughs in basic research and key technologies, the space force is just a pipe dream, and subsequent confusion about the importance of its present work; being satisfied simply with completing tasks related to establishing this military branch; lacking innovation.

"Three. Harboring unrealistic fantasies: requesting to use hibernation technology to leap four centuries into the future and take part in the Doomsday Battle directly. A number of younger comrades have already expressed this wish, and one has even submitted a formal application. On the surface, this is a positive state of mind, a desire to throw oneself onto the front lines, but it is essentially just another form of defeatism. Lacking confidence in victory and doubting the significance of our present work, a soldier's dignity becomes the only pillar sustaining work and life.

"Four. The opposite of the above: doubts about the dignity of the soldier, the belief that the military's traditional moral code is no longer suitable for the battlefield, and that fighting to the end

has no meaning; the belief that a soldier's dignity only exists when there is someone to see it, and when a battle ends in defeat and no humans are left in the universe, then this dignity loses its significance. Although only a minority hold this notion, the abrogation of the very worth of the space force is exceedingly harmful."

Here Zhang Beihai looked out at the assembly and saw that although his speech had attracted some interest, it still hadn't managed to shake the fatigue from the meeting hall. He was confident that what he had to say next would change the situation.

"I'll give you a specific example of a comrade who exhibits a typical form of defeatism. I am referring to Colonel Wu Yue." Zhang Beihai held out his hand in the direction of Wu Yue's seat at the conference table.

The tiredness of the room was swept away and the attendees pricked up their ears. Everyone looked nervously at Zhang Beihai and then at Wu Yue, who gazed placidly back, the picture of calmness.

"Wu Yue and I have worked together in the navy for quite some time and we know each other very well. He has a strong technology complex, and as a captain he is a technical type, or, if you want, an engineer. This in itself isn't a bad thing, but unfortunately, his military thinking is over-reliant on technology, and while he doesn't come out and say it, he subconsciously believes that technological advancement is the primary and perhaps sole determinant of combat effectiveness. He completely neglects the human role in battle, particularly in his lack of understanding of the unique advantages formed in our army by difficult historical conditions. When he learned of the Trisolar Crisis, he lost all confidence in the future, and once he joined the space force, this despair only became more pronounced. Comrade Wu Yue's defeatist sentiment is so heavy and ingrained that we have no hope of pulling him out of it. We must adopt strong measures as soon as possible to arrest the spread of defeatism in the troops, and therefore I believe that Comrade Wu Yue is no longer suitable for work in the space force."

All eyes were on Wu Yue, who was now looking at the space force emblem on his hat lying on the table. He remained calm as before.

Throughout the course of his speech, Zhang Beihai had not even glanced in Wu Yue's direction. He continued: "Commander, Comrade Wu Yue, and the rest of you, I ask for your understanding. I say this only out of concern for the present ideological state of the troops. Of course, I also hope to engage Wu Yue in face-to-face, frank, and open discussion."

Wu Yue raised a hand requesting permission to speak, and at a nod from Chang Weisi, he said, "What Comrade Zhang Beihai has said about my mental state is accurate, and I accept his conclusion: I am no longer fit to serve in the Space Force. I will abide by whatever the organization arranges."

The atmosphere turned tense. Several officers looked at the notebook in front of Zhang Beihai, wondering who else its contents might concern.

One senior colonel in the air force got up and said, "Comrade Zhang Beihai, this is an ordinary work meeting. You ought to go through the proper organizational channels instead of bringing up issues like this. Do you think it's appropriate to talk about this openly?"

His words were immediately echoed by many of the other officers.

Zhang Beihai said, "I know that my remarks violate organizational principles, and I am prepared to accept all responsibility. However, I do believe that I must, by whatever means, bring the seriousness of our current situation to your attention."

Chang Weisi raised a hand to prevent any other replies. "First, the sense of responsibility and urgency that Comrade Zhang Beihai has shown in his work must be commended. The existence of defeatism amongst the troops is a fact, and we must face it rationally. So long as a technology gap exists between our two sides, defeatism will not vanish. It is not a problem that can be solved through simple methods but will require long and painstaking work, as well as more interaction and discussion. However, I also agree with the suggestion proposed by the colonel: matters concerning personal ideology should be resolved primarily through communication and

exchange, and if a report is necessary, it should be made through the proper channels."

The officers let out a sigh of relief. At this meeting, at least, Zhang Beihai would not be mentioning their names.

Imagining the boundless night sky above the cloud layer, Luo Ji struggled to collect his thoughts. Involuntarily, his mind drifted to thoughts of the woman: her voice and laughing face appeared in the dimness, and a sorrow he had never felt before weighed upon his heart. This was followed closely by self-reproach, a disdain he had felt on countless prior occasions, but never so intensely. Why was she on his mind now? Up to this point, his only reaction to her death apart from fear and astonishment had been self-absolution, and only now that he knew her role in the situation was negligible did he spare her any of his precious sorrow. What sort of a person was he?

But what could be done? That's just the sort of person he was.

In his bed, the minute oscillations of the plane gave Luo Ji the feeling of being in a cradle. He had slept in a cradle as a baby, he remembered, and one day in his parents' basement he had seen, covered in dust under an old kid's bed, the rockers of a cradle. Now when he closed his eyes and imagined the couple rocking his cradle, he asked himself, *From the day you left that cradle, have you ever cared about anyone else besides those two people? Have you ever made even a small, permanent bit of room in your heart for anyone else?*

Yes, he had made room, once. Five years before, the golden light of love had inhabited his heart. But that had been an unreal experience.

Everything had started with Bai Rong, an author of young-adult novels. She wrote them in her spare time but had gained enough of a following to bring her more in royalties than she made in salary. Out of all the women he had met, he had spent the most time with Bai Rong, and had even reached the point of considering

marrying her. Their relationship was the ordinary sort, not particularly intense or unforgettable, but they felt it suited them to be relaxed and happy together. Despite a certain dread of marriage, they felt giving it a try was the responsible thing to do.

At Bai Rong's behest, he had read all of her work, and while he wouldn't say he appreciated it, it wasn't as torturous as the other works in the genre he had flipped through. She had an elegant style, and a mature lucidity that her peers lacked. But this style was not complemented by the novels' content. Reading them was like looking at dewdrops on the undergrowth: pure and transparent, but distinguished from each other only by the way the light reflected and refracted through them and how they rolled about on the leaves, fusing together where they met and separating when they fell, until they evaporated entirely within the space of a few minutes after sunrise. Every time he read one of her books, beneath the graceful style he was left with one question: What do these people live on if they spend twenty-four hours a day in love?

"That love you write about—do you think it exists in the real world?" he asked one day.

"I do."

"Something you've seen, or something you've experienced yourself?"

She squeezed his neck. "Either way, I'm telling you that it exists," she said cryptically into his ear.

Sometimes he would give her suggestions for the novels she was working on, or even help her revise them.

"It's like you're more talented than I am," she said once. "You're not revising plot, but character, and that's the hardest thing to do. Every time, you're adding the touches that make the characters most vivid. Your skill at creating literary figures is first rate."

"You've got to be kidding. My background's in astronomy."

"Wang Xiaobo[9] studied mathematics, remember."

9 *Translator's Note*: Wang Xiaobo (1952–1997) was an influential novelist, essayist, and screenwriter whose work became enormously popular after his untimely death.

On her birthday last year, she had asked him for a specific present: "Can you write a novel for me?"

"A whole novel?"

"Well, at least fifty thousand characters long."

"With you as the protagonist?"

"No. I saw a really interesting exhibition of paintings by male artists of the most beautiful women they could imagine. The protagonist of your novel should be the same. You can leave reality behind and create an angel based entirely on your dream of feminine perfection."

To this day he had no idea of the motivation for her request. Maybe she didn't know herself. Thinking back now, it seemed her mood at the time had been a mixture of craftiness and ambivalence.

So he began constructing a character. He first imagined her face, and then designed her clothes, and then thought of her environment and the people around her, and finally placed her in that environment and had her move about and speak, letting her live. But this soon turned tedious, and he told Bai Rong about the difficulties he had encountered: "She's like a puppet on a string. Every word and action arises from the design but lacks the spark of life."

She said, "Your approach is wrong. You're writing an essay rather than creating a literary figure. What a literary character does in ten minutes might be a reflection of ten years' experience. You can't be limited to the plot of a novel—you've got to imagine her entire life, and what actually gets put into words is just the tip of the iceberg."

So he followed her advice. He threw out everything he wanted to write and instead imagined the character's entire life and every detail of it. He imagined her nursing at her mother's breast, her tiny mouth sucking energetically and burbling with satisfaction; chasing a red balloon tumbling down the street but making it just one step before falling to the ground, wailing as she watched the balloon drift away without realizing that she had just taken her first step; walking in the rain and impulsively folding up her umbrella to feel the raindrops; her first day at elementary school, sitting alone in a strange classroom, unable to see her parents through the

windows or door, and nearly starting to cry, only to realize that her best friend from kindergarten was at a nearby desk, and crying in joy instead; her first night at college, lying on her dorm bunk and watching the shadows of trees thrown by streetlamps onto the ceiling. . . . He imagined every one of her favorite foods, the color and style of every item of clothing in her dresser, the decorations on her mobile phone, the books she read, the music on her media player, the Web sites she visited, the movies she liked; but never her makeup, because she didn't need makeup. . . . Like a creator outside of time, he wove the different stages of her life together and gradually came to discover the endless pleasure of creation.

One day at the library, he imagined her standing by a row of shelves, reading. He put her in his favorite outfit, so her petite form would stand out more vividly in his mind. Suddenly, she looked up from the book and over at him, and flashed him a smile.

He was taken aback: Had he told her to smile? The smile had already imprinted itself on his memory like a stain on ice, never to be wiped away.

The real turning point came the following night. The snow and wind picked up, temperatures plummeted, and he watched from the warmth of his dorm the bluster that blanketed the other sounds of the city, the buffeting of the snowflakes on the widow like the patter of sand. A huge carpet of snow covered everything outdoors. The city seemed to no longer exist, leaving the faculty dormitory standing on an infinite snowy plain. He went back to bed, but before he drifted off to sleep he had a sudden thought: If she were outside in this awful weather, she would be terribly cold. Then he reminded himself: It doesn't matter, she won't be outside unless you put her there. But this time his imagination failed, and she continued walking outside in the blizzard like a blade of grass that could blow away at any moment. She still wore that white coat and that red scarf, which was all he could make out, vaguely, through the swirling snow, like a tiny flame fighting against the storm.

It was impossible for him to sleep. He sat up in his bed, then threw on some clothes and sat on the sofa. He wondered if he should

have a smoke but, remembering that she detested the smell, instead made a cup of coffee and drank it slowly. He had to wait for her. The blizzard and the cold night weighed on his heart. This was the first time he had felt such heartache for someone, or such yearning.

As his mind was sputtering to life, she came quietly, her small frame wrapped in a layer of cold from the outdoors, but with a breath of spring amid the chilliness. The snowflakes in her hair quickly melted into gleaming droplets as she unwrapped her scarf and put her hands to her mouth to blow on them. He folded her hands in his to warm the icy softness, and she looked at him with excitement and asked the question he was about to ask her: "Are you okay?"

He could only nod dumbly. Then, as he helped her out of her coat, he said, "Come and get warm." He rubbed her soft shoulders and guided her to the fireplace.

"It's really warm. Wonderful . . ." She sat on the rug in front of the fireplace, laughing happily as she watched the firelight.

Damn it! What's wrong with me? he said to himself, in the middle of the empty room. Wouldn't it be enough to just come up with any fifty thousand words, print them on high-grade bond, Photoshop a gorgeous cover and flap, have it professionally bound, have it gift-wrapped, and then give it to Bai Rong on her birthday? Why had he fallen so deep into this trap? He was amazed to find that he had tears in his eyes. And then another realization: *A fireplace? When the hell did I get a fireplace? Why would I think of a fireplace?* But then he understood: What he wanted wasn't a fireplace, but the glow of the fire, for it is in firelight that a woman is most beautiful. He recalled how she had looked just then against the glow of the fire. . . .

No! Don't think about her. It will be a disaster! Go to sleep!

Contrary to his expectations, he did not dream of her the entire night. He slept well, imagining the single bed as a small boat floating on a rosy sea. When he awoke the next morning, he felt reborn, like he was a candle that had been covered in dust for years before being lit by that tiny flame in last night's snowstorm. He walked

excitedly down the road to the classroom building, and though the air was hazy after the snowfall, he felt like he could see a thousand miles. There was no snow on the poplar trees lining the road, their bare branches poking up toward the cold sky, but to him they were more alive than in springtime.

He took the podium, and just as he had hoped, there she was again, seated in the back of the amphitheater, the only one in an empty row, at a distance from the other students. Her pure white coat and red scarf were on the seat beside her, and she was wearing a beige turtleneck sweater. She did not have her head down, flipping pages in her textbook like the other students. Instead, she watched him, and flashed him another snowy-sunrise of a smile.

He grew nervous. His pulse increased, and he had to leave through a side door to stand on the balcony and calm himself in the cold air. The only other times he had been in a similar state were during his two doctoral thesis defenses. In his lecture he did his utmost to show off, and his extensive citations and impassioned language won a rare burst of applause from the auditorium. She didn't join in, but merely smiled at him and nodded.

After class, he walked side by side with her along the tree-lined avenue that offered no shade, listening to the crunch of her blue boots in the snow. The two lines of winter poplars listened in silence to their heartfelt conversation.

"You lecture quite well, but I didn't really understand."

"You're not in this major, are you?"

"No, I'm not."

"Do you often sit in on classes in other majors?"

"Only the past few days. I'll go into a lecture hall at random and sit for a while. I just graduated and will be leaving soon. I suddenly realized that it's great here, and I'm afraid of the outside. . . ."

Over the next three or four days, he spent the majority of his time with her, although to others, it looked as if he was spending most of his time alone, strolling on his own. It was quite easy to explain to Bai Rong: He was thinking about her birthday gift. And indeed, this was no lie.

On New Year's Eve, he bought a bottle of red wine, which he had never drunk before, returned to his dorm room, shut off the light, and lit some candles on the table next to the sofa. When all three candles were burning, she sat down wordlessly next to him.

"Oh, look," she exclaimed, pointing at the wine bottle with childlike excitement.

"What?"

"Look at it from here, where the candles shine through. The wine is lovely."

Shining through the wine, the candlelight was a deep, crystalline red, the stuff of dreams.

"Like a dead sun," he said.

"Don't think like that," she said, with a sincerity that melted his heart. "I think it's like . . . the eyes of twilight."

"Why not the eyes of dawn?"

"I like twilight better."

"Why?"

"When twilight fades, you can see the stars. When dawn fades, all that's left is . . ."

"All that's left is the harsh light of reality."

"Yes, that's right."

They spoke about everything, sharing a common language in even the most trivial of things, until the bottle that had contained the eyes of twilight had been emptied into his stomach.

He lay drowsily in bed and watched the candles still burning on the table. She had vanished from the candlelight, but he was not worried. So long as he was willing, she could reappear at any time.

Then there was a knock on the door. He knew the knock came from reality and had nothing to do with her, so he ignored it. The door opened and Bai Rong entered. When she turned on the light it was like switching on the gray of reality. She glanced at the table with the candles, then sat down at the head of his bed and sighed lightly. "It's still okay."

"What is?" He used a hand to block the harsh light.

"You haven't gotten to the point of leaving a glass for her, too."

He covered his eyes but said nothing. She pulled away his hands, and then, looking straight at him, asked, "She's alive, isn't she?"

He nodded and sat up. "Rong, I used to think that a character in a novel was controlled by her creator, that she would be whatever the author wanted her to be, and do whatever the author wanted her to do, like God does for us."

"Wrong!" she said, standing up and beginning to pace the room. "Now you realize you were wrong. This is the difference between an ordinary scribe and a literary writer. The highest level of literary creation is when the characters in a novel possess life in the mind of the writer. The writer is unable to control them, and might not even be able to predict the next action they will take. We can only follow them in wonder to observe and record the minute details of their lives like a voyeur. That's how a classic is made."

"So literature, it turns out, is a perverted endeavor."

"It was like that for Shakespeare and Balzac and Tolstoy, at least. The classic images they created were born from their mental wombs. But today's practitioners of literature have lost that creativity. Their minds give birth only to shattered fragments and freaks, whose brief lives are nothing but cryptic spasms devoid of reason. Then they sweep up these fragments into a bag they peddle under the label 'postmodern' or 'deconstructionist' or 'symbolism' or 'irrational.' "

"So you mean that I've become a writer of classic literature?"

"Hardly. Your mind is only gestating an image, and it's the easiest one of all. The minds of those classic authors gave birth to hundreds and thousands of figures. They formed the picture of an era, and that's something that only a superhuman can accomplish. But what you've done isn't easy. I didn't think you'd be able to do it."

"Have you ever done it?"

"Just once," she said simply, and dropped the subject. She grabbed his neck, and said, "Forget it. I don't want that birthday present anymore. Come back to a normal life, okay?"

"And if all this continues—what then?"

She studied him for a few seconds, then let go of him and shook

her head with a smile. "I knew it was too late." Picking up her bag from the bed, she left.

Then he heard people outside counting down, four, three, two, one. From the classroom building, which until then had been resounding with music, came peals of laughter. On the athletic field people lit fireworks. Looking at his watch, he saw that the final second of that year had just passed.

"It's a holiday tomorrow. Where should we go?" he asked. He lay on the bed, but knew his character had already appeared beside the nonexistent fireplace.

"You're not taking *her*?" she asked in all innocence, pointing toward the still-open door.

"No. Just the two of us. Where would you like to go?"

She drank in the dancing flames in the fireplace and said, "It's not important where we go. I think it's a wonderful feeling just being on a journey."

"Then we'll set out and see where we end up?"

"Excellent."

The next morning, he drove his Accord off campus and headed west, a direction he chose purely because it avoided the headaches of having to traverse the entire city. He felt for the first time the wonderful freedom of traveling with no destination in mind. As the buildings outside slowly thinned out and fields began to appear, he cracked his window to let the cold winter air in. He sensed her long hair catching the wind, and strands of it blew over to tickle his right temple.

"Look, mountains." She pointed off in the distance.

"Visibility is good today. Those are the Taihang Mountains. They run parallel to this road, and then bend around to form a block in the west, where the road goes into them. I'd say that right now we're—"

"No, no. Don't say where we are! Once we know where we are, then the world becomes as narrow as a map. When we don't know, the world feels unlimited."

"Okay. Then let's do our best to get lost." He turned onto an

emptier road, and before they had gone very far, turned a second time. On both sides of them were now endless fields where the snow had not yet melted completely, the snowy patches and snow-free ground roughly equal. No green anywhere, although the sunlight was brilliant.

"A classic northern scene," he said.

"This is the first time I've ever felt that land without the slightest bit of green could be beautiful."

"The green is buried in the fields and is waiting for springtime. The winter wheat will sprout while it's still very cold, then this will be a sea of green. Imagine, all this expanse . . ."

"It doesn't need green. It's beautiful right now. Look, doesn't the land look like a big milk cow asleep under the sun?"

"What?" He looked in surprise, first at her and then through the windows at the patchy snow on either side of the car. "Oh, there really is a resemblance! So, what's your favorite season?"

"Autumn."

"Why not spring?"

"Spring . . . has so many sensations squashed together. It gets tiring. Autumn is better."

He stopped the car and went out with her to the edge of the field to look at the magpies, which foraged on the ground until they got quite close, at which point they flew off to some trees in the distance. Then they went down a riverbed that was practically dried up, with only a thin stream of water flowing down the center. But it was a northern river all the same, and so they picked up small chilly smooth stones from the riverbed and pitched them in, watching the cloudy yellow water gush out of the holes they broke in the thin ice. They passed a small town and spent a while at the market there. She knelt down by a goldfish vendor, the fish in their glass bowls like liquid flames under the sun, and wouldn't leave. He bought her two and put them, water and all, in plastic bags on the backseat of the car. They entered a hamlet, but found nothing that felt like the countryside. The houses and compounds were brand new, cars were parked outside of many of the gates,

the cement roads were wide, and people were dressed no differently than in the cities—a few girls were even stylish. Even the dogs were the same long-haired, short-legged parasites found in the cities. More interesting was the large stage at the entrance to the village—they marveled at how such a small village could have such an immense stage. It was empty, so with some effort he climbed up and—looking down at his lone audience member— sang a verse from "*Tonkaya Ryabina*" about the slender hawthorn tree. At noon, they ate in another town, where the food was more or less the same as in the city, only the portions were about twice as large. After lunch, they sat drowsily in the warmth of the sun on a bench outside the town hall, and then drove onward with no direction in mind.

Before they knew it, the road had entered the mountains, which were plain and ordinary in shape and devoid of vegetation apart from withered grasses and vitex vines in the crevices of the gray rocks. Over the course of hundreds of millions of years, the mountains, weary of standing, had lain down, sunken into flatness amid time and sunlight, and turned anyone walking among them just as indolent. "The mountains here are like old villagers basking in the sun," she said, but they hadn't seen any of those old men in the villages they passed through; none more at ease than the mountains. More than once their car had been stopped by a flock of sheep crossing the road. Beside the road there at last appeared the kind of villages they had imagined, with cave houses and persimmon and walnut trees and stone-tiled low buildings, roofs piled high with stripped corn cob. Even the dogs were larger and more fierce.

They started and stopped as they went through the mountains, and before they knew it the entire afternoon was spent. The sun was setting, and the road had entered the shadows long ago. He drove along a dirt road pitted with potholes up onto a high ridge where the sun still shone, and they decided that this would be the terminus of their journey: They would watch the sun set and then head back. Her long hair blew in the light evening breeze, seemingly striving to seize hold of the last golden rays.

They had only just turned onto the highway when the car broke down. The rear axle had broken, meaning they had to call for help. A while later he was able to learn the name of the place from the driver of a small passing truck. He was comforted by the fact that his phone had a signal. When he gave his location to the person at the repair station, he was informed that the repair truck would take at least four or five hours to get there.

The mountain air chilled quickly after sunset. After their surroundings began to grow dusky, he collected some corn stalks from a nearby terraced field and started a fire.

"Nice and warm," she said, gazing into the fire, as happy as she had been that first night in front of the fireplace. Again he was transfixed by her appearance in the firelight, drowned in emotions he had never felt before, as if he was a bonfire himself and the only purpose of his existence was to give her warmth.

"Are there wolves?" she asked, looking around at the growing darkness.

"No. Northern China is still in the interior. It just looks desolate, but it's actually one of the most densely populated regions. Look at the road. A car drives past every two minutes, on average."

"I was hoping you'd say there were wolves," she said with a sweet smile, then looked off at the cloud of sparks flying off like stars into the night.

"Okay. There are wolves, but I'm right here."

They said nothing more, but sat silently before the fire, occasionally feeding it another bunch of straw.

Later—he didn't know how much later—his phone rang. Bai Rong.

"Are you with her?" she asked gently.

"No, I'm alone," he said as he looked up. He wasn't lying. He truly was by himself, next to a bonfire along a road in the Taihang Mountains. The firelight revealed stones around him, and overhead was only a starry sky.

"I know you're alone. But are you with her?"

He paused and softly said, "Yes," and when he looked beside

89

him, there she was, feeding straw into the fire and smiling at the flames that lit up the area where they sat.

"Now do you believe that the love I write about in my novels really exists?"

"Yes, I believe it."

When he said those four words, he immediately realized how great the distance between the two of them really was. They were silent for a long time, during which radio waves spun their gossamer strands through the mountains to sustain this final contact.

"You have one of your own, don't you?" he asked.

"Yes. For a long time."

"Where is he now?"

He could hear her laugh softly. "Where else would he be?"

He laughed too. "Yes, where else?"

"Well. Take it easy. Good-bye." Bai Rong hung up, snapping the thread that stretched across the night sky and leaving the people at the two ends a little saddened, but nothing more than that.

"It's too cold outdoors. Let's sleep in the car," he said to her.

She gently shook her head. "I want to be with you here. You like me by the fire, right?"

It was midnight by the time the repair truck arrived from Shijia-zhuang. The repairmen were surprised to find him sitting beside a fire. "Sir, you've gotta be freezing. The engine's not busted. Wouldn't it be warmer to sit in the car with the heat turned on?"

After the car was repaired, Luo Ji dashed home through the night, out of the mountains and back onto the plain, reaching Shijiazhuang by dawn. It was already ten in the morning by the time he got back to Beijing.

Rather than returning to school, he drove straight to the psychologist.

"You may need a bit of adjustment, but it's nothing serious," the doctor said, after listening to his lengthy narrative.

"Nothing serious?" Luo Ji opened his bloodshot eyes wide. "I'm madly in love with a fictional person from a novel of my own creation. I've been with her, I've traveled with her, and I've even

broken up with my real-life girlfriend over her. Is that nothing serious to you?"

The doctor smiled tolerantly.

"Don't you get it? I've given my most profound love to an illusion!"

"Are you under the impression that the object of everyone else's love actually exists?"

"Is that even a question?"

"Sure. For the majority of people, what they love exists only in the imagination. The object of their love is not the man or woman of reality, but what he or she is like in their imagination. The person in reality is just a template used for the creation of this dream lover. Eventually, they find out the differences between their dream lover and the template. If they can get used to those differences, then they can be together. If not, they split up. It's as simple as that. You differ from the majority in one respect: You didn't need a template."

"So this isn't a sickness?"

"Only in the way your girlfriend pointed out: You've got natural literary talent. If you want to call that a sickness, go right ahead."

"But isn't imagining to this degree a little excessive?"

"There's nothing excessive about imagination. Especially where love is concerned."

"So what should I do? How can I forget about her?"

"It's impossible. You can't forget her, so don't make the effort. That will only lead to side effects, and maybe even mental disorders. Let nature take its course. Once more, for emphasis: Don't try to forget about her. It won't work. But as time passes, her influence on your life will decrease. And you're actually quite lucky. Whether or not she really exists, you're fortunate to be in love."

This was Luo Ji's most deeply felt romantic experience, a love that only comes around once in a man's life. After that, he took to an insouciant lifestyle, going where life took him, just like the day they had set out in the Accord. And like the psychologist had said, her influence in his life decreased. When he was with a real

woman, she didn't appear, and eventually she rarely appeared even when he was alone. But he knew that the most secluded part of his soul belonged to her, and she would be there for life. He even saw clearly the world she inhabited, a still snowscape where the sky was forever graced with silver stars and a crescent moon, the snow falling steadily. In the silence you could practically hear the snowflakes coming to rest on the ground like smooth white sugar. In her exquisite cabin in the snow, the Eve that Luo Ji had formed out of one of his mind's ribs sat before an ancient fireplace quietly watching the dancing flames.

Now that he was alone on this ominous plane flight, he wanted to have her companionship, to guess with her what lay at the journey's end. But she didn't appear. He could still see her in a far-off region of his soul, sitting silently before the fireplace, never feeling lonely, because she knew her world was within him.

Luo Ji reached out a hand to the medicine bottle by the bed with the thought of using a sleeping pill to force himself to sleep, but the instant his fingers touched the bottle it flew off the cabinet and up to the ceiling, as did the clothing that he had flung onto the chair. They remained on the ceiling for a couple seconds. He felt himself leave the bed, but since the sleeping bag was attached, he didn't fly away, and when the bottle landed, he fell heavily back into the bed. For a few seconds his body felt like it was being pressed down by a heavy object, and he couldn't move. The sudden weightlessness and hypergravitation made him dizzy, a condition that continued for less than ten seconds before everything returned to normal.

He heard the soft swish of footsteps on the carpet outside the door. A number of people were in motion, and then the door opened and Shi Qiang poked his head in. "Luo Ji, are you okay?"

When Luo Ji said he was fine, he closed the door without coming in. Outside, a dialogue continued in low voices.

"It looks like a misunderstanding during the escort change. Nothing to worry about."

"What did the higher-ups say on the call earlier?" That was Shi Qiang's voice.

"They said that the escort formation would require a midair refueling in half an hour, and that we shouldn't be alarmed."

"The plan doesn't mention this interruption, does it?"

"Not even close. In the chaos just now, seven of the escort planes jettisoned their secondary fuel tanks."

"Why all the jumpiness? Forget it. You should go back to sleep. Don't get too worked up."

"How are we supposed to sleep in a state like this?"

"Leave someone on watch. What good are you if you're tired out? They may try to keep us on high alert all the time, but I maintain my own opinion of security work: When you've thought of everything you should, and done everything you need to, then let whatever happens happen. There's nothing more anyone can do, you know? Don't psych yourselves out."

At the mention of "escort change," Luo Ji reached over, opened the cover to the window, and looked outside. There was still a sea of clouds in the night sky. The moon was inclining toward the horizon, and he could see the trails of the fighter formation, now with an additional six lines. He inspected the tiny aircraft heading up those trails and noticed that they were a different model than the four he'd seen earlier.

The bedroom door opened and Shi Qiang poked his torso in to say, "Luo, my man, just a small issue. Don't worry. Nothing else from now on. Go back to sleep."

"There's still time to sleep? How many hours have we been flying?"

"We've still got a few more hours. Go to sleep." He closed the door and left.

Luo Ji turned over in the bed and picked up the pill bottle. Shi had been thorough: It contained just one pill. He took it, looked at the small red light beneath the window, imagining it was the light of a fireplace, and drifted off to sleep.

When Shi Qiang woke Luo Ji up, he had been sleeping dream-free for more than six hours and was feeling pretty good.

"We're nearly there. Get up and get ready."

Luo Ji went to the washroom to wash up, and when he returned to the office for a simple breakfast, he became aware of the plane's descent. Ten minutes later, after a flight of fifteen hours, the charter plane was resting on the ground.

Shi Qiang had Luo Ji wait in the office and went out himself. He brought back a man with a European face who was tall and immaculately dressed, and who seemed like a high-level official. "Is this Dr. Luo?" the official ventured as he looked at him. Noticing Shi Qiang's difficulty with English, he repeated his question in Chinese.

"He's Luo Ji," answered Shi Qiang, and then briefly introduced the man to Luo Ji. "This is Mr. Kent. He's here to welcome you."

"I am honored," Kent said with a bow.

When they shook hands, Luo Ji sensed that the man was incredibly experienced. So much was hidden behind his decorum, but the gleam in his eyes betrayed the presence of secrets. Luo Ji was fascinated by the man's gaze, like a devil and an angel, like an atom bomb and an identical-size precious stone. . . . In the complex information conveyed by those eyes, Luo Ji could make out just one thing: This moment was immensely important to the man's whole life.

Kent turned to Shi Qiang. "You've done very well. Your segment was the most cleanly done. The others had a bit of trouble on their way over."

"We listened to our superiors. The principle we observed was to minimize the total number of stages," Shi Qiang said.

"Absolutely correct. In the present circumstances, minimizing the stages makes for maximum security. And now we'll follow the same principle and head straight for the conference hall."

"When does the session start?"

"In one hour."

"We've cut it that close?"

"The start of the session is set by the arrival of the final candidate."

"That's pretty good. Shall we hand off, then?"

"No. You are still responsible for the security of this one. Like I said before, you are the best."

Shi Qiang was silent for a second or two as he looked at Luo Ji. Then he nodded. "As we've been getting acquainted with the situation over the past few days, our people have run into quite a few obstacles."

"I guarantee that nothing of the sort will happen from now on. You have the full cooperation of the local police and military. Well then," Kent said, looking at the two men. "We can set off."

It was still nighttime, Luo Ji realized as he stepped through the door of the aircraft. Thinking back to their takeoff time, he had a pretty good idea of which general area of the globe they were in. The fog was thick, and the lights shone a dim yellow as events from their takeoff seemed to be replaying before their eyes: the patrol helicopters in the air, only dimly visible through the fog as shadows with glowing lights; the plane quickly surrounded by a ring of military vehicles and outward-facing soldiers; and several officers with radios clustered in a group discussing something and occasionally throwing a glance in the direction of the airstair. A buzzing from somewhere overhead set Luo Ji's scalp on fire, and even the imperturbable Mr. Kent covered his ears. Looking up, they could see an indistinct light flying low overhead: the escort formation, still circling above them, its exhaust tracing a large circle in the air that was hazily visible through the fog, as if a cosmic giant had tagged the Earth with chalk at this very spot.

The four of them boarded an obviously bulletproofed car waiting at the end of the airstair and sped off. The window curtains were drawn, but judging from the light that came in, Luo Ji knew that they were smack in the middle of a convoy. Silence reigned on the ride, a road to the ultimate unknown. Although it took only forty minutes, this part of the journey felt terribly long.

When Kent said they had arrived, Luo Ji could make out a shape through the curtains, backlit by the even light from the building to its rear that cast its silhouette onto the curtain. He could never mistake such a distinctive shape: a giant revolver with a knot tied

in its barrel. Luo Ji knew exactly where he was: the United Nations building in New York.

He was surrounded as soon as he got out by people who seemed like security personnel: they were tall, and many of them wore dark glasses despite the night. He couldn't make out his surroundings, but was pushed forward by the cluster, squeezed with such force that his feet practically left the ground, the scraping of footsteps the only sound that broke the silence. Just as the bizarre tension had pushed him almost to the breaking point, the men in front of him gave way. Light flashed before his eyes, and then the rest of them halted in their steps, leaving him, Shi Qiang, and Kent to continue forward. They were walking in a large quiet hall, empty but for a few black-clothed guards who spoke quietly into a handheld radio each time the three of them passed one of them. They crossed a hanging balcony in the direction of a stained-glass panel whose riot of colors and intricate lines described the distorted shapes of humans and animals. Turning left, they entered a small room. After the door closed, Kent and Shi Qiang exchanged a smile, and a look of relief came over them.

Luo Ji glanced around him and discovered that the room was fairly peculiar. The wall at one end was entirely covered by an abstract painting made up of yellow, white, blue, and black geometric shapes, which overlapped randomly and seemed suspended atop an ocean of pure blue. But the strangest thing was the large stone in the shape of a rectangular prism sitting right in the center of the room and illuminated by several weak lamps. A closer look revealed that the stone bore rust lines. The abstract painting and the stone were the only furnishings, and apart from them the room was empty.

"Dr. Luo, do you need to change clothes?" Kent asked in English.

"What's he saying?" Shi Qiang asked, and when Luo Ji translated, he shook his head firmly. "No, just wear this."

"But this is a formal occasion," Kent struggled out in Chinese.

"No," said Shi Qiang with another shake of his head.

"The hall is only open to national representatives, not the media. It should be fairly secure."

"I said no. If I've understood correctly, I'm in charge of his safety now."

Kent relented. "Very well. It's not a big issue."

"You really should give him a general explanation," Shi Qiang said, jerking his head in Luo Ji's direction.

"I'm not authorized to explain anything."

"Just say anything," Shi Qiang said with a laugh.

Kent turned toward Luo Ji, his dignified face suddenly tense, and subconsciously adjusted his tie. Luo Ji then realized that he had been avoiding looking directly at him. He also noticed that Shi Qiang seemed like a different person. The ever-present smirk was gone, replaced by a solemn expression, and he looked at Kent in a rare posture of attention. Then Luo Ji knew that everything Shi Qiang had said to him before was correct: He really had no idea of the purpose of the visit.

Kent said, "Dr. Luo, all I can tell you is this: You are about to take part in an important meeting at which there will be an important announcement. And at this meeting, you do not need to do anything."

Then they were silent. The room was completely quiet. Luo Ji could clearly hear the beating of his heart. This, he realized, was the Meditation Room. The centerpiece was a six-ton rock made of the purest raw iron, symbolizing timelessness and strength. It had been a gift from Sweden. But right now, far from wanting to meditate, he tried as hard as possible to think of nothing, convinced of what Shi had said: Any thinking is liable to go off the rails. He counted the shapes in the painting.

The door opened, and the head that poked in signaled to Kent, who then turned to Luo Ji and Shi Qiang: "Time to go in. No one knows Dr. Luo, so there won't be any disruption if he and I go in together."

Shi Qiang nodded, then waved a hand at Luo Ji with a smile: "I'll wait for you outside." It warmed his heart. Right then Shi Qiang was his sole spiritual support.

Then he followed Kent out of the Meditation Room and into the United Nations General Assembly Hall.

The hall was full and the people seated in it buzzed with conversation. He didn't attract attention at first when Kent led him up along the aisle, but heads began to turn once they got close to the front. Depositing him in an aisle seat in the fifth row, Kent went on ahead and sat down in the second row.

Luo Ji looked around him at the place he had seen countless times on television. Based on these glimpses, he had been wholly unable to appreciate the meaning the building's architects wanted to express. Straight ahead of him, the tall yellow wall inset with the UN insignia that served as a backdrop for the podium was tilted forward at an acute angle, like a cliff face that was liable to collapse at any time. The dome, built to resemble a starry sky, was structurally separate from the yellow wall and did nothing to stabilize it, acting instead as an immense weight bearing down from above, adding to the wall's instability and lending the whole environment the overpowering feeling of being ready to tumble down at any moment. Under the present circumstances, however, it seemed as if the eleven architects who had designed the building in the mid-twentieth century had wonderfully predicted humanity's present predicament.

Turning his attention away from the distant wall, he heard two people talking next to him. He couldn't make out their nationality, but they were speaking idiomatic English.

"Do you really believe in the decisive role of the individual in history?"

"Well, I think it's a question that can't be proven or disproven, unless we restart time, kill off a few great men, and see how history proceeds. Of course, you can't rule out the possibility that the course of history was determined by the rivers carved out and dammed up by those great figures."

"But there's another possibility: Those great figures of yours might be no more than swimmers in history's river. They may have left their names in history because of the world records they set

and the praise and renown they won, but they had no effect on the river's flow. . . . Ah, with things the way they are, what's the point of thinking about all that?"

"The problem is that throughout the entire decision-making process, no one thought about issues on this level. The countries are all tangled up in stuff like candidate equality and resource rights."

The hall grew quiet as Secretary General Say walked to the podium. The administration of this Filipino politician had straddled the pre- and postcrisis eras. If the vote had come just a little bit later, she never would have been elected, because a refined Asian lady didn't project the sense of power the world was looking for in the face of the Trisolar Crisis. Now her small frame seemed tiny and helpless against the sloping cliff wall. As she was ascending the podium, Kent stopped her and whispered something in her ear. She looked down, nodded, and then continued walking.

Luo Ji was certain that the secretary general had looked in the direction of his seat.

On the rostrum, she surveyed the assembly, and then said, "The nineteenth meeting of the Planetary Defense Council has arrived at the final item on its agenda: the disclosure of the Wallfacer candidates and the announcement of the start of the Wallfacer Project.

"Before we move on to that agenda item, I believe it is necessary to take a brief look back at the Wallfacer Project.

"At the start of the Trisolar Crisis, the permanent members of the former Security Council held emergency negotiations and conceived the Wallfacer Project.

"The countries took note of the following facts: After the first two sophons appeared, burgeoning evidence demonstrated that additional sophons were constantly reaching the Solar System and coming to Earth, a process that continues even now. Therefore, as far as the enemy is concerned, the Earth is a completely transparent world. To them, everything is an open book, one they can read at any time. Humanity has no secrets at all.

"The international community has recently launched a mainstream defense program which, in both overall strategic thinking

and the tiniest of technological and military details, is completely exposed to the enemy's eyes. Every meeting room, every file cabinet, the hard drives and memory of every computer—there is nowhere the sophons do not see. Every plan, program, and deployment, no matter the size, will be visible to the enemy command four light-years away the moment they take shape on the Earth. Human communication in any form will result in leaks.

"We should be aware of this one fact: Strategic and tactical tricks do not advance in proportion to technological progress. Precise intelligence has proven that the Trisolarans communicate through direct, open thoughts, making them highly deficient at tricks, camouflage, and deception, and giving human civilization a huge advantage over the enemy. This is one advantage we can't afford to lose. The founders of the Wallfacer Project believe that a number of other strategic plans should proceed in parallel to the mainstream defense program, and that these plans should be secret, not transparent to the enemy. A number of proposals were put forward, but ultimately only the Wallfacer Project is feasible.

"One correction to what I just said: Humanity still has secrets, in the inner world that each of us possesses. The sophons can understand human language, and they can read printed texts and information on every kind of computer storage media at ultrahigh speeds, but they can't read human thoughts. So long as we do not communicate with the outside world, every individual keeps things secret forever from the sophons. This is the basis of the Wallfacer Project.

"At its heart, the project consists of selecting a group of people to formulate and direct strategic plans. They will develop their plans entirely in their own minds, with no communication of any kind with the outside world. The true strategy of these plans, the necessary steps for completion, and the ultimate aims will remain hidden inside the brain. We shall call them the Wallfacers because that ancient Eastern name for meditators mirrors the unique characteristics of their work. As they direct the execution of their strategic plans, the thoughts and behaviors these Wallfacers present to the outside world will be entirely false, a carefully crafted

mélange of disguise, misdirection, and deception. The subject of this misdirection and deception will be the entire world, both enemy and ally, until a huge, bewildering maze of illusions is erected to make the enemy lose its judgment, and to delay as long as possible the moment it works out our true strategic intent.

"These Wallfacers will be granted extensive powers that will enable them to mobilize and exploit a portion of Earth's existing military resources. As they carry out their strategic plans, the Wallfacers need not make any explanation for their actions and commands, regardless of how incomprehensible their behavior may be. Monitoring and control of the Wallfacer activity will be undertaken by the UN Planetary Defense Council, the sole institution granted the authority to veto Wallfacer commands under the UN Wallfacer Act.

"To guarantee the continuity of the Wallfacer Project, the Wallfacers will take advantage of hibernation technology to bridge the centuries to the Doomsday Battle. When and under what circumstances they will awaken, and for how long, will be decided by the Wallfacers themselves. Over the next four centuries, the UN Wallfacer Act will exist under international law on a level equal to the UN Charter and will act in concert with the national laws to guarantee the execution of the Wallfacers' strategic plans.

"The Wallfacers are undertaking the most difficult mission in human history. They will truly be on their own, their souls closed off to the world, to the entire universe. Their only communication partner and sole spiritual support will be themselves. Shouldering this great responsibility, they will pass through the long years alone, so let me speak for all humanity and offer them our deepest respect.

"Now, on behalf of the United Nations, I will announce the final four Wallfacer candidates as chosen by the UN Planetary Defense Council."

Luo Ji, like the entire assembly, had been listening to the secretary general's speech with rapt attention, and he held his breath for the announcement of the list of names. He wanted to find out what sort of person would be tasked with this unimaginable mission.

His own fate was completely forgotten for the time being, because nothing that could happen to him would amount to more than a speck when measured against this historic moment.

"The First Wallfacer: Frederick Tyler."

When the secretary general uttered his name, Tyler stood up from his seat in the first row and walked with deliberate steps up to the rostrum, where he looked down at the assembly without expression. There was no applause as everyone sat in silence and stared at the First Wallfacer. Tyler's tall, thin body and square-framed glasses were well known across the world. The recently retired US secretary of defense, he had exerted a deep influence on his country's national strategy. His ideological focus was expressed in a book titled *The Truth of Technology,* in which he argued that small countries are the ultimate beneficiaries of technology, and that the unstinting efforts toward technological development on the part of larger countries was in fact paving the way for world dominance by the smaller ones. This was because technological progress rendered the population and resource advantages of larger countries unimportant, but provided small countries with leverage to move the world. One consequence of nuclear technology was that it allowed a country of just a few million people to pose a substantial threat to one with a hundred million, something that at one time had been practically impossible. One of his key points was that the advantages of a large country were only truly advantageous in low-technology eras and would ultimately be weakened by the swift pace of technological progress, which would meanwhile enhance the strategic weight of small countries. Some might experience a sudden rise, gaining world dominance like Spain and Portugal once did. There was no question that Tyler's thinking provided a theoretic foundation for the United States' global war on terror. But he was not just a strategist. He was also a man of action, and on multiple occasions had won popular acclaim for demonstrating courage and foresight in the face of major threats. Hence, as far as both the depth of his thinking and his leadership were concerned, Tyler made a worthy Wallfacer.

"The Second Wallfacer: Manuel Rey Diaz."

When this brown-skinned, stocky South American with a stubborn look in his eyes ascended the rostrum, Luo Ji was surprised: It was highly unusual for this man to even appear at the UN. But on second thought, it stood to reason. He even wondered why it hadn't already occurred to him. Rey Diaz was the current president of Venezuela, which, under his leadership, had aptly demonstrated Tyler's theory about the rise of small countries. He carried forward the Bolivarian Revolution instigated by Hugo Chavez: In a contemporary world ruled by capitalism and market economics, he promoted in Venezuela what Chavez called Socialism of the Twenty-First Century, founded on lessons drawn from the experience of the international socialist movements of the previous century. Surprisingly, he had achieved considerable success, boosting the country's power across the board and—for a time—turning Venezuela into a city on a hill, a symbol of equality, justice, and prosperity for the world. The other countries in South America followed suit, and socialism briefly caught fire on the continent. Rey Diaz inherited not only Chavez's socialist ideology but his strong anti-Americanism, which reminded the United States that its Latin American backyard could become a second Soviet Union if left unchecked. A rare opportunity presented by an accident and a misunderstanding gave the United States the excuse to launch a full-scale invasion of Venezuela that sought to overthrow the Rey Diaz government along the Iraq model. But with this war, the post–Cold War streak of victories by major western powers over small Third World countries had finally broken. When the US Army entered Venezuela, it discovered that the uniformed military was nowhere to be found. The entire army had been divided by squad into guerilla teams concealed among the people, and their sole combat objective was killing the enemy's vital forces. Rey Diaz's basic approach to warfare was built atop a single, clear idea: Modern high-tech weapons might be useful against point targets, but, for area targets, their performance is no better than conventional weapons and their cost and limited quantity make

them essentially nonfactors. He was a genius at low-cost, high-tech exploits. At the turn of the century, an Australian engineer had built a cruise missile for five thousand dollars with the aim of boosting vigilance against terrorists, but Rey Diaz's thousands of guerilla teams were armed with a total of two hundred thousand of them, mass produced for just three thousand dollars apiece. Although the missiles were made out of parts that were cheap and widely available on the market, they were fully equipped with a radar altimeter and GPS and could hit targets within a five-kilometer radius at an accuracy of within five meters. Their hit rate may have been less than 10 percent during the war, but they caused enormous destruction to the enemy. Other mass-produced high-tech gadgets, like proximity-fuse sniper rifle bullets, had a similarly brilliant track record during the war. During its short time in Venezuela, the US Army suffered casualties that approached Vietnam War levels, and it eventually had to withdraw. The defeat of the strong at the hands of the weak made Rey Diaz a hero for the twenty-first century.

"The Third Wallfacer: Bill Hines."

A debonair Englishman ascended the rostrum, a picture of refinement next to Tyler's coldness and Rey Diaz's stubbornness. He gave the assembly a graceful salute. He, too, was well known to the world, although he lacked the aura of the other two men. Hines's life was split into two entirely distinct stages. As a scientist, he was the only person in history to be nominated for the Nobel Prize in two sciences simultaneously for the same discovery. During research conducted with the neuroscientist Keiko Yamasuki, he discovered that brain activity for thoughts and memories operated on the quantum level rather than on the molecular level as previously believed. This discovery pushed brain mechanisms downward to the microstate of matter, rendering all prior research nothing more than superficial attempts that merely skimmed the surface of neuroscience. This discovery also demonstrated that the animal brain's capacity to process information was several orders of magnitude higher than previously imagined, which lent credence to long-held speculation that the brain had a holographic

structure. Hines was nominated for Nobel Prizes in both Physics and Physiology or Medicine for the discovery. Although his work was too radical for him to win either award, Keiko Yamasuki—who by this time was his wife—won the prize in Physiology or Medicine that year for her application of the theory to the treatment of amnesia and mental illness.

In the second stage of his life, he was a politician and served as president of the EU for two years. Hines was recognized as a prudent and experienced politician, but his term in office was not marked by many challenges that tested his political skills. The nature of the EU's work at the time, which was largely transactional coordination, meant that his qualifications to face a major crisis stacked up rather poorly compared to the other two men. Still, the choice of Hines evidently took into account both his scientific and political credentials, a perfect combination that was quite rare indeed.

Seated in the very last row of the hall, Keiko Yamasuki, the world authority in neuroscience, gazed lovingly down at her husband on the rostrum.

The assembly remained silent as all waited for the announcement of the final Wallfacer. The first three, Tyler, Rey Diaz, and Hines, represented balance and compromise among the political powers of the United States, Europe, and the Third World, so there was considerable interest in the final selection. As he watched Say turn back to the paper in the folder, world-famous names flashed through Luo Ji's mind. The final Wallfacer would be one of them. He looked ahead four rows and surveyed the backs of the first-row occupants. That's where the first three Wallfacers had been before they ascended the rostrum, but from behind he couldn't make out whether any of the people he had in mind were seated there. Still, the Fourth Wallfacer would definitely be there.

Say slowly raised her right hand, and he watched as it pointed to a spot not in the first row.

She was pointing at him.

"The Fourth Wallfacer: Luo Ji."

———

"It's my Hubble!" shouted Albert Ringier, clapping his palms together. The tears brimming in his eyes reflected the distant blazing ball of fire that rumbled for a few seconds before passing on. He and the cheering crowd of astronomers and physicists behind him ought to have been watching the launch from a VIP platform closer in, but a damn NASA official said they lacked proper qualifications for access, because the object being sent heavenward did not belong to them. Then the official had turned back to the group of uniformed, ramrod-straight generals and, groveling like a dog, had led them past the sentry post to the viewing platform. Ringier and his colleagues were forced to remain at this far-off spot where, in the previous century, a countdown clock had been built across a lake from the launch site. It was open to the public, but on this late night, there were no other observers apart from scientists.

Viewed from this distance, the blastoff looked like a spedup sunrise. The floodlights did not follow the rocket as it lifted off, leaving its massive body indistinct except for the spurting flames. From its hiding place in the dark of night, the world burst forth into a magnificent light show, and golden waves whipped up on the inky black surface of the lake as if the flames had ignited the water itself. They watched the rocket ascend. When it passed through the clouds, it turned half the sky the kind of red only found in dreams before it disappeared into the Florida sky, the brief dawn once again swallowed up by the night.

The Hubble II Space Telescope was a second-generation model, its diameter enlarged to 21 meters from its predecessor's 4.27 meters, which enhanced its observational capability by a factor of fifty. It used a compound lens technology consisting of lens components manufactured on the ground and assembled in orbit. To put the whole lens into space required eleven launches, and this was the final one. The assembly of Hubble II in the vicinity of the International Space Station was nearing completion. In two months, it would be able to turn its gaze to the depths of the universe.

"You pack of thieves! You've stolen another thing of beauty," Ringier said to the tall man beside him, the only one in the group

unaffected by the sight before them. George Fitzroy had seen too many of the launches, and spent the entire process leaning against the countdown clock smoking a cigarette. He had become the military's representative after Hubble II's requisition, but since he wore civilian clothes most of the time, Ringier didn't know his rank and never called him sir. Calling a thief by his name worked just fine.

"Doctor, in wartime the military has the right to requisition all civilian equipment. Besides, you people didn't grind a single lens component or design a single screw of the Hubble II. You're just there to enjoy its success, so it's not your place to complain." Fitzroy yawned, as if it was tiring work dealing with this pack of nerds.

"But without us, it wouldn't have any reason to exist! Civilian equipment? It can see the edge of the universe, but you shortsighted types only want to use it to look at the nearest star!"

"Like I've said before, this is wartime. A war to defend all humanity. Even if you've forgotten that you're an American, you at least remember you're human, right?"

Ringier groaned and nodded, then shook his head with a sigh. "But what do you want Hubble II to see? You've got to be aware that it won't be able to see the Trisolaran planet."

Fitzroy said with a sigh, "It's worse than that. The public thinks that it will be able to see the Trisolaran Fleet."

"Great," Ringier said. Though his face was indistinct in the darkness, Fitzroy could sense the schadenfreude in Ringier's expression, which made Fitzroy as uncomfortable as the acrid odor that now wafted over from the launch platform and filled the air.

"Doctor, you ought to know the consequences."

"If the public has placed its hope in Hubble II, then they probably won't believe the enemy really exists until they have seen the Trisolaran Fleet with their own eyes."

"And you find this acceptable?"

"You've explained it to the public, right?"

"Of course we've explained it! We've held four press conferences, and I've repeatedly explained that although Hubble II is orders of magnitude more powerful than the largest telescopes currently

available, there's no way it can detect the Trisolaran Fleet. It's too small! Detecting a planet in another star system from our Solar System is like detecting a mosquito on a lamp on the East Coast from the West Coast, but the Trisolaran Fleet is only as big as the bacteria on one of that mosquito's legs. How much clearer can I be?"

"That's pretty clear."

"But what else can we do? The public will believe whatever it wants. I've been in this job for a while now, and I haven't seen any major space project that they haven't misinterpreted."

"I said long ago that the military has lost all credibility as far as space projects are concerned."

"But they're willing to believe you. Don't they call you a second Carl Sagan? You've made a mint off those popular cosmology books of yours. Give us a hand. That's what the military wants, and now I'm formally passing on their request."

"Is this a private negotiation of terms?"

"There aren't any terms! It's your duty as an American. As a citizen of Earth."

"Assign me a bit more observational time. I don't need much. Bump me up to twenty percent, okay?"

"You're doing quite well at twelve point five percent right now, and no one can say if those allotments can be guaranteed in the future." Fitzroy waved a hand in the direction of the launch pad, where the dissipating smoke left by the rocket smeared a dirty patch across the night sky. Illuminated by the launch pad lights, it looked like a milk stain on a pair of jeans. The odor had grown more unpleasant. The rocket's first stage was fueled by liquid oxygen and liquid hydrogen and shouldn't have had that odor, so something nearby had probably been burnt by the stream of flames diverted by the launch pad. Fitzroy said, "I'm telling you, all of this is definitely going to get worse."

Luo Ji felt the weight of the slanted cliff face pressing down on him, and for a moment he was paralyzed. The hall was totally silent,

until a voice behind him said softly, "Dr. Luo, if you please." He stood up stiffly and walked with mechanical steps to the rostrum. On the short journey, it was like he had returned to a child's sense of helplessness and wanted someone to hold his hand and guide him forward. But no one extended a hand. He ascended the platform and stood next to Hines, then turned to face the assembly and the hundreds of pairs of eyes focused on him, eyes that represented six billion people from more than two hundred countries on Earth.

As for what went on during the rest of the session, Luo Ji had absolutely no idea. All he knew was that after standing there for a while, he was led off to a seat in the middle of the first row alongside the other three Wallfacers. In a haze, he had missed the historic moment of the announcement of the launch of the Wallfacer Project.

Some time later, when the session seemed to have ended and people, including the three Wallfacers sitting to Luo Ji's left, had begun to disperse, a man, perhaps Kent, whispered something into his ear before leaving. Then the hall was empty except for the secretary general, still standing on the rostrum, her petite figure in far-off opposition to his against the sloping cliff.

"Dr. Luo, I imagine you have some questions." Say's gentle feminine voice echoed in the empty hall like a spirit descending from the heavens.

"Has there been some mistake?" Luo Ji said. His voice, sounding similarly ethereal, didn't feel like his own.

From the rostrum, Say gave a laugh that clearly meant, *Do you really think that's possible?*

"Why me?" he asked.

"You need to find your own answer to that," she said.

"I'm just an ordinary man."

"In the face of this crisis, we are all ordinary people. But we all have our own responsibilities."

"No one solicited my opinion in advance. I was totally in the dark about this."

Say laughed again. "Doesn't your name mean 'logic' in Chinese?"

"That's right."

"Then you should be able to work out that it would have been impossible to solicit the opinions of the people undertaking this mission before it was handed to them."

"I refuse," he said firmly, without even thinking over what Say had just said.

"You may."

The swiftness of this reply, right on the heels of his refusal, left him at a loss for a moment. After a few seconds of silence, he said, "I reject the position of Wallfacer, I reject all the powers granted it, and I will not undertake any responsibility you force upon me."

"You may."

The simple, immediate reply to his statement, light as a dragonfly touching on the water, shut down his brain's ability to think and made his mind a total blank.

"So am I free to leave?" was all he could ask.

"You may, Dr. Luo. You are free to do anything."

Luo Ji turned and walked out past the rows of empty seats. The ease with which he was able to discard the Wallfacer identity and its responsibilities did not give him the slightest shred of comfort or release. Filling his mind now was an absurd sense of unreality, as if all of this was part of some postmodern play devoid of all logic.

He looked back at the exit and saw Say watching him from the rostrum. She seemed small and helpless against the cliff, but when she saw him looking back, she nodded and smiled at him.

He continued onward, past the Foucault Pendulum at the entrance that showed the rotation of the Earth, and ran into Shi Qiang, Kent, and a group of black-suited security personnel who looked inquiringly at him. In their eyes he saw a new respect and awe. Even Shi Qiang and Kent, who had always behaved naturally toward him, made no attempt to mask their expressions. Luo Ji passed through their midst, saying nothing. He walked through the bare lobby, occupied as on his arrival only by black-clothed guards. As before, whenever he passed one, they spoke softly into a radio. When he came to the exit, Shi Qiang and Kent stopped him.

"It may be dangerous outside. Do you need security?" Shi Qiang asked.

"No, I don't. Get out of my way," Luo Ji said, keeping his eyes straight ahead.

"Very well. We can only do as you tell us," Shi Qiang said as he moved aside. Kent did the same. Luo Ji went out the door.

The cool air hit him in the face. It was still nighttime, but the outside was clearly lit by the bright lamps. The delegates to the special session had driven off, and the few people left in the plaza were tourists or locals. The historic meeting had not yet made the news, so no one recognized him, and his presence did not attract any attention.

And so Luo Ji the Wallfacer walked as if sleepwalking through absurd fantastic reality. In his trance, he had lost the capacity for rational thought and was unaware of where he came from, much less where he was going. Unwittingly, he walked onto the lawn and came to a statue. When his gaze passed over it, he noticed that it was of a man hammering a sword: *Let Us Beat Swords into Plowshares*. It had been a gift to the UN from the former Soviet Union, but to his mind the powerful composition formed by the hammer, the bulky man, and the sword being bent beneath him imbued the work with hints of violence.

And then the man with the hammer was smacking Luo Ji savagely in the chest with a fierce blow that sent him tumbling to the ground and knocked him out before he even hit the grass. But the shock passed quickly, and soon partial consciousness returned amid pain and dizziness. He had to shut his eyes against the blinding flashlights that were all around him. Then the rings of light receded and he could make out a circle of faces over him. In the black cloud of haze and agony he recognized Shi Qiang the moment he heard his voice:

"Do you need security protection? We can only do as you tell us!"

Luo Ji nodded weakly. Then everything happened in a flash. He felt himself lifted onto what seemed like a stretcher, and then the stretcher was hoisted up. He was surrounded by a tight clutch of people, as if he was in a narrow pit with walls formed by human bodies. The only thing visible out of the mouth of the pit was the

black night sky, and it was only from the motion of the legs of the people surrounding him that he could tell he was being carried. Soon the pit vanished, as did the sky above him, replaced by the lit ceiling panels of an ambulance. He tasted blood in his mouth and then emptied his stomach in a bout of nausea. Someone beside him caught his vomit—blood and what he had eaten on the plane—in a plastic bag with a practiced hand. After he vomited, someone strapped an oxygen mask to his face. When he could breathe easier he felt a little better, although his chest still hurt. He felt his clothes getting cut off at the chest, and imagined in a panic that fresh blood was spurting from a wound, but that didn't seem to be right, since no bandaging seemed to be taking place. He was covered in a blanket. Not long after that, the vehicle stopped. He was carried out, and the night sky and the lit ceilings of hospital corridors passed over him, then the ceiling of an emergency room, and then, moving slowly overhead, the glowing red slit of the CT scanner. Faces of doctors and nurses occasionally popped into view and caused him pain with their inspections and manipulation of his chest. Finally, when he could see the ceiling of the ward overhead, everything settled down.

"One broken rib and minor internal bleeding. It's not serious. You're not badly injured, but you need rest due to the bleeding," the bespectacled doctor looking down at him said.

This time Luo Ji didn't refuse sleeping pills, but took them with a nurse's help and quickly fell asleep. Two scenes alternated in his dreams: the rostrum of the UN assembly hall looming above him, and the man from *Let Us Beat Swords into Plowshares* swinging a hammer into him over and over. Later, he came to the quiet patch of snow deep in his heart and entered the simple, exquisite cabin. The Eve of his own creation stood up from the fireplace, her beautiful eyes brimming with tears. . . . Then he woke up and felt tears in his own eyes and a spot of wetness on the pillow. They had dimmed the lights for him, and since she didn't appear while he was awake, he fell back to sleep in the hope of returning to the cabin. But this time he slept without dreaming.

When he woke next, he knew that he had been asleep for a long time. He felt refreshed, and although there was still intermittent pain in his chest, he could believe now that his injuries weren't serious. When he tried to sit up, the blond nurse didn't stop him, but simply adjusted his pillow for him to lean on. After a while, Shi Qiang came in and sat down by his bed.

"How are you feeling? I've been shot three times while wearing a bulletproof vest. This shouldn't be anything serious," he said.

"Da Shi, you saved my life," Luo Ji said weakly.

Shi Qiang waved a hand. "This happened because we fell down on the job. We didn't take timely and effective protection measures. We have to do what you say. It's over now, though."

"And the other three?"

Shi Qiang knew immediately who he was referring to. "They're fine. They weren't as careless as you, walking out alone."

"Does the ETO want to kill us?"

"Probably. The assailant has been detained. It's a good thing we set up a snake-eye behind you."

"A what?"

"A precise radar system that can quickly determine the shooter's position from the path of the bullet. The assailant's identity has been confirmed. He's a professional guerilla in the ETO militia. We never imagined he would dare to attack in a downtown area like this. His actions were practically suicidal."

"I'd like to see him."

"Who? The assailant?"

Luo Ji nodded.

"Sure. But that's not within the scope of my authority. I'm only in charge of security protection. I'll put in a request." Having said this, Shi Qiang turned and left. He seemed more careful and cautious now, different from the lackadaisical image he used to project. Luo wasn't used to it.

Shi Qiang quickly returned and said, "You may, either here or somewhere else. The doctor says walking isn't an issue."

Luo Ji wanted to tell him that he'd like to change venues.

He even started to get up, but then the thought struck him that a sickly appearance better suited his purpose, so he lay back down again. "I'll see him here."

"They're on their way over, so you'll have to wait for a while. Why don't you have something to eat? It's been a day since you ate on the plane. I'll set it up." Then he went out again.

The assailant was brought in right after Luo Ji had finished eating. He had a handsome European face, but his most prominent feature was his slight smile, a smile that seemed so plastered on it never went away. He was not in cuffs, but when he entered, two people who looked like professional escorts sat down on chairs, and two others stood at the doorway. They were wearing badges that identified them as PDC officers.

He tried to look as close to death's door as possible, but the assailant saw through him. "Doctor, surely it's not as serious as all that?" He smiled as he said this, a different smile appearing over his permanent one like an ephemeral oil slick floating on water. "I'm very sorry."

"You're sorry for trying to kill me?" Luo Ji raised his head off the pillow to look at his attacker.

"Sorry I didn't kill you, sir. I thought you wouldn't be wearing a vest to a meeting like this. Never imagined you would be so scrupulous with protecting your life. Otherwise I'd have used armor-piercing bullets, or simply aimed for your head. Then I would have completed my mission, and you would be freed from yours, this unnatural mission no normal person can shoulder."

"I'm already free of it. I submitted my refusal to the secretary general, rejecting the Wallfacer position and all of its rights and responsibilities, and she agreed on behalf of the UN. Of course, you didn't know this when you were trying to kill me. The ETO wasted an assassin."

The smile on the assailant's face grew brighter, like a monitor whose brightness had been turned up. "You're a funny man."

"What do you mean? I'm telling you the honest truth. If you don't believe me—"

"I believe you, but you're still a funny man," the assailant said, the bright smile still on his face. It was a smile that Luo Ji noted in passing but that would soon be imprinted on his consciousness as if by liquid metal, marking him for life.

He shook his head and, with a sigh, lay back down on the bed. He did not speak.

The assailant said, "Doctor, I don't think we have much time. I presume you did not call me here purely to tell this infantile joke."

"I still don't understand what you mean."

"If that's the case, then your intelligence does not qualify you to be a Wallfacer, Dr. Luo Ji. You're not as logical as your name suggests. My life really has been wasted, it appears." The assailant looked at the two people standing on alert behind him and said, "Gentlemen, I think we can leave."

The two cast an inquiring glance at Luo Ji, who waved a hand at them, and then the assailant was led out.

Luo Ji sat up in bed and thought over the assailant's words. He had the odd feeling that something wasn't right, but he didn't know what it was. He got out of bed and took a couple of steps: no impediments apart from the dull pain in his chest. When he went to the door and looked out, the guards armed with rifles sitting beside it stood up immediately, and one of them spoke into the radio on his shoulder. Luo Ji saw a bright and clean hallway that was completely empty except for two more armed guards at the very end. He shut the door, went over to the window, and drew back the curtain. Looking down from this height he saw that guards armed to the teeth were posted all over the hospital entrance, and two green military vehicles were parked out front. Apart from the occasional white-clothed hospital staffer hurrying in or out, he saw no one else. Looking more carefully, he noticed that on the roof of the building opposite were two people surveying the surroundings through binoculars next to a sniper rifle, and he was instinctively certain that similar snipers were on the roof of his own building.

The guards weren't police. They looked like military. He called for Shi Qiang.

"The hospital is still under heavy security, correct?" he asked.

"Yes."

"And if I asked you to dismiss all of the security, what would happen?"

"We would do as you asked. But I advise you not to do so. It's dangerous at the moment."

"What department are you with? What are you in charge of?"

"I belong to the Planetary Defense Security Department, and I'm in charge of your safety."

"But I'm no longer a Wallfacer. I'm just an ordinary citizen, so even if my life is in danger, the duty ought to fall to the ordinary police. Why should I still enjoy this degree of protection from planetary defense security? And to have them dismissed or recalled if I so desire? Who gave me that power?"

Shi Qiang's face remained expressionless, like a rubber mask. "These are the orders we were given."

"Then . . . where's Kent?"

"Outside."

"Call him in!"

Kent came in shortly after Shi Qiang left. His manner had returned to the gracious demeanor of a UN official.

"Dr. Luo, I wanted to wait to see you until you had recovered."

"What are you doing now?"

"I'm your day-to-day liaison with the Planetary Defense Council."

"But I'm not a Wallfacer anymore!" Luo Ji shouted. Then he asked, "Has the media announced the Wallfacer Project?"

"To the entire world."

"And my refusing to be a Wallfacer?"

"It's in there too, of course."

"What did it say?"

"It was quite simple. 'After the conclusion of the UN special session, Luo Ji declared his refusal of the Wallfacer position and mission.' "

"Then what are you still doing here?"

"I'm in charge of your day-to-day liaisons."

Luo Ji looked at him blankly. Kent seemed to be wearing the same rubber mask as Shi. He was unreadable.

"If there's nothing else, then I'll be going. Rest well. Call for me at any time," Kent said, and then started to leave. Just as he stepped through the door, Luo Ji called for him to stop.

"I want to see the secretary general."

"The Planetary Defense Council is the specific agency in charge of the direction and execution of the Wallfacer Project. The supreme leader is the PDC's rotating chair. The UN secretary general exercises no direct leadership over the PDC."

Luo Ji thought this over. "I'd still like to see the secretary general. I ought to have that power."

"Very well. Wait one moment." Kent left the room, but soon returned and said, "The secretary general is waiting for you in her office. Shall we be off, then?"

All along the way to the secretary general's office on the thirty-fourth floor of the Secretariat Building, Luo Ji remained under security so tight he was practically shut up in a movable safe. The office was smaller than he had imagined, and simply furnished, with a fair bit of space taken up by a UN flag standing behind the desk. Say came around the desk to welcome him.

"Dr. Luo, I'd wanted to visit you in the hospital yesterday, but you see . . ." She gestured to the pile of papers on the desk, whose only personal touch was a finely crafted bamboo pencil holder.

"Ms. Say, I have come to reiterate the statement I made to you at the close of the meeting," he said.

Say nodded but said nothing.

"I want to go home. If I am in danger, please notify the New York Police Department and have them be responsible for my safety. I am just an ordinary citizen. I don't need PDC protection."

Say nodded again. "That certainly can be done, but I advise you to accept your current protection, because it is more specialized and reliable than the NYPD."

"Please answer me honestly. Am I still a Wallfacer?"

Say returned to her desk. Standing beside the UN flag, she

smiled slightly at Luo Ji. "What do you think?" Then she motioned for him to take a seat on the sofa.

The slight smile on Say's face was familiar. He had seen the same smile on the face of the young assailant, and in the future he would see it in the eyes and on the face of everyone he met. The smile would come to be called "the Wallfacer smile," and it would be as famous as the smile of the *Mona Lisa* or the grin of the Cheshire cat. Say's smile calmed him down at last, the first time he had been truly calm since before she had stood on the rostrum and announced to the world that he was a Wallfacer. He sat slowly down on the sofa, and by the time he got situated, he understood everything.

My god!

It took just an instant for Luo Ji to comprehend the true nature of his status as Wallfacer. Like Say had said, before the mission was handed down, the ones who would undertake it could not have been consulted. And once the Wallfacer mission and identity were granted, they could not be refused or abandoned. This impossibility was not due to any individual's coercion, but because cold logic, as determined by the project's very nature, meant that once someone became a Wallfacer, an invisible and impenetrable screen was immediately thrown up between them and ordinary people that made their every action significant. And that was what the smiles directed at Wallfacers meant:

How are we supposed to know whether or not you have already started work?

He now understood that the Wallfacers had a mission far weirder than any in history, its logic cold and twisted, yet unyielding as the chains that bound Prometheus. It was an unliftable curse impossible for the Wallfacers to break under their own strength. No matter how he struggled, the totality of everything would be greeted with the Wallfacer smile and imbued with the significance of the Wallfacer Project:

How are we supposed to know whether or not you are working?

His heart surged with a towering fury such as he had never before experienced. He wanted to shout hysterically, to inquire

after Say's mother and the UN's mother, to inquire after the mothers of all of the delegates at the special session and on the PDC, to inquire after the mothers of the entire human race, and finally to inquire after the nonexistent mothers of the Trisolarans. He wanted to jump up and down and smash things, to sweep aside the documents, globe, and bamboo pencil holder on Say's desk, and then tear the blue flag to shreds. . . . But in the end he understood where he was and who he was facing, controlled himself, and stood up, only to fall heavily back upon the sofa again.

"Why was I chosen?" Luo Ji began, hands covering his face. "Next to the three of them, I have no qualifications. I have no talent and no experience. I've never seen war, much less led a country. I'm not a successful scientist. I'm just a university professor who muddles through by throwing together crappy papers. I'm someone who lives for today. I don't want kids of my own, and I could care less about the continuation of human civilization. . . . Why was I picked?" By the end of this speech, he had jumped up from the sofa.

Say's smile vanished. "To tell you the truth, Dr. Luo, we're baffled by this too. And that's the reason you have access to the fewest resources out of all of the Wallfacers. Choosing you is the greatest gamble in history."

"But there's got to be a reason why I was chosen!"

"Yes, but only indirectly. No one knows the real reason. Like I said, you have to find your own answer."

"Then what about the indirect reason?"

"I'm sorry. I'm not authorized to tell you. But I do believe that you'll know when the time is right."

Luo Ji sensed that they had reached the end of their conversation, so he turned to leave, only realizing when he reached the door that he hadn't said good-bye. He turned around. Like in the assembly hall, Say nodded at him with a smile. Only this time, he knew the meaning behind that smile.

She said, "It's a pleasure to meet you again. But in the future, your work will be conducted within the framework of the PDC, so you will report directly to the PDC rotating chair."

"You don't have any confidence in me, do you?" Luo Ji asked.

"I said that choosing you was a huge gamble."

"Then you're right."

"Right to have gambled?"

"No. Right to have no confidence in me."

Again with no good-bye, he walked straight out of the office. Relapsing to the state he had been in just after being declared a Wallfacer, he walked aimlessly. At the end of the hallway, he entered an elevator and rode it down to the hall on the ground floor, then exited the Secretariat Building and came once more to the United Nations Plaza. He was surrounded by security guards the entire way, and though he pushed them impatiently a few times, they stuck to him like magnets and followed him wherever he went. It was daytime now, and Shi Qiang and Kent walked up to him in the sunny square and asked him to either go back inside or enter a vehicle as quickly as possible.

"I'm never going to see the sun again my entire life, am I?" he asked Shi Qiang.

"It's not that. They've cleared the vicinity, so it's relatively safe here. But there are lots of visitors who all recognize you. Crowds are hard to handle, and you probably don't want that either."

Luo Ji looked around him. At least for now, no one paid any attention to their small group. He headed toward the General Assembly Building and entered quickly for a second time. His goal was clear and he knew where he had to go. Past the empty balcony, he saw the colorful stained-glass panel. Turning right, he entered the Meditation Room, closing the door to keep Shi Qiang, Kent, and the guards outside.

When he saw the oblong slab of iron ore for a second time, his first instinct was to dash himself into it headfirst and put an end to everything. Instead he lay down on the stone's smooth surface, whose coolness drained off some of the irritation from his mind. With his body, he felt the hardness of the ore and, weirdly, thought

of a problem put forth by his high school physics teacher: How can you make a marble bed as soft as a Simmons mattress? The answer: Dig out a depression in that marble the exact size and shape of a human body. Then when you lie in that depression, the pressure will be evenly distributed and it would feel incredibly soft. He closed his eyes and imagined that the warmth of his body was melting the iron ore beneath him and forming that kind of depression. . . . Gradually, this calmed him. After a time, he opened his eyes and looked up at the bare ceiling.

The Meditation Room had been designed by Dag Hammarskjöld, second secretary general of the UN, who believed that the UN ought to have a place for meditation removed from the history-making decisions of the General Assembly Hall. Luo Ji didn't know whether any head of state or ambassador to the UN had actually meditated here, but surely when Hammarskjöld died in 1961 he never imagined that a Wallfacer like himself would be daydreaming here.

Luo Ji felt himself getting snared once again in a logical trap, and once again was convinced that he could not extricate himself.

So he turned his attention to the power in his hands. The least of all the Wallfacers, Say had said, but he would certainly be able to make use of a terrifying amount of resources. Most importantly, he didn't have to justify his use of them to anyone. In fact, an important part of his mandate was to act in such a way as to keep others guessing, and furthermore, to do as much as possible to engender misunderstandings. Never in human history had there been such a thing! Maybe the absolute monarchs of old had been able to do whatever they wished, but even they ultimately had to account for their actions.

If all I'm left with is this peculiar power, why not make use of it? Luo Ji thought to himself, and sat up. After a short time thinking it over, he decided what his next step would be.

He got off the hard bed of stone, opened the door, and asked to see the chair of the PDC.

The incumbent chair, a Russian named Garanin, was a burly, white-bearded old man. The chair's office was one floor below the

secretary general's. He was sending off a few visitors, half of them in uniform, when Luo Ji entered.

"Oh, Dr. Luo. I heard you had some minor problems, so I wasn't in a hurry to get in touch with you."

"What are the other three Wallfacers doing?"

"They're busy setting up general staff departments, a task I'd advise you to get on with immediately. I'll send some advisors to assist you in the initial stages."

"I don't need a general staff department."

"Oh? If you think it would be better that way. . . . If you do have the need, one can be set up at any time."

"May I have a pen and paper?"

"Of course."

Looking at the paper, Luo Ji asked, "Mr. Chair, have you ever had a dream?"

"What sort?"

"For instance, have you ever dreamt of living in some perfect place?"

Garanin shook his head with a wry smile. "I just flew in from London yesterday. I worked the entire trip, and when I arrived I slept less than two hours before I had to rush to work. When today's regular PDC meeting finishes, I'll have to fly overnight to Tokyo. . . . My whole life is rushing around, and I'm at home no more than three months out of the year. What's the point of that kind of dream for me?"

"In my dreams, I've got lots of those places. I've chosen the most beautiful." Luo Ji picked up the pencil and began sketching on the paper. "This isn't colored, so you've got to imagine it. See these snowcapped mountains here? They're steep like the swords of the gods or the tusks of the earth, and they shine a satiny silver against the blue sky. Utterly dazzling . . ."

"Ah," Garanin said, watching with careful attention. "That's a very cold place."

"Wrong! The land beneath the snowcaps must not be cold. It's a subtropical climate. This is important! In front of the mountains

there's a broad lake, and the water is even bluer than the sky, as blue as your wife's eyes. . . ."

"My wife's eyes are black."

"Well, the lake water is a blue so deep it looks black. That's even better. Surrounding the lake are swaths of forest and grasslands, but remember that there have to be both, not just one of the two. This is the place: snow peaks, a lake, forests, and grasslands. And everything is in its untouched, primeval state. When you see the place, you would imagine that man had never set foot on the Earth. Here, on the grass beside the lake, build a house. It doesn't need to be large, but it should be fully equipped for modern living. The style can be either classical or modern, but it should complement its natural surroundings. And the necessary facilities—fountains, a swimming pool—should be provided so that its master can live the comfortable life of the aristocracy."

"And who will its master be?"

"Myself."

"What are you going to do there?"

"Live out my days in peace."

Luo Ji waited for Garanin to say something rude, but the chair simply nodded gravely, and said, "After an audit by the commission, we will carry this out at once."

"You and your commission won't raise any questions about my motivation?"

Garanin shrugged. "The commission can question the Wallfacers in two areas: use of resources exceeding the set scope, and harm caused to human lives. Apart from these, all questions are in violation of the spirit of the Wallfacer Project. And truth be told, Tyler, Rey Diaz, and Hines have left me disappointed. Looking at their strategizing over the past two days, you can tell immediately what they are up to with their grand strategic plans. You're different from them. Your behavior is baffling. That's what a Wallfacer should be like."

"Do you really believe the place I described exists?"

Garanin smiled, winked, and made an "okay" sign. "The world

is big enough to have a place like that. Besides, to tell you the truth, I've seen it before."

"That's wonderful, truly. And make sure that I can live a comfortable aristocrat's life. This is part of the Wallfacer Project."

Garanin nodded gravely.

"Oh, and one other thing. When you find a suitable place, never tell me where it is."

No, you can't say where it is! Once I know where I am, then the world becomes as narrow as a map. When I don't know, the world feels unlimited.

Garanin nodded again, seemingly pleased this time. "Dr. Luo, you've got another trait that satisfies my notion of being a Wallfacer: Your project requires the smallest investment of the four, at least for the time being."

"If that's the case, then mine will never have the largest investment."

"Then you'll be a blessing to all my successors. Money is a real headache. . . . The specific departments in charge of executing this may consult with you on some details. The house, in particular, I think."

"Oh, the house," Luo Ji said. "I forgot one very important detail."

"Go on."

Luo Ji imitated Garanin's wink and smile. "It needs a fireplace."

After his father's funeral, Zhang Beihai went with Wu Yue one more time to the carrier dry dock, where construction on *Tang* had been suspended entirely. The welding sparks had vanished from the hull, and there were no signs of life anywhere on the giant ship lying in the noonday sun. The overarching impression it gave was one of the passage of time.

"It's dead," Zhang Beihai said.

"Your father was one of the wisest generals among the navy's top brass. If he were still with us, I might not have gotten so thoroughly stuck," Wu Yue said.

Zhang Beihai said, "Your defeatism is built on a rational basis, or at least it's your own reasoning, so I don't believe there's anyone who can truly cheer you up. I'm not here to apologize, Wu Yue. I know you don't hate me over this."

"I'd like to thank you, Beihai. You got me out."

"You can return to the navy. Working there should suit you quite well."

Wu Yue shook his head slowly. "I've submitted my discharge application. What would I do if I went back? Construction on new destroyers and frigates has stopped, and I no longer have any place in the fleet. Sit in an office in Fleet Command? Forget it. Besides, I'm not a good soldier at all. A soldier who's only willing to engage in a winnable war is unqualified to be one."

"Victory or defeat is not for us to see."

"But you have faith in victory, Beihai. I envy you, really, to the point of jealousy. Faith like yours is the height of happiness for a military man these days. You truly are your father's son."

"So do you have any plans?"

"No. I feel like my life is over." Wu Yue pointed at *Tang* in the distance. "Just like that, over before it even launched."

A low rumble came from the direction of the shipyard, and *Tang* slowly started to move. To vacate the dock, it had to take to the water ahead of schedule and be towed to another dock for demolition. When *Tang*'s sharp prow split the seawater, Zhang Beihai and Wu Yue sensed a trace of anger in the massive hull. Quickly, it entered the sea, tossing up huge waves that caused the other boats in the port to rock, as if paying tribute. *Tang* crept slowly forward in the water, quietly enjoying the sea's embrace. In its brief and aborted career, this giant ship had at least met the ocean once.

In the virtual *Three Body* world, it was the dead of night. Apart from scraps of starlight, all was immersed in an inky blackness, so that even the horizon was invisible, and the empty land and sky blended together in the dark.

"Administrator, start up a Stable Era. Can't you see we're holding a meeting?" shouted a voice.

The administrator's voice seemed to come from the sky itself. "I can't do that. The era is run randomly along the core model and can't be set externally."

Another voice in the darkness said, "Then increase the speed and find some stable daylight. It won't take too long."

The world flashed. Suns flew across the sky, and soon time returned to normal. One stable sun illuminated the world.

"Okay. I don't know how long this will last," the administrator said.

The sun shone in the wilderness on a group of people, some familiar faces among them: King Wen of Zhou, Newton, Von Neumann, Aristotle, Mozi, Confucius, and Einstein. Sparsely distributed, they faced Qin Shi Huang, who stood on a rock with a sword across his shoulders.

"I am not alone," he said. "This is the core leadership of seven speaking."

"You shouldn't be talking about a new leadership before it's been finalized," someone said, and a clamor rose among the rest.

"Enough," Qin Shi Huang said, struggling to raise the sword. "Setting aside the leadership controversy for the moment, we shall turn to more pressing matters. We all know of the launch of the Wallfacer Project, humanity's attempt to use closed-off, private strategic thinking to resist sophon surveillance. Since the Lord's transparent mind cannot possibly thread that labyrinth, humanity has regained its edge through this plan, and the four Wallfacers pose a threat to the Lord. In accordance with the resolution of the previous offline meeting, we must launch the Wallbreaker Project immediately."

At those last words, silence reigned, and no one voiced any objections.

Then Qin Shi Huang said, "We will appoint a Wallbreaker for each Wallfacer. Like the Wallfacers, the Wallbreakers will be authorized to tap all of the organization's resources, but their greatest

resource will be the sophons, which will render the Wallfacers' every action utterly exposed. The only secret will be their thoughts. The Wallbreakers' mission, then, is to analyze the Wallfacers' open and clandestine actions, with the help of the sophons, and decipher the true nature of their strategic aims as early as possible. The leadership will now appoint the Wallbreakers."

Qin Shi Huang extended the sword and, as if conferring knighthood, touched it to Von Neumann's shoulder. "You are the First Wallbreaker," he said. "You are Frederick Tyler's Wallbreaker."

Von Neumann knelt down and placed his left hand to his right shoulder in a salute. "I accept the mission."

Qin Shi Huang touched the sword to Mozi's shoulder. "You are the Second Wallbreaker. You are Manuel Rey Diaz's Wallbreaker."

Mozi did not kneel, but stood straight and nodded haughtily. "I will be the first to break a wall."

The sword touched Aristotle's shoulder. "You are the Third Wallbreaker. You are Bill Hines's Wallbreaker."

Aristotle did not kneel either, but shook his robe and said thoughtfully, "Yes, I'm the only one who can break his wall."

Qin Shi Huang returned the sword to his own shoulder and swept his gaze across the crowd. "Good. We now have Wallbreakers. You, like the Wallfacers, are the elite of the elite. The Lord be with you! Assisted by hibernation, you will start the long journey to the end of days together with the Wallfacers."

"I don't think hibernation is necessary," Aristotle said. "I can complete the Wallbreaker mission before we finish our normal lifespan."

Mozi nodded in agreement. "When I break the wall, I will face my Wallfacer in person, and I will savor how his spirit collapses in anguish and despair. Devoting the rest of my life to this is well worth it."

The final Wallbreaker likewise stated his intent to break their Wallfacers in person. Von Neumann said, "We will unmask the last traces of every secret that humanity harbors from the sophons. This is the final thing we can do for the Lord, for afterward there will be no reason for us to exist."

"What about Luo Ji's Wallbreaker?" someone asked.

The question seemed to touch something in Qin Shi Huang's mind. He planted the sword into the ground and fell deep in thought. The sun suddenly sped up its descent to the Earth, lengthening the shadows until they extended to the horizon. When it had set halfway, it abruptly changed direction and rose and fell a few times along the horizon, like the gleaming back of a whale cresting out of the black ocean, pulling the vast wilderness and the small group of people that made up this stark world back and forth between light and darkness.

"Luo Ji is his own Wallbreaker. He needs to find out what threat he poses to the Lord," Qin Shi Huang said.

"Do we know whether or not he is a threat?" someone asked.

"I don't know, but the Lord knows, and Evans knew. Evans taught the Lord how to keep this secret, and he's dead. We can't know."

"So of all the Wallfacers, is Luo Ji the greatest threat?" someone hesitantly asked.

"We don't know that either. Only one thing is clear," Qin Shi Huang said, looking up at the canopy of the sky as it changed from blue to black. "Out of the four Wallfacers, he is the only one in direct contest with the Lord."

Work meeting, Space Force Political Department

Chang Weisi stayed silent for a long while after opening the meeting, something he had never done before. He swept his eyes across the two rows of political officers at the conference table, then looked into the infinite distance while gently tapping his pencil on the tabletop, a light tapping that seemed to mark time for his thoughts. At last, he pulled himself out of his reverie.

"Comrades, by an order announced yesterday by the Central Military Commission, I am now serving as commander of the Political Department of the Armed Forces. I accepted the appointment one week ago, but only now that we are seated together do

I feel conflicted. I have suddenly realized that in front of me is the most beleaguered group of people in the space force, and now I am one of your number. I didn't realize this before, and for this I apologize to you." He opened the document in front of him. "This portion of the meeting will be off the record. Comrades, let us have a candid exchange of views. Let us be Trisolarans for once and open our thoughts to each other. This is crucial for our future work."

Chang Weisi's gaze lingered on the face of each officer for a second or two, but they remained silent. Then he stood up and paced along the table behind the row of seated officers.

"Our duty is to build in our forces the faith that we will be victorious in the future war. So, do we have that faith ourselves? Please raise your hands if you do. Remember, we are speaking our minds."

No one raised a hand. Nearly everyone was staring at the table. But Chang Weisi noticed one man's gaze was fixed straight ahead: Zhang Beihai.

He went on, "Do you believe that victory is possible? By possible, I mean not an accidental few tenths of a percent, but an actual, meaningful possibility."

Zhang Beihai raised a hand. His was the only hand raised.

"First let me thank all of you for your honesty," Chang Weisi said, and then turned to Zhang Beihai. "Excellent, Comrade Zhang. Tell us, on what do you base your confidence?"

Zhang Beihai stood up, but Chang Weisi motioned for him to sit down. "This is not a formal meeting," he said. "It's just a heart-to-heart chat."

Still standing at attention, Zhang Beihai said, "Commander, I can't answer your question sufficiently in just a few words, because building faith is a long and complicated process. First of all, I'd like to make note of the mistaken thinking among the troops at the present time. We all know that prior to the Trisolar Crisis, we had been advocating for the examination of the future of war from scientific and rational perspectives, and a powerful inertia has sustained this mentality to the present day. This is particularly

the case in the present space force, where it has been exacerbated by the influx of a large number of academics and scientists. If we use this mentality to contemplate an interstellar war four centuries in the future, we'll never be able to establish faith in a victory."

"What Comrade Zhang Beihai says is peculiar," a colonel said. "Is steadfast faith not built upon science and reason? No faith is solid that is not founded on objective fact."

"Then let's take another look at science and reason. Our own science and reason, remember. The Trisolarans' advanced development tells us that our science is no more than a child collecting shells on the beach who hasn't even seen the ocean of truth. The facts we see under the guidance of our science and reason may *not* be the true, objective facts. And since that's the case, we need to learn how to selectively ignore them. We should see how things change as they develop, and we shouldn't write off the future through technological determinism and mechanical materialism."

"Excellent," Chang Weisi said, and nodded at him to continue.

"We must establish faith in victory, a faith that is the foundation of military duty and dignity! When the Chinese military once faced a powerful enemy under extremely poor conditions, it established a firm faith in victory through a sense of responsibility to the people and the motherland. I believe that today, a sense of responsibility to the human race and to Earth civilization can encourage the same faith."

"But how are we supposed to go about specific ideological work?" asked an officer. "The space force is made up of complicated parts, which means that its ideology is complex. We've got our work cut out for us."

"I think that for the time being, at least, we should start with the mental condition of the troops," Zhang Beihai said. "Big picture: Last week I visited troops from the air force and naval air force that have just been brought under our branch, and I discovered that day-to-day training for these forces is incredibly slack. Small picture: Problems with military discipline are cropping up with increasing frequency. There was supposed to be a total switch

to summer uniforms, but lots of people in headquarters are still wearing their winter uniforms. This state of mind must be changed as quickly as possible. Look, the space force is turning into an academy of sciences. Of course, we can't deny that its present mission is that of an academy of military sciences, but we ought to be conscious that we are an army, and we're an army in a state of war!"

The conversation went on for a while longer, and then Chang Weisi returned to his seat. "Thank you. I hope that we will be able to continue having frank conversations. Now, let's move on to the contents of the formal meeting." As he spoke, he looked up and once again saw Zhang Beihai's steady gaze, which revealed a determination that warmed his heart a little.

Zhang Beihai, I know you have faith. With a father like that, it would be impossible for you not to. But things are definitely not as simple as you say. I don't know what you base your faith on, and I don't even know what else your faith encompasses. Just like your father. I admired him, but I have to admit that in the end I couldn't figure him out.

Chang Weisi flipped open the document in front of him. "Research on space warfare theory is in full swing at present, but one problem has already cropped up: The study of interplanetary warfare needs to be founded on a certain level of technological development, no doubt about it. But right now, basic research has only just begun, and technological breakthroughs will occur far in the future. This means our research has no support. Headquarters has revised the research plan in light of the circumstances, and has divided unified research on the theory of space warfare into three parts, to cater to the possible technological levels that the human world may reach in the future. Namely: a low-tech strategy, a mid-tech strategy, and a high-tech strategy.

"Work is currently in progress to define these three levels of technology, as well as to define a large number of index parameters in every major scientific discipline, but the core parameter will be the speed and range of a ten-kiloton-class spaceship.

"The Low-Tech Level: Spacecraft speed achieves fifty times the third cosmic velocity,[10] or roughly eight hundred kilometers per second. Spacecraft are not equipped with life support. Under these conditions, the craft has a combat radius limited to the inner Solar System. That is, within Neptune's orbit, or thirty AU from the sun.

"The Mid-Tech Level: Spacecraft speed achieves three hundred times the third cosmic velocity, or forty-eight hundred kilometers per second. Spacecraft are equipped with partial life support. Under these conditions, the combat radius of the craft extends beyond the Kuiper Belt, and includes all space within one thousand AU of the sun.

"The High-Tech Level: Spacecraft speed achieves one thousand times the third cosmic velocity, or sixteen thousand kilometers per second, which is five percent of the speed of light. Spacecraft are fully equipped with life support. Under these conditions, the combat radius extends to the Oort Cloud,[11] with preliminary interstellar navigation capabilities.

"Defeatism is the greatest threat to the armed forces in space, so political and ideological workers will shoulder an extremely important responsibility in the space force. Political departments in the military will participate fully in the study of space warfare theory to eradicate the stain of defeatism and guarantee the correct direction of research.

"Those of you present today will become members of a space warfare theory task force. Although there will be some overlap among members of the three branches, the research institutions are independent, and will tentatively be known as the Institute for Low-Tech Strategy, the Institute for Mid-Tech Strategy, and the

10 *Translator's Note:* First cosmic velocity is the initial velocity a body needs to achieve orbit, second cosmic velocity the amount needed to leave an object's gravitational pull, and third cosmic velocity the amount needed to leave the Solar System.

11 *Translator's Note:* The Oort Cloud is a collection of icy objects in a spherical distribution that surrounds the Solar System at a distance of 50,000 to 100,000 AU and is believed to be the source of long-period comets.

Institute for High-Tech Strategy. At today's meeting, I'd like to hear from each of you which one you would choose, as a reference for the Political Department's next round of work appointments. Let's share our selections."

Of the thirty-two political officers at the meeting, twenty-four selected low-tech and seven selected mid-tech. Just one officer chose high-tech: Zhang Beihai.

"Looks like Comrade Beihai wants to get into science fiction," someone said, to scattered laughter.

"My choice is the only hope for victory. That's the only level of technology that gives humanity any chance of building an effective defensive system for the Earth and Solar System," Zhang Beihai said.

"We haven't even mastered controlled nuclear fusion. Sending a ten-thousand-ton warship to five percent of the speed of light? Ten thousand times faster than the truck-sized spacecraft humanity has today? It's not even science fiction. It's fantasy!"

"But don't we have four more centuries? We've got to keep potential progress in mind."

"But progress in fundamental physics is impossible."

"We haven't even tapped one percent of the potential applications of existing theories," Zhang Beihai said. "My feeling is that the biggest problem right now is the technology sector's approach to research. They're wasting too much time and money on low-end technology. In propulsion, for example, there's no reason at all to work on the fission drive, but right now they're not only throwing huge amounts of R&D at it, they're even putting the same amount of effort into studying next-gen chemical propulsion! We should focus our resources on studying fusion engines, and move directly to the development of media-free fusion engines, leapfrogging media-based fusion. The same problem exists in other areas of research. Sealed ecosystems, for instance, are a necessary technology for interstellar spacecraft, one that is not particularly dependent on fundamental theory, but research in this area is very limited."

Chang Weisi said, "Comrade Zhang Beihai has posed at least one question worthy of attention: The military and scientific

communities are all busy starting their own work, but there is insufficient communication among them. Fortunately, both sides are aware of the situation and are organizing a joint conference, and the military and the scientific communities have each established special agencies to strengthen communication between the two sides and establish a fully interactive relationship between space strategy and scientific research. The next step is to dispatch military representatives to the various research areas and to involve a large group of scientists in studying the theory of space warfare. Again, we can't sit and wait for technological breakthroughs. We ought to form our own ideological strategy as soon as possible and then promote it in every field.

"Next, I'd like to talk about another layer of relationships: that between the space force and the Wallfacers."

"The Wallfacers?" someone asked in wonder. "Are they going to interfere in space force work?"

"There's no sign of that at the moment, although Tyler has proposed paying an inspection visit to the military. But we ought to realize that they do have that power, and any interference that does take place may have unanticipated effects. We need to be mentally prepared for it. When such a situation does occur, we should maintain a balance between the Wallfacer Project and mainstream defense."

After the meeting, Chang Weisi sat alone in the empty conference room smoking a cigarette. The smoke wafted into a beam of sunlight shining through the window and seemed to catch fire.

Whatever happens, at least it's begun, he thought to himself.

For the first time, Luo Ji felt that a dream had come true. He had imagined that Garanin was only boasting—of course he could find a stunning, untouched place, but it was certain to be quite different from the place in his imagination. But when he got off the helicopter, it was like he had stepped into a dream world: the distant snow peaks, the lake in front of him, the grassy plain and

forest beside the lake, all of it laid out exactly as he had sketched it for Garanin. And he hadn't dared permit himself to imagine such an immaculate environment. Everything seemed to have sprung out of a fairy tale. There was a slight sweetness to the fresh air, and even the sun seemed to be cautious, sending the softest and most exquisite part of its glow into this place. The most incredible thing was the small estate beside the lake and the villa at its heart. Kent, who was traveling with him, said the house was built in the mid-nineteenth century, but it looked older, and the passage of time had made it blend in with its environment.

"Don't be surprised. Sometimes people dream of places that really exist," Kent said.

"Does anyone live here?" Luo Ji asked.

"No one in a five-kilometer radius. Beyond that there are a few small villages."

Luo Ji guessed that the place might be in northern Europe, but he didn't ask.

Kent led him into the house. With his first glance at the spacious European-style living room, Luo Ji saw a fireplace, with fruitwood stacked neatly next to it that gave off a fresh fragrance.

"The former master of the house bids you welcome. He is proud to have a Wallfacer living here." Kent went on to tell him that the estate contained more than just the facilities he had requested: stables with ten horses, because the best way to get to the mountains was by walking and riding; a tennis court and a golf course; a wine cellar; and, on the lake, a motorboat and a few sailboats. Beneath its old exterior, the house had been fully modernized. Every room was equipped with a computer, broadband, and satellite television, and there was a digital projection room as well. In addition to all of this, Luo Ji had noticed a helipad when he arrived. It was clearly not built at the last minute.

"The man's got money."

"Not just money. He doesn't want to disclose his identity, but you would probably recognize his name if I told you. He donated the land to the UN, a far larger gift than Rockefeller's. Just so

you're clear, the land and all of the real estate on it belong to the UN. You only have right of residence. But you're not getting nothing. When the owner left, he said that he had taken away all of his personal belongings and that whatever is left is yours. These paintings alone must be worth quite a bit."

Kent took Luo Ji on a tour of every room in the house. He noticed that the original owner had good taste and had furnished every room with a sense of elegant tranquility. A considerable portion of the books in the library were old Latin editions. The paintings were mostly in the modernist style, but they did not seem out of place in rooms with a rich classical atmosphere. One thing in particular that struck him was the total absence of landscapes, the mark of a mature aesthetic sensibility: hanging landscape paintings in a house situated in the Garden of Eden would be as pointless as pouring a bucket of water into the ocean.

Returning to the living room, Luo Ji sat down on the deliciously comfortable chair in front of the fireplace. He stretched out his hand and brushed against an object, which he then picked up and inspected. A churchwarden pipe, the kind with a long, thin stem, used indoors by the leisure class. He looked toward the wall and its empty shelves and imagined what had been taken down.

Then Kent came in and introduced a few people: the housekeeper, cook, driver, groom, and boat master, all of whom had been in the previous owner's service. When they had gone, Kent introduced him to a lieutenant colonel in civvies, who was responsible for security. After he left, Luo Ji asked Kent where Shi Qiang was.

"He's handed over your security detail and has probably returned home."

"Let him take the place of that guy just now. I think he'll do a better job."

"I feel the same way, but he doesn't speak English. It would be hard for him to do his job."

"Then bring in Chinese guards to replace the ones here."

Kent agreed and left to make the call. Luo Ji also left the room and walked across the manicured lawn onto a pier leading out

into the middle of the lake. He held the railing at the end and gazed at the reflection of the snowcaps in the lake's mirror surface. Surrounded by sweet air and sunshine, he said to himself, "Compared to life today, what does the world four centuries from now matter?"

Screw the Wallfacer Project.

"How did that bastard get in?" the researcher at the terminal said softly.

"Wallfacers are naturally free to enter," his neighbor answered quietly.

"It's pretty dull, isn't it? I expect you're disappointed, Mr. President," Dr. Allen, director of the Los Alamos National Laboratory, said to Rey Diaz as he led him past the rows of computer terminals.

"I'm no longer president," Rey Diaz said severely, as he surveyed his surroundings.

"This is our nuclear weapons simulation center. Los Alamos has four of these centers, and Lawrence Livermore has three."

Two objects caught Rey Diaz's eye as being not entirely dull. They looked new, with large displays and consoles with lots of fine knobs. He headed over to take a closer look, but Allen pulled him back. "That's a game machine. The terminals here aren't for gaming, so we brought in two machines for relaxation."

Rey Diaz noticed another two not-entirely-dull objects. Transparent and structurally complicated, they contained a bubbling liquid. Again, he started over to take a look, and this time Allen shook his head with a smile and did not stop him. "That one's a humidifier. The climate is dry in New Mexico. The other one's just a coffee machine. Mike, pour Mr. Rey Diaz a cup of coffee. . . . No, wait, not from that. I'll brew you a cup of top-shelf roast in my office."

The only thing left for Rey Diaz to do was to examine the blownup black-and-white photographs hanging on the wall. He recognized the skinny man wearing a hat and smoking a pipe as

Oppenheimer, then Allen directed his attention back to the bland terminals.

"These displays are obsolete," Rey Diaz said.

"But behind them is the most powerful computer in the world, operating at thirty petaFLOPS."

An engineer came up to Allen. "Doctor, the AD4453OG is operational."

"Excellent."

The engineer lowered his voice. "We've suspended the output module," he said, and glanced at Rey Diaz.

"Run it," Allen said, then turned to Rey Diaz: "See, we've got nothing to hide from the Wallfacers."

Then Rey Diaz heard tearing sounds and saw the people at the terminals ripping paper apart. Assuming that they were destroying documents, he muttered, "Don't you even have a shredder?" But then he noticed that they were tearing up blank copy paper. Then someone shouted, "Over!" and everyone cheered and tossed the shredded paper into the air, making the cluttered floor even more like a garbage dump.

"This is a simulation center tradition. When the first atom bomb was exploded, Dr. Fermi tossed torn paper into the air, and according to the distance the pieces drifted in the shock wave, he was able to accurately compute the yield of the bomb. Now we do the same thing for every simulation we run."

Rey Diaz brushed the paper from his head and shoulders, and said, "You run nuclear tests every day, but to you it's as easy as playing a video game. It's not like that for us. We don't have super-computers. We've got to do real tests. . . . We do the same things, but the poor always end up being the nuisance."

"Mr. Rey Diaz, no one here is interested in politics."

Rey Diaz leaned in to take a closer look at the terminals, but saw only scrolling data and shifting curves. When he finally did locate some graphics, they were so abstract he couldn't make anything out. When he leaned toward another terminal, the physicist seated in front of it looked up and said, "Mr. President, if you're

looking for a mushroom cloud, it's not there."

"I'm not the president," Rey Diaz repeated, as he accepted the coffee Allen handed him.

Allen said, "Then we ought to talk about what we can do for you."

"Design a nuclear bomb."

"Of course. Los Alamos may be a multidisciplinary institution, but I suspected you wouldn't be here for any other reason. Can you give me any specifics? What type? What yield?"

"The PDC will send you the completed technical requirements before long, so I'll just brief you on the key points. Large yield, the largest possible. As large as you can make it. Two hundred megatons at an absolute minimum."

Allen stared at him for a moment, and then bent his head in thought. "That will require some time."

"Don't you have mathematical models?"

"Of course we do. We have models for everything from five-hundred-ton shells to large twenty-megaton bombs, from neutron bombs to EMP bombs, but the explosive yield you're asking for is far too large. It's more than ten times the world's largest thermo-nuclear device. It would have to have a totally different trigger and staging from a conventional nuclear weapon, and it might even require an entirely new structure. We don't have a model that fits."

They spoke some more about the general planning of various research projects, and when it came time to leave, Allen said, "Mr. Rey Diaz, I know you have the best physicists on your staff at the PDC. I assume they've told you about the applications of nuclear weapons to space warfare?"

"You're permitted to be redundant."

"Very well. In space warfare, nuclear bombs may be low-efficiency weapons, since nuclear explosions produce no shock wave in the vacuum of space and only negligible pressure from the light they generate, so they don't produce the mechanical impact found in explosions in the atmosphere. All their energy is released in the form of radiation and electromagnetic pulses, and, at least for humans, radiation and

EM shielding on spacecraft is a fairly mature technology."

"And if the target is directly hit?"

"That's a different thing altogether. In that case, heat will be a decisive factor, and the target may be melted or even vaporized. But one bomb of a few hundred million tons will probably be as big as a building, so I'm afraid it won't be easy to score a direct hit. . . . In fact, the mechanical impact of nuclear weapons doesn't measure up to kinetic weapons, their radiation is less intense than particle beam weapons, and their thermal destruction can't compare to gamma-ray lasers."

"But those weapons aren't combat ready. Nuclear bombs are humanity's most powerful mature weapons. And as for the performance issues you mention in space combat, ways can be found to improve them. Adding a medium to create a shock wave, for example, like putting ball bearings in a grenade."

"That's an intriguing idea. Your STEM background shows through."

"My studies were in nuclear energy, which is why I like nuclear bombs. I've got a good feeling about them."

Allen laughed. "I almost forgot: It's ridiculous to discuss issues like this with a Wallfacer."

The two men laughed, but Rey Diaz quickly grew serious and said, "Dr. Allen, like everyone else, you're treating the Wallfacer strategy as something mysterious. The most powerful combat-ready weapon available to mankind right now is the hydrogen bomb. Focusing on that is only natural, isn't it? I believe my approach is the correct one."

The two men stopped on the quiet path through the woods they had been walking along. Allen said, "Fermi and Oppenheimer walked down this road countless times. After Hiroshima and Nagasaki, most of the architects of the first generation of nuclear weapons spent the rest of their lives mired in depression. They would be gratified if they knew the mission that humanity's nuclear weapons are now facing."

"No matter how frightening they might be, weapons are a

good thing. . . . Just to let you know, the next time I come, I hope I won't see you throwing scrap paper around. We should make a tidy impression on the sophons."

Keiko Yamasuki woke up in the middle of the night to find herself alone, the sheets beside her cool. She got up, dressed, and went out the door. At first glance she saw her husband's shadow in the bamboo grove in the yard, as usual. They had homes in England and in Japan, but Hines preferred his Japanese home. He said that the moonlight of the East calmed his heart. There was no moon tonight. The bamboo and his kimono-clad figure lost their dimensionality and looked like paper cuttings hung beneath the stars.

Hines heard Keiko Yamasuki's footsteps but did not look back. Strangely, Keiko wore the same shoes in England as in Japan. Even in her hometown she never wore geta. But it was only here, never in England, that he could hear her footsteps.

"My love, you haven't slept properly for days," she said. Her voice was soft, but the summer insects stopped chirping and peace flooded like water over everything.

She heard her husband sigh. "Keiko, I can't do it. I can't think of anything. Really, I can't come up with anything at all."

"No one can. I say an ultimate victory plan doesn't exist." She took two steps forward but was still separated from Hines by a few stalks of bamboo. The grove was their place for contemplation, and the inspiration for most of their previous research had its source here. They rarely brought intimacy to this sacred place, but always addressed each other courteously, as befitted an atmosphere seemingly imbued with Eastern philosophy. "Bill, you should relax. Doing the best you can is enough."

He turned around, but in the darkness of the grove his face was indistinct. "How is that possible? Every step I take consumes a massive amount of resources."

"Then why not adopt this approach?" Keiko's answer came

swiftly. She had obviously been thinking about the question. "Choose a direction that, even if you're unsuccessful, will do something beneficial while it is being carried out."

"Keiko, that's exactly what I've been thinking about. Here's what I've decided to do: Even if I can't come up with a plan, I can help other people think of one."

"What other people? The other Wallfacers?"

"No, they're not much better off than I am. I mean our descendants. Keiko, have you ever considered this fact? The outcome of natural biological evolution requires at least twenty thousand years to manifest itself, but human civilization has just five thousand years of history, and modern technological civilization just two hundred. That means that the study of modern science today is being done by the brain of primitive man."

"You want to use technology to accelerate the brain's evolution?"

"We've been doing brain research, and we ought to put more effort into expanding it to a scale that can tackle a planetary defense system. If we work hard for a century or two, we might be able to increase human intelligence and allow the science of the future to break out of the sophons' prison."

"Intelligence is a vague term in our field. What in particular—"

"I mean intelligence in the broadest sense of the word. Not just the traditional meaning of logical reasoning, but learning ability, imagination, and innovation as well. And also the ability to accumulate common sense and experience while preserving intellectual vigor. And enhancing mental endurance, so that a brain can think continuously without fatigue. And we can even consider the possibility of eliminating sleep. And so forth."

"What will it take? Do you have even a rough idea?"

"No. Not yet. Perhaps the brain can be connected directly to a computer, which can use its computing power to amplify human intelligence. Or maybe we can achieve a direct interface between human brains and blend different people's thoughts. Or inherit memories. But whatever avenue we ultimately take to increase

human intelligence, we must first begin from a fundamental understanding of the mechanisms of the human brain."

"And that's precisely our area of interest."

"We can continue in the same career as before. The difference will be that we can tap huge resources to do it!"

"Love, I'm truly happy. I'm ecstatic! There's just one thing. As a Wallfacer, don't you think this plan is a little . . ."

"A little indirect? Maybe. But think about it, Keiko. Human civilization ultimately comes down to humans themselves. If we start by elevating humans, doesn't that make this a far-reaching plan? Besides, what else can I do?"

"Bill, you're wonderful!"

"So think about this for a moment: If we turn neuroscience and thought research into a world engineering project, and can invest an inconceivably enormous amount of money in it, how long will we have to wait for success?"

"About a century, more or less."

"Let's be a little more pessimistic and say two centuries. Then the highly intelligent humans will still have two centuries left, and if they use one century to develop fundamental science and another to turn those theories into technology . . ."

"Even if it fails, we'll have done what we wanted to do."

"Keiko, come with me to the end of days," Hines murmured.

"Yes, Bill. We certainly have the time."

The insects in the grove seemed to have grown accustomed to their presence and resumed their musical chirping. When a soft wind blew through the bamboo and the stars in the night sky flashed through the gaps between the leaves, it was as if the insect chorus was issuing from those stars.

It was day three of the PDC's first Wallfacer Project Hearing. Rey Diaz and Hines had spoken about the first phase of their respective projects, which were put to preliminary discussion by representatives of the PDC permanent members.

Rey Diaz and Hines had both submitted their plans at the previous hearing, but Tyler had delayed his first disclosure until this session, leaving representatives particularly eager for details.

Tyler started with a brief introduction: "I need to establish an armed force in space that will supplement Earth's fleet but be under my command."

Just one sentence in, the hands of the other two Wallfacers shot up.

"Mr. Hines and I have been accused of overuse of resources in our plans," Rey Diaz broke in. "But this is absurd. Mr. Tyler wants to have his own space force!"

"I didn't say it was a space force," Tyler said calmly. "The intent is not to construct warships or large spaceships, but to establish a fleet of space fighters. They'll each be roughly the size of a conventional Earth-based fighter and will carry a single pilot. They'll be like mosquitoes in space, so I've dubbed this the 'mosquito swarm plan.' The formation needs to be at least equal to the size of the invading Trisolaran Fleet. A thousand ships."

"You would attack a Trisolaran warship with a mosquito? That's not even going to raise a welt," a hearing member said dismissively.

Tyler raised a finger. "Not if each of those mosquitoes is equipped with a hundred-megaton-class hydrogen bomb. So I'm going to need the latest superbomb technology. . . . Don't turn me down immediately, Mr. Rey Diaz. You can't turn me down, in fact. According to the principles of the Wallfacer Project, that technology isn't your proprietary property. Once it's been developed, I have the right to requisition it."

Rey Diaz glanced up at him. "My question is, do you intend to plagiarize my plan?"

Tyler smiled sardonically. "If a Wallfacer's plan can be copied, is he still a Wallfacer?"

"Mosquitoes can't fly very far," said Garanin, the PDC rotating chair. "These toy space fighters can only engage in combat within the orbit of Mars, I believe."

"Watch out. His next request might be for a space carrier," Hines said with a chuckle.

Tyler answered with aplomb. "That will be unnecessary. These space fighters can be networked to turn the entire squadron into a single entity, a mosquito group, that acts as a space carrier and is propelled by an external engine or by the engines of a small portion of its member fighters. At cruising speed, the group will possess the long-range space navigation capabilities of large spacecraft. Once it reaches the battlefield, the huge entity will disassemble and go into battle as a fleet of independent fighters."

"Your mosquito group will take years to reach the defensive zone at the perimeter of the Solar System. A fighter pilot can't spend such a long journey in a cockpit that doesn't even permit them to stand up. Will there even be room for supplies in such a small craft?" someone asked.

"Hibernation," Tyler said. "They'll have to hibernate. My plan relies on the realization of two technologies: miniaturized super-bombs and miniaturized hibernation units."

"Hibernating for a few years in a metal coffin, then waking up, only to launch a suicide attack. Clearly, the job of a mosquito pilot is not one to be envied," Hines said.

Tyler's enthusiasm disappeared, and he remained silent for a moment. Then he nodded. "Yes. Finding pilots is the hardest part of the mosquito swarm plan."

Details of Tyler's plan were distributed to the members of the hearing, but there was no interest in discussion. The chair declared the hearing adjourned.

"Luo Ji still hasn't arrived?" asked the annoyed US representative.

"He won't be coming," said Garanin. "He declared that his seclusion and nonparticipation in the PDC hearing is part of his plan."

At this, the attendees whispered among themselves. Some of them seemed annoyed, while others flashed cryptic smiles.

"He's a deadbeat, a waste!" Rey Diaz said.

"Then what are *you*?" Tyler asked rudely, even though his

mosquito swarm plan relied on Rey Diaz's super hydrogen bomb technology.

Hines said, "I'd rather express my regard for Dr. Luo. He knows himself and knows his own abilities, so he doesn't want a pointless waste of resources." He turned graciously to Rey Diaz. "I think Mr. Rey Diaz should learn something from him."

Everyone could see that Tyler and Hines were not defending Luo Ji, but that their enmity toward Rey Diaz was far deeper by comparison.

Garanin rapped the gavel on the table. "First of all, Wallfacer Rey Diaz has spoken out of order. I remind you to show respect to the other Wallfacers. Similarly, I remind Wallfacers Hines and Tyler that your words are also inappropriate for this meeting."

Hines said, "Mr. Chair, what Wallfacer Rey Diaz has demonstrated in his plan is nothing but the crudeness of a soldier. Following in the footsteps of Iran and North Korea, his country fell under UN sanctions because of its nuclear weapons program, and this has given him a twisted complex for the bomb. There is essentially no difference between Mr. Tyler's mosquito swarm program and Rey Diaz's giant hydrogen bomb plan. Both are disappointments. The two straightforward plans will have their strategic intent exposed right from the start. Neither exhibits the canniness that's the strategic advantage of the Wallfacer Project."

Tyler shot back, "Mr. Hines, your plan is like some sort of naïve daydream."

When the hearing ended, the Wallfacers went to the Meditation Room, their favorite place in UN Headquarters. It now seemed to them that this room designed for silence was built especially for Wallfacers. Gathered there, they waited in silence, each of them feeling that they would never be able to exchange thoughts until the final war came. The slab of iron ore lay silently in their midst, as if absorbing and collecting their thoughts and silently bearing witness.

Hines said softly, "Have you heard about the Wallbreakers?"

Tyler nodded. "The ETO just announced it on their public Web site, and it's been verified by the CIA."

The Wallfacers lapsed into silence again, each one conjuring in his mind an image of his own Wallbreaker. It was an image that would appear countless times in their nightmares, for the day a Wallbreaker actually appeared would likely spell the end of that Wallfacer.

When Shi Xiaoming saw his father enter, he edged toward the corner, but Shi Qiang simply sat down quietly next to him.

"Don't be afraid. I won't hit you or curse at you this time. I don't have the energy." He brought out a pack of cigarettes, took out two, and offered one to his son. Shi Xiaoming hesitated before accepting it. They lit up and smoked for a while in silence. Then Shi Qiang said, "I've got a mission. I'll be leaving the country soon."

"What about your illness?" Shi Xiaoming looked up through the smoke and gave his father a worried look.

"Let's talk about you first."

Shi Xiaoming's expression turned pleading. "Dad, there's going to be a heavy sentence for this—"

"Any other crime, and I'd be able to work it out for you, but that's not how this is going to work. Ming, we're both adults. We need to be responsible for our actions."

Shi Xiaoming bowed his head in despair and took a silent draw on his cigarette.

Shi Qiang said, "I'm half to blame. I never had any concern for you when you were growing up. I came home late every night, so tired I'd just have a drink and then go to bed. I never went to a parents' meeting at school, and I never had a good talk with you about anything. . . . It's the same thing again: We have to be responsible for our own actions."

Tears in his eyes, Shi Xiaoming ground the cigarette back and forth repeatedly on the edge of the bed, like he was extinguishing the latter half of his life.

"Prison is like a criminal training course. Forget about reform when you go in, just don't get mixed up with the other prisoners.

And learn how to protect yourself a little. Take these—" Shi Qiang placed a plastic bag on the bed. Inside were two cartons of ordinary Yun Yan cigarettes. "And if you need anything else, your mother will send it to you."

Shi Qiang went to the door, then turned and said to his son, "Ming, you may still meet your dad again. You'll probably be older than me at that point, and then you'll understand what's in my heart right now."

Through the small window in the door, Shi Xiaoming watched his father exit the detention center. From the back, he looked quite old.

In an era where anxiety had taken hold of everything, Luo Ji was now the world's most laid-back man. He strolled beside the lake, took a boat out into the water, had the chef turn the mushrooms he picked and the fish he caught into tasty delicacies, browsed through the library's rich collection, and when he tired of that, went outside and golfed with the guards. He rode on horseback through the grassland and on the forest path in the direction of the snow peak, but he never reached the foot of the mountain. Oftentimes, he would sit on a bench on the lakeside and look at the mountain's reflection in the water, doing and thinking nothing as an entire day passed unknowingly.

He was alone during this time, with no connection to the outside world. Kent was in the manor, too, but he had his own small office and rarely bothered him. Luo Ji had only spoken once to the officer in charge of security, to ask that the security detail not trail along behind him, and if they absolutely had to, to make sure that he could not see them.

He felt like the boat in the water, floating quietly with its sail furled, ignorant of where it was moored and not caring where it floated. Now and then when he thought about his former life, he was surprised to discover that in the short space of a few days, he could no longer recognize it. This state satisfied him.

He was particularly interested in the wine cellar. He knew that the dust-covered bottles lying horizontally on the racks held nothing but the best. He drank in the living room, he drank in the library, and sometimes he drank on the boat; but never too much, just enough to keep him in that perfect, half-drunk, half-sober state, and then he would take out that long-stemmed pipe left by the previous owner and puff away.

Even when it rained and the living room grew chilly, Luo Ji never had the fireplace lit. He knew it wasn't yet time.

He never went online here, but he sometimes watched television, skipping over the news and watching programs that had nothing to do with current events or even the present day. This sort of content was still possible to find, although it was growing increasingly rare in the last ebbs of the Golden Age.

Late one night, he got carried away by a bottle of cognac that, from the label, was thirty-five years old. Wielding the remote, he skipped past the several news stations on the high-definition television, but one English-language news item caught his eye. It concerned the salvage of a mid-seventeenth-century wreck, a clipper that had sailed from Rotterdam to Faridabad and had sunk off Cape Horn. Among the objects that divers had retrieved from the wreck was a small, sealed cask of fine wine that experts speculated was still drinkable. Not only that, but after three centuries in storage at the bottom of the ocean, its taste would be unparalleled. Luo Ji recorded most of the program, and then called for Kent.

"I want that cask. Buy it for me," he said.

Kent went to make a call. Two hours later he told Luo Ji that the price of the cask was astonishingly high: Bidding would start at three hundred thousand euros.

"That amount is nothing to the Wallfacer Project. Buy it. It's part of the plan."

And thus, the Wallfacer Project produced a second idiom after the "Wallfacer smile." Anything that was clearly absurd but which had to be done anyway was called "part of the Wallfacer plan," or simply, "part of the plan."

Two days later, the cask, its aged surface covered in shells, was placed in the villa's living room. Luo Ji took out a tap with a twist drill specially made for wooden casks, which he found in the cellar, and carefully drilled it into the side to pour out the first glass. The liquid was a tempting emerald green. He sniffed it, and then put the glass to his lips.

"Doctor, is this part of the plan too?" Kent asked softly.

"That's right. It's part of the plan." Luo Ji was about to drink, but seeing the people present in the room, he said, "All of you, out."

Kent and the rest of them did not move.

"Sending you out is part of the plan too. Out!" He glared at them. Kent gently shook his head and led the others out.

Luo Ji took a sip. Although he did his utmost to convince himself that the flavor was heavenly, in the end he did not have the guts to take a second sip. But that one sip didn't let him go unscathed. That night he was sick out both ends until he spat up bile the color of the wine and his body was so weak he couldn't get out of bed. Later, after doctors and experts opened the cask lid, they found that it had a rather large brass label on the inside wall, as was the custom in those days. Over time there had been some sort of reaction between the normally peacefully coexisting copper and the wine, and some sort of substance had dissolved into the wine. . . . When the cask was carried off, Luo Ji could see the schadenfreude on Kent's face.

Deeply exhausted, he lay in bed watching his IV drip, and an intense loneliness seized him. He knew that his recent leisure was merely the weightlessness of tumbling into the abyss of loneliness, and now he had reached the bottom. But he had anticipated this moment, and he had been prepared. He was waiting for someone, and then the next step of the plan would begin. He was waiting for Da Shi.

Tyler stood holding an umbrella against the Kagoshima drizzle. Behind him, two meters away, stood defense chief Koichi Inoue, whose umbrella remained unopened. The past two days he had

maintained the same separation from Tyler, both physically and mentally. They were at the Chiran Peace Museum for Kamikaze Pilots, and in front of them was a statue of a special attack unit next to a white plane, call sign 502. A light layer of rain painted the surface of the statue and the aircraft and made them deceptively lifelike.

"Isn't there any room for discussion of my proposal?" Tyler asked.

"I strongly advise you not to speak of this to the media. It will cause trouble." Koichi Inoue's words were as icy as the rain.

"Is it still that sensitive, even today?"

"What's sensitive isn't the history, but your proposal to restore the kamikaze special attack units. Why don't you do it in the US or some other place? Are the Japanese people the only ones in the world who can die out of duty?"

Tyler closed up his umbrella and drew closer to Koichi Inoue, who—although he didn't recoil—seemed to have a force field surrounding him that prevented Tyler from getting close. "I've never said that the future kamikaze forces would be made up only of Japanese members. It's an international force, but since it originated in your great country, isn't it only natural to revive it here?"

"In interplanetary war, does this mode of attack really have any significance? You should realize that victories for those special attack units were limited, and they didn't turn the tide of battle."

"Commander, sir, the space force I have established is a fleet of fighters equipped with super hydrogen bombs."

"Why do you need humans? Can't computer-controlled fighters get close enough to attack?"

This question seemed to give Tyler the opportunity he was waiting for, and he grew excited. "That's exactly the problem! Today's computers are unable to replace human brains, and advancements in fundamental theory would be necessary for quantum and other next-gen computers. But that's been locked up by the sophons. So four centuries from now, computing intelligence will still be limited, and human-controlled weapons will be indispensable. . . . To tell you the truth, reviving the kamikaze squads only has moral

significance now, because it will be ten generations before any of them go to their death. But establishing that spirit and faith means starting now!"

Koichi Inoue turned around to face Tyler for the first time. His wet hair was plastered against his forehead and the raindrops on his face looked like tears. "That approach violates the basic moral principles of modern society: Human lives come first, and the state and the government can't require any individual to take up a death mission. I seem to remember a line Yang Wenli said in *Legend of the Galactic Heroes*:[12] 'In this war lies the fate of the country, but what does it matter next to individual rights and freedoms? All of you just do your best.'"

Tyler sighed. "You know what? You have thrown away your most precious resource." Then he snapped open his umbrella and turned and walked angrily away. When he reached the gate of the memorial, he looked back and saw Koichi Inoue still standing in the rain before the statue.

As Tyler walked in the sea breeze, his mind returned to a sentence from a suicide note from a kamikaze pilot to his mother that he had seen in the exhibit:

Mom, I'm going to be a firefly.

"It's worse than I imagined," Allen said to Rey Diaz. They were standing next to a black obelisk made of lava rock, the monument marking ground zero of humankind's first atom bomb.

"Is its structure really that different?" Rey Diaz asked.

"Totally different from today's nuclear bombs. Constructing its mathematical model might be more than a hundred times more complicated than today's bombs. This is an enormous under-taking."

"What do I need to do?"

"Cosmo's on your staff, right? Get him to come to my lab."

12 *Translator's Note:* Yang Wenli is one of the protagonists of *Legend of the Galactic Heroes*, a series of Japanese science fiction novels launched in 1982 by Yoshiki Tanaka, and followed by manga and anime adaptations.

"William Cosmo?"

"Yes."

"But he's . . . he's . . ."

"An astrophysicist. An authority on stars."

"What's he going to do?"

"That's what I'm gonna tell you. To your mind, a nuclear bomb is detonated and then explodes, but the actual process is more like burning. The greater the yield, the longer the combustion. A twenty-megaton nuclear explosion, for example, has a fireball that can last for over twenty seconds. The superbomb we're designing is two hundred megatons, and its fireball will burn for several minutes. Think about that. What will it look like?"

"A small sun."

"Correct! Its fusion structure is very like that of a star, and it reproduces stellar evolution over a very abbreviated period. So the mathematical model we need to construct is essentially the model of a star."

White sands stretched out in front of them. In the moments just before dawn, the details of the dark desert couldn't be made out. As they gazed at the scenery, they were involuntarily reminded of the basic setting of *Three Body*.

"I'm very excited, Mr. Rey Diaz. Please forgive me for our lack of enthusiasm at the start. Looking at the project now, the significance far exceeds the construction of a superbomb itself. Do you know what we're doing? We're creating a virtual star!"

Rey Diaz shook his head in disapproval. "What does that have to do with the defense of Earth?"

"Don't be limited by planetary defense. Me and my colleagues in the lab are scientists, after all. Besides, this thing is not without practical significance. So long as you input the appropriate parameters, the star could be a model for our sun. Think about it. It's always useful to have the sun in your computer memory. It's the biggest presence that's close to us in the cosmos, but we could take more advantage of it. The model may have many more discoveries lying in wait."

Rey Diaz said, "One previous use of the sun is what brought humanity to the brink, and brought you and me to this place."

"But new discoveries might bring humanity back. So today, I've invited you here to watch the sunrise."

The rising sun was now just peeking its head over the horizon. The desert in front of them came into focus like a developing photograph, and Rey Diaz could see that this place, once blasted by the fires of hell, was now covered in sparse undergrowth.

"I am become death, the destroyer of worlds," Allen exclaimed.

"What?" Rey Diaz whipped his head around, as if someone had shot him from behind.

"Oppenheimer said that when he watched the first nuclear explosion. I think it's a quote from the Bhagavad Gita."

The wheel in the east expanded rapidly, casting light across the Earth like a golden web. The same sun was there on that morning when Ye Wenjie had tuned the Red Shore antenna, and even before that, the same sun had shone upon the dust settling after the first bomb blast. Australopithecus a million years ago and the dinosaurs a hundred million years ago had turned their dull eyes upon this very sun, and even earlier than that, the hazy light that penetrated the surface of the primeval ocean and was felt by the first living cell was emitted by this same sun.

Allen went on, "And then a man called Bainbridge followed up Oppenheimer's statement with something completely nonpoetic: 'Now we are all sons of bitches.'"

"What are you talking about?" Rey Diaz said. Watching the rising sun, his breathing became ragged.

"I'm thanking you, Mr. Rey Diaz, because from now on we're not sons of bitches."

In the east, the sun rose in overarching solemnity, as if declaring to the world, "Everything is as fleeting as a shadow before me."

"What's the matter, Mr. Rey Diaz?" Allen saw that Rey Diaz had fallen into a crouch, one hand on the ground, and was convulsing in dry heaves. His face had turned pale and was covered in a cold sweat, and he had no strength to move his hand from the

clump of thorns it was pressing on.

"Go, go to the car," he said weakly. He turned his head in the direction opposite the sun, and he raised his other hand to block the sunlight. He was unable to get up. Allen tried to assist but couldn't budge his stocky body. "Drive the car over. . . ." Rey Diaz wheezed out, while pulling his hand back to cover his eyes. When Allen drove over to him, he had fallen to the ground. With difficulty, Allen helped him into the backseat. "Sunglasses. I need sunglasses. . . ." He half-reclined into the backseat, his hands clawing at the air. Allen handed Rey Diaz a pair of sunglasses he found on the dashboard. After he put them on his breathing grew smoother. "I'm all right. Let's get out of here. Quickly," he said feebly.

"What on earth happened? What's wrong?"

"It might be the sun."

"Uh . . . when did you start having this sort of reaction?"

"Just now."

The peculiar phobia for the sun that afflicted Rey Diaz pushed him to the edge of mental and physical breakdown whenever he saw it and kept him confined indoors from then on.

"Was the flight very long? You look like you don't have any energy," was the first thing Luo Ji said after Shi Qiang arrived.

"Yeah. You'll never find a plane as comfortable as that one we were on," Shi Qiang said as he appraised his surroundings.

"Not bad, eh?"

"It's awful," Shi Qiang said, shaking his head. "Woods on three sides, so it's easy to hide close to the house. And there's a lake. With the shore this close to the house, it would be difficult to defend against divers coming from the woods on the other side. But the surrounding grassland is pretty good, and provides some open space."

"Can't you be any more romantic?"

"I'm here to work, my boy."

"It's romantic work I'm thinking of." Luo Ji led Shi Qiang into

the living room. He surveyed it, but did not seem much impressed by the luxury and elegance. Luo Ji poured him a drink in a crystal goblet, but Shi Qiang turned it down with a wave of his hand.

"It's thirty-year-old aged brandy."

"I can't drink right now. . . . Tell me of this romantic work of yours."

Luo Ji sipped his brandy and sat down next to him. "Da Shi, I'm asking you to do me a favor. In your old job, did you ever have to look across the entire country for a particular person, or even around the world?"

"Yes."

"Were you good at it?"

"At finding people? Of course."

"Great. Help me find a person. A woman in her early twenties. This is part of the plan."

"Nationality? Name? Address?"

"None. The possibility that she even exists in the world is low."

Shi Qiang looked at him, and after a few seconds said, "You dreamed her?"

Luo Ji nodded. "Daydreams, too."

Shi Qiang nodded, too, then said something Luo Ji had not expected him to say. "Okay."

"What?"

"Okay, so long as you know what she looks like."

"She's, well, she's Asian, so let's say Chinese." As Luo Ji spoke, he took out a paper and pencil. "Her face is like this. Her nose, like this. And her mouth . . . geez, I can't draw. And her eyes . . . damn it, how can I draw her eyes? Do you have one of those things, a piece of software that will let you pull up a face and then adjust the eyes and nose and so on according to the eyewitness's description to come up with an accurate depiction of the person the witness saw?"

"Sure. I've got one right here on my laptop."

"Then get it out and let's draw!"

Shi Qiang stretched out on the sofa and situated himself comfortably. "Not necessary. You don't need to draw her. Just keep

156

talking. Put aside her appearance, and first talk about what sort of person she is."

Something in Luo Ji's mind caught fire, and he stood up and began to pace restlessly in front of the fireplace. "She . . . how should I put it? She came into this world like a lily growing out of a rubbish heap, so . . . so pure and delicate, and nothing around her can contaminate her. But it can all harm her. Yes, everything around her can hurt her! Your first reaction when you see her is to protect her. No, to care for her, to let her know that you are willing to pay any price to shield her from the harm of a crude and savage reality. She . . . she's so . . . ah, I've got a clumsy tongue. I can't say anything clearly."

"It's always like that," Shi Qiang said with a laugh. His laugh, which had seemed crude and silly the first time Luo Ji heard it, felt full of wisdom now, and it soothed him. "But you've been clear enough."

"Okay. Well, I'll go on, then. She . . . but what am I saying? No matter what I say, I can't express what she's like in my heart." He grew irritated, and seemed to want to tear out his heart to show to Shi Qiang.

Shi Qiang calmed him with a wave. "Forget it. Just talk about what happens when the two of you are together. The more detailed the better."

Luo Ji's eyes widened in amazement. "How did you know about the two of us?"

Shi Qiang laughed again. Then he looked around. "There wouldn't happen to be any cigars in this place, would there?"

"Yes, there are!" Luo Ji grabbed an elegant wooden box from the mantel, took out a thick Davidoff, and used an even more elegant guillotine-style cigar cutter to slice off the end. Then he passed it to Shi Qiang, and lit it for him with a cedar strip specially designed for cigars.

Shi Qiang took a puff and nodded his head, pleased. "Go on."

Luo Ji overcame his earlier language barrier and grew garrulous. He described how she had come alive for the first time in

the library, how she appeared in his classroom during a lecture, how the two of them had met in front of the imaginary fireplace in his dormitory, the beauty of the firelight shining onto her face through the bottle of wine like the eyes of twilight. He recalled with pleasure their road trip, describing every last detail: the fields after the snow, the town and village under the blue sky, the mountains like old villagers basking in the sun, and the evening and bonfire at the foot of the mountain. . . .

After he finished, Shi Qiang stubbed out his cigar. "Well, that's about enough. I'll guess a few things about the girl, and you see if I'm right."

"Great!"

"Education: She's got at least a bachelor's, but less than a doctorate."

Luo Ji nodded. "Yes, yes. She's knowledgeable, but not to the point where it calcifies her. It only makes her more sensitive to life and to the world."

"She was probably born into a highly educated family and lived a life that wasn't too rich but more affluent than most families. Growing up she enjoyed her parents' love, but she had little contact with the community, particularly the lower rungs of society."

"Right, absolutely right! She never told me about her family circumstances, or actually anything about herself, but I think that ought to be the case."

"Now, if any of the following speculations are wrong, let me know. She likes to wear—how would you put it—simple, elegant clothing, a little plainer than other women her age." Luo Ji nodded dumbly, over and over. "But there's always something white, like a shirt or a collar, that contrasts sharply with the dark colors of the rest of the outfit."

"Da Shi, you're . . ." Luo Ji said, admiration in his eyes, as he watched Shi Qiang speak.

Brushing him aside, Shi Qiang went on, "Finally, she's not tall, one hundred and sixty centimeters or so, and her body is . . . well, I guess you could say slender, as if a gust of wind could blow her

away, so she doesn't seem so short. . . . I can come up with more, of course. Not far off, is it?"

Luo Ji was ready to fall on his knees before Shi Qiang. "Da Shi, I throw myself on the ground before you. You're the reincarnation of Sherlock Holmes!"

Shi Qiang stood up. "Now I'll sketch her on the computer."

That night, he brought the computer to Luo Ji. When the woman's portrait appeared onscreen, Luo Ji stared, not moving a muscle, like he had been struck by a curse. Shi Qiang had evidently expected this, and retrieved another cigar from the mantel, clipped it with the guillotine, lit it, and began to smoke. When he had taken a few puffs, he came back to find Luo Ji still staring at the screen.

"Tell me what's off and I'll adjust it for you."

With difficulty, Luo Ji tore his gaze from the screen, stood up, and walked to the window, where he watched the moonlight shining on the distant snow peak. He murmured, dreamlike, "Nothing."

"I thought so," Shi Qiang said, and closed the computer.

Still gazing into the distance, Luo Ji uttered a phrase that others had used to evaluate Shi Qiang: "Da Shi, you're a devil."

Shi Qiang sat down on the sofa, exhausted. "There's nothing supernatural about it. We're both men."

Luo Ji turned to him. "But every man's dream lover is quite different!"

"Dream lovers are basically the same for men of a certain type."

"Still, getting it so close should be impossible!"

"Remember, you told me a lot of stuff."

Luo Ji walked over to the computer and opened it up again. "Send me a copy." Then, as Shi Qiang worked on copying the image, he asked, "Can you find her?"

"All I can say now is that it's quite likely. But I can't rule out not finding her."

"What?" Luo Ji's hands stopped their movements and he turned to look at Shi Qiang in astonishment.

"With this sort of thing, how can you guarantee one hundred percent success?"

"No, that's not what I mean. The total opposite, in fact. I thought you would say that it's practically impossible, but you wouldn't rule out a random, one-ten-thousandth of a percent chance of finding her. And if you had said that, I'd have been satisfied." He turned back to the picture on the screen, and murmured again, "Can such a person really exist in the world?"

Shi Qiang smiled scornfully. "Dr. Luo, how many people have you seen?"

"Not as many as you, of course, but I know that there's no perfect person in the world, much less a perfect woman."

"Like you said earlier, I'm often able to find a particular individual out of tens of thousands, and I can tell you from the experience of most of my life that there are all kinds of people out there. All kinds, my boy. Perfect people, perfect women. You just haven't met them."

"That's the first time I've heard anyone say that."

"It's because someone who's perfect in your mind isn't necessarily perfect in the minds of others. This girl of your dreams—to me, she's got obvious, well, imperfections. So there's a good chance of finding her."

"But directors can search for an ideal actor out of tens of thousands of people and not find them in the end."

"Those directors can't match our professional search capabilities. We're not just looking at tens of thousands, or even hundreds of thousands or millions of people. The tools and techniques we use are more sophisticated than any director's. The computers at the police analysis center, say, can find a match out of upwards of a hundred million faces in just half a day. . . . The only catch is that this is beyond the scope of my duties, so I'll need to report to the higher authorities first. If they approve and assign the task to me, then of course I'll do my best."

"Tell them that it's an important part of the Wallfacer Project and must be taken seriously."

Shi Qiang chuckled opaquely and then took his leave.

———

"What? The PDC needs to find him . . . ?" Kent groped for the Chinese term. "A dream lover? The guy's been indulged too much. I'm sorry. I can't pass along your request."

"Then you are in violation of the Wallfacer Project principle: No matter how incomprehensible a Wallfacer's order is, it must be reported and executed. Any veto belongs to the PDC."

"But we can't use society's resources to allow a person like him to live the life of an emperor! Mr. Shi, we haven't been working together long, but I really respect you. You're an experienced and insightful man, so tell me the truth. Do you really think Luo Ji is carrying out the Wallfacer Project?"

Shi Qiang shook his head. "I don't know." He raised a hand to stop Kent from arguing. "However, sir, that's just my ignorance, not the opinion of our superiors. This is the biggest difference between you and me: I'm just someone who faithfully carries out orders. You, you're someone who always has to ask why."

"Is that wrong?"

"It's not about right or wrong. If everyone had to be clear about why before they executed an order, then the world would have plunged into chaos long ago. Mr. Kent, you do outrank me, but when you get down to it, we're both people who carry out orders. We ought to understand that some things aren't for people like us to think over. It's enough to do our duty. If you can't do that, then I'm afraid you'll have a rough time."

"I'm already having a rough time! We just wasted gobs of money buying that sunken wine. I just think . . . look, does he look like a Wallfacer at all?"

"What should a Wallfacer look like?"

Kent was speechless for a moment.

"Even if there were a template for a Wallfacer, Luo Ji is not entirely inconsistent with it."

"What?" asked Kent, a little taken aback. "You're not saying that you see a certain amount of quality in him?"

"That I am."

"Well, damn it, what do you see?"

Shi Qiang clapped a hand to Kent's shoulder. "You, for example. If the Wallfacer mantle descended upon you, you would be an opportunistic hedonist just like him."

"I'd have broken down long before now."

"That's right. But Luo Ji's carefree. Nothing bothers him. Kent, old fellow, do you think what he's doing is easy? Open-mindedness, is what this is, and anyone who wants to do great things needs to be open-minded. Someone like you won't accomplish great things."

"But he's so . . . I mean . . . if he's just carefree like that, how does it relate to the Wallfacer Project?"

"I've been explaining it all this time and you still don't get it? I said that I don't know. How do you know that what the guy's doing right now isn't part of the plan? Once again, this isn't something for you or I to judge. Taking a step back, even if we're correct in what we think,"—Shi Qiang drew close to Kent and lowered his voice—"some things require time."

Kent stared at Shi Qiang for a long moment, and at last shook his head, unsure whether or not he understood that last sentence. "Fine. I'll make the report. But can you let me see that dream lover of his first?"

When he saw the woman on the screen, Kent's old face grew gentle for an instant. He rubbed his jaw and said, "Oh . . . my god. I don't believe for a moment that anyone like that exists, but I hope you find her soon."

"Colonel, do you find it a little abrupt for me to inspect the political and ideological work of your military in my capacity?" Tyler said when he met Zhang Beihai.

"No, Mr. Tyler. There's precedent for it. Rumsfeld once visited the Central Military Commission's Party School when I was studying there." Zhang Beihai lacked the curiosity, caution, and distance that Tyler had observed in the other officers. He appeared sincere, and that made the conversation easier.

"You've got good English. You must be from the navy."

"That's right. The US Space Force drew an even larger proportion from the navy than we did."

"That venerable old branch of the services would never have imagined that its warships would be sailing into space. . . . I'll be frank. When General Chang Weisi introduced you as the finest political cadre in the space force, I thought you would be army, because the army is the soul of your military."

Zhang Beihai clearly did not agree, but he laughed graciously. "The same soul is found throughout the different branches of the military. In every country's nascent space force, the military culture bears the imprint of its various branches."

"I'm quite interested in your political and ideological work. I was hoping I could do some in-depth investigation."

"Not a problem at all. My superiors have instructed me to hold nothing back, within the scope of my work."

"Thank you!" Tyler hesitated before going on. "My purpose in this trip is to obtain an answer. I'd like to ask you first."

"Of course. Go ahead."

"Colonel, do you believe that we can restore the spirit of armies of the past?"

"What do you mean by 'past'?"

"A wide range of time, from perhaps ancient Greece through the Second World War. What's key is the spiritual commonalities I mentioned: duty and honor above all, and, in time of need, to unhesitatingly lay down one's life. You may have noticed that after the Second World War, this spirit vanished from the military in democratic and authoritarian countries alike."

"The army is drawn from society, so it would mean that the past spirit you speak of would need to be restored throughout society."

"Our views agree on this point."

"But, Mr. Tyler, that is impossible."

"Why? We have four hundred years. In the past, human society used exactly that amount of time to evolve from the era of

163

collective heroism to one of individualism, so why can't we use the same amount of time to evolve back?"

Zhang Beihai considered this for a moment, then said, "This is a profound question, but I think that society has grown up and can never return to its childhood. In the four hundred years that led to the formation of modern society, we see no cultural or mental preparation for this sort of crisis."

"Then from what do you draw your confidence? As far as I'm aware, you are a committed triumphalist. How will a space fleet brimming with defeatism face a powerful enemy?"

"Didn't you just say we have four hundred years? If we can't go backward, then we must move resolutely forward."

Zhang Beihai's answer was opaque. Tyler obtained nothing else from the ensuing conversation but a feeling that the man's thoughts went deeper than a brief visit could reveal.

Tyler passed a sentry as he left the space force headquarters. When their eyes met, the sentry greeted him with a shy smile. It was something he hadn't seen in other countries' militaries, whose sentries stared intently straight ahead. Looking at the young man's face, Tyler once again repeated that line to himself:

Mom, I'm going to be a firefly.

It began to rain that evening for the first time since Luo Ji had arrived at the estate, and the living room was quite cold. He sat beside the unlit fireplace and listened to the rain outside, feeling that the house was located on a lonely island in the middle of a dark ocean. He wrapped himself in the boundless solitude. With Shi Qiang gone, he had been restlessly waiting, and this lonely wait was itself a kind of happiness. Then he heard a car pull up to the porch and caught snatches of conversation. The soft, gentle voice of a woman saying "Thank you" and "Good-bye" jolted him like an electric shock.

Two years ago, he had heard the same sound day and night in his dreams. The ethereal sound, a wisp of gossamer floating

through the blue sky, brought a fleeting sunshine to the gloomy evening.

Then there was a light knock at the door. He sat stiffly in place and only after a long while did he finally open his mouth and say, "Come in." The door opened. A slender figure floated in on a breath of rain. The sole light in the living room was a floor lamp with an old-fashioned lampshade that cast a circle of illumination beside the fireplace but lit the rest of the room only dimly. Luo Ji couldn't make out her face, but noticed that she wore white trousers and a dark jacket that stood in stark contrast to her white collar and made him think of lilies.

"Hello, Mr. Luo," she said.

"Hello," he said, standing up. "Is it cold outside?"

"Not in the car." Although he couldn't see her clearly, he knew she was smiling. "But here"—she looked around her—"here it's a little cold. . . . Er, I'm Zhuang Yan, Mr. Luo."

"Hello, Zhuang Yan. Let's light the fireplace."

And so Luo Ji knelt down and put some of the neatly stacked fruitwood into the fireplace. He said, "Have you ever seen one before? Here, come have a seat."

She came over and sat on the sofa, still in the shadows. "Oh . . . only in the movies."

Luo Ji struck a match and lit the fire-starter under the wood pile. The flame stretched like it was alive, and the woman gradually took shape in its soft golden glow. Luo Ji gripped tightly to the match with two fingers as it burnt down. He needed the pain to tell him this wasn't a dream. It was like he had ignited the sun, which now shone on a dreamworld-turned-reality. Outside, the sun could remain forever hidden by clouds and night, so long as his world had her and the firelight in it.

Da Shi, you really are a devil. Where did you find her? How the hell were you able to find her?

Luo Ji looked away, back into the fire, and tears came unbidden to his eyes. This made him a little scared to look at her, until he realized there was no reason to hide—she would probably think it was the

165

smoke that made him cry. He rubbed his tears away with a hand.

"It's really warm, and nice . . ." she said with a smile as she watched the flames.

Her words and her smile made Luo Ji's heart tremble.

"Why is it like this?" She looked up and glanced around the dim living room a second time.

"It's not the same as you imagined?"

"It's not the same."

"It's not . . ." He thought about her name. "It's not 'dignified' enough for you?"

She smiled at him. "My name is the 'yan' that means color, not dignity."

"Oh, I see. Perhaps you think there ought to be lots of maps, and a large screen, and clusters of uniformed generals, and I'd be here pointing at things with a stick?"

"That's it exactly, Mr. Luo." Delighted, her smile blossomed like a rose in bloom.

Luo Ji stood up. "You must be tired from the journey. Have some tea." He hesitated. "Or would you care for some wine? It'll ward off the cold."

She nodded. "Okay." She accepted the goblet with a quiet "Thank you," and took a small sip.

Looking at her innocently holding the wineglass stirred the most delicate parts of his mind. She drank when invited. She trusted the world and had no wariness about it at all. Yes, everything in the world was lying in wait to hurt her, except here. She needed to be cared for here. This was her castle.

He sat down and looked at her, and then said, as calmly as he could, "What did they tell you before you came?"

"That I'd be coming to work, of course." She flashed him that innocent smile that dashed his heart to pieces. "Mr. Luo, what will I be working on?"

"What did you study?"

"Traditional painting, at the Central Academy of Fine Arts."

"Ah. Have you graduated?"

"Yes. I just graduated, and have been looking for work while I prepare for grad school."

Luo Ji considered this for a while, but he couldn't come up with anything for her to do. "Well, as for work, we'll talk about that tomorrow. You must be tired. First you must sleep well. . . . Do you like it here?"

"I don't know. There was a lot of fog when I came from the airport, and then it got dark, so I couldn't see anything. . . . Mr. Luo, where is this?"

"I don't know either."

She nodded and chuckled to herself, clearly not believing him.

"I really don't know where we are. The land looks like Scandinavia. I could call and ask right now." He reached for the phone next to the sofa.

"No, don't, Mr. Luo. It's nice not knowing."

"Why?"

"Once you know, the world turns narrow."

My god, he exclaimed to himself.

All of a sudden, she exclaimed, "Mr. Luo, look at how lovely the wine is in the firelight."

The wine, soaked in the light of the fire, shone with a glistening crimson found only in dreams.

"What do you think it looks like?" he asked nervously.

"Well, I think it looks like eyes."

"The eyes of twilight, no?"

"The eyes of twilight? That's a marvelous way to put it, Mr. Luo."

"Dawn or twilight? You prefer twilight, do you?"

"That's right. How did you know? I love painting the twilight." Her eyes shone crystalline in the firelight, as if asking, *What's wrong with that?*

The next morning, after the rain had cleared, Luo Ji felt as if God had washed out this Garden of Eden to prepare for Zhuang Yan's arrival. When she saw its true appearance for the first time, what Luo Ji heard was not the squeals and fussing and exclamations that young women like her usually made. No, in the face of

167

such a magnificent vista, she fell into an awed and breathless state and was unable to speak even one word of praise. He could tell that she was far more sensitive to natural beauty than other women.

"So you really like to paint?" he asked.

She stared speechless at the distant snow peak, and it was some time before she recovered her senses. "Oh, yes. But if I'd grown up here, I probably wouldn't."

"Why's that?"

"I've imagined lots of wonderful places, and when I paint them it's like I've been there. But this place has everything from my dreams and imagination, so what would a painting do?"

"That's true. When the beauty in your imagination becomes reality, it's really . . ." He trailed off, and glanced at Zhuang Yan against the sunrise, the angel who had stepped out of his dream. The happiness in his heart rippled like the waves on the lake sparkling in the light. The UN and the PDC never imagined that this would be a consequence of the Wallfacer Project. If he died now, he wouldn't care.

"Mr. Luo, if it rained so much yesterday, why hasn't the snow on that mountain been washed away?" she asked.

"The rain fell below the snowline. That mountain has snow year-round. The climate here is very different from back in China."

"Have you been to the mountain?"

"No. I haven't been here very long." He noticed that the girl's eyes never left the mountain. "Do you like snowcaps?"

She nodded.

"Then let's go."

"Really? When?" she exclaimed in excitement.

"We can set off now. There's a simple roadway that runs to the foot of the mountain, and if we go now, we can be back by evening."

"What about work?" Zhuang Yan tore her eyes from the mountain and looked at Luo Ji.

"Work can be set aside for now. You just arrived," he said perfunctorily.

"Well . . ." She tilted her head, giving his heart a jolt. The naïve

expression was one he had seen on her countless times before. "Mr. Luo, I've got to know what it is I'm doing."

He looked into the distance and thought for a few seconds, then said with finality, "I'll tell you when we've reached the mountain."

"Great! Then we should be off, shouldn't we?"

"Right. It's easier if we take the boat to the other side of the lake and then drive from there."

They walked to the end of the pier. Luo Ji noted that the wind was favorable, so they could take the sailboat. The direction would change at night so they would be able to catch it again coming back. He took her by the hand to help her into the boat. It was the first time he had touched her, and her hands were exactly like the ones he had first clasped on that winter night in his imagination, so soft and cool. She was pleasantly surprised when he raised the white spinnaker. When the boat left the pier, she plunged a hand into the water.

"The lake water is very cold," he said.

"But it's so clean and clear!"

Like your eyes, he said to himself. "Why do you like snowcaps?"

"I like traditional painting."

"What's that got to do with snowcaps?"

"Mr. Luo, are you aware of the difference between traditional painting and oil painting? Oil paintings are brimming with rich colors. A master once said that in oil painting, white is as precious as gold. But it's different with traditional painting. There's lots and lots of blank space, and blank space forms the painting's eyes. The scenery is just the border for that blank space. Look at that snowy peak. Doesn't it look like the blank space in a traditional painting?"

This was the most she had ever said to him. She lectured the Wallfacer, pouring out words and turning him into an ignorant schoolboy, without any sense of being out of line.

You're like the blank space in a traditional painting: pure, but to a mature appreciation, infinitely appealing, he thought as he looked at her.

The boat docked at a pier on the opposite shore, where an

open-top Jeep was parked next to the trees. The driver who had parked it there was gone.

"Is this a military car? I saw troops around when I arrived, and had to go past three sentry points," she said as they got into the car.

"That doesn't matter. They won't bother us," he said, starting the engine.

The road passing through the forest was narrow and rough, but the car drove smoothly on it. In the forest, where the morning mist had not yet lifted, the sun penetrated the tall pines with shafts of light, and even through the engine sound they could hear the calls of birds in the trees. A sweet breeze whipped up Zhuang Yan's hair and tossed it about on Luo Ji's face, and the itching made him think of the winter road trip two years ago.

Everything about their surroundings was completely remote from Mount Taihang and the snowy northern China plains, but his dreams from that trip were so seamlessly connected to today's reality that he found it hard to believe that it was actually happening to him.

He turned to look at Zhuang Yan and found her looking back at him. She had been for a long time, it seemed. The look in her eyes was one of slight curiosity mixed with goodwill and innocence. Sunbeams flickered over her face and body. When she saw Luo Ji looking at her, she did not turn away.

"Mr. Luo, do you really have the ability to defeat the aliens?" she asked.

He was completely overcome by her childlike nature. The question was one that no one but her would ever ask a Wallfacer, and they had known each other so briefly.

"Zhuang Yan, the core meaning of the Wallfacer Project is to encapsulate humanity's real strategy in the mind of one person, the only place in the world that's safe from sophon spying. They had to choose a few people, but that doesn't mean those people are supermen. Superman doesn't exist."

"But why were you chosen?"

That question was even more abrupt and outrageous than the previous one, but it sounded natural coming from Zhuang Yan's

lips, because in her transparent heart, every sunbeam was transmitted and refracted with crystalline clarity.

Luo Ji slowed the car to a stop. She looked at him in surprise as he stared straight ahead at the patches of sun on the roadway.

"Wallfacers are the most untrustworthy people in history. The world's greatest liars."

"That's your duty."

He nodded. "But, Zhuang Yan, I'm going to tell you the truth. Please believe me."

She nodded. "Mr. Luo, please continue. I believe you."

He was silent for a long while, increasing the weight of the words he then uttered. "I don't know why I was chosen." He turned to her. "I'm just an ordinary man."

She nodded again. "It must be very hard."

Those words and Zhuang Yan's look of innocence again brought tears to his eyes. It was the first time he had received such an acknowledgement since becoming a Wallfacer. The girl's eyes were his paradise, and in that clear gaze he saw no trace of the expression that everyone else directed at the Wallfacers. Her smile was paradise for him, too. It wasn't the Wallfacer smile, but a pure, innocent smile, like a sun-drenched dewdrop falling softly into the driest part of his soul.

"It'll be hard, but I'd like to make it easier. . . . That's all. Here endeth the truth. We now return to the Wallfacer state," he said, as he restarted the engine.

They drove on in silence, until the trees grew sparse and the deep blue sky emerged overhead.

"Mr. Luo, look at that eagle!" Zhuang Yan shouted.

"And that over there looks like deer!" He pointed, fast enough to distract her attention, because he knew that the object in the sky wasn't an eagle but a circling sentry drone. This reminded him of Shi Qiang. He took out his phone and dialed.

Shi Qiang answered. "Hey, brother Luo. So now you remember me, eh? First, tell me: How's Yan Yan doing?"

"Fine. Excellent. Wonderful. Thank you!"

"That's good. So it turns out I've completed my final mission."

"Final mission? Where are you?"

"Back home. I'm getting ready for hibernation."

"What?"

"I've got leukemia. I'm going to the future to cure it."

Luo Ji slammed his foot down on the brakes and stopped short. Zhuang Yan yelped. He looked at her in concern, but, seeing that nothing was wrong, he resumed talking to Shi Qiang.

"Er . . . when did this happen?"

"I got irradiated on a previous mission and then got ill last year."

"My god! I didn't delay you, did I?"

"With this sort of thing, delay isn't relevant. Who knows what medicine will be like in the future?"

"I'm truly sorry, Da Shi."

"Oh, it doesn't matter. It's all part of the job. I didn't bother you about it because I figured we would be able to meet again sometime. But I'd like to tell you something in case we can't."

"Please."

After a lengthy silence, Shi Qiang said, " 'Three things are unfilial, and having no issue is the greatest.'[13] Brother Luo, the lineage of the Shi family four hundred years from now is in your hands."

The call disconnected. Luo Ji looked up at the sky, where the drone had disappeared. The empty blue wash of the sky was his heart.

"You were talking to Uncle Shi?" Zhuang Yan asked.

"Yes. Did you meet him?"

"I met him. He's a nice man. The day I left he accidentally broke the skin on his hand and it wouldn't stop bleeding. It was pretty scary."

"Oh . . . Did he say anything to you?"

"He said you were doing the most important thing in the world, and he asked me to help you."

13 *Translator's Note:* This famous quote about filial piety appears in *Mencius*, a collection of conversations and anecdotes related to the Confucian philosopher of the same name, who lived in the late fourth century BC.

Now the forest had entirely disappeared, leaving only grassland between them and the mountain. In silver and green, the composition of the world had turned simple and pure, and, to Luo Ji's mind, more and more like the girl sitting beside him. He noticed a hint of melancholy in her eyes, and he became aware that she was sighing softly.

"Yan Yan, what's wrong?" he asked. It was the first time he had called her that, but he thought, *If Da Shi can call her that, why can't I?*

"It's such a beautiful world, but when you think about how someday there may be no one here to see it, it's quite sad."

"Won't the aliens be here?"

"I don't think they appreciate beauty."

"Why?"

"My dad said that people who are sensitive to beauty are good by nature, and if they're not good, then they can't appreciate beauty."

"Yan Yan, their approach to humans is a rational choice. It's the responsible thing to do for the survival of their species, and has nothing to do with good or evil."

"That's the first I've heard of it. Mr. Luo, you're going to see them, aren't you?"

"Perhaps."

"If they're really like you say, and you defeat them in the Doomsday Battle, then, well, could you . . ." She tilted her head to look at him, and hesitated.

He was about to say that the possibility of that was practically nil, but he controlled himself, and said, "Could I what?"

"Why do you have to drive them out into space to die? Give them a plot of land, and let them coexist with us? Wouldn't that be wonderful?"

Luo Ji dealt silently with his emotions for a moment, then pointed up to the sky and said, "Yan Yan, I'm not the only one who heard what you just said."

Zhuang Yan looked up nervously. "Oh, right. There must be tons of sophons around us."

"It might have been the Trisolar High Consul himself who heard you."

"And you're all laughing at me, aren't you?"

"No. Yan Yan, do you know what I'm thinking right now?" He had a strong impulse to take hold of her slender left hand, which was lying next to the steering wheel, but he controlled himself. "I'm thinking that the person who might actually have a chance of saving the world is you."

"Me?" She burst out laughing.

"You, except that you're not enough. Or, rather, there aren't enough people like you. If a third of humanity was like you, then Trisolaris might negotiate with us about the possibility of coexisting on the world. But now . . ." He let out a long sigh.

Zhuang Yan flashed a helpless smile. "Mr. Luo, it hasn't been easy for me. Going out into the world after graduation, I was like a fish swimming into the sea, where the water was muddy and I couldn't see anything at all. I wanted to swim to clearer waters, but all that swimming got tiring. . . ."

I wish I could help you swim to those waters, he said to himself.

The road began to climb the mountain, and as the altitude increased, the vegetation grew sparse, exposing the naked black rock. For one stretch of road, they seemed to be driving on the surface of the moon. But soon they crossed the snowline and were surrounded by white, and a crisp chill filled the air. He grabbed down jackets from the travel bag in the backseat, and they put them on and continued ahead.

Before long they reached a roadblock, a conspicuous sign in the middle of the road that warned, DANGER: AVALANCHE SEASON. ROAD AHEAD CLOSED. So they got out of the car and walked to the snow at the roadside.

The sun had started its descent, casting shadows around them on the snowy slope. The pure snow was pale blue in color, almost weakly fluorescent. The jagged peaks in the distance were still lit and shone silver in all directions, a light that seemed to issue from

the snow itself, as if it was this mountain and not the sun that had been illuminating the world all along.

"Okay, now the painting's entirely blank," he said, sweeping his hands about him.

Zhang Yan drank in the white world around her. "Mr. Luo, I actually did do a painting like this once. From a distance, it was a white sheet of paper, almost entirely blank, but closer in you would see fine reeds in the lower left corner, and in the upper right the traces of a disappearing bird. In the blank center, two infinitesimally tiny people. . . . It's the painting I'm proudest of."

"I can imagine it. It must be magnificent. . . . So, Zhuang Yan, now that we're in this blank world, are you interested in learning about your job?"

She nodded, but looked anxious.

"You know about the Wallfacer Project, and you know that its success relies on its incomprehensibility. At its highest level, no one on Earth or Trisolaris, apart from the Wallfacer himself, understands it. So, Zhuang Yan, no matter how inexplicable you find your work, it definitely has meaning. Don't try to understand it. Just do it as best you can."

She nodded nervously. "Yes, I understand." Then she laughed and shook her head. "I mean, I get it."

Looking at her amid the snow, the whiteness lost all dimension, and the world faded around her, leaving her its only presence. Two years before, when the literary image he had created had come to life in his imagination, he had tasted love. Now, in the blank space of this grand natural painting, he understood love's ultimate mystery.

"Zhuang Yan, your work is to make yourself happy."

Her eyes widened.

"You must become the happiest woman on Earth. This is part of the Wallfacer plan."

The light of the peak that illuminated their world was reflected in her eyes, and complex feelings drifted across the purity of her

gaze. The snowy peak absorbed all sound from the outside world, and he waited patiently in the silence, until finally she said, in a voice that seemed to come from a great distance, "Then . . . what should I do?"

Luo Ji grew animated. "Whatever you want to! Tomorrow, or when we go back tonight, you can go wherever you want and do whatever you wish, and live life as you please. As a Wallfacer, I can help you realize all of it."

"But I . . ." She looked at him helplessly. "Mr. Luo, I . . . I don't need anything."

"That's not possible. Everyone needs something! Aren't young people always chasing after something?"

"Have I ever chased after anything?" She slowly shook her head. "No, I don't think so."

"Ah, yes. A carefree young woman like you might not need to. But you've got to have a dream, at least. You like painting, so have you ever thought of having an individual exhibition at the world's largest gallery or art museum?"

She laughed, as if Luo Ji had turned into a foolish child. "Mr. Luo, I paint for myself. I've never thought about that stuff."

"Well then. You must have dreamed of love," he said without hesitation. "You've got the means now, so why not go find it?"

The sunset was draining its light from the snowy peak. Zhuang Yan's eyes darkened, and her expression softened. She said gently, "Mr. Luo, that's not something you can go in search of."

"True." He calmed himself down and nodded. "Then, how about this: Don't think long term, just think about tomorrow. Tomorrow, you know? Where do you want to go tomorrow? What do you want to do? What will make you happy tomorrow? You're able to come up with something, surely."

She thought earnestly for a while, and finally said, hesitantly, "If I tell you, can you really make it happen?"

"Of course. Tell me."

"Then, Mr. Luo, can you take me to the Louvre?"

When Tyler removed the blindfold, his eyes weren't adjusted to the light and he had to squint. Despite the bright lights affixed to the rock walls of this mountain cave, it was dark here—quite dark, in fact—because the light was absorbed by the walls. He smelled antiseptic, and noticed the cave was set up like a field hospital, with lots of open aluminum cases containing neatly packed drugs, as well as oxygen tanks, small UV disinfectant cabinets, mobile shadowless operating lamps, and several portable medical devices that looked like X-ray machines and defibrillators. It looked like it had just been unpacked and could be re-boxed at any time. Tyler saw two assault rifles hanging on a rock wall, but their similarity in color to the rock behind made them easy to miss. A stony-faced man and woman walked past him. They weren't in white lab coats, but they were definitely a doctor and a nurse.

The bed, near the cave entrance, was a sea of white: the curtains behind it, the old man under the bedsheets, the old man's long beard, the scarf around his head, and even his face—all white. The light in that area was more like candlelight, obscuring some of the whiteness and casting a weak golden sheen across the remainder, turning the place into a classical oil painting of a saint.

Tyler spat inwardly. "Damn it to hell. How did it come to this?"

As he walked over to the bed, he tried to overcome the pain in his hip and inner thigh by adopting a stately, steady pace. He stopped at the bedside, before the man that he and his government had dreamed of finding for so many years. He could hardly believe he was real. He looked at the old man's pale face, and it was like the media always said: This was the kindliest face in the world.

Man truly was a peculiar animal.

"I'm honored to meet you," Tyler said with a slight bow.

"As am I," the old man said politely. He didn't move, but while his voice was reed-thin, it could render power inert but never snap, like spider silk. The old man gestured to the end of the bed, and Tyler sat down gingerly, not knowing whether or not it was intended as kindness. There was no chair, after all. The old man said, "You must be tired. Was it your first time on a mule?"

"Ah, no. I rode one when I visited the Grand Canyon." Although his legs hadn't hurt so much back then. "Are you doing well?"

The old man slowly shook his head. "Surely you can see that I don't have long to live." A playful light suddenly entered his deep eyes. "You're about the least likely person to want me to die of illness. I am truly sorry."

The irony in this last sentence pricked Tyler, but it was the truth. One of his greatest fears had once been that the man would die of illness or old age. The secretary of defense had prayed on many an occasion that an American cruise missile or Special Forces bullet would drop on the man's head before he died of natural causes, even if it happened just a minute before death. Natural death would be the man's greatest triumph, and mark the failure of the war on terror. Even now, the man was edging close to glory. There had been opportunities, of course: Once a Predator drone had snapped his picture in the courtyard of a mosque in the mountains of northern Afghanistan. Simply crashing the drone into him would have made history, not to mention the fact that it had been carrying Hellfire missiles that day. But the young officer on duty lacked the courage to make a unilateral decision once he made the positive ID. Instead, he had reported it up the command chain, and when they checked again the target was gone. Tyler, roused from his bed, had erupted in anger and shattered a precious piece of Chinese porcelain he had at home.

Tyler wanted to avoid the awkward subject, so he brought out his briefcase and set it on the bed. "I have a small gift for you," he said, opening the case. He took out a set of hardcover books. "This is the latest Arabic version."

With effort, the old man reached out a hand as thin as kindling and plucked out the bottommost volume. "Ah, I've only read the first trilogy. I had someone buy the others, but I never had the time to read them, and then I lost them. . . . Excellent, thank you. I like them very much."

"There's a legend that says you named your organization after these novels."[14]

The old man set the book gently to one side and smiled. "Let it stay a legend. You have your wealth and technology. Legends are all we have."

Tyler picked up the book the old man had set down, and faced him like a pastor holding a Bible. "I've come to make you into Seldon."

The same playful light returned to the old man's eyes. "Oh? What do I need to do?"

"Let your organization be preserved."

"Preserved until when?"

"Until four centuries from now. Until the Doomsday Battle."

"And you think that's possible?"

"Yes, if it continues to develop. Let its soul and spirit permeate the space force so that your organization will be part of it forever."

"And you value that so highly because?" The sarcasm in the old man's voice grew stronger.

"Because it's one of the few armed forces available to humanity that uses lives as a weapon. You know, fundamental science has been frozen by the sophons, and this imposes corresponding limitations on advances in computer science and artificial intelligence. In the Doomsday Battle, space fighters will still be piloted by humans, and that requires an army who possesses that spirit. Ball lightning requires a close-range attack."

"What else have you brought with you besides those books?"

Tyler stood up excitedly from the bed. "That depends on what you need. So long as you can ensure the preservation of your organization, I can give you anything."

The old man motioned for Tyler to sit down. "I sympathize with you. After so many years, you still don't know what our needs truly are."

"You can tell me."

14 *Translator's Note:* "Al-Qaeda" is translated into Chinese rather than transliterated, and is known as *Jīdì*, the same term used for the title of Asimov's *Foundation* novels.

"Weapons? Money? No, no. What we need is far more precious. The organization doesn't exist because of Seldon's ambitious goals. You can't get a sane, rational person to believe in and die for that. It exists because it possesses something, something that's its air and blood, and without which the organization would wither away immediately."

"What's that?"

"Hatred."

Tyler was silent.

"On the one hand, thanks to our common enemy, our hatred of the West has faded. On the other, the human race that the Trisolarans want to wipe out includes the hated West, so to us, perishing together would be a joy. So we don't hate the Trisolarans." The old man spread his hands. "You see, hatred is a treasure more precious than gold or diamonds, and a weapon keener than any in the world, but now it's gone. It's not yours to give back. So the organization, like me, does not have long to live."

Tyler remained silent.

"As for Seldon, I'd say his plan is an impossible one."

Tyler let out a sigh and sat back down on the bed. "You mean you've read the ending?"

The old man raised an eyebrow in surprise. "No, I haven't read it. That's just what I think. What? Does the Seldon Plan fail in the book? The author is an exceptional man, if that's the case. I'd imagined he wrote a happy ending, may Allah protect him."

"Asimov's been dead for many years."

"Ah, the wise always die young. May he find heaven, whichever one it is. . . ."

For most of the way back, Tyler was not blindfolded, giving him the opportunity to see the steep, barren mountains of Afghanistan. The young man who led his mule even trusted him enough to leave his assault rifle hanging from the saddle, right next to Tyler's hand.

"Have you killed anyone with that gun?" he asked.

The young man didn't understand, but an older, unarmed man

riding next to them answered for him. "No. There hasn't been any fighting for a long time."

The young man looked up questioningly at Tyler. He had no beard on his childlike face, and his eyes were as clear as the blue sky of western Asia.

Mom, I'm going to be a firefly.

At the Fourth PDC Wallfacer Hearing, Tyler appeared fatigued from his long journey as he submitted revisions to his mosquito swarm plan. "I want every fighter in the mosquito fleet to be equipped with two control systems: a pilot-operated mode and a drone mode. Switching to drone mode will allow me to control all of the fighters in the fleet."

"You're very hands-on." Hines snickered.

"I'll be able to instruct the fleet to form a mosquito group and voyage to the battle zone, then tell it to disassemble and reenter formation. When it engages the enemy fleet, I will command the weapons module on each fighter to select its own target and attack automatically. I'd imagine that even with the lockdown on the fundamentals of physics, current AI technology will develop enough in the next three centuries to permit that."

"Do you mean that you plan to hibernate until the Doomsday Battle, and then directly engage the Trisolaran Fleet?"

"Do I have a choice? You know I've just been to Japan, China, and Afghanistan and didn't find what I'm looking for there."

"And you paid someone a visit," the US representative said.

"That's right. I saw him. But . . ." Tyler gave a long, dejected sigh. "Nothing. I'll keep trying to establish a force of dedicated space fighters, but if I can't, then I'll have to guide them into the final attack myself."

No one spoke. Where the Doomsday Battle was concerned, people usually chose to be silent.

Tyler continued, "I have another supplement to the mosquito swarm plan. I want to conduct my own studies, of certain bodies

in the solar system, in areas of my choosing. These bodies include Europa, Ceres, and several comets."

"How is this related to the space fighter fleet?" someone asked.

"Do I need to answer that?" Tyler asked, looking at the rotating chair.

No one spoke. Of course he didn't have to answer.

"Finally, I have a recommendation. The PDC and every nation on Earth should scale back their attacks on the ETO."

Rey Diaz jumped out of his chair. "Mr. Tyler, even if you claim that this is part of the plan, I strongly oppose this outrageous proposal!"

Tyler shook his head. "This is not part of the plan. It's totally unconnected to the Wallfacer Project. The reason for my suggestion is obvious: If we persist in our attacks on the ETO, in two or three years we may wipe it out, and we will lose the only direct channel for communication between Earth and Trisolaris. We'll have lost the most important source of enemy intelligence. I'm sure you understand what the consequences would be."

Hines said, "I agree. But this proposal shouldn't be made by a Wallfacer. The three of us are a unit in the minds of the public, so please keep *our* reputation in mind."

The hearing ended in unresolved arguments, but an agreement was reached for the PDC to conduct further study of the three revisions to Tyler's plan and put them to a vote at the next hearing.

Tyler remained seated until he was the last one in the assembly hall. He was exhausted and drowsy after his lengthy travels, and as he looked around the empty room, he suddenly realized a risk he had overlooked: He needed to find a doctor or a psychologist, and a specialist in sleep medicine.

He had to find someone to stop him from talking in his sleep.

Luo Ji and Zhuang Yan walked toward the main entrance of the Louvre at ten p.m. Kent had advised them to visit at night to facilitate more convenient security.

The first thing they saw was the glass pyramid, shielded from the nighttime din of Paris by the U-shaped palace building, and standing quietly under the watery moonlight as if it were made of silver.

"Mr. Luo, don't you get the feeling that it flew in from outer space?" Zhuang Yan asked, pointing to the pyramid.

"Everyone has that feeling," Luo Ji said.

"At first it feels a little out of place, but the more you look at it, the more it seems to be an integral part of the place."

The meeting of two vastly different worlds, Luo Ji thought, but did not say.

Then the whole pyramid lit up, turning from moonlit silver to a brilliant gold. At the same time the fountains came on in the surrounding pools, sending tall columns of water and light skyward. Zhuang Yan glanced at Luo Ji in alarm, unsettled by the Louvre's awakening at their arrival. Accompanied by water sounds, they made their way down the pyramid into the Hall Napoléon, and then into the palace.

Their first destination was the largest exhibition hall. It was two hundred meters long and softly lit, and their footsteps echoed down the emptiness. Luo Ji quickly realized that it was only his footsteps echoing, for Zhuang Yan walked lightly on catlike steps, like a child in a fairy tale who enters a magic castle and is afraid of waking what slumbers there. He slowed his pace—not for the artwork, which didn't interest him at all, but to let the distance between them grow and allow him to appreciate her among this world of art, gazing upon the beauty of this Eastern woman along with the full-figured Greek gods, angels, and the Blessed Virgin in the surrounding classical oil paintings. Like the glass pyramid in the courtyard, she soon blended into the environment and became part of the sacred realm of art. Without her, this place would be missing something. In a reverie or a dream or a vision, he let time pass by quietly.

After a time, Zhuang Yan finally remembered Luo Ji's presence and flashed a smile back at him. His heart quaked at what felt to

him like a bolt of light sent to the mortal realm from a painting of Mount Olympus.

"I've heard that with a trained eye, it would take you a whole year to see all of the pieces here," he said.

"I know," was her simple reply, but her eyes said, *What should I do?* Then she turned her attention to the paintings. In all this time she had seen only five of them.

"It doesn't matter, Yan Yan. I can look at them with you every night for a year." The words slipped out.

She turned to look at him, visibly excited. "Really?"

"Really."

"Well . . . Mr. Luo, have you ever been here before?"

"No. But I went to the Centre Pompidou when I came to Paris three years ago. At first I thought you would be more interested in going there."

She shook her head. "I don't like modern art."

"Then, all this—" He glanced around at the gods, angels, and Blessed Virgin. "You don't think it's too old?"

"I don't like it too old. I just like the paintings of the Renaissance."

"Those are pretty old, too."

"But they don't feel old to me. Those painters were the first to discover human beauty, and they painted God as a pleasing person. Looking at these works, you can sense their joy in painting, the same joy I felt when I first saw the lake and the snow peak."

"That's good, but the humanistic spirit pioneered by the Renaissance masters has become a stumbling block."

"You mean, in the Trisolar Crisis?"

"Yes. You must have seen what's been happening lately. Four centuries from now, the post-disaster world might return to the Middle Ages, with humanity once again subjected to extreme repression."

"And art will enter a long winter's night, right?"

Looking at her innocent eyes, he smiled wryly to himself. *Silly kid, you talk about art, but if humanity does manage to survive, regressing to a primitive society would be a small price to pay.* But he said, "When that time comes, there may be a second Renaissance,

and you could rediscover forgotten beauty and paint it."

She smiled a smile tinged with sadness, clearly understanding the meaning behind Luo Ji's consoling words. "I'm just thinking: After doomsday, what will happen to these paintings and artworks?"

"You're worried about that?" he asked. When she mentioned doomsday, his heart ached, but if his last attempt at comfort had failed, he was confident that he would succeed this time. So he took her hand and said, "Come on, let's go to the Asian Art exhibit."

Before the pyramid lobby was built, the Louvre was a giant maze. Getting to any particular gallery meant a long and winding detour. But now you could go directly from the Hall Napoléon beneath the pyramid to any point in the museum. Luo Ji and Zhuang Yan returned to the entrance hall, followed the signs leading to the Arts of Africa, Asia, Oceania, and the Americas, and wound up in an entirely different world from the galleries of classical European paintings.

Luo Ji pointed out the sculptures, paintings, and old documents from Asia and Africa, and said, "These were taken by an advanced civilization from a backward one. Some were looted, others were stolen or defrauded, but look at them now: They're all well preserved. Even during the Second World War, these objects were transferred to a safe place." They stood before a Dunhuang mural sealed in a glass case. "Think about how much turmoil and war that land of ours has seen since the time Abbot Wang gave these to the Frenchman.[15] If the murals were left there, can you be certain they would have been this well preserved?"

"But will the Trisolarans preserve humanity's cultural heritage? They have no regard for us at all."

15 *Translator's Note:* Dunhuang, an oasis on the Silk Road in what is now Gansu province, was home to spectacularly decorated Buddhist grottoes inhabited from the fourth to fourteenth centuries. In 1900, Wang Yuanlu, a Taoist abbot at Dunhuang's Mogao Caves, discovered a sealed-up Library Cave containing a cache of ancient documents that he subsequently sold to Hungarian-British archeologist Aurel Stein and French sinologist Paul Pelliot.

"Because they said we're bugs? But that's not what that means. Yan Yan, do you know what the greatest expression of regard for a race or civilization is?"

"No, what?"

"Annihilation. That's the highest respect a civilization can receive. They would only feel threatened by a civilization they truly respect."

They passed silently through the twenty-four galleries housing Asian art, walking through the distant past while imagining a gloomy future. Without realizing it, they reached the Egyptian Antiquities gallery.

"Do you know who I'm thinking of here?" Luo Ji stood beside a glass case containing the golden mask of a mummified pharaoh and tried out a lighter topic of conversation. "Sophie Marceau."

"Because of *Belphegor, Phantom of the Louvre,* right? Sophie Marceau is gorgeous. She's got Eastern looks, too."

For some reason, right or wrong, Luo Ji sensed traces of jealousy and offense in her voice.

"Yan Yan, she's not as beautiful as you. That's the truth." He also wanted to say, *One might be able to find her beauty among these works of art, but yours eclipses them,* but he didn't want to come off as sarcastic. The hint of a shy smile flitted across her face like a cloud, the first time he had seen this smile he remembered from his dreams.

"Let's go back to the oil paintings," she said softly.

They returned to the Hall Napoléon, but forgot which entrance to use. The most visible signs pointed to the three jewels of the palace: the *Mona Lisa,* Venus de Milo, and Winged Victory.

"Let's see the *Mona Lisa,*" he suggested.

As they headed in that direction, she said, "Our teacher said that after he visited the Louvre, he was a little disgusted with the *Mona Lisa* and Venus de Milo."

"Why was that?"

"Because tourists come for those two objects but have no interest in less famous but equally great works of art."

"I'm one of the great uncultured."

They arrived at the mysterious smile, which was behind a thick wall of protective glass and much smaller than Luo Ji had imagined. Even Zhuang Yan didn't seem particularly excited.

"Seeing her reminds me of all of you," she said, pointing at the figure in the painting.

"All of us?"

"The Wallfacers, of course."

"What's she got to do with the Wallfacers?"

"Well, I wonder—and this is just speculation, so don't laugh—I wonder whether we could find a form of communication that only humans can comprehend, but which the sophons never will. That way, humanity can be free of sophon monitoring."

Luo Ji looked at her for several seconds, and then stared at the *Mona Lisa*. "I get what you mean. Her smile is something that the sophons and the Trisolarans will never understand."

"That's right. Human expressions, and people's eyes in particular, are subtle and complex. A gaze or a smile can transmit so much information! And only humans can understand that information. Only humans have that sensitivity."

"True. One of the biggest problems in artificial intelligence is identifying facial and eye expressions. Some experts even say that computers may never be able to read the eyes."

"So is it possible to create a language of expressions and then speak with the face and the eyes?"

Luo Ji thought this over seriously, then shook his head with a smile. He pointed at the *Mona Lisa*. "We can't even read *her* expression. When I stare at her, the meaning of her smile changes every second and never repeats itself."

Zhuang Yan jumped up and down excitedly, like a child. "But that means that facial expressions really can convey complex information!"

"And if the information is: 'The spacecraft have left Earth, destination Jupiter'? How would you convey that using facial expressions?"

"When primitive man began to speak, surely it was only to

convey simple meanings. It may even have been less complex than birdcalls. Language gradually grew in complexity after that."

"Well, let's try to convey a simple meaning through facial expressions."

"Okay!" She nodded her head excitedly. "Here, let's each think of a message, and then exchange them."

Luo Ji paused for a moment. "I've thought of mine."

Zhuang Yan thought for a much longer time, and then nodded. "Then let's begin."

They stared at each other, but held that pose for less than half a minute before they burst out laughing at practically the same instant.

"My message was, 'Tonight I'd like to invite you to have supper on the Champs-Élysées,'" he said.

She doubled over with laughter. "Mine was, 'You . . . need to shave!'"

"These are grave matters concerning the fate of humanity, so we ought to remain serious," Luo Ji said, holding in his laughter.

"This time, no laughing allowed!" she said, as serious as a child redefining the rules of a game.

They stood back to back, each thinking of a message, and then turned around and locked eyes once again. Luo Ji felt the urge to laugh and strove to suppress it, but the task soon became much easier, for Zhuang Yan's clear eyes had begun to pluck at his heartstrings again.

And so it was that the Wallfacer and the young woman stood, gazes locked, in front of the smile of *Mona Lisa* in the Louvre in the dead of night.

The dam in Luo Ji's soul had sprung a tiny leak, and this trickle eroded it, expanding the tiny fissure into a turbulent stream. He grew afraid and strove to patch the crack in the dam, but was unable to. A collapse was inevitable.

Then he felt like he was standing on a towering cliff top, and the girl's eyes were the vast abyss beneath, covered in a pure white sea of clouds. But the sun shone down from all directions and turned the clouds into a brilliance of color that surged endlessly. He felt

himself sliding downward, a very slow slide, but one he could not arrest under his own power. In a panic, he shook his limbs to try to find a place to hold on. But beneath his body was nothing but slick ice. His slide accelerated, until, finally, with a burst of vertigo, he began to fall into the abyss. In an instant, the joy of falling reached the upper limit of pain.

The *Mona Lisa* was deforming. The walls were deforming, melting like ice as the Louvre collapsed, its stones turning to red-hot magma as they fell. When the magma passed over their bodies, it felt cool as a clear spring. They fell with the Louvre, passing through a melted Europe toward the center of the Earth, and when they reached it, the world around them exploded in a shower of gorgeous cosmic fireworks. Then the sparks extinguished, and in the twinkling of an eye, space became crystal clear. The stars wove crystal beams into a giant silver blanket, and the planets vibrated, emitting beautiful music. The starfield grew dense like a surging tide. The universe contracted and collapsed, until at last everything was annihilated in the creative light of love.

"We need to observe Trisolaris right now!" General Fitzroy said to Dr. Ringier. They were in the control room of the Hubble II Space Telescope, a week after its assembly was completed.

"General, I'm afraid that's not possible."

"I have the feeling that the observations in progress right now are actually private work that you astronomers are doing on the side."

"I'd have done my own work if it were possible, but Hubble II is still in the testing phase."

"You're working for the military. Carrying out orders is all you need to do."

"No one here is military apart from you. We're following NASA's testing plan."

The general's tone softened. "Doctor, can't you just use Trisolaris as a test target?"

"Test targets have been carefully selected according to distance

and brightness classes, and the test plan has been formulated to be maximally economical, so that the telescope completes all tests after just one rotation. In order to observe Trisolaris now, we would need to rotate through an angle of nearly thirty degrees and back, and spinning this bad boy uses up propellant. We're saving the military money, General."

"Let's have a look at how you're saving it, then. I just found this on your computer," Fitzroy said as he brought a hand out from behind his back. He held a printout of a photograph, an overhead shot of a group of people looking upward excitedly. They were recognizably the crew from this very control room, Ringier in their midst, along with three women in sexy poses who might have been the girlfriends of some in the group. The location of the photo was evidently the roof of the control room building, and the photo was very clear, as if it had been shot from ten or twenty meters above. Where it differed from an ordinary photograph was in the complicated numbers overlaid atop it. "Doctor, you're standing on the highest point of the building. It doesn't have a rocker arm like a movie set, does it? You're telling me that rotating Hubble II thirty degrees costs money. Well, how much does it cost to rotate it three hundred sixty degrees? Besides, that ten-million-dollar investment wasn't made so you could snap photos of you and your girlfriends from space. Should I add that sum to your bill?"

"General, your order must of course be carried out," Ringier said hastily, and the engineers immediately went to work.

Coordinate data was quickly called up from the target database. In space, the enormous cylinder, over twenty meters in diameter and more than a hundred meters long, slowly started to turn, panning across the starfield displayed on the screen in the control room.

"This is what the telescope sees?" asked the general.

"No, this is just the image returned by the positioning system. The telescope returns still photos that need to be processed before they're viewable."

Five minutes later, the panning stopped. The control system reported that positioning had been achieved, and after another five

minutes, Ringier said, "Good. Now return to the test position."

In surprise, Fitzroy asked, "What? Is it done?"

"Yes. Now the images are being processed."

"Can't you take a few more?"

"General, we've captured two hundred ten images at multiple focal lengths." At that moment the first observation image finished processing, and Ringier pointed to the screen. "Look, General. There's the enemy world you want to see so badly."

Fitzroy saw nothing but a group of three halos against a dark background. They were diffuse, like streetlights through fog. These were the three stars that would decide the fate of two civilizations.

"So we really can't see the planet." Fitzroy couldn't hide his disappointment.

"Of course we can't. Even when the hundred-meter Hubble III is finished, we'll only be able to observe Trisolaris at a very few set positions, and we'll only be able to make it out as a dot, with no detail at all."

"But there's something else here, Doctor. What do you think this is?" asked one of the engineers, pointing to a spot close to the three halos.

Fitzroy leaned in but saw nothing. It was so faint that only an expert could catch it.

"It's got a diameter larger than a star," an engineer said.

After enlarging the area several times, the thing covered the entire screen.

"It's a brush!" shouted the general in alarm.

The layman always comes up with better names than the expert, which is why when experts name things they, too, work from an outsider's perspective. And thus "brush" became the figure's name, because the general's description was accurate: It was a cosmic brush. Or, to be more precise, a set of cosmic bristles without a handle. Of course, you could also see it as hair standing on end.

"It must be a scratch in the coating! I mentioned in the feasibility study that a pasteup lens would cause problems," Ringier said, shaking his head.

"All the coatings have been through stringent testing. A scratch of this sort wouldn't happen. And it's not generated by any other lens flaw, either. We've already returned tens of thousands of test images, and it's never come up before," said an expert from Zeiss, the lens's manufacturer.

A hush fell over the control room. They all gathered to stare up at the image on the screen until it got so crowded that some of them called up the image on other terminals. Fitzroy sensed the change in the room's atmosphere: People who had grown lazy from the fatigue of lengthy tests were anxious now, like they had been hit by a curse that rooted everything in place but their eyes, which grew ever brighter.

"God!" exclaimed several people at the same time.

The frozen formation abruptly turned into excited activity. The snatches of dialogue Fitzroy picked up were a bit too technical for him.

"Any dust around the target's position? Check it—"

"No need. I completed that item. Observing the absorption of the background stellar radial movement, there's an absorption peak at two hundred millimeters. It may be a carbon microparticle, F-class density."

"Any opinions on the effect of high-speed impact?"

"The wake diffuses along the impact axis, but the diffusion scope . . . Do we have a model of that?"

"Yes. One moment. . . . Here it is. Impact speed?"

"A hundred times third cosmic velocity."

"Is it already that high?"

"That's a conservative figure. . . . For the impact cross section, use . . . Right, that's right. That's just about it. Just a rough estimate."

With the experts busy, Ringier stood next to Fitzroy. "General, can you try your best to count the bristles in the brush?"

The general nodded, and then bent over a terminal and began counting.

The computer needed four or five minutes to complete every

calculation, but there were a number of errors, so it was half an hour before the results were ready.

"The wake diffuses the dust to a maximum diameter of two hundred forty thousand kilometers, or twice the size of Jupiter," the astronomer running the mathematical model said.

"That makes sense," Ringier said. He raised his arms and looked up at the ceiling, as if looking through it to the heavens. "And that confirms it." There was a tremble to his voice, and then, as if to himself, he said, "So it's been confirmed. Nothing wrong with that."

Silence fell over the control room again, heavy and oppressive this time. Fitzroy wanted to ask a question, but at the sight of the solemn, bowed heads, he couldn't open his mouth. After a while, he heard gentle sobs and saw a young man trying to hide his tears.

"Knock it off, Harris. You're not the only skeptic here. It's hard for everyone," someone said.

The young man, Harris, lifted his teary eyes and said, "I know skepticism is just a way to comfort myself, but I wanted to live out my life in comfort. God, now I'm not even lucky enough for that."

Silence returned.

At last Ringier remembered Fitzroy. "General, let me explain. The three stars are surrounded by interstellar dust. Previously, a number of bodies moving at high speed crossed that dust, and their high-speed impact with the dust left behind a wake. The wake continued to expand and has now reached a diameter twice that of the planet Jupiter. There are only subtle differences between the wake and the surrounding dust, so they are undetectable at close range. Only here, four light-years away, are they observable."

"I've counted the bristles. There are about a thousand," General Fitzroy said.

"Of course. That number confirms our intelligence reports. General, we're looking at the Trisolaran Fleet."

Hubble II's discovery, the final confirmation of the reality of the

Trisolaran invasion, extinguished the last of humanity's fantasies. The descent of a new round of despair, panic, and confusion ushered the human race into life under the Trisolar Crisis. Then the hard times began. With a rocky change of direction, the vehicle of time veered off along a new track.

The only constant in a world of tremendous change is the swift passage of time. Five years passed like a blur.

PART II

THE
SPELL

Year 8, Crisis Era

Tyler had been jumpy lately. Despite the setbacks, the mosquito swarm plan eventually won PDC approval. Development of the space fighters began, but progress was slow due to a lack of advanced technologies. Humanity continued to improve on the technology of its stone age axes and clubs, inventing chemically propelled rockets. Tyler's supplemental project, the study of Europa, Ceres, and various comets, was odd enough that some people suspected that he had come up with it purely to add a sense of mystery to the overly direct main plan. However, since it could be incorporated into the mainstream defense program, he was allowed to start working on that as well.

So Tyler had to wait. He went home and, for the first time in his five years as a Wallfacer, led the life of a normal person.

The Wallfacers were subject to increasing scrutiny from the community. Whether they had asked for the role or not, they had been set up in the eyes of the masses as messiah figures. Accordingly, a Wallfacer cult sprang up. No matter how many explanations the UN and PDC issued, legends of their supernatural abilities circulated widely and grew increasingly fanciful. In science fiction movies, they were shown as superheroes, and, in the eyes of many, they were the sole hope for humanity. This gave the Wallfacers an enormous amount of popular and political

capital that guaranteed things would go smoothly when they tapped huge amounts of resources.

Luo Ji was the exception. He remained in seclusion, never showing his face. No one knew where he was or what he was doing.

One day, Tyler had a visitor. Like the other Wallfacers, his home was under heavy guard, and all visitors had to pass stringent background checks. But when he first saw the visitor in the living room, he knew that the man would pass through easily, because it was obvious at a glance that he posed no threat to anyone. On this hot day he wore a wrinkled suit, a similarly wrinkled tie, and, more annoyingly, the sort of bowler hat no one wore anymore. He evidently wanted to present a more formal appearance for his visit, since he had probably never attended a formal occasion before. Pale and emaciated, he looked malnourished. His glasses sat heavily on his skinny, pale face, his neck hardly seemed able to support the weight of his head, and his suit looked practically empty, as if it was hanging on a rack. As a politician, Tyler saw at a glance that he belonged to one of those mean social classes whose poverty was more spiritual than material, like Gogol's petty bureaucrats who, despite their lowly social station, still worry about preserving that status and spend their whole lives engaged in uncreative, exhausting random tasks that they carry out exactingly. In everything they do, they fear making mistakes; with everyone they meet, they fear causing displeasure; and they dare not take the slightest glance through the glass ceiling to a higher plane of society. Tyler detested those people. They were utterly dispensable, and when he thought about how they made up the majority of the world that he wanted to save, it left a bad taste in his mouth.

The man walked gingerly through the living room door, but did not dare venture further. He seemed afraid of marking the carpet with the dirty soles of his shoes. He took off his hat and looked at the master of the house through his thick glasses as he bowed repeatedly. Tyler made up his mind to send him off as soon as he spoke his first sentence, for even if what the man had to say was important to him, to Tyler it was meaningless.

In a frail voice, the pitiful man uttered his first sentence. It struck Tyler like a bolt of lightning and so dazed him that he practically sat down on the ground. Every word was like a thunderclap.

"Wallfacer Frederick Tyler, I am your Wallbreaker."

"Who would have thought we'd one day be facing a battle map like this," Chang Weisi exclaimed as he looked at a one-to-one-trillion-scale chart of the Solar System displayed on a monitor large enough to be a movie screen. It was almost entirely dark, except for the tiny spot of yellow in the center that was the sun. The chart radius reached the middle of the Kuiper Belt. When it was displayed in its entirety, it was like looking down on the Solar System from a distance of fifty AU above the ecliptic plane. The chart accurately marked the orbits of planets and satellites, as well as the conditions of known asteroids, and it could display a precise sectional layout of the Solar System for any point in the next millennium. Now that positional markings for celestial bodies had been turned off, the chart display was bright enough that you could make out Jupiter if you looked closely enough. It was just an indistinct, tiny bright spot, but from this distance the other seven major planets were invisible.

"Yes, we are facing major changes," Zhang Beihai said. The military had just completed a meeting to assess its first space map, and now only the two of them remained in the spacious war room.

"Commander, I wonder if you noticed the eyes of our comrades when they saw this map," he said.

"Of course I noticed. It's understandable. They would have imagined a space map to be like what you find in popular science books. A couple of colored billiard balls rotating around a fireball. It's only when they're faced with one drawn to an accurate scale that they come to an appreciation of the vastness of the Solar System. And, whether they're air force or navy, the furthest their air and water craft can go doesn't even amount to one pixel on the big screen."

"It seems that looking at the battlefield of the future did not inspire a stitch of confidence or passion for battle in our comrades."

"And now we're back to defeatism."

"Commander, I don't want to talk about the reality of defeatism today. That's a subject for a formal meeting. What I'd like to discuss is . . . well . . ." He faltered, and smiled, a rare thing for someone who was usually so outspoken.

Chang Weisi turned away from the map and smiled back at him. "Seems you've got something highly unorthodox to say."

"Yes. Or something unprecedented, at least. I'm making a recommendation."

"Proceed. Get right down to the topic. Of course, you don't need encouragement for that."

"Yes, Commander. Over the past five years, little progress has been made in basic planetary defense and space travel research. The preliminary technology in those two programs—controlled nuclear fusion and the space elevator—are still at square one, with no hope in sight, and there are all kinds of problems with higher-thrust chemical rockets. If things continue in this vein, then I fear a space fleet, even at the low-tech level, will remain science fiction forever."

"You chose high-tech, Comrade Beihai. You ought to be well aware of the rules of scientific research."

"Of course I'm aware of them. Research is a process of leaping forward, and qualitative change is only produced by long-term quantitative accumulation. Breakthroughs in theory and technology are mostly achieved in concentrated bursts. . . . Still, Commander, how many people understand the problem like I do? It's very likely that in ten or twenty or fifty years, or even a century, we still won't have any major breakthroughs in any scientific or technical field, and at that point, how far will defeatist thinking have developed? What spiritual and mental state will have taken hold in the space force? Commander, am I really taking this too far?"

"Beihai, what I most admire about you is that you always keep the long term in mind as you work. It's a rare thing among political cadres in this military. Please go on."

"Well, I can only speak from the scope of my own work. Working under the above assumptions, what sort of difficulties and pressures will be faced by our future comrades engaged in political and ideological work in the space force?"

"A grimmer question is, how many ideologically qualified political cadres will be left in the forces?" added Chang Weisi. "To contain defeatism, we first need to have a firm faith in victory ourselves. But this is certain to be more difficult in your hypothetical future."

"That's where my worry lies, Commander. When that time comes, political work in the space force won't be up to the task."

"Your recommendation?"

"Send reinforcements!"

Chang Weisi looked at Zhang Beihai for a few seconds, then turned back to the big screen. He moved the cursor and enlarged the sun until their epaulets reflected the sunlight.

"Commander, what I mean is . . ."

He raised a hand. "I know what you mean." Then he pulled back until the entire map was displayed, plunging the war room back into gloom, and then brought the sun forward again . . . and again and again as he thought, until at last he said, "Has it ever occurred to you that if political and ideological work in the space force is a complex and difficult task right now, it will considerably weaken today's work to hibernate the most outstanding political officers and send them to the future?"

"I realize that, Commander. I'm just voicing a personal suggestion. Big-picture thinking is, of course, up to my superiors."

Chang Weisi stood up and turned on the lights, illuminating the war room. "No, Comrade Beihai, this is a job for you now. Drop everything else. Starting tomorrow, you will focus on the Space Force Political Department, do some research into the other branches, and draft a preliminary report for the Central Military Commission as soon as possible."

The sun was setting behind the mountains when Tyler arrived. Exiting the car, he faced a vision of paradise: the softest light of the day shining on the snow peaks, the lake, and the forest, and Luo Ji and his family enjoying the otherworldly evening in the grass on the lakeshore. What first caught his eye was the mother, so young-looking, like an older sister to the one-year-old child. From a distance it was hard to make her out, but as he drew closer, his attention shifted to the child. If he hadn't seen it with his own eyes, he wouldn't have believed that such an adorable little being actually existed. Like a stem cell of beauty, the embryonic state of all that is beautiful. Mother and child were drawing on a large sheet of white paper as Luo Ji stood off to one side watching with interest as he had in the Louvre, gazing from a distance at his beloved, now a mother. Moving closer still, Tyler saw in his eyes an infinite bliss, a happiness that seemed to permeate everything between mountain and lake in this Garden of Eden. . . .

Having just arrived from the grim outside world made the scene before his eyes feel unreal. He had been married twice but was now single, and the joys of family had meant little to him in his pursuit of a man's glory. Now, for the first time ever, he felt he had lived an empty life.

Luo Ji, captivated by his wife and child, only noticed Tyler when he had gotten quite close. Due to the psychological barriers erected by their common situation, there had been no personal contact between Wallfacers up to this point. But having spoken with him on the phone, Luo Ji showed no surprise at Tyler's arrival, and met him with polite warmth.

"Madam, please excuse the interruption," Tyler said with a slight bow to Zhuang Yan, who had come over with the child.

"Welcome, Mr. Tyler. We seldom have guests, so we are pleased that you could come." Her English was strained, but her voice retained a childlike softness and she still had that cool spring of a smile, which stroked his weary soul like an angel's hands. "This is our daughter, Xia Xia."

He wanted to hug the child, but was afraid of losing control

of his feelings, so he simply said, "Seeing you two angels is worth the trip."

"We'll let you talk. I'll go and prepare dinner," she said as she smiled at the two men.

"No, that's not necessary. I just want to have a brief chat with Dr. Luo. I won't take up too much time."

Zhuang Yan warmly insisted that he stay for dinner, then left with the child.

Luo Ji motioned for Tyler to sit on a white chair in the grass. When he sat down, his whole body went limp, as if his tendons had been removed. He was a traveler who had at last reached his destination after a long voyage. "Doctor, it seems like you've been lost to the world for the past two years," Tyler said.

"Yes." Luo Ji remained standing. He swept a hand about him. "This is my everything."

"You are truly a smart man, and at least from one perspective, a more responsible man than me."

"What do you mean by that?" Luo Ji asked, with a puzzled smile.

"At least you haven't wasted resources. . . . So she doesn't watch TV either? I mean, your angel."

"Her? I don't know. She's always with Xia Xia these days, so I don't think she watches much."

"Then you really don't know what's happened out there over the past few days?"

"What happened? You don't look well. Are you tired? What can I get you to drink?"

"Anything," Tyler said, watching the last golden rays of the setting sun on the lake dazedly. "Four days ago, my Wallbreaker appeared."

Luo Ji stopped pouring the wine, and after a moment's silence, said, "So soon?"

Tyler nodded heavily. "That's the first thing I said to him, too."

"So soon?" Tyler said to the Wallbreaker. He tried to keep his voice calm but it ended up sounding feeble.

"I'd like to have come sooner, but I thought I'd collect more comprehensive evidence, so I'm late. I am sorry," the Wallbreaker said. He stood behind Tyler like a servant and spoke slowly, with a servant's humility. His final sentence even contained a meticulousness and thoughtfulness, the understanding that an executioner shows to his victim.

Then a suffocating silence took hold. At last Tyler screwed up the courage to look at the Wallbreaker, who then asked respectfully, "Sir, shall I go on?"

Tyler nodded but averted his gaze. He sat down on the sofa and did his best to calm down.

"Thank you, sir." The Wallbreaker bowed again, his hat still in hand. "First, I'll briefly describe the plan you've shown to the outside world: Using a fleet of nimble space fighters carrying hundred-megaton-class superbombs, your fighters will assist Earth's fleet by executing a suicide strike on the Trisolaris Fleet. Perhaps I've oversimplified, but that's basically it, right?"

"There's no point in discussing this with you," Tyler said. He had been considering whether to terminate the conversation. The moment the Wallbreaker revealed himself, Tyler's intuition as a politician and strategist informed him that the other man was the victor, but at this point he would be lucky if his mind had not been laid entirely bare.

"If that's the case, sir, then I don't have to go on, and you can arrest me. But you surely must know that regardless of what happens, your true strategy, and all of the evidence used to prove my hypothesis, will make the news across the world tomorrow, or maybe even tonight. At the cost of the rest of my life I stand before you today, and I hope that you will value my sacrifice."

"You may continue," Tyler said with a wave of his hand.

"Thank you, sir. I am truly honored, and I will not use up too much time." The Wallbreaker bowed again. A humble respect so rarely seen among modern people seemed to be in his blood, able to manifest at any time, like a noose gradually tightening around Tyler's neck. "Then, sir, was my rendition of your strategy just now correct?"

"It was."

"It was not," the Wallbreaker said. "Sir, pardon my saying it, but it was not correct."

"Why?"

"Given humanity's technological capabilities, the most powerful weapons we are likely to possess in the future are super hydrogen bombs. In a spacebattle environment, the bombs must be detonated in direct contact with their target to be capable of destroying enemy ships. Space fighters are nimble and can be deployed in large numbers, so sending the fighter fleet in for swarmlike suicide strikes is undoubtedly the best option. Your plan is eminently reasonable. All of your behavior, including trips to Japan, China, and even the mountains of Afghanistan in search of space kamikaze pilots with a spirit of self-sacrifice, and your plan to put the mosquito fleet under your direct control once that search failed, was also entirely reasonable."

"What's wrong with that?" Tyler asked, sitting up on the sofa.

"Nothing's wrong with that. But that's just the strategy you presented to the outside." The Wallbreaker bent down, drew near to Tyler's ear, and continued speaking in a soft voice. "Your true strategy had small alterations. For quite a long time, you had me stumped. It was agonizing for me, and I nearly gave up."

Tyler realized that he had a death grip on a sofa handle, and tried to relax.

"But then you gave me the key to unlock the whole puzzle. It was such a good fit that for a moment I doubted my good fortune. You know what I'm referring to: Your study of several bodies in the solar system, Europa, Ceres, and the comets. What do they have in common? Water. They all possess water, and in large quantities! On their own, Europa and Ceres have more water than in all of the oceans on Earth. . . .

"Rabies sufferers fear the water and can go into spasms at the mere mention of the word. I imagine you have similar feelings right now."

The Wallbreaker drew close to Tyler and spoke directly into his

ear. His breath was not the least bit warm, but felt like a ghostly wind flavored with the grave. "Water," he whispered, as if talking in his sleep. "Water . . ."

Tyler remained silent, his face like a statue's.

"Is there any need for me to continue?" the Wallbreaker asked, standing up.

"No," Tyler said in a low voice.

"But I'll continue anyway," the Wallbreaker said, almost gleefully. "I'll leave historians with a complete record, even if history won't endure for much longer. And an explanation for the Lord as well, of course. Not everyone has the keen intellect of the two of us, able to grasp the whole from the merest part. Particularly the Lord, who may not even understand a complete explanation." He raised up a hand, as if to acknowledge the Trisolaran listeners, and laughed. "Forgive me."

Tyler's features slackened, and then his bones seemed to melt. He slumped into the sofa. He was finished, and his spirit no longer inhabited his body.

"Now then. Setting aside the water, let's talk about the mosquito swarm. Its first attack target will not be the Trisolaran invaders, but Earth's own space force. This hypothesis is a bit of a reach based on the barest of signs, but I maintain that it is correct. You went around the world seeking to establish a kamikaze force for humanity, but your efforts failed. You anticipated this, but from this failure you were able to obtain two things you desired. One was total despair in humanity—this, you have achieved fully. The second I'll discuss in a moment."

The blade fell.

"After traveling the world you became utterly disillusioned with modern humanity's dedication. You also became convinced that Earth's space-force did not stand a chance of defeating Trisolaris via standard combat. You therefore hatched a strategy even more extreme. In my opinion, this is a very faint hope, and an immense risk. Nevertheless, the principles of the Wallfacer Project dictate that in this war, the safest bet is to take a risk.

"Of course, this was only the beginning. Your betrayal of humanity would be a long process, but you had time on your side. In the following months and years, you were prepared to engineer events that would add to the wall you erected between yourself and the human race. Your despair would gradually grow and your sorrow intensify, and you would leave the human world further and further behind, growing closer and closer to the ETO and Trisolaris. In fact, you took your first steps on this road when you urged mercy for the ETO at the PDC hearing not long ago. That wasn't just for show, though. You truly need them to endure. You need members of the ETO to pilot your space fighters in the Doomsday Battle. It is a matter of time and patience, but you would succeed, because the ETO also needs you. It needs your assistance, and the resources you possess. It wouldn't be difficult to turn over the mosquito fleet to the ETO, so long as it was kept a secret from the outside world. And if it were discovered, you could claim that it was all part of the plan."

Tyler did not seem to be listening to the Wallbreaker. He sat on his sofa with his eyes half-closed, looking fatigued, as if he had already given up and was beginning to relax.

"Very well. Let's talk about the water now. In the Doomsday Battle, the ETO-controlled mosquito fleet would likely launch a sneak attack on Earth's fleet and then flee to the Lord's fleet. Because they had just demonstrated their disloyalty to Earth, Trisolaris might be willing to let them join the fleet, but the Lord would not be so fast to accept the turncoat army. A sufficiently meaningful gift would be required to win them over. What would the Lord need that the Solar System possesses? Water. On their four-century voyage, most of the water in the Trisolaran Fleet would be used up. As they approached the Solar System, dehydrated Trisolarans on board would need to be rehydrated. Since the water used for this would become part of their bodies, clean water would certainly be preferred to the stale water that had been recycled innumerable times on the ship. The mosquito fleet would offer the Lord an iceberg formed out of huge quantities of water

obtained from Europa, Ceres, and the comets. I'm not certain of the specifics—I expect you don't know right now either—but let's say tens of thousands of tons.

"This giant chunk of ice would be propelled by the mosquito group. The mosquito fleet would likely draw very close to the Lord's fleet when presenting the gift, at which point the second consequence of the failure of your attempt to build a kamikaze force would be put to use. That failure prompted your very logical request for independent control of the entire mosquito fleet. When Earth's fleet draws close to the Lord's fleet, you would take over control of the fighters from the ETO pilots and switch them to drone mode, ordering the fighters to strike their chosen targets. The superbombs would be detonated at point-blank range, annihilating all of the Lord's ships."

The Wallbreaker straightened up and, leaving Tyler's side, approached the floor-to-ceiling windows that overlooked the garden. The hellish wind he had blown into Tyler's ear dissipated, but not before the chill had penetrated his body.

"An outstanding plan. That's not a lie. But certain oversights are inexplicable. Why were you so eager to pursue the study of water-bearing heavenly bodies? The technology to extract and transport water in quantity does not exist right now, and engineering-side R&D could take years or even decades. Even if you felt you had to start right away, why not toss in a few targets that don't contain water—the moons of Mars, for instance? If you had done so, although it wouldn't have prevented me from eventually exposing your plan, it would have vastly increased the difficulty. How could a great strategist such as yourself overlook such simple tricks? On the other hand, I do recognize the pressure you are under."

The Wallbreaker placed a gentle hand on Tyler's shoulder, and Tyler felt a flash of tenderness, as of an executioner for his victim. He was even a little moved.

"Don't beat yourself up. You did well enough, really. I hope history remembers you." The Wallbreaker removed his hand, a flush

of restored energy on his formerly wan and sickly face. He stretched out his arms. "Well, Mr. Tyler, I'm done. Call your people."

Tyler, his eyes still shut, said without energy, "You may leave."

When the Wallbreaker opened the door, Tyler croaked out a final question: "If what you say is true, so what?"

The Wallbreaker turned back toward him. "So nothing. Mr. Tyler, regardless of whether or not I've broken your plan, the Lord does not care."

Luo Ji was rendered speechless for a long while after hearing Tyler's account.

When an ordinary person spoke with one of them, they would always be thinking, *He's a Wallfacer, his words can't be trusted,* and those suggestions would present a barrier to communication. But when two Wallfacers spoke with each other, the suggestions that existed in both minds cross-multiplied those communication barriers. Such an exchange, in fact, rendered anything either side said meaningless, so that communication itself lost all significance. This was why there had been no private interaction between Wallfacers.

"How do you evaluate the Wallbreaker's analysis?" Luo Ji asked to break the silence, even though he knew there was no point to the question.

"He guessed right," Tyler said.

Luo Ji wanted to say something, but what? What could be said? They were both Wallfacers.

"That was my true strategy," Tyler went on. He evidently had a strong desire to speak and didn't care whether or not his listener believed him. "Of course, it's still in the preliminary stages. The technology alone is quite difficult, although I expected a gradual resolution to all of the theoretic and technical issues over the course of four centuries. But judging from the enemy's attitude toward the plan, it wouldn't make any difference. They don't care, and that's the height of contempt."

"And that was . . . ?" Luo Ji felt like a machine for meaningless dialogue.

"The day after the Wallbreaker's visit, a complete analysis of my strategy was posted online. The material ran into the millions of words, most of it obtained through sophon monitoring, and it caused a sensation. The day before yesterday, the PDC called a hearing on the issue, at which it resolved the following: 'Wallfacer Plans may not contain anything that poses a threat to human life.' If my plan actually existed, then its execution would be a crime against humanity. It must be stopped, and its Wallfacer punished by law. Notice how they invoke crimes against humanity, a term that's being thrown around more than ever these days? But the resolution concluded by saying, 'According to the basic principles of the Wallfacer Project, the evidence available to the outside world may just be a part of the Wallfacer's strategy of deception and cannot be used to prove that the Wallfacer has actually developed and is executing this plan.' So I won't be charged."

"I'd thought as much," Luo Ji said.

"But at the hearing, I declared that the Wallbreaker's analysis was correct, and that my strategy was indeed the mosquito swarm. I asked to be tried in accordance with national and international law."

"I can imagine their reaction."

"The PDC's rotating chair and all the permanent member representatives looked at me with that Wallfacer smile on their face, and the chair declared the meeting adjourned. Those bastards!"

"I know the feeling."

"I had a total breakdown. I fled out of the hall and into the square outside, shouting, 'I am Wallfacer Frederick Tyler! My Wallbreaker exposed my strategy! He was right! I'm going to attack the Earth fleet with the mosquito swarm! I'm anti-human! I'm a devil! Punish me and kill me!'"

"That was a meaningless act, Mr. Tyler."

"What I hate the most is the expression people have when they look at me. A crowd of people surrounded me in the square, their eyes revealing the fantasies of children, the reverence of the

middle-aged, and the concern of the elderly. All of their eyes said, 'Look, he's a Wallfacer. He's at work, but he's the only one in the world who knows what he's doing. See what a great job he's doing? He's pretending so well. How will the enemy know what his real strategy is? That great, great, great strategy that only he knows and that will be the salvation of the world . . .' Complete and utter crap! Those idiots!"

At last Luo Ji decided to remain silent, and merely smiled wordlessly at Tyler.

As Tyler stared at him, a thin smile wavered on his pale face and then developed into full-blown hysterical laughter. "Ha! You're smiling the Wallfacer smile! A smile from one Wallfacer to another! You think I'm at work. You believe I'm acting the part, and you think I'll save the world!" He cackled again. "How did we end up in such a hilarious situation?"

"This is a vicious cycle we'll never be free of, Mr. Tyler," Luo Ji said, and sighed softly.

Tyler's laughter stopped abruptly. "Never be free? No, Dr. Luo, there's a way out. There really is a way, and I'm here today to tell it to you."

"You need a break. Rest here for a few days," Luo Ji said.

Tyler nodded slowly. "Yeah, I need a break. We're the only ones who understand each other's pain, Doctor. That's why I've come." He looked up. The sun had set a while ago, and the Garden of Eden had grown indistinct in the twilight. "This is paradise. Can I go for a walk alone by the lake?"

"You may do whatever you like here. Take it easy, and I'll call you to dinner in a while."

Tyler walked down to the lake, leaving Luo Ji to sit down, sunken in heavy thoughts.

For five years, he had bathed in an ocean of happiness. The birth of his Xia Xia in particular had made him forget everything about the outside world. The love of his wife and child blended together and intoxicated his soul, and, in this gentle home isolated from the rest of the world, he had fallen deeper and deeper into an

illusion: Perhaps the outside world really was something akin to a quantum state, and did not exist unless he observed it.

But it was a state that could no longer endure now that the abominable outside world had burst into his Garden of Eden to confuse and frighten him. His thoughts shifted to Tyler, whose last words still resounded in his ears. Was it really possible for Wallfacers to break free of the vicious cycle, to shatter the iron shackles of logic . . . ?

He jerked to his senses and ran toward the lake. He wanted to shout, but was afraid of scaring Zhuang Yan and Xia Xia, so he just ran as fast as he could through the quiet twilight, the swish of his feet against the grass on the hillside the only sound. But into this rhythm a soft *crack* inserted itself.

The sound of a gunshot from the lake.

Luo Ji returned home late that evening after the child was sound asleep. Zhuang Yan asked softly, "Did Mr. Tyler leave?"

"Yes. He's gone," he said wearily.

"He seemed worse off than you."

"Yes. That's because he didn't take an easy path. . . . Yan, have you watched TV recently?"

"No. I . . ." She paused, and Luo Ji knew what she was thinking. With the outside world growing more serious by the day, and the gap widening between life here and life outside, the difference made her uneasy. "Is our life really part of the Wallfacer plan?" she asked, looking at him with that same innocent face.

"Of course. What is there to doubt?"

"But can we truly be happy when all humanity is unhappy?"

"My love, your responsibility when all of humanity is unhappy is to make yourself happy. With Xia Xia, your happiness gains a point, and the Wallfacer plan gains a point toward its success."

Zhuang Yan stared silently at him. The language of facial expressions she had envisioned in front of the *Mona Lisa* five years ago seemed to have been partially realized between her and Luo Ji. More and more, he could read her mind through her eyes, and what he read now was, *How can I believe that?*

Luo Ji pondered this for a long time, and finally said, "Yan, everything has an ending. The sun and the universe will die one day, so why should humanity believe that it ought to be immortal? Listen, this world is paranoid. Fighting a hopeless war is a fool's errand, so look at the Trisolar Crisis from a different perspective and leave your cares behind. Not just the ones involving the crisis, but everything else from before that. Use the time that's left to enjoy life. Four hundred years! Or, if we refuse the Doomsday Battle, then nearly five hundred. That's a fair amount of time. Humanity used the same period to go from the Renaissance to the information age, and in the same space could create a carefree, comfortable life. Five idyllic centuries without needing to worry about the distant future, where the sole responsibility is to enjoy life. How wonderful. . . ."

He realized that he had spoken unwisely. Claiming that the happiness of her and the child were part of the plan added another layer of protection to her life by making her happiness into a responsibility. This was the only way to ensure that she maintained a balanced mind in the face of the cruel world. He could never resist her eternally innocent eyes, so he didn't dare look at her when she questioned him. But now, because of the Tyler factor, he had involuntarily told the truth.

"When you say that, are you being a Wallfacer?" she asked.

"Yes, of course I am," he said, to fix the situation.

But her eyes said, *You really did seem to believe that!*

UN Planetary Defense Council, Wallfacer Project Hearing #89

At the start of the hearing, the rotating chair spoke to strongly urge that Luo Ji be required to attend the next hearing, arguing that refusal to participate was not part of the Wallfacer plan because the PDC's supervisory authority over the Wallfacers trumped the Wallfacers' own strategic plans. The proposal was unanimously adopted by all permanent member representatives, and with the

emergence of the first Wallbreaker and the suicide of Wallfacer Tyler in mind, the other two Wallfacers attending the meeting heard the unspoken implications of the chairman's words.

Hines spoke first. His neuroscience-based plan was still in its infancy, but he described the equipment he was envisioning as a basis for further research. He called it the Resolving Imager. Based on computed tomography and nuclear magnetic resonance, it operated by scanning in all cross sections of the brain at once, which required cross sectional accuracy on the scale of the internal structure of brain cells and neurons. This would bring the number of simultaneous CT scans to several million, to be synthesized by computer into a digital model of the brain. Other technical requirements were even greater: The scan needed to be conducted at a rate of twenty-four frames per second to produce a dynamic synthetic model that could capture all brain activity at a neuron-level resolution, making it possible to precisely observe thought activity in the brain, or even replay all neural activity throughout the thinking process.

Then Rey Diaz described the progress of his plan. After five years of research, the digital star model for super-high-yield nuclear weapons had been completed and was now being thoroughly debugged.

Next, the PDC scientific advisory panel presented a report on its feasibility study of the two Wallfacers' plans.

The advisory panel felt that although there were in theory no obstacles to Hines's Resolving Imager, the technical difficulties far exceeded current conditions, and modern CT scanning was about as far from RI technology as black-and-white film was from modern high-definition cameras. Data processing presented the biggest technical hurdle to the RI device, because scanning and modeling an object the size of the human brain with neuron-level precision required power that was unavailable to modern computers.

The obstacle to Rey Diaz's stellar bomb was the same: present computing power was insufficient. After inspecting the calculations required by the completed portion of the model, the panel's expert group felt that the most powerful of today's computers

would take twenty years to model a hundredth of a second of the fusion process. Since the model would need to be run repeatedly in the course of research, practical application was an impossibility.

The panel's chief computer scientist said, "Right now, computer technology based on traditional integrated circuits and Von Neumann architecture is nearing the limit of its technological development. Moore's law is going to collapse. Of course, we can still squeeze out the last few drops of lemonade from these traditional electronic and technological lemons. In our opinion, even given the present deceleration in supercomputer progress, the computing power required by the two plans is still achievable. It just requires time. Optimistically, twenty to thirty years. Those goals, if they are reached, will represent the peak of human computing technology, and any further progress will be difficult. With frontier physics under sophon lockdown, the next-gen and quantum computers that we once dreamed of are now very unlikely to be realized."

"We've reached the wall that the sophons have erected across our scientific road," the chair said.

"Then there's nothing that we can do for twenty years," Hines said.

"Twenty years is the most optimistic estimate. As a scientist, you ought to know what cutting-edge research is like."

"Then the only thing to do is hibernate and wait the arrival of capable computers," Rey Diaz said.

"I've decided to hibernate, too," Hines said.

"If that's the case, then I will ask the two of you to greet my successor in twenty years," the chair said with a smile.

The mood of the hearing relaxed. Now that the two Wallfacers had decided to enter hibernation, the hearing's participants sighed with relief. The emergence of the first Wallbreaker and his Wallfacer's suicide had dealt a heavy blow to the entire project. Tyler's suicide in particular had been a foolish act. If he had lived, people would still be in doubt about whether the mosquito swarm had really been his plan. His death was tantamount to a final confirmation of the existence of the terrible plan. He had vaulted out of the vicious

cycle at the cost of his life, prompting increasing murmurs of criti-cism of the Wallfacer Project among the international community. Public opinion demanded further restrictions on Wallfacer power, but the very nature of the Wallfacer Project meant that too many restrictions would make it difficult for the Wallfacers to conduct their strategic deceptions, rendering the entire project meaningless. The Wallfacer Project possessed a leadership structure that human society had never before seen, and it required time to adjust and adapt to it. It was clear that the hibernation of the two Wallfacers would provide a buffer period for that to take place.

A few days later, in a top-secret underground structure, Rey Diaz and Hines entered hibernation.

Luo Ji found himself in an ominous dream. He dreamt he was walking the halls of the Louvre. It was a dream he had never had before, because the past five years of bliss had given him no cause to dream of previous joys. In this dream, he was alone with the loneliness that had been absent for five years. His every footstep reverberated through the palace halls, and something seemed to leave him with every reverberation, until at last he dared not take another step. In front of him was the *Mona Lisa*. She no longer smiled, but looked on him with compassion in her eyes. When his footsteps stopped, the sound of the outdoor fountains trickled in and gradually grew louder, at which point he awoke to find that the sound was coming from the real world. It was raining.

Luo Ji reached out to hold his beloved's hand, and discovered that his dream had become a reality.

Zhuang Yan was gone.

He rolled out of bed and entered the nursery, where a lamp was softly glowing, but Xia Xia wasn't there. On the little bed, tidily made up, was one of Zhuang Yan's paintings, a favorite of both of theirs. It was practically blank, and from a distance it looked like a sheet of paper. Closer in, you could see fine reeds in the lower left, and in the upper right the traces of a vanishing goose. In the blank

center were two infinitesimally tiny people. But now, a graceful line of text had been added to it:

My love, we're waiting for you at doomsday.

It was bound to happen sooner or later. Could such a dream life last forever? *It was bound to happen, so don't worry. You're mentally prepared for it,* Luo Ji told himself, but a wave of dizziness came over him. As he picked up the painting and went toward the living room, his legs quavered and he felt as if he was floating.

The living room was empty, but the embers in the fireplace glowed a hazy red that made everything look like melting ice. The rain continued outside. It was to the same sound of rain that she had walked out of his dreams five years ago, and now she had returned to them, taking their child with her.

He picked up the phone to call Kent, but then he heard soft footsteps outside. A woman's footsteps, but not Zhuang Yan's. Even so, he tossed the phone down and went outside.

Luo Ji immediately recognized the slender figure standing on the porch in the rain, even though he could only see a silhouette.

"Hello, Dr. Luo," Secretary General Say said.

"Hello . . . Where are my wife and child?"

"They're waiting for you at doomsday," she said, repeating the words in the painting.

"Why?"

"This is a PDC resolution, to let you work and fulfill your Wallfacer responsibilities. No harm will come to them, and children are better suited to hibernation than adults."

"You've kidnapped them! That's criminal!"

"We did not kidnap anyone."

Luo Ji's heart quaked at the implications of Say's statement, and he pushed them out of his mind rather than face that reality. "I said that having them here was part of the plan!"

"But after a thorough investigation, the PDC decided that it was not part of the plan, and so took steps to prompt you to get to work."

"Even if it's not kidnapping, you took away my child without my consent, and that's against the law." When he realized who he

was including in "you," his heart quaked again and he leaned back feebly against the pillar behind him.

"True, but it is well within acceptability. Do not forget, Dr. Luo, that this and all of the resources you have tapped do not fall under existing legal frameworks, so the UN's actions in the present time of crisis can be justified under the law."

"Are you still working on behalf of the UN?"

"Yes."

"You were reelected?"

"Yes."

He wanted to change the subject to avoid facing the cold facts, but he failed. *What will I do without them? What will I do without them?* his heart asked over and over. Finally it slipped out of his mouth as he slid down the pillar to the ground. It felt like everything was collapsing around him, turning to magma from the top down, except that this time the magma was burning and pooled inside his heart.

"They're still here, Dr. Luo. They're waiting for you safe and sound in the future. You've always been a sober person, and you must become even more sober now. If not for all humanity, then for your family." Say looked down at the ground, where Luo Ji sat beside the column on the brink of a breakdown.

Then a gust of wind blew rain onto the porch. Its refreshing chill and Say's words managed to cool the fire raging in Luo Ji's heart to an extent.

"This was your plan from the beginning, wasn't it?"

"Yes, but this step was taken only when there was no other choice."

"So she was . . . When she came, was she really a woman who did traditional painting?"

"Yes."

"From the Central Academy of Fine Arts?"

"Yes."

"Then was she . . ."

"Everything you saw was the real her. Everything you knew

about her was true. Everything that made her *her*: Her past life, her family, her personality, and her mind."

"You mean she really was that kind of woman?"

"Yes. Do you really think she could have faked it for five years? That's how she really was. Innocent and gentle, like an angel. She didn't fake anything, including her love for you, which was very real."

"Then how could she carry out such a cruel deception? To never let anything slip for five years?"

"How do you know she never let anything slip? Her soul was shrouded in melancholy from the first time you saw her on that rainy night five years ago. She didn't hide it. That melancholy stayed with her for five years like an ever-present background music that never stopped the whole time, and that's why you didn't notice."

Now he understood. When he first saw her, what had it been that had touched the softest place in his heart? That made him feel like the entire world was an injury to her? That made him willing to protect her with his life? It was that gentle sadness concealed within her clear, innocent eyes—a sadness that, like the light in the fireplace, shone gently through her beauty. It was indeed an imperceptible background music that had quietly permeated his subconscious and pulled him step by step into the abyss of love.

"I can't find them, can I?" he asked.

"That's right. Like I said, this is a PDC resolution."

"Then I'll go with them to doomsday."

"You may."

Luo Ji had imagined he would be turned down, but—just as when he had given up his Wallfacer status—there was practically no space between his statement and Say's reply. He knew that things weren't as easy as that. He asked, "Is there a problem?"

"No. This time it really is fine. You know, since the birth of the Wallfacer Project there has always been dissent within the international community. Out of their own interests, most countries have supported some of the Wallfacers while opposing others, so there was always going to be a side that wants to be rid of you.

Now that the first Wallbreaker is out and Tyler has failed, forces opposed to the project have grown more powerful and have driven its supporters to a stalemate. If at this point you proposed going directly to doomsday, it would be a compromise plan acceptable to both sides. But, Dr. Luo, are you truly willing to do that while humanity is fighting for survival?"

"You politicians sound off about humanity at the drop of a hat, but I can't see humanity. I can only see individuals. I'm just one individual, an ordinary person, and I can't take on the responsibility of saving all of humanity. I just want to live my own life."

"Very well. But Zhuang Yan and Xia Xia are two of those individuals. Don't you want to fulfill your responsibility to them? Even if she hurt you, I can see you still love her. And there's the child, too. From the moment Hubble II finally confirmed the Trisolaran invasion, one thing has been certain: Humanity will fight to the end. When your beloved and your child awaken in four centuries, doomsday and the flames of war will be upon them, but by that time you'll have lost your Wallfacer status and will be powerless to protect them. They will only be able to share a hellish existence with you while you await the final annihilation of the world. Is that what you want? Is that the life you want to give your wife and child?"

Luo Ji said nothing.

"If you won't think of anything else, then just imagine that Doomsday Battle four centuries from now, and the look in their eyes when they see you! What sort of a person will they see? A man who abandoned the woman he loves most, together with all of humanity? A man unwilling to save all of the world's children? A man who wouldn't even save his own child? Are you, as a man, capable of withstanding their gaze?"

Luo Ji bent his head in silence. The sound of the nighttime rain falling on grass and lake was like myriad entreaties from another time and space.

"Do you really believe that I can change all of that?" Luo Ji asked, raising his head.

"Why not try? Of all the Wallfacers, you may have the greatest hope of success. I've come today to tell you that."

"Go on, then. Why?"

"Because out of all of humanity, you are the only person that Trisolaris wants dead."

Leaning against the pillar, Luo Ji stared at Say, but saw nothing. He struggled to remember.

Say went on. "That car crash was meant for you. It just accidentally hit your girlfriend."

"But that really was an accident. That car changed direction because two other cars collided."

"They had been planning that for a long time."

"But I was just an ordinary person back then, with no special protection. It would've been simple to kill me. Why go to such lengths?"

"To make the murder look like an accident, so as not to attract any attention. They almost succeeded. There were fifty-one traffic accidents that killed five people in the city that day. But a scout hidden within the ETO provided an intelligence report confirming that the ETO had orchestrated the attempt on your life. And what's most frightening is this: The order came from Trisolaris itself, conveyed to Evans through the sophons. To this date, that is the only assassination they've ever ordered."

"Me? Trisolaris wants to kill me? For what reason?" Again, Luo Ji felt displaced from himself.

"I don't know. No one knows, now. Evans may have known, but he's dead. He was evidently the one who added the requirement to the assassination order that it not attract attention. That only reinforces your importance."

"Importance?" Luo Ji shook his head with a wry smile. "Look at me. Do I really look like someone with superpowers?"

"You don't have superpowers, so don't let your thoughts go in that direction. It'll only lead you astray," Say said, gesturing emphatically. "You had no special powers in your prior research, be they supernatural abilities or extraordinary technical skills within the known laws of nature. Or, at least, none that we have

been able to discover. That Evans required that the assassination not attract attention demonstrates this point as well, because it proves that your ability can be acquired by others."

"Why didn't you tell me?"

"We were afraid of influencing whatever it is you have. Too many unknowns. We felt it best to let things ride."

"I'd once had a notion to work on cosmic sociology, because . . ." Then a small voice deep within him said, *You're a Wallfacer!* This was the first time he had heard that voice. He also heard another nonexistent sound: the buzzing of the sophons as they flew about him. He even thought he saw a few blurry, firefly-like points of light. So for the first time, he acted like a Wallfacer and swallowed his words, saying only, "Is that relevant?"

Say shook her head. "Probably not. As far as we are aware, that's just the topic of a research application that never actually went forward, much less obtained any results. Besides, even if you had done the research, we wouldn't expect you to come up with results any more valuable than any other researcher."

"And why is that?"

"Dr. Luo, we're speaking frankly here. As I understand it, you're a failure of a scholar. You perform research not out of any thirst for exploration, nor out of a sense of duty and mission, but simply as a way to make a living."

"Isn't that the way things are these days?"

"There's nothing wrong with that, of course, but you exhibit all kinds of behaviors unbecoming a serious and dedicated scholar. Your research is utilitarian, your techniques opportunistic, you seek out sensationalism, and you have a history of embezzling funding. Character-wise, you're cynical and irresponsible, and you harbor a mocking attitude toward a scholar's vocation. . . . We're actually well aware of the fact that you don't care about the fate of the human race."

"And that's why you would stoop to such despicable means to coerce me. You've despised me all along, haven't you?"

"Under normal circumstances, a man like you would never be

tasked with such an important duty, but there is this one overriding detail: Trisolaris is afraid of you. Be your own Wallbreaker. Find out why."

When Say finished, she stepped off the porch, got into the waiting car, and disappeared into the rainy mist.

Standing there, Luo Ji lost his sense of time. Gradually, the rain stopped and the wind picked up, blowing the night sky free of clouds, revealing the snow peaks, and letting the bright round moon bathe the world in silvery light.

Before going back inside, Luo Ji took one last look at the silver Garden of Eden, and his heart said to Zhuang Yan and Xia Xia, *My love, wait for me at doomsday.*

Standing in the giant shadow cast by the space plane *High Frontier* and looking up at its massive body, Zhang Beihai was involuntarily reminded of the carrier *Tang,* now long dismantled, and even wondered if the hull of *High Frontier* could contain a few steel plates from *Tang.* Over the course of more than thirty reentries, the burning heat had left scorch marks on the body of the space plane, and it really did look the way *Tang* had when it was under construction. The body had the same sense of age, but the two cylindrical booster rockets beneath the wings were new, making it resemble repairs to ancient architecture in Europe: The newness of the patches stood in stark contrast to the coloring of the original building, reminding visitors that those parts were modern additions. But if the boosters were removed, *High Frontier* would look like a big old transport plane.

The space plane was a very new thing, one of the few breakthroughs in aerospace technology over the last five years, and quite possibly the last generation of chemically propelled spacecraft. The concept had been proposed the previous century as a replacement for the space shuttle that could take off from a runway like an ordinary plane and fly conventionally to the top layer of the atmosphere, at which point the rockets would be turned on for

spaceflight and it would enter orbit. *High Frontier* was the fourth such space plane in operation, and many more were under construction. They would, in the near future, take on the task of building the space elevator.

"I once imagined that we would never get the chance to go to space in our lifetime," Zhang Beihai said to Chang Weisi, who had come to see him off. He and twenty other space force officers, all of them members of the three strategic institutes, would take *High Frontier* to the ISS.

"Are there naval officers who've never been to sea?" Chang Weisi said, smiling.

"Of course there are. Lots of them. Some people in the navy sought exactly that. But I'm not that sort of person."

"Beihai, be aware of one thing: The active-duty astronauts are still air force personnel, so you are the first representatives of the space force to go into space."

"It's a shame there's no specific mission."

"Experience is the mission. A space strategist ought to have a consciousness of space. This wasn't feasible before the space plane, since sending up one person cost tens of millions, but it's much cheaper now. We'll try to put more strategists into space soon, since we're the space force, after all. Right now we're more like a college of bullshit, and that just won't do."

Then the boarding call was issued, and the officers began climbing the airstair to the plane. They wore uniforms but not space suits, and looked no different than if they were taking standard air travel. It was a sign of progress, demonstrating that going to space was a little more normal than it had been. From the uniforms, Zhang Beihai noticed that there were people from other departments boarding the plane as well.

"Ah, Beihai, there's another important thing," Chang Weisi said as Beihai was about to pick up his carryon. "The CMC has studied the report we submitted on sending political cadres to the future as reinforcements, and the brass feel that conditions are still premature."

Zhang Beihai squinted, as if warding against a glare, though

they were still in the space plane's shadow. "Commander, my feeling is that we ought to keep the entire four-century period in mind when making plans, and to be clear about what's urgent and what's important. . . . But please be assured that I won't say that in any formal setting. I know very well that our superiors are considering the bigger picture."

"The higher-ups have affirmed your long-term thinking and commend you for it. The document stresses one point: The plan to send reinforcements to the future has not been denied. Research and planning will continue, but present conditions are still premature for execution. I feel—and this is of course my personal opinion—that we need additional qualified political cadres in our ranks to lessen the current work pressures before we can consider it."

"Commander, surely you are aware of what 'qualified' means in the context of the Space Force Political Department, and what the basic requirements are. Qualified people are becoming increasingly rare."

"But we've got to look forward. If there are breakthroughs in the two key technologies of phase one, the space elevator and controlled fusion—and there's hope of this in our lifetimes—then things will be better. . . . Okay then. Off with you."

Zhang Beihai saluted him and then stepped onto the stairs. His first feeling upon entering the cabin was that it wasn't much different than a civilian airliner, except the seats were wider, having been designed to accommodate space suits. During the first flights of the space plane, all passengers had to wear space suits as a precaution, but there was no need for that now.

He had a window seat, and the seat immediately next to his was also occupied. A civilian, judging from his clothing. Zhang Beihai nodded to him in greeting before turning his attention to fastening the seat's complicated safety belt.

There was no countdown. *High Frontier* started its air engines and began taxiing. Because of its weight, it spent longer on the ground during takeoff than an ordinary plane, but at last it lifted ponderously off the ground and embarked on its voyage into space.

"This is the thirty-eighth flight of the space plane *High Frontier*. The aviation phase has started and will last approximately thirty minutes. Please do not unfasten your safety belts," said a voice over the intercom.

As he watched the ground recede through the cabin window, Zhang Beihai's thoughts turned to the past. During training to become a carrier captain, he had completed naval aviation pilot training and had passed the level three fighter pilot exam. On his first solo trip he had watched Earth recede like this and suddenly discovered that he loved the sky even more deeply than the ocean. Now, his longing was for the space beyond the sky.

He was a man destined to fly high and fly far.

"Not much different from civil aviation, you think?"

He turned to see the speaker sitting in the next seat, and recognized him at last. "You must be Dr. Ding Yi. I've been wanting to meet you."

"But it's going to get rough in just a little bit," the man said, ignoring Zhang Beihai's salutation. He went on, "The first time, I didn't take off my glasses after the aviation phase, and they crushed my nose with the weight of a brick. The second time I took them off, but then they flew off after gravity went away. It wasn't easy for the guy to find them for me in the air filter in the plane's tail."

"I thought you went up on the space shuttle the first time. On TV, that didn't look like a very nice trip," Zhang Beihai said with a grin.

"Oh, I'm talking about taking the space plane. If we count the shuttle, then this is my fourth time. On the shuttle, they took away my glasses before takeoff."

"Why are you going to the station this time? You've just been put in charge of a controlled fusion project. The third branch, isn't it?"

Four branches had been set up for the controlled fusion project, each pursuing a different direction of research.

Restrained by the safety belt, Ding Yi lifted a hand to point at Zhang Beihai. "You study controlled fusion and you can't go to space? You sound the same as those guys. The ultimate goal of

our research is spaceship engines, and the real power held by the aerospace industry today remains to a large degree in the hands of the people who used to make chemical rocket engines. They're saying now that we're just supposed to devote ourselves to controlled fusion on the ground, and that we basically have no say in the general plan of the space fleet."

"Dr. Ding, your views are identical to mine." Zhang Beihai loosened his safety belt and leaned over. "For a space fleet, space travel is an entirely different concept from chemical rocketry. Even the space elevator is different from today's aerospace techniques. But right now the aerospace industry of the past still holds too much power. Its people are ideologically ossified and legalistic, and if things continue, there will be all kinds of trouble."

"There's nothing to be done. At least they've managed to come up with this in the course of five years." He pointed around him. "And this gives them the capital to squeeze out outsiders."

The cabin intercom started up. "Please take care: We are approaching an altitude of twenty thousand meters. Due to the thin atmosphere we will now be flying through, there may be sharp drops in altitude that will produce momentary weightlessness. Please do not panic. Again, please keep your safety belts fastened."

Ding Yi said, "But our trip to the station this time is unrelated to the controlled fusion project. It's to recover those cosmic ray catchers. That's some expensive stuff."

"The space-based high-energy physics research project has been stopped?" asked Zhang Beihai, retightening his safety belt.

"It's stopped. Knowing that there's no need to waste effort in the future counts as a kind of success."

"The sophons won."

"That's right. So humanity only has a few reserves of theory remaining: classical physics, quantum mechanics, and a still-embryonic string theory. How far their applications can be pushed is up to fate."

High Frontier continued to climb, its aviation engines rumbling under the strain as if it were struggling up a tall mountain, but

there were no sudden drops. The space plane was now approaching thirty thousand meters, the limit of aviation. Looking out, Zhang Beihai saw that the blue of the sky was fading as it got dark, even though the sun became even more dazzling.

"Our current flight altitude is thirty-one thousand meters. The aviation phase is complete and the spaceflight phase is about to begin. Please adjust your seats according to the illustration onscreen to minimize the discomfort of hypergravitation."

Then Zhang Beihai felt the plane rise gently, as if it had discarded a burden.

"Aircraft engine assembly separated. Aerospace engine ignition countdown: ten, nine, eight . . ."

"For them, this is the real launch. Enjoy," Ding Yi said, and closed his eyes.

When the countdown reached zero, there was a huge roar, as if the entire sky outside was shouting, and then hypergravity came like a giant, slowly tightening fist. With effort, Zhang Beihai twisted his head to look out the window. He was unable to see the flames spurting from the engine, but a wide swath of the rarefied air of the sky outside was painted red, as if *High Frontier* was floating through a sunset.

Five minutes later, the boosters detached, and after another five minutes of acceleration, the main engine cut off. *High Frontier* had entered orbit.

The giant hand of hypergravity suddenly let go and Zhang Beihai's body bounced back from the depths of his seat. Although the restraint of his safety belt kept him from floating away, to his senses he and the *High Frontier* were no longer parts of the same whole. The gravity that had once bonded them together was gone, and he and the plane were now flying in parallel paths through space. Out the window were the brightest stars he had ever seen in his life. Later, when the space plane adjusted its attitude, the sun streamed in through the windows and myriad points of light danced in its beams: dust particles that had weightlessly taken to the air. As the plane gradually rotated, he saw the Earth.

From this low orbital position he couldn't see the entire sphere, only the arc of the horizon, but he could clearly make out the shapes of the continents.

Then the starfield, that long-awaited sight, finally came into view, and he said in his heart, *Dad, I've taken the first step.*

For five years, General Fitzroy had felt like a Wallfacer in the actual sense of the word, in that the wall he faced was the big screen with the image of the stars between Earth and Trisolaris. At first glance it was entirely black, but closer inspection of the screen revealed points of starlight. He had grown so well acquainted with those stars that when he had attempted to sketch their position on a piece of paper at a dull meeting the previous day and compared it to the actual photo afterward, he was basically correct. The three stars of Trisolaris lying inconspicuously at the center looked like a single star in the standard view, but every time he magnified them he found that their positions had changed. This chaotic cosmic dance so fascinated him that he forgot what he was looking for in the first place. The brush that had been observed five years ago had gradually faded away, and no second brush had appeared. The Trisolaran Fleet left a visible wake only when it passed through interstellar dust clouds. Earth's astronomers had verified through observations of the absorption of background starlight that during the fleet's four-century-long voyage through space, it would pass through five of them. People dubbed these "snow patches" after the way that passersby left tracks on snowy ground.

If the Trisolaran Fleet had maintained a constant acceleration over the past five years, it would pass the second snow patch today.

Fitzroy arrived at the Hubble II Space Telescope Control Center early. Ringier laughed when he saw him. "General, why do you remind me of a child who wants another present so soon after Christmas?"

"Didn't you say that they would cross the snow patch today?"

"That's right, but the Trisolaran Fleet has only traveled 0.22 light-years, so it's still four light-years away. Light reflected from

its passage through the snow won't reach Earth for another four years."

"Oh, I'm sorry. I forgot about that," Fitzroy said with an embarrassed shake of his head. "I really wanted to see them again. This time, we'll be able to measure their speed and acceleration at the time of passage, and that's very important."

"I'm sorry. We're outside the light cone."

"What's that?"

"It's what physicists call the cone shape that light describes as it emanates along the time axis. It's impossible for people outside the cone to comprehend events taking place inside the cone. Think about it: Information about who-knows-how-many major events in the universe is flying toward us right now at the speed of light. Some of it has been traveling for hundreds of millions of years, but we're still outside the light cones of those events."

"Fate lies within the light cone."

Ringier considered this, then gave him an appreciative nod. "General, that's an excellent analogy! But sophons outside the light cone can see events on the inside."

"So the sophons have changed fate," Fitzroy said with feeling, and turned back to an image-processing terminal. Five years before, the young engineer Harris had started to cry at the sight of the brush, and afterward had suffered from depression so severe that he became practically useless at his job and was let go. No one knew where he had ended up.

Fortunately, there weren't many people like him.

Temperatures were cooling rapidly these days, and it had started to snow, causing the green to gradually disappear from the surrounding area and a thin layer of ice to freeze on the surface of the lake. Nature lost its bright coloring, like a color photograph turned black-and-white. Warm weather here had always been short-lived, but to Luo Ji, the Garden of Eden felt like it had lost its aura since the departure of his wife and child.

Winter was a season for thinking.

When Luo Ji began to think, he was surprised to find that his thoughts were already in progress. He remembered back to middle school and a lesson a teacher had taught him for language arts exams: First, take a look at the final essay question, then start the exam from the top, so that as you work on the exam, your subconscious will be thinking over the essay question, like a background process in a computer. Now he knew that from the moment he became a Wallfacer, his thinking had started up and had never stopped. The entire process was subconscious and he had never been aware of it.

He quickly retraced the steps his thoughts had already completed.

He was now certain that everything about his current situation stemmed from his chance encounter with Ye Wenjie nine years ago. Afterward, he had never spoken of the meeting with anyone for fear of causing unnecessary trouble for himself, but with Ye Wenjie gone, the meeting was a secret known only to him and Trisolaris. In those days, only two sophons had reached Earth, but he could be certain that on that evening, they had been there by Yang Dong's grave, listening to their every word. And the fluctuation in their quantum formation that instantly crossed the space of four light-years meant that Trisolaris had also been listening.

But what had Ye Wenjie said?

Secretary General Say had been wrong about one thing. Luo Ji's never-begun research into cosmic sociology *was* quite likely the immediate reason why Trisolaris wanted to kill him. Of course, Say didn't know that the project had been Ye Wenjie's suggestion, and although it had just seemed to Luo Ji like an excellent opportunity to make scholarship entertaining, he had been looking for just such an opportunity. Prior to the Trisolar Crisis, the study of alien civilization was indeed a sensational project that would have garnered easy media attention.

The aborted research project wasn't important in and of itself. What mattered was the instruction that Ye Wenjie had given him, so that's where Luo Ji's mind was stuck.

Over and over again he recalled her words: *Suppose a vast number of civilizations are distributed throughout the universe, on the order of the number of detectable stars. Lots and lots of them. The mathematical structure of cosmic sociology is far clearer than that of human sociology.*

The factors of chaos and randomness in the complex make-ups of every civilized society in the universe get filtered out by the immense distance, so those civilizations can act as reference points that are relatively easy to manipulate mathematically.

First: Survival is the primary need of civilization. Second: Civilization continuously grows and expands, but the total matter in the universe remains constant.

One more thing: To derive a basic picture of cosmic sociology from these two axioms, you need two other important concepts: chains of suspicion and the technological explosion. I'm afraid there won't be that opportunity. . . . Well, you might as well just forget I said anything. Either way, I've fulfilled my duty.

He had returned countless times to these words, analyzing each sentence from every angle and chewing over every word. The component words had been strung into a set of prayer beads, and like a pious monk he stroked them time and again; and unstrung them, scattered them, and restrung them in different orders until a layer of each had been worn away.

Try as he might, he couldn't extract the clue from those words, the clue that made him the only person that Trisolaris wanted to destroy.

During his lengthy contemplation he strolled aimlessly. He walked along the desolate lakeside, walked through the wind as it grew ever colder, oftentimes completing a circuit of the lake unawares. Twice he even walked to the foot of the snow peak, where the patch of exposed rock that looked like a moonscape was blanketed with snow, becoming one with the snowcap ahead of him. Only then did his mood leave the track of his thoughts, Zhang Yan's eyes appearing before his own in the boundless blank white of the natural painting. But he was now able to keep his mood in check and continue turning himself into a thinking machine.

A month went by without him knowing it, and then winter came in full force. But he still conducted his lengthy thought process outside, sharpening his mind on the cold.

By this time, most of the prayer beads had been worn faint, except for twenty-one of them. These ones seemed only to get newer the more he polished them, and now emitted a faint light:

Survival is the primary need of civilization.

Civilization continuously grows and expands, but the total matter in the universe remains constant.

He fixated on these two sentences, the axioms Ye Wenjie had proposed for cosmic civilization. Although he did not know their ultimate secret, his long meditation told him that the answer lay within them.

But it was too simple a clue. What could he and the human race gain from two self-evident rules?

Don't dismiss simplicity. Simple means solid. The entire mansion of mathematics was erected on a foundation of this kind of irreducibly simple, yet logically rock-solid, axiom.

With this in mind, he looked around him. All that surrounded him was huddled up against the icy cold of winter, but most of the world still teemed with life. It was a living world brimming with a complex profusion of oceans, land, and sky as vast as the foggy sea, but all of it ran according to a rule even simpler than the axioms of cosmic civilization: survival of the fittest.

Luo Ji now saw his problem: Where Darwin had taken the boundless living world and made a rule to sum it up, Luo Ji had to use the rules he knew to uncover a picture of cosmic civilization. It was the opposite road to Darwin's, but a more difficult one.

So he began sleeping in the daytime and thinking at night. Whenever the perils of his mental roadway terrified him, he found comfort in the stars overhead. Like Ye Wenjie had said, the distance hid the complex structure of each star, making them just a collection of points in space with a clear mathematical configuration. It was a thinker's paradise, his paradise. To Luo Ji, at least, it felt like the world in front of him was far clearer and more concise than Darwin's.

But this simple world held a perplexing riddle: The entire galaxy was a vast empty desert, but a highly intelligent civilization had appeared on the star nearest to us. In this mystery, his thoughts found an entry point.

Gradually, the two concepts Ye Wenjie had left unexplained came into focus: chains of suspicion and the technology explosion.

The weather that day was colder than usual, and from Luo Ji's vantage point on the lakeshore, the cold seemed to make the stars into an even purer silver lattice against the black sky, solemnly displaying for him their clear mathematical configuration. All of a sudden, he found himself in a state that was entirely new. In his perception, the entire universe froze, all motion stopped, and everything from stars down to atoms entered a state of rest, with the stars just countless cold, dimensionless points reflecting the cold light of an outside world. . . . Everything was at rest, waiting for his final awakening.

The distant bark of a dog brought him back to reality. Probably a service canine belonging to the security forces.

Luo Ji was beside himself with excitement. Although he hadn't actually glimpsed that final mystery, he had clearly felt its presence just now.

He collected his thoughts and tried to reenter that state, but was unsuccessful. Though the stars remained the same, the world around him interfered with his thinking. All was shrouded in darkness, but he could make out the distant snowcap, the lakeside forest and grassland, and the house behind him, and through the house's half-open door he could see the dark glow of the fire. . . . Next to the simple clarity of the stars, everything in the vicinity represented a complexity and chaos that mathematics would be forever unable to grasp, so he attempted to remove them from his perception.

He walked out onto the frozen lake—cautiously, at first, but when he found that the icy surface seemed solid, he walked and slid ahead more quickly, until he reached a point where he could no longer make out the lakeshore through the night around him. Now he was surrounded on all sides by smooth ice. This distanced

him somewhat from earthly complexity and chaos, and by imagining that the icy plane extended infinitely in every direction, he obtained a simple, flat world; a cold, planar mental platform. Cares vanished, and soon his perception reentered that state of rest, where the stars were waiting for him. . . .

Then, with a crunch, the ice beneath Luo Ji's feet broke and his body plunged straight into the water.

At the precise instant the icy water covered Luo Ji's head, he saw the stillness of the stars shatter. The starfield curled up into a vortex and scattered into turbulent, chaotic waves of silver. The biting cold, like crystal lightning, shot into the fog of his consciousness, illuminating everything. He continued to sink. The turbulent stars overhead shrank into a fuzzy halo at the break in the ice above his head, leaving nothing but cold and inky blackness surrounding him, as if he wasn't sinking into ice water, but had jumped into the blackness of space.

In the dead, lonely, cold blackness, he saw the truth of the universe.

He surfaced quickly. His head surged out of the water and he spat out a mouthful. He tried crawling onto the ice at the edge of the hole but could only bring his body up halfway before the ice collapsed again. He crawled and collapsed, forging a path through the ice, but progress was slow and his stamina began to give out from the cold. He didn't know whether the security team would notice anything unusual on the lake before he drowned or froze to death. Stripping off his soaked down jacket to lessen the burden on his movement, he had the idea that if he spread out the jacket on the ice, it might distribute the pressure and allow him to crawl onto it. He did so, and then, with just enough energy left for one last attempt, he used every last ounce of strength to crawl onto the down jacket at the edge of the ice. This time the ice didn't collapse, and at last his entire body was lying on top of it. He crept carefully ahead, daring to stand up only after putting a fair distance between him and the hole. Then he saw flashlights waving on the shore and heard shouts.

He stood on the ice, his teeth chattering in the cold, a cold that

seemed to come not from the lake water or icy wind, but from a direct transmission from outer space. He kept his head down, knowing that from this moment on, the stars were not like they once were. He didn't dare look up. As Rey Diaz feared the sun, Luo Ji had acquired a severe phobia of the stars. He bowed his head, and through chattering teeth, said to himself:

"Wallfacer Luo Ji, I am your Wallbreaker."

"Your hair's turned white over the years," Luo Ji said to Kent.

"For many years to come, at least, it's not going to get any whiter," Kent said, laughing. In Luo Ji's presence, he had always worn a courteous, studied face. This was the first time Luo Ji had seen him with such a sincere smile. In his eyes, he saw the words that remained unspoken: *You've finally begun to work.*

"I need someplace safer," he said.

"Not a problem, Dr. Luo. Any particular requests?"

"Nothing apart from safety. It must be absolutely secure."

"Doctor, an absolutely safe place does not exist, but we can come very close. I'll have to warn you, though, these places are always underground. And as for comfort . . ."

"Disregard comfort. However, it'd be best if it's in China."

"Not a problem. I'll take care of it immediately."

When Kent was about to leave, Luo Ji stopped him. Pointing out the window at the Garden of Eden, which was now completely blanketed in snow, he said, "Can you tell me the name of this place? I'm going to miss it."

Luo Ji traveled more than ten hours under tight security before reaching his destination. When he exited the car, he knew immediately where he was: It was here, in the broad, squat hall that looked like an underground parking garage, that he had embarked on his fantastic new life five years before. Now, after five years of dreams alternating with nightmares, he had returned to the starting point.

Greeting him was a man named Zhang Xiang, the same young man who—along with Shi Qiang—had sent him off five years ago, and who now was in charge of security. He had aged considerably in five years and now looked like a middle-aged man.

The elevator was still operated by an armed soldier—not the one from back then, of course, but Luo Ji still felt a certain warmth in his heart. The old-style elevator had been swapped for one that was completely automated and did not require an operator, so the soldier merely pressed the "10" button and the elevator started its descent.

The underground structure had clearly undergone a recent renovation: The ventilation ducts in the hallways had been hidden, the walls coated with moisture-proof tile, and all traces of the civil air defense slogans had disappeared.

Luo Ji's living quarters took up the whole of the tenth basement floor. While it was no match in comfort for the house he had just left, it was equipped with comprehensive communications and computer equipment, along with a conference room set up with a remote video conferencing system, giving the place the feel of a command center.

The administrator made a particular point of showing Luo Ji a set of light switches in the room, each of which bore a small picture of the sun. The administrator called them "sun lamps" and said they needed to be turned on for no fewer than five hours a day. Originally intended as labor-safety products for mine workers, they could simulate sunlight, including UV rays, as supplementary daylight for people spending long periods underground.

The next day, as Luo Ji had requested, the astronomer Albert Ringier visited the tenth basement.

When he saw him, Luo Ji said, "You were the first to observe the flight path of the Trisolaran Fleet?"

Ringier looked a little unhappy to hear this. "I've repeatedly issued statements to reporters, but they insist on forcing this honor on my head. It should be credited to General Fitzroy. He was the one who demanded that Hubble II observe Trisolaris during

237

testing. Otherwise we might have missed the chance, since the wake in the interstellar dust would have faded."

"What I'd like to talk to you about isn't connected to that. I did a bit of astronomy once, but not in much depth, and I'm no longer familiar with the subject. My first question is this: If, in the universe, there exists another observer apart from Trisolaris, has Earth's position been revealed to them?"

"No."

"You're sure of that?"

"Yes."

"But Earth has exchanged communication with Trisolaris."

"That low-frequency communication would reveal only the general direction of Earth and Trisolaris in the Milky Way Galaxy, and the distance between the two worlds. That is, if there's a third-party recipient, the communication would make it possible for them to know of the existence of two civilized worlds 4.22 light-years apart in the Orion Arm of the Milky Way, but they would still be ignorant of the precise position of those two worlds. In fact, determining each other's position through this kind of exchange is only feasible for stars in close proximity, like the sun and the stars of Trisolaris. For a slightly more distant third-party observer, however, even if we communicate directly with them, we wouldn't be able to determine each other's position."

"Why is that?"

"Marking the position of a star for another observer in the universe is hardly as easy as people imagine. Here's an analogy: You're taking a plane through the Sahara Desert and a grain of sand below you shouts 'Here I am!' You hear the shout, but can you fix a location for that grain of sand from the plane? There are nearly two hundred billion stars in the Milky Way. It's practically a desert of stars."

Luo Ji nodded in apparent relief. "I understand. So that's it, then."

"What is?" Ringier asked in confusion.

Luo Ji didn't answer, but asked instead, "Using our present

level of technology, is there a way to indicate the position of a star in the universe?"

"Yes, by using directed very high frequency electromagnetic waves, equal to or higher in frequency than visible light, and then harnessing stellar power to transmit information. In simple terms, you'd make the star flash, like a cosmic lighthouse."

"This far exceeds our present technical capabilities."

"Oh, I'm sorry. I overlooked your precondition. At our present technical capabilities, it would be fairly difficult to show a star's position to the far reaches of the universe. There's still a way, but interpreting the positional information requires a level of technology far beyond that of humanity, and even, I believe, beyond that of Trisolaris."

"Tell me about that approach."

"The key information is the relative position of stars. If you specify a region of space in the Milky Way that contains a sufficient number of stars—perhaps a few dozen would be sufficient—their relative arrangement in three-dimensional space would be totally unique, like a fingerprint."

"I'm starting to understand. We send out a message containing the position of the star we wish to point out, relative to the surrounding stars, and the recipient compares the data to its star map to determine the star's location."

"Right. But things aren't that simple. The recipient must possess a three-dimensional model of the entire galaxy that precisely indicates the relative position of every one of a hundred billion stars. Then, after receiving our message, they would have to search through that enormous database to find an area of space that matches the pattern of positions we sent out."

"No, it's not simple at all. It's like recording the relative position of every grain of sand in the desert."

"Even harder than that. The Milky Way, unlike the desert, is in motion, and the relative positions of its stars are constantly changing. The later the position information is received, the greater the error caused by these changes. This means the database has to be

able to predict the changes in position of each of those hundred billion stars. In theory, it's not a problem, but to actually do it . . . God . . ."

"Would it be hard for us to send that positional information?"

"No, because we would only need to have a position pattern for a limited number of stars. And now that I've had time to think about it, given the average stellar density of the outer arm of the galaxy, a position pattern with no more than thirty stars should be sufficient. That's a small amount of information."

"Good. Now I'll ask a third question: Outside the Solar System, there are other stars with planets. You've discovered several hundred, right?"

"More than a thousand to date."

"And the closest to the sun?"

"244J2E1, sixteen light-years from the sun."

"As I remember it, the serial numbers are set like this: the prefix digits represent the order of discovery; the letters J, E, and X stand for Jupiter-type planets, Earth-type planets, and other planets, respectively; and the digits following the letter indicate the number of that type of planet in the system."

"That's right. 244J2E1 is a star with three planets, two of them Jupiter-type and one Earth-type."

Luo Ji thought for a moment, then shook his head. "That's too close. How about a little farther, like . . . around fifty light-years?"

"187J3X1, 49.5 light-years from the sun."

"That one's fine. Can you draw up a position pattern for that star?"

"Of course I can."

"How long would it take? Would you need help?"

"I can do it here if there's a computer with Internet. For a pattern of, say, thirty stars, I can give it to you tonight."

"What time is it now? It's not nighttime already?"

"I'd say it's probably morning, Dr. Luo."

Ringier went to the computer room next door, and Luo Ji called in Kent and Zhang Xiang. He first explained to Kent that

he wanted the PDC to hold the next Wallfacer hearing as soon as possible.

Kent said, "There are lots of PDC meetings these days. Once you've submitted the application, you'll probably only have to wait a few days."

"Then I'll have to wait. But I'd really like it as soon as possible. Also, I have a request: to attend the hearing here via video rather than go to the UN."

Kent looked reluctant. "Dr. Luo, don't you think that's a little inappropriate? For such a high-level international meeting . . . It's a question of respect for the participants."

"It's part of the plan. All those bizarre requests I made in the past were fulfilled, but this one's over the line?"

"You know . . ." Kent faltered.

"I know that a Wallfacer's status isn't like it once was, but I insist on this." When he continued, it was in a softer voice, even though he knew that the sophons hanging in the vicinity could still hear. "There are two possibilities now: One, if everything is like it used to be, I wouldn't mind going to the UN. But there's another possibility: I may be in a very dangerous situation, and I can't take that risk."

Then he said to Zhang Xiang, "That's why I've brought you here. We may become a target for a concentrated enemy attack, so security must be strengthened."

"Don't worry, Dr. Luo. We're located two hundred meters below ground. The area above us is under lockdown, an antimissile system has been deployed, and a state-of-the-art subterranean warning system has been installed to detect the digging of a tunnel from any direction. I guarantee to you that our security is foolproof."

When the two men left, Luo Ji took a walk down the hallway, his thoughts turning involuntarily to the Garden of Eden (he knew its name now, but still called it that in his heart) and its lake and snow peak. He knew that it was quite likely he would spend the rest of his life underground.

He looked around at the sunlamps in the hallway ceiling. The light they emitted was nothing like the sun.

Two meteors moved slowly across the starfield. All was dark on the ground, and the distant horizon blended into one with the night sky. A burst of whispers sounded through the dark, although the speakers remained unseen, as if the voices themselves were invisible creatures floating in the darkness.

With a clink, a small flame appeared in the darkness, its dim light revealing three faces: Qin Shi Huang, Aristotle, and Von Neumann. The flame came from a lighter in Aristotle's hand. When a few torches were extended, he lit one, which then passed fire among the others to form a shaky light in the wilderness and illuminate a group of people drawn from every era. Their whispers continued.

Qin Shi Huang leapt up on a stone and brandished his sword, and the crowd fell silent.

"The Lord has issued a new command: Destroy Wallfacer Luo Ji," he said.

"We too have received this command. This is the second assassination order that the Lord has issued for Luo Ji," Mozi said.

"But it will be difficult to kill him now," someone said.

"Difficult? It's impossible!"

"If Evans hadn't added that condition to the first assassination order, he would have been dead five years ago."

"Perhaps Evans was right to do so. After all, we don't know his reasons. Luo Ji was lucky to escape a second time in the UN Plaza."

Qin Shi Huang stopped the debate with a wave of his sword. "Shall we talk instead about what to do?"

"There's nothing we can do. Who can even get anywhere near a bunker two hundred meters deep, much less get inside? It's guarded too tightly."

"Shall we consider nuclear weapons?"

"The place is an antinuke bunker from the Cold War, damn it."

"The only viable option is sending someone to infiltrate security."

"Can that be done? We've had years. Has there ever been a successful infiltration?"

"Infiltrate his kitchen!" This prompted some laughter.

"Cut the crap. The Lord ought to tell us the truth, and maybe we can come up with a better option."

Qin Shi Huang answered the last speaker: "I also made that request, but the Lord said the truth was the most important secret in the universe and could not be revealed. The Lord spoke of it with Evans under the impression that humanity already knew but later learned otherwise."

"Then ask the Lord to transfer technology!"

Many other voices echoed this. Qin Shi Huang said, "This was another request I made. To my surprise, the Lord uncharacteristically did not reject it entirely."

A commotion took hold of the crowd, but Qin Shi Huang's next words quieted the excitement: "But once the Lord learned the location of the target, the request was swiftly rejected. It said that as far as the target's location was concerned, any technology It could transfer to us would be ineffective."

"Is he really that important?" Von Neumann asked, unable to conceal a note of jealousy in his voice. As the first successful Wallbreaker, he had risen rapidly in the organization.

"The Lord is afraid of him."

Einstein said, "I have thought this over for a long time, and I believe that the Lord's fear of Luo Ji has only one possible reason: He is the mouthpiece of certain power."

Qin Shi Huang shut down further discussion of the subject: "Don't get into that. Instead, let's think of how to fulfill the Lord's command."

"It can't be done."

"It really can't be done. It's a mission that can't be completed."

Qin Shi Huang clanged his sword on the rock beneath his feet. "This mission is crucial. The Lord may really be under threat.

Besides, if we complete it, the organization will be greatly elevated in the Lord's eyes! Gathered here are the elite of every sphere throughout the world, so how can we fail to think of something? Go back and think it over, and send your plans here to me through other channels. We've got to get on this!"

The torches burned out in succession and darkness swallowed everything. But the whispering went on.

The PDC Wallfacer Project Hearing did not convene for two weeks. After Tyler's failure and the hibernation of the other two Wallfacers, the PDC's main priority and attention had turned to mainstream defense.

Luo Ji and Kent awaited the start of the meeting in the video-conference room. The conference video connection had been made, and the big screen displayed the PDC auditorium, where the circular table familiar from the Security Council days was still completely empty. Luo Ji had arrived early as something of an apology for not attending in person.

While they waited, he chatted with Kent and asked him how he was managing. Kent said that he had lived in China for three years when he was younger, so he was quite accustomed to it and was doing well. At any rate, he didn't have to spend all day underground like Luo Ji, and his rusty Chinese had recently regained its fluency.

"You sound like you have a cold," Luo Ji said.

"I've just caught the bed flu," he replied.

"Bird flu?" Luo Ji said in alarm.

"No. Bed flu. That's what the media's calling it. It started going around in a nearby city a week ago. It's infectious, but symptoms are light. There's no fever, just a runny nose, and some patients get a sore throat. There's no need for medication, and it goes away on its own in three days or so after a little bed rest."

"The flu is usually more serious than that."

"Not this time. A lot of soldiers and staff here have already been infected. Haven't you noticed that they replaced the caretaker?

She caught the bed flu too, but was afraid of giving it to you. But as your liaison, I can't be replaced for the time being."

Onscreen the national delegates had begun to enter the auditorium. They sat down and started talking in low voices, as if they hadn't noticed Luo Ji's presence. The incumbent rotating chair of the PDC opened the meeting, saying, "Wallfacer Luo Ji, the Wallfacer Act was amended at the special session of the UN General Assembly that just adjourned. You've seen it?"

"Yes," he answered.

"Then you must have noticed that the Act strengthens the examinations and restrictions on Wallfacer resource allocation. I hope that the plan you will submit to the hearing today will comply with the Act's requirements."

"Mr. Chair," Luo Ji said, "the other three Wallfacers have allocated an enormous amount of resources to the execution of their own strategic plans. To limit my plan's resources in this way is unfair."

"Resource allocation privileges depend on the plan itself, and you must be aware that the other three Wallfacer plans are not in conflict with mainstream defense. In other words, the research and engineering they are conducting would have been carried out even without the Wallfacer Project. I hope that your strategic plan is also of this nature."

"I'm sorry to say that my plan is not of this nature. It has absolutely nothing to do with mainstream defense."

"Then I'm sorry, too. Under the new Act, the resources you can allocate to this plan are very limited."

"Even under the old plan, I couldn't allocate all that much. However, this isn't a problem, Mr. Chair. My strategic plan consumes practically no resources at all."

"Just like your previous plans?"

The chair's remark prompted snickers from several participants.

"Even less than in the past. Like I said, it consumes practically no resources at all," he said simply.

"Then let's have a look," the chair said, nodding.

"The specifics of the plan will be introduced by Dr. Albert

Ringier, although I presume you all received the corresponding file. To sum up, using the radio wave magnification capabilities of the sun, a message will be sent into the cosmos containing three simple images, along with additional information to demonstrate that these images have been sent by an intelligence as opposed to occurring naturally. The images are included in the file."

The sound of rustling paper filled the auditorium as the attendees located the three sheets. The images were also displayed on the screen. They were quite simple. Each consisted of black dots, seemingly scattered at random, but they all noticed that each image contained one conspicuously larger dot that was marked with an arrow.

"What is it?" asked the US representative, who, like the rest of the attendees, was inspecting the images carefully.

"Wallfacer Luo Ji, according to the basic principles of the Wallfacer Project, you do not need to answer that question," the chair said.

"It's a spell," he said.

The rustling and murmuring in the auditorium stopped abruptly. Everyone looked up in the same direction, so that Luo Ji now knew the location of the screen displaying his feed.

"What?" asked the chair, with narrowed eyes.

"He said it's a spell," someone seated at the circular table said loudly.

"A spell against whom?"

Luo Ji answered, "Against the planets of star 187J3X1. Of course, it could also work directly against the star itself."

"What effect will it have?"

"That's unknown right now. But one thing is certain: The effect of the spell will be catastrophic."

"Er, is there a chance these planets have life?"

"I consulted repeatedly with the astronomical community on that point. From present observational data, the answer is no," Luo Ji said, narrowing his eyes like the chair had. He prayed silently, *May they be right.*

"After the spell is sent out, how long will it take to work?"

"The star is around fifty light-years from the sun, so the spell will be complete in fifty years at the earliest. But we won't be able to observe its effects for one hundred years. This is just the earliest estimate, however. The actual time it takes might stretch out much farther."

After a moment of silence in the auditorium, the US representative was the first to move, tossing the three sheets and their printed black dots onto the table. "Excellent. We finally have a god."

"A god hiding in a cellar," added the UK representative, to peals of laughter.

"More like a sorcerer," sniffed the representative of Japan, which had never been admitted to the Security Council, but had been accepted immediately once the PDC was established.

"Dr. Luo, you have succeeded in making your plan weird and baffling, at least," said Garanin, the Russian representative who had held the rotating chair on several occasions during Luo Ji's five years as a Wallfacer.

The chair banged the gavel, silencing the commotion in the auditorium. "Wallfacer Luo Ji, I have a question for you. Given that this is a spell, why don't you direct it at the enemy's world?"

Luo Ji said, "This is a proof of concept. Its actual implementation will wait for the Doomsday Battle."

"Can't Trisolaris be used as the test target?"

Luo Ji shook his head with finality. "Absolutely not. It's too close. It's close enough that the effects of the spell might reach us. That's why I rejected any planetary star system within fifty light-years."

"One final question: Over the next hundred or more years, what do you plan on doing?"

"You'll be free of me. Hibernation. Wake me when the effects of the spell on 187J3X1 are detected."

As he was preparing for hibernation, Luo Ji came down with the bed flu. His initial symptoms were no different from everyone else, just a runny nose and a slight throat inflammation, and neither he

nor anyone else paid it any attention. But two days later his condition worsened and he began to run a fever. The doctor found this abnormal and took a blood sample back to the city for analysis.

Luo Ji spent the night in a fevered torpor, haunted endlessly by restless dreams in which the stars in the night sky swirled and danced like grains of sand on the skin of a drum. He was even aware of the gravitational interaction between these stars: It wasn't three-body motion, but the 200-billion-body motion of all of the stars in the galaxy! Then the swirling stars clustered into an enormous vortex, and in that mad spiral the vortex transformed again into a giant serpent formed from the congealed silver of every star, which drilled into his brain with a roar. . . .

At around four in the morning, Zhang Xiang was awakened by his phone. It was a call from the Planetary Defense Council Security Department leadership who, in severe tones, demanded that he report immediately on Luo Ji's condition, and ordered the base to be put under a state of emergency. A team of experts was on its way over.

As soon as he hung up the phone, it rang again, this time with a call from the doctor in the tenth basement, who reported that the patient's condition had sharply deteriorated and he was now in a state of shock. Zhang Xiang descended the elevator at once, and the panicked doctor and nurse informed him that Luo Ji had begun spitting up blood in the middle of the night and then had gone unconscious. Zhang Xiang saw Luo Ji lying on the bed with a pale face, purple lips, and practically no signs of life in his body.

The team, consisting of experts from the Chinese Center for Disease Control and Prevention, doctors from the general hospital of the PLA, and an entire research team from the Academy of Military Medical Sciences soon arrived.

As they observed Luo Ji's condition, one expert from the AMMS took Zhang Xiang and Kent outside and described the situation to them. "This flu came to our attention a while ago. We felt that its origin and characteristics were highly abnormal, and it's clear now that it's a genetic weapon, a genetic guided missile."

"A guided missile?"

"It's a genetically altered virus that is highly infectious, but only causes mild flu symptoms in most people. However, the virus has a recognition ability which allows it to identify the genetic characteristics of a particular individual. Once the target has been infected, it creates deadly toxins in his blood. We now know who the target is."

Zhang Xiang and Kent glanced at each other, first in incredulity and then in despair. Zhang Xiang blanched and bowed his head. "I accept full responsibility."

The researcher, a senior colonel, said, "Director Zhang, you can't say that. There's no defense against this. Although we had begun to suspect something odd about the virus, we never even considered this possibility. The concept of genetic weapons first appeared in the last century, but no one believed that anyone would actually produce one. And although this one's imperfect, it truly is a frightening tool for assassination. All you need to do is spread the virus in the target's general vicinity. Or, rather, you don't even need to know where the target is: You could just spread it across the globe, and because the virus causes little to no illness in ordinary people, it will spread quickly and would probably strike its target in the end."

"No, I accept full responsibility," Zhang said, covering his eyes. "If Captain Shi was here, this wouldn't have happened." He dropped his hand and his eyes shone with tears. "The last thing he said to me before hibernation was to warn me of what you said about no defense. He said, 'Xiao Zhang, in this job of ours we need to sleep with one eye open. There's no certainty of success, and some things we can't defend against.'"

"So what do we do next?" Kent asked.

"The virus has penetrated deep. The patient's liver and cardiopulmonary functions have failed, and modern medicine is helpless. Hibernate him as soon as possible."

After a long while, when Luo Ji recovered a little of the consciousness that had totally disappeared, he had sensations of cold,

a cold that seemed to emanate from within his body and diffuse outward like light to freeze the entire world. He saw a snow-white patch in which there first was nothing but infinite white. Then a small black dot appeared at its very center, and he could gradually make out a familiar figure, Zhuang Yan, holding their child. He walked with difficulty through a snowy wilderness so empty that it lost all dimension. She was wrapped in a red scarf, the same one she had worn seven years ago on the snowy night he first saw her. The child, red-faced from the cold, waved two small hands at him from her mother's embrace, and shouted something that he couldn't hear. He wanted to chase them through the snow, but the young mother and child vanished, as if dissolved into snow. Then he himself vanished, and the snowy white world shrank into a thin silver thread, which in the unbounded darkness was all that remained of his consciousness. It was the thread of time, a thin, motionless strand that extended infinitely in both directions. His soul, strung on this thread, was gently sliding off at a constant speed into the unknowable future.

Two days later, a stream of high-power radio waves was sent off from Earth toward the sun, penetrating the convection zone and reaching the energy mirror in the radiation zone, where its reflection, magnified hundreds of millions of times, carried Wallfacer Luo Ji's spell into the cosmos at the speed of light.

Year 12, Crisis Era

Distance of the Trisolaran Fleet from the Solar System:
4.18 light-years

Another brush had appeared in space. The Trisolaran Fleet had crossed the second patch of interstellar dust, and because Hubble II had been closely monitoring the area, the fleet's wake was captured as soon as it appeared. This time, it looked nothing like a brush. Rather, it resembled a patch of grass that had just begun to sprout in the dark abyss of space. Those thousand blades of grass grew with a speed that was perceptible to the naked eye, and they were much clearer than the wake had been nine years before, due to nine years of acceleration that had greatly increased the fleet's speed and had made its impact on the interstellar dust more dramatic.

"General, look closely here. What can you see?" Ringier said to Fitzroy as he pointed to the magnified image on the screen.

"There still seem to be about a thousand."

"No, look closer."

Fitzroy looked carefully for a long moment, then pointed to the middle of the brush. "It looks like . . . one, two, three, four . . . ten bristles are longer than the others. They're extended out."

"Right. Those ten wakes are quite weak. They're only visible after image enhancement."

Fitzroy turned to Ringier, wearing the same expression he had when the Trisolaran Fleet had been discovered a decade earlier. "Doctor, does this mean that those ten warships are accelerating?"

"All of them are accelerating. But those ten show a greater acceleration. But they're not ten warships. The number of wakes has increased by ten, to one thousand and ten. An analysis of the morphology of those ten wakes shows that they are far smaller than the warships behind them: about one ten-thousandth the size, or about the size of a truck. But due to their high speed, they still produce detectable wakes."

"So small. Are they probes?"

"Yes, they must be probes."

This was another of Hubble II's shocking discoveries: Humanity would make contact with Trisolaran entities ahead of schedule, even if they were just ten small probes.

"When will they reach the Solar System?" Fitzroy asked nervously.

"We can't say for certain. It depends on the acceleration, but they will definitely arrive before the fleet. A conservative estimate would be half a century earlier. The fleet acceleration is evidently at a maximum, but for some reason we don't understand, they want to reach the Solar System as quickly as possible, so they launched probes that can accelerate even faster."

"If they have sophons, then what's the need for probes?" one engineer asked.

This question made them all stop and think, but Ringier soon broke the silence. "Forget it. This isn't something we can figure out."

"No," Fitzroy said, raising a hand. "We can figure out at least a part of it. . . . We're looking at events from four years ago. Can you determine the exact date that the fleet launched the probes?"

"We're fortunate that the fleet launched them on the snow . . . I mean, in the dust . . . allowing us to pinpoint the time from our observations of the intersection of the probe wakes and the fleet tracks." Then Ringier told him the date.

Fitzroy was speechless for a moment, then lit a cigarette and sat down to smoke. After a while, he said, "Doctor, you're not politicians. Just like I couldn't make out those ten longer bristles, you can't tell that this is a crucial fact."

"What's so special about that date?" Ringier asked, uncertainly.

"On that day four years ago, I attended the PDC Wallfacer Hearing, at which Luo Ji proposed using the sun to send a spell out into the universe."

The scientists and engineers glanced at each other.

Fitzroy went on, "And it was right around that time that Trisolaris issued a second command to the ETO calling for Luo Ji's elimination."

"Him? Is he really that important?"

"You think he was first a sentimental playboy and then a pretentious sham sorcerer? Of course. We thought so too. Everyone did, except for Trisolaris."

"Well . . . what do *you* think he is, General?"

"Doctor, do you believe in God?"

The suddenness of the question left Ringier momentarily speechless. ". . . God? That's got a variety of meanings on multiple levels today, and I don't know which you—"

"I believe, not because I have any proof, but because it's relatively safe: If there really is a God, then it's right to believe in him. If there isn't, then we don't have anything to lose."

The general's words prompted laughter, and Ringier said, "The second half is untrue. There is something to lose, at least as far as science is concerned. . . . Still, so what if God exists? What's he got to do with what's right in front of us?"

"If God really exists, then he may have a mouthpiece in the mortal world."

They all stared at him for ages before they understood the implication of his words. Then one astronomer said, "General, what are you talking about? God wouldn't choose a mouthpiece from an atheist nation."

Fitzroy ground out his cigarette end and spread out his hands. "When you have eliminated the impossible, whatever remains, no matter how improbable, must be the truth. Can you think of a better explanation?"

Ringier mused, "If by 'God' you mean a force of justice in the universe that transcends everything—"

Fitzroy stopped him with a raised hand, as if the divine power of what they had just learned would be reduced if it were stated outright. "So believe, all of you. You can now start believing." And then he made the sign of the cross.

The trial run of *Tianti III* was airing on television. Construction on three space elevators had begun five years ago, and since *Tianti I* and *Tianti II* had been put into operation at the start of the year, the test of *Tianti III* did not cause much of a commotion. All space elevators were currently being built with just a single primary rail, giving them a far smaller carrying capacity than the four-rail models still under design, but this was already an altogether different world from the age of chemical rockets. Setting aside construction, the cost of going into space by elevator was substantially lower than by civilian aircraft. This in turn had led to an increase in the number of bodies in motion in Earth's night sky: These were humanity's large-scale orbiting structures.

Tianti III was the only space elevator based on the ocean. Its base was located on the Equator on an artificial floating island in the Pacific Ocean that could navigate at sea under its own nuclear power, which meant that the elevator's position on the Equator could be adjusted if necessary. The floating island was a real-life version of the Propeller Island Jules Verne had described, and so it had been dubbed "Verne Island." The ocean wasn't even visible on the television, which was showing a shot of a metal, pyramid-shaped base surrounded by a steel city, and—at the bottom of the rail—the cylindrical transport cabin that was ready to launch. From this distance, the guide rail extending into space was invisible due to its sixty-centimeter diameter, although at times you could catch a glint of reflected light from the setting sun.

Three old men, Zhang Yuanchao and his two old neighbors, Yang Jinwen and Miao Fuquan, were watching this on television. All of them were now past seventy, and while no one would call

them doddering, they were now definitely old. For them, recalling the past and looking toward the future were both burdens, and since they were powerless to do anything about the present, their only option was to live out their waning years without thinking about anything in this unusual era.

Zhang Yuanchao's son Zhang Weiming led his grandson Zhang Yan through the door. He was carrying a paper sack, and said, "Dad, I've picked up your ration card and your first batch of grain tickets." Then he took out a pack of colorful tickets from the bag and gave them to his father.

"Ah, just like in the old days," Yang Jinwen said, as he watched from the side.

"It's come back. It always comes back," Zhang Yuanchao murmured emotionally to himself, as he took the tickets.

"Is that money?" asked Yan Yan, looking at the bits of paper.

Zhang Yuanchao said to his grandson, "It's not money, child. But, from now on, if you want to buy nonquota grain, like bread or cake, or want to eat at a restaurant, you'll need to use these along with money."

"This is a little different from the old days," Zhang Weiming said, taking out an IC card. "This is a ration card."

"How much is on it?"

"I get twenty-one and a half kilos, or forty-three *jin*. You and Xiaohong get thirty-seven *jin*, and Yan Yan gets twenty-one *jin*."

"About the same as back then," the elder man said.

"That should be enough for a month," Yang Jinwen said.

Zhang Weiming shook his head. "Mr. Yang, you lived through those days. Don't you remember? It might be fine now, but very soon there'll be fewer nonstaples, and you'll need numbers to buy vegetables and meat. So this paltry bit of grain really won't be enough to eat!"

"It's not that serious," Miao Fuquan said with a wave of his hand. "We've been through times like these a few decades ago. We won't starve. Drop it, and watch TV."

"Oh, and industrial coupons[16] may be coming soon, too," Zhang Yuanchao said, putting the grain tickets and ration card on the table and turning his attention to the television.

On the screen, the cylindrical cabin was rising from the base. It ascended quickly and accelerated rapidly, then disappeared into the evening sky. Because the guide rail was invisible, it looked like it was ascending on its own. The cabin could reach a maximum speed of five hundred kilometers per hour, but even at that speed it would take sixty-eight hours to reach the space elevator's terminus in geostationary orbit. The scene cut to a downward-facing camera installed beneath the cabin. Here, the sixty-centimeter rail occupied the larger part of the screen. Its slick surface made motion practically undetectable, except for the fleeting scale markings that showed the camera's upward velocity. The rail quickly tapered into nothing as it extended downward, but it pointed at a spot far below where Verne Island, now visible in total, seemed like a giant platter suspended from the lower end of the rail.

Something occurred to Yang Jinwen. "I'll show you two a real rarity," he said, as he got up and walked somewhat less nimbly out the door, perhaps to his own home. He soon returned with a thin slice of something about the size of a cigarette box and laid it on the table. Zhang Yuanchao picked it up and looked at it: The object was gray, translucent, and very lightweight, like a fingernail. "This is the material *Tianti* is made out of!" Yang Jinwen said.

"Great. Your son stole strategic materials from the public sector," Miao Fuquan said, pointing at the slice.

"It's just a leftover scrap. He said that when *Tianti* was under construction, thousands upon thousands of tons of this stuff was shot into space, and it was made into the guide rail there and then hung back down from orbit again. . . . Soon, space travel will be

16 *Translator's Note:* China instituted a ration system for grain and cooking oil in the early 1950s, and expanded it in 1961 to include goods ranging from shoes and scissors to home appliances and electronics. With the transition from planned economy to market economy in the 1980s, use of the ration system declined, and it was terminated in the early 1990s.

popularized. I've asked my son to hook me up with business in that area."

"You want to go to space?" asked Zhang Yuanchao, surprised.

"It's not such a big deal. I've heard there's not even hypergravity when you go up. It's just like taking a long-distance sleeper train," Miao Fuquan said dismissively. In the many years he had been unable to operate his mines, his family had gone into decline. He had sold off his villa four years ago, leaving this as his only residence. Yang Jinwen, whose son worked on the space elevator project, had in a single bound become the wealthiest of the three, and this sometimes made old Miao jealous.

"I'm not going to space," Yang Jinwen said, looking up, and when he saw that Weiming had taken the boy to another room, he went on. "But my remains will. Hey, you two fellows don't have any taboos about talking about this, do you?"

"What's taboo about it? Still, why do you want to put your remains up there?" Zhang Yuanchao asked.

"You know there's an electromagnetic launcher at the end of *Tianti*. When it's time, my casket will be fired off at the third cosmic velocity and will fly out of the Solar System. It's called a cosmic burial, you know. After I die, I don't want to stay on an alien-occupied Earth. It's a form of Escapism, I guess."

"And if the aliens are defeated?"

"That's practically impossible. Still, if it really happens, it's no great loss. I get to roam the universe!"

Zhang Yuanchao shook his head. "You intellectuals with your weird ideas. They're pointless. The fallen leaf returns to the root. I'm going to be buried in the yellow soil of the Earth."

"Aren't you afraid that the Trisolarans will dig up your grave?"

At this, Miao Fuquan, who had been silent, suddenly grew excited. He motioned for the others to draw closer, and lowered his voice, as if afraid that the sophons would hear: "Don't tell anyone, but I've thought of something. I have lots of empty mines in Shanxi. . . ."

"You want to be buried there?"

"No, no. They're all small pit mines. How deep can they be? But in several places they're connected to major state-owned mines, and by following their abandoned works, you can get all the way down to four hundred meters below ground. Is that deep enough for you? Then we blast the shaft wall. I don't think the Trisolarans will be able to dig down there."

"Sheesh. If Earthlings can dig that far, why can't the Trisolarans? They'll find a tombstone and just keep digging down."

Looking at Zhang Yuanchao, Miao Fuquan was unable to hold back his laughter. "Lao Zhang, have you gone stupid?" Seeing him still at a loss, he pointed to Yang Jinwen, who had grown bored with their conversation and was watching the television broadcast again. "Let an educated man tell it to you."

Yang Jinwen chuckled. "Lao Zhang, what do you want a tombstone for? Tombstones are meant for people to see. By then, there won't be any people left."

All along the way to the Third Nuclear Fusion Test Base, Zhang Beihai's car drove through deep snow. But as he neared the base, the snow melted entirely, the road turned muddy, and the cold air turned warm and humid, like a breath of springtime. On the slopes lining the road he noticed patches of peach flowers blooming, unseasonable in this harsh winter. He drove on toward the white building in the valley ahead, a structure that was merely the entrance for the majority of the base, which was underground. Then he noticed someone on the hillside picking peach flowers. Looking closer, he saw it was the very person he had come to see, and he stopped his car.

"Dr. Ding!" he called to him. When Ding Yi came over to the car carrying a bunch of flowers, he laughed and asked, "Who are those flowers for?"

"They're for myself, of course. They're flowers that have bloomed from fusion heat." He practically beamed under the influence of the brightly colored flowers. Evidently he was still

in the throes of excitement at the breakthrough that had just been achieved.

"It's pretty wasteful, letting all this heat disperse." Zhang Beihai got out of the car, took off his sunglasses, and took stock of the mini-spring. He couldn't see his breath, and he could feel the heat of the ground even through the soles of his shoes.

"There's no money or time to build a power plant. But that doesn't matter. From now on, energy is not something that Earth needs to conserve."

Zhang Beihai pointed at the flowers in Ding Yi's hands. "Dr. Ding, I really was hoping that you had gotten distracted. This breakthrough would have happened later without you."

"Without me here, it would've happened even earlier. There are over a thousand researchers at the base. I just pointed them in the right direction. I've felt for a long time that the tokamak approach[17] is a dead end. Given the right approach, a breakthrough was a certainty. Me, I'm a theoretician. I don't get experimentation. My blind pointing probably only delayed the progress of research."

"Can't you postpone the announcement of your results? I'm being serious here. And I'm also informally conveying the wish of Space Command."

"How could we postpone it? The media has been actively tracking the progress of all three fusion test bases."

Zhang Beihai nodded and let out a sigh. "That's bad news."

"I know a few of the reasons, but why don't you tell me why."

"If controlled nuclear fusion is achieved, spacecraft research will begin immediately. Doctor, you know about the two current research forks: media-propelled spacecraft and non-media radiation-drive spacecraft. Two opposing factions have formed around these two directions of research: the aerospace faction advocates research into media-propelled spacecraft, while the space force is pushing

17 *Translator's Note:* In a tokamak, plasma is confined to a torus shape by a toroidal electromagnetic field surrounding the torus and a current induced in the plasma itself. Developed by Soviet scientists in the 1950s, they produced better results than other plasma containment devices.

radiation-drive spacecraft. The projects will consume enormous resources, and if the two directions can't progress simultaneously on equal footing, then one direction must take the mainstream."

"The fusion people and I are in favor of the radiation drive. For my part, I feel that it's the only plan that enables interstellar cosmic voyages. Of course, I'll grant that Aerospace has its logic, too. Media-propelled spacecraft are actually a variant of chemical rockets that use fusion energy, so the prospects are a little safer for that line of research."

"But there's nothing safe in the space war of the future! As you said, media-propelled spacecraft are just huge rockets. They have to devote two-thirds of their carrying capacity to their propulsion media, and it's consumed very quickly. That type of spacecraft requires planetary bases in order to navigate through the Solar System. We do that, and we would be reenacting the tragedy of the Sino-Japanese War, with the Solar System as Weihaiwei."[18]

"That's a keen analogy," Ding Yi said, raising his bouquet at Zhang Beihai.

"It's a fact. A navy's front line defenses ought to be at the enemy's ports. We can't do that, of course, but our defensive line ought to be pushed out as far as the Oort Cloud, and we should ensure that the fleet possesses sufficient flanking capabilities in the vast reaches outside the Solar System. This is the foundation of space force strategy."

"Internally, Aerospace isn't entirely monolithic," Ding Yi said. "It's the old guard left over from the chemical rocket era that's pushing for media spacecraft, but forces from other disciplines have entered the sector. Take the people on our fusion system. They're mostly pushing for radiation spacecraft. These two forces are evenly matched, and all that's needed is three or four people in

18 *Translator's Note:* The Battle of Weihaiwei was the last major battle of the First Sino-Japanese War. In February 1895, the ships of the Beiyang Fleet, the Qing Dynasty's northern navy, were anchored in the harbor at Weihaiwei, Shandong province, their home base, for safety from the advancing Imperial Japanese Navy. When Japanese land forces seized shore fortifications, the Chinese fleet was forced to surrender.

key positions to break the equilibrium. Their opinions will decide the ultimate course of action. But those three or four key people are, I'm afraid, all part of the old guard."

"This is the most critical decision in the entire master strategy. If it's a misstep, the space fleet will be built atop a mistaken foundation, and we might waste a century or two. And by that time, I'm afraid there will be no way to change direction."

"But you and I aren't in a position to fix it."

After lunching with Ding Yi, Zhang Beihai left the fusion base. Before he had driven very far, the moist ground was again covered with wet snow that glowed white under the sun. As the air temperature plummeted, his heart also chilled.

He was in dire need of a spacecraft capable of interstellar travel. If other roads led nowhere, then just one was left. No matter how dangerous it might be, it had to be taken.

When Zhang Beihai entered the home of the meteorite collector, situated in a courtyard house in the depths of a *hutong* alleyway, he noticed that the old, dimly lit home was like a miniature geological museum. Each of its four walls was lined with glass cases in which professional lights shone on rock after unremarkable rock. The owner, in his fifties, hale in spirit and complexion, sat at a workbench examining a small stone with a magnifying lens, and he greeted the visitor warmly when he saw him. He was, Zhang Beihai noticed immediately, one of those fortunate people who inhabited a beloved world of his own. No matter what changes befell the larger world, he could always immerse himself in his own and find contentment.

In the old-fashioned atmosphere unique to old houses, Zhang Beihai was reminded that he and his comrades were fighting for the survival of the human race, while the majority of people were still clinging to their existing lives. This gave him a sense of warmth and peace of mind.

The completion of the space elevator and the breakthrough in controlled fusion technology were two enormous encouragements

to the world, and eased defeatist sentiment to a considerable extent. But sober leaders were aware that this was only the beginning: If the construction of the space fleet was analogous to naval fleets, then humanity had just now arrived at the seashore, carrying tools. Not even the shipbuilding dockyards had been built yet. Apart from the construction of the main spacecraft body, research into space weapons and recirculating ecosystems, as well as the construction of space ports, represented an unprecedented technological frontier for humanity. Just getting the foundations in place might take a century.

Human society faced another challenge aside from the terrifying abyss: The construction of a space defense system would consume an enormous amount of resources, and this consumption would likely drag the quality of life back a century, which meant that the greatest challenge to the human spirit was still to come. With that in mind, the military leadership had decided to begin implementing the plan to use political cadres from the space force as future reinforcements. As the initial proponent of the plan, Zhang Beihai had been named commander of the Special Contingent of Future Reinforcements. Upon accepting the mission, he proposed that all of the officers in the special contingent ought to undergo at least a year of space-based training and work before entering hibernation in order to provide them with the necessary preparations for their future work in the space force. "The brass won't want their political commissars to be landlubbers," he said to Chang Weisi. This request was swiftly approved, and one month later, he and the first special contingent of thirty comrades went to space.

"You're a soldier?" the collector asked as he served tea. After receiving a nod, he went on: "Soldiers these days aren't much like soldiers used to be, but you, I could tell at a glance."

"You were a soldier once too," Zhang Beihai said.

"Good eye. I spent most of my life serving in the General Staff Department's Surveying and Mapping Bureau."

"How did you get interested in meteors?" Zhang Beihai asked as he looked appreciatively at the rich collection.

"Over a decade ago I went with a survey team to Antarctica in

search of meteorites buried beneath the snow, and I got hooked. They come from outside of Earth, from distant space, so naturally they've got that attraction. Whenever I pick one up, it's like I'm going to a new and alien world."

Zhang Beihai shook his head with a smile. "That's just a feeling. The Earth itself is formed out of aggregated interstellar matter, so it's basically just a giant meteorite. The stone beneath our feet is meteorite. This teacup I'm holding is meteorite. Besides, they say that the water on Earth was brought here by comets, so"—he raised the teacup—"what's contained in this cup is meteorite, too. There's nothing particularly special about what you have."

The collector pointed at him and laughed. "You're sharp. You've already started to bargain. . . . Still, I trust my feelings."

The collector couldn't resist taking Zhang Beihai on a tour, and he even opened a safe to show him the treasure of his house: a Martian achondrite the size of a fingernail. He had him view the small round pits on the meteorite's surface and said that they might be microbial fossils. "Five years ago, Robert Haag wanted to buy her for a thousand times the price of gold, but I didn't agree."

"How many of these did you collect on your own?" asked Zhang Beihai, pointing around the room.

"Only a small part. The majority were bought from the private sector or traded from the community. . . . So, let's hear it. What sort do you want?"

"Nothing too valuable. It should be high density, shouldn't break easily under impact, and should be easily workable."

"I see. You want to engrave it."

He nodded. "You could say that. It would be great if I could use a lathe."

"Then an iron meteorite," the collector said as he opened a glass case and took out a dark-colored stone the size of a walnut. "This one. It's composed mainly of iron and nickel, with cobalt, phosphorus, silicon, sulfur, and copper. You want dense? This one's eight grams to the cubic centimeter. It's easily workable, and highly metallic, so the lathe won't be a problem."

"Good. It's just a little too small."

The collector took out another piece the size of an apple.

"Do you have anything even bigger?"

The collector looked at him and said, "This stuff's not sold by weight. The big ones are expensive."

"Well, do you have three the size of this one?"

The collector brought out three iron meteorites of roughly the same size and began to lay the groundwork for his asking price: "Iron meteorites are not very common. They represent just five percent of all meteorites, and these three are fine specimens. See here—this one's an octahedrite. Look at the crisscross pattern on the surface. They're called Widmanstätten patterns. And here's a nickel-rich ataxite. These parallel lines are called Neumann lines. This piece contains kamacite, and this one is taenite, a mineral not found on Earth. This piece is one I found in the desert using a metal detector, and it was like fishing a needle out of the ocean. The car got stuck in the sand and the drive shaft snapped. I almost died."

"Name your price."

"On the international market, a specimen of this size and grade would have a price of about twenty USD per gram. So how's this: sixty thousand yuan per piece, or three for one hundred eighty thousand?"[19]

Zhang Beihai took out his phone. "Tell me your account number. I'll pay right away."

The collector said nothing for quite some time. When Zhang Beihai looked up, he gave a slightly embarrassed laugh. "Actually, I was ready for you to counter-offer."

"No. I accept."

"Look. Now that space travel is for everyone, the market price has dropped somewhat even though it's not as easy to get meteorites in space as it is on the ground. These, well, they're worth—"

Zhang Beihai cut him off decisively. "No. That's the price. Treat it as a sign of respect for their recipients."

19 *Translator's Note:* Roughly $10,000 per piece, or a total of $30,000.

After leaving the collector's house, Zhang Beihai took the meteorites to a modeling workshop in a research institute belonging to the space force. Work had let out and the workshop, which contained a state-of-the-art CNC mill, was empty. First, he used the mill to slice the three meteorites into cylinders of equal diameter, about the thickness of a pencil lead, and then cut them into small segments of equal length. He worked very carefully, trying to minimize waste as much as possible, and ended up with thirty-six small meteorite rods. When this was done, he carefully collected the cutting debris, removed the special blade he had selected for cutting the stone from the machine, and then left the workshop.

The remainder of the work he conducted in a secret basement. He set thirty-six 7.62 mm pistol cartridges on the table before him and removed each projectile in turn. If they had been old-style brass cartridges, this would have required a lot of effort, but two years ago the entire military had updated its standard guns to use caseless ammunition, whose projectile was glued directly to the propellant and was easy to detach. Next, he used a special adhesive to affix a meteorite rod onto each propellant. The adhesive, originally developed to repair the skin of space capsules, ensured that the bond would not fail in the extreme hot and cold temperatures of space. In the end he had thirty-six meteorite bullets.

He inserted four meteorite bullets into a magazine, which he then loaded into a P224 pistol and fired at a sack in the corner. The gunshot was deafening in the narrow basement room and left behind a strong scent of gunpowder.

He carefully examined the four holes in the sack, noting that they were small, which meant that the meteorite had not shattered upon firing. He opened the sack and withdrew a large hunk of fresh beef, and with a knife carefully extracted the meteorite that had penetrated it. The four meteorite rods had shattered completely, leaving a small pile of rubble that he poured onto his palm. It showed practically no sign of having been worked. This outcome satisfied him.

The sack that held the beef was made out of materials used in space suits. To make the simulation even more realistic, it had

been arranged in layers that sandwiched insulation sponges, plastic tubing, and other material.

He carefully packed up the remaining thirty-two meteorite bullets and exited the basement, heading off to make preparations for his visit to space.

Zhang Beihai hung in space five kilometers out from Yellow River Station, a wheel-shaped space station that lay three hundred kilometers above the space elevator terminus as a counterweight. It was the largest structure humanity had ever constructed in space and it could house over a thousand long-term residents.

The region of space within a five-hundred-kilometer radius of the space elevator was home to other space facilities, all of them much smaller than Yellow River Station and scattered about like the nomadic tents that dotted the prairie during the opening of the American West. These formed the prelúde of humanity's large-scale entrance into space. The shipyards that had just commenced construction were the largest yet and would eventually cover an area ten times greater than Yellow River Station, but right now, all that had been put up was scaffolding that looked like the skeleton of a leviathan. Zhang Beihai had come from Base 1, a separate space station eighty kilometers away and just one-fifth the size of Yellow River Station, the space force's base in geostationary orbit. He had been living and working with the other members of the first Special Contingent of Future Reinforcements for three months now and had only been back to Earth once.

At Base 1, he had been waiting for an opportunity, and now an opportunity presented itself: the aerospace faction was holding a high-level work conference on Yellow River Station, and all three of his targets for elimination would be attending. Once Yellow River Station went into operation, Aerospace had held quite a few meetings there, as if to make up for the regrettable fact that most of the people in the aerospace sector had never gotten the chance to go to space.

Before leaving Base 1, Zhang Beihai had dropped his space

266

suit's positioning unit in his own cabin so the surveillance system would not be aware that he had left the base and there would be no record of his movements. Using the thrusters on his suit, he flew eighty kilometers through space to the position he had selected. Then he waited.

The meeting was over, but he was waiting for the participants to come out and take a group photo.

It was a tradition for all meeting participants to take a group photo in space. Usually, the photograph would be taken against the sun, because that was the only way to get a clear shot of the space station. Since every person in the group shot had to turn their helmet visors to transparent to expose their face during the photo, they would have to keep their eyes shut against the sun's intense rays if they faced it, not to mention the fact that the inside of their helmets would get intolerably hot. So the best time for a group shot was when the sun was just about to rise or fall over the horizon of the Earth. In geosynchronous orbit, one sunrise and one sunset took place every twenty-four hours, although the night was very short. Zhang Beihai was waiting for the sun to set.

He knew that Yellow River Station's surveillance system was able to detect his presence, but that wouldn't attract any attention. As the point of origin for space development, the region was littered with construction materials both unused and abandoned, as well as an even greater quantity of garbage. Much of this floating material was roughly the size of a human. Moreover, the space elevator and the surrounding facilities had a relationship like a metropolis and its surrounding villages, with the supplies for the latter coming entirely from the former, so traffic between them was quite busy. As people became used to the environment of space, they gradually adopted the habit of crossing solo. Using space suits as a sort of space bicycle with thrusters that could push them to speeds of up to five hundred kilometers per hour was the easiest means of travel within a few hundred kilometers of the space elevator. By this point, people were flying between the space elevator and the surrounding stations all the time.

But right now, Zhang Beihai knew the surrounding space was empty. Apart from the Earth (which was visible as a complete sphere from geosynchronous orbit) and the sun, about to dip below its edge, everything in all directions was a pitch-black abyss, and the myriad stars were shining dust that was powerless to alter the emptiness of the universe. He knew that his suit's life-support system would only hold up for twelve hours, and before that time ran out he had to make it eighty kilometers back to Base 1, now just a shapeless point far off in the distance of the abyss of space. The base itself would not survive very long, either, if it left the umbilical cord of the space elevator. But now, as he floated in the vast void, he felt like his contact with the blue world down below had been cut off. He was an independent presence in the universe, unattached to any world, dangling in the cosmos, no ground beneath his feet and surrounded by empty space on all sides, with no origin or destination, like the Earth, the sun, and the Milky Way. He simply existed, and he liked this feeling.

He even sensed that his father's departed spirit might share this very same feeling.

The sun made contact with the edge of the Earth.

Zhang Beihai raised one hand. The glove of his suit held a telescopic sight which he used to observe one of Yellow River Station's exits, ten kilometers distant. On the large, curved-metal exterior wall, the round air lock door was still sealed.

He turned his head toward the sun, which had now set halfway and looked like a glittering ring atop the Earth.

Looking back through the scope at the station, this time he saw that the beacon light next to the exit had turned from red to green, indicating that the air inside the air lock had been emptied. Immediately afterward, the hatch slid open and a group of figures wearing white space suits filed out. There were about thirty of them. As they flew off in a group, the shadow they cast on the outer wall of Yellow River Station expanded.

They had to fly a considerable distance to fit the entire station into frame, but before long they slowed down and began their

weightless lineup under the photographer's direction. By now the sun had sunk by two-thirds. The remainder looked like a luminous object inlaid into the Earth above a smooth sea mirror that was half blue and half orange-red, its top covered by sun-soaked clouds that looked like pink feathers.

As the light dropped in intensity, the people in the distant group photo began to turn their visors transparent, revealing the faces in the helmets. Zhang Beihai increased his scope's focal length and quickly found his targets. Just as he had expected, due to their rank, they were in the center of the front row.

He released the scope, leaving it suspended in front of him, and with his left hand he twisted the metal retaining ring of his right glove to detach it. Now that his right hand was wearing just a thin cloth glove, he immediately felt the minus-one-hundred-degree temperature of space, so to avoid a quick freeze he turned his body to an angle that let the weak sunlight shine on his hand. He extended the hand into a side pocket of his suit and withdrew a pistol and two magazines. Then, with his left hand, he grasped the floating scope and affixed it to the pistol. The scope had been a rifle sight that he had modified with a magnetic attachment so it could be used on a pistol.

The vast majority of firearms on Earth could shoot in space. The vacuum was not a problem, because the bullet's propellant contained its own oxidizer, but you did need to worry about the temperature of space: Both extremes differed greatly from atmospheric temperatures and had the potential to affect the gun and ammunition, so he was afraid to leave the pistol and magazines exposed for too long. To shorten that time, over the past three months he had drilled repeatedly in taking out the gun, mounting the sight, and changing magazines.

He started to aim, and captured his first target in the cross hairs of the scope.

In Earth's atmosphere, even the most sophisticated sniper rifles couldn't hit a target at a distance of five kilometers, but an ordinary pistol could in space. The bullets moved in a zero-gravity

vacuum, free of any outside interference, so as long as their aim was true, they would follow an extremely stable trajectory directly to the target. Zero air resistance, meanwhile, meant that the bullets would not decelerate during flight and would strike the target with the initial muzzle velocity, ensuring a lethal blow from a distance.

He pulled the trigger. The pistol fired in silence, but he saw the muzzle flash and felt the recoil. He fired ten rounds at the first target, then quickly replaced the magazine and fired another ten rounds at the second target. Replacing the magazine again, he fired the last ten rounds at the third target. Thirty muzzle flashes. If anyone in the direction of Yellow River Station had been paying attention, they would have seen a firefly against the dark backdrop of space.

Now the thirty meteorites were speeding toward their targets. The Type 2010 pistol had a muzzle velocity of five hundred meters per second, so they would take around ten seconds to cross the distance, during which Zhang Beihai could only pray that his targets did not change position. This hope wasn't groundless, because the two back rows had not yet gotten situated for the group photo, and even when they were all situated, the photographer had to wait until the mist sprayed out by the space suit thrusters dissipated, so the leaders in the front row had to wait. But since the targets were, after all, floating in space and weightless, they could easily drift, causing the bullets to not only miss their targets but possibly hurt innocents.

Innocent? The three people he was about to kill were innocent, too. In the years before the Trisolar Crisis, they had made what, looking back now, seemed like particularly meager investments, and had crept carefully over the thin ice toward the dawn of the space age. That experience had imprisoned their thinking. They had to be destroyed for the sake of interstellar-capable spacecraft. Their deaths could be viewed as their final contribution to the cause of humanity's endeavors in space.

As a matter of fact, Zhang Beihai had deliberately sent a few bullets wide of the mark in the hope of hitting people other than his targets. Ideally he would only wound them, but if he happened

to kill an extra person or two, that didn't matter. That would only serve to reduce any potential suspicion.

He lifted the empty gun and looked soberly through the scope. He was prepared for failure. In that eventuality, he would dispassionately begin the search for a second opportunity.

Time passed second by second, and at last there were signs that a target had been hit. Zhang Beihai did not see the hole in the space suit, but a white gas spurted out. Immediately afterward, an even larger burst of white steam erupted from between the first and second rows, perhaps because the bullet had passed out the target's back and penetrated his thruster pack. He was confident of the bullets' power: When the meteorite projectiles struck their targets with practically no decrease in speed, it would be like being shot at gunpoint. Cracks suddenly appeared across the helmet visor of one target, rendering it opaque, but he could still see the blood that splashed up on the inside before mixing with leaking gases and spraying out of the bullet hole, where it quickly froze into snowflake-like crystals. His observations soon confirmed that five people, including the three targets, had been hit, and each target had been struck at least five times.

Through their visors he saw everyone in the crowd screaming in terror, and from the shape of their lips he knew that their words included the ones he was expecting:

"Meteor shower!"

Everyone in the photo group turned their thrusters to full power and sped back to the station, trailing tails of white mist behind them, and then they were through the round hatch and back inside Yellow River Station. Zhang Beihai saw that the five who had been hit were dragged back with them.

He activated his own thruster pack and accelerated toward Base 1. His heart was now as cold and calm as the empty space around him. He knew that the death of the three key aerospace figures did not guarantee that the non-media radiation drive would become the mainstream of spacecraft research, but he had done all he could. No matter what happened next, as far as the watchful eyes of his father in the beyond were concerned, he could now relax.

At practically the same time as Zhang Beihai was returning to Base 1, back on Earth's Internet, a group of people hastily assembled in the wilderness of the virtual *Three Body* world to discuss what had just happened.

"This time, the information transmitted via sophon was very thorough, or we wouldn't have believed he actually did it," Qin Shi Huang said as he waved the sword about him in his uneasiness. "Look at what he did, and then look at our three attempts on Luo Ji." He sighed. "Sometimes we're just too nerdy. We don't have that kind of cool competency."

"Are we just going to sit by and let him do this?" Einstein asked.

"In accordance with the Lord's intentions, that's all we can do. The man is an extremely stubborn holdout and a triumphalist, and the Lord doesn't want us to interfere unnecessarily with that type of human. Our attention must be focused on Escapism. The Lord believes that defeatism is more dangerous than triumphalism," Newton said.

"If we are to work sincerely and seriously in the service of the Lord, we can't wholly believe the Lord's strategy. After all, it's just the counsel of a child," Mozi said.

Qin Shi Huang knocked his sword on the ground. "Nevertheless, nonintervention is correct as far as this matter is concerned. Let them turn their development in the direction of radiation-drive spacecraft. With physics under sophon lockdown, that will be a technological peak that's practically unsurpassable. Not to mention a bottomless abyss into which humanity will pour all of their time and energy and end up with nothing."

"We are agreed on this point. But I believe this man is critical. He's dangerous," Von Neumann said.

"Precisely!" Aristotle said, nodding repeatedly. "We used to think he was a pure soldier, but is this the behavior of a soldier who acts in accordance with strict discipline and rules?"

"He is indeed dangerous. His faith is rock-solid, he's farsighted

and dispassionately ruthless, and he acts with calm resolve. Ordinarily he's precise and serious, but when there's a need he can go outside the lines and take extraordinary action," Confucius said with a sigh. "Just like the First Emperor said, this is the sort of person we lack."

"He won't be hard to deal with. All we have to do is denounce his murders," Newton said.

"It's not that simple!" Qin Shi Huang said, flipping a sleeve at him. "It's all your fault. You've been using the information you receive from the sophons to sow discord in the space force and the UN, so how did this happen? Denunciation would be an honor, or even a symbol of loyalty!"

"And we don't have any conclusive evidence," Mozi said. "His plans were thorough. The bullets shattered when they hit, so any autopsy would retrieve only authentic meteorites from the bodies of the dead and wounded. Everyone is going to think they died in a meteor shower. The truth is so bizarre that no one would believe it."

"It's a good thing he's going to reinforce the future. At least he won't be making trouble for us for a while."

Einstein let out a long sigh. "Gone. Everyone's gone. Some of us should go to the future too."

Although they said they would meet again, everyone knew in their hearts that this was a final farewell.

When the Special Contingent of Future Reinforcements headed to the hibernation center, Chang Weisi and a number of other senior space force generals came to the airport to see them off. He handed a letter to Zhang Beihai.

"This letter is for my future successor. In it, I explain your circumstances and strongly recommend you to the future Space Command. You'll awaken no sooner than fifty years in the future, possibly longer than that, at which time you may be faced with a more challenging work environment. You'll have to adapt to the future first, even as you preserve the spirit of the soldiers of our

time. You must be cognizant of our working methods today, and know which are obsolete and which should be carried on. This may turn out to be your greatest advantage in the future."

Zhang Beihai said, "Commander, for the first time I feel a bit of regret that I'm an atheist. Otherwise, we'd have the hope of meeting again at some other time and place."

Chang Weisi was a little taken aback at this sentiment coming from the ordinarily sober man, and the words resonated in the hearts of everyone else. But, as soldiers, they kept the beating of their hearts deeply hidden.

"I'm gratified that we've been able to meet in this lifetime. Be sure to greet our future comrades for us," Chang Weisi said.

After a final salute, the special contingent boarded the plane.

Chang Weisi's eyes did not leave Zhang Beihai's back for a moment. A steadfast soldier was leaving, and there might never be another like him. Where did his firm faith come from? The question had always lain hidden in the depths of his mind, and sometimes it even prompted a bit of jealousy. A soldier with faith in victory was fortunate. In the Doomsday Battle, those lucky people would be few and far between. As Zhang Beihai's tall frame disappeared inside the cabin door, Chang Weisi had to admit that, up to the very end, he had never really understood him.

The plane took off, carrying those who would perhaps have the chance to see humanity's final outcome, then disappeared behind thin, pale clouds. It was a bleak winter's day. The sun that shone listlessly behind a shroud of gray clouds and the chilly wind that blew across the empty airport gave the air the feel of solidified crystal, conjuring up the sense that the springtime might never really arrive. Chang Weisi tightened the collar of his army coat. He turned fifty-four years old today, and in the dreary winter wind he saw his own end, and the end of the human race.

Year 20, Crisis Era

Rey Diaz and Hines were awakened from hibernation at the same time to the news that the technology they awaited had appeared.

"So soon?!" they exclaimed upon learning that just eight years had passed.

They were informed that due to unprecedented investment, technology had progressed with amazing speed over the past few years. But not everything was optimistic. Humanity was simply making a final sprint across the distance between them and the sophon barrier, so the progress they were making was purely technological. Cutting-edge physics remained stopped up like a pool of stagnant water, and the reservoir of theory was being drained. Technological progress would begin to decelerate and eventually come to a complete halt. But, for the time being at least, no one knew when the end of technology would arrive.

On feet that were still stiff from hibernation, Hines walked into a stadium-like structure whose interior was shrouded in a white fog, although it felt dry to him. He couldn't identify what it was. A soft moonlight glow illuminated the fog, which was fairly sparse at the height of a person but grew dense enough up above that the roof was obscured. Through the fog, he saw a petite figure whom

he recognized at once as his wife. When he ran to her through the fog, it was like chasing a phantom, except that in the end they came together in an embrace.

"I'm sorry, love. I've aged eight years," Keiko Yamasuki said.

"Even so, you're still a year younger than me," he said as he looked her over. Time seemed to have left no mark on her body, but she looked pale and weak in the fog's watery moonlight. In the fog and moonlight, she reminded him of that night in the bamboo grove in their yard in Japan. "Didn't we agree that you would enter hibernation two years after me? Why have you waited all this time?"

"I wanted to work on preparations for our post-hibernation work, but there was too much to do, so that's what I've been doing," she said as she brushed a strand of hair from her forehead.

"Was it hard?"

"It was very hard. Six next-gen supercomputer research projects were launched not long after you went into hibernation. Three of them employed traditional architecture, one used non–Von Neumann architecture, and the other two were quantum and biomolecular computing projects. But two years later, the lead scientists of those six projects told me that the computing power we desired was impossible. The quantum computing project was the first to be terminated, because it failed to find sufficient support in current theoretic physics: Research had run into the sophon barrier. Next, the biomolecular project was discontinued. They said it was only a fantasy. The last to end was the non–Von Neumann computer. Its architecture was actually a simulation of the human brain, but they said it was a shapeless egg that would never turn into a chicken. Only the three traditional architecture projects were still ongoing, but for a long time there was never any progress."

"So that's it. . . . I ought to have been with you the whole time."

"It would have been no use. You only would have wasted eight years. It was only recently, during a period of time when we were totally discouraged, that we came up with the crazy idea of simulating the human brain in a practically barbaric way."

"And what was that?"

276

"To put the previous software simulation into hardware by using a microprocessor to simulate one neuron, letting all the microprocessors interact, and allowing for dynamic changes to the connection model."

Hines thought about this for a few seconds, then realized what she meant. "Do you mean manufacturing a hundred billion microprocessors?"

She nodded.

"That's . . . that's practically the sum total of all the microprocessors that have been manufactured in human history!"

"I didn't run the numbers, but it's probably more than that."

"Even if you really had all those chips, how long would it take to connect them all together?"

Keiko Yamasuki smiled wearily. "I knew it wasn't workable. It was just a desperate idea. But we really thought about doing it back then, and making as many as we could." She pointed around her. "This here is one of the thirty virtual brain assembly shops we had planned. But it's the only one that got built."

"I really should have been here with you," Hines repeated with more emotion.

"Fortunately we still got the computer we wanted. Its performance is ten thousand times better than when you entered hibernation."

"Traditional architecture?"

"Traditional architecture. A few more drops squeezed out of the lemon of Moore's law. It astonished the computing community—but this time, my love, we've really come to the end."

A peerless computer. If humanity failed, it would never be equaled, Hines thought, but did not say it out loud.

"With this computer, research on the Resolving Imager became much easier." Then she suddenly asked, "Love, do you have any idea of what a hundred billion looks like?" When he shook his head, she smiled and stretched out her hands around her. "Look. This is a hundred billion."

"What?" At a loss for words, Hines looked at the white fog around him.

"We're in the middle of the supercomputer's holographic display," she said as she manipulated a gadget hanging at her chest. He noticed a scroll wheel on it, and thought it might be something like a mouse.

As she adjusted it, he felt a change in the surrounding fog. It thickened in what was clearly a magnification of a particular region. Then he noticed that it was made up of an uncountable number of tiny glowing particles, and these particles were emitting the moonlike illumination rather than scattering light from an outside source. As the magnification continued, the particles became shining stars, but instead of seeing the starry sky over Earth, it was like he was situated at the heart of the Milky Way, where the stars were dense and left practically no room for darkness.

"Every star is a neuron," she said. Their bodies were plated in silver by the ocean formed from a hundred billion stars.

As the hologram continued to enlarge, he noticed innumerable thin tentacles extending radially from every star to form intricate connections, wiping out the starfield and situating him inside an infinitely large network structure.

The image enlarged further, and every star began to exhibit a structure that was familiar to him from electron microscopy, that of brain cells and synapses.

She pressed the mouse and the image returned instantly to the white fog state. "This is a full view of the structure of the brain captured using the Resolving Imager scanning three million cross sections simultaneously. Of course, what we're seeing now is the processed image—for the convenience of observation, the distance between neurons has been magnified by four or five orders of magnitude so it looks like we vaporized a brain. However, the topology of the connections between them has been preserved. Now, let's take a look at a dynamic view. . . ."

Disturbances appeared in the fog, glittering points in the mist that looked like a pinch of gunpowder sprinkled onto a flame. Keiko Yamasuki enlarged the image until it resembled a starfield, and Hines saw the surging of startide in a brain-universe, the

disturbances in the ocean of stars appearing in different forms at different locations: some like streams, others like vortexes, and others like the sweeping tides, all of it instantly mutable and giving rise to stunning pictures of self-organization within the teeming chaos. Then the image changed again to resemble a network, and he saw myriad nerve signals busily passing messages along thin synapses, like flashing pearls within the flow of an intricate network of pipes. . . .

"Whose brain is this?" he asked in wonder.

"Mine," she said, looking lovingly at him. "When this thought picture was taken, I was thinking of you."

Please note: When the light turns green, the sixth batch of test propositions will appear. If the proposition is true, press the right-hand button. If the proposition is false, press the left-hand button.

Proposition 1: Coal is black.

Proposition 2: $1 + 1 = 2$.

Proposition 3: The temperature in winter is lower than in summer.

Proposition 4: Men are generally shorter than women.

Proposition 5: A straight line is the shortest distance between two points.

Proposition 6: The moon is brighter than the sun.

The statements were displayed in succession on the small screen in front of the test subject. Each proposition was displayed for four seconds, and the subject pressed the left-hand or right-hand buttons according to his own judgment. His head was encased in a metal cover that allowed the Resolving Imager to capture a holographic view of his brain, which the computer would process into a dynamic neural network model for analysis.

In this, the initial stage of Hines's research project, the subject

engaged in only the simplest of critical thinking, and the test propositions had concise and clear answers. During such simple thoughts, the operation of the cerebral neural network was relatively easy to identify and provided a starting point for a more in-depth study of the nature of thought.

The research teams led by Hines and Keiko Yamasuki had made some progress. They discovered that critical thinking was not produced in any specific location in the cerebral neural network but used a particular mode of nerve impulse transmission, and that with the powerful computer's assistance, this model could be retrieved and located from among the vast network of neurons using a method quite similar to the star positioning the astronomer Ringier had provided to Luo Ji. Unlike finding a particular position pattern in a starfield, in the universe of the brain the pattern was dynamic and was only identifiable by its mathematical characteristics. It was a little like looking for a small whirlpool in an expansive ocean, which meant that the computing power it required was many orders of magnitude greater than that of the starfield and was only feasible on this latest machine.

Hines and his wife strolled through the cloud map of the brain in the holographic display. Every time a point of critical thinking was identified in the subject's brain, the computer would indicate its position on the image with a flashing red light. This was actually just a way to provide a more intuitive feast for the eyes and was not strictly required by the study. The important thing was the analysis of the internal structure of nerve impulse transmission at the point of thought, for there lay hidden the mysteries of the essence of the mind.

Just then the research team's medical director came in and said that Subject 104 was experiencing problems.

When the Resolving Imager had just been developed, scanning such a huge quantity of cross sections generated powerful radiation that was fatal to any life being scanned, but successive improvements had brought the radiation below the danger line, and a large number of tests had demonstrated that so long as filming was kept

below a set length of time, the Resolving Imager would not cause any damage to the brain.

"He seems to have caught hydrophobia," the medical director said, as they hurried toward the medical center.

Hines and Keiko Yamasuki stopped in their tracks in surprise. Hines stared at the medical director: "Hydrophobia? Did he somehow get rabies?"

The medical director raised a hand and tried to sort out his thoughts: "Oh, I'm sorry. That wasn't accurate. He doesn't have any physical problems, and his brain and other organs have not been damaged at all. It's just that he's afraid of the water, like someone with rabies. He refuses to drink, and he won't even eat moist food. It's an entirely psychological effect. He just believes that water is toxic."

"Persecutory delusion?" Keiko Yamasuki asked.

The medical director waved a hand. "No, no. He doesn't think that anyone put poison in the water. He just believes the water itself is toxic."

Again, Hines and his wife stopped still, and the medical director shook his head helplessly. "But psychologically, he's completely normal in every other way. . . . I can't explain it. You've got to see it for yourselves."

Subject 104 was a volunteer college student who had come to earn some pocket money. Before they entered the patient's room, the director told Hines and his wife, "He hasn't had a drink in two days. If this continues, he'll become severely dehydrated and we'll have to hydrate him by force." Standing at the door he pointed to a microwave oven, and said, "You see that? He wants bread and other food baked completely dry before he'll eat it."

Hines and his wife entered the patient's room. Subject 104 looked at them with fear in his eyes. His lips were cracked and his hair disheveled, but otherwise he looked entirely normal. He tugged at Hines's sleeve and said in a hoarse voice, "Dr. Hines, they want to kill me. I don't know why." Then he pointed a finger at a glass of water sitting on the cabinet next to the head of the bed. "They want me to drink water."

Hines looked at the glass of clear water, certain that the subject did not have rabies, because true hydrophobia would cause spasms of terror at the mere sight of it. The sound of running water would induce madness, and there might even be an intense fear response if others simply talked about it.

"From his eyes and speech, he ought to be in a normal psychological state," Keiko Yamasuki said to Hines in Japanese. She had a degree in psychology.

"Do you really believe that water is toxic?" Hines asked.

"Is there any question? Just like the sun has light and the air has oxygen. You can't deny this basic fact, can you?"

Hines leaned on his shoulder and said, "Young man, life was born in the water and can't exist without it. Your own body is seventy percent water."

Subject 104's eyes darkened, and he slumped back in bed, clutching his head. "That's right. This question tortures me. It's the most incredible thing in the universe."

"Let me see Subject 104's experiment record," Hines said to the medical director after they left the patient's room. When they reached the director's office, Keiko Yamasuki said, "Look at the test propositions first."

The test propositions displayed on the computer screen one by one:

Proposition 1: Cats have a total of three legs.
Proposition 2: Rocks are not living.
Proposition 3: The sun is shaped like a triangle.
Proposition 4: Iron is heavier than cotton of the same volume.
Proposition 5: Water is toxic.

"Stop," Hines said, pointing to Proposition 5.

"His answer was 'false,'" the director said.

"Look at all parameters and operations following the answer to Proposition 5."

The records indicated that once Proposition 5 was answered,

the Resolving Imager increased the strength of its scan of the critical thinking point in the subject's cerebral neural network. To improve the accuracy of the scan of this area, the intensity of the radiation and the magnetic field were increased in this small region. Hines and Keiko Yamasuki carefully examined the long list of recorded parameters on the screen.

"Has this enhanced scan been done to other subjects and on other propositions?" Hines asked.

The director said, "Because the effect of the enhanced scan was not particularly good, it was canceled after four tries due to fears of excessive localized radiation. The previous three . . ." He consulted the computer, and then said, "were all benign true propositions."

"We should use the same scanning parameters and repeat the experiment for Proposition 5," Keiko Yamasuki said.

"But . . . who will do it?" asked the director.

"I will," Hines said.

Water is toxic.

Proposition 5 appeared in black text on a white background. Hines pressed the left "False" button, but he felt nothing apart from a slight sensation of heat produced by the intensive scanning at the back of his head.

He exited the Resolving Imager lab and sat down at a table, as a crowd, which included Keiko Yamasuki, watched. On the table stood a glass of clear water. He picked up the glass and slowly drew it to his lips and took a sip. His movements were relaxed and he wore an expression of quiet calm. Everyone began to sigh with relief, but then they noticed that his throat wasn't moving to swallow the water. The muscles of his face stiffened and then twitched slightly upward, and into his eyes came the same fear Subject 104 exhibited, as if his spirit was fighting with some powerful, shapeless force. Finally he spat out all of the water in his mouth and knelt down to vomit, but nothing came out. His face turned purple.

Hugging Hines to her, Keiko Yamasuki clapped him on the back with one hand.

When he had recovered his senses, he held out a hand: "Give me some paper towels," he said. He took them and carefully wiped off the droplets of water that had splashed on his shoes.

"Do you really believe that water is toxic, love?" Yamasuki asked, tears in her eyes. Prior to the experiment she had asked him repeatedly to replace the proposition with a false one that was entirely harmless, but he had refused.

He nodded. "I do." He looked up at the crowd, helplessness and confusion in his eyes. "I do. I really do."

"Let me repeat your words," she said, clapping him on the shoulder. "Life was born in the water and can't exist without it. Your own body is seventy percent water!"

Hines bowed his head and looked at the water stains on the floor. Then he shook his head. "That's right, dear. This question tortures me. It's the most incredible thing in the universe."

Three years after the breakthrough in controlled nuclear fusion, new and unusual heavenly bodies had taken their place in the Earth's night sky, up to five of them now simultaneously visible in one hemisphere. The bodies changed dramatically in luminance, outshining Venus at their brightest, and often blinked rapidly. Sometimes one of them would suddenly erupt with a rapid increase in brightness, then go out after two or three seconds. They were fusion reactors undergoing tests in geosynchronous orbit.

Non-media radioactive propulsion had won out as the research path for future spacecraft. This type of propulsion required high-powered reactors that could only be tested in space, leading to these glowing reactors thirty thousand kilometers out in space known as nuclear stars. Every time a nuclear star erupted, it represented a disastrous defeat. But contrary to what most people believed, nuclear star eruptions were not explosions in the nuclear reactor, but the exposure of the core when the outer

hull of the reactor melted from the heat produced by fusion. The fusion core was like a small sun, and because it melted Earth's most heat-tolerant materials as if they were wax, it had to be contained by an electromagnetic field. These restraints frequently failed.

On the balcony of the top floor of Space Command, Chang Weisi and Hines had just witnessed one such eruption. Its moonlike glow cast its shadows onto the wall before disappearing. Hines was the second Wallfacer that Chang Weisi had met, after Tyler.

"The third time this month," Chang Weisi said.

Hines looked out at the now-darkened night sky. "The power of these reactors only reaches one percent of what's needed for future spacecraft engines, and they don't operate stably. And even *if* the required reactors were developed, engine technology will be even more difficult. We're sure to encounter the sophon block there."

"That's true. The sophons are blocking our every path," Chang Weisi said as he looked off into the distance. The sea of lights in the city seemed even more brilliant now that the light in the sky had disappeared.

"A glimmer of hope fades as soon as it is born, and one day it will be destroyed forever. It's like you said: The sophons block our every path."

Chang Weisi said, with a laugh, "Dr. Hines, you're not here to talk defeatism with me, are you?"

"That's precisely what I want to talk about. The resurgence of defeatism is different this time. It's based on the drastically reduced living conditions in the general population and has an even greater impact in the military."

Chang Weisi looked back from the distance but said nothing.

"I understand your difficulties, General, and I'd like to help you."

Chang Weisi looked at Hines in silence for a few seconds, his expression unreadable to the other man. Then, without replying to his offer, he said, "The evolution of the human brain needs twenty thousand to two hundred thousand years to achieve noticeable changes, but human civilization has a history of just five thousand years. So what we're using right now is the brain of primitive

man. . . . Doctor, I really applaud your unique ideas, and perhaps this is where the real answer lies."

"Thank you. All of us are basically Flintstones."

"But is it really possible to use technology to enhance mental ability?"

This got Hines excited. "General, you're not so primitive, at least compared to others! I notice you said 'mental ability' rather than 'intelligence.' The former is much broader than the latter. To overcome defeatism, for example, we can't simply rely on intelligence. Given the sophon block, the higher your intelligence, the more trouble you have establishing a faith in victory."

"So give me an answer. Is it possible?"

Hines shook his head. "How much do you know about my and Keiko Yamasuki's work before the Trisolar Crisis?"

"Not too much. I believe it was: The essence of thought is not on the molecular level but is carried out on the quantum level. I wonder, does that imply—"

"It implies that the sophons are waiting for me. Just like we're waiting for them," Hines said pointing at the sky. "But right now, our research is still quite a ways from our goal. Still, we've come up with an unexpected by-product."

Chang Weisi smiled and nodded, showing cautious interest.

"I won't talk about the details. Basically, we discovered the mind's mechanism for making judgments in the cerebral neural network, as well as the ability to have a decisive impact on them. If we compare the process by which a human mind makes judgments to a computer's process, there's the input of external data, calculation, and then the final outcome. What we're able to do is omit the calculation step of the process and directly produce an outcome. When a certain piece of information enters the brain, it exerts an influence on a particular part of the neural network, and we can cause the brain to render a judgment—to believe that the information is genuine—without even thinking about it."

"Has this already been achieved?" Chang Weisi asked softly.

"Yes. It started with a chance discovery, which we subjected

to in-depth research, and now we've done it. We call it the 'mental seal.'"

"And if the judgment—or if you will, faith—is at odds with reality?"

"Then the faith will eventually be overturned. But the process will be quite painful, because the judgment produced in the mind by the mental seal is particularly stubborn. Once, this had me convinced that water was toxic, and it was only after two months of psychotherapy that I was able to drink unimpeded. That process is . . . not something I want to remember. But the toxicity of water is an extremely clear false proposition. Other beliefs may not be. Like the existence of God, or whether humanity will be victorious in war. These don't have a clearly determined answer, and in the normal course of establishing these beliefs, the mind is slightly tilted in a certain direction by all sorts of choices. If the belief is established by the mental seal, it will be rock-solid and absolutely unshakeable."

"That is truly a great achievement." Chang Weisi grew serious. "I mean, for neuroscience. But in the real world, Dr. Hines, you have created a truly troublesome thing. Really. The most troublesome thing in history."

"You don't want to use this thing, the mental seal, to create a space force possessing an unshakeable faith in victory? In the military, you have political commissars and we have chaplains. The mental seal is just a technological means of accomplishing their work more efficiently."

"Political and ideological work establishes faith through rational, scientific thinking."

"But is it possible to establish faith in a victory in this war on the basis of rational, scientific thought?"

"If not, Doctor, we'd rather have a space force that lacks faith in victory yet retains independent thought."

"Apart from this one belief, the rest of the mind would of course be entirely autonomous. We would just be performing a tiny intervention in the mind, using technology to leapfrog thought

to implant a conclusion—just one alone—into the mind."

"But one is enough. Technology is now capable of modifying thoughts just like modifying a computer program. After the modifications, are people still people, or are they automatons?"

"You must have read *A Clockwork Orange*."

"It's a profound book."

"General, your attitude is what I expected," Hines said with a sigh. "I'll continue my efforts in this area, the efforts a Wallfacer must exert."

At the next PDC Wallfacer Project Hearing, Hines's introduction of his mental seal triggered rare emotion in the assembly. The US representative's concise evaluation expressed the feeling of the majority of the attendees: "With their extraordinary talent, Dr. Hines and Dr. Yamasuki have opened up a great door into darkness for humanity."

The French representative left his seat in his excitement. "Which is more tragic for humanity: the loss of the ability and right to think freely, or defeat in this war?"

"Of course the latter is more tragic!" Hines retorted, standing up. "Because under the first condition, humanity at least has the chance of regaining independent thought!"

"I have doubts about that. If this thing really does get used . . . Look at all you Wallfacers," the Russian representative said, raising his hands toward the ceiling. "Tyler wanted to deprive people of their lives, and you want to deprive them of their minds. What are you trying to do?"

His words caused a commotion.

The UK representative said, "Today we are merely proposing a motion, but I believe that the governments of all countries will be unanimous in banning this thing. Regardless of what happens, nothing is more evil than thought control."

Hines said, "Why is it that everyone gets so sensitive at the mention of thought control? From commercial advertising to

Hollywood culture, thought control is everywhere in modern society. You are, to use a Chinese phrase, mocking people for retreating a hundred paces when you've retreated fifty yourselves."

The US representative said, "Dr. Hines, you haven't gone just one hundred paces. You've walked up to the threshold of darkness and are threatening the very foundations of modern society."

Another commotion swept through the assembly, and Hines knew that now was the time to seize control of the situation. He raised his voice and said, "Learn from the little boy!"

Sure enough, there was a lull in the noise after his utterance. "What little boy?" asked the rotating chair.

"I think we're all familiar with this story: In a forest, a little boy got his leg caught under a fallen tree. He was alone at the time, and his leg was bleeding uncontrollably. It would have killed him, except that he made a decision that would shame every one of you delegates: He took up his saw and sawed off the leg that was pinned, then climbed into a car and found a hospital. He saved his own life."

Hines saw with satisfaction that no one in the meeting room had attempted to interrupt him, at least. He went on. "Humanity is now facing a life-and-death problem. The life or death of our species and civilization as a whole. In these circumstances, how can we not give up a few things?"

Two light thumps sounded. The chair was banging the gavel, even though there wasn't much noise in the assembly. The attendees were reminded that the German man had maintained an unusual silence during the course of the hearing. In a gentle voice, the chair said, "First of all, I hope that each of you can take a good look at the current situation. Investment in building a space defense system is constantly increasing, and the world economy is experiencing a sharp recession during this time of transition. The prediction that the standard of living will retreat a century may come to pass in the not-too-distant future. Meanwhile, space defense–related scientific research is running up against the sophon block, and technological progress is slowing. This will trigger a new wave of

defeatism in the international community, and this time, it may cause the total collapse of the Solar System Defense Program."

The chair's words calmed the assembly completely. After a silence of nearly half a minute, he continued. "Like each of you, when I learned of the existence of the mental seal, I felt the kind of fear and loathing I'd get from seeing a poisonous snake. But the most rational approach to take right now is to calm down and seriously consider it. When the devil does actually appear, the best option is calmness and rationality. At this hearing, we are simply putting forward a votable motion."

Hines saw a thread of hope. "Mr. Chair, Representatives, since my initial proposal is unable to be put to an assembly vote, maybe we all can take a step back."

"No matter how many steps back you take, thought control is absolutely unacceptable," the French representative said, but in a slightly softer tone than before.

"And if it weren't thought control? Perhaps something in between control and freedom?"

"The mental seal equals thought control," the Japanese representative said.

"Not so. In thought control, there must be a controller and a subject. If someone voluntarily places a seal in their own mind, then tell me, where is the control in that?"

The assembly fell silent again. Feeling that success was near, Hines went on, "I propose that the mental seal be opened up, like a public facility. It would have but one proposition: belief in a victory in the war. Anyone willing to gain that faith through the use of the seal could, totally voluntarily, take advantage of the facility. Of course, all of this would be conducted under strict supervision."

The assembly opened up a discussion and added to Hines's basic proposal a fair number of new restrictions on the use of the mental seal. The most crucial of these was the one limiting its use to the space forces, because it was relatively easy for people to accept the idea of uniform thinking in the military. The hearing continued for nearly eight hours, the longest ever, and eventually formulated

a motion to be voted on at the next meeting, and which the permanent member states would take back to their own governments.

"Shouldn't we come up with a name for this facility?" asked the US representative.

"How about calling it the Faith Relief Center?" the UK representative said. The British humor of the odd name drew a burst of laughter.

"Take out 'relief,' and call it the Faith Center," Hines said, in all earnestness.

At the gate to the Faith Center stood a reduced-scale replica of the Statue of Liberty. Its purpose was unknown—perhaps it was an attempt to use "liberty" to dilute the feeling of "control"—but the most notable thing about the statue was the altered poem on its base:

> *Give me your hopeless souls,*
> *Your fearful crowds that thirst for victory,*
> *The dazed refuse of your treacherous shoals.*
> *Send these, the downcast, wand'ring ones to me,*
> *For lo, my lamp of golden faith consoles.*

The golden faith of the poem was prominently inscribed in many different languages on a black granite stone called the Faith Monument that stood beside the statue:

In the war of resistance against the invasion from Trisolaris, humanity will be victorious. The enemy invading the Solar System will be destroyed. Earth will endure in the cosmos for ten thousand generations.

The Faith Center had been open for three days, during which time Hines and Keiko Yamasuki had been waiting in the majestic foyer. The smallish building erected near the United Nations Plaza had

become the latest tourist attraction, with people constantly coming up to take photos of the Statue of Liberty and the Faith Monument, but no one had entered. They all seemed to be maintaining a cautious distance.

"Do you get the feeling we're running a struggling mom-and-pop store?" she said.

"My dear, one day this will be a sacred place," Hines said solemnly.

On the afternoon of the third day, someone finally walked into the Faith Center. The bald, melancholy-looking, middle-aged man walked unsteadily and smelt of alcohol when he approached. "I've come to get faith," he slurred out.

"The Faith Center is only open to members of national space forces. Please show your ID," Keiko Yamasuki said while bowing. She seemed to Hines like a polite waitress at the Tokyo Plaza Hotel.

The man fished out his ID. "I'm a space force member. Civilian personnel. Is that okay?"

After inspecting the ID, Hines nodded. "Mr. Wilson, do you want to do it now?"

"That would be great," he said, and nodded. "The . . . the thing you call a belief proposition. I've written it here. I want to believe this." He pulled a neatly folded piece of paper from his breast pocket.

Keiko Yamasuki wanted to explain that according to the PDC resolution, the mental seal was only permitted to operate on one proposition, the one written on the monument at the gate. It had to be done exactly as written, and any alteration was prohibited. But Hines gently stopped her. He wanted to take a look at the proposition the man had submitted first. Unfolding the paper, he read what was written on it:

Katherine loves me. She has never and will never have an affair!

Keiko Yamasuki stifled a laugh, but Hines angrily crumpled up the paper and tossed it in the drunken man's face. "Get the hell out!"

After Wilson left, another man passed the Faith Monument,

the boundary beyond which ordinary tourists maintained their distance. As the man paced behind the monument, he soon came to Hines's attention. Hines called Keiko Yamasuki over and said, "Look at him. He must be a soldier!"

"He looks mentally and physically exhausted," she said.

"But he's a soldier. Believe me," he said. He was about to go out and talk to the man when he saw him heading up the steps. The man looked about Wilson's age and, though his Asian features were handsome, it was like Keiko Yamasuki had said: He seemed a little melancholy, but in a different way from the previous hardluck case. His melancholy looked lighter, but also deeper, as if it had been with him for years.

"My name is Wu Yue. I'd like to get belief," the visitor said. Hines noticed how he referred to "belief" instead of "faith."

Keiko Yamasuki bowed and repeated her earlier line: "The Faith Center is only open to members of every country's space force. Please show your ID."

Wu Yue did not move, but he said, "Sixteen years ago, I spent a month serving in the space force, and then I retired."

"You served for one month? Well, if you don't mind my asking, what was your reason for retiring?" Hines asked.

"I'm a defeatist. My superiors and I felt that I was no longer suited to work in the space force."

"Defeatism is a common mentality. You're evidently just an honest defeatist, and stated your own ideas forthrightly. Your colleagues who continued serving may have harbored an even stronger defeatist complex, but they just kept it hidden," Keiko Yamasuki said.

"Maybe. But I've been lost all these years."

"Because you left the service?"

Wu Yue shook his head. "No. I was born into a family of scholars, and the education I received made me treat humanity as a single unit, even after I became a soldier. I always felt that a soldier's highest honor would be to fight for the entire human race. This opportunity came, but it was a war that we were destined to lose."

Hines was about to say something, but was interrupted by Keiko Yamasuki. "Permit me to ask a question. How old are you?"

"Fifty-one."

"If you are really able to return to the space force after obtaining faith in victory, don't you think that at your age it's a little late to start up in the service again?"

Hines could see that she didn't have the heart to refuse him directly. No doubt this deeply melancholy man was very attractive to a woman's eyes. But this didn't worry him, because the man was obviously so consumed by his despair that nothing else had any meaning for him.

Wu Yue shook his head. "You misunderstand. I don't want to gain faith in victory. I'm just looking for peace for my soul."

Hines wanted to speak, but again Keiko Yamasuki stopped him.

Wu Yue went on. "I met my present wife when I was studying at the naval academy in Annapolis. She was a fervent Christian and faced the future with a calmness that made me jealous. She said that God had everything planned out, from the past to the future. We children of the Lord did not need to understand his plans. We just needed to firmly believe that this plan was the most reasonable one in the universe, and then live peacefully according to the Lord's will."

"So you mean that you've come to gain a belief in God?"

Wu Yue nodded. "I've written out my belief proposition. Please have a look." He reached into his shirt pocket as he spoke.

Again Keiko Yamasuki stopped Hines from saying anything. She said to Wu Yue, "If that's the case, then just go and believe. There's no need to resort to such extreme, technological means."

The former space force captain showed a trace of a wry smile. "I grew up under a materialist education. I'm a staunch atheist. Do you think gaining this belief would be easy for me?"

"Absolutely not!" Hines said, getting out in front of Keiko Yamasuki. He decided to clear things up as quickly as he could. "You ought to know that according to the UN resolution, the mental seal can only operate on one proposition." As he spoke, he took out a large, exquisitely fashioned red card case and opened it up for

Wu Yue to see. There, on the black velvet lining, in letters engraved in gold, was the victory oath from the Faith Monument. He said, "This is a faith book." He took out a set of cases in different colors. "These are faith books in different languages. Mr. Wu, let me tell you how stringent the supervision is for use of the mental seal. To guarantee safe and reliable operation, the proposition is not put up on a display but is given to the volunteer to read from this primitive faith book. As a reflection of the voluntary principle, the specific procedure is completed by the volunteer. He opens up this faith book, then presses the Start button on the mental seal device. Prior to actually performing the procedure, the system will give three confirmation opportunities. Before each procedure, the faith book is inspected by a panel of ten special commissioners from the members of the UN Human Rights Commission and the permanent member states of the PDC. During the operation of the mental seal device, the ten-member panel will be on site to strictly supervise the entire affair. So, sir, your request can't be fulfilled. Forget about your proposition for religious belief. Changing even one word in the faith book is a crime."

"Then I'm sorry to have troubled you," Wu Yue said, nodding. He appeared to have anticipated this outcome. As he turned to walk out, he appeared lonely and old from the back.

"The rest of his life will be hard," Keiko Yamasuki said softly, with a voice full of tenderness.

"Sir!" Hines called, stopping Wu Yue just outside the door. He ran out to where the light of the setting sun was reflecting like fire off the Faith Monument and the glass-walled UN building in the distance. He squinted his eyes against the flames and said, "You might not believe me, but I nearly did the exact opposite."

Wu Yue looked puzzled. Hines looked back and, seeing that Keiko Yamasuki had not followed him, took out a piece of paper from his pocket and opened it for Wu Yue. "This is the mental seal I wanted to apply to myself. I was hesitant, of course, and in the end didn't do it." The bold text on the paper read:

God is dead.

"Why?" asked Wu Yue, raising his head.

"Isn't it obvious? Isn't God dead? Screw the Lord's plan. Screw his mild yoke!"

Wu Yue looked at Hines in silence for a moment, then turned and walked down the steps.

When Wu Yue walked into the shadow cast by the Faith Monument, Hines called after him, "Sir, I wish I could disguise my contempt for you, but I can't."

The next day, the people Hines and Keiko Yamasuki were waiting for finally started to arrive. In the bright sunshine that morning, four people walked in, three men with European faces and one woman with Asian features. Young, standing straight and tall, and walking at a steady pace, they looked confident and mature. But Hines and Keiko Yamasuki saw in their eyes something familiar, the same melancholy confusion that had been in Wu Yue's.

They set their documents neatly down on the reception desk, and their leader said solemnly, "We're space force officers, and we've come to get faith in victory."

The mental seal process was quite fast. After the faith books were passed among the ten members of the oversight panel, each of whom carefully checked the contents, they signed their names to the notary certificate. Then, under their supervision, the first volunteer received the faith book and sat down in front of the mental seal scanner. In front of him was a small platform on which he placed the book, and which had a red button in the lower right-hand corner. When he opened the faith book, a voice asked, "Are you certain that you want to obtain a faith in this proposition? If so, please press the button. If not, please leave the scanning area."

The question was repeated three times, and each time it was asked, the button glowed red. A positioning apparatus slowly contracted to fix the volunteer's head in place, and then the voice said, "The mental seal procedure is ready to start. Please read the proposition silently and then press the button."

When the button was pressed, it turned green, and after about half a minute, it went out. The voice said, "The mental seal

procedure is complete." The positioning apparatus separated, and then the volunteer got up and left.

After all four officers completed the procedure and returned to the foyer, Keiko Yamasuki carefully looked them over, confirming almost immediately that her perception of their improved moods was not just her imagination. The melancholy and confusion had disappeared from the four pairs of eyes, which now were serene as water.

"How do you feel?" she asked, smiling.

"Excellent," one young officer said, returning her smile. "How it ought to be."

When they left, the Asian woman turned around and added, "Doctor, I really feel great. Thank you."

At that moment, the future was certain, at least in the minds of those four young people.

From that day forward, members of the space force came without pause to obtain faith—at first mostly on their own, but eventually in larger groups. They wore civilian clothes at first, but later most of them wore military uniforms. If more than five people came at a time, the supervisory panel convened a review meeting to verify that no one had been coerced.

One week later, more than a hundred space force members had obtained faith in victory through the mental seal. They ranged in rank from private to senior colonel, the highest rank permitted by national space forces to use the mental seal.

That night, in the moonlight at the Faith Monument, Hines said to Keiko Yamasuki, "Dear, we need to go."

"To the future?"

"That's right. We're not any better than other scientists in the study of the mind, and we've accomplished everything we needed to. We have pushed forward the wheel of history, so now let's go to the future and wait for it."

"How far?"

"Very far, Keiko. Very far. To the day when the Trisolaran probes reach the Solar System."

"Before we do that, let's go back to that house in Tokyo for a while. After all, this age is going to be buried forever."

"Of course, dear. I miss it too."

Six months later, as Keiko Yamasuki sank into the deepening cold and was about to enter hibernation, the cold froze and filtered out the riot of noise in her mind. This brought the thread of her focused thoughts into sharp relief in the lonely darkness, like the moment ten years before when Luo Ji plunged into the icy lake. All of a sudden, her hazy thoughts became unusually clear, like the chilly sky in the dead of winter.

She wanted to shout for the hibernation to stop, but it was too late. The ultra-low temperatures had seeped into her body and she had lost the ability to produce sound.

The operators and doctors noticed that just as she was entering hibernation, her eyes suddenly opened a crack, revealing an expression full of horror and despair. If the cold hadn't frozen her eyelids, her eyes would have been wide open. But this was just a normal reflex during the process that had been seen on previous hibernators, so they paid it no mind.

The UN PDC Wallfacer Project Hearing deliberated the stellar hydrogen bomb test.

The giant breakthrough in computing technology meant that computers were at last capable of handling the theoretical stellar model of a nuclear explosion developed over the past decade, and the manufacture of large-yield stellar hydrogen bombs could begin forthwith. The projected yield of the first bomb was the equivalent of 350 megatons of TNT, or seven times more powerful than the largest hydrogen bomb ever manufactured by humanity. It was impossible for this superbomb to be tested in the atmosphere, and a detonation in an underground shaft of the depth previously used would eject the surrounding rock into the air, so testing on Earth

would require digging an ultra-deep shaft. But even detonating in an ultra-deep shaft would cause powerful shock waves to spread across the world and might have an unanticipated effect on a broad range of geological structures, possibly touching off disasters including earthquakes and tsunamis. Therefore, the stellar hydrogen bomb could only be tested in space. Yet it was impossible in high orbit, because at that distance, the electromagnetic pulse the bomb generated would have a catastrophic effect on Earth's telecommunications and power systems. The ideal test location, then, was on the back side of the moon. However, Rey Diaz chose differently.

"I've decided to conduct the tests on Mercury," he said.

This proposal surprised the representatives in attendance, and they voiced questions about the meaning of the plan.

"According to the basic principles of the Wallfacer plan, I do not have to explain," he answered icily. "The tests should be conducted underground. We need to dig ultra-deep shafts on Mercury."

The Russian representative said, "We can consider tests on the surface of Mercury, but underground tests are too expensive. Digging deep shafts there could cost a hundred times what a similar engineering project would cost on Earth. Besides, the effects of a nuclear bomb on the environment of Mercury would tell us nothing useful."

"Even a surface test on Mercury is impossible!" the US representative said. "To date, Rey Diaz has consumed the most resources of all of the Wallfacers. The time has come to stop him!" This sentiment was echoed by representatives from the UK, France, and Germany.

Rey Diaz said with a laugh, "Even if I used as few resources as Dr. Luo, you'd still be keen to veto my plan." He turned to the rotating chair. "I would ask the chair and each representative to remember that out of all the strategies proposed by the Wallfacers, my plan is most closely in harmony with mainstream defense, to the point that you could view it as part of the mainstream. In absolute numbers the consumption of resources might look large, but a considerable portion of that overlaps the mainstream. Therefore—"

The UK representative cut him off. "You still ought to explain why you need to conduct underground tests on Mercury. Unless you're just doing it to spend money. We can't find any explanation for it."

"Mr. Chair, Representatives," Rey Diaz countered calmly, "you may have noticed that the PDC no longer has even the barest respect for Wallfacers or for the Wallfacer principle. If we have to explain every detail of our plans, then how is the Wallfacer Project meaningful?" One by one, he turned his scorching gaze on every representative, forcing them to turn away.

He went on, "Even so, I am willing to offer an explanation of the issue just raised. The goal of conducting deep underground tests on Mercury is to blast out a large cave on the planet to serve as a future Mercury base. This is clearly the most economical way of conducting an engineering project of this kind."

His words stirred up whispers, and one representative asked, "Wallfacer Rey Diaz, do you mean you want to use Mercury as the launch base for stellar hydrogen bombs?"

With confidence, Rey Diaz answered, "Yes. Current strategic theory in mainstream defense holds that emphasis should be placed on the outer planets, and so the inner planets, which are not believed to be defensively significant, have not been given sufficient attention. The Mercury base I have planned is intended to mend this weak link in mainstream defense."

"He's afraid of the sun, but he wants to go to the planet closest to it. Isn't that a little strange?" the US representative said. There was a bit of laughter, followed by a warning from the chair.

"It doesn't matter, Mr. Chair. I've grown accustomed to this lack of respect. I was used to it even before I became a Wallfacer," Rey Diaz said with a wave of his hand. "But all of you should respect the facts at hand. When the outer planets and Earth have fallen, the Mercury base will be the last bastion of humanity. Backed by the sun and situated amid the cover of radiation, it will be the most rugged of positions."

"Wallfacer Rey Diaz, does this mean that your plan's entire significance lies in a last stand when humanity's situation is already

hopeless? This is quite consistent with your character," the French representative said.

"Gentlemen, we can't simply refuse to consider the final resistance," Rey Diaz said gravely.

"Very well, Wallfacer Rey Diaz," the chair said. "Now, would you be able to tell us, in your overall deployment scenario, how many stellar hydrogen bombs you'll need, all told?"

"The more the better. Manufacture as many as the Earth has capacity to produce. The specific number depends on the yield that hydrogen bombs will be able to achieve in the future, but according to current figures, the first batch in the deployment plan requires at least a million."

Laughter shook the auditorium at Rey Diaz's words.

"Evidently Wallfacer Rey Diaz doesn't just want to make a small sun. He wants to make a small galaxy!" the US representative said loudly. Then he leaned toward Rey Diaz. "Do you really think that the ocean's protium, deuterium, and tritium were prepared just for you? Because of your perverted affection for the bomb, the Earth should be turned into a bomb workshop?"

By this point Rey Diaz was the only one in the assembly with a straight face. He waited quietly until the clamor he had sparked died down, and then said, one word at a time, "This is the ultimate war of the human race, so the number I ask for is not at all large. But I did anticipate today's outcome. Nevertheless, I will work hard. I will build bombs. I will build as many as I can, I tell you. I will work hard and I won't stop."

In response, the representatives of the US, UK, and France put forth a joint proposal, P269, to terminate the strategic plan of Wallfacer Rey Diaz.

Only two colors were visible on the surface of Mercury: black and gold. The black was the planet's land, and its low reflectance meant that even under close illumination from the fierce sun, it remained a sheet of black. The gold was the sun, which occupied

a considerable portion of the sky. In its broad wheel you could clearly see the surging of its fiery seas and the sunspots drifting by like black clouds, and, at its edges, the graceful dance of solar prominences.

And on this hard chunk of rock suspended atop the sun's fiery sea, humanity was planting another small sun.

With the completion of the space elevator, humanity had begun the large-scale exploration of the other planets in the Solar System. Manned spacecraft landings on Mars and the moons of Jupiter had not caused much of a stir because people knew that the purpose of these expeditions was much clearer and more practical than in the past: They were purely intended to establish bases for the defense of the Solar System. These voyages, which relied mainly on chemical-propulsion rockets and spacecraft, were merely the tiniest of steps toward that goal. Initial explorations focused primarily on the outer planets, but as the study of space strategy deepened, neglecting the strategic value of the inner planets was increasingly called into question. Hence the exploration of Venus and Mercury was stepped up, and so it was that the PDC narrowly passed Rey Diaz's plan to test the stellar hydrogen bomb on Mercury.

Excavating the shaft through the rock of Mercury was the first large-scale engineering project humanity had undertaken on another planet in the Solar System. Because construction could only take place during Mercury's night, in stretches of eighty-eight Earth days, the project would take three years to complete. However, in the end it only reached one-third of the projected depth, due to the discovery of an unusually hard layer farther down, a mixture of metal and rock. Continued excavation would be much slower and far more costly. Ultimately, it was decided to terminate the project. If tests were carried out at the present depth, the surrounding rock would most certainly be ejected by the blast and would form a crater, making it basically a watered-down atmospheric test. And because of the interference from the surrounding crust, it would be far harder to observe the test's outcome than with a purely atmospheric test. But Rey Diaz thought that if a cover were fitted onto

this crater, it could still serve as a base, and insisted on conducting the test underground at the current depth.

The test was carried out at dawn. Sunrise on Mercury was a process that took over ten hours, and a faint light had just appeared on the horizon. When the detonation countdown reached zero, rings of ripples centered on ground zero spread outward, and the ground on Mercury seemed momentarily to become soft as satin. Then, at the blast site, a mountain slowly rose like the back of a waking giant. When the peak had risen to around three thousand meters, the entire mountain exploded, sending billions of tons of mud and rock flying into the air in a towering display of rage by the ground toward the sky. And alongside the surging ground came the radiant light of the underground nuclear fireball, which shone on the rock and earth flying through the air to cause a grand spectacle of fireworks in the black Mercury sky. The fireball lasted for five minutes, as chunks of rock fell to the ground amid a nuclear glow, before it went out.

Ten hours after the conclusion of the blast, observers noticed that a ring had appeared around Mercury. This was due to the considerable amount of rock that had achieved cosmic velocity in the violent explosion and had turned into myriad satellites of various sizes. They spread out evenly in orbit, making Mercury the first ringed terrestrial planet. The ring was thin, and as it sparkled in the harsh light of the sun, it looked almost like someone had taken a highlighter to the planet.

Another proportion of the rocks achieved escape velocity and left Mercury behind entirely, becoming satellites of the sun in their own right and forming an extremely sparse asteroid belt in Mercury's orbit.

Rey Diaz lived underground not out of any concern for security, but because of his heliophobia. The claustrophobic environment, far removed from the sunshine, made him feel a little more comfortable. He watched the live broadcast of the Mercury test from the basement where he lived. It wasn't actually live, since the

images took about seven minutes to reach Earth. When the blast on Mercury had concluded and the rock rain was still falling in the post-fireball darkness, he received a telephone call from the rotating chair of the PDC, who said that the tremendous power of the stellar hydrogen bombs had made a deep impression on the PDC leadership, and that the permanent member states had requested that the next Wallfacer hearing be held as soon as possible to discuss the bombs' manufacture and deployment. The chair said that although the number of bombs Rey Diaz had requested was an impossibility, the major powers were indeed interested in the production of this weapon.

Over ten hours after the conclusion of the Mercury test, as he was watching Mercury's new ring sparkling on the television, a guard's voice came over the intercom to tell him that his psychiatrist had arrived for an appointment.

"I never asked for any psychiatrist. Send him away!" He felt exasperated, like he had suffered some great indignity.

"Don't be like that, Mr. Rey Diaz," said another, calmer voice, evidently the visitor's. "I can let you see the sun . . ."

"Get the hell out," he shouted, but then immediately changed his mind. "No. Seize that idiot and find out where he came from."

". . . because I know the cause of your condition," the voice continued, still calm. "Mr. Rey Diaz, please believe me. You and I are the only ones in the world who know."

At this, Rey Diaz suddenly grew alert, and said, "Let him in." He stared at the ceiling for a few seconds through haggard eyes, then got up slowly and picked up a tie from the cluttered sofa, only to toss it back again. He walked over to the mirror, straightened his collar, and combed his hair with his hands, like he was preparing for a solemn event.

He knew that it was indeed a solemn event.

The visitor was a handsome middle-aged man who walked in but did not introduce himself. He frowned slightly at the room's heavy odor of cigars and alcohol, then simply stood there calmly as Rey Diaz looked him over.

"Why do I have the feeling I've seen you before?" he said, as he looked at the visitor.

"That's not strange, Mr. Rey Diaz. Everyone says I look like Superman, from the old movies."

"Do you really believe you're Superman?" Rey Diaz said. He sat down on the sofa, picked up a cigar, bit off the end, and began to light it.

"That question shows that you already know what kind of man I am. I'm not Superman, Mr. Rey Diaz. Nor are you." As he spoke, the younger man took a step forward. Rey Diaz found that the man was standing directly in front of him, peering down at him through the cloud of smoke he had just exhaled. So he stood up.

The visitor said, "Wallfacer Manuel Rey Diaz, I am your Wallbreaker."

Gloomily, Rey Diaz nodded.

"May I sit down?" the Wallbreaker asked.

"You may not," Rey Diaz said, slowly blowing smoke in the other man's face.

"Don't be depressed," the Wallbreaker said with a considerate smile.

"I'm not," Rey Diaz said, his voice cold and hard like stone.

The Wallbreaker walked over to the wall and flipped a switch. Somewhere, ventilator fans started humming.

"Don't mess with things around here," Rey Diaz warned.

"You need a little fresh air. And, more than that, you need sun. I'm quite familiar with this room, Wallfacer Rey Diaz. In the images sent by the sophons I have often watched you pace back and forth like a caged beast. No one in the world has stared at you for as long as I have, and on those days, believe me, it wasn't any easier for me."

The Wallbreaker looked straight at Rey Diaz, whose expression was as blank as an ice sculpture, and then he went on. "Compared to Frederick Tyler, you are a brilliant strategist. A competent Wallfacer. Please trust that this is not flattery. I must admit that for quite some time, for nearly a decade, you had me fooled. Your

mania for the superbomb, such an inefficient weapon in a space battle, successfully concealed your own strategic direction, and for a long while I couldn't find any clue to crack your true strategy. I struggled in the maze that you laid down, and at one point almost despaired." The Wallbreaker looked up at the ceiling, overcome by the memory of those difficult times. "Later, I thought of checking out information from before you became a Wallbreaker, but this wasn't easy, because the sophons were unable to help. You know, in those days, only a limited number of sophons had reached Earth, and as a South American head of state you had not attracted their attention. So I had to resort to conventional means to gather materials. This took three years. In those materials, one man stood out: William Cosmo. You met him in secret on three occasions. The sophons did not record the content of your conversations, so I will never know, but for the head of a small, undeveloped country to meet three times with a Western astrophysicist is highly unusual. We now know that at that time you had already been preparing to become a Wallfacer.

"No doubt what interested you was the fruit of Dr. Cosmo's research. How those results first came to your attention I am not clear on at this time, but you had a background in engineering, and you had the successful experience of your socialism-loving predecessor, who had equal enthusiasm for a nation ruled by engineers. This was a major reason why you became his successor. So you ought to have had the capability and sensitivity to notice the potential significance of Cosmo's research.

"Once the Trisolar Crisis began, Dr. Cosmo's research team worked on studying the atmosphere of the Trisolaran stellar system. They speculated that the atmosphere had been produced by a former planet that had collided with a star. As it collided, it broke apart the outer layers, its photosphere and troposphere, causing the stellar matter inside to be ejected into space and form a surrounding atmosphere. Due to the total irregularity of the system's motion, there are times when the stars pass each other quite closely, and at those times, one star's atmosphere is dispersed by the gravity of the other star, only to be replenished by eruptions on the stellar

surface. These aren't constant eruptions, more like volcanoes that experience sudden outbreaks. This is the reason for the continual contraction and expansion of the stars' atmosphere. To prove this hypothesis, Cosmo searched the universe to find another star with an atmosphere that was ejected following a collision with a planet. In the third year of the Crisis Era, he succeeded.

"Dr. Cosmo's team discovered planetary system 275E1, about eighty-four light-years from the Solar System. Hubble II had not gone into operation at that time, so they used the wobble method. By observing and calculating the wobble frequency and light mask, they learned that the planet was quite close to its parent star. At first, this discovery did not attract too much attention because the astronomy community had by then discovered more than two hundred planetary systems, but further observations revealed a shocking fact: The distance between planet and star was continually shrinking, and the rate of shrinkage was accelerating. This meant that humanity would, for the first time, observe a planet falling into a star. One year later—or, rather, eighty-four years prior to observation—it happened. Observational conditions at the time meant that the collision could only be determined based on the gravitational wobble and the periodic light mask. But then something wondrous happened: A spiral of matter appeared around the star, and this spiral flow continued to expand. It looked like a mainspring slowly unwinding with the star as its center. Cosmo and his colleagues realized that the material flow had been ejected from the planet's crash point. The chunk of rock had crashed through the shell of that distant sun and ejected its stellar matter into space, where, due to the star's own rotation, it formed a spiral.

"There were several key pieces of data here, sir. The star is a yellow G2 class with an absolute magnitude of 4.3 and a diameter of 1.2 million kilometers. Quite similar to our sun. The planet was about four percent of the mass of Earth, or a little smaller than Mercury, and the spiral cloud of material produced from the collision had a radius of up to three AU, more than the distance between our sun and the asteroid belt.

"And it was in this discovery that I found the crack with which to break open your real strategic plan. Now, as your Wallbreaker, I will explain your grand strategy.

"Supposing that you are ultimately able to obtain those million or more stellar hydrogen bombs, you will, as you promised to the PDC, stockpile them all on Mercury. If the bombs are detonated in the rock of Mercury, they'll be like a turbo-engine decelerating the planet. Eventually its speed will no longer be able to keep it in low orbit and it will fall into the sun. Next, what happened on 275E1 eighty-four light-years away is reenacted here: Mercury punctures the sun's convective shell and ejects a huge amount of stellar matter from its radiation layer into space at high speed; which, as the sun rotates, forms a spiral atmosphere similar to that in 275E1. The sun differs from the Trisolaran system in that, as a lone star, it will never cross paths with another star, and therefore its atmosphere will continue to increase uninhibited until it becomes even thicker than the atmosphere of those stars. This was also confirmed by observations of 275E1. When the spiral flow of ejected matter expands outward from the sun like an unwound mainspring, its thickness eventually passes Mars's orbit, at which point a magnificent chain reaction begins.

"First, three terrestrial planets—Venus, Earth, and Mars—pass through the sun's spiraling atmosphere, losing speed due to the atmospheric friction and turning into three giant meteors that eventually crash into the sun. But well before this happens, the Earth's atmosphere is stripped away by the intense friction of the solar matter. The oceans evaporate, and the lost atmosphere and evaporated oceans turn the Earth into a giant comet whose tail extends along its orbit to wrap all the way around the sun. The surface of the Earth returns to the fiery magma sea of its birth, where no life can survive.

"When Venus, Earth, and Mars crash into the sun, it exacerbates the sun's ejection of solar matter into space. The single spiral flow of matter increases to four flows. Because the total mass of those three planets is forty times that of Mercury, and because their higher orbits mean they impact the sun at a much

higher speed, each new spiral is ejected with a ferocity tens of times greater than Mercury's. The existing spiral atmosphere rapidly expands until its edge approaches the orbit of Jupiter.

"Friction produces only a very small deceleration effect on the huge mass of Jupiter, so it is quite some time before the spiral has a noticeable effect on Jupiter's orbit. But Jupiter's satellites meet one of the following two fates: friction strips them away from Jupiter and they lose speed and fall into the sun, or they lose speed in Jovian orbit and fall into the liquid planet.

"As the chain reaction continues, the decrease in speed from the spiral atmosphere, though small, is still present, and Jupiter's orbit gradually decays. This causes it to pass through an increasingly dense atmosphere whose friction accelerates its loss in speed, thereby causing the orbit to decay even more quickly. . . . In this way, Jupiter eventually falls into the sun, too. Its mass is six hundred times that of the previous four planets, and the impact that such a massive body makes on the sun will, even according to the most conservative reasoning, produce an even more violent ejection of stellar matter, increasing the density of the spiral atmosphere and exacerbating the bitter cold of Uranus and Neptune. But another possibility is more likely: The fall of the Jovian giant pushes the edge of the spiral atmosphere out to the orbit of Uranus or even Neptune, and though the atmosphere is quite thin at the top, friction's decelerating effects pull these two planets and their satellites toward the sun, too. What state the sun will be in and how the Solar System will have been transformed after the chain reaction finishes and the four dense terrestrial planets and four gas giants are consumed is unknowable. But one thing is certain: For life and for civilization, this will be a hell even crueler than attack by Trisolaris.

"As for Trisolaris, the Solar System is their only hope before their planet is engulfed by their stars. There is no other world they can migrate to in time, and therefore, their civilization will follow humanity into total destruction.

"This is your strategy: death for both sides. Once everything

is prepared, with all of the stellar hydrogen bombs in place on Mercury, you will use it to coerce Trisolaris to surrender and gain the ultimate victory for humanity.

"What I've just presented is the outcome of the years of work that I, your Wallbreaker, have performed. I am not seeking your opinion or critique, because I know that all of this is true."

As the Wallbreaker spoke, Rey Diaz had been listening quietly. The cigar in his hand was more than halfway gone, and he now turned it about as if appreciating the glow of the tip.

The Wallbreaker sat down on the sofa, close beside him. Like a teacher evaluating a student's homework, he continued unfatigued: "Mr. Rey Diaz, I said you are a brilliant strategist, or at least you demonstrated many excellent qualities in the formulation and implementation of this plan.

"For one thing, you took advantage of your own background. Right now, people clearly remember the humiliations you and your country suffered when the Orinoco nuclear facility was forced to be taken down as you were developing nuclear energy. The whole world saw your gloomy face, and you took advantage of outside perceptions of your paranoia about nuclear weapons to reduce or even eliminate any possible suspicion.

"But every detail in the execution of your plan demonstrates your talent as well. I will mention but one example: During the Mercury test, you wanted the rock to be blasted into the sky, but you insisted on excavating an ultra-deep shaft in a farsighted gambit. You quite precisely understood the tolerance of the PDC's permanent member states for the cost of this enormous undertaking, and that is admirable.

"But you had one major slipup. Why did the first test have to be carried out on Mercury? There would have been plenty of time to bring the bombs there in a later phase, but maybe you got impatient and wanted to see the outcome of a stellar hydrogen bomb blast there. You saw it: lots of rock matter blasted to escape velocity, perhaps even exceeding your expectations. You were satisfied. But this provided the final confirmation of my hypothesis.

"Yes, Mr. Rey Diaz, even given all my previous work, without that final event I might never have been able to determine your true strategic intentions. The notion was too mad. But it was grand, and even beautiful. If the chain reaction triggered by Mercury's fall actually took place, then it would be the most magnificent movement of the entire symphony of the Solar System . . . although, unfortunately, humanity would only be able to enjoy the first section. Mr. Rey Diaz, you are a Wallfacer with the makings of a god. It is my honor to become your Wallbreaker."

The Wallbreaker stood up and offered Rey Diaz a genial bow.

Rey Diaz did not look at him. He took a puff of his cigar and blew out the smoke as he continued to examine it. "Fine. Then I'll ask the question that Tyler asked."

The Wallbreaker asked the question for him. "If what I say is true, then so what?"

Rey Diaz stared at the lit end of the cigar and nodded.

"My answer is the same as Tyler's Wallbreaker's: The Lord does not care."

Rey Diaz lifted his eyes from the cigar and looked questioningly at his Wallbreaker.

"You look crude, but your mind is sharp. Yet in the depths of your soul, you're still crude. Your nature is that of a crude man. And this crudeness is revealed in the basis of this strategic plan. It's greedy. Humanity doesn't have the ability to manufacture so many stellar hydrogen bombs. Even if all of Earth's industrial resources were exhausted, it wouldn't produce even one-tenth of that number. And a million stellar hydrogen bombs is far from enough to decelerate Mercury into the sun. With a soldier's recklessness, you formulated this impossible plan, and then stubbornly carried it forward step by step with the wily calculations of a superior strategist. Wallfacer Rey Diaz, this is truly a tragedy."

As Rey Diaz looked at the Wallbreaker, his expression gradually filled with an elusive softness, and hints of convulsions showed on his coarsely lined face, gradually taking shape, until at last his suppressed laughter erupted.

"Ha ha ha ha ha . . ." he laughed, pointing at the Wallbreaker. "Superman! Ha ha ha ha. I remember now. That . . . that old Superman. He could fly, and he could reverse the rotation of the Earth, but when he was riding a horse . . . ha ha ha ha . . . when he was riding a horse, he fell and broke his neck . . . ah ha ha ha . . ."

"It was Christopher Reeve, the actor who played Superman, who fell and broke his neck," the Wallbreaker corrected him, quietly.

"Do you imagine . . . imagine that your fate will be better than his? Ha ha ha ha . . ."

"Since coming here, I have no regard for my fate. I've lived a full life," the Wallbreaker said evenly. "But you, Mr. Rey Diaz, ought to think about your own fate."

"You'll die first," Rey Diaz said, smiling with his entire face as he pressed the cigar end directly between the Wallbreaker's eyes. Then, when the Wallbreaker was covering his face with his hands, Rey Diaz took up a military-issue belt from the sofa, wrapped it around the Wallbreaker's neck, and strangled him with every ounce of his strength. Although the Wallbreaker was young, he had no way to defend himself against Rey Diaz's agile strength, and was thrown to the floor by his neck. Rey Diaz bellowed, "I'll wring your neck! You bastard! Who sent you here to play smart? Who the hell are you? Bastard! I'll wring your neck!" He tightened the belt and slammed the Wallbreaker's head into the ground repeatedly, to the crunch of teeth smacking into the floor. When the guards burst in to separate them, the Wallbreaker's face was purple, he was foaming at the mouth, and his eyes were protruding like a goldfish's.

Rey Diaz, still in a fury, struggled with the guards as he continued to shout, "Wring his neck! String him up and hang him! Right now! This is part of the plan! Do you fucking hear me? Part of the plan!"

But the three guards did not carry out his order. One of them held Rey Diaz tightly while the other two lifted up the Wallbreaker, who had recovered his breath somewhat, and started to carry him out.

"Just wait, you bastard. You won't die easy," he said, abandoning his efforts to escape the guard and have another go at the Wallbreaker. He let out a long sigh.

The Wallbreaker looked back over the guard's shoulder, a smile on his bruised and swollen face. He opened up a mouth that was missing several teeth and said, "I've lived a full life."

PDC Wallfacer Hearing

As the meeting commenced, the United States, United Kingdom, France, and Germany put up another proposition, this one demanding the immediate suspension of Rey Diaz's position as Wallfacer and his trial before the International Court of Justice for crimes against humanity.

The US representative declared, "After substantial investigation, we believe that Rey Diaz's strategic intent as disclosed by the Wallbreaker is credible. What we are facing now is a person whose crime dwarfs all of the crimes ever committed in human history. We were unable to find a single law applicable to his crime, so we recommend that the crime of Extinction of Life on Earth be added to international law, and that Rey Diaz be tried under it."

Rey Diaz appeared quite relaxed at the hearing. Sneering, he said to the US representative, "You've been trying to get rid of me, haven't you? Ever since the Wallfacer Project began, you have all applied a double standard to the Wallfacers. I'm the one you like least."

The UK representative retorted, "Wallfacer Rey Diaz's claim is baseless. In fact, the countries he is accusing are the ones who invested the most money into his plan, far exceeding what they invested in the other three Wallfacers."

"Sure," Rey Diaz said with a nod, "but the real reason you invested so heavily in my plan is because you wanted to get your hands on the stellar hydrogen bombs."

"Ridiculous! What would we do with them?" the US representative shot back. "They're incredibly inefficient weapons in a space battle, and on the Earth, there's no practical significance even for those old twenty-megaton hydrogen bombs, much less a three-hundred-megaton monster."

Rey Diaz responded calmly, "But the bombs will be the most

effective weapon in battles on other planets, particularly in wars among humans. On the desolate surface of other planets, there's no need to be concerned with civilian casualties or environmental damage, so you're free to carry out wide-area destruction, or even a devastating sweep of the entire surface. Here's where the stellar hydrogen bombs will prove useful. You must have anticipated that, as humanity expands into the Solar System, Earth's conflicts will expand outward as well. This won't change even with Trisolaris as a common enemy, and you're preparing for it. Right now, it's politically indefensible to develop superweapons for use against humans, so you took advantage of me to make them."

The US representative said, "That's the preposterous logic of a terrorist and a dictator. Rey Diaz is the kind of man who, granted the status and power of a Wallfacer, turns the Wallfacer Project into as big a danger as the Trisolaran invasion. We must take decisive action to correct this mistake."

"They're as good as their word," Rey Diaz said, turning to Garanin, the incumbent rotating chair. "The CIA has men waiting outside to arrest me as soon as I go outside after this hearing."

The rotating chair glanced in the direction of the US representative, who was fiddling intently with his pen. Garanin had first taken office at the start of the Wallfacer Project, and even he had forgotten the number of short terms in office he had served during the ensuing two decades. But this was the last time. Now white-haired, he was about to retire.

"Wallfacer Rey Diaz, if what you say is true, then that is inappropriate. So long as the principles of the Wallfacer Project still hold, Wallfacers have legal immunity, and none of their words and actions can be used as evidence to charge them of a crime," he said.

"Additionally, please remember that this is international territory," the Japanese representative said.

"So does that mean," the US representative said, raising a pencil, "that even when Rey Diaz is about to detonate the million superbombs he's buried on Mercury, society still won't be able to charge him with a crime?"

"According to the relevant provisions in the Wallfacer Act, placing limitations and curbs on the strategic plans of Wallfacers who exhibit dangerous tendencies is an entirely separate matter from the Wallfacer's own legal immunity," Garanin said.

"Rey Diaz's crimes have crossed outside the boundary of legal immunity. He must be punished. This is a precondition for the continued existence of the Wallfacer Project," the UK representative said.

"May I remind the chair and the representatives," Rey Diaz said, rising from his seat, "that this is a PDC Wallfacer hearing, and that I'm not on trial."

"You'll stand in court soon," the US representative said, with a chilly smile.

"I agree with Wallfacer Rey Diaz. We should return to the discussion of his strategic plan," Garanin said, seizing the opportunity to temporarily bypass the thorny issue.

The Japanese representative broke his silence. "From the way it looks now, the representatives have reached a consensus on the following point: Rey Diaz's strategic plan exhibits dangerous tendencies toward clear violations of human rights, and according to the relevant principles in the Wallfacer Act, it should be stopped."

"Then Proposition P269, proposed at the previous Wallfacer hearing, regarding halting Rey Diaz's strategic plan, can now be put to a vote," Garanin said.

"Mr. Chair, wait one moment." Rey Diaz raised his hand. "Before the vote, I hope I might be able to offer a final explanation of some of the details of my plan."

"If they're just details, is this really necessary?" someone asked.

"Save it for court," the UK representative said sarcastically.

"No, these details are important," Rey Diaz persisted. "Right now, let us assume that what the Wallbreaker has disclosed about my strategic intentions is true. One representative spoke of the moment when the million hydrogen bombs deployed on Mercury are ready to be detonated, at which point I will face the omnipresent sophons and declare to Trisolaris humanity's intent to die with them. What will happen then?"

315

"The Trisolarans' reaction can't be predicted, but on Earth, it's certain that billions of people will want to wring your neck, just like you did to that Wallbreaker," the French representative said.

"Exactly. So I took certain measures to deal with such a situation. Take a look at this." Rey Diaz raised his left hand and displayed his wristwatch to the assembly. It was entirely black, and the dial was twice as large and thick as a normal men's watch, although it didn't appear large on his thick wrist. "This is a transmitter sending a signal through a space link directly to Mercury."

"You'll use it to send the detonation signal?" someone asked.

"Precisely the opposite. It sends a non-detonation signal."

His words focused the attention of the entire assembly. He went on: "The system is code-named 'cradle,' meaning that when the cradle stops rocking, the baby will wake. It sends a continuous signal, received continuously on Mercury. If the signal is interrupted, then the system will immediately detonate the hydrogen bomb."

"It's called a dead-man's switch," the US representative said stoically. "In the Cold War there was research into using anti-triggers and dead-man's switches on strategic nukes, but they were never implemented. Only a madman would actually do it."

Rey Diaz brought down his left hand and covered the cradle with his sleeve. "I was taught this wonderful idea not by an expert in nuclear strategy but by an American film. In it, a man has one of these gadgets that sends out a continuous signal, but if his heart stops beating, the signal is terminated. Another man has a bomb strapped to him that's impossible to remove, and if the bomb doesn't receive the signal, it'll explode. So even though this hapless fool doesn't like the first guy, he has to do everything he can to protect him. . . . I like watching American blockbusters. Even today I can still recognize the old version of Superman."

"Do you mean that this device is tied to your heartbeat?" the Japanese representative asked. He reached over to Rey Diaz, who was standing next to him, to touch the device under his sleeve, but Rey Diaz moved his arm and stood a bit farther away.

"Of course. But the cradle is more advanced and refined than

that. It monitors not just the heartbeat but lots of other physiological indicators such as blood pressure, body temperature, and so forth, and conducts a comprehensive analysis of these parameters. If they're not normal, then it immediately stops the anti-trigger signal in the dead-man's switch. It can also recognize many of my simple voice commands."

A nervous-looking man entered the auditorium and whispered something into Garanin's ear. Before he had finished whispering, Garanin glanced up at Rey Diaz with a peculiar look in his eyes, which did not escape the keen-eyed representatives.

"There's a way to disarm your cradle. Countermeasures for anti-triggers were studied during the Cold War, too," the US representative said.

"It's not my cradle. It's the cradle for those hydrogen bombs. If the cradle stops rocking, they'll wake up," Rey Diaz said.

"I've thought of the same technique," the German representative said. "When the signal is transmitted from your watch to Mercury, it must pass through a complicated communications link. Destroying or shielding any node, then using a false signal source to continue to transmit the anti-trigger signal farther down the chain, will render your cradle system useless."

"That is indeed a problem," Rey Diaz said, with a nod at the German representative. "Without the sophons, the problem is easily solved. All the nodes are loaded with an identical encryption algorithm that generates every signal sent. To the outside world, it looks as if the signal values are random and different every time, but the cradle's sender and recipient produce a sequence of values that are identical. Only when the recipient receives a signal corresponding to its own sequence is the signal considered valid. Without this encryption algorithm, the signal sent out by your false source won't match the recipient's sequence. But the damn sophons can detect the algorithm."

"You've perhaps come up with another approach?" someone asked.

"A crude approach. Me, all my approaches are clumsy and crude,"

Rey Diaz said, with a self-mocking laugh. "I have increased the sensitivity of each node's monitoring of its own state. Specifically, each communication node is composed of several units that may be separated by a large distance, but are connected into a whole by continuous communication. If any one unit fails, the entire node will issue a command terminating the anti-trigger, after which, even if the false signal source resumes sending a signal to the next node, it will not be acknowledged. The monitoring of every unit can achieve a microsecond level of accuracy, which means that—using the German representative's approach—every unit of a node must be simultaneously destroyed and the signal resumed from the false signal source within the space of a microsecond. Every node is composed of at least three units, but may have dozens of them. These units are separated by a distance of about three hundred kilometers. Each one is built to be extremely rugged, and it will issue its warning upon any outside touch. Causing these units to fail within the space of a microsecond might be possible for the Trisolarans, but it's not currently possible for humans."

His final sentence put everyone on alert.

"I have just received a report that the thing on Rey Diaz's wrist has been sending out an electromagnetic signal," Garanin said. The atmosphere of the assembly turned tense at the news. "I'd like to ask you, Wallfacer Rey Diaz: Is the signal from your wristwatch being sent to Mercury?"

Rey Diaz chuckled a few times, then said, "Why would I be sending it to Mercury? There's nothing there but a giant pit. Besides, the cradle's space communication link hasn't been set up yet. No, no, no. You don't need to worry. The signal isn't going to Mercury. It's going somewhere in New York City, very close to us."

The air froze, and everyone in the assembly, apart from Rey Diaz, stood as shocked as wooden chickens.

"If the signal sustaining the cradle is terminated, what will it trigger?" the UK representative asked sharply, no longer attempting to mask his tension.

"Oh, something will be triggered, all right," Rey Diaz said to

him with a broad laugh. "I've been a Wallfacer for more than twenty years, and I've always been able to get a few things of my own."

"Well then, Mr. Rey Diaz, would you be able to answer an even more direct question?" the French representative said. He looked entirely calm, but there was a tremble in his voice. "How many lives will you, or will we, be responsible for?"

Rey Diaz widened his eyes at the Frenchman, as if he thought the question bizarre. "What? The number of people makes a difference? I thought all of you here were respectable gentlemen who prize human rights above all. What's the difference between one life and 8.2 million? If it's the former, then you don't have to respect it?"

The US representative stood up and said, "More than twenty years ago when the Wallfacer Project began, we pointed out what he was." Pointing a finger at Rey Diaz and spraying saliva as he spoke, he strove to contain himself, but ended up losing control. "He's a terrorist. An evil, filthy terrorist! A devil! You unstopped the bottle and let him loose, and you must take responsibility! The UN must be held responsible!" he shouted hysterically, sending his papers flying.

"Calm down, Mr. Representative," Rey Diaz said with a slight smile. "The cradle is very sensitive to my physiological indices. If I were to go into hysterics like you, if my mood wavered, it would immediately stop sending the anti-trigger signal. So you, and all of you sitting here, shouldn't make me too upset. It would be better for all of us if you could try and keep me happy."

"What are your conditions?" Garanin asked softly.

A bit of sadness crept into the smile on Rey Diaz's face as he turned toward Garanin and shook his head. "Mr. Chair, what other conditions could I name? To leave here and return to my own country. A charter plane is waiting for me at Kennedy Airport."

The assembly was silent. Unconsciously, they had all gradually turned their attention from Rey Diaz to the US representative, who, unable to stand all the eyes on him, threw himself back into his chair and hissed, "Get the hell out."

Rey Diaz slowly nodded, then stood up and walked out.

"Mr. Rey Diaz, I'll take you home," Garanin said, leaving the rostrum.

Rey Diaz stood waiting for Garanin as he walked over, less nimbly than before. "Thank you, Mr. Chair. I thought you might like to get out of here too."

The two were at the door when Rey Diaz grabbed Garanin and turned with him back toward the auditorium. "Gentlemen, I won't miss this place. I've wasted these two decades, and no one here understands me. I want to go back to my homeland, back to my people. Yes, my homeland and my people. I miss them."

To everyone's surprise, the big man's eyes shone with tears. At last he said, "I want to go back to my homeland. This is not part of the plan."

When he walked out the door of the UN General Assembly building, Rey Diaz opened his arms wide to the sun and called out with relish, "Ah, my sun!" His two-decade-long heliophobia had vanished.

Rey Diaz's flight took off, and crossed the eastern coastline to fly over the vast Atlantic Ocean.

In the cabin, Garanin said to him, "With me here, this aircraft is safe. Please tell me the location of the device you have connected to the dead-man's switch."

"There's no device. There's nothing. It was just a trick to escape." Rey Diaz took off his watch and handed it to Garanin. "This is just a simple transmitter converted from a Motorola phone. It's not connected to my heartbeat, either. It's been turned off. Keep it as a souvenir."

For a long time neither of them spoke. Then Garanin sighed and said, "How did this happen? The Wallfacers' privilege of sealed-off strategic thinking was meant to be used against the sophons and Trisolaris. But you and Tyler both used it against humanity."

"There's nothing strange about that," Rey Diaz said. He sat next to the window, enjoying the sunlight shining in from the outside. "Right now, the greatest obstacle to humanity's survival comes from itself."

Six hours later, the plane touched down at Caracas International Airport on the Caribbean coast. Garanin did not get off. He would be taking the plane back to the UN.

When they parted, Rey Diaz said, "Don't abort the Wallfacer Project. It really is a hope amid this war. There are still two Wallfacers. Please wish them the best for me."

"I won't be seeing them, either," Garanin said, with emotion. By the time Rey Diaz walked off, leaving him alone in the cabin, he was in tears.

The sky over Caracas was as clear as in New York. Rey Diaz walked down the airstair and smelled the familiar tropical atmosphere, then bent down and gave a long kiss to the ground of his homeland. Then, guarded by a large detachment of military police, he took a motorcade to the city. After half an hour on a winding mountain road, they entered the capital and drove up to the city center and Plaza Bolívar. At the statue of Simón Bolívar, Rey Diaz got out of the car and stood on the statue's base. Above him on horseback was the great armor-clad hero who had defeated the Spanish and tried to establish a unified Republic of Gran Colombia in South America. In front of him, a crowd of frenetic people boiled under the sun, swelling forward, only to be met with the vigorous resistance of the military police. Shots were fired into the air, but the tide of people eventually surged past the police line and poured toward the living Bolívar at the foot of the statue.

Rey Diaz held up his hands, and, with tears in his eyes, called out to the crowd in a voice dripping with emotion, "Ah, my people!"

The first stone thrown by his people struck him on his outstretched left hand, the second hit him in the chest, and the third smashed into his forehead and nearly knocked him out. After that, the people's stones came like raindrops, and had practically buried his lifeless body by the end. The last stone that hit Wallfacer Rey Diaz was thrown by an old woman, who struggled to carry it up to his corpse, then said, in Spanish, "Evildoer! You would kill everyone. My grandson would have been there. You'd have killed my grandson!"

Then, using all the strength in her trembling hands, she slammed her stone against Rey Diaz's broken skull, where it lay exposed beneath the pile of rocks.

Time is the one thing that can't be stopped. Like a sharp blade, it silently cuts through hard and soft, constantly advancing. Nothing is capable of jolting it even the slightest bit, but it changes everything.

The same year as the Mercury test, Chang Weisi retired. In his final media appearance, he frankly acknowledged that he himself had no confidence in victory, but this did not affect history's high opinion of the work of the space force's first commander. Working for so many years in a state of anxiety had damaged his health, and he died at the age of sixty-eight. The general was lucid on his deathbed and mentioned Zhang Beihai's name many times.

After leaving her second term in office, Secretary General Say launched the Human Memorial Project, whose goal was the comprehensive collection of data and commemorative artifacts of human civilization that would ultimately be sent out into the cosmos on unmanned spacecraft. The project's most influential component was called the Human Diary, a Web site that was set up to allow as many people as possible to record their lifetimes in the form of text and images from their everyday lives, to become part of the data of civilization. The Human Diary Web site eventually grew to have more than two billion users and formed the largest-ever body of information on the Internet. Later, the PDC, believing that the Human Memorial Project contributed to defeatism, passed a resolution stopping its further development, and even equated it with Escapism. But Say continued to pour her individual efforts into the project until she passed away at the age of eighty-four.

After retirement, Garanin and Kent made the same choice: to seclude themselves in that Garden of Eden in northern Europe where Luo Ji had lived for five years. They were never again seen by the outside world, and no one even knew the exact date they

died. But one thing was certain: They lived a long time. Some said that the two of them reached the century mark before dying a natural death.

Just as Keiko Yamasuki had predicted, Wu Yue spent the remainder of his life in depression and confusion. He worked for more than a decade on the Human Memorial Project but was unable to find any solace in it, and he passed away in loneliness at the age of seventy-seven. Like Chang Weisi, Wu Yue had Zhang Beihai's name on his lips in his final moments. They pinned their shared hopes for the future on the stalwart warrior now hibernating through time.

Dr. Albert Ringier and General Fitzroy both lived into their eighties and saw the completion of the hundred-meter Hubble III Space Telescope, which they used to look at the planet Trisolaris. But they never again saw the Trisolaran Fleet or the probes now flying ahead of it. They did not live long enough for them to cross the third patch of snow.

The lives of ordinary people continued and ended as well. Out of the three old Beijing neighbors, Miao Fuquan was the first to depart, passing away at the age of seventy-five. He really did have his son bury him two hundred meters down an abandoned mine, and his son obeyed his last wishes to blow up the mine wall and erect a tombstone to remember him. According to his father's will, the last generation before the Doomsday Battle was supposed to clear out the tombstone, and if humanity won, then it could be restored to its original location. But, in fact, less than half a century after his death, the area over the mine shaft became a desert. The tombstone disappeared, the mine's location was lost, and the Miao family's descendants couldn't be bothered to look for it.

Zhang Yuanchao died of illness like an ordinary person at the age of eighty, and, like an ordinary person, he was cremated. His ashes were laid in an ordinary rectangular slot on a long rack in a public cemetery.

Yang Jinwen lived till ninety-two, and the alloy vessel containing his remains headed out of the Solar System and into the

vast cosmos at the third cosmic velocity. This consumed all of his savings.

But Ding Yi lived on. After the breakthrough in controlled fusion technology, he turned his attention to theoretical physics, looking for ways to escape sophon interference in high-energy particle physics experiments. He had no success. When he reached his seventies, he had, like other physicists, abandoned all hope of the possibility of a breakthrough. He entered hibernation and planned to wake at the Doomsday Battle. His sole desire was to be able to see with his own eyes the superior technology of Trisolaris.

In the century following the start of the Trisolar Crisis, everyone who had lived through the Golden Age passed away. It was an era that was constantly recalled, and the old folks who had lived through those grand times chewed over their memories of it like ruminants, savoring the flavors. They always closed with one line: "Ah, if only we knew how to cherish things back then." Young people would listen to their stories with a mixture of envy and skepticism. That fabled peace, prosperity, and happiness, that ideal utopia free from care: Did it ever really exist?

As the elderly passed away, the departed Golden Shore vanished into the smoke of history. The ship of human civilization floated alone in the vast ocean, surrounded on all sides by endless, sinister waves, and no one knew if there even was an opposite shore.

PART III

THE
DARK
FOREST

Year 205, Crisis Era

Distance of the Trisolaran Fleet from the Solar System:
2.10 light-years

Darkness. Before the darkness there was nothing but nothingness, and the nothingness was without color. Nothing was in the nothingness. Darkness at least meant that there was space. Soon, disturbances appeared in the darkness of space, penetrating every thing like a gentle breeze. It was the sensation of time passing, for the nothingness was without time, but now time took shape in a glacial thaw. Only much later was there light, at first as a shapeless blob of brightness, and then, after another long wait, the shape of the world gradually emerged. The newly resurrected consciousness struggled to make sense of it, at first managing to work out a few thin, transparent tubes, then a human face behind them, which quickly disappeared, exposing the creamy-white light of the ceiling.

Luo Ji awoke from hibernation.

The face reappeared. It belonged to a man with a gentle expression who looked at Luo Ji and said, "Welcome to our era." As he spoke, a field of vibrant roses flashed on his white lab coat, then gradually faded and disappeared. As he continued speaking, the coat displayed a continuous assortment of delightful images that matched his expressions and emotions: seas, sunsets, and woods in the drizzle. He told Luo Ji that his illness had been cured during hibernation, and that his reawakening had gone smoothly.

Recovery would take just three days or so, and then he would completely regain normal bodily functions. . . .

Luo Ji's mind, still sluggish and only partially awake, caught just one piece of information out of everything the doctor said: This was year 205 of the Crisis Era, and he had been in hibernation for 185 years.

He found the doctor's accent peculiar at first, but he soon discovered that although the sounds of standard Mandarin hadn't changed much, it had been stuffed with a large quantity of English words. As the doctor spoke, the text of what he said was displayed on the ceiling, apparently through voice recognition. Perhaps to help the newly awakened better understand, the English words were replaced with Chinese characters.

At last the doctor said that Luo Ji could be transferred from the revival room to the general ward. His coat showed an evening scene in which a setting sun rapidly turned into a starry sky to say farewell. As this was going on, Luo Ji felt his bed begin to move. Just out the door, he heard the doctor call out, "Next." Twisting his head back to look, he saw another bed enter the revival room bearing someone who had obviously just been taken out of the hibernation chamber. The bed was quickly wheeled to a bank of monitors, and the doctor, his coat now a pure white, tapped on the wall with a finger, causing one-third of it to display complex curves and data that he began to manipulate intensely.

Luo Ji realized that his own reawakening was probably not a major event at all, but rather just a part of day-to-day work here. The doctor was friendly, but in his eyes Luo Ji was nothing more than an ordinary hibernator.

Like the revival room, the hallway had no lamps. The walls themselves emitted light, and although it was soft, Luo Ji still had to squint. But as he did so, the walls in the section of corridor he was in dimmed, and the dimmed segment followed him as his bed moved. Once his eyes grew accustomed to the light, he opened them again, at which point the hallway brightened again, remaining in his comfort zone. Evidently the hallway's

brightness adjustment system was able to monitor the changes in his pupils.

Judging by that, he had to be in a personalized age.

This far exceeded his expectations.

As the walls passed slowly by, he saw lots of activated displays of different sizes randomly distributed on them. Some of them were moving images that he didn't have the time to look at clearly, and might have been left behind by users who forgot to turn them off.

Sometimes, his automatic bed crossed paths with people walking down the hallway. He noticed that both the soles of their feet and the bed's wheels made luminous, watery waves of pressure where they contacted the ground, like what used to happen when you pressed a finger onto an LCD in his own time. The long corridor gave him an intense sense of cleanliness, as clean as a 3-D computer animation, although he knew all of it was real. He moved through it with a sense of tranquility and comfort he had never known before.

But what impressed him most about the people he saw was that everyone—doctors, nurses, and nonstaff alike—appeared clean and elegant, and smiled warmly at him or waved when they approached. Their clothes displayed gorgeous images, a different style for each person, some abstract, others concrete. He was won over by their expressions, because he knew that the eyes of ordinary people were the best reflection of the level of civilization in a time and place. He had once seen a set of photos taken by European photographers in the late Qing Dynasty, and his deepest impression had been of the dull expressions of the people in the photographs. Officials and commoners alike had eyes that revealed only numbness and stupidity, lacking the slightest shred of vitality. When the people of this new era looked at Luo Ji's eyes, they might be having the same feeling about him. The gazes that crossed his own were full of a vigorous wisdom, and a sincerity, understanding, and love that he had rarely perceived in his own age. But what impressed him most was the confidence in their expressions. The sunny confidence that filled every pair of eyes had evidently become the spiritual backdrop for the people of this new era.

This did not seem to be an age of despair, and that was another unexpected surprise.

Luo Ji's bed moved soundlessly into the general ward, which held two more reawakened hibernators. One of them was lying on a bed. The other, next to the door, was packing his things with a nurse's help and seemed about ready to leave. From the look in their eyes, Luo Ji knew that both of them were from his own era. Their eyes were like the windows of time, and through them he had another glance of that gray era he had come from.

"How can they be that way? I'm their great-grandfather!" Luo Ji heard the hibernator who was about to leave complaining.

"You can't pull seniority in front of them. It's the law: Hibernation doesn't count as age, so in the presence of the elderly, you're the younger generation. . . . Let's go. They've waited in the reception room long enough," the nurse said. Although she tried to avoid English words, sometimes she stumbled over Chinese words, as if speaking an ancient tongue, and was forced to use the modern language. Then the wall would display a translation into Chinese.

"I can't even understand it when they talk. All that bird-speak mixed in!" the hibernator said, as he and the nurse each picked up a bag and went out the door.

"In this age, you've got to keep learning. Otherwise, you'll just have to go live up top," Luo Ji heard the nurse say. By now he could understand the modern language without difficulty, but he was still unclear what the nurse meant by her last sentence.

"Hello. Did you hibernate due to illness?" the hibernator in the bed beside Luo Ji asked. He was young, and looked to be in his early twenties.

Luo Ji opened his mouth but no sound came out. The young man smiled at him encouragingly. "You can speak. Try harder!"

"Hello," Luo Ji managed hoarsely.

The young man nodded. "The one who just left did. I didn't. I came here to escape from reality. Oh, and my name's Xiong Wen."

"Here . . . how is it?" Luo Ji asked, much more easily this time.

"I don't really know. I've only been here five days. Still, it's

330

definitely a good era. But for us, it's bound to be difficult to integrate into society. Mostly because we woke up too soon. A few years later would have been better."

"A few years later? Wouldn't that be even harder?"

"No. It's still a state of war now, so society can't take care of us. In a few decades, after the peace talks, there'll be peace and prosperity."

"Peace talks? With whom?!"

"Trisolaris, of course."

Shaken by Xiong Wen's final statement, Luo Ji strove to sit up. A nurse entered and helped him up to a half-sitting position in bed.

"They said they want peace talks?" he asked anxiously.

"Not yet. But they'll have no other choice," Xiong Wen said, nimbly getting out of his bed and coming over to sit down on Luo Ji's. He had clearly been anticipating the pleasure of introducing someone newly awakened to this era. "Don't you know? Humanity is amazing now. Simply amazing!"

"How?"

"Our spacecraft are incredibly powerful. Far more powerful than Trisolaran ships!"

"How is that possible?"

"Why wouldn't it be? Put the superweapons aside and look purely at speed. They can reach fifteen percent of the speed of light! Tons faster than the Trisolarans!"

When Luo Ji turned a skeptical eye toward the nurse, he noticed that she was exceptionally pretty. Everyone in this age seemed to be attractive. She nodded with a smile. "It's true."

Xiong Wen went on, "And do you know how many ships there are in the space fleet? I'll tell you: two thousand! Twice as many as the Trisolarans! And the number's still growing!"

Luo Ji glanced again at the nurse, who nodded.

"You know how badly off the Trisolaran Fleet is now? In two centuries they've passed through the, ah, the space dust they call the snow patch three times. I heard someone say that the most recent time was four years ago, and the telescope observed that

their formation has become sparser. They're not holding together. More than half of the ships stopped accelerating long ago, and they decelerated considerably when they crossed the dust. They're crawling now, and they won't reach the Solar System for more than eight hundred years. They might already be broken hulks. Projecting from their current speed, no more than three hundred ships will arrive on time two centuries from now. However, one Trisolaran probe will reach the Solar System soon. This year. The other nine are following afterward and will get here three years later."

"The probe . . . What's that?" Luo Ji asked in confusion.

The nurse said, "We don't encourage the exchange of practical information. When the previous reawakened hibernator learned about these things, it took him many days to calm down. It's not conducive to recovery."

"It makes me happy, so what's it to you?" Xiong Wen said with a shrug. Then he returned to his own bed to lie down. As he lay watching the soft light emitted by the ceiling, he sighed, "The kids are all right. They're really all right."

"Who's a kid?" the nurse sniffed. "Hibernation doesn't count as age. You're the kid." To Luo Ji's eyes, she actually looked younger than Xiong Wen, although he knew that his appearance-based judgment of age might not be accurate in this era.

The nurse said to him, "The people from your time are all pretty despairing. But things aren't really all that serious."

To Luo Ji, this was the voice of an angel. He felt like he had turned into a child who had just awakened from a nightmare, and all the frightening things he had experienced were taken care of by a smile from an adult. When she spoke, her nurse's uniform shone a fast-rising sun, and under its golden light, the dry yellow earth turned green, and flowers bloomed in wild abandon. . . .

When the nurse had gone, Luo Ji asked Xiong Wen, "What about the Wallfacer Project?"

Xiong Wen shook his head in confusion. "Wallfacer . . . ? Never heard of it."

Luo Ji asked when Xiong Wen had entered hibernation. It had been before the Wallfacer Project had started, when hibernation was very expensive. His family must have had money. But if he hadn't heard anything about the Wallfacer Project in the five days he had been awake, that meant that even if the program hadn't been forgotten in this era, it was no longer important.

Next, Luo Ji personally experienced the level of technology of this new age in two trivial areas.

Soon after he entered the ward, the nurse carried in his first meal after reawakening, a very small quantity of milk and bread and jam, because his stomach functions were still recovering. He took a bite of bread and felt like he was chewing sawdust.

"Your sense of taste is still recovering, too," the nurse said.

"It'll taste even worse once you've recovered," Xiong Wen said.

The nurse laughed. "Of course, it's not as good as the food grown on the surface in your era."

"Then where does this come from?" Luo Ji asked, through his full mouth.

"It's produced in a factory."

"You're able to synthesize grain?"

Xiong Wen answered for the nurse. "There's no other option but to synthesize it. The land won't grow any crops anymore."

Luo Ji felt sorry for Xiong Wen. There had been people in his era who had become immune to technology and were indifferent to any sort of technological wonder, and Xiong Wen was apparently one of them. He was unable to properly appreciate this new age.

The next discovery was an incredible shock to Luo Ji, although the thing itself was still quite plain. The nurse pointed to the cup of milk and told him that it had been put into a heating cup especially for hibernators, because the people of this era generally did not drink hot liquids. Even coffee was taken cold. If he wasn't used to drinking cold milk, he could heat it up simply by moving a slider near the bottom of the cup to the desired temperature. When he finished drinking, he inspected the cup. It looked like an ordinary glass cup apart from a thick, opaque base which must contain the

heat source. But no matter how hard he looked, he couldn't find any controls but the slider, and when he tried to twist the base, he found it was integrated with the rest of the cup.

"Don't mess around with the supplies. You don't understand them yet. It's dangerous," the nurse said after watching Luo Ji's efforts.

"I'd like to know where it gets recharged."

"Re . . . charged?" The nurse awkwardly repeated the word, evidently hearing it for the first time.

"*Charge. Recharge,*" Luo Ji said in English, but the nurse just shook her head in confusion.

"What happens when the batteries run out?"

"Batteries?"

"*Batteries,*" he said in English. "You don't have batteries anymore?" When the nurse shook her head again, he said, "Then where does the electricity in the cup come from?"

"Electricity? There's electricity everywhere," the nurse said disapprovingly.

"The electricity in the cup won't run out?"

"It won't run out."

"It's inexhaustible?!"

"Inexhaustible. How could electricity run out?"

When the nurse left, Luo Ji still was unable to let go of the cup. He ignored Xiong Wen's ridicule, for his surging emotions told him that he was holding a sacred object, the age-old dream of humanity: a perpetual motion machine. If humanity had really achieved inexhaustible energy, then they could achieve practically everything. Now he believed the words of the pretty nurse: Things might not be so serious.

When the doctor came into the ward for a routine checkup, Luo Ji asked him about the Wallfacer Project.

"I know of it. It's an ancient joke," the doctor replied offhandedly.

"What happened to the Wallfacers?"

"I think one of them committed suicide, and another was

stoned to death. . . . It all happened in the project's early days, and it's been nearly two centuries since then."

"And the other two?"

"I don't know. They're probably still in hibernation."

"One of them was Chinese. Do you remember him?" Luo Ji ventured, staring nervously at the doctor.

"You mean the one who cast a spell on a star? I think he was mentioned in premodern history class," the nurse interjected.

"Right. And now he's . . ." Luo Ji said.

"I don't know. I think he's still in hibernation. I don't pay much attention to that stuff," the doctor said absently.

"And the star? The one he cursed, the star with a planet? What happened to it?" he asked, his heart tensing up.

"What do you think happened? It's probably still there. That spell? What a joke!"

"So nothing at all happened to that star?"

"Nothing I've heard, at any rate. You?" he asked the nurse.

"Me neither," she said, shaking her head. "The world was scared to death back then and lots of silly things happened."

"And then?" Luo Ji said with a sigh.

"Then there was the Great Ravine," the doctor said.

"The Great Ravine? What was that?"

"You'll find out later. For now, rest up," the doctor said with a gentle sigh. "But it's probably better that you don't know about it." As he turned to leave, his white coat displayed billowing dark clouds, and the nurse's uniform displayed lots of pairs of eyes, some of them frightened, some brimming with tears.

When the doctor had left, Luo Ji sat motionless on his bed for a long while, mumbling to himself, "A joke. An ancient joke." Then he began laughing, silently at first, and then in great guffaws, trembling on his bed and frightening Xiong Wen, who wanted to call the doctor.

"I'm fine. Go to sleep," Luo Ji told him. Then he lay down and soon fell asleep for the first time since his reawakening.

He dreamed of Zhuang Yan and the child. As before, Zhuang Yan walked through the snow, the child asleep in her arms.

When he awoke, the nurse walked in and said good morning to him. Her voice was soft so as not to wake the still-sleeping Xiong Wen.

"Is it morning? Why aren't there any windows in this room?" Luo Ji asked, looking around.

"Any place on the wall can turn transparent. But the doctors feel that you aren't ready to look outside. It's too unfamiliar, and it will distract you and affect your rest."

"I've been revived for a while now, but I still don't know what the outside world is like. This affects my rest." Luo Ji pointed at Xiong Wen, and said, "I'm not that kind of person."

The nurse laughed. "That's okay. I'm about to go off shift. Shall I take you out for a look around? You can have breakfast after you get back."

Excitedly, Luo Ji followed the nurse to the on-call room. Looking it over, he could guess what about half of the furnishings were, but he had no idea what the rest were for. There was no computer or similar equipment, but because a display could be activated anywhere on the walls, this was to be expected. Three umbrellas lined up outside the door caught his attention. They were in different styles, but from their shape, they were definitely umbrellas. What surprised him was their bulk. Weren't there folding umbrellas in this age?

The nurse came out of the changing room dressed in her own clothes. Aside from the flashing movies on the fabric, changes to women's fashion in this age were well within the scope of Luo Ji's imagination. Compared to his own era, the major difference was their conspicuous asymmetry. He was pleased that after 185 years had passed, he could still find beauty in women's clothing. The nurse picked up one of the umbrellas, which must have been fairly heavy, because she had to carry it over her shoulder.

"Is it raining out?"

She shook her head. "You think I'm carrying an . . . umbrella?" she said, unfamiliar with the last word.

"If it's not an umbrella, then what is it?" Luo Ji pointed to the

device on her shoulder, imagining that she would say some peculiar name for it.

But she didn't. "It's my bicycle," she said.

When they arrived in the corridor, Luo Ji asked, "Is your home far from here?"

"If you're talking about where I live, it's not far. Ten or twenty minutes biking," she said. Then, standing still and fixing him with her charming eyes, she said something that shocked him: "There are no homes now. No one has them. Marriage, family, they went away after the Great Ravine. That will be the first thing you'll have to get used to."

"That first thing is something I won't be able to get used to."

"Oh, I don't know. In history class I learned that marriage and family had already begun to disintegrate in your own time. Lots of people didn't want to be tied down. They wanted free lives." This was the second time she had mentioned history class.

I was like that once, but then . . . Luo Ji said to himself. From the moment he'd reawakened, Zhuang Yan and the child had never really left his mind. They were the desktop wallpaper of his consciousness, perpetually on display. But no one here recognized him, and with the situation so uncertain, he couldn't just rashly ask about their whereabouts, even though he was tormented by longing.

They walked a ways down the corridor. Then, after they'd passed through an automatic door, Luo Ji's eyes lit up as he saw a narrow platform extending into the distance and felt fresh air blowing toward him. He sensed that he was now outside.

"What a blue sky!" was the first thing he shouted to the outside world.

"Really? It can't compare to the blue skies of your era."

Definitely bluer. Much bluer. Luo Ji didn't say that out loud, just reveled in the boundless blue embrace and let his soul melt. Then he had a flash of doubt: Was this heaven? In his memory, he had only ever seen such a pure blue sky during the five years he had spent apart from the world, secluded in his Garden of Eden. But this blue sky had fewer white clouds, just a couple of pale wisps in

the western sky, like someone had unintentionally left a smudge. The sun that had just risen in the east shone like crystal in the entirely transparent air, with its edge rimmed in dew.

Luo Ji turned his eyes downward and immediately became dizzy. From high up, it took him a long moment to realize that what he saw from here was the city. At first he thought he was looking at a giant forest, the slender tree trunks stretching straight up toward the sky, each one sprouting perpendicular branches of varying lengths. The city's buildings were the leaves hanging off these branches. The layout of the city looked random, and different trees had different densities of leaves. The Hibernation and Reawakening Center formed a part of one of those large trees, and the leaf that contained his bed hung from the narrow platform that now extended out in front of him.

Looking back, the tree trunk his branch was connected to extended so far upward that it disappeared out of view. The branch they were on was located in the middle to upper section of the tree, and above and below them he could see other branches, and the structural leaves that hung on them. On closer inspection, the branches formed an intricate network of bridges in space, bridges with one end left floating in midair.

"What is this place?" Luo Ji asked.

"Beijing."

He looked at the nurse, even prettier now in the morning sun. Looking back at the place she called Beijing, he asked, "Where's the city center?"

"In that direction. We're outside the West Fourth Ring, in Tree 179, Branch 23, Leaf 18, so you're almost able to see the entire city."

Luo Ji looked for a bit into the distance where she pointed, and then exclaimed, "Impossible! How is there nothing left?"

"What would be left? In your day, there was absolutely nothing here!"

"Nothing? The Imperial Palace? Jingshan Park? Tiananmen? The China World Trade Center? It hasn't even been two hundred years. It can't all have been torn down."

"All those things are still there."

"Where?"

"On the surface."

Seeing Luo Ji's terrified look, she burst out laughing so hard that she had to lean on the railing for support. "Ah, haha. I forgot. I'm really sorry. I've forgotten so many times. Look, we're underground here. A thousand meters beneath the surface . . . If I ever get to time travel to your time, you can get back at me and forget to tell me that the city's on the surface, and I'll be as terrified as you are now. Ha ha ha . . ."

"But . . . this . . ." He held up his hands.

"The sky is fake. The sun is fake, too," the woman said, trying to suppress a smile. "Of course, saying it's fake isn't right, either, because it's an image taken from an altitude of ten thousand meters and displayed down here, so maybe it counts as real, too."

"Why build the city below ground? And a thousand meters— that's really deep."

"For the war, of course. Think about it. When the Doomsday Battle comes, won't the surface be an ocean of fire? Yeah, that battle is another outdated idea now, but when the Great Ravine ended, all the world's cities developed underground."

"So all the cities in the world are underground now?"

"The majority of them."

Luo Ji took stock of the world again. Now he understood that the trunks of the great trees were the pillars supporting the vault of the underground world, and also served as the columns from which the city's buildings were suspended.

"You won't be claustrophobic. Look at how broad the sky is! Up on the surface, the sky's not nearly this wonderful."

Luo Ji looked again at the blue sky, or rather the projection of the blue sky. He now noticed a few small objects—just some scattered bits, at first, but once his eyes got used to looking, he saw that there were so many that they covered the entire sky. Strangely, the objects in the sky reminded him of someplace completely unrelated, the showcase of a jewelry store. Before he became a Wallfacer, back

when he had fallen in love with the Zhuang Yan of his imagination, he had once been so obsessed that he wanted to buy his imaginary angel a present. He went to the jewelry store and looked at all the platinum pendants in the showcase, every one of them exquisite, lying there on the black velvet and twinkling under the spotlights. If the black velvet had been blue, then it would have been just like the sky he saw today.

"Is that the space fleet?" he asked excitedly.

"No. The fleet isn't visible from here. It's beyond the asteroid belt. Those, well, they're everything. The ones with a visible shape are space cities, and the points of light are civilian spacecraft. But sometimes there are warships in orbit, too. Their engines are very bright, so you can't stare at them. . . . Okay, I've got to get going. You should head back soon. It gets windy here."

Luo Ji turned around to say good-bye, but was so surprised he couldn't speak. The woman had her umbrella—or, rather, her bicycle—positioned on her back like a backpack, and then it stood up in back of her and opened overhead to form two coaxial propellers that started up silently, turning in opposition to offset rotational torque. Then she lifted slowly up into the air and hopped over the railing beside her into the abyss that had so dazzled him.

Suspended there, she called to him: "You can see how this is a pretty decent age. Think of your past as a dream. See you tomorrow!"

She flew gracefully, the small propellers churning the sunlight, until she turned into a tiny dragonfly between two giant trees in the distance. Swarms of these dragonflies flew between the giant trees of the city. More notable still were the streams of flying cars like schools of fish navigating endlessly among the plants on the ocean floor. The rising sun shone onto the city and was cut into shafts of light by the trees, coating the traffic with a layer of gold.

Tears streamed down Luo Ji's face at the sight of this brave new world, and the sensation of newborn life permeated his every cell. The past really was a dream.

———

When he saw the European man in the reception room, Luo Ji got the feeling that there was something different about him. Later, he realized that it was because the formal suit he wore didn't flash or display any image, but resembled the clothing of a bygone era. Perhaps this was an expression of solemnity.

After Luo Ji shook his hand, the visitor introduced himself. "I'm Special Commissioner Ben Jonathan from the Solar Fleet Joint Conference. I arranged your reawakening at the committee's behest, and now, we're going to attend the final hearing of the Wallfacer Project. Oh, can you understand me? English has changed quite a bit."

Luo Ji *could* understand what Jonathan said, but listening to him speak, the sense of Western cultural invasion that Luo Ji had felt over the past few days because of the changes to modern Chinese disappeared, because Jonathan's English was peppered with Chinese vocabulary. He said "Wallfacer Project" in Chinese, for example. English, formerly the most widely used language, and Chinese, spoken by the largest population, had blended with each other without distinction to become the world's most powerful language. Luo Ji learned later that the other languages of the world were undergoing the same fusion.

The past isn't a dream, Luo Ji thought. *The past catches up with you.* Then he recalled that Jonathan had said the word "final" and wondered if there was hope of a quick resolution after all.

Jonathan looked back, as if to make sure the door had been closed, and then walked over to the wall and activated an interface. He gave a few simple taps on the surface, and then all four walls and the ceiling disappeared into a holographic display.

Now Luo Ji found himself in an auditorium. Although everything was greatly changed, and the walls and table glowed softly, the designers had clearly tried to replicate the style of the old era. Everything from the great circular table and the rostrum to the overall layout embodied a nostalgia that allowed him to know at once where he was. The auditorium was empty but for two staffers laying out documents on the tables. Luo Ji was astonished to see

that paper documents were still being used. Just like Jonathan's clothes, this seemed to be an expression of solemnity.

"Remote meetings are a common practice now. Taking part in this way won't affect the meeting's importance or seriousness," Jonathan said. "There's still some time before the hearing begins, and you look like you don't know much about the outside world. Do you need me to tell you a bit about the basics?"

Luo Ji nodded. "Of course. Thank you."

Jonathan pointed to the auditorium and said, "I'll be brief. First, the countries. Europe is a single country, called the European Commonwealth, and it includes both eastern and western Europe, but not Russia. Russia and Belarus unified into a country still called the Russian Federation. Canada's French-speaking and English-speaking areas split into two countries. There have been some changes in other regions, too, but these are the major ones."

Luo Ji was shocked. "Those are the only changes? It's been nearly two centuries. I'd have thought the changes would have made the world unrecognizable."

Jonathan turned back from the auditorium and nodded solemnly at Luo Ji. "Unrecognizable, Dr. Luo. The world is indeed unrecognizable."

"No, there were early signs of those changes in our era."

"But there's one thing you never anticipated: There are no longer any great powers. All countries have declined in political power."

"All the countries? Then who rose up?"

"A suprastate entity: the space fleet."

Luo Ji thought this over for a while before realizing what Jonathan meant. "You mean the space fleet is independent?"

"Yes. The fleets do not belong to any country. They form independent political and economic entities that, like countries, are members of the UN. Right now, there are three major fleets in the Solar System: the Asian Fleet, the European Fleet, and the North American Fleet. Their names refer only to their primary region of origin, but the fleets themselves are no longer subordinate to those

regions. They are entirely independent. Each one possesses the political and economic might of a superpower of your era."

"My god," Luo Ji exclaimed.

"But please don't misunderstand. Earth is not ruled by a military government. The territory and sovereignty of the space fleets is in space, and they rarely interfere with the internal affairs of terrestrial society. This is stipulated by the UN charter. So right now the human world is divided into two international spheres: the traditional Earth International, and the newly emerged Fleet International. The three fleets of Fleet International—the Asian, European, and North American—make up the Solar Fleet, and the former Planetary Defense Council evolved into the Solar Fleet Joint Conference, nominally the highest command body in the Solar Fleet. However, as with the UN, it has a coordinating function, but no real power. In fact, it's a Solar Fleet in name only. The actual power of humanity's space-based armed forces lies in the hands of the supreme command of the three major fleets.

"Well, then, you now know enough to take part in today's hearing. It was convened by the SFJC, which inherited the Wallfacer Project."

Then a window opened up on the holographic display, and an image of Bill Hines and Keiko Yamasuki appeared in it. They looked unchanged. Hines greeted Luo Ji with a smile, but Yamasuki sat impassively next to him, giving only a slight nod of acknowledgement at Luo Ji's greeting.

Hines said, "I just woke up, Dr. Luo. I was quite sorry to learn that that planet you cursed is still orbiting its star fifty light-years away."

"Heh. A joke. An ancient joke," Luo Ji said self-mockingly, with a wave of his hand.

"But compared to Tyler and Rey Diaz, you're pretty lucky."

"You appear to be the only successful Wallfacer. Perhaps your strategy really has elevated human intelligence."

Hines displayed the same self-mocking smile that Luo Ji had just exhibited, and he shook his head. "No, it really hasn't. I know

now that after we entered hibernation, research into the human mind quickly encountered an insurmountable obstacle. Going forward meant approaching the quantum level of the brain's thought mechanisms. But at that point, like all other science, they hit the impassible sophon barrier. We didn't elevate human intelligence. If I did anything at all, it was just to increase some people's confidence."

When Luo Ji entered hibernation, the mental seal had not yet been developed, so he didn't really understand the last thing Hines said. But he noticed that when he said it, a mysterious smile flashed across Keiko Yamasuki's frosty face.

The window vanished, and then Luo Ji realized that the auditorium was full of people. Most of them were dressed in military uniforms whose styles hadn't changed all that much. None of the attendees had pictures decorating their clothing, but their lapel pins and epaulets all glowed.

The SFJC still used a rotating chair system. It was currently held by a civilian officer. As Luo Ji looked at him, he was reminded of Garanin. The thought struck him that he was an ancient man from two centuries ago, but he was at least fortunate compared to those of his own age who had been annihilated by the river of time.

Once the meeting opened, the chair spoke. "Representatives, at this hearing, we will hold the final vote on Proposition 649, put forth by the North American Fleet and the European Fleet at the forty-seventh Joint Conference this year. First, let me read the proposition.

"In the second year of the Trisolar Crisis, the UN's Planetary Defense Council established the Wallfacer Project. It was adopted unanimously by the permanent members of the UN and was implemented the following year. At its core, the Wallfacer Project attempted to develop hidden strategies for resisting the Trisolaran invasion by tasking four Wallfacers nominated by permanent member states with formulating and executing strategic plans in the seclusion of their own minds, out of reach of the sophons' omnipresent surveillance. The UN promulgated the Wallfacer

344

Act to guarantee privileges to the Wallfacers for formulating and executing their plans.

"The Wallfacer Project has been going on for two hundred five years to date, a time frame that has included more than a century's hiatus. During this time, leadership of the project passed from the former PDC to the present SFJC.

"The Wallfacer Project arose out of a unique historical background. The Trisolar Crisis had just begun, and in the face of a devastating crisis unheard of in human history, the international community had descended to unprecedented levels of fear and despair. This was the climate into which the Wallfacer Project was born. It was not a rational choice, but a struggle of desperation.

"The facts of history have proven that, as a strategic plan, the Wallfacer Project was a complete and utter failure. It is no exaggeration to say that it was the most naïve and foolish action that human society as a whole has ever taken. The Wallfacers were granted unprecedented power without any legal oversight, and even possessed the freedom to deceive the international community. This violated the basic moral and legal norms of human society.

"During the execution of the Wallfacer Project, enormous quantities of strategic resources were exhausted for no reason. Wallfacer Frederick Tyler's mosquito swarm was proven to have no strategic significance, while Wallfacer Manuel Rey Diaz's Mercury-chain-reaction plan was unrealizable, even given humanity's present capabilities. Moreover, both of those plans were criminal. Tyler sought to attack and wipe out Earth's fleet, while Rey Diaz's even more sinister goal was to hold every life on the planet hostage.

"The other two Wallfacers were similarly disappointing. The true strategic intent of Wallfacer Hines's mental upgrade plan has not yet been revealed, but the use in the space forces of its preliminary result, the mental seal, is also a crime. It is a serious violation of freedom of thought, which is the foundation of the survival and further progress of human civilization. As for Wallfacer Luo Ji, he

first irresponsibly squandered public funds on his own hedonistic lifestyle and then played to the crowds with ridiculous mysticism.

"We believe that given the decisive growth in humanity's strength and its seizure of the initiative in the war, the Wallfacer Project no longer has any meaning. The time has come to bring the problem that history has passed down to us to an end. We propose that the SFJC immediately terminate the Wallfacer Project and abolish the UN Wallfacer Act.

"Here ends the proposition."

The chair slowly set down the proposal document, and, glancing around the auditorium, said, "We will commence the vote on SFJC Proposition 649. All in favor?"

All of the representatives raised their hands.

Voting in this era was still done by primitive methods. Staffers walked through the auditorium solemnly verifying the number of votes, and when they reported the result to the chair, he announced, "Proposition 649 has passed unanimously and is effective immediately." The chair raised his head. Luo Ji didn't know whether he was looking at Hines or himself, because, like at the first remote hearing he had attended 185 years before, he still didn't know where in the auditorium his and Hines's images were displayed. "Now that the Wallfacer Project is terminated, the Wallfacer Act is abolished as well. On behalf of the SFJC, I hereby notify Wallfacers Bill Hines and Luo Ji that your Wallfacer status has been revoked. All associated rights granted you by the Wallfacer Act, as well as the corresponding legal immunity, are no longer in effect. You have recovered your identity as ordinary citizens of your respective countries."

The chair declared the hearing adjourned. Jonathan stood up and switched off the holographic image, switching off Luo Ji's two-century-long nightmare in the process.

"Dr. Luo, as far as I am aware, this is the outcome you were hoping for," Jonathan said to him with a smile.

"Yes. It's just what I wanted. Thank you, Mr. Commissioner. And I thank the SFJC for restoring my ordinary status," Luo Ji said, from the depths of his heart.

"The hearing was simple. Just a vote on a proposition. I've been empowered to discuss matters with you in more detail. You may start with your biggest concern."

"What about my wife and child?" Luo Ji asked, unable to hold back the question that had been tormenting him since reawakening. It was a question he had wanted to ask when he first met Jonathan, before the start of the meeting.

"Don't worry. They're both fine. They're still in hibernation. I can give you their files, and you can apply to reawaken them whenever you'd like."

"Thank you. Thank you." Luo Ji's eyes grew moist, and once again he had that feeling of arriving in heaven.

"However, Dr. Luo, I have a small piece of advice," Jonathan said as he slid closer to Luo Ji on the couch. "It's not easy for a hibernator to get used to life in this age. I advise you to stabilize your own life first before you wake them up. The UN funds are enough to keep them in hibernation for another two hundred thirty years."

"Well, how am I supposed to live out there?"

The commissioner laughed off his question. "Don't worry about that. You might not be used to the times, but living won't be an issue. In this age, social welfare is excellent, and a person can enjoy a comfortable life even if they don't do anything at all. The university you used to work at is still there, right in this city. They said they would consider the question of your work, and they'll contact you later on."

A thought suddenly occurred to Luo Ji, and it nearly made him shudder. "What about my security when I go out? The ETO wants to kill me!"

"The ETO?!" Jonathan burst into laughter. "The Earth-Trisolaris Organization was completely wiped out a century ago. There's no social foundation for them to exist in the world anymore. Of course, there are still people who have those ideological tendencies, but they aren't able to organize. You'll be absolutely safe outside."

347

As he was about to leave, Jonathan dropped his official attitude, and his suit started shining with an exaggerated, distorted image of the sky. He smiled and said to Luo Ji, "Doctor, out of all the historical figures I've seen, you've got the greatest sense of humor. A spell. A spell on a star. Ha ha ha . . ."

Luo Ji stood alone in the reception room, ruminating in silence over the reality before him. After two centuries as a messiah, he was once again an ordinary person. A new life was waiting before him.

"You're a commoner, my boy," a gruff voice loudly intruded on Luo Ji's thoughts. When he looked back toward the door, he saw Shi Qiang coming in. "Heh. I heard it from the guy who just left."

It was a happy reunion. They traded experiences, and Luo Ji learned that Shi Qiang had reawakened two months before. His leukemia had been cured. The doctors had also discovered that he was at high risk of liver disease, probably due to drinking, so they had taken care of that, too. To the two of them, it didn't really feel like they had been apart for very long. No more than four or five years, since there was no sense of time in hibernation. But meeting in a new era two centuries in the future added a deeper level to their friendship.

"I've come to pick you up when you're discharged. There's no reason to stay here," Shi Qiang said as he took a set of clothes out of his backpack and had Luo Ji put them on.

"Isn't it . . . a little big?" Luo Ji asked, opening up the jacket.

"Look at you. Two months late waking up, and you're a yahoo next to me. Try it on."

Shi Qiang pointed out an object on the front of the shirt and told him that he could use it to adjust the sizing. When Luo Ji put on the clothes, he heard a hissing sound, and the clothing slowly shrank to fit the dimensions of his body. It was the same with the trousers.

"Hey, you're not wearing that same set of clothes you wore two centuries ago, are you?" Luo Ji asked, looking at Shi Qiang. He remembered quite clearly that the leather jacket Shi Qiang was wearing now was the same one he had on the last time he saw him.

"Most of my belongings got lost in the Great Ravine, but my family did keep that set of clothes for me. But it wasn't wearable. You've got some things left over from that era too, and when you're settled down you can go pick them up. I tell you, my boy, when you see how that stuff has changed, that's when you'll really know that nearly two hundred years isn't a short length of time." As he spoke, Shi Qiang pressed something somewhere on his jacket and his outfit turned entirely white. The leather texture had just been an image. "I like it like the past."

"Can mine do that too? Can it put up images like theirs?" Luo Ji asked, looking at his own clothes.

"They can, but it's a little hard to get it set up. Let's go."

Luo Ji and Shi Qiang took the elevator in the trunk down to the ground floor, passed through the tree's large foyer, and out into the new world.

When the commissioner shut off the holographic image of the hearing, the meeting had not actually concluded. Luo Ji had in fact noticed that when the chair declared the meeting adjourned, a sudden voice had rung out. It was a woman's voice, and while he hadn't been able to make it out clearly, everyone in the assembly had turned in a particular direction. Then Jonathan had turned off the image. He must have noticed it, too, but once the chair had adjourned the meeting, Luo Ji, now an ordinary citizen without Wallfacer status, was not eligible to participate even if it was still in progress.

The speaker was Keiko Yamasuki. She said, "Mr. Chair, I have something to say."

The chair said, "Dr. Yamasuki, you are not a Wallfacer. You are allowed to attend today's meeting due to your special status, but you do not have the right to speak."

None of the representatives seemed interested in her. They were getting up to leave. For them, the entire Wallfacer Project was nothing but a footnote in history that they had to spend energy

dealing with. But what she said next stopped them in their tracks. She turned to Hines and said, "Wallfacer Bill Hines, I am your Wallbreaker."

Hines, who was getting up to leave, felt his legs buckle at Yamasuki's words, and he sat down in his chair again. The people in the auditorium glanced at each other, and then began to whisper, as the blood gradually drained from Hines's face.

"I hope you have not all forgotten the significance of that title," Yamasuki said imperiously to the assembly.

The chair said, "Yes, we know what a Wallbreaker is. But your organization does not exist anymore."

"I know." She appeared totally calm. "But as the last member of the ETO, I will fulfill my duty for the Lord."

"I should have known it, Keiko. I should have known," Hines said, his voice trembling. He looked weak. He had known that his wife was a devotee of the ideas of Timothy Leary, and he had seen her fanatical desire to alter the human mind through technological means, but he had never connected it with a deeply hidden hatred of humanity.

"First off, I'd like to say that the true goal of your strategic plan was not the elevation of human intelligence. You more than anyone are aware that it is utterly impossible for human technology to accomplish this in the foreseeable future, because you were the one who discovered the quantum structure of the brain. You know that when the study of the mind reaches the quantum level, the sophon lockdown on fundamental physics means that scientific research will be like water with no source: It's got no grounding, and will never succeed. The mental seal was not just a chance by-product of your study of the mind. It was the thing you always wanted. That was the ultimate goal of your research." She turned to the assembly. "Now, what I'd like to know from all of you is this: In the years that we've been in hibernation, what happened to the mental seal?"

"It didn't have much of a history," the representative of the European Fleet said. "Nearly fifty thousand people from national space forces voluntarily accepted faith in victory through the mental

seal, and they formed a special class in the military known as the 'Imprinted.' Later on, about ten years after you went into hibernation, the use of the mental seal was found by the International Court of Justice to be a crime, an infringement on the freedom of thought, and the sole mental seal device—the one in the Faith Center—was put into storage. The manufacture and use of that type of equipment was placed under a worldwide ban nearly as strict as nuclear nonproliferation. And, in fact, the mental seal was even harder to obtain than nuclear weapons, primarily because of the computer it used. By the time you entered hibernation, computing technology had basically stopped moving forward. The computer used by the mental seal is still a supercomputer today and is inaccessible to ordinary individuals and organizations."

Then Keiko Yamasuki revealed her first piece of substantive information: "What you don't know is that there was more than one mental seal device. Five were made, each with its own accompanying supercomputer. The other four, Hines secretly handed over to people who had already accepted the seal, the ones you call the Imprinted. There were only around three thousand of them at that time, but they had already formed a tightly knit supranational organization within the militaries of individual countries. Hines did not tell me this. I learned it from the sophons. The Lord does not care about staunch triumphalism, so we didn't take action."

"And how is this significant?" the chair asked.

"Let's hypothesize, shall we? The mental seal device is not a continuously operating piece of equipment. It's only activated when necessary. Each device can be used for quite a long time, and if they're properly maintained, it would be no problem for them to be used for half a century. If the four devices were used in turn, one run into the ground before the next one is started up, they would have been able to last for two centuries. Which means that the Imprinted may not have died off, but might have endured from generation to generation up to the present day. It's a religion that believes in faith hardened by the mental seal, and its induction ceremony is the voluntary use of the mental seal on your own mind."

The representative of the North American Fleet said, "Dr. Hines, you have lost your Wallfacer status and no longer have the legal power to deceive the world. Would you please tell the Joint Conference the truth: Is your wife, or, rather, your Wallbreaker, telling the truth?"

"It's true," Hines said, with a heavy nod.

"That's a crime!" the representative of the Asian Fleet said.

"Perhaps it is," Hines said, and nodded again. "But just like all of you, I don't know whether the Imprinted have endured to the present day."

"That's not important," the representative of the European Fleet said. "I think the next step should be to find the mental seal devices that are still around and seal them up or destroy them. As for the Imprinted, if they voluntarily accepted the mental seal, then that doesn't appear to have violated the laws of the time. If they applied the mental seal to other volunteers, then they were under the dominance of the faith or belief that they had already received through technical means, so they should not be subjected to punishment. So the only thing we need to do is find the mental seals. The matter of the Imprinted might not need to be pursued at all."

"That's right. It's not a bad thing for there to be a few people in the Solar Fleet who have absolute faith in victory. At least, it won't cause any harm. It should remain a matter of personal privacy, and no one needs to know who they are. Although it's hard to understand why anyone would voluntarily undergo the mental seal today, because humanity's victory is so apparent," the representative of the European Fleet said.

Keiko Yamasuki smiled derisively, revealing a seldom-seen expression that conjured up for the assembly an ancient picture of moonlight reflecting off the scales of a snake in the grass.

"You're being naïve," she said.

"You're being naïve," Hines echoed his wife, and deeply bowed his head.

She turned once again to her husband. "Hines, you've always hidden your thoughts from me. Even before you became a Wallfacer."

"I was afraid you'd despise me," he said, head still down.

"How many times did we look silently into each other's eyes in the bamboo grove in the quiet of the Kyoto night? From your eyes I saw a Wallfacer's loneliness, and I saw your desire to speak. How many times did you almost tell me the truth? You wanted to bury your head in my arms, put everything into words through your tears, and obtain total release. But the duty of a Wallfacer prevented you. Deceit, even toward the one you loved the most, was one of your responsibilities. So I could only look into your eyes in the hope of finding some trace of your true thoughts. You don't know how many sleepless nights I spent waiting next to you as you slept soundly, waiting for you to talk in your sleep. . . . More often, I carefully observed you, studying your every move and capturing your every look, including the years you were first in hibernation. I recalled every detail about you, not out of longing but because I wanted to see your true thoughts. For a very long time, I failed. I knew you wore a mask, but I knew nothing of what was below the mask. The years passed, until finally, when you had just awakened and walked through the neural-network cloud to my side, and I looked into your eyes, I finally understood. I'd matured eight years, while you were still the you of eight years before. And so you were exposed.

"From that moment, I knew the real you: a deep-rooted defeatist and a staunch Escapist. Both before and after you became a Wallfacer, your sole goal was to achieve an exodus of humanity. Compared to the other Wallfacers, your genius lay not in strategic deception, but in concealing and disguising your true worldview.

"But I still didn't know how you would achieve this goal through your research into the brain and thoughts. I was confused even when the mental seal came out, all the way up until the moment I entered hibernation, when I remembered their eyes. The eyes of those people who had been given the mental stamp . . . they were like yours. And all of a sudden I understood an expression of yours that I'd never been able to read before. That was when I broke through to your real strategy, but it was too late to say anything."

The representative of the North American Fleet said, "Ms. Keiko Yamasuki, I don't think there's anything unusual here.

We know the history of the mental seal. In the first group of fifty thousand volunteers, the procedure was carried out under the strictest of supervision."

"That's right," she said. "But the supervision was only absolutely effective so far as the content of the faith proposition was concerned. The mental seal itself was much harder to supervise."

"But the literature indicates that the supervision of the technical details of the mental seal was very strict as well, and it underwent a large number of tests before it was put into operation," the chair said.

Yamasuki shook her head. "The mental seal is an incredibly complicated piece of equipment. Any supervision will have gaps. Specifically, one tiny minus sign out of hundreds of millions of lines of code. Even the sophons didn't detect it."

"A minus sign?"

"When the neural circuit model for judging a proposition to be true was discovered, Hines also discovered the model for judging a proposition to be false. That was what he needed. He concealed this discovery from everyone, including me. It wasn't difficult, because the two models were highly similar. It manifested as the direction of flow of a key signal in the neuron transmission model, and in the mathematical model of the mental seal, it was represented by a sign. Positive for true, negative for false. Working in extreme secrecy, Hines manipulated this sign in the mental seal's control software. In all five devices, the sign was negative."

A deathly silence fell over the auditorium, a silence that had manifested only once before during a PDC Wallfacer Hearing two centuries ago, when Rey Diaz had shown off the "cradle" on his wrist and had told the assembly that the device receiving the anti-trigger signal was nearby.

"Dr. Hines, what have you done?" The chair turned toward him in anger.

Hines raised his head, and everyone could see that his pallid face had returned to normal. His voice was calm and even. "I admit that I underestimated the power of humanity. The progress

that you've made is truly unbelievable. I have seen it, and I believe it, and I also believe that victory in the war belongs to humanity. This faith is as steadfast as if it had been imprinted by the mental stamp. The defeatism and Escapism of two centuries ago is truly ridiculous. However, Mr. Chair and representatives, I would like to say to the world that it is impossible to make me repent of what I have done."

"You still think you shouldn't repent?" the representative of the Asian Fleet demanded angrily.

Hines raised his head. "It's not a question of 'should.' It's an impossibility. I used the mental seal to imprint this proposition on myself: Everything about my Wallfacer plan is entirely correct."

The assembly exchanged amazed glances, and Yamasuki even turned to her husband with the same expression.

Hines flashed her a small smile and nodded. "Yes, dear, if you'll permit me to call you that. Only by doing that could I obtain the spiritual strength necessary to execute the plan. Yes, right now I believe all I've done is correct. I absolutely believe it, regardless of what reality says. I used the mental seal to turn myself into my own god, and God can't repent."

"In the not-too-distant future, when the Trisolaran invaders surrender to a more powerful human civilization, will you still think that?" the chair asked, with a look in his eyes that was more curious than amazed.

Hines nodded earnestly. "I'll still think that I'm right. Everything about my Wallfacer plan is entirely correct. Of course, in the face of the facts, I'll be put through a hell of a torture." He turned to his wife. "Dear, you know I've already suffered that torture once, when I believed that water was toxic."

"Let's come back to the present day," the representative of the North American Fleet said, interrupting everyone's whispered discussions. "It's just speculation that the Imprinted have endured. It's been over one hundred seventy years, after all. If a class or organization with such an absolute faith in defeatism exists, why haven't there been any signs of it?"

"There are two possibilities," the representative of the European Fleet said. "One is that the mental seal vanished long ago, and this is just a false alarm. . . ."

The representative of the Asian Fleet completed his thought. "But there's another possibility: The most frightening thing about the situation is the fact that there aren't any signs."

Luo Ji and Shi Qiang walked through the underground city shaded by the tree-shaped structures as streams of cars flew through the gaps in the sky above them. Because the buildings were "leaves" hanging in the air, the ground was wide open, and the widely spaced trunks of the giant trees meant there was no sense of streets, just a rolling plaza dotted with tree trunks. The environment was wonderful: The wide swaths of grasses, forests of actual trees, and fresh air all made it look at first glance like beautiful countryside. Pedestrians passed through in shining clothes like glowing ants. Luo Ji was impressed to no end by the urban design that elevated modern noise and crowdedness into the air and let the ground return to nature. Here, there was no shadow of the war, only human comforts and pleasures.

Before they had gotten far, he heard a woman's gentle voice. "Is that Mr. Luo Ji?" He looked around and found that the voice was coming from a billboard on the grass at the side of the road. An attractive woman dressed in a uniform was looking at him from the moving image.

"I am," he said with a nod.

"Hello. I am Financial Counselor 8065 of the General Banking System. Welcome to our era. I will now inform you of your current financial situation." As she spoke, a table of data appeared beside her. "These are your financial records for Year 9 of the Crisis Era, including deposits at the Industrial and Commercial Bank of China and the China Construction Bank. There are investments in quoted securities as well, but those items may have been partially lost during the Great Ravine."

"How does she know I'm here?" he whispered.

Shi Qiang said, "A chip's been implanted in your left arm. Don't worry, these days everyone's got one. It's like an ID card. All billboards can recognize you. Ads are all personalized now, so no matter where you go, everything on the billboards is showing just for you."

Apparently hearing Shi Qiang's words, the counselor said, "Sir, this isn't an advertisement. It's a service from the General Banking System."

"How much do I have on deposit?" Luo Ji asked.

A highly complicated chart appeared next to the counselor. "This is the status of all your interest-bearing accounts since Year 9 of the Crisis Era. It's fairly complicated, but you can access it in your personal information area from now on." Another, simpler chart popped up. "This is your current financial situation in all of the various subsystems of the General Banking System."

Luo Ji had no concept of what those figures meant, and asked blankly, "That's . . . how much?"

"My boy, you're a rich man!" Shi Qiang said, slapping him vigorously. "I may not have as much as you, but I've still got money. Heh, two centuries of interest—it's a real long-term investment. Pauper to tycoon. I only regret not saving a little more."

"Well . . . are you sure there's nothing wrong?" Luo Ji asked, skeptically.

"Hmm?" The big eyes of the counselor looked at Luo Ji quizzically.

"It's been more than one hundred eighty years. Wasn't there any inflation? Did the finance system really just continue on smoothly?"

"You're overthinking it," Shi Qiang said, taking a pack of cigarettes out of his pocket. Luo Ji knew then that tobacco was still around. But when Shi Qiang took one out, he was able to puff out clouds of smoke without lighting it.

The counselor replied, "There were many rounds of inflation during the Great Ravine, and the finance and credit systems came close to collapse. But according to current laws, interest on the

deposits of hibernators is calculated according to a special formula that excludes the Great Ravine, and instead transfers the deposit amount over to the financial level of the post-Ravine period and resumes calculating interest from there."

"Wow, that's some preferential treatment!" Luo Ji exclaimed.

"My boy, these are good times," Shi Qiang said, blowing out smoke. Then, raising his still-burning cigarette, he said, "Except the cigarettes are terrible."

"Mr. Luo Ji, this is just an opportunity for us to get acquainted. When it's convenient for you, we can discuss your personal financial arrangements and investment plan. If there's nothing else, then I'll say good-bye." The counselor smiled and waved good-bye.

"I've got one question," he said quickly. He didn't know what to call young women in this era, and didn't want to risk making a mistake by addressing her improperly. So he simply said, "I'm not too familiar with this era, so please forgive me if my question is offensive to you."

The counselor smiled, and said, "Not a problem. Our responsibility is to help you get acquainted with this era as quickly as possible."

"Are you a real person or a robot? Or are you a program?"

The question didn't faze the counselor. She replied, "Of course I'm a real person. Could a computer handle services as complicated as this?"

After the woman on the billboard disappeared, Luo Ji said to Shi Qiang, "Da Shi, there are some things I find hard to understand. This is an age that has invented perpetual motion and can synthesize grain, but computer technology doesn't seem to have advanced at all. Artificial intelligence can't even handle personal finance."

"What perpetual motion? You mean a perpetual motion machine?" Shi Qiang said.

"Yeah. It signifies unlimited energy."

Shi Qiang looked around him. "Where?"

Luo Ji pointed up to the stream of traffic. "Those flying cars. Do they consume oil or batteries?"

Shi Qiang shook his head. "Neither. Earth's oil was pumped dry. Those cars can fly forever without batteries and they'll never run out of power. They're pretty awesome. I'm thinking of getting one myself."

"How can you be so unmoved by a technological miracle? Unlimited power for humanity. This is as big an event as when Pangu created the heavens and the Earth! Don't you realize what a magnificent age this is?"

Shi Qiang tossed aside the cigarette butt; then, thinking better of it, reached down and retrieved it from the grass and threw it into a nearby garbage can. "I'm unmoved? You're an intellectual whose imagination has gotten away from him. The technology is something we actually had in our era."

"You've got to be kidding."

"I don't understand most tech, but I do know a bit about this one thing in particular because, as it happens, I once had occasion to use a police bug that had no batteries but never ran out of power. You know how it worked? It was powered remotely by microwaves. That's what electricity is today, although the methods are a little different from our day."

Luo Ji stopped and stared at Shi Qiang for a long while, then up at the flying cars in the air. He thought about the heating glass, and finally understood: It was just a wireless power supply. The power source emitted electricity in the form of microwaves or other EM radiation to form an electric field over a certain space, allowing any equipment within it to draw power through an antenna or resonant coil. Like Shi Qiang had said, even two centuries ago, this technology was entirely ordinary. The only reason it hadn't been commonplace was because the power loss was too great. Only a small portion of the power emitted into a space could be used, but the majority was lost. In this era, however, mature controlled fusion technology meant that energy sources had been greatly enriched, to the point that losses from wireless power supplies were acceptable.

"And the synthetic grain? Can't they synthesize grain?" Luo Ji asked.

"I'm not really sure about that. Grain is still grown from seed, it's just that it's grown in factories in those cultivation tank things. Crops are all genetically modified, and I've heard that wheat grows just an ear, with no stalk. And it grows pretty quickly because of the strong artificial sunlight, and other things like intense, growth-inducing radiation. A season of wheat and rice can be harvested in a week, so from the outside it looks just like it's produced on a production line."

"Oh—" Luo Ji punctuated his thought with an extended sigh as the gorgeous bubbles before his eyes burst to reveal the true face of the world, and he knew that in this great new era, sophons still floated everywhere and human science was still deadlocked. Existing technology could never cross the line set down by the sophons.

"And the spacecraft that can reach fifteen percent of light speed?"

"Well, that's true. When those warships mobilize, it's like a tiny sun in the sky. And their space weapons—the day before yesterday I saw a news report on TV about an Asian Fleet exercise. A laser cannon swept a target ship as big as a carrier. Half of that iron guy evaporated like a chunk of ice, and the other half exploded like fireworks in a shower of sparkling molten steel. And there are rail-guns that can fire a hundred iron spheres a second, each the size of a football, at tens of kilometers per second. In a few minutes they can flatten a mountain on Mars. . . . So even though there isn't any of your perpetual motion, with these technologies, humanity is more than capable of putting down the Trisolaran Fleet."

Shi Qiang handed Luo Ji a cigarette and taught him how to twist the filter tip to light it. They smoked and watched the snow-white swirls drift upward. "Anyway, my boy, these are good times."

"Yes. Good times."

Luo Ji had hardly finished speaking when Shi Qiang pounced on him and the two of them tumbled onto the grass a few meters away, hearing a loud noise at their heels as a flying car smashed into the spot where they had just been standing. Luo Ji felt the

impact of the blast, and metal debris whizzed overhead, taking out half the billboard and sending the transparent glass tubes of the display crashing to the ground. While he was still on the ground with a dizzy head and a black eye, Shi Qiang leapt up and ran over to the flying car. Its disc-shaped body was entirely broken and deformed, but due to the lack of onboard fuel, it hadn't caught fire. There was only the sound of sparks crackling in the twisted metal.

"There's no one in the car," Shi Qiang said to Luo Ji, who was limping over.

"Da Shi, you saved my life again," Luo Ji said, leaning on his shoulder and massaging his injured leg.

"I don't know how many times I'll have to. You really ought to grow some sense, and a few more eyes." He pointed to the totaled flying car. "Remind you of anything?"

Luo Ji thought about that occasion two centuries before and shivered involuntarily.

Lots of pedestrians crowded round, the scenes of terror on their clothing flashing as one. Two police cars landed, sirens blaring, and several officers got out to form a line around the broken car. Their uniforms flashed like the police light, drowning out the crowd's clothing with their brightness. The one officer who came over to Shi Qiang and Luo Ji had clothing so bright they had to shut their eyes.

"You were right here when the car fell. You aren't hurt, are you?" he said with concern. He evidently could see that the two of them were hibernators, because he made an effort to speak "ancient Chinese."

Before Luo Ji could answer, Shi Qiang pulled the officer who had asked the question across the tape and out of the crowd. Once they had gotten away, the officer's uniform stopped flashing.

"You need to check up on this. It might be an assassination attempt," he said.

The officer laughed. "Really? It's just a traffic accident."

"We want to report it."

"Are you sure?"

"Of course. We're reporting it."

"You're making a big deal out of it. You may have been startled, but it really was a traffic accident. However, according to the law, if you insist on reporting it . . ."

"We insist."

The officer pressed a display area on his sleeve. It popped up an information window, which he looked over, and then said, "It's been reported. For the next forty-eight hours, the police will track you, but this requires your agreement."

"We agree. We might still be in danger."

The officer laughed again. "It's really a common occurrence."

"A common occurrence? Let me ask you: On average, how many traffic accidents of this kind take place in this city every month?"

"There were six or seven all of last year!"

"I'll have you know, officer: In our time, this city had more than that every day."

"Cars all ran on the ground in your day. I can't even imagine how dangerous that was. Well, you're now in the police surveillance system. You'll be notified of any progress on your case, but, please believe me, this is an ordinary traffic accident. Whether or not you filed a report, you would still receive compensation."

After they left the police and the scene of the accident behind, Shi Qiang said to Luo Ji, "We'd better get back to my place. I don't feel at ease when I'm outside. It's not far. We probably should walk back. Taxis are unmanned, so it's not safe."

"But hasn't the ETO been destroyed?" Luo Ji asked, looking about him. Off in the distance, the fallen car had been lifted up by a larger flying car. The crowd had dispersed, and the police car had left. A municipal works vehicle had landed, and several workmen had gotten out to gather scattered debris and begin repairs to the ground, which had been damaged by the crash. Following the small commotion, the city had returned to its normal, pleasing calm.

"Perhaps it has. But you've got to trust my intuition, my boy."

"I'm no longer a Wallfacer."

"That car didn't seem to think so. . . . While we're walking, pay attention to the cars above you."

They kept to the "shade" of the treelike buildings as much as possible, and crossed any open spaces they reached at a run. Soon they arrived at a broad plaza, and Shi Qiang said, "My place is just opposite. It's too far to go around, so we'll have to make a run for it."

"Isn't that being a little paranoid? Maybe it was just a traffic accident."

"That's a 'maybe,' though. There's nothing wrong with being careful. . . . See that sculpture in the center of the plaza? If anything happens, we can hide there."

There was a square sandy area in the center of the plaza, like a miniature desert. The sculpture that Shi Qiang mentioned, located right in the center of the sand, was a group of black pillar-like objects, each two or three meters tall. From a distance, it looked like a grove of withered black trees.

Luo Ji ran across the plaza behind Shi Qiang. When they neared the sandy area, he heard Shi Qiang call, "Hurry. Get in there!" and he was dragged skidding across the sand and then headlong into the withered grove. Lying on the grove's warm sand, he looked up between the black pillars at the sky and saw a flying car zoom down and buzz the grove before pulling up and accelerating away. The gust of wind it left in its wake blew a burst of sand into the air, which hit the pillars with a whoosh.

"Maybe it wasn't headed for us."

"Hmm. Maybe," Shi Qiang said, as he sat up and dumped the sand out of his shoes.

"Will they laugh at us for this?"

"Don't be afraid of that crap. Who's going to recognize you? Besides, we're from two centuries ago, so even if we're entirely normal, people are still gonna laugh. My boy, nothing's lost by being careful. What if the thing really was headed for you?"

Only then did Luo Ji turn his attention to the sculpture they were inside. He noticed that the pillars weren't withered trees, but arms extending out of the desert. The skinny arms were just skin and bones, so at first glance they looked like dead tree trunks. The

hands atop them made a variety of distorted gestures to the sky and seemed to express a kind of endless pain.

"What kind of sculpture is this?" Within this group of struggling arms, Luo Ji felt a chill, even though he was still sweating from the run. At the sculpture's edge, he saw a solemn obelisk, on which was carved a line of large golden characters: MAKE TIME FOR CIVILIZATION, FOR CIVILIZATION WON'T MAKE TIME.

"The Great Ravine Memorial," Shi Qiang said. He did not seem interested in explaining further, but led Luo Ji out of the sculpture and across the other half of the plaza at a fast clip. "Okay, my boy. This tree's where I live," Shi Qiang said, pointing to the massive architectural tree in front of them.

Luo Ji looked around him as he walked. All of a sudden he heard the floor creak, and then the ground fell away under his feet and he plummeted downward. Shi Qiang grabbed hold of him when his chest was already at ground level and struggled to haul him up. After he had his footing, the two of them stared at the hole in the ground. It was the mouth of a sewer, and its cover had slid aside just as Luo Ji was about to step on it.

"My god! Are you all right, sir? That's really dangerous!" said a voice issuing from a small billboard next to them. The billboard was attached to a small pavilion containing a machine selling drinks and such, and the speaker was a young man dressed in a blue uniform. His face was pale, and he seemed even more frightened than Luo Ji. "I'm with the Office of Evacuation and Drainage at the Third Municipal Administration Company. That cover opened automatically. It might be a software failure."

"Does this happen often?" Shi Qiang asked.

"Oh, no, no. At least, this is the first time I've ever seen it."

Shi Qiang picked up a small round stone from the grass next to the road and tossed it down the hole. It was quite some time before they heard any sound. "Damn. How deep is it?" he asked the man in the billboard.

"Around thirty meters. So, like I said, it's really dangerous! I've inspected the surface drainage system. The sewers in your day were

all pretty shallow. This accident has been recorded. You . . ." He glanced at his sleeve as he spoke. "Ah, Mr. Luo. You can go to the TMAC to be compensated."

At last they reached the lobby leading to Shi Qiang's tree, #1863. He said that he lived on branch 106, near the top, and advised Luo Ji to eat down below before going up. They went into a restaurant on one side of the lobby. Aside from being as clean as a 3D rendering, one characteristic of this age was even more obvious here than when he first saw it in the reawakening center: Dynamic information windows were everywhere, on the walls, tabletops, chairs, the floor and ceiling, and even on small objects like the glasses and napkin holders on the table. Everything had an interface and display with scrolling text or moving images. It was as if the entire restaurant was a giant computer display showing off a diverse and glittering splendor.

Not many people were dining. They chose a table by the window and sat down. Shi Qiang tapped the tabletop to activate an interface and then ordered a few dishes. "I can't read the foreign writing, so I've only ordered Chinese ones."

"The world seems like it's built using bricks made from displays," Luo Ji sighed.

"That's right. Anything smooth can light up." As Shi Qiang spoke he took out a pack of cigarettes and passed it to Luo Ji. "Look at this. Just a pack of cheap cigarettes." As soon as Luo Ji held the pack in his hands, it started displaying an animated image of several miniature pictures that seemed like an options menu.

"This . . . it's just a film that can display images," Luo Ji said as he looked at the pack.

"A film? You can go online with this gadget!" Shi Qiang reached over and tapped the pack, and one of the miniature pictures sank in like a button. Then the advertisement he selected took over the entire pack.

In the picture, Luo Ji saw a family with one child sitting in a living room. The picture obviously came from the past, and a shrill voice sounded from the pack: "Mr. Luo, this is the era you used to live in. We know that in that age, owning a house in the capital was

the grand dream of every person. Now, the Greenleaf Group can help you achieve that dream. As you can see, this is a wonderful age. Houses have turned into leaves on a tree, and the Greenleaf Group can provide you with every kind of leaf." Here the picture showed a scene of leaves being added to a tree branch, and then a dazzling variety of hanging homes, one of which was even completely transparent, with furnishings inside that seemed suspended in midair. "Of course, we can also build you a traditional home on the surface to return you to the warmth of the Golden Age, and build you a warm . . . family . . ." A lawn and detached home, perhaps another old photo, appeared onscreen. The voice artist in the ad spoke in fluent "ancient Chinese," but paused momentarily before the word "family," then said it with particular emphasis. After all, it was something the speaker didn't have, something that belonged to the past.

Shi Qiang took the cigarette pack out of Luo Ji's hands, withdrew the last two cigarettes, passed one to him, and then crumpled the empty pack into a ball and tossed it onto the table. On the crumpled ball, the images still flashed, but the sound had disappeared. "Whenever I go anywhere, the first thing I do is to turn off every screen that's around me. They're so annoying," Shi Qiang said, turning off the tabletop and floor displays with his hands and feet. "But the people here can't be away from them." He pointed around them. "There aren't any computers anymore. Anyone who wants to go online or something can just tap any smooth surface. Clothing and shoes can be used as computers, too. Believe it or not, I've even seen toilet paper that you can go online with."

Luo Ji pulled out a napkin. It was just ordinary, non-wired paper, but the paper box activated, and the pretty woman on it hawked bandages to Luo Ji, evidently aware of today's experiences and guessing that his arms and legs might have gotten scraped up.

"God," Luo Ji sighed, and stuffed the napkin back in the box.

"This is the information age. Our times were pretty damn primitive," Shi Qiang said with a laugh.

While they waited for their food, Luo Ji asked Shi Qiang about

366

his life. He felt a little guilty for only asking now, but looking back on how the day had gone, he had been something of a clockwork machine ticking relentlessly forward. Only now did he have a bit of free time.

"They had me retire. It's not a bad deal," Shi Qiang said simply.

"Was it the Public Security Bureau, or the unit you were at later? Are they still around?"

"They're around. And the PSB is still the PSB. But even before hibernation I wasn't connected to it anymore. The unit I was with later now belongs to the Asian Fleet. You know, the fleet is like a big country, so I'm a foreigner now." Saying this, he exhaled a long cloud of smoke. He watched the cloud ascend, as if he was trying hard to unravel a mystery.

"Countries don't have the significance they used to. . . . The world's changed. It's confusing. Fortunately, Da Shi, you and I are the kind of indifferent people who can live, and live well, no matter what happens."

"Luo, my boy, to tell you the truth, I'm not as open-minded as you in certain things. I'm not as uninvolved. If I'd been through everything you have, I'd have fallen apart long ago."

Luo Ji picked up the crumpled cigarette pack from the table, opening it to reveal the image that was still showing, with only a little discoloration. It was playing the Greenleaf Group advert. He said, "Whether as messiah, or as refugee, I can always use what resources I have to try and live a happy life. You might think I'm selfish, but to be honest, this is the only thing I respect about myself. Da Shi, let me say something about you. You look like a careless person, but deep in your bones you're someone who prizes responsibility. Leave that responsibility completely behind now. Look at this age. Who needs us? Carpe diem is our most sacred duty."

"Sure, but if I gave up all responsibility, you wouldn't have much of an appetite at all right now." Shi Qiang tossed his cigarette into the ashtray, activating a cigarette advert.

Luo Ji realized he had misspoken. "Oh, no, Da Shi, you've still got to carry out your responsibility to me. I'll die if I leave you.

Already today you've saved me one, two, three times. Or at least two and a half!"

"I can't just leave someone to die, you mean? That's the life I've got, a life of saving yours," Shi Qiang said disapprovingly as he cast his eyes about him, probably looking for someplace selling cigarettes. Then he looked back, leaned in to Luo Ji, and whispered, "But you really were a messiah for a little while, my boy."

"It's impossible for anyone in that position to be of sound mind. Fortunately, I'm now back to normal."

"How did you come up with the idea of putting a spell on that star?"

"I was seriously paranoid back then. I don't want to think about it. Believe it or not, Da Shi, I'm certain that while I was asleep, they not only cured my illness, but also conducted psychiatric treatment. Really, I'm not the same person now that I was back then. How could I have been so stupid as to have that kind of idea? That sort of delusion?"

"What delusion? Let me hear it."

"It's difficult to explain briefly. Besides, there's no point. In your work, you must have run into delusional patients, people who were always thinking someone wanted to kill them. Is there any point to listening to those people talk?" Luo Ji methodically tore the cigarette pack into pieces. This time the display was destroyed, but the scraps still flashed in a grotesquely colored heap.

"Okay. We'll talk about something happy. My son is still alive."

"What?" Luo Ji asked, practically jumping up in his surprise.

"I just learned about it two days ago. He looked me up. We haven't met, just spoken by phone."

"He's not . . ."

"I don't know how long he spent in prison, but afterward he went into hibernation. He said it was to come to the future to see me. Who knows where the kid got the money. Now he's on the surface, and he's arranged to come over tomorrow."

Luo Ji stood up excitedly, sweeping flashing scraps of paper to the floor. "Oh, Da Shi, that's just . . . We've got to drink to that."

"A drink, then. The alcohol in this age tastes awful, but it's still the same strength."

Then the food came. Luo Ji didn't recognize anything, and Shi Qiang said, "Nothing's good. There are restaurants supplied by traditional farms, but those are all high-end places. We'll eat at one when Xiaoming comes."

But Luo Ji's attention had shifted to the server. Her face and body were unrealistically beautiful, and he saw that the other servers sliding between the tables had the same angelic appearance.

"Hey, don't stare like an idiot. They're fake," Shi Qiang said, without looking up.

"Robots?" Luo Ji asked. At last the future had something he had seen in one of his childhood science fiction stories.

"Sort of."

"What do you mean, 'sort of'?"

Shi Qiang pointed to a robot server and said, "This silly girl only knows how to serve food. They travel fixed paths. How stupid is that? Once I saw a table that had been temporarily moved, but they kept bringing dishes to the original location, so everything crashed to the ground."

When the robot server had laid out the food, it smiled sweetly and wished them a good meal. Its voice did not sound robotic, but was incredibly lovely. Then, it extended a slender hand and picked up the dinner knife in front of Shi Qiang. . . .

Like lightning, Shi Qiang's eyes shot from the knife in the server's hands to Luo Ji across the table from him. He leapt up, vaulted the table, and pulled Luo Ji violently off his chair to the floor. Almost simultaneously, the robot stabbed the knife right where Luo Ji's heart would have been. The knife went through the back of the chair, activating its information interface. The robot retracted the knife and stood beside the table with a serving tray in its other hand, still with the sweet smile on its unrealistically beautiful face. Panicked, Luo Ji struggled to stand up, then hid behind Shi Qiang. But Shi Qiang just waved his hand, saying, "Don't worry. It's not that agile."

The robot stood motionless, holding the knife and smiling, and once again wished them a good meal in its gentle voice.

The startled diners had clustered around them looking at the scene in amazement. Then the duty manager came rushing over. When she heard Shi Qiang accusing the restaurant's robot of attempted murder, she shook her head. "Sir, that's impossible! Their eyes don't see people. They only see the sensors on the tables and chairs!"

"I'll testify that it picked up a dinner knife and tried to kill that man. We saw it with our own eyes!" one man said in a loud voice. The other onlookers added their proof.

While the duty manager was considering how to rebut this, the robot stabbed the knife at the chair a second time, putting it precisely through the hole punctured the first time and eliciting a few screams.

"Have a pleasant meal," it said with a smile.

A number of other people arrived, including the restaurant's engineer. When he pressed the back of the robot's head, the smile left her face and she said, "Forced shutdown. Breakpoint data backed up." Then she froze in place.

"It's probably a software failure," the engineer said, wiping away cold sweat.

"Does this happen often?" Shi Qiang said with a sarcastic smile.

"No, no. I swear, I've never even heard of anything like this," the engineer said, then directed two assistants to haul the robot out.

The duty manager energetically explained to the customers that until the cause of the failure was identified, the restaurant would use real human servers, but about half of the customers left anyway.

"You both reacted pretty fast," one bystander said admiringly.

"Hibernators. In their era, people had experience with this kind of sudden incident," someone else said. His clothing displayed a swordsman.

The duty manager said to Luo Ji and Shi Qiang, "Sirs, this was truly . . . Anyway, I guarantee that you'll receive compensation."

"Good. Now let's eat." Shi Qiang beckoned Luo Ji to retake his seat, and a human server brought over new dishes to replace those that had spilled.

Sitting there, his shock not yet abated, Luo Ji felt the uncomfortable hole in the chair back. "Da Shi, it seems the whole world is against me. I used to have a favorable impression of it."

Shi Qiang considered one of the dishes in front of him, then said, "I've got some ideas about this." He looked up and poured Luo Ji a drink. "Ignore it for now. I'll tell you in detail later."

"Here: to carpe diem, to living one day at a time. One hour at a time, even," Luo Ji said as he raised his glass. "Here's to your still-living son."

"Are you really okay?" Shi Qiang said, shooting him a smile.

"I've been a messiah. Nothing scares me." He shrugged, then drained his glass. The taste of the alcohol made him wince. "This is like rocket fuel."

"You kill me, my boy. That attitude of yours has always killed me," Shi Qiang said, sticking up a thumb.

The leaf where Shi Qiang lived was at the top of the tree. It was a spacious house, and was fully equipped with facilities for comfortable living. It had a gym, and even an indoor garden with a fountain.

He said, "The fleet gave me these temporary living quarters. They said I can buy a better leaf with my retirement money."

"Does everyone have so much space to live in these days?"

"Probably. This kind of structure is the best use of space. A big leaf is equivalent to an entire building from our era. But mainly it's because there are fewer people. Far fewer, ever since the Great Ravine."

"But Da Shi, your country is in space."

"I won't be going there. I'm already retired, you know."

Luo Ji's eyes felt more comfortable here, largely because most of the information windows in Shi Qiang's house were closed, although there were scattered flashes in the walls and on the floor. Shi Qiang tapped an interface on the floor with his foot, turning one wall entirely transparent and unfurling the night city before

their eyes. It was a dazzling, giant forest of Christmas trees chained together by the lights of the traffic.

Luo Ji went over to the sofa, which was hard as marble to the touch. "Is this for sitting?" he asked. At Shi Qiang's affirmative, he sat gingerly down on it, only to feel like he was sinking into soft clay. The sofa's cushions and backrest adapted to a person's body, forming a mold completely in sync with their body shape, keeping pressure to a minimum.

His vision from the slab of iron ore in the Meditation Room of the UN Building two centuries ago had become reality.

"Do you have any sleeping pills?" he asked. Now that he was in a space that felt safe, exhaustion hit him.

"No, but you can buy them here," Shi Qiang said, and operated the wall again. "Here. Nonprescription sleeping pills. This one, River of Dreams."

Although Luo Ji thought he would witness some sort of high-tech hardware-over-the-network transmission, the reality was much simpler than he imagined. In a few minutes, a small, flying delivery van pulled up outside the transparent wall and delivered the medicine through the portal that had just opened up with a slender mechanical arm. Luo Ji took the medicine from Shi Qiang. It was a traditional box without any active display. The instructions said to take one pill, so he opened the pack, took one out, and reached out for the glass of water on the coffee table.

"Wait a moment," Shi Qiang said, taking the box out of Luo Ji's hands and reading it carefully before returning it to him. "What does this say? The one I asked for was called River of Dreams."

Luo Ji saw a long string of complicated English-language drug names. "I don't recognize it. But it's certainly not River of Dreams."

Shi Qiang activated a window on the coffee table and began looking for a medical consult. With Luo Ji's help, they found one, a white-clothed consulting physician who examined the box, then looked from the box to Shi Qiang with a peculiar expression.

"Where did this come from?" the doctor asked warily.

"I bought it. Right here."

"Impossible. This is a prescription drug. It's only for use in the hibernation center."

"What's it got to do with hibernation?"

"It's short-term hibernation medicine. It can make someone hibernate for ten days to a year."

"You just swallow it?"

"No. It requires a whole set of external systems to sustain internal bodily circulatory functions before short-term hibernation can be achieved."

"And if you take it without them?"

"Then you'd die for sure. But you'd die comfortably. So it's often used for suicide."

Shi Qiang closed the window and tossed the box onto the table. He looked straight at Luo Ji for a while, then said, "Damn it."

"Damn it," Luo Ji said, pitching back onto the sofa. Then he was subjected to the final attempt on his life that day.

When his head touched back against the sofa, the hard headrest quickly adapted to the back of his head and began to form an impression of its shape. But the process didn't stop there. His head and neck continued to sink, until the headrest on either side formed a pair of tentacles that squeezed tight around his neck. He had no time to cry out, but could only open his mouth and eyes and scramble with his hands.

Shi Qiang bounded into the kitchen and returned with a knife, which he used to hack at the tentacles a few times, then resorted to his own hands to pry them from Luo Ji's neck. When Luo Ji left the sofa and pitched forward onto the floor, the sofa's surface lit up and displayed a large string of error messages.

"How many times have I saved your life today, my boy?" Shi Qiang asked, rubbing his hands.

"This is . . . the . . . sixth," Luo Ji said, through gasps. He vomited onto the floor. When he finished, he leaned back weakly against the sofa, but then pulled back immediately, as if shocked. He didn't know where to put his hands. "How long will it be before I can be as agile as you and save my own life?"

"Probably never," Shi Qiang said. A vacuum cleaner–like machine glided over to clean up the vomit on the floor.

"Then I'm dead meat. This is a twisted world."

"It's not that bad. I've got an idea about the whole situation, at least. The first attempt on your life failed, and then there were five more attempts. This is stupidity, not professional behavior. Something somewhere must have gone wrong. . . . Let's contact the police immediately. We can't wait for them to crack the case."

"Who made a mistake, and where? Da Shi, it's been two centuries. Don't just apply your mind-set from our time."

"It's the same thing, my boy. Certain things are the same no matter the age. As for whose mistake it is, I really don't know. I even wonder whether such a 'who' actually exists. . . ."

The doorbell rang. Shi Qiang opened it to see several people standing outside. They wore civilian clothes, but Shi Qiang identified them before the leader had even flashed his ID.

"Wow. So there are actual footbeats in this society. Come on in, officers."

Three of them entered the house, leaving two others outside to guard the door. The officer in charge, who looked about thirty years old, surveyed the room. Like Shi Qiang and Luo Ji, he had all the displays on his clothes turned off, which put them at ease, and he spoke a pure, fluent "ancient Chinese" without any English words.

"I'm Officer Guo Zhengming with the PSB's Digital Reality Department. I apologize for our tardy arrival. That was negligent. The last time there was a case like this was half a century ago." He bowed to Shi Qiang. "I pay my respects to my senior officer. Aptitude like yours is very rare in the force these days."

As Officer Guo was speaking, Luo Ji and Shi Qiang noticed that all of the information windows in the house had switched off. The leaf had evidently been cut off from the external hyper-information world. The other two officers were hard at work. They were holding something he hadn't seen in ages: a notebook computer. But the computer was as thin as a sheet of paper.

"They're installing a firewall for this leaf," Officer Guo explained. "Rest assured, you're safe now. And I'll guarantee that you'll receive compensation from the municipal PSB system."

"Today," Shi Qiang said, counting off on his fingers, "we've been guaranteed compensation four times."

"I know. And lots of people in lots of departments have lost their jobs over this. I beg for your cooperation, so that I don't join them. Thanks in advance," he said, bowing to them.

Shi Qiang said, "I understand that. I've been in that position. Do you need us to brief you on the situation?"

"No. We've actually been tracking you all along. It's just negligence."

"Can you tell us what's happening?"

"Killer 5.2."

"What?"

"It's a network virus. The ETO first released it about a century into the Crisis Era, and then there were lots of subsequent variants and upgrades. It's a murder virus. First it establishes the identity of the target by a variety of methods including the chip everyone has implanted in their body. When it locates the target, the Killer virus manipulates every possible piece of external hardware to carry out the murder. Its concrete manifestation is what you experienced today. It seems like everything in the world wants to kill you. So, at the time, people called it a 'modern hex.' For a while, the Killer software was even commercialized and sold on the online black market. You entered the personal ID number of your target and uploaded the virus. Then, even if that person was able to evade death, they would still have a hard time living in society."

"The industry developed as far as that? Incredible!" Shi Qiang exclaimed.

"Software from a century ago can still run today?" Luo Ji asked incredulously.

"Sure it can. Computer technology stopped advancing long ago. When the Killer virus first appeared, it killed quite a few people, including a head of state, but eventually it was controlled

by firewalls and antivirus software and gradually faded away. This version of Killer is programmed specifically to attack Dr. Luo, but because the target was in hibernation, it never had the opportunity to take any concrete action. It stayed dormant and wasn't detected or recorded by the information security system. It was only when Dr. Luo emerged into the world today that Killer 5.2 activated itself and carried out its mission. It's just that its creators were wiped out a century ago."

"They were still trying to kill me a century ago?" Luo Ji said. A mood he thought was gone forever returned, and he struggled to dispel it again.

"Yes. The key thing about this version of the Killer virus is that it was programmed specifically for you. It was never activated, which is why it was still lurking in wait today."

"Then what are we supposed to do now?" Shi Qiang asked.

"The entire system will be cleaned of Killer 5.2, but that will take some time. Before it's completed, you have two choices. First, Dr. Luo can be given a temporary false identity, but this will not totally guarantee his safety and might lead to other more serious consequences. Due to the technological sophistication of the ETO software, Killer 5.2 might have already recorded other characteristics of its target. In one case that caused a sensation a century ago, when a protected individual was given a false identity, Killer used fuzzy recognition to simultaneously kill over a hundred people, target included. The other choice, and my personal recommendation, is for you to live up on the surface for a while. Killer 5.2 won't have any hardware to manipulate up there."

Shi Qiang said, "I agree. Even without this situation, I've been wanting to go up to the surface."

"What's on the surface?" Luo Ji asked.

Shi Qiang explained, "Most of the reawakened hibernators live on the surface. It's hard for them to adapt down here."

"That's right. So you ought to spend at least some time up there," Officer Guo said. "Many aspects of modern society—politics, economics, culture, lifestyle, and relations between the sexes—

have changed greatly in two centuries, so it takes some time for us to adapt."

"But you've adapted well enough," Shi Qiang said, looking him over. He and Luo Ji had both noticed that the officer had said "us."

"I went into hibernation because of leukemia, and I was quite young when I reawakened, just thirteen years old," Guo Zhengming said with a laugh. "But people still don't understand the difficulties I've had. I don't know how many times I've gone for psychological treatment."

"Are there many other hibernators like you who have totally adapted to modern life?" Luo Ji asked.

"Lots. But you can still live quite well on the surface."

"Special Contingent of Future Reinforcements commander Zhang Beihai reporting," Zhang Beihai said, and saluted.

Behind the commander of the Asian Fleet flowed the brilliant Milky Way. Fleet Command was in orbit around Jupiter and rotated continuously to produce artificial gravity. Zhang Beihai noticed that the room lights were relatively dim, and the wide windows seemed intended to integrate the interior environment with space outside as closely as possible.

The commander saluted back. "Greetings, predecessor." He looked quite young, his Asian features illuminated by the glow of his epaulets and cap insignia. When he was issued a uniform on the sixth day after he reawakened, Zhang Beihai had noticed the familiar emblem of the space force: a silver star shining rays in four directions, the rays in the shape of sword. Two centuries had passed, and while the insignia had not changed much, the fleet had become an independent country, with a president as its supreme leader. The commander was just in charge of the military.

Zhang Beihai said, "That's too much, Commander. We're all just new recruits now, who have to learn everything."

The commander smiled and shook his head. "You can't say

that. You've already learned everything there is to know here. And the knowledge you've got, we'll never be able to learn. That's why we awakened you now."

"Commander Chang Weisi of the Chinese Space Force asked me to convey his greetings."

Zhang Beihai's words touched something in the commander's heart. He turned and looked out through the window at the river of stars, like the upper reaches of a long river. "He was an exceptional general, one of the founders of the Asian Fleet. Today's space strategy still uses the framework he established two centuries ago. I wish that he could have seen this day."

"Today's achievements are far beyond anything he ever dreamed."

"But all of this began in his . . . in your time."

Then Jupiter appeared, at first as a sliver of an arc that quickly took over the entire field of view in the window, bathing the office in its orange light. The dreamlike patterns of hydrogen and helium in its vast gaseous ocean were on a breathtaking scale and fascinating in their detail. The Great Red Spot moved into view. The superstorm that could hold two Earths looked like the giant, pupilless eye of this blurry world. The three fleets had put their primary base on Jupiter because its hydrogen-helium ocean held an inexhaustible supply of fusion fuel.

Zhang Beihai was transfixed by the Jovian scene. Countless times he had dreamed of the new domain that now presented itself before his eyes. He waited until Jupiter had moved out of the window before speaking. "Commander, the great achievements of this age are what make our mission unnecessary."

The commander turned to him and said, "No, that's not right. The Future Reinforcement Plan was a farsighted initiative. During the Great Ravine, when the space armed forces were on the brink of collapse, the special reinforcement contingents played a major role in stabilizing the overall situation."

"But our contingent arrived too late to be of assistance."

"I'm sorry, but that's how things are," the commander said. The lines on his face turned gentle. "After you left, they sent more

special reinforcement contingents to the future, and the last to be sent out were the first to be reawakened."

"That's understandable, Commander, since their knowledge framework was closer to that era's."

"Right. Eventually your contingent was the only one left in hibernation. The Great Ravine ended and the world entered a period of rapid development. Defeatism had practically vanished, so there was no need to reawaken you. At the time, the fleet made the decision to keep you until the Doomsday Battle."

"Commander, this was actually what we all hoped for," Zhang Beihai said excitedly.

"And it's the highest honor of all space servicemen. They were well aware of this when they made that decision. But present circumstances are totally different, as you of course know." The commander pointed at the river of stars behind him. "The Doomsday Battle might never even take place."

"That's excellent, Commander. My small regret as a soldier counts for nothing compared with the great victory humanity is about to welcome. I just hope you'll be able to fulfill our one request: to let us join the fleet at the lowest level, as ordinary soldiers, to do whatever work we can."

The commander shook his head. "The length of service for all special contingent personnel will resume from the date of reawakening, and ranks will be elevated one or two levels."

"Commander, that shouldn't be. We don't want to spend our remaining years in an office. We want to go to the fleet's front lines. Two centuries ago, the space force was our dream. Without it, our lives have no meaning. But even at our present ranks, we are unqualified for work in the fleet."

"I never said I wanted you to leave the fleet. Precisely the opposite. You will all be working in the fleet to complete a highly important mission."

"Thank you, Commander. But what mission can there be for us today?"

The commander did not answer him. Instead, as if it had only just

379

occurred to him, he said, "Are you okay with talking while standing like this?" The commander's office had no chairs, and the table had been designed to be high enough to work at while standing. Fleet Command's rotation produced one-sixth of Earth's gravity, which meant there wasn't much difference between standing and sitting.

Zhang Beihai smiled and nodded. "Not a problem. I spent a year in space."

"And the language? Do you have any communication problems in the fleet?"

The commander was speaking standard Chinese, but the three fleets had formed a language of their own, similar to the modern Chinese and modern English on Earth, but with the two languages blended more closely. Chinese and English words each accounted for half of the vocabulary.

"At first—mostly because I couldn't distinguish between Chinese and English vocabulary—but I was able to understand it pretty quickly. Speaking is more difficult."

"That doesn't matter. If you just use English or Chinese when you speak, we'll be able to understand you. So that means that the General Staff Department has fully briefed you?"

"That's right. In the first few days on base, they gave us a comprehensive introduction to everything."

"Then you must be aware of the mental seal."

"That's right."

"Recent investigations still haven't discovered any signs of the Imprinted. What's your read?"

"I believe that one possibility is that the Imprinted have disappeared. Another possibility is that they've been deeply hidden. If a person has an ordinary defeatist mentality, they will speak of it to others. But a one-hundred-percent unshakeable technologically hardened faith will inevitably produce a corresponding sense of mission. Defeatism and Escapism are intimately related, and if the Imprinted really exist, then their ultimate mission is bound to be accomplishing an escape into the universe. But to achieve this goal, they have to deeply conceal their true thoughts."

The commander nodded with approval. "An excellent analysis. This is the opinion of General Staff."

"Commander, the second alternative is very dangerous."

"Yes, it is, particularly with the Trisolaran probe so close to the Solar System. The fleet is divided by command system classifications into two major groups. The first, a distributed command system, is a traditional structure akin to the naval craft you once commanded. The captain's orders are carried out by various operating personnel. The second is a centralized command system. The captain's orders are carried out automatically by the ship's computer. The most recently built advanced space warships, as well as those currently under construction, fall into this category. It is mainly against this category of warship that the mental seal poses a threat, because the captain wields enormous power in the command system. He can unilaterally control when the ship leaves and returns to port, its speed and course, and even a large portion of its weapons systems. Under this command system, you could call the ship an extension of the captain's body. Right now, 179 of the 695 stellar-class warships in the fleet have a centralized command system. The commanding officers on board these ships will be the focus of review. Originally, all the warships involved in the review process were supposed to be docked and sealed up, but present circumstances no longer permit this, because the three fleets are preparing to intercept the Trisolaran probe when it arrives. This will be the first actual engagement between the Space Fleet and the Trisolaran invaders, so all warships must be on standby."

"So, Commander, the command authority for centrally commanded warships must be turned over to reliable individuals," Zhang Beihai said. He had been speculating about his mission but had not guessed it yet.

"Who is reliable?" the commander asked. "We don't know the extent of the mental seal, and we have no information about the Imprinted. In these circumstances, no one can be trusted, not even me."

The sun appeared outside the window. Although its light was far weaker than on Earth from this distance, the commander's body

was hidden in a glare when the disc passed behind him, leaving only his voice: "But you are all reliable. When you entered hibernation, the mental seal didn't exist. And one of the most important factors for your selection two centuries ago was your loyalty and faith. You are the only trustworthy group available to us in the fleet right now. So the fleet has decided to put the authority of the centralized command system into your hands, to appoint you as acting captains, through whom every order issued by the former captains must pass before being issued to the command system."

Two tiny suns ignited in Zhang Beihai's eyes. He said, "Commander, I'm afraid that's not possible."

"Saying no to an order is not our tradition."

The commander's use of "our" and "tradition" warmed Zhang Beihai, letting him know that the bloodline of the military of two centuries ago still endured in the space fleet of today.

"Commander, we're from two centuries ago, after all. In the context of the navy of our time, it's like using an official in the Beiyang Fleet to command a twenty-first-century destroyer."

"Do you think that the Qing admirals Deng Shichang and Liu Buchan[20] would really be unable to command your destroyers? They were educated, and their English was good. They would have learned. Today, captaining a space warship doesn't involve technical details. Captains issue general commands, but the warship is a black box to them. Besides, the warships will be docked at base while you serve as acting captain. They won't be navigating. Your duty will be to convey the former captains' commands to the control system once you've determined whether or not the commands are normal. You'll be able to pick that up as you learn."

"We'll have too much power in our hands. You could let the former captains retain a portion of that power, and we could supervise their orders."

"If you think about it carefully, you'll realize that won't work. If the Imprinted really do occupy key battle positions, they'll take

20 *Translator's Note:* Liu Buchan commanded the Beiyang Fleet's flagship, the battleship *Dingyuan*, in the aforementioned Battle of Weihaiwei in February 1895.

any necessary measures to evade your supervision, including assassinating their supervisors. A centrally supervised ship on standby requires just three commands to take off, after which it's too late to do anything. The system must only acknowledge commands from the acting captain."

As the personnel craft flew past the Asian Fleet's Jupiter base, Zhang Beihai felt he was flying over a range of towering mountains, except each was a docked warship. The naval base had entered nightside orbit around Jupiter, and the steel mountain clusters slept silently under the surface phosphorescence and the silvery moonlight from Europa overhead. A moment later, a ball of white light rose from the edge of the mountain range, lighting the moored ships in perfect clarity in an instant. To Zhang Beihai, it looked like a sunrise over the mountains, casting a moving shadow of the fleet upon the turbulent Jovian atmosphere down below. When a second light rose over the other side of the fleet, he realized it wasn't the sun, but two warships that were entering the dock and turning their fusion engines toward the base to decelerate.

The fleet's chief of staff, who was delivering Zhang Beihai to his new post, told him that more than four hundred warships, representing two-thirds of the Asian Fleet, were now moored at the base. The remainder of the fleet's ships now cruising the Solar System and beyond were also expected to return to port.

Zhang Beihai had to tear himself away from the grand spectacle of the fleet and return to reality. "Sir, won't recalling all of the ships provoke any Imprinted there are to immediate action?"

"Hmm. No, the order recalling the ships was given for another reason—a real one, not an excuse, although it does sound a little ridiculous. You haven't been watching the news lately, I take it?"

"No. I've been reading materials on *Natural Selection*."

"Don't worry about that. You've got a good grasp of things, judging from the last phase of basic training. Your task now is to familiarize yourself with the systems to the point that everything

can proceed in an orderly manner once you go aboard. It's not as hard as you think. . . . Competition among the three fleets for the task of intercepting the Trisolaran probe has turned into bickering, but a preliminary agreement was hammered out by the Joint Conference yesterday: Each fleet's ships will assemble back at base. A special committee will supervise the execution of the maneuver to avoid any ships being dispatched without authorization to carry out the interception."

"Why has it come to that? Any technological information and intelligence obtained from a successful interception would be shared."

"Yes, but it's a question of honor. There's considerable political capital to be gained by the fleet that makes first contact with Trisolaris. Why did I call it ridiculous? Because it's cheap and absolutely risk-free. The worst thing that could happen is if the probe self-destructs during the interception process, so everyone's gunning for it. If it was a battle with the main Trisolaran Fleet, then all sides would try to preserve their strength. Politics today isn't all that different from your time. . . . Look, there's *Natural Selection*."

As the personnel craft approached *Natural Selection* and the sheer bulk of the iron mountain gradually became clear, the image of *Tang* floated up in Zhang Beihai's mind. *Natural Selection*, comprised of a disc-shaped body and a separate cylindrical engine, looked entirely different from that seagoing aircraft carrier of two centuries before. When *Tang* met its untimely end, it was like he had lost his spiritual home, even though he had never moved in. Now, this giant spaceship gave him a new feeling of home. On *Natural Selection*'s stalwart hull, his spirit found a place to live after two centuries of wandering, like a child enfolded in the embrace of some enormous power.

Natural Selection was the flagship of the third squadron of the Asian Fleet, and in gross tonnage and performance it was second to none. Possessing the latest non-media fusion propulsion system, at full thrust it could accelerate to 15 percent of the speed of light, and its impeccable internal ecological systems could sustain a long-term voyage. In fact, an experimental version of this system

was first put into use on the moon seventy-five years ago and had not yet exhibited any major defects or faults. *Natural Selection*'s weapons were the most powerful in the fleet, too. Its gamma-ray lasers, railguns, high-energy particle beams, and stellar torpedoes made up a four-way weapons system that could obliterate the surface of an Earth-sized planet.

Natural Selection now occupied Zhang Beihai's entire field of view so that only part of it was visible from the personnel craft. He noticed that the outer walls of the ship were mirror-smooth, a broad mirror that perfectly reflected the atmospheric ocean of Jupiter, as well as the gradual approach of the personnel craft.

An oval opening appeared in the outer wall of the ship. The craft flew straight inside and came to a halt. The chief of staff opened the cabin door and exited first. Although Zhang Beihai was slightly nervous because he hadn't seen the craft pass through an air lock, he immediately sensed the influx of fresh air from the outside. The technology to maintain a pressurized compartment opening directly into space without allowing air to leak out was not something he had seen before.

Zhang Beihai and the chief of staff were inside a giant sphere the diameter of a soccer field. Spaceship compartments typically adopted a spherical structure, because during acceleration, deceleration, or change of direction, any point on the sphere could serve as a floor or ceiling, and during weightlessness, the center of the sphere would be the crew's main activity space. In Zhang Beihai's time, cabins had been modeled on the structure of Earth buildings, so he was not at all used to this entirely new cabin structure. The chief of staff told him that this was the fighter hangar, but since there were no fighters right now, a formation of *Natural Selection*'s two thousand officers and soldiers was floating in the center of the sphere.

Before Zhang Beihai entered hibernation, national space forces had begun conducting drills in the weightlessness of space. They had developed specifications and drill books as a result, but implementation had been particularly difficult. Personnel could use their space

suits' microthrusters to move about outside the cabin, but since they lacked propulsion equipment inside, they had to maneuver by pushing against bulkheads and paddling the air. Under such conditions, it was very difficult to form neat lines. Now, he was astonished at the sight of more than two thousand people floating in space in such a neat formation without any supports. These days, personnel moved through weightless cabins primarily by using magnetic belts, fabricated from superconductors and containing a circuit that generated a magnetic field that interacted with the magnetic field that was always present in the cabins and corridors of the spacecraft. With a tiny controller in hand, they could move freely inside the ship. Zhang Beihai was now putting on such a belt, but it would require skill to master.

He watched the formation of space soldiers, a generation that had grown up in the fleet. Their tall, slender bodies had none of the clumsy sturdiness of people growing up under Earth's gravity, but possessed the light agility of spacers. Three officers were in front of the formation, and his gaze eventually rested on the young woman in the center with four glittering stars on her shoulder— *Natural Selection*'s captain, no doubt. A typical representative of new space humanity, taller even than Zhang Beihai, who was himself quite tall. She drifted easily over from the formation, her slender body floating through space like an elegant musical note. When she reached Zhang Beihai and the chief of staff she stopped, and the hair that had been floating behind her rippled around the fair skin of her neck. Her eyes were full of sunshine and vitality, and Zhang Beihai immediately trusted her, because the Imprinted would never wear such an expression.

"Dongfang Yanxu, captain of *Natural Selection*," she said, saluting him. A note of playful challenge appeared in her eyes. "On behalf of the entire crew, I offer a gift to my forbear." She extended her hand, and he saw that, although the object she held in it had changed quite a bit, it was still recognizably a pistol. "If you really find that I have defeatist thinking and Escapist goals, you may use this to kill me."

Getting to the surface was easy. The trunk of every giant tree building was a pillar supporting the dome of the underground city, and from the trunk you could take an elevator directly to the surface, passing through more than three hundred meters of rock. When Luo Ji and Shi Qiang exited the elevator, they felt nostalgic, a feeling prompted by one thing: The walls and floor of the exit hall did not have activated display windows. Information was displayed on actual display screens that hung from the ceiling. It looked like an old subway station, and most of the handful of people in it wore clothes that didn't flash.

When they passed through the hall air lock, they were met by a hot wind blowing dusty air.

"There's my boy!" Shi Qiang shouted, pointing at a man bounding up the steps. From this distance, Luo Ji could make out only that the man was in his forties, so he was a little surprised at Shi Qiang's certainty. As Shi Qiang hurried down the stairs to welcome his son, Luo Ji turned his eyes from the reunion to the surface world before him.

The sky was yellow. He now realized why the image of the sky showing in the underground city was shot from a height of ten thousand meters, because, from the ground, the sun was only visible as a hazy outline. Sand covered everything on the ground, and cars passed by on the streets dragging dusty tails. It was another sight from the past for Luo Ji: cars that traveled on the ground. They didn't seem to run on gasoline. They came in all kinds of weird shapes, and some were new and some old, but they all shared one feature: Every car had a flat sheet installed on the roof, like an awning. Across the street, he saw an old-era building with sand-covered windowsills and windows that were either boarded up or glassless black holes. However, people were evidently living in some of the rooms, because he saw clothing hanging outside to dry and even some potted flowers on the windowsills. Though the airborne sand and dust kept visibility low, he soon located a couple of familiar building outlines

farther away and knew for certain that he was in the same city where he had spent half his life two centuries ago. He walked down the steps to the two men who were hugging and pounding each other in their excitement. Seeing the middle-aged man up close, he knew that Shi Qiang hadn't made a mistake.

"Dad, when you figure it, I'm only five years younger than you," Shi Xiaoming said, wiping tears from the corners of his eyes.

"Not bad, kiddo. I was afraid some damn white-bearded old man would be calling me Dad," Shi Qiang said with a chuckle. Then he introduced Luo Ji to his son.

"Oh, Dr. Luo. You used to be world famous," Shi Xiaoming said, as he looked Luo Ji up and down.

The three of them headed toward Shi Xiaoming's car, which was parked at the side of the road. Before they got in, Luo Ji asked about the thing on the roof.

"It's an antenna. Up on the surface, we have to use whatever electricity leaks through from the underground city, so the antennas are a little larger, and the power is only enough to run the cars on the ground. They can't fly."

The car wasn't fast, due either to the power or the sand on the road. Luo Ji looked out the window at the sandy city. He had a belly full of questions, but Shi Xiaoming and his father kept talking and he couldn't get a word in.

"Mom passed away in Year 34 of the Crisis. Me and your granddaughter were with her then."

"Oh, good. . . . You didn't bring my granddaughter with you?"

"After the divorce, she went with her mom. I looked up her file. She lived into her eighties and died in Year 105."

"Too bad I never met her. . . . How old were you when your sentence ended?"

"Nineteen."

"What did you do then?"

"Everything. At first, with no other way out, I kept up the swindles, but then I did a bit of legitimate business. After I had the money, I saw the signs of the Great Ravine and went into

hibernation. I didn't know then that things would get better later on. I just wanted to see you."

"Is our house still there?"

"Land-use rights were extended past the original seventy-year period, but I only got to stay a short time before it was demolished. The one we bought later is still there, but I haven't been to see it." Shi Xiaoming pointed outside. "The city population isn't even one percent of what it was in our day. Do you know what the most worthless thing is? That house. You dedicated your entire life to it, Dad, but everything's empty now. You can live wherever you like."

Finally Luo Ji managed to seize a gap in their conversation to ask, "Do all reawakened hibernators live in the old city?"

"No way! They live outside. There's too much sand in the city. But mostly, it's because there's nothing to do. Of course, you can't go too far from the underground city, or you can't get electricity."

"What do all of you do?" Shi Qiang asked.

"Think: What can we do that the kids can't? Farming!" Shi Xiaoming, like other hibernators, no matter their age, had the habit of calling modern people "kids."

The car left the city and drove east. As the sand lessened to reveal the highway, Luo Ji recognized it as the old expressway between Beijing and Shijiazhuang, although both sides were piled high with sand now. The old buildings still stood there amid the sand, but what brought a spark of life to this desertified plain of northern China were the small oases ringed by sparse trees, which Shi Xiaoming said were hibernator settlements.

They drove into one oasis, a small residential community surrounded by a sand-break of trees that Shi Xiaoming called New Life Village #5. When he got out of the car, Luo Ji felt time flowing backward: rows of six-story apartments fronted by open space, old men playing chess on stone tables, mothers pushing baby carriages, and a few children playing soccer on the sparse lawn growing on the sand. . . .

Shi Xiaoming lived on the sixth floor with a wife nine years younger than him. She had entered hibernation in Year 21 due

to liver cancer, but was completely healthy now. They had a four-year-old son who called Shi Qiang "Grampa."

A sumptuous lunch had been laid out to welcome Luo Ji and Shi Qiang: local farm produce, chicken and pork produced at other nearby farms, and even home-brewed alcohol. They called three of their neighbors to join them, three men who—like Shi Xiaoming—had entered hibernation relatively early, back when it was expensive and available only to rich members of the upper class or their sons and daughters. Now, gathered here after a span of more than a century, they were all just ordinary people. Shi Xiaoming introduced one neighbor as Zhang Yan, the grandson of Zhang Yuanchao, the man he had cheated back in the day.

"Remember how you made me return the money I cheated him out of? I began the day I got out, and that's how I met Yan. He had just graduated from college. Taking inspiration from his two neighbors, we went into the funeral business and called our firm the High and Deep Company. 'High,' for space burials. We shot ashes into the Solar System, and later on we were able to launch entire bodies. For a price, of course. 'Deep,' for mine burials. At first we used abandoned shafts, and later on we dug new ones, since they would work equally well as anti-Trisolaris tombs too."

The man called Yan was a little older—he looked to be in his fifties or sixties. Shi Xiaoming explained that Yan had been reawakened once before and lived for more than thirty years before going back into hibernation.

"What's our legal status here?" Luo Ji asked.

Shi Xiaoming said, "Completely equivalent to modern residential areas. We count as the city's distant suburbs, and we have a proper district government. It's not just hibernators who live here. We also have modern people, and people from the city often come out here for fun."

Zhang Yan took over: "We call the modern people 'walltappers,' because when they first get here they're always touching the wall out of habit, trying to activate something."

"So life's okay?" Shi Qiang asked.

They all said it was pretty good.

"But along the road I saw the fields you plant. Can you really support yourselves by growing crops?"

"Why not? In the cities these days, agricultural products are luxury items. . . . The government's actually quite good to hibernators. Even if you don't do anything, you can still live comfortably off government subsidies. But you've got to have something to do. The idea that hibernators all know how to farm is nonsense. No one was a farmer at first, but this is all we can do."

The conversation quickly turned to the history of the past two centuries.

"So what was the deal with the Great Ravine?" Luo Ji brought up the question he had long been wanting to ask.

Instantly their faces grew serious. Seeing that the meal was almost over, Shi Xiaoming allowed the topic to continue. "You've probably learned a little about it over the past few days. It's a long story. For more than a decade after you went into hibernation, life was pretty good. But later on, when the pace of economic transformation picked up, the standard of living declined by the day and the political climate constricted. It really felt like wartime."

A neighbor said, "It wasn't just a few countries. The entire Earth was like that. Society was on edge, and if you said something wrong they would say you were ETO, or a traitor to humanity, so nobody felt safe. And film and television from the Golden Age began to be restricted, and then was banned worldwide. Of course, there was too much of it to ban effectively."

"Why?"

"They were afraid of eroding the fighting spirit," Shi Xiaoming said. "Still, so long as there was food to eat, you could make do. But later on, things got worse, and the world began to starve. This was about twenty years after Dr. Luo went into hibernation."

"Because of the economic transition?"

"Right. But environmental deterioration was also a major factor. The environmental laws were there, but in those pessimistic times, the general attitude was, 'What the hell is environmental

protection for? Even if Earth turns into a garden, isn't it all going to the Trisolarans anyway?' Eventually, environmental protection was seen as no less treasonous to humanity than the ETO. Organizations like Greenpeace were treated like ETO branches and suppressed. Work on the space forces accelerated the development of highly polluting heavy industry, which made environmental pollution unstoppable. The greenhouse effect, climate anomalies, desertification . . ." He sighed.

"When I entered hibernation, desertification was just starting," another neighbor said. "It's not what you imagine, like the desert advancing from the Great Wall. No! It was patchwork erosion. Perfectly fine plots of land in the interior began turning to desert simultaneously, and it spread from those points, like how a damp cloth dries in the sun."

"Then agricultural production plummeted, and grain reserves were exhausted. And then . . . and then came the Great Ravine."

"Did the prediction that the standard of living would go backward a hundred years come true?" Luo Ji asked.

Shi Xiaoming gave a few bitter chuckles. "Ah, Dr. Luo. A hundred years? In your dreams! A hundred years back from that time would have been . . . around the 1930s or so. A paradise compared to the Great Ravine! No way the two are the same. For one thing, there were so many more people than in the Great Depression— 8.3 billion!" He pointed at Zhang Yan. "He saw the Great Ravine when he reawakened for a while. You tell them."

Zhang Yan drained his glass. Eyes blank, he said, "I have seen the grand march of hunger. Millions of people fleeing famine on the great plains through sand that blocked out the sky. Hot sky, hot earth, and hot sun. When they died, they were divided up on the spot. . . . It was hell on Earth. There are tons of videos to watch if you want. You think of that time, and you feel lucky to be alive."

"The Great Ravine lasted for about half a century, and in those fifty-odd years, the world population dropped from 8.3 billion to 3.5 billion. Think about what that means!"

Luo Ji got up and went over to the window. From here he could

see the desert across the protective tree line, its yellow covering of sand extending silently to the horizon under the noonday sun. The hand of time had smoothed over everything.

"And then?" Shi Qiang asked.

Zhang Yan let out a long breath, as if no longer having to talk about that period of history had taken a burden off his shoulders. "After that, well, some people came to terms with it, and then more and more people did. They wondered whether it was worth it to pay so high a price, even if it was for victory in the Doomsday Battle. Think about what's more important: the child dying of starvation in your arms, or the continuation of human civilization? Right now you might think the latter choice is more important, but you wouldn't have in that day and age. No matter what the future might bring, the present is most important. Of course, that mind-set was outrageous at first, the classic thinking of a traitor to humanity, but you couldn't stop people from thinking it. And very soon the entire world thought so. There was a popular slogan back then, which soon became a famous historical quote."

" 'Make time for civilization, for civilization won't make time,' " Luo Ji contributed, without looking back from the window.

"Right, that one. Civilization is meant for us."

"And after that?" Shi Qiang asked.

"A second Enlightenment, a second Renaissance, a second French Revolution . . . You can find all that stuff in the history books."

Luo Ji turned back in surprise. The predictions he had made to Zhuang Yan two centuries before had come to pass. "A second French Revolution? In France?!"

"No, no. That's just a saying. It was the entire world! After the revolution, the new national governments terminated their space strategies and poured their attention into improving people's lives. And then critical technology emerged: Genetic engineering and fusion technology were harnessed for large-scale food production, ending the age of weather-dependent food. From then on, the world would no longer be hungry. Everything moved quickly after

that—there were fewer people, after all—and in the space of just two decades, life returned to pre-Great Ravine levels. Then Golden Age levels were restored. People had set their hearts on this road of comfort, and no one wanted to go back."

"There's another term you might find interesting, Dr. Luo," said the first neighbor, drawing closer to him. An economist before hibernation, he had a deeper understanding of the issues. "It's called civilization immunity. It means that when the world has suffered a serious illness, it triggers civilization's immune system, so that something like the early Crisis Era won't happen again. Humanism comes first, and perpetuating civilization comes second. These are the concepts that today's society is based on."

"And after that?" Luo Ji asked.

"After that came the freaky stuff." Shi Xiaoming grew excited. "Originally, the countries of the world had planned to live in peace and push the Trisolar Crisis onto the back burner, but what do you think happened? There was swift progress everywhere. Technology sped forward and broke through all the technical obstacles that had stood in the way of space strategy before the Great Ravine, one after the other!"

"That's not freaky," Luo Ji said. "Emancipation of human nature inevitably brings with it scientific and technological progress."

"After about half a century of peace following the Great Ravine, the world turned its thoughts back to the Trisolaran invasion and felt it ought to reconsider the war. With humanity's power now on a completely different plane than before the Great Ravine, a global state of war was again declared, and construction was begun on a space fleet. But unlike the first time, national constitutions were clear about one thing: Resource expenditure for the space strategy had to be kept within a specified range, and must not have a disastrous impact on the world economy and on community life. And that's when the space fleets became independent countries. . . ."

"You don't actually have to think about any of this, though," the economist said. "From now on, just think about how to live a good life. That old revolutionary slogan is just an adaptation of the

old saying from the Golden Age: 'Make time for life, or life won't make time.' To new life!"

When they had drained their last glass, Luo Ji praised the economist for putting things so well. Now his mind had space only for Zhuang Yan and the child. He wanted to get settled as soon as possible, and then go wake them.

Make time for civilization, make time for life.

After boarding *Natural Selection,* Zhang Beihai found that the modern command system had evolved far beyond what he had imagined. The giant spacecraft, equal in volume to three of the largest seagoing carriers of the twenty-first century, was practically a small city, but it had no bridge or command module, or even a captain's room or operations room. In fact, it had no specific functional compartments whatsoever. All of them were identical, regular spheres that differed only in size. At any location inside the ship, you could just use a data glove to activate a holographic display, which, due to the high cost, was a rarity even in Earth's super-wired society. And at any location, so long as you had the appropriate system permissions, you could pull up a complete command console, including a captain's interface, which effectively made the entire ship, even the passageways and bathrooms, a bridge, command module, captain's room, and operations room! To Zhang Beihai, it felt like the evolution from a client-server model to a browser-server model in late-twentieth-century computer networks. With the former, you could only access the server through specific software installed on a computer, but using the latter, you could access the server from any computer on the network so long as you had the right permissions.

Zhang Beihai and Dongfang Yanxu were situated in an ordinary cabin that, like every other one, had no special instruments or screens. It was just a spherical compartment whose bulkheads were white most of the time, making it feel like the inside of a giant Ping-Pong ball. When gravity was produced by ship acceleration,

any part of the spherical bulkhead could be transformed into a shape suitable for use as a chair.

For Zhang Beihai, this was another aspect of modern technology that few people had imagined: the elimination of single-purpose facilities. Only the first tendrils of this trend had appeared on Earth, but it was part of the fundamental structure of the far more advanced world of the fleet. This world was spare and simple. Devices were no longer permanently installed, but would appear when necessary at any location required. The world, made complex by technology, was becoming simple again, its technology hidden deeply behind the face of reality.

"Now we come to your first onboard lesson," Dongfang Yanxu said. "Of course, you really shouldn't be getting this lesson from a captain who's under review, but no one in the fleet is more trustworthy than I am. Today, we'll demonstrate how to launch *Natural Selection* and put it into navigation mode. And, in fact, so long as you remember what you see today, you'll have closed off the primary opening for the Imprinted." As she spoke, she used her data glove to call up a holographic star chart in the air. "This may be a little different from the spatial maps of your time, but it still uses the sun as the origin."

"I studied this in training, so I can read it fine," Zhang Beihai said, looking at the star chart. His memory of the ancient Solar System map he and Chang Weisi had stood in front of two centuries ago was still fresh. This chart, however, precisely marked out the positions of all celestial bodies within a radius of one hundred light-years of the sun, at a scale more than a hundred times greater than the older one.

"You don't really need to understand much. In the present state, navigation to any position on the map is prohibited. . . . If I were Imprinted, and wanted to hijack *Natural Selection* to flee into the cosmos, I'd first need to select a heading, like this." She activated a point on the map, turning it green. "Of course, we're just in simulation mode right now, because I no longer have permissions. When you obtain captain's permissions, I'll have to go through you

to perform the operations. But if I really submitted this operation request, it would be a dangerous act, and you should refuse it. You should also report me."

Once the heading was activated, an interface appeared in the air. Zhang Beihai was already quite familiar with the appearance and operations from his training, but he still listened patiently to Dongfang Yanxu's explanation and watched how she brought the huge ship from complete shutdown to hibernation, then to standby, and finally to Slow Ahead.

"If these were real operations, *Natural Selection* would now leave port. What do you think? Simpler than spaceship operations in your day?"

"Yes. Much simpler." When he and the other special contingent members first saw the interface, they were surprised at its simplicity, and the total lack of technical detail.

"The operation is totally automatic, leaving the technical process entirely hidden from the captain."

"This display only shows general parameters. How do you see the ship's operational status?"

"Operational status is monitored by officers and noncommissioned officers at lower levels. Their displays are more complex—the further down you go, the more complicated the interface becomes. As captain and vice-captain, we must focus our attention on more important matters. . . . Very well, let's continue. If I were Imprinted . . . There I go with that supposition again. What do you think?"

"Given my position, any response would be irresponsible."

"Fine. If I were Imprinted, then I'd set the throttle directly to Ahead Four. No other ship in the fleet can catch *Natural Selection* under Ahead Four acceleration."

"But you couldn't do that, even if you had the permissions, because the system will only proceed to Ahead Four if it detects that all passengers are in a deep-sea state."

Under maximum propulsion, the ship's acceleration could reach 120 gs, but this exerted a force more than ten times what a human could tolerate under normal conditions. To go to maximum,

they had to enter a "deep-sea state," which consisted of the cabins being filled with an oxygen-rich "deep-sea acceleration fluid" that trained personnel could breathe directly. As they breathed, it would fill their lungs and then the rest of their organs. First dreamed up in the first half of the twentieth century, the liquid was intended at the time to facilitate ultra-deep dives. Pressure was in equilibrium inside and outside of a human body filled with deep-sea acceleration fluid, meaning it could sustain high pressures like a deep-sea fish. The environment of a liquid-filled cabin in a rapidly accelerating spacecraft was like that of the deep sea, so the liquid was now being used to protect human bodies against the ultra-high acceleration of space travel. Hence the term "deep-sea state."

Dongfang Yanxu nodded. "But you should know that there's a way to get around that. If you set the spacecraft to remote control, then it will assume that no one is on board and won't perform the check. This setting is part of the captain's permissions."

"Let me try it and you tell me if I've got it right." Zhang Beihai activated an interface in front of him and began setting up remote control mode for the spacecraft, looking at a small notebook from time to time as he did so.

Dongfang Yanxu smiled at the notebook. "There are more efficient recording methods now."

"Oh, it's just habit. For particularly important things, it's always more reassuring to write them down like this. It's just that I can't find a pen now. I brought two with me into hibernation, but only the pencil was still usable."

"You've learned quickly."

"That's because the command system retains a lot of the navy's style. After all these years, the names of things haven't even changed. The engine orders, for example."

"The space fleet did have its origins in the navy. . . . Okay, you'll soon be receiving system permissions as the acting captain of *Natural Selection*. This warship is in class-A standby, or, as they called it in your time, 'fired up and ready to go.'" She extended her slender arms and turned a circle in the air.

Zhang Beihai had not been able to figure out how to perform that action using the superconducting belt. "We didn't 'fire up' in those days. But you evidently know quite a bit of naval history," he said, changing the subject from the sensitive issue that was liable to make her hostile to him.

"A grand old branch of the service."

"Doesn't the space fleet inherit that grandeur?"

"Yes. But I'm going to leave it. I plan on resigning."

"Because of the review?"

She turned to look at him, her thick black hair leaping again from the lack of gravity. "You encountered this sort of thing all the time back then, didn't you?"

"Not necessarily. But if we did, every comrade would understand, because undergoing review is one of the duties of a soldier."

"Two centuries have passed. This is no longer your time."

"Dongfang, don't deliberately widen the gap. There are similarities between the two of us. Soldiers in all ages have to bear up under humiliation."

"Are you advising me to stay?"

"No."

"Ideological work. That's the word, isn't it? Wasn't that your duty once?"

"Not anymore. I have a new duty."

She floated easily around him, as if carefully studying him. "Is it that we're children to you? Half a year ago I went to Earth, and in one hibernator district, a six- or seven-year-old boy called me a kid."

He laughed.

"Are we kids to you?"

"In our day, seniority was very important. In the countryside, there were adults who called children Aunt and Uncle because of family seniority."

"But your seniority is unimportant to me."

"I can see that in your eyes."

"Your daughter, and your wife—they didn't come with you?

Special Contingent family members were allowed to hibernate, too, as far as I'm aware."

"They didn't come, and they didn't want me to go. You know, trends at the time pointed toward a very bleak future. They criticized me for being irresponsible. She and her mother moved out, and in the dead of night the day after they left, the Special Contingent received the order. I didn't even have time to see them again. It was on a late winter's night, a cold one, that I left home carrying my bags. . . . Of course, I'm not expecting you to understand any of this."

"I understand. . . . What happened to them?"

"My wife died in Year 47. My daughter in Year 81."

"They saw the Great Ravine." She lowered her eyes and remained silent for a while. Then she activated a holographic window and switched to an external display mode.

The bulkheads of the white sphere melted like wax and *Natural Selection* vanished, leaving them suspended in infinite space, facing the misty starfield of the Milky Way. They were now two independent beings in the universe, unattached to any world, with nothing but the abyss surrounding them. They hung in the universe like the Earth, the sun, and the galaxy itself, with no origin and no destination. Simply existing . . .

Zhang Beihai had experienced this feeling before, 190 years ago, when he floated in space wearing nothing but a space suit, holding a pistol loaded with meteorite bullets.

"I like it this way, where you can ignore the spacecraft and the fleet and everything outside your own mind," she said.

"Dongfang," he called softly.

"Hmm?" The captain turned around, her eyes shining with the starlight of the Milky Way.

"If the day comes when I have to kill you, please forgive me," he said gently.

She met his words with a smile. "Do I look to you like I'm Imprinted?"

He looked at her in the sunlight coming from five AU away. She was a lithe feather floating against the backdrop of the starfield.

"We belong to the Earth and the sea, you belong to the stars."

"Is that bad?"

"No. It's very good."

"The probe's gone out!"

The report from the duty officer came as a shock to Dr. Kuhn and General Robinson. They knew that once the news got out it would make waves in both the Earth International and the Fleet International, particularly since the latest observations of the probe's speed meant that it would cross the orbit of Jupiter in just six days.

Kuhn and Robinson were on the Ringier-Fitzroy Station that orbited the sun along the outside rim of the asteroid belt. Floating in space five kilometers away from the station were the most peculiar objects in the Solar System: a set of six giant lenses, the top one 1,200 meters in diameter, and the five below it slightly smaller in size. This was the latest incarnation of the space telescope, but unlike the previous five generations of the Hubble, this space telescope had no barrel, or any connecting material at all between the six giant lenses. They floated independently, the rim of each lens equipped with multiple ion thrusters that could precisely adjust the distance between them or change the orientation of the entire group. Ringier-Fitzroy Station was the control center for the telescope, but even from this close, the transparent lenses were practically invisible. When technicians and engineers would fly between them during maintenance, the universe on either side would be grossly distorted, and if they were at the proper angle, the protective iris on the surface would reflect the sunlight and reveal the entire giant lens, whose curved surface would then resemble a planet covered in bewitching rainbows. The telescope broke with the Hubble series naming convention and was dubbed the Ringier-Fitzroy Telescope, to commemorate the two men who discovered the tracks of the Trisolaran Fleet. Although their discovery had no scholarly significance, the name was fitting, because the primary purpose of this

massive telescope, a joint project of the three major fleets, was the continued monitoring of the Trisolaran Fleet.

A team like Ringier and Fitzroy—a lead scientist from Earth and a head of military affairs from the fleet—had always been in charge of the telescope, and in every such team there were the same differences of opinion that Ringier and Fitzroy had. Right now, Kuhn wanted to squeeze in some observation time for his own study of the cosmos, while Robinson worked to stop him, so as to safeguard the fleet's interests. They argued about other things, too: For example, Kuhn reminisced over the wonderful way that Earth's superpowers, headed up by the United States, were leading the world, in contrast to the fleets' current inefficient bureaucracy; but every time he did so, Robinson would ruthlessly dismantle Kuhn's ridiculous historical fantasies. But the most heated argument was over the station's rotation speed. The general insisted on a slow rotation for minimal gravity, even to the point of keeping the station in an entirely weightless state with no rotation at all, while Kuhn stumped for a fast rotation and Earth standard gravity.

But what was happening now overwhelmed all of that. The probe having "gone out" meant that its engines had turned off. Two years before, far beyond the Oort Cloud, the probe had begun to decelerate, which meant that its engine had started up in a sun-facing direction, enabling the space telescope to track the probe by engine light. Now that the light had gone out, tracking was no longer possible, because the probe itself was far too small—probably no bigger than a truck, based on the wake it left crossing the interstellar dust. An object that small out on the periphery of the Kuiper Belt, no longer emitting its own light and reflecting the weak light of the distant sun even more weakly—even a telescope as powerful as Ringier-Fitzroy couldn't see such a tiny dark object so far off in the darkness of space.

"The three fleets don't know how to do anything but struggle over power. This is just perfect—the target's been lost. . . ." Kuhn grumbled, waving his arms for emphasis. He forgot the station

was now in a weightless state, and his movements caused him to perform a somersault.

For the first time, General Robinson did not defend the fleet. The Asian Fleet had originally dispatched three light, high-speed ships to track the probe at close range, but after the dispute erupted among the three fleets over the right to intercept, the Joint Conference had issued a resolution recalling all craft to base. The Asian Fleet repeatedly protested that the three fighter-class spaceships had been stripped of all weapons and external equipment and were carrying a crew of just two people each to achieve maximum acceleration for tracking the target, and even so, they could not possibly intercept the probe. However, the European and North American Fleets were unconvinced, and insisted that all spaceships in transit be recalled and replaced by three spaceships dispatched by Earth International as a fourth party. If not for that, the fleet ships would already have made close contact with the probe and begun tracking it. Earth's ships, dispatched by the European Commonwealth and China, had not even passed the orbit of Neptune.

"Perhaps. Its engines might start up again," the general said. "It's still traveling pretty fast, and if it doesn't decelerate it won't be able to rest in solar orbit. It'll pass right through the Solar System."

"Are you the Trisolaran commander? Maybe the probe wasn't ever planning on remaining in the Solar System, but was just going to pass through anyway!" Kuhn said. Then a thought suddenly struck him. "If the engines are off, then it can't change course! Can't you just figure out where it's headed and send the tracking spacecraft to wait for it?"

The general shook his head. "That's not precise enough. It's not like an air force search in Earth's atmosphere. One minuscule error, and you'll be hundreds of thousands or even millions of kilometers off course. In such a huge area, the tracking craft won't be able to find such a tiny, dark target. . . . But we've got to come up with a way somehow."

"What can we do? Let the fleet figure it out."

The general turned tough. "Doctor, you've got to realize the

nature of the situation. Even though this isn't our fault, the media won't care. The Ringier-Fitzroy system was, after all, responsible for tracking the probe in deep space, so a good portion of that dirty water is going to land on our heads."

Kuhn said nothing, but remained with his body perpendicular to the general's for a while. Then he asked, "Is there anything else outside Neptune's orbit that could be useful?"

"For the fleet, probably nothing. For Earth . . ." The general turned to ask the duty officer and soon learned that the UN Environmental Protection Organization had four large ships near Neptune, working on the early stages of the Fog Umbrella Project. The three small craft newly tasked with tracking the probe had been dispatched from those ships.

"And they're there to mine oil film?" Kuhn asked. The reply was affirmative. Oil film was a substance found in Neptune's rings. At high temperatures, it turned into a rapidly diffusing gas that then condensed into nanoparticles in space, forming space dust. It was so called because when it evaporated, it became highly diffusive, so a small quantity of the substance could form a large patch of dust, like a tiny droplet of oil spreading into an oil film of molecular thickness across a large area of water. Dust formed from this oil film had another property: Unlike other types of space dust, "oil-film dust" was not easily dispersed by the solar wind.

It was the discovery of oil film that made the Fog Umbrella Project possible. The plan was to use nuclear blasts in space to evaporate and spread the oil-film substance into a cloud of oil-film dust between the sun and Earth as a means of decreasing the sun's radiation on Earth and alleviating global warming.

"I remember there's supposed to be a stellar bomb near Neptune orbit from before the wars," Kuhn said.

"There is. And the Fog Umbrella spaceships brought along a few, too, for blasting Neptune and its satellites. I'm not sure of the precise number."

"I'd say one is enough," Kuhn said excitedly.

Like Wallfacer Rey Diaz had predicted two centuries prior when

he developed the stellar hydrogen bomb for his Wallfacer plan, although the weapon would be of limited use in the Doomsday Battle, the major powers wanted it to prepare for the possible outbreak of interplanetary war between humans. More than five thousand bombs had been manufactured, mostly during the Great Ravine, when international relations grew volatile due to lack of resources, and humanity was pushed to the brink of war. When the new era dawned, the horrifying weapons became dangerous nonessentials that were kept in storage in outer space, although they still belonged to countries on Earth. A few of them were blown up in planetary engineering projects, and another set was sent into orbit in the remote Solar System with the notion that the fusion materials could supplement the fuel of long-range spacecraft. However, because of the difficulty involved in dismantling the bombs, this idea was never realized.

"Do you think it'll work?" Robinson asked, his eyes aglow. He was a little rueful that he hadn't thought up such a simple idea himself, and that Kuhn had snatched the opportunity to go down in history.

"Give it a try. It's the only thing we've got."

"If your idea works, Doctor, then the Ringier-Fitzroy Station will forever revolve fast enough to generate Earth gravity."

"It's the biggest thing humanity has ever made," the commander of *Blue Shadow* said, as he looked out the spacecraft's window into the pitch-black of space. Nothing was visible, but he tried to convince himself that he could see the dust cloud.

"Why isn't it lit by the sun, like the tail of a comet?" the pilot said. He and the commander were the only crew on *Blue Shadow*. He knew the density of the dust cloud was as thin as a comet's tail, or about the same as a vacuum created in an Earth-based laboratory.

"Maybe the sunlight is too weak." The commander looked back at the sun, which, in the lonely space between Neptune's orbit and the Kuiper Belt, looked like a large star, its disc shape

only barely distinguishable. Still, even the weak sunlight could still cast shadows on the bulkhead. "Besides, a comet tail is only visible from a certain distance away. We're just at the edge of the cloud."

The pilot tried to conjure up a mental image of the thin yet gigantic cloud. A few days ago, he and the commander had seen with their own eyes how small the cloud was when compressed into a solid. At the time, the giant spaceship *Pacific* had arrived from Neptune and left behind five things when it stopped in this section of space. The *Blue Shadow*'s mechanical arm first retrieved a stellar hydrogen bomb from the early days of the war, a cylinder five meters long and a meter and a half in diameter. Next it picked up four large spheres between thirty and fifty meters in diameter. The four spheres, the oil film harvested from Neptune's rings, were placed at points several hundred meters from the bomb. Once *Pacific* had departed the vicinity, the bomb exploded, forming a small sun whose light and heat surged into the cold abyss of space and instantly vaporized the surrounding spheres. The gaseous oil film diffused rapidly under the typhoon of H-bomb radiation, then cooled into countless tiny particles of dust, forming a cloud. The cloud had a diameter of two million kilometers, greater than that of the sun.

The dust cloud was located in the region that the Trisolaran probe was expected to pass through, according to path observations made prior to its engine shutting off. Dr. Kuhn and General Robinson hoped to precisely determine the probe's path and position by the tracks it left in the man-made dust cloud.

Following the formation of the cloud, *Pacific* returned to Neptune base, leaving behind three small spaceships that would track the probe closely once its wake showed. *Blue Shadow* was one of them. The small high-speed ship had been dubbed a "space racer." With a small capsule that could seat five as its only payload, its remaining volume was entirely occupied by a fusion engine, giving it high acceleration and maneuverability. Once the dust cloud took shape, *Blue Shadow* flew through the entire area to test whether wakes would be left, with quite satisfactory results. Of course, the wakes could only be observed by the space telescope

more than one hundred AU distant. From *Blue Shadow* itself, its own wake was invisible, and the surrounding space was as deserted as it always had been. Still, after passing through the cloud, the pilot insisted that the sun looked a little dimmer, that its formerly sharp circumference had gone a bit blurry. Instrument observations confirmed the sole visual impression they had of this giant creation.

"Less than three hours to go," the commander said, looking at his watch. The dust cloud was actually a giant, thin satellite in orbit around the sun, its position constantly changing. When it eventually moved out of the space where the probe might pass through, another dust cloud would have to be created behind it.

"Do you really hope we'll catch up to it?" the pilot asked.

"Why not? We're making history!"

"Won't the thing attack us? We're not soldiers. This really ought to be done by the fleet."

Then their spacecraft received a message from the Ringier-Fitzroy Station reporting that the Trisolaran probe had entered the dust cloud and left a wake, and that precise parameters had been calculated for its trajectory. *Blue Shadow* was ordered to move immediately to rendezvous with and closely track the target. The station was more than one hundred AU away from *Blue Shadow,* meaning the message was delayed more than ten hours in transit, but the key had made an impression in the mold. Orbital calculations had even taken into account the effect of the thin dust cloud, so a rendezvous was just a matter of time.

Blue Shadow set a course in accordance with the probe's path and once again entered the invisible dust cloud, this time heading in the direction of the Trisolaran probe. It was a long flight this time, and over the course of more than ten hours, both pilot and commander grew sleepy. But the continuously shrinking distance between them and the probe kept them on edge.

"I see it! I see it!" the pilot shouted.

"What are you talking about? There's still over fourteen thousand kilometers to go!" rebuked the commander. The naked eye could not possibly see a truck at a distance of fourteen thousand

kilometers, even given the transparency of space. But soon he saw it for himself: On the trajectory described by the parameters, against the silent backdrop of space, a point of light was in motion.

After a moment's thought, the commander understood: The cloud of dust larger than the sun had been unnecessary, since the Trisolaran probe had restarted its engines and was continuing to decelerate. It did not intend to skip through the Solar System. It would remain here.

Because it was only a temporary measure in the fleets, the ceremony for handing over captain's permissions on *Natural Selection* was a simple and low-key affair attended only by Captain Dongfang Yanxu, Acting Captain Zhang Beihai, First Vice-Captain Levine, and Second Vice-Captain Akira Inoue, as well as a special team from the General Staff Department.

Despite this era's technological development, they had still not managed to overcome the stagnation of fundamental theory, so *Natural Selection*'s permissions transfer was done via means Zhang Beihai was familiar with: three-factor retina, fingerprint, and pass-phrase authentication.

Once the General Staff team had finished resetting the pupil and fingerprint data that identified the captain in the system, Dongfang Yanxu surrendered her pass phrase to Zhang Beihai: "Men always remember love because of romance only."

"You don't smoke," he replied calmly.

"And the brand was lost during the Great Ravine," she said with a trace of disappointment, and lowered her eyes.

"But the password's a good one. Not many people knew it back then either."

The captain and vice-captains exited, leaving Zhang Beihai alone to update the password and obtain complete control over *Natural Selection*.

"He's clever," Akira Inoue said when the door to the spherical cabin vanished.

"Ancient wisdom," Dongfang Yanxu said, watching the spot where the door had disappeared, as if trying to see through it. "We'll never be able to learn the stuff he brought from two centuries ago, but he can learn what we know."

Then the three of them remained silent and waited. Five minutes passed, clearly too long for changing a password, especially since Captain-in-waiting Zhang Beihai had come through training as the most skilled command system operator out of all the members of his Special Contingent. Five more minutes passed. The two vice-captains began swimming impatiently in the corridor, but Dongfang Yanxu remained silent and motionless.

At last the door reappeared. To their surprise, the spherical cabin had turned black. Zhang Beihai had a holographic star map pulled up on which the labels had been blocked, leaving only the twinkling stars. From the doorway, he seemed to be suspended outside the spaceship, with his interface floating alongside him.

"I'm done," he said.

"Why did it take so long?" Levin grumbled.

"Were you relishing the thrill of gaining *Natural Selection*?" Akira Inoue asked.

Zhang Beihai said nothing. He didn't look at the interface, but gazed off instead at a star in a distant part of the map. Dongfang Yanxu noticed that a green light was flashing in the direction he was looking.

"That would be ridiculous," Levin said, picking up from Akira Inoue. "May I remind you that the captainship still belongs to Colonel Dongfang? The acting captain is just a firewall. I'm sorry to be rude about it, but that's pretty much the truth."

Akira Inoue said, "And this state won't last for very long. The investigation of the fleet is nearing an end, and it's basically been proven that the Imprinted don't exist."

He was about to go on, but was stopped by a low gasp of surprise from the captain. "Oh, god!" she said, and the two vice-captains, following her eyes, noticed *Natural Selection*'s current status on Zhang Beihai's interface.

The warship had been set into remote control mode, thereby bypassing the check for deep-sea state prior to Ahead Four. Outside communication had been severed. And, finally, most of the captain's settings for putting the ship into maximum propulsion were in place. With the push of just one more button, *Natural Selection* would head off at maximum speed to the target selected on the map.

"No, this can't be happening," Dongfang Yanxu said, her voice so low only she could hear it. It was for her own ears, in response to her earlier "god" exclamation. She had never believed in the existence of God, but now her prayers were real.

"Are you insane?" Levin shouted. He and Akira Inoue rushed toward the cabin, only to crash into the bulkhead. There was no door, just an oval-shaped section of wall that had turned transparent.

"*Natural Selection* is about to proceed to Ahead Four. All crew must enter deep-sea state immediately," Zhang Beihai said, every word in his solemn, calm voice lingering in the air like an ancient anchor standing in the chill wind.

"This is impossible!" Akira Inoue said.

"Are you Imprinted?" Dongfang Yanxu asked, quickly calming herself.

"You know that's not possible."

"ETO?"

"No."

"Then who are you?"

"A soldier carrying out his duty to fight for humanity's survival."

"Why are you doing this?"

"I'll explain after acceleration is complete. I repeat: All crew must enter deep-sea state immediately."

"This is impossible!" Akira Inoue repeated.

Zhang Beihai turned around and, without so much as looking at the two vice-captains, stared straight at Dongfang Yanxu. His eyes instantly reminded her of the emblem of the Chinese Space Force, bearing swords and stars alike.

"Dongfang, I said that I would be sorry if I had to kill you. There's not much time."

Then the deep-sea acceleration fluid appeared within Zhang Beihai's spherical compartment, forming into balls in the weightless environment. Each liquid globe, containing his distorted reflection along with the interface and the star map, began to combine into larger ones. The two vice-captains looked at Dongfang Yanxu.

"Do as he says. The whole ship will enter deep-sea state," the captain said.

The two vice-captains stared at her. They knew what the consequences were for proceeding to Ahead Four outside of the deep-sea protective state: The body would be plastered to the bulkhead by a force 120 times that of Earth gravity. First blood would burst out under the immense weight, spreading into a thin layer of impossibly huge, radially patterned blood stains, and then the organs would be squeezed out, forming another thin layer that would be pressed together with the body into an ugly Dali painting. . . .

As they left for their cabins, they issued orders to the entire ship to enter a deep-sea state.

"You're a well-qualified captain." Zhang Beihai nodded at Dongfang Yanxu. "This shows maturity."

"Where are we going?"

"Wherever we're going, it's a more responsible choice than staying here."

And then he was submerged in the deep-sea acceleration fluid, and Dongfang Yanxu could only make out a murky body through the liquid now filling the spherical compartment.

Floating in the translucent liquid, Zhang Beihai recalled his diving experience in the navy two centuries before. He had never imagined that the ocean would be so dark a few dozen meters down, but that undersea world gave him the same feeling he later found in space. The ocean was space in miniature on Earth. He tried breathing, but his reflexes made him violently cough up liquid and residual gas, and his body shifted with the recoil. Still, there wasn't the suffocation that he had anticipated, and as cool liquid

filled his lungs, the oxygen it contained was supplied to his blood. He could breathe freely, like a fish.

On the interface suspended in the liquid, he saw that the deep-sea acceleration fluid was filling each occupied compartment in the spaceship in turn. The process continued for more than ten minutes. His consciousness began to blur as the breathing liquid was injected with a hypnotic component that put everyone aboard ship into a state of sleep so as to avoid damage to the brain from the high pressure and relative hypoxia generated by acceleration at Ahead Four.

Zhang Beihai felt his father's spirit alight on the spaceship from the beyond, becoming one with it. He pressed the button on the interface, issuing in his mind the command that he had been working toward his entire life:

"*Natural Selection,* Ahead Four!"

A small sun appeared in Jovian orbit, its bright light washing out the phosphorescence of the planet's atmosphere. Dragging the sun behind it, the stellar-class warship *Natural Selection* eased out of the Asian Fleet base and accelerated rapidly, casting shadows of the other warships—each dark spot big enough to contain the Earth—onto the Jovian surface. Ten minutes later, a larger shadow was flung onto Jupiter like a curtain drawn across the giant planet. *Natural Selection* was passing Io.

It was at this point that the Asian Fleet High Command confirmed the incredible fact that *Natural Selection* had defected.

The European and North American Fleets issued protests and warnings to the Asian Fleet under the initial impression that it was an unauthorized move to intercept the Trisolaran probe, but they soon realized from *Natural Selection*'s heading that this was not the case. It was headed in the opposite direction from the Trisolaran invasion.

The various systems hailing *Natural Selection* gradually let up after receiving no response. The high commands began to deploy pursuit and intercept ships, although they soon realized that little could be done about the defector warship. Bases on four of

Jupiter's moons possessed sufficient firepower to destroy *Natural Selection,* but they would not take that path, because it was quite likely that only a small minority of those on board, or even a single individual, had actually defected, and the two thousand-odd soldiers in deep-sea state were merely hostages. Commanders at the gamma-ray laser base on Europa could only watch as the small sun flew across the sky and into outer space, sprinkling Europa's vast ice sheets with light like burning phosphorus.

Natural Selection crossed the orbits of sixteen Jovian moons, and achieved escape velocity by the time it reached Callisto. Seen from the Asian Fleet base, the small sun gradually shrank, turning into a bright star that remained faintly visible for a week, as a reminder from the stars of the lasting pain of the Asian Fleet.

Since the pursuing force had to enter deep-sea state, it took forty-five minutes after *Natural Selection* left for those ships to launch, lighting up Jupiter with another six suns.

At Asian Fleet Command, which had stopped rotating, the commander silently faced the giant dark side of Jupiter as lightning flashed in the atmosphere ten thousand kilometers below him. Powerful radiation from the fusion engines of *Natural Selection* and the pursuing force had caused atmospheric ionization and lightning. The fleeting lightning strikes illuminated the surrounding atmosphere, visible at this distance as halos in constantly changing locations, turning the surface of Jupiter into a pond spattered with fluorescent rain.

Natural Selection accelerated in silence to one-hundredth the speed of light, the point of no return for its fusion fuel consumption. Now unable to return to the Solar System under its own power, it had become a lonely boat bound to forever wander in outer space.

The commander of the Asian Fleet gazed at the stars trying unsuccessfully to find one in particular, for all there was in that direction was the faint light of the pursuers' fusion engines. A report soon came in: *Natural Selection* had stopped accelerating. A while later, *Natural Selection* restored communication with the fleet.

Then the following communication took place, with delays of more than ten seconds between transmissions due to the fact that the ship was now over five million kilometers away:

NATURAL SELECTION: *Natural Selection* calling Asian Fleet! *Natural Selection* calling Asian Fleet!

ASIAN FLEET: *Natural Selection*, Asian Fleet reads you. Report your status.

NATURAL SELECTION: This is acting captain Zhang Beihai. I'll speak directly to the fleet commander.

FLEET COMMANDER: I'm listening.

ZHANG BEIHAI: I take full responsibility for *Natural Selection*'s breakaway voyage.

FLEET COMMANDER: Is anyone else responsible?

ZHANG BEIHAI: No. Responsibility is mine alone. The situation has nothing at all to do with anyone else aboard *Natural Selection*.

FLEET COMMANDER: I want to talk to Captain Dongfang Yanxu.

ZHANG BEIHAI: Not now.

FLEET COMMANDER: What is the ship's current status?

ZHANG BEIHAI: All is good. Every crew member is still in deep-sea state, apart from me. Power systems and life support are operating normally.

FLEET COMMANDER: And your reasons for this treason?

ZHANG BEIHAI: I may have deserted, but I am no traitor.

FLEET COMMANDER: Your reasons?

ZHANG BEIHAI: Humanity is certain to lose on the battlefield. I only want to save one of Earth's stellar-class spaceships to preserve a seed of human civilization in the universe, a scrap of hope.

FLEET COMMANDER: That makes you an Escapist.

ZHANG BEIHAI: I'm just a soldier fulfilling his duty.

FLEET COMMANDER: Have you received the mental seal?

ZHANG BEIHAI: You know that's not possible. That technology wasn't around when I went into hibernation.

FLEET COMMANDER: Then your unusually resolute defeatist beliefs are baffling.

ZHANG BEIHAI: I don't need the mental seal. I am the master of my beliefs. My faith is resolute because it doesn't come from my own intelligence. At the beginning of the Trisolar Crisis, my father and I began to seriously consider the most basic questions about this war. Gradually, a group of deep-thinking scholars, including scientists, politicians, and military strategists, gathered around him. They called themselves the Future Historians.

FLEET COMMANDER: Was it a secret organization?

ZHANG BEIHAI: No. They studied very basic questions, and their discussions were always conducted in the open. The government and military even came forward and held several academic conferences on Future History. And it was from their research that I arrived at the mind-set that humanity is doomed.

FLEET COMMANDER: But the theories of Future History have since been proven incorrect.

ZHANG BEIHAI: Sir, you underestimate them. They not only predicted the Great Ravine but the Second Enlightenment and Second Renaissance as well. What they predicted for today's era of prosperity is virtually indistinguishable from the real thing. And, finally, they predicted that humanity would be totally defeated, wiped out in the Doomsday Battle.

FLEET COMMANDER: Have you forgotten that you're on a spaceship capable of traveling at fifteen percent of the speed of light?

ZHANG BEIHAI: Genghis Khan's cavalry attacked with the speed of twentieth-century armored units. The mounted crossbow of the Song Dynasty had a range of up to fifteen hundred meters, comparable to twentieth-century assault rifles. But it's impossible for ancient cavalry and crossbows to compete with modern forces. Fundamental theory determines everything. The Future Historians clearly saw this point. You, on the other hand, have been blinded by the dying radiance of low-level technology and are luxuriating in the nursery of modern civilization, without any mental preparation whatsoever for the coming ultimate battle that will determine the fate of humanity.

FLEET COMMANDER: You come from a great army, one that was

victorious over an enemy with far more advanced equipment. It won victory in one of the largest land wars in the world, relying solely on seized weapons. Your behavior is a disgrace to that army.

ZHANG BEIHAI: My dear commander, I'm more qualified than you to speak of that army. Three generations of my family served in it. During the Korean War, my grandfather attacked a Pershing tank armed with a grenade. The grenade hit the tank and slid off before exploding. The target was barely scratched, but my grandfather was hit by machine-gun fire from the tank, had both legs broken under its treads, and spent the rest of his life an invalid. But compared to two of his comrades, who were crushed to a pulp, he was lucky. . . . It's that army's history that so clearly taught us the significance of a technological gap during wartime. The glory you know is what you've read in the history books, but our trauma was cemented by the blood of our fathers and grandfathers. We know more than you do what war means.

FLEET COMMANDER: When did you conceive of your treasonous plan?

ZHANG BEIHAI: I repeat: I may have deserted, but I am not a traitor. I conceived of the plan the last time I saw my father. I saw in his eyes what I needed to do, and it took me two centuries to realize my plan.

FLEET COMMANDER: And to do this you disguised yourself as a triumphalist. A very successful disguise.

ZHANG BEIHAI: General Chang Weisi almost saw through me.

FLEET COMMANDER: Yes. He was keenly aware that he had never worked out the foundation of your triumphalist faith, and his suspicions were only aggravated by your unusual enthusiasm for radiation propulsion systems capable of interstellar travel. He had always been opposed to you joining the Special Contingent of Future Reinforcements, but he couldn't breach his superiors' orders. He warned us in the letter he sent, but did so in your era's subtle way, and we overlooked it.

ZHANG BEIHAI: In order to obtain a spacecraft capable of fleeing into space, I killed three people.

FLEET COMMANDER: We did not know that. Maybe no one did. But one thing is certain: The research direction chosen at that time was crucial for the subsequent development of spaceflight technology.

ZHANG BEIHAI: Thank you for saying so.

FLEET COMMANDER: I will also say that your plan will fail.

ZHANG BEIHAI: Perhaps. But it hasn't yet.

FLEET COMMANDER: *Natural Selection*'s fusion fuel is only at one-fifth capacity.

ZHANG BEIHAI: But I had to act immediately. There would be no other opportunity.

FLEET COMMANDER: What it means is that you're only able to accelerate to one percent of light speed now. You can't consume excess fuel, because the spaceship's life-support systems still need power to maintain operations for a timespan that could be as short as a few decades or as long as a few centuries. But at that speed, the pursuing force will catch up to you quite soon.

ZHANG BEIHAI: I still control *Natural Selection*.

FLEET COMMANDER: True. And of course you know our concern: that pursuit will drive you to continue accelerating, expending fuel until life support fails and *Natural Selection* becomes a dead ship at near-absolute zero. That's why the pursuit force won't draw near *Natural Selection* for the time being. We have confidence that the commander and soldiers aboard will solve their own warship's problems.

ZHANG BEIHAI: I'm also convinced that all problems will be resolved. I will shoulder my responsibility, but I still firmly believe that *Natural Selection* is headed in the right direction.

When Luo Ji jerked awake, he recognized something else that had endured from the past: firecrackers. It was dawn, and through the window the desert glowed white in the early light, illuminated by

bursts of firecrackers and fireworks. Then came an urgent knock at the door. Without waiting for it to be answered, Shi Xiaoming opened it up and charged in, his face red with excitement as he urged Luo Ji to watch the news.

Luo Ji watched television only rarely. Since arriving in New Life Village #5, he had returned to a life in the past. After the post-awakening impact of the new era, this was a precious feeling for him, and, for the time being, he didn't want to be disturbed by information about the present day. He spent most of his time immersed in memories of Zhuang Yan and Xia Xia. All of the paperwork had been filed for their reawakening, but government controls on hibernators meant that it would not happen for two months.

The television news broadcast the following: Five hours ago, the Ringier-Fitzroy Telescope observed the Trisolaran Fleet cross yet again into an interstellar dust cloud. This was the seventh time since its launch two centuries ago that the fleet had revealed itself by passing through a dust cloud. The fleet had lost its rigorous formation, so that the brush shape it had formed on passing through the first cloud was now altered beyond all recognition. But just as in its second crossing, a bristle was observed extending out in front. What was different this time, however, was that the shape of the track indicated that the bristle was not a probe, but a warship of the fleet. Having completed the acceleration and cruising legs of their journey to the Solar System, some of the ships in the Trisolaran Fleet had been observed decelerating as early as fifteen years ago. Ten years ago, the majority of them had begun to slow down. It was clear now that this particular ship had never reduced speed. In fact, judging from its path through the dust cloud, it was still accelerating. At its current rate of acceleration, it would arrive in the Solar System half a century before the rest of the fleet.

A lone ship charging into Solar System territory and in range of Earth's powerful fleet would be suicide, if it was an invasion. This left just one possible conclusion: It was coming to negotiate. Observations of the Trisolaran Fleet over the course of two centuries had determined the maximum acceleration of every ship,

and projections indicated that this advance ship would be unable to decelerate sufficiently, so it would pass right through the Solar System in 150 years. That meant just two possibilities. The first was that the Trisolarans wanted Earth to assist in deceleration. More likely was that, before the ship passed out of the Solar System, it would drop a smaller craft that could decelerate more easily, a ship that would be carrying the Trisolaran negotiation delegation.

"But if they desired to negotiate, wouldn't they notify humanity by sophon?" Luo Ji asked.

"That's easy to explain!" Shi Xiaoming said excitedly. "It's a different way of thinking. The Trisolarans have totally transparent minds, so they imagine that we already know what they're thinking!"

Even though the explanation was unconvincing, Luo Ji shared Shi Xiaoming's feeling, like the sun outside was rising early.

When the sun rose for real, the revelry reached a climax. This was just a small corner of the world, and the center of the activity was in the underground cities, where people left their trees and crowded into the streets and plazas, their clothing turned up to maximum brightness to form a glowing sea of light. Virtual fireworks blossomed in the vaults overhead, and at times a colorful burst covered the entire sky, its brilliant light a match for the sun.

News continued to arrive. The government was cautious at first, and its spokespersons stated repeatedly that there was no conclusive evidence to demonstrate that Trisolaris had the intent to negotiate. But, at the same time, the UN and the SFJC convened an emergency summit to formulate strategies for negotiation procedures and terms. . . .

In New Life Village #5, a short interlude paused the revelry: A city legislator came to make a speech. He was a fanatical supporter of what was called Project Sunshine and was taking this opportunity to win the support of the hibernator community.

Project Sunshine was a UN proposal whose main thrust was that, in the event of a human victory in the Doomsday Battle, defeated Trisolarans ought to be provided with space in the Solar System. There were various versions of the project. The Weak

Survival Plan set up Pluto, Charon, and the moons of Neptune as Trisolaran reservations that would grant admission only to those aboard the defeated Trisolaris ships. The living conditions on these reservations would be very poor, and they would rely on fusion energy and the support of human society to sustain themselves. The Strong Survival Plan would use Mars for the Trisolaran sojourn and would eventually admit all Trisolaran immigrants, in addition to members of the fleet. This plan would provide Trisolaran civilization with the Solar System's best living conditions apart from Earth. The other versions were more or less situated between these two, but there were also a few more extreme ideas, such as accepting Trisolarans into Earth society. Project Sunshine had won broad support from Earth International and Fleet International, and preliminary studies and planning had already begun, with many nongovernmental forces in both Internationals pushing for it. Yet it had encountered fierce resistance from the community of hibernators, who had even coined a name for supporters of the project: "Dongguo," after the soft-hearted scholar in the fable who saved a wolf's life.[21]

As soon as the legislator's speech began, he was met with strong pushback from the audience, which tossed tomatoes at him. Ducking, he said, "I'd like to remind you that we're in a humanitarian age following the Second Renaissance. The life and civilization of every race are accorded the greatest respect. You are bathed in the light of this age, are you not? Hibernators in modern society enjoy citizenship in complete equality and suffer no discrimination. This principle is recognized in the constitution and in the law, but more importantly, it exists in everyone's heart. I trust you can appreciate this. Trisolaris, too, is a great civilization. Human

21 *Translator's Note:* In the fable "The Wolf of Zhongshan," attributed to the Ming Dynasty writer Ma Zhongxi, the bookish scholar Master Dongguo takes pity on a hunted, starving wolf and hides it in a bag as hunters pass by. When he lets the wolf out, it threatens to eat him but is persuaded to put the issue to a third party. An old farmer, after hearing the situation, protests that the wolf could not possibly fit in the bag. The wolf climbs back in, whereupon the farmer ties up the bag and bashes the wolf to death with his hoe.

society must acknowledge its right to exist. Project Sunshine is not a charity. It is an acknowledgement and an expression of humanity's own value! If we . . . Hey, jerks. Focus on your work!"

The legislator's final line was addressed to his team, who were busily gathering up the tomatoes that had fallen to the ground—they were quite expensive underground, after all. When the hibernators saw this, they began tossing cucumbers and potatoes onto the stage as well, and thus the minor confrontation was resolved in mutual merriment.

At noon, every household feasted. On the grass, a sumptuous meal of unadulterated agricultural products was laid out for the city folk who had come to join in the fun, including Mr. Dongguo the legislator and his entourage. The festivities continued tipsily through the afternoon and until sunset, which was exceptionally beautiful that evening. The sandy plains outside the neighborhood looked creamily soft and delicate under the red-orange sun, and the rolling dunes looked like the bodies of sleeping women. . . .

By nighttime, one news item pushed their flagging spirits to new heights of excitement: the Fleet International had made the decision to combine the stellar-class warships of the Asian Fleet, the European Fleet, and the North American Fleet into a single fleet of 2,015 ships to sally forth in unison and intercept the Trisolaran probe as it crossed the orbit of Neptune!

The news propelled the revelry to a renewed climax, and fireworks filled the night sky. But it also elicited some disdain and mockery.

"Mobilizing two thousand warships for a tiny probe?"

"It's like using two thousand butcher knives to kill a chicken!"

"That's right! Two thousand cannons to hit a mosquito! It's not that tough!"

"Hey, everyone, we should be more understanding of the Fleet International. You know, it might be the only chance they'll get to fight Trisolaris."

"Right. If this can be called fighting."

"It's okay. Just think of it as a military parade for humanity. Let's see what this superfleet's got. It'll scare the Trisolarans to

death! They'll be so frightened they won't be able to pee. If they even have pee."

Laughter.

Close to midnight, more news came: The combined fleet had set off from Jupiter base! Viewers were informed that in the southern sky, the fleet could be seen with the naked eye. At this, the revelers quieted down for the first time and searched the sky for Jupiter. It wasn't easy, but under the guidance of the expert on the television, they soon located the planet in the southwest. At this point, the light of the combined fleet was moving in Earth's direction from a distance of five AU. Forty-five minutes later, the brightness of Jupiter suddenly increased, soon surpassing Sirius to become the brightest object in the night sky. Then a brilliant shining star separated from Jupiter, like a soul leaving a body. The planet returned to its original brightness as the star moved slowly away from it. That was the launch of the combined fleet.

At practically the same time, live images of Jupiter base reached Earth. On the television, people saw the sudden appearance of two thousand suns in the blackness of space. Standing out awesomely in the eternal night of space, their clean rectangular formation put one thought in everyone's mind: *God said, Let there be light, and there was light*. Under the light of those two thousand suns, Jupiter and its moons seemed to have caught fire. The planet's atmosphere, ionized by the radiation, produced lightning that filled the entire fleet-facing hemisphere and covered it in a giant blanket of electric light. The fleet accelerated with no disruption to its formation, its huge wall blocking out the sun, and then made a stately advance into space with the force of a thundercloud, declaring to the universe the dignity and invincibility of the human race. The human spirit that had been repressed since the first appearance of the Trisolaran Fleet two centuries ago had finally found total liberation. At this moment, all the stars in the galaxy silently held back their light, and Human and God stepped out proudly into the universe as one.

The people wept and cheered, and many of them were moved to loud wails. Never before in history had there been such a moment,

in which every single person felt fortunate and proud to be a member of the human race.

But there were some who kept their heads. Luo Ji was one of them. Surveying the crowd, he noticed that someone else was calm: Shi Qiang was off by himself, leaning against one side of the giant holographic television, smoking a cigarette and watching the revelers indifferently.

Luo Ji went over and asked, "What are you . . ."

"Ah, hello my boy. I've got a duty to fulfill." He indicated the ebullient crowd. "Extreme joy easily turns to grief, and now's the best time for something to happen. Like when Mr. Dongguo lectured this morning. If I hadn't come up with the tomatoes and such in a timely fashion, they would have used stones."

Shi Qiang had recently been appointed chief of police for New Life Village #5. To the hibernators, the fact that someone belonging to the Asian Fleet, someone who no longer was a Chinese citizen, had been given an official post in the national government was a little strange. However, his work had been universally acclaimed among the villagers.

"Besides, I'm not the type to get carried away," he continued, clapping Luo Ji across the shoulders. "Neither are you, my boy."

"No, I'm not." Luo Ji nodded. "I was always out for instant gratification. The future had nothing to do with me, even though for a while there I was forced to become a messiah. Maybe my present state is a sort of compensation for the harm from that. I'm going to bed. Believe it or not, Da Shi, I'll actually be able to get to sleep tonight."

"Go and see your colleague. He just arrived. Humanity's victory might not be a good thing for him."

Luo Ji was slightly taken aback by this remark. Looking at the man Shi Qiang pointed to, he realized with surprise that it was the old Wallfacer Bill Hines. His face was ashen and he seemed to be in a trance. He had been standing not far off from Shi Qiang and had only just now noticed Luo Ji. When they hugged each other in greeting, Luo Ji felt that Hines's body seemed to tremble with weakness.

"I came looking for you," he said to Luo Ji. "Only the two of us, history's rubbish, understand each other. But now, I'm afraid even you don't understand me."

"What about Keiko Yamasuki?"

"Remember the Meditation Room in the UN Assembly Building?" Hines said. "It was always deserted. Tourists only visited occasionally. . . . Do you remember the chunk of iron ore? She committed seppuku on top of it."

"Oh . . ."

"Before she died, she cursed me, saying that my life would be worse than death, since I'm marked with the mental seal of defeatism even as humanity is victorious. She was right. I'm in real pain right now. Of course I'm happy for the victory, but it's impossible for me to believe any of it. It's like there are two gladiators fighting in my mind. You know, it's far harder than trying to believe that water is drinkable."

After he and Shi Qiang had gotten Hines set up with a room, Luo Ji returned to his own room and soon fell asleep. Once again he dreamed of Zhuang Yan and the child. When he woke, the sun was shining through the window and the revelries were still going on outside.

Natural Selection flew at 1 percent of the speed of light on a course between Jupiter and the orbit of Saturn. Behind it, the sun was now small, although it was still the brightest of the stars, while up ahead, the Milky Way shone with an even greater brilliance. The ship's heading was more or less in the direction of Cygnus, but in the expanse of outer space, its speed was imperceptible. To a nearby observer, *Natural Selection* would have seemed suspended in deep space. From its own vantage point, in fact, all movement throughout the universe had been erased, leaving the ship seemingly in a static state, with the Milky Way ahead and the sun behind. Time seemed to have stopped.

"You have failed," Dongfang Yanxu said to Zhang Beihai. All personnel aboard the ship but the two of them were still in deep-sea sleep state. Zhang Beihai remained shut inside the spherical

compartment, and Dongfang Yanxu, unable to enter, had to talk with him through the communication system. Through the section of bulkhead that was still transparent, she could see the man who had hijacked humanity's most powerful warship floating quietly in the center of the compartment, head bent, intent on writing in a notebook. In front of him floated an interface that showed the ship on standby for Ahead Four, ready to go at the press of a button. Around him floated several globs of liquid deep-sea acceleration fluid that hadn't yet been evacuated. His uniform had dried, but its wrinkles made him look much older.

He ignored her and continued to write, head bent.

"The pursuing force is only 1.2 million kilometers away from *Natural Selection*," she said.

"I know," he said without looking up. "You were wise to keep the entire ship in deep-sea state."

"It had to be this way. Otherwise, agitated officers and soldiers would have attacked this cabin. And if you took *Natural Selection* to Ahead Four at will, you would have killed them all. That's also the reason why the pursuers haven't closed in."

He said nothing. Flipping a page in the notebook, he continued writing.

"You wouldn't do that, would you?" she asked softly.

"You never imagined I'd do what I'm doing now." He paused a few seconds, then added, "The people of my time have our own ways of thinking."

"But we're not enemies."

"There are no permanent enemies or comrades, only permanent duty."

"Then your pessimism about the war is totally unfounded. Trisolaris has just shown signs of wanting talks, and the combined Solar Fleet has set off to intercept the Trisolaran probe. The war will end with a victory for humanity."

"I've seen the news that came in . . ."

"And you still persist in your defeatism and Escapism?"

"I do."

She shook her head in frustration. "Your way of thinking really is different from ours. For instance, you knew from the start that your plan would be unsuccessful, because *Natural Selection* has only a fifth of its fuel and is certain to be caught."

He set down his pencil and looked out of the cabin at her. His eyes were calm as water. "We're all soldiers, but do you know what the biggest difference between soldiers from my time and soldiers now is? You determine your actions according to possible outcomes. But for us, we must carry out our duty regardless of the outcome. This was my only chance, so I took it."

"You're saying that to comfort yourself."

"No. It's my nature. I don't expect you to understand, Dongfang. We're separated by two centuries, after all."

"So you've carried out your duty, but there's no hope for your Escapist endeavor. Surrender."

He smiled at her, then looked back at his writing. "It's not time yet. I need to write down all that I've experienced. Everything across two centuries needs to be written down, so that it might be of assistance to a few sober-minded people in the next two centuries."

"You can dictate to the computer."

"No, I'm used to writing by hand. Paper lasts longer than a computer. Don't worry. I'll bear full responsibility."

Ding Yi looked out through *Quantum*'s broad porthole. Even though the holographic display in the spherical cabin provided a better view, he still liked seeing things with his own eyes. What he saw was that he was situated on a large plane consisting of two thousand small, dazzling suns whose light seemed to set his gray hair aflame. The sight had grown familiar to him in the days since the launch of the combined fleet, but its grandeur still shook him each time he looked. The fleet was not just in this configuration as a show of force or majesty. In a traditional naval configuration of staggered columns, the radiation produced by the engine of every warship would have an effect on the ships to the rear. In this

rectangular formation, the ships were separated by about twenty kilometers. Even though each of them was an average of three to four times the size of a naval aircraft carrier, from that distance they were practically dots, with only the glow of the fusion engines to prove their existence in space.

The combined fleet was in a dense formation, one that had only ever been used in fleet review. In a normal cruising formation, the ships ought to have been spaced at roughly three hundred to five hundred kilometers, so a twenty-kilometer spacing was basically like sailing hull-to-hull through the ocean. Many of the generals in the three fleets disagreed with this dense formation, but conventional formations presented a number of thorny problems. First of all, there was the principle of fairness in battle opportunity. If the probe were approached in a standard formation, then the ships at the edge would still be tens of thousands of kilometers away from the target when the formation reached minimum distance. If combat broke out during the capture, a fair number of the ships could not have been considered to have taken part, leaving them nothing in the history books but eternal regret. But the three fleets couldn't break off into their own subformations, because it was impossible to coordinate which of them would occupy the most advantageous position in the overall formation. So the formation had to be made as dense as possible, a review formation that placed all ships within combat distance of the probe. A second reason for selecting this formation was that the Fleet International and the United Nations both desired stunning visuals, not so much to show off for Trisolaris as to give the masses something to look at. The visual impact held enormous political significance for both groups. With the main enemy force still two light-years away, the dense formation was certainly not in danger.

Quantum was located in a corner of the formation, giving Ding Yi a view of the majority of the fleet. When they crossed the orbit of Saturn, all the fusion engines turned toward the forward direction and the fleet began to decelerate. Now, as the fleet closed in on the Trisolaran probe, its velocity was negative—it was traveling

back toward the sun as it closed the distance separating it from its target.

Ding Yi put a pipe to his lips. With no loose tobacco in this age, it was an empty pipe that dangled there, the lingering flavor of two-century-old tobacco faint and indistinct, like a memory of the past.

He had been reawakened seven years earlier and had been teaching in the Peking University physics department since then. Last year he had put in a request to the fleet asking to be one of the people who would examine the Trisolaran probe up close when it was intercepted. Although Ding Yi was held in high regard, his request had been refused until he declared that he would kill himself in front of the three fleet commanders if they did not comply. Then they said they would think about it. In fact, selection of the first person to contact the probe was a knotty problem, because first contact with the probe meant first contact with Trisolaris. According to the fairness principle to be observed during interception, none of the three fleets could be permitted to enjoy this honor alone, but sending someone from each of them presented operational problems and could complicate matters. So the mission had to be undertaken by someone outside Fleet International. Ding Yi was naturally the most suitable candidate, although another unstated reason lay at the core of his request's ultimate approval: Neither the Fleet International nor the Earth International had much confidence in obtaining the probe, because it was practically certain to self-destruct during or after intercept. Before it did so, close-range observation and contact were imperative if they wanted to obtain as much data as possible. As the discoverer of the macro-atom and the inventor of controlled fusion, the veteran physicist was completely qualified in this area. At any rate, Ding Yi's life was his own, and at eighty-three, his unparalleled qualifications naturally gave the old man the power to do anything he wanted.

At the final meeting of *Quantum* command before the intercept began, Ding Yi saw an image of the Trisolaran probe. Three tracking craft had been dispatched by the three fleets to replace Earth International's *Blue Shadow*. They had captured an image at a

distance of five hundred kilometers from the target, the closest that any human spacecraft had come to the probe. The probe was about as large as expected, 3.5 meters long, and when Ding Yi saw it, he had the same impression as everyone else: a droplet of mercury. The probe was a perfect teardrop shape, round at the head and pointy at the tail, with a surface so smooth it was a total reflector. The Milky Way was reflected on its surface as a smooth pattern of light that gave the mercury droplet a pure beauty. Its droplet shape was so natural that observers imagined it in a liquid state, one for which an internal structure was impossible.

Ding Yi remained silent after he saw the image of the probe. He did not speak at the meeting, and his expression was downcast.

"Master Ding, you seem to have something on your mind," the captain said.

"I don't feel good," he said softly, and pointed at the holographic probe with his pipe.

"Why? It looks like a harmless work of art," an officer said.

"And that's why I don't feel so good," Ding Yi said, shaking his gray head. "It looks like a work of art rather than an interstellar probe. It's not a good sign when something's so far removed from our own mental concept."

"It is peculiar. Its surface is entirely sealed. Where's the engine nozzle?"

"Yet its engine lights up. We've observed that. When it went out for a second time, *Blue Shadow* wasn't close enough to capture an image in time, so we don't know where the light came from."

"What is its mass?" Ding Yi asked.

"We don't have an exact value right now. A rough value, obtained through high-precision gravitational instruments, is less than ten tons."

"Then at least it's not made of matter from a neutron star."

The captain put an end to the officers' discussion and continued with the meeting. He said to Ding Yi, "Master Ding, this is how the fleet has planned out your visit: After the unmanned craft completes its capture of the target and carries out an observation

period, if nothing unusual is found, you will enter the capture craft on a shuttle and conduct a closeup observation of the target. You may not stay longer than fifteen minutes. This is Major Xizi. She will represent the Asian Fleet and accompany you as you carry out your examination."

A young officer saluted Ding Yi. Like the other women in the fleet, she was tall and slender, the very epitome of New Space Humanity.

With only a glance at the major, Ding Yi turned to the captain. "Why does there have to be someone else? Can't I go alone?"

"Of course not, sir. You're unfamiliar with the space environment, and you need assistance throughout the entire process."

"In that case, I'd better not go. Does someone really need to follow me . . ." He broke off without uttering "to death."

The captain said, "Master Ding, this trip is dangerous, to be sure, but not completely so. If the probe self-destructs, then it will most likely occur during the intercept. The likelihood of it self-destructing two hours after the intercept is very low, so long as the examination process does not use destructive instruments."

In point of fact, the primary reason the Earth and Fleet Internationals decided to send a human to the probe was not for an inspection. When the world saw the probe for the first time, everyone was captivated by its magnificent exterior. The mercury droplet was just so beautiful, so simple in shape yet masterfully styled, with each point on its surface in exactly the right place. It was imbued with a graceful dynamism, as if at every moment it was dripping endlessly in the cosmic night. It inspired the feeling that even if human artists tried out every possible smooth closed shape, they wouldn't come up with this one. It transcended every possibility. Not even in Plato's Republic was there such a perfect shape: straighter than the straightest line, more circular than a perfect circle, a mirrored dolphin leaping out of the sea of dreams, a crystallization of all the love in the universe. . . . Beauty is always paired with good, so if there really existed a demarcation between good and evil in the universe, this object would fall on the good side.

So a hypothesis was quickly worked out: The object might not even be a probe. Further observation confirmed this hypothesis, to an extent. People first noticed its exterior, the highly smooth finish that made it a total reflector. The fleet conducted an experiment on the probe using a large quantity of monitoring equipment: Its entire surface was irradiated with different wavelengths of high-frequency electromagnetic waves, and the reflectance was measured. To their shock, they discovered that at every frequency, including visible light, the reflection was practically 100 percent. No absorption was detected. This meant that the probe could not detect any high-frequency waves—or, in layman's terms, it was blind. There must be a particular significance to a blind design. The most reasonable guess was that it was a token of goodwill from Trisolaris to humanity, expressed through its nonfunctional design and beautiful form. A sincere desire for peace.

So the probe was given a new name inspired by its shape: "the droplet." On both Earth and Trisolaris, water was the source of life and a symbol of peace.

Public opinion maintained that a formal delegation ought to be sent to make contact with the droplet, rather than an expedition team made up of a physicist and three ordinary officers. But after careful consideration, Fleet International decided to keep its original plan unchanged.

"Can't you at least swap in someone else? Letting this young lady . . ." Ding Yi said, gesturing at Xizi.

Xizi smiled at him and said, "Master Ding, I am *Quantum*'s science officer. I'm in charge of off-ship scientific expeditions during our voyages. This is my duty."

"And women make up half the fleet," the captain said. "Three people will accompany you. The other two are science officers sent by the European and North American Fleets. They'll be reporting shortly. Master Ding, let me reiterate one point: According to the decision of the SFJC, you must be the first to make direct contact with the target. Only then are they permitted to make contact."

"Pointless." Ding Yi shook his head again. "Humanity hasn't

changed at all. So eager to chase after vanity. . . . But, rest assured, I'll do as you wish. I just want to have a look, is all. What I'm really interested in is the theory behind this super-technology. But I'm afraid that this life is . . . ah."

The captain floated over to him and said with concern, "Master Ding, you can go rest now. The intercept will be starting soon, and you need to preserve your energy before setting off on your expedition."

Ding Yi looked up at the captain. For a moment he didn't realize that the meeting was going to continue after he left. Then he looked back at the image of the droplet, noticing now how its round head reflected a regular row of lights that gradually deformed toward the rear, merging into the reflected pattern of the Milky Way. That was the fleet. He looked again at *Quantum*'s commanders floating before him, all of them so very young. Just children. They looked so noble and perfect, from the captain to the lieutenants, and their eyes shone with a godlike wisdom. The light of the fleet streaming in through the portholes was tinted like a golden sunset by the auto-darkening glass, enveloping them all in gold. Behind them floated the image of the droplet like a supernatural silver symbol, making the place otherworldly and transcendent, and turning them into a host of gods atop Mount Olympus. . . . Something stirred deep within him, and he grew excited.

"Master Ding, do you have something else to add?" the captain asked.

"Er, I'd like to say . . ." His hands moved aimlessly, and he let his pipe float in the air. "I'd like to say that you kids have been great to me over the past few days. . . ."

"You're the man we admire the most of all," a vice-captain said.

"Oh . . . so there are a few things I'd really like to say. Just . . . the nonsense of an old fool. You don't have to take it seriously. Still, children, as someone who's crossed two centuries, I've been through a bit more than you. . . . Of course, like I said, don't take it seriously. . . ."

"Master Ding, if you've got something to say, then just say it. You really have our highest respect."

432

Ding Yi slowly nodded. Then he pointed upward. "If this spaceship has to go to maximum acceleration, everyone here will need to . . . be immersed in a liquid."

"That's right. Deep-sea state."

"Yes, right. The deep-sea state." Ding Yi hesitated again, and ruminated for a moment before resolving to go on. "When we go out for our examination, could this ship, ah, *Quantum,* be put into a deep-sea state?"

The officers looked at each other in surprise, and the captain said, "Why?"

Ding Yi's hands began fluttering again. His hair glowed white under the fleet's light. Like someone had noticed when he first came aboard, he looked quite a bit like Einstein. "Um . . . well, at any rate there's no harm in doing it, right? You know, I don't have a good feeling."

After saying this, he remained silent, his eyes locked onto the infinite distance. At last he reached out, plucked the pipe out of the air, and put it into his pocket. Without saying good-bye, he awkwardly worked his superconductor belt to float toward the door as the officers watched him.

When he was halfway out, he slowly turned back around. "Children, do you know what I've been doing all these years? Teaching physics at a university and advising doctoral students." As he looked out at the galaxy, an inscrutable smile played on his face—tinted with, the officers noticed, a hint of sadness. "Children, a man from two centuries ago is still able to teach university physics today." With that, he turned and left.

The captain wanted to say something to him, but now that he was gone, the words didn't come out. He remained deep in thought. Some of the officers looked at the droplet, but more of them turned their attention to the captain.

"Captain, you're not going to take him seriously, are you?" one lieutenant asked.

"He's a wise scientist, but he's still an ancient man. Their thoughts about modern things are always . . ." someone else added.

"But in his field, humanity hasn't made any progress. It's still stuck at his era's level."

"He spoke of intuition. I think his intuition may have discovered something," an officer said, in a voice full of awe.

"Also . . ." Xizi blurted out. But looking at the surrounding officers who outranked her, she swallowed the rest of her words.

"Major, please continue," the captain said.

"Also, like he said, there's no harm in doing it," she said.

"Think about it this way," a vice-captain said. "According to present battle plans, if the capture fails and the droplet unexpectedly escapes, then the fleet can only deploy fighters as a tracking force. But long-range tracking needs to be stellar-class, so the fleet ought to have warships prepared. This is an oversight in the plan."

"Make a report to the fleet," the captain said.

The fleet's approval was swift: When the examination team had set off, *Quantum* and the neighboring stellar-class warship *Bronze Age* would enter a deep-sea state.

To capture the droplet, the fleet's formation maintained a distance of one thousand kilometers from the target, a figure decided after careful calculation. There were various hypotheses about the manner in which the droplet might self-destruct, but the maximum release of energy would come from self-destruction by antimatter annihilation. Since the droplet had a mass of less than ten tons, the largest energy burst that needed to be considered was that produced by the annihilation of five tons each of matter and antimatter. That annihilation, if it occurred on Earth, would be enough to destroy all life on the planet surface, but in space, the energy would be released entirely in the form of light radiation. For stellar-class warships, with their super anti-radiation capacity, one thousand kilometers was far enough to allow for a sufficient margin of safety.

The capture would be accomplished by *Mantis,* a small unmanned craft that had previously been used for collecting mineral specimens in the asteroid belt. Its key feature was an extra-long robotic arm.

At the start of the operation, *Mantis* crossed the five-hundred-kilometer line held by the previous monitoring craft and carefully approached the target, flying slowly and pausing for several minutes every fifty kilometers so that the dense omnidirectional surveillance system behind it could perform a complete scan of the target. Only after confirming that there were no abnormalities did it proceed.

At one thousand kilometers from the target, the combined fleet had matched speed with the droplet, and most of the warships had turned off their fusion engines to drift silently in the abyss of space, their giant metal hulls reflecting the weak sunlight. They were like abandoned space cities, the whole fleet array a silent, prehistoric Stonehenge. The 1.2 million people in the fleet held their breath as they watched *Mantis* on its brief voyage.

The images seen by the fleet traveled at the speed of light for three hours before reaching Earth, where they were transmitted to the eyes of three billion people similarly holding their breath. All activity in the human world had stopped. The flying cars had disappeared from among the giant trees, and a stillness had fallen over the underground metropolises. Even the global information network, busy since its birth three centuries before, emptied out. The majority of data transmissions were images from twenty AU away.

Mantis's stop-and-go advance took half an hour to cover a distance that was hardly even a step through space. Finally, it hung in place fifty meters from the target. Now the *Mantis*'s distorted reflection could be clearly seen in the droplet's mercury surface. The ship's many instruments began a close-range scan of the target, first confirming prior observations: The droplet's surface temperature was even lower than the surrounding space, close to absolute zero. Scientists had thought that there might be powerful cooling equipment inside the droplet, but *Mantis*'s instruments were still unable to detect anything about the target's internal structure.

Mantis extended its extra-long robot arm toward the target, starting and stopping over the fifty-meter distance. But the dense monitoring system did not pick up anything abnormal. The grueling

process lasted half an hour before the tip of the arm finally reached the target's position and touched it, an object that had come from four light-years away on a nearly two-century-long trek through space. When the robot arm's six digits grasped hold of the droplet at last, a million hearts in the fleet beat as one, echoed three hours later by three billion hearts on Earth.

Holding the droplet, the mechanical arm waited motionless. When the target still showed no response or abnormality after ten minutes, it began to pull it back.

It was at this point that people noticed a strange contrast: The mechanical arm was obviously designed purely as a functional object, with a rugged steel frame and exposed hydraulics that felt complicatedly technological and crudely industrial. But the droplet was perfect in shape, a smoothly gleaming, solid drop of liquid whose exquisite beauty erased all functional and technical meaning and expressed the lightness and detachment of philosophy and art. The steel claw of the robot arm clutched the droplet like the hairy hand of *Australopithecus* clutching a pearl. The droplet looked so fragile, like a glass thermos liner in space, that everyone was afraid it would shatter in the claw. But that did not occur, and the robot arm began to retract.

It took another half hour for the arm to retract and pull the droplet into *Mantis*'s main cabin, after which the two bulkheads gradually came together. If the target were to self-destruct, this would be the most likely time. The fleet and Earth behind it waited quietly, as if through the silence they could hear the sound of time flowing through space.

Two hours later, nothing had happened.

The fact that the droplet had not self-destructed was final proof of what people had guessed: If it was a military probe, it surely would have self-destructed after falling into enemy hands. It was now certain that this was a gift from Trisolaris to humanity, a sign of peace sent in that civilization's baffling mode of expression.

Once again the world erupted with joy. This time the revelry wasn't as wild and abandoned as the last, because humanity's victory and the end of the war were no longer anything unanticipated. Taking a thousand steps back, even if the coming negotiations broke down and the war continued, humanity would still ultimately be the victors, because the presence in space of the combined fleet had given the masses a visual impression of human power. Earth now had the calm confidence to face any sort of enemy.

With the arrival of the droplet, people's feelings toward Trisolaris slowly began to change. They increasingly began to recognize that the race marching toward the Solar System was a great civilization, one that had experienced two-hundred-odd cyclic catastrophes and had endured with unbelievable tenacity. Their arduous journey of four light-years across the vastness of space was all for the sake of finding a stable star, a home in which to live out their lives. . . . The public's feelings toward Trisolaris began to change from enmity and hatred to sympathy, compassion, and even admiration. People also realized another fact: Trisolaris had sent out the ten droplets two centuries ago, but humanity had only just realized their true significance. This was no doubt because the behavior of Trisolaris was overly subtle, as well as a reflection of the fact that humanity's state of mind had been distorted by its own bloody history. In a global online referendum, citizen support for Project Sunshine rose rapidly, increasingly inclined toward the Strong Survival Plan that offered Mars as a Trisolaran reservation.

The UN and the fleets accelerated their preparations for negotiations, and the two internationals began organizing delegations.

All of this took place in the day after the droplet was captured.

But what excited people most of all was not the facts before their eyes, but the rudimentary outline of a bright future: What sort of fantastic paradise would the Solar System become after the union of Trisolaran technology and human power?

At about the same distance on the other side of the sun, *Natural Selection* coasted silently at 1 percent the speed of light.

"Message just received: The droplet didn't self-destruct upon capture," Dongfang Yanxu said to Zhang Beihai.

"What's a droplet?" he asked. They faced each other through the transparent bulkhead. His face was haggard.

"The Trisolaran probe. Now we have confirmation that it's a gift to the human race, an expression of the Trisolaran wish for peace."

"Is that so? That's very good."

"You don't seem to care very much."

He didn't reply. Instead he lifted the notebook up in front of him with both hands. "I've finished." Then he put it into a close-fitting pocket.

"So can you hand over control of *Natural Selection* now?"

"I can, but first I'd like to know what you plan on doing once you've gained control."

"Decelerating."

"To rendezvous with the pursuing force?"

"Yes. *Natural Selection*'s fuel store is below return capacity, so it needs to refuel before being able to return to the Solar System. But the pursuing force doesn't have enough fuel for us. Those six ships are only half the tonnage of *Natural Selection,* and in their pursuit they've accelerated to five percent of light speed and decelerated a similar amount. They've got enough fuel for a return. So *Natural Selection*'s personnel will have to return aboard the pursuing force. Later, a ship carrying enough fuel will be sent after *Natural Selection* to take it back to the Solar System, but that will require time. We need to decelerate as much as possible before leaving to minimize that time."

"Don't decelerate, Dongfang."

"Why?"

"Deceleration will consume all of *Natural Selection*'s remaining fuel. We can't become a powerless ship. No one knows what will happen. As captain, you ought to keep that in mind."

"What can happen? The future is clear: The war will end and humanity will win, and you'll be proven totally wrong!"

He smiled at her excitement, as if trying to quell it. As he looked at her, there was a softness in his eyes that had never been there before. It rocked her emotions. She found his defeatism unbelievable, and suspected him of having other motivations for defecting. She had even wondered about his sanity. But for some reason she felt a certain attachment to him. She had left her father when she was very young, certainly not anything unusual for a child of that era. Fatherly love was something ancient. But in this ancient soldier from the twenty-first century, she had come to understand it.

He said, "Dongfang, I come from troubled times. I'm a realist. All I know is that the enemy is still there and it's still approaching the Solar System. As a soldier knowing this, I can't be happy until everyone is at peace. . . . Don't decelerate. This is the condition under which I'll relinquish control. Of course, the only guarantee I have is your character."

"I promise that *Natural Selection* will not decelerate."

Zhang Beihai turned and floated to the interface panel, where he called up the permissions-transfer interface and entered his password. After a series of taps, he turned it off.

"*Natural Selection*'s captain's privileges have been transferred to you. The password is still Marlboro," he said, without looking back at her.

Dongfang Yanxu called up an interface in the air and quickly confirmed this. "Thank you. But I ask you not to come out of that cabin for the time being, or open the door. The ship's personnel are awakening from deep-sea state and I'm afraid they might act aggressively toward you."

"Will they make me walk the plank?" At her mystified expression, he laughed. "It's a form of the death penalty on ancient ships. If it had really carried on through to today, you would have to shove a criminal like me right out into space. . . . Okay. I'd quite like to be alone."

The shuttle that sailed out of *Quantum* seemed as small as a car leaving a city compared to its mother ship. The light of its engine illuminated only a small part of the ship's hull, like a candle beneath a cliff. It eased out of *Quantum*'s shadow into the sunlight, its engine nozzle glowing like a firefly as it flew toward the droplet a thousand kilometers away.

The expedition team consisted of four people: a major and a lieutenant colonel from the European and North American Fleets, Ding Yi, and Xizi.

Through the porthole, Ding Yi looked back at the receding fleet formation. *Quantum,* situated in a corner, still appeared large, but its nearest neighbor, the warship *Cloud,* was so small that its shape could only barely be made out. Farther away, the ranks of warships were just rows of points across his field of view. Ding Yi knew that the rectangular array was a hundred ships in length by twenty in width, with an additional fifteen ships maneuvering outside of the formation. But when he counted along the length, by the time he reached thirty he couldn't see clearly, and that was just six hundred kilometers away. It was the same looking up, where the short side extended vertically. The warships that could be made out in the far distance were just fuzzy points of light under the weak sunlight, nearly indistinguishable from the starry background. Only when their engines started up would the fleet array be totally visible to the naked eye. The combined fleet was a one-hundred-by-twenty matrix in space. He imagined another matrix being multiplied with it, the horizontal elements from one multiplied in turn with vertical elements from the other to form an even larger matrix, although in reality the only important constant for the matrix was one tiny point: the droplet. He didn't like extreme asymmetry in mathematics, so this attempt to calm himself through mental gymnastics failed.

When the force of acceleration subsided, he struck up a conversation with Xizi, who was sitting next to him. "Child, are you from Hangzhou?"

Xizi was staring straight ahead, as if trying to locate *Mantis,* which was still hundreds of kilometers away. Then she recovered

and shook her head. "No, Master Ding. I was born in the Asian Fleet. I don't know whether my name has anything to do with Hangzhou.[22] I've been there, though. It's a nice place."

"It was a nice place back in our day. But West Lake has now turned into Crescent Lake, and it's in a desert. . . . Still, even though the desert's everywhere, today's world still reminds me of the south, and the age in which the women were as graceful as the water." As he said this, he looked at Xizi, whose enchanting silhouette was set off by the soft light of the distant sun that streamed in through the porthole. "Child, looking at you, I'm reminded of someone I once loved. Like you, she was a major, and although she wasn't as tall as you, she was just as beautiful. . . ."

"In the old days, lots of girls must have been in love with you," Xizi said to Ding Yi, turning back to him.

"I wouldn't usually bother the girls I liked. I believed in what Goethe said: 'If I love you, what business is it of yours?' "

Xizi laughed.

He went on, "Oh, if only I had the same attitude toward physics! My life's biggest regret is that we've been blinded by the sophons. But here's a more positive way of thinking about it: If we're exploring laws, what business is that of the laws? One day, perhaps, humanity—or maybe someone else—will explore the laws so thoroughly that they'll be able to alter not only their own reality, but perhaps the entire universe. They'll be able to turn every star system into whatever shape they require, like kneading a ball of dough. But so what? The laws still won't have changed. Yes, she'll still be there, the one unchanging presence, forever young, like how we remember a lover. . . ." As he spoke, he pointed out the porthole at the brilliant Milky Way. "And when I think about that, my worries go away."

Xizi said nothing, and they fell into a heavy silence. *Mantis* soon came into view, albeit as a point of light two hundred kilometers

22 *Translator's Note:* Xīzǐ is another name for Xi Shi, one of the Four Beauties of ancient China, who lived near Hangzhou. West Lake (Xīhú) in Hangzhou has a particular association with Xi Shi.

away. The shuttle rotated 180 degrees, and the engine nozzle, now pointing ahead of them, began their deceleration.

The fleet was now directly ahead of the shuttle, around eight hundred kilometers away, a trivial distance in space, but one that turned the massive warships into barely visible points. The fleet itself was distinguishable from the starry background only by its neatly arranged ranks. The entire rectangular array seemed like a grid covering the Milky Way, its regularity standing in stark contrast to the chaos of the starfield. With its great size made tiny by the distance, the power of the formation was made apparent. Many people in the fleet and the distant Earth behind it who were watching this image sensed that it was a visual display of what Ding Yi had just been talking about.

The shuttle reached *Mantis* and the force of deceleration cut off. To the shuttle's passengers, the speed of the process made it feel as if *Mantis* had suddenly popped up in space.

Docking was completed quickly. Since *Mantis* was unmanned, there was no air in the cabin, so the four members of the expedition team put on light space suits. Upon receiving final instructions from the fleet, they filed weightlessly through the docking hatch and into *Mantis*.

The droplet floated dead center in *Mantis*'s one spherical main cabin. Its colors were entirely different from the image seen aboard *Quantum,* paler and softer, evidently due to differences in the scene reflected on its surface—the droplet's total reflectance meant that it had no color of its own. Arranged in the main cabin of *Mantis* was the folded robotic arm, an assortment of equipment, and several piles of asteroid rock samples. Floating in a mechanical and stony environment, the droplet once again presented a contrast between exquisiteness and crudeness, aesthetics and technology.

"It's the tear of the blessed mother," Xizi said.

Her words were transmitted from *Mantis* at the speed of light, first to the fleet and then resonating three hours later throughout the entire human world. Xizi, the lieutenant colonel, and the major from the European Fleet—ordinary people on the expedition team

placed, by unexpected circumstance, in a central position at the pinnacle moment in the history of civilization—shared a common feeling now that they were so close to the droplet: All sense of the distant world's unfamiliarity vanished, replaced by an intense desire for recognition. Yes, in the cold expanse of the universe, all carbon-based life shared a common destiny, one that might take billions of years to cultivate, but a destiny that cultivated feelings of love that transcended time and space. And now, they sensed that love in the droplet, a love that could bridge the chasm of any enmity. Xizi's eyes were wet, and three hours later, the eyes of billions of people like her would fill with tears.

But Ding Yi watched all of this dispassionately from the rear. "I see something else," he said. "Something far more sublime. A realm where both self and other are forgotten, an effort to encompass everything by shutting out everything."

"That's too much philosophy for me to understand," Xizi laughed through her tears.

"Dr. Ding, we don't have much time." The lieutenant colonel motioned for Ding Yi to come forward to be the first to touch the droplet.

Ding Yi floated slowly toward the droplet and placed a hand on its surface. To avoid frostbite from the cold mirror surface, he had to touch it with a gloved hand. Then the three officers touched it, too.

"It looks so fragile. I'm afraid of breaking it," Xizi said softly.

"I can't feel any friction at all," the lieutenant colonel marveled. "It's so smooth."

"How smooth is it?" Ding Yi asked.

To answer that question, Xizi took out a cylindrical instrument, a microscope, from a pocket in her space suit. She touched the lens to the droplet, and they could see a magnified image of the surface on the instrument's small display. Displayed on the screen was a smooth mirror.

"What's the magnification?" Ding Yi asked.

"A hundred times." Xizi pointed to a number in the corner of the screen, then adjusted the magnification to one thousand.

The enlarged surface remained a smooth mirror.

"Your device is broken," the lieutenant colonel said.

Xizi removed the microscope from the droplet and placed it against her space suit visor. The other three drew closer to look at the screen, where the visor—a surface which, to the naked eye, looked as smooth as the droplet—was a rough and rocky beach on the screen under one-thousand-times magnification. Xizi returned the microscope to the surface of the droplet, and the screen once again displayed a smooth mirror, no different from the surrounding, unmagnified surface.

"Increase it by another factor of ten," Ding Yi said.

This was beyond the capabilities of optical magnification, so Xizi carried out a series of operations to switch the microscope from optical to electron tunneling mode. Now the magnification power stood at ten thousand.

The magnified surface remained a smooth mirror. The smoothest surface that human technology could produce revealed itself as rough at just one thousand times magnification, like Gulliver's impression of the face of the beautiful giantess.

"Adjust to a hundred thousand times," the lieutenant colonel said.

Still they saw a smooth mirror.

"A million times."

A smooth mirror.

"Ten million times."

Macromolecules would be visible at this magnification, but what they saw on the screen remained a smooth mirror without the slightest sign of roughness, no difference in smoothness from the surrounding unmagnified surface.

"Push it up again!"

Xizi shook her head. This was the electron microscope's highest level of magnification.

More than two centuries before, in his novel *2001: A Space Odyssey,* Arthur C. Clarke had described a black monolith left on the moon by an advanced alien civilization. Surveyors had measured its dimensions with ordinary rulers and had found a ratio of one to four

to nine. When these were rechecked using the most high-precision measurement technology on Earth, the ratio remained an exact one to four to nine, with no error at all. Clarke described it as a "passive yet almost arrogant display of geometrical perfection."

Now, humanity was facing a far more arrogant display of power.

"Can an absolutely smooth surface really exist?" Xizi gasped.

"Yes," Ding Yi said. "The surface of a neutron star is nearly absolutely smooth."

"But this has a normal mass!"

Ding Yi considered this, then looked about him. "Hook up to the spaceship computer and find the spot that the robot arm gripped during capture."

This was accomplished remotely by a fleet surveillance officer. The *Mantis* computer projected thin red laser beams to mark the position on the droplet surface that had been gripped by the steel claw. Xizi examined one of the spots with the microscope, and at a magnification of ten million times, she still saw a smooth, flawless mirror.

"How high was the pressure at the point of contact?" the lieutenant colonel asked, and soon received a reply from the fleet: approximately two hundred kilograms per square centimeter.

Smooth surfaces are easily scratched, but the strong metal clamp did not leave any scratches on the droplet's surface.

Ding Yi floated away in search of something within the cabin. He returned with a rock pick, perhaps dropped in the cabin by someone during collection of rock samples. Before anyone could stop him, he slammed it forcefully into the mirror surface. There was a clang, crisp and melodious, like the pick had smashed into jade-paved ground. The sound traveled through his body, but the other three didn't hear it because of the vacuum. With the handle of the pick, he pointed out the spot he had struck, and Xizi examined it with the microscope.

At ten million times magnification, it was still a smooth mirror.

Ding Yi tossed the pick aside dejectedly and looked away from

the droplet, deep in thought. The eyes of the three officers, and the eyes of the million people in the fleet, were all focused on him.

"All we can do is guess," he said, looking up. "The molecules in this thing are neatly arranged, like an honor guard, and they're mutually solidifying. Do you know how solid it is? It's as if the molecules are nailed into place. Even their own vibrations are gone."

"That's why it's at absolute zero!" Xizi said. She and the other two officers understood what Ding Yi was getting at: At normal densities of matter, the separation between atomic nuclei is quite large. It would be no easier to fix them all in place than it would be to join the sun to the eight planets with rods to form a stationary truss.

"What force would allow that?"

"There's only one option: strong interaction."[23] Through his visor, it was obvious that Ding Yi's forehead was covered in sweat.

"But . . . that's like shooting the moon with a bow and arrow!"

"Indeed, they've shot the moon with a bow and arrow. . . . The tear of the blessed mother?" He gave a chilly laugh, a mournful sound that made them shiver, and the three officers knew what it meant: The droplet wasn't fragile like a tear. Entirely the opposite: Its strength was a hundred times greater than the sturdiest material in the Solar System. All known substances were as fragile as paper by comparison. It could pass through the Earth like a bullet through cheese, without even the slightest harm to its surface.

"Then . . . what's it here for?" the lieutenant colonel blurted out.

"Who knows? Maybe it really is just a messenger. But it's here to give humanity a different message," Ding Yi said, turning his gaze away from the droplet.

"What?"

"If I destroy you, what business is it of yours?"

The words were followed by a momentary silence as the three other members of the expeditionary team and the million members

23 *Translator's Note:* Strong interaction is the strongest of the four fundamental interactions, and is responsible for the strong nuclear force that binds together subatomic particles. It is roughly 100 times more powerful than electromagnetism, but is only effective at distances of less than a femtometer.

of the combined fleet ruminated over their meaning. Then, all of a sudden, Ding Yi said, "Run." The word was uttered softly, but then he raised his hands and shouted hoarsely, "Stupid children. Run!"

"Run where?" Xizi asked in fright.

Just seconds after Ding Yi, the lieutenant colonel realized the truth. Like Ding Yi, he shouted desperately: "The fleet! Evacuate the fleet!"

But it was too late. Powerful interference had already wiped out their communication channels. The image being transmitted from *Mantis* vanished, and the fleet was unable to hear the lieutenant colonel's final call.

A blue halo emerged from the tip of the droplet's tail. It was small at first, but very bright, and cast a blue shroud over its surroundings. Then it dramatically expanded, turning from blue to yellow and finally to red. It almost seemed as if the droplet wasn't producing the halo, but had just drilled out from within it. The halo weakened in luminosity as it expanded, and when it had reached a diameter twice that of the largest part of the droplet, it vanished. The instant it vanished, a second small blue halo emerged from the tip. Like the first one, it expanded, changed color, weakened, and quickly disappeared. The halos continued to emerge from the droplet's tail at a rate of two or three a second, and under their propulsion, the droplet began to move forward, and then rapidly accelerated.

But the four members of the expedition team never saw the second halo emerge, because the first one was accompanied by ultra-high temperatures approaching that of the sun's core, which vaporized them instantly.

The hull of *Mantis* glowed red, resembling from the outside a paper lantern whose candle had just been lit. Its metal body melted like wax, but no sooner had the ship begun to melt than it exploded, dispersing into space as an incandescent liquid with hardly any solid fragments left behind.

From a thousand kilometers away, the fleet had a clear view of *Mantis*'s explosion, but the initial analysis was that the droplet had

self-destructed. Everyone felt sorrow for the sacrifice of the four expedition team members, followed by disappointment that the droplet was not a messenger of peace. But the human race did not have even the slightest bit of psychological preparation for what was about to happen.

The first anomaly was identified by the fleet's space surveillance computer, which discovered during the course of processing images of *Mantis*'s explosion that one of the fragments was abnormal. Most of the pieces were molten metal that flew uniformly through space following the explosion, but this one was accelerating. Of course, only a computer was able to find a tiny object among the massive quantity of flying fragments. From an immediate search of its database and knowledge bank, which included an enormous amount of information on *Mantis,* it arrived at several dozen possible explanations for the peculiar debris, but none was correct.

Neither computer nor human realized that the explosion had destroyed only *Mantis* and the four-member expedition team, but not the droplet.

As for the accelerating fragment, the fleet's space surveillance system issued only a level-three attack alarm, because the approaching object was not a warship and was headed toward one corner of the rectangular formation. On its current heading, it would pass outside the formation and would not strike any warship. Due to the large number of level-one alarms issued following the *Mantis* explosion, this level-three alarm was completely ignored. The computer had, however, also noted the fragment's high rate of acceleration. By three hundred kilometers it had already passed the third cosmic velocity and was continuing to gain speed. The alert was upgraded to level two, but was still ignored.

By the time the fragment had flown roughly 1,500 kilometers from the explosion site toward the corner of the formation, only fifty-one seconds had elapsed. By the time it reached the corner, it was traveling at a speed of 31.7 kilometers per second. Now it was on the periphery of the formation, 160 kilometers away from *Infinite Frontier,* the first warship in this corner of the array. The fragment

did not pass by the formation, but executed a thirty-degree turn, and, without slowing down, sped straight toward *Infinite Frontier.* In the roughly two seconds it took to cover that distance, the computer actually dropped its alert from level two back to level three, concluding that the fragment wasn't actually a physical object due to the fact that its motion was impossible under aerospace mechanics. At twice the third cosmic velocity, executing a sharp turn without a drop in speed was like slamming into an iron wall. If it was a vessel containing a metal block, the change in direction would have exerted such force as to flatten that metal block into a thin film. So the fragment had to be an illusion.

In that manner, the droplet struck *Infinite Frontier* at twice the third cosmic velocity, at a heading straight along the first row of the fleet rectangle.

The droplet struck *Infinite Frontier* in its rear third and passed through with no resistance, as if penetrating a shadow. The extreme speed of the impact meant that two highly regular entry and exit holes roughly the diameter of the droplet's thickest part appeared in its hull. But no sooner had they appeared than the holes deformed and vanished as the surrounding hull melted under the heat produced by the high-speed impact and the ultra-high temperature of the droplet's trailing halo. The part of the ship that had been hit turned red-hot, and the redness spread from the point of impact until it covered half the ship, like a chunk of iron that had just been taken out of the forge.

After passing through *Infinite Frontier,* the droplet continued onward at a speed of thirty kilometers per second. In the space of three seconds it had crossed ninety kilometers, passing first through *Yuanfang, Infinite Frontier*'s neighbor in the first row, and then through *Foghorn, Antarctica,* and *Ultimate,* leaving their hulls red-hot, as if the warships were giant lamps lined up.

Then *Infinite Frontier* exploded. It and the four warships after it were hit in the fusion fuel tanks. But unlike *Mantis*'s conventional, high-temperature explosion, this explosion was a fusion reaction triggered in *Infinite Frontier*'s fuel. No one ever figured out whether

the fusion reaction had been sparked by the droplet's ultra-high-temperature propulsive halo or some other factor. The fireball of the thermonuclear explosion appeared at the point of impact with the fuel tank and swiftly expanded until it illuminated the entire fleet against the velvety background of space, outshining the Milky Way.

Nuclear fireballs then took shape on *Yuanfang, Foghorn, Antarctica,* and *Ultimate* in succession.

In the next eight seconds, the droplet passed through ten more stellar-class warships.

By this point, the expanding nuclear fireball had engulfed the entirety of *Infinite Frontier* and had begun to shrink, while more fireballs were lighting up and expanding on other ships that had been struck.

The droplet continued to traverse the length of the array, penetrating one stellar-class warship after another at intervals of less than a second.

The fusion fireball on *Infinite Frontier* had gone out, leaving the ship's hull totally melted. Now it exploded, spewing a million tons of glowing, dark-red metallic liquid like a bud bursting into bloom, the molten metal scattering unimpeded in an omnidirectional storm of burning metallic magma.

The droplet continued its advance, following a straight line through more warships and leaving a line of ten nuclear fireballs behind it. The entire fleet shone in the flames of these burning small suns as if it had been set ablaze and turned into a sea of light. Behind the line of fireballs, the melted warships continued to fling waves of hot molten metal into space, as if massive rocks were being pitched into a magma sea.

In one minute and eighteen seconds, the droplet had completed a two-thousand-kilometer course, passing through each of the hundred ships in the first row of the combined fleet's rectangular formation.

By the time the last ship in the row, *Adam,* was swallowed up in a nuclear fireball, the bursts of metallic magma at the opposite end had scattered, cooled, and spread out, leaving the heart of the

explosion—the spot where *Infinite Frontier* had been a minute before—empty of practically everything. *Yuanfang, Foghorn, Antarctica, Ultimate* . . . all of them vanished one after another into metallic magma. When the last nuclear fireball in the line went out and darkness fell upon space once more, the gradually cooling magma that had barely been visible reappeared as dark red lights in the blackness of space, like a two-thousand-kilometer-long river of blood.

After punching through *Adam,* the droplet flew a short distance of about eighty kilometers through empty space, then executed another sharp turn unexplainable by humanity's aerospace mechanics. This time the angle it described was even smaller: just fifteen degrees off a total reversal, executed nearly instantaneously even as it maintained a constant speed. Then, after a small heading adjustment that brought it in line with the second row of warships in the fleet's array—or what was now the first row, in light of the recent destruction—it sped toward the first ship in that row, *Ganges,* at thirty kilometers per second.

Until this point, Fleet Command had not made any response.

The fleet's battle information system had faithfully carried out its mission and captured through its massive monitoring network a complete record of all battle information over the course of that one minute and eighteen seconds. The sheer amount of information was for the time being only analyzable by the computerized battlefield decision-making system, which had arrived at the following conclusion: A powerful enemy space force had appeared in the vicinity and had launched an attack on the fleet. However, the computer did not provide any information about that enemy force. Only two things were certain: 1. The enemy space force was located at the position occupied by the droplet, and 2. The force was invisible to every means of detection they possessed.

By this time, fleet commanders were in a state of numb shock. For nearly two centuries, research into space strategy and tactics had dreamed up every possible kind of extreme battle condition, but witnessing a hundred warships blowing up like a string of

firecrackers in under a minute was beyond what their minds could comprehend. The tide of information surging out of the battle information system meant that they were forced to rely on the analyses and judgments of the computer battlefield decision-making system and focus their attention on detecting an invisible enemy fleet that didn't even exist. All battle monitoring capacity was directed into the distant regions of space, ignoring the danger right in front of them. A fair number of people even believed that the powerful invisible enemy might be a third-party alien force distinct from humanity and Trisolaris, because in their subconscious minds, Trisolaris remained the weaker, losing side.

The fleet's battle monitoring system did not detect the droplet's presence any earlier primarily because it was invisible to radar at all wavelengths and could only be located through analysis of visible spectrum images, but visible images were treated with far less importance than radar data. Most of the fragments scattered through space in storms of exploded debris were liquid metal melted by the high-temperature nuclear blasts, upward of a million tons melted in the destruction of each ship. A fair proportion of this massive amount of molten debris was roughly the same size and shape as the droplet, which presented the computer image analysis system with the difficult task of distinguishing the droplet from the debris. Besides, practically all of the commanders believed that the droplet had self-destructed inside *Mantis,* so no one issued specific instructions to perform such an analysis.

Meanwhile, other circumstances were exacerbating the confusion of battle. Debris ejected from the explosions of the first row of warships soon reached the second row, prompting their battle defense systems to respond with high-energy lasers and railguns to intercept the debris. These flying fragments, consisting largely of metal melted by the nuclear fireballs, were irregular in size, and although they had been partially cooled in flight by the low temperatures of space, only their outer shells had solidified. Their insides were still in a fiery liquid state, and when struck, they scattered in a brilliant explosion of fireworks. It was not long before

the second row turned into a flaming barrier parallel to the dull "river of blood" left behind by the exploded warships in the first, roiling with explosions as if washed in a tide of fire surging from the direction of that invisible enemy. Debris flew thick as hail, more than defensive systems could block, and when fragments slipped through and struck the warships, the impact of these jets of solid-liquid metal possessed considerable destructive power. A number of the ships in the fleet's second row suffered major hull damage, and some were even punctured. Shrill decompression alarms blared. . . .

Although the dazzling battle with debris did receive notice, given the circumstances, it was hard for the computers and humans in the command system to avoid the misconception that the fleet was engaged in a fierce exchange of fire with an enemy space force. Neither person nor machine noticed the tiny figure of Death that had begun to destroy the second row of ships.

And so, when the droplet charged at *Ganges*, the hundred warships in the second row were still assembled in a straight line. A death formation.

The droplet surged like lightning, and in the space of just ten seconds, it passed through twelve warships: *Ganges, Columbia, Justice, Masada, Proton, Yandi, Atlantic, Sirius, Thanksgiving, Advance, Han, and Tempest.* As in the destruction of the first row, each warship turned red-hot after penetration, before being engulfed in a nuclear fireball that left a million tons of dark red, glowing, metallic magma that then exploded. In this brutal destruction, the lined-up warships were like a two-thousand-kilometer fuse that burned with such intensity that it left behind nothing but ash glowing a dull, dark red.

One minute and twenty-one seconds later, the hundred ships in the second row had been completely annihilated.

After passing through the last ship, *Meiji*, the droplet reached the end of the row and turned another acute angle to charge straight at the first ship in the third row, *Newton*. During the destruction of the second row, debris from the explosions had raged into the third.

The tide of debris included molten metal flung from explosions in the second row as well as mostly cooled metal fragments from the ships of the first. Most of the third-row ships had by now started up their engines and defensive systems and had begun maneuvering, which meant that this time, the ships were not situated along a perfectly straight line, as had been the case for the first and second rows. Nevertheless, the hundred ships were still roughly in line. After the droplet passed through *Newton*, it sharply adjusted direction and, in a twinkling, crossed the twenty kilometers separating *Newton* from *Enlightenment*, now at a three-kilometer offset from the line. From *Enlightenment*, it turned sharply again, raced toward *Cretaceous*, which was moving toward the other side, and penetrated it. Following this broken path, the droplet drilled through the ships in the third row one after the other, never dropping its speed below thirty kilometers per second.

When analysts subsequently observed the droplet's route, they were amazed to discover that its every turn was a sharp corner, not the smooth curve of a human spacecraft. The diabolical flight path demonstrated a space drive entirely beyond human comprehension, as if the droplet was a shadow without mass, unconcerned with the principles of dynamics, moving at will like the nib of God's pen. During the attack on the fleet's third row, the droplet's sharp changes of direction occurred at a rate of two or three per second, a deathly embroidery needle sewing a thread of destruction through the row's hundred ships.

The droplet took two minutes and thirty-five seconds to destroy the third row of ships.

By this time, all of the warships in the fleet had started their engines. Although the array had lost its shape entirely, the droplet continued to strike the evacuating ships. The pace of destruction slowed, but, at any given time, three to five nuclear fireballs were burning among the ships. Their deathly flames drowned out the glow of the engines, turning them into a cluster of terrified fireflies.

The fleet command system still had no clue about the true source of the attack and continued to focus its energies on searching for

the imaginary invisible enemy fleet. However, subsequent analysis of the massive clouds of vague information transmitted by the fleet revealed that it was at this point that the earliest analysis to come close to the truth was performed by two low-ranking officers in the Asian Fleet. One was Ensign Zhao Xin, an assistant targeting screener on *Beifang,* and the other was Captain Li Wei, an intermediate EM weapons system controller on *Wannian Kunpeng.* A transcript of their conversation follows:

ZHAO XIN: This is *Beifang TR317* calling *Wannian Kunpeng EM986*! This is *Beifang TR317* calling *Wannian Kunpeng EM986*!

LI WEI: This is *Wannian Kunpeng EM986*. Please be advised, transmitting ship-to-ship voice communication at this information level is a violation of wartime regulations.

ZHAO XIN: Is that Li Wei? This is Zhao Xin! You're who I'm trying to find!

LI WEI: Hi! I'm glad to know you're still alive.

ZHAO XIN: Captain, here's the thing. I've discovered something that I'd like to transmit to the shared command level, but my privileges are too low. Could you help me out?

LI WEI: My privileges are too low, too. But shared command has plenty of information right now. What do you want to transmit?

ZHAO XIN: I've analyzed a visual image of the battle—

LI WEI: Shouldn't you be analyzing radar information?

ZHAO XIN: That's a system fallacy. When I analyzed the visual image and extracted only the speed characteristic, do you know what I found? Do you know what's been going on?

LI WEI: You seem to know.

ZHAO XIN: Don't think I've gone crazy—you know me, we're friends.

LI WEI: You're a stone-cold beast. You'll be the last to go crazy. Go ahead.

ZHAO XIN: Listen, it's the fleet that's gone crazy. We're attacking ourselves!

LI WEI: . . .

ZHAO XIN: *Infinite Frontier* attacked *Yuanfang*, and *Yuanfang* attacked *Foghorn*, and *Foghorn* attacked *Antarctica*, and *Antarctica* . . .

LI WEI: You're out of your damn mind!

ZHAO XIN: That's what's happening. A attacks B; and after B is attacked, but before it explodes, it attacks C; and after C is attacked but before it explodes, it attacks D. . . . It's like every warship that was hit attacked the next warship in the row—like an infection, damn it, or a game of pass the parcel, but to the death. It's insane!

LI WEI: What weapons are they using?

ZHAO XIN: I don't know. I picked up a projectile in the image, so frickin' tiny and so frickin' fast, way the hell faster than your rail-guns. And incredibly precise. It hit the fuel tanks every single time!

LI WEI: Send me the analysis.

ZHAO XIN: I've sent it over, the original data and vector analysis both. Take a look, god damn it!

Ensign Zhao Xin's analysis, though unconventional, was pretty close to the truth. Li Wei took half a minute to study the information he sent over. In that time, another thirty-nine warships were destroyed.

LI WEI: I've noticed something about the speed.

ZHAO XIN: What speed?

LI WEI: The speed of the small projectile. Its speed when it's launched from each warship is slightly slower. Then it accelerates to thirty kilometers per second during flight. Then it strikes the next warship, and when it launches from that warship prior to the explosion, its speed is a little slower. Then it accelerates. . . .

ZHAO XIN: That doesn't mean anything. . . .

LI WEI: What I mean is . . . it's a little like drag.

ZHAO XIN: Drag? How so?

LI WEI: Every time this projectile passes through a target, the drag slows it down.

ZHAO XIN: I see what you're doing. I'm not stupid. You said "this projectile" and "passes through a target." . . . Is it a single object?
LI WEI: Take a look outside. Another hundred ships have exploded.

This conversation took place not in the modern language of the fleet but in twenty-first-century Mandarin. From the mode of speech, it was obvious that the two were hibernators. There were few hibernators serving in the fleet, and although most of them had awakened while still very young, they still lacked a modern person's capacity to absorb information, which meant that most of them carried out relatively low-level duties. It was later discovered that the vast majority of officers and soldiers who recovered their senses and good judgment the earliest during the grand destruction were hibernators. These two officers, for instance, despite being at a level that did not even permit them the use of the ship's advanced systems, were nonetheless able to perform a remarkable piece of analysis.

Zhao Xin and Li Wei's information was not passed up the fleet command system, but the system's analysis of the battle was headed in the right direction. Realizing that the invisible enemy force posited by the computer decision-making system didn't exist, attention was now focused on analyzing the aggregated battle information. After a search and match on massive amounts of data, the system finally discovered the continued existence of the droplet. The image of the droplet extracted from battle recordings was unchanged apart from the addition of a propulsion halo at the tail. It was still a perfect droplet shape, only this time what was reflected as it sped onward was the glow of nuclear fireballs and metal magma, glaring brightness alternating with dark red. It looked like a drop of burning blood. Further analysis arrived at a model of the droplet's attack path.

Various scenarios for the Doomsday Battle had been concocted during two centuries of the study of space strategy, but in the minds of strategists, the enemy had always been big. Humanity would meet the main part of the mighty Trisolaran force on a space battlefield, with every warship a fortress of death the size of

a small city. They had imagined every extreme form of weapons and tactics the enemy could possibly possess, the most terrifying of which involved the Trisolaran Fleet launching an attack using antimatter weapons, and obliterating a stellar-class battleship with antimatter the size of a rifle bullet.

But now the combined fleet had to face facts: Their only enemy was a tiny probe, one drop of water out of the enormous ocean of Trisolaran strength, and this probe attacked using one of the oldest and most primitive tactics known to human navies: ramming.

Roughly thirteen minutes passed from the moment the probe started its attack until the fleet command system arrived at the correct assessment. Given the complex and grim battlefield conditions, this was fairly quick, but the droplet was quicker. In twentieth-century naval battles, there might have been time for commanders to be summoned to the flagship for a conference once the enemy fleet appeared on the horizon. But space battles were measured in seconds, and in that thirteen-minute span, more than six hundred warships were destroyed by the probe. Only then did humanity realize that command of a space battle was beyond their reach. And due to the sophon block, it was beyond the reach of their artificial intelligence as well. Purely in terms of command, humanity might *never* have the capacity to engage in a space battle with Trisolaris.

The speed of the droplet's strikes and its invisibility to radar meant that defensive systems on the first ships hit never responded. But as the distance between the warships grew and the droplet's striking distance increased, defensive systems on all warships were recalibrated based on the droplet's target characteristics. This meant that *Nelson* was the first ship to attempt to intercept, using laser weapons to increase the accuracy of firing on the small, high-speed target. When struck by the multiple beams, the droplet emitted a powerful visible light, even though the *Nelson* had fired gamma-ray lasers that were invisible to the naked eye. The droplet's imperceptibility to radar had never been understood, since it had a completely reflective surface and a shape that was perfectly diffuse, but perhaps the ability to alter the frequency of

reflected electromagnetic waves was the secret to this invisibility. The light emitted from the droplet when it was struck was so bright it drowned out the nuclear fireballs going off all around it, forced the monitoring systems to dim their images to avoid damage to their optical components, and caused sustained blindness to anyone who looked directly at it. In other words, this superpowerful light was indistinguishable from darkness in its effect. The droplet, wrapped in this all-engulfing light, entered *Nelson* and was extinguished, plunging the battlefield into pitch darkness. Moments later, the nuclear fireballs reestablished their dominance and the droplet emerged from *Nelson* unscathed and sped straight for *Green,* eighty-odd kilometers away.

Green's defense system switched over to EM-based kinetic weapons to intercept the attacking droplet. The metal shells fired by the railgun possessed enormous destructive power, and the kinetic energy inherent in their high speed meant that every shell that struck the target hit with the force of a bomb. Against ground targets, they would flatten a mountain in no time at all. The droplet's relative velocity only added to the shells' energy, but when they struck, the droplet slowed only slightly before it adjusted its propulsion and recovered its speed. Under a dense hail of shells, it flew straight at *Green* and penetrated it. Under the ultra-high magnification microscope, the droplet's surface would still be mirror-smooth and totally scratch-free.

Strong-interaction material differs from ordinary matter like solid differs from liquid. The attacks on the droplet by human weapons were like waves striking a reef. Damaging it was impossible, which meant that nothing in the Solar System could destroy it. It was untouchable.

The fleet command system had just stabilized itself, only to be plunged once again into chaos. This time, its despair over the loss of every weapon available to it meant it would not recover from this collapse.

The merciless slaughter in space continued. As the distance between ships grew, the droplet accelerated and had soon doubled

its speed to sixty kilometers per second. Exhibiting a cool and precise intelligence in its continuous attacks, it solved the traveling salesman problem in local regions with perfect accuracy, hardly ever retracing its path. With its targets in constant motion, the droplet accomplished a huge range of accurate measurements and complex calculations effortlessly and at high speed. In the course of its intensely focused massacre, it would occasionally veer off to the edges of the group of ships to quickly dispatch a few outliers and arrest the fleet's inclination to flee in that direction.

The droplet usually made precise strikes on the ships' fuel tanks—whether it found them by real-time location detection or with the use of a stored database of every ship's structure provided by the sophons was unknown. However, in around 10 percent of the targets, the droplet did not strike the tanks. The destruction of those ships did not involve fusion in the nuclear material, so it took a comparatively long time for the red-hot ships to finally explode, a brutal situation in which the crew suffered under high temperatures before burning to death.

The evacuation of the ships did not go smoothly. It was too late to enter deep-sea state, so the warships could only evacuate at Ahead Three acceleration, which made scattering impossible. Like a sheepdog racing alongside a flock, the droplet executed occasional blocking strikes at different positions at the fleet's edges to keep it in shape.

Space was full of cooled or still-molten debris and large chunks of warships, so ship defense systems had to continually sweep their flight path with lasers or railguns. The fragments formed glittering, flaming arcs that wrapped each ship in a brilliant canopy. Yet some debris still slipped through the defenses and caused serious hull damage and even loss of navigational capability when they struck the ships directly. Collision with larger fragments was fatal.

Despite the collapse of the fleet command system, High Command remained in charge during evacuation, but the density of the initial formation meant collisions between ships were unavoidable. *Himalaya* and *Thor* collided headon at high speed

and were smashed to bits. *Messenger* rear-ended *Genesis,* and the air that leaked like a hurricane through the gashes tore into both ships and blew personnel and other objects out into space, forming tails that dragged along in the wake of the two giant wrecks.

Most horrifying of all was what happened to *Einstein* and *Xia,* whose captains bypassed system protections via remote control mode and entered Ahead Four acceleration. None of their personnel was protected by deep-sea state. Images transmitted from *Xia* showed a hangar emptied of fighters but occupied by over a hundred people who were flattened against the deck by the high gs once acceleration began. From this vantage point, observers saw crimson flowers of blood bloom on the white space the size of a football field, forming extremely thin layers that spread out and ultimately merged into one under the immense force. . . . Spherical cabins presented the ultimate horror: At the beginning of hypergravitation everyone inside slid to the bottom, and then the devil's weighty hand squished them all into a lump, as if balling up a pile of clay men, with no time for anyone to even scream. The only sound was of shattering bones and viscera squeezing out. Then the pile of flesh and bones was submerged in a bloody liquid that turned eerily clear once the solids were precipitated out by the high gs, its surface flat and motionless as a mirror under the intense force. It seemed solid, and the formless pile of flesh, bone, and organs lay within it like rubies sealed in crystal. . . .

Afterward, people initially thought that putting *Einstein* and *Xia* into Ahead Four had been a mistake made during the chaos, but further analysis repudiated this view. Using the remote control mode to bypass the stringent procedures required by the warship control system prior to executing Ahead Four acceleration, including the confirmation that all personnel were in deep-sea state, involved a complicated series of operations that were unlikely to have been made in error. In the information transmitted from the two ships, it was also found that, prior to entering Ahead Four, *Einstein* and *Xia* had been using fighters and smaller craft to transport personnel outside. They did not enter Ahead Four until the

droplet drew nearer and neighboring warships began to explode. This suggested that they intended to escape the droplet at top acceleration to preserve humanity's warships, but even *Einstein* and *Xia* were unable to evade the droplet's clutches. The keen-eyed death god noticed that two ships were accelerating far faster than the average rate of the group and swiftly caught up to them and destroyed the ships and their lifeless cargo.

But two other warships successfully accelerated at Ahead Four and escaped the droplet's attack: *Quantum* and *Bronze Age,* which had both entered deep-sea state prior to the battle, at Ding Yi's behest. As soon as the third row of ships had been destroyed, the two of them entered Ahead Four and made an emergency escape in the same direction. Their position in a corner of the array, with the entire fleet separating them from the droplet, gave them sufficient time to escape into the depths of space.

More than a thousand ships, over half the fleet, had been destroyed in a twenty-minute attack.

Space was chock-full of debris in a cluster ten thousand kilometers in diameter, a rapidly expanding metallic cloud whose edges were illuminated time and again by the nuclear fireballs of exploding warships, as if a giant, stony face were flickering in and out of the cosmic night. In between the fireballs, the glow of metallic magma turned the cloud into a blood-red sunset.

The remaining warships were scattered widely, but nearly all of them were still within the metallic cloud. The majority had exhausted their railguns and had to rely on lasers to open up a path through the cloud, but the energy drain made the lasers under-powered and left the ships to wend a slow, torturous path through the debris. Most of them moved at a speed practically the same as the cloud's rate of expansion, turning it into a death trap from which evacuation and flight were impossible.

The droplet's speed was now ten times the third cosmic velocity, or roughly 170 kilometers per second. Its course took it smashing through debris that liquefied under impact, splashing away at high speed to collide with other debris and giving the droplet a brilliant

tail. First it resembled a comet bristling with rage, but as the tail lengthened, it turned into a huge silver dragon that stretched ten thousand kilometers. The entire metallic cloud glowed with the dragon's light as it whipped to and fro in its mad dance. The warships penetrated by the dragon's head began to explode along its body, so that it was dotted with the nuclear explosions of four or five small suns at any given time. Further back, molten battleships became million-ton metallic magma explosions that dyed its tail a bewitching bloodred. . . .

The brilliant dragon was still flying thirty minutes later, but the nuclear fireballs on its body had disappeared, and its tail was no longer bloodred. Not a single warship remained in the metallic cloud.

When the dragon flew out of the cloud, its body vanished at the cloud's edge, its head followed by its tail. Then it began taking out the remnants of the fleet. Only twenty-one warships had cleared the cloud, most of them suffering enough damage in the process that they retained minimal acceleration or were even coasting unpowered. These were quickly caught and destroyed by the droplet. The metallic clouds formed from the newly exploded ships expanded and merged into the larger cloud.

The droplet had to spend a bit more time destroying the five mostly intact ships because they had already picked up speed and were headed in different directions. The final ship to be destroyed, *Ark,* had traveled a considerable distance from the cloud, so when the fireball of its explosion lit up space for a few seconds before going out, it was like a solitary lamp in the wind of the wilderness.

Humanity's space-based armed forces had been annihilated.

The droplet briefly accelerated in the direction *Quantum* and *Bronze Age* had fled, but soon abandoned the chase because the two targets were too far away and had picked up too much speed. And thus, *Quantum* and *Bronze Age* became the only survivors of the tremendous destruction.

The droplet left the field of slaughter and set its heading in the direction of the sun.

Apart from those two complete warships, a small number of

people in the fleet had survived the holocaust by boarding fighters or other small craft before the destruction of their ships. Although the droplet could have destroyed them effortlessly, it had no interest in small spacecraft. The biggest threat to these vessels, which lacked defensive systems and couldn't survive an impact, was from high-speed metal fragments, and some of them were destroyed by debris after leaving their mother ships. They had the greatest chance of survival at the beginning and the end of the attack, because at the start the metallic cloud had not yet formed, and by the end the cloud had grown far less dense as it expanded.

The surviving small craft and fighters drifted for a few days beyond the orbit of Uranus and were eventually rescued by civilian spacecraft plying that region of space. The survivors numbered around sixty thousand, and included the two hibernator officers who had made the first correct assessment of the droplet's attack: Ensign Zhao Xin and Captain Li Wei.

The region eventually became still, and the metallic cloud lost its luster in the coldness of the cosmos and disappeared into darkness. Over the years, under the pull of the sun's gravity, the cloud stopped its expansion and began to lengthen, ultimately forming a long strip that turned into an extremely thin metallic belt around the sun, as if a million restless souls were floating endlessly in the cold outer reaches of the Solar System.

The destruction of the entirety of humanity's space force was accomplished by just one Trisolaran probe, and nine like it were three years away from the Solar System. The ten of them together weren't even one ten-thousandth the size of a single warship, and Trisolaris had a thousand of those that even now were flying onward toward the Solar System.

"If I destroy you, what business is it of yours?"

Awakening from a long sleep, Zhang Beihai looked at the time: He had been asleep fifteen hours, perhaps the longest he had ever slept apart from his two centuries in hibernation. Now he felt a

new feeling. Examining his mind, he realized where this feeling came from.

He was on his own.

In the past, even when floating alone in the endlessness of space, he had never had the feeling of being on his own. His father's eyes were watching him from the beyond with a gaze that was present every moment of every day. Like the sunlight during daytime and the starlight at night, it had become a part of his world. Now his father's gaze had disappeared.

Time to go out, he said to himself as he adjusted his uniform. He had slept weightless, so no part of his hair or clothing was out of place. Taking a last look at the spherical cabin in which he had spent more than a month, he opened the door and drifted out, prepared to calmly face the fury of the crowd, to face the countless expressions of disdain and condemnation, to face the final judgment . . . and to face, as a conscientious soldier, a life whose duration he did not know. Whatever happened, the rest of his life was sure to be calm.

The corridor was empty.

He advanced slowly, passing compartments on either side, all of them open. They were all identical to his own spherical cabin, their snow-white walls resembling pupilless eyes. The environment was clean, and he saw no open information windows. The ship's information system had probably been restarted and reformatted.

He recalled a movie he had seen in his youth, in which the characters lived in a Rubik's Cube world made up of countless identical cubic rooms, each of which contained a different sort of death mechanism. They passed from one room to the next, endlessly. . . .

The free rein of his thoughts surprised him. This used to be a luxury, but now that his nearly two-century-long mission was at an end, his mind could walk a leisurely path.

He turned a corner, and ahead of him was another, longer corridor that was just as empty. The bulkheads emitted an even, milky-soft light that was enough to make him lose his sense of depth. The world felt compact. Again, the doors to the spherical cabins on

either side were all open, and each one was an identical white space.

Natural Selection looked abandoned. To Zhang Beihai's eyes, the massive ship he occupied was one enormous yet concise symbol, a metaphor for some law hidden beneath reality. He had the illusion that these identical white spherical spaces extended endlessly into space around him, repeating infinitely through the universe.

An idea popped into his mind: holography.

Every spherical cabin could achieve total manipulation and control of *Natural Selection,* so, at least from an informatics perspective, every cabin was the totality of *Natural Selection*. That meant *Natural Selection* was holographic.

The ship itself was a metal seed carrying the total information of human civilization. If it germinated somewhere in the universe, then it might grow into a complete civilization. The part contained the whole, hence human civilization might be holographic as well.

He had failed. He had not managed to spread these seeds, and for this he felt regret. But not sadness, and not just because he'd done everything he could to carry out his duty. His mind, now freed, took flight, and he imagined the universe as holographic, every point containing the whole, so that the entire universe endured so long as one atom remained. Suddenly he had an all-encompassing sense of focus, the same feeling that Ding Yi had just over ten hours ago at the other end of the Solar System on the last stage of his approach toward the droplet, while Zhang Beihai was still asleep.

He reached the end of the corridor and opened the door to enter the warship's largest spherical hall, the one he had arrived at when he first entered *Natural Selection* three months ago. As before, a formation of fleet officers and soldiers was floating in the center of the sphere, but their numbers were several times greater and made up three layers in the formation. The two-thousand-strong crew of *Natural Selection* formed the center layer, which he realized was the only real layer. The other two were holograms.

Looking closer, he saw that the hologram formations were made up of the officers and soldiers from the four pursuing ships. Right in the center of the three-layer formation was a row of five

colonels: Dongfang Yanxu and the captains of the four other ships. All but Dongfang Yanxu were holograms that were evidently being transmitted from the pursuing ships. When he entered the hall, the eyes of five thousand people focused on him with an expression clearly not directed at a defector. The captains saluted in order.

"*Blue Space,* of the Asian Fleet!"

"*Enterprise,* of the North American Fleet!"

"*Deep Space,* of the Asian Fleet!"

"*Ultimate Law,* of the European Fleet!"

Dongfang Yanxu was the last to salute him. "*Natural Selection,* of the Asian Fleet! Sir, the five stellar-class warships you have preserved for humanity are all that is left of Earth's space fleet. Please accept your command!"

"It's a collapse. Everything's collapsed. It's a collective mental breakdown!" Shi Xiaoming sighed and shook his head. He had just returned from the underground city. "The whole city's out of control. It's chaos."

The administrative officials had all come to a meeting of the neighborhood government. Hibernators made up two-thirds, with modern people accounting for the rest. They were easily distinguishable now: Although they were in a state of extreme depression, the hibernator officials kept their composure despite their low spirits, while the moderns manifested signs of breakdown to varying degrees and lost control on multiple occasions during the course of the meeting. Shi Xiaoming's words plucked at their fragile nerves once again. The neighborhood chief executive's eyes were wet with tears, and when he covered his face to weep, it prompted several other modern officials to weep with him. The official in charge of education laughed hysterically, and several other moderns began to snarl, before tossing their cups on the ground. . . .

"Quiet down," Shi Qiang said. His voice wasn't loud, but it had a dignity that quieted the modern officials. The executive and the

others who were crying struggled to hold back their tears.

"They're just kids," Hines said, shaking his head. Attending the meeting as a people's representative, he was perhaps the only person who had benefited from the destruction of the combined fleet, because now that reality was in line with his mental seal, he had returned to normal. Previously, he had been tormented day and night by the mental seal in the face of what seemed like an all-but-certain victory, and he had nearly suffered a mental breakdown. He had been sent to the largest hospital in the city, where expert psychiatrists had been powerless to help him, although they had proposed a novel idea, which Luo Ji and the suburban officials helped carry out. As in Daudet's "The Siege of Berlin," or the old Golden-Age film *Good Bye, Lenin!*, why not fabricate a fictional environment in which humanity had failed? Fortunately, at the pinnacle of modern virtual technology, it wasn't at all hard to create such an environment. Every day at his residence, Hines watched news that was broadcast especially for him, accompanied by lifelike three-dimensional images. He saw a portion of the Trisolaran Fleet accelerate and arrive at the Solar System early, and humanity's combined fleet suffer heavy losses in a battle at the Kuiper Belt. Then the three fleets were unable to hold the line at Neptune's orbit, and they were forced to stage a difficult resistance at Jupiter's orbit. . . .

The neighborhood official in charge of manufacturing this false world got quite wrapped up in it, and when the crushing defeat actually took place, he was the first to suffer a mental breakdown. He had exhausted his imagination painting humanity's defeat in the most disastrous way possible, both for Hines's needs and for his own personal pleasure, but cruel reality far outstripped anything he had imagined.

When the images of the fleet's destruction twenty AU away reached Earth after a three-hour delay, the public behaved like a gang of desperate children, turning the world into a nightmare-plagued kindergarten. Mass mental breakdown spread rapidly, and everything went out of control.

In Shi Qiang's neighborhood, all the officials ranked higher than him either resigned or simply broke down and did nothing, so the higher-level authorities gave him an emergency appointment to take over the duties of the local chief executive. It may not have been all that important a post, but the fate of this hibernator neighborhood was in his hands during this crisis. Fortunately, compared to the underground city, the hibernator societies remained relatively stable.

"I would ask everyone to remember the situation we're in," Shi Qiang said. "If there's ever a problem with the artificial environmental system in the underground city, the place will turn to hell and everyone there will flood out to the surface. If that happens, this place won't be fit for survival. We had better consider migration."

"Migration where?" someone asked.

"To somewhere sparsely populated, like the northwest. Of course, we would have to send people to check it out first. Right now, no one can say what will happen to the world, or whether there will be another Great Ravine. We have to make preparations to survive totally on agriculture."

"Will the droplet attack Earth?" someone else asked.

"What's the point of fretting?" Shi Qiang shook his head. "No one can do anything about it, at any rate. And until it punches through the Earth, we've still got to live, right?"

"That's right. Worrying is pointless. I'm quite clear on that point," Luo Ji said, breaking his silence.

Humanity's seven remaining spaceships flew away from the Solar System, split into two groups: five ships comprised of *Natural Selection* and its pursuers and another group of two ships, *Quantum* and *Bronze Age,* which had survived the droplet's devastation. The two small fleets were at opposite ends of the Solar System, separated by the sun. They were on headings that took them in almost opposite directions, and gradually getting farther apart.

On *Natural Selection,* after Zhang Beihai heard the account of the combined fleet's annihilation, his expression didn't change. His eyes remained calm as water, and he said lightly, "A dense formation is an unforgivable error. Everything else was to be expected."

"Comrades," he said, sweeping his eyes over the five captains and the three layers of assembled officers and soldiers, "I call you by that ancient title because I want us all to share a common will from this day forward. Each of you must understand the reality we are facing, and must envision the future that we will face. Comrades, we can't go back."

Indeed, there was no going back. The droplet that had destroyed the combined fleet was still in the Solar System, and nine others would arrive in three years. For this small fleet, their former home was now a death trap. From the information they had received, human civilization would totally collapse even before the main Trisolaran Fleet arrived, so Earth's doomsday was not far off. The five ships had to accept the responsibility of carrying civilization forward, but all they could do was to fly onward, and fly far. The spaceships would be their home forever, and space would be their final resting place.

Together, the 5,500 crewmembers were like an infant who had been cut from its cord, then cruelly tossed into the abyss of space. Like that infant, there was nothing they could do but cry. Yet Zhang Beihai's calm eyes were a strong force field that upheld the stability of the formation and helped them maintain their military poise. Children cast aside into the endless night needed a father most of all, and now, like Dongfang Yanxu, they found the power of that father in the person of this ancient soldier.

Zhang Beihai went on. "We will be a part of humanity forever, but we are an independent society and must rid ourselves of our psychological dependence on Earth. Now we need to choose a new name for this world of ours."

"We come from Earth, and we may be the sole inheritors of Earth civilization, so let's call ourselves Starship Earth," Dongfang Yanxu said.

"Excellent." Zhang Beihai nodded approvingly, then turned to the formation. "From now on, we are each of us citizens of Starship Earth. This moment might be a second starting point for human civilization. There are many things we need to do, so I would ask all of you to return to your posts now."

The two hologram formations vanished, and *Natural Selection*'s formation began to disperse.

"Sir, should our four ships rendezvous?" the captain of *Deep Space* asked. The captains had not vanished.

Zhang Beihai shook his head firmly. "That's not necessary. You are currently around two hundred thousand kilometers from *Natural Selection,* and although that's close, a rendezvous would expend nuclear fuel. Energy is the foundation of our survival, and with what little we have, we must conserve as much as we can. We are the only humans in this part of space, so I understand your desire to gather together, but two hundred thousand kilometers is a short distance. From now on, we have to think about the long term."

"Yes, we have to think about the long term," Dongfang Yanxu repeated softly, her eyes still staring at the horizon as if surveying the long years ahead of them.

Zhang Beihai continued, "A citizens' assembly must be convened immediately to set down basic issues, then the majority of the people need to be put into hibernation as soon as possible so that the ecological systems can be operated at a minimum. . . . Whatever transpires, the history of Starship Earth has begun."

Zhang Beihai's father's eyes emerged from the beyond once again, like rays from the edge of the cosmos that penetrated everything. He felt the gaze, and in his heart he said, *No, Dad. You really can't rest. It's not over. It's started up again.*

The next day, still keeping Earth time, Starship Earth convened its first plenary Citizens' Assembly, held in a venue formed from the combination of five holographic subvenues. The citizens in attendance numbered around three thousand, and the remainder who were unable to leave their posts networked in.

First off, the assembly identified an urgent matter: the destination of Starship Earth's voyage. Maintaining the current heading unchanged was passed by unanimous vote. This target was the one Zhang Beihai had set for *Natural Selection,* a heading in the direction of Cygnus—or, more precisely, the star NH558J2, one of the planetary systems closest to the Solar System. It had two planets,

both of which were gaseous like Jupiter and not suitable for human life, but could provide supplemental nuclear fuel. It now appeared that the choice of destination had been made after considerable thought, because along a different heading, at a distance just 1.5 light-years farther than their present destination, there was another planetary system which, according to observations, contained a planet whose natural environment was similar to Earth's. But that system had just one planet, and if it turned out to be an inhospitable world—the conditions for a hospitable world were more exacting than the rough observations from light-years away could reveal—then Starship Earth would miss the chance to refuel. After reaching NH558J2 and refueling, they could fly at even higher speeds toward their next target.

NH558J2 was eighteen light-years away from the Solar System. At their present speed, taking into account various uncertainties in the voyage, Starship Earth would reach it in two thousand years.

Two millennia. The grim number presented another clear picture of the present and the future. Even taking hibernation into account, most of the citizens of Starship Earth would never live to see their destination. Their lives would last just a small part of the twenty-century-long voyage, and even for their descendants who would reach it, NH558J2 was just a way station. No one knew what their next destination would be, much less when Starship Earth would finally reach its true, hospitable home.

In fact, Zhang Beihai had been exceptionally rational in his thinking. He clearly knew that Earth's suitability for human life was no coincidence, much less an effect of the anthropic principle, but rather was an outcome of the long-term interaction between the biosphere and the natural environment, an outcome that would not likely be repeated on another planet around some far-flung star. His choice of NH558J2 implied another possibility: Perhaps a hospitable world would never be found, and the new human civilization would forever voyage on a starship.

But he did not make this idea explicit. It might take the next generation born on Starship Earth to truly be able to accept a starship

civilization. The present generation would have to live their lives sustained by the thought of a home on an Earth-like planet.

The assembly also determined Starship Earth's political status. It decided that the five ships would remain part of the human world forever, but under the present circumstances, it was impossible for Starship Earth to be politically subordinate to Earth or the three fleets, so it would become a totally independent country.

When this resolution was transmitted back to the Solar System, the UN and the SFJC were silent for quite some time before replying. Without taking a position, they merely sent their tacit blessing.

And thus the human world was divided into three internationals: the ancient Earth International, the Fleet International of the new era, and the Starship International that was voyaging into the depths of the cosmos. The last group had just over five thousand people, but it carried with it all the hope of human civilization.

At the second meeting of the Citizens' Assembly, they began discussing the issue of Starship Earth's leadership structure.

When the meeting began, Zhang Beihai said, "I think it's too early for this agenda item. We've got to determine the shape of society on Starship Earth before we can decide what sort of governing bodies we need."

"You mean, we need to draft a constitution first," Dongfang Yanxu said.

"At least the basic principles for a constitution."

So the meeting continued along those lines. The inclination of the majority was that because Starship Earth was a highly fragile ecosystem traveling through the harsh environment of space, a disciplined society had to be established to guarantee a unified will to survive under these conditions. Someone proposed maintaining the present military system, and the idea received majority support.

"You mean a totalitarian society," Zhang Beihai said.

"Sir, there ought to be a nicer name for it. We're military, after all," the captain of *Blue Space* said.

"I don't think it'll work." Zhang Beihai shook his head decisively. "Staying alive is not enough to guarantee survival. Development is the best way to ensure survival. During our voyage, we'll have to develop our own science and technology to expand the size of our fleet. The historical facts of the Middle Ages and the Great Ravine prove that a totalitarian system is the greatest barrier to human progress. Starship Earth requires vibrant new ideas and innovation, and this can only be accomplished through the establishment of a society that fully respects freedom and individuality."

"Are you talking about establishing a society like the modern Earth International, sir? Starship Earth has certain intrinsic conditions," a low-ranking officer said.

"That's right." Dongfang Yanxu nodded at the speaker. "Starship Earth may have few people, but it possesses a highly refined information system through which any problem can easily be put to discussion and vote by all citizens. We can establish the first truly democratic society in human history."

"That won't work either." Zhang Beihai shook his head again. "Like those citizens said before, Starship Earth is traveling through the harsh environment of space, where catastrophes that threaten the entire world might occur at any time. Earth's history during the Trisolar Crisis has demonstrated that, in the face of such disasters, particularly when our world needs to make sacrifices in order to preserve the whole, the humanitarian society you have in mind is especially fragile."

All of those in attendance at the meeting glanced at each other, their eyes holding the same question: *So what should we do?*

Smiling, Zhang Beihai said, "I'm thinking too simply. There's never been an answer to this question throughout human history, so how can we solve it in one meeting? It will, I think, require a long process of practice and exploration before we can find the social model most suitable for Starship Earth. After the meeting, discussions should be opened up on the issue. . . . Please forgive me for disrupting the meeting's agenda. We should continue with the original topic."

Dongfang Yanxu had never seen Zhang Beihai smile like that. He rarely smiled, and when he occasionally did, it was confident and forgiving. But this smile had shown an apologetic shyness that she had never seen before. Even though interrupting the meeting wasn't a big deal, he was a man with an especially discreet mind, and this was the first time he had put forth an opinion only to retract it. She noticed his distraction. He hadn't taken notes during this meeting, unlike the careful recording he had done at the previous one. He was the only one on board who still used an ancient pen and paper, and it had become an emblem for him.

So what was occupying his thoughts now?

The meeting turned toward the matter of governing bodies. The citizens tended to feel that conditions were not yet right for holding elections, so the ships' present chains of command should not be changed. Captains would lead their respective ships, and a Starship Earth Authority Committee formed from the five of them would discuss and decide upon major affairs. Zhang Beihai was unanimously elected as chair of the committee, to serve as supreme commander of Starship Earth. The resolution was put to the entire assembly, and passed with 100 percent of the votes.

But he refused the appointment.

"Sir, it's your responsibility," the captain of *Deep Space* said.

"On Starship Earth, you're the only one with the prestige to command all the ships," Dongfang Yanxu said.

"I feel I've fulfilled my responsibility. I'm tired, and I've reached retirement age," Zhang Beihai said softly.

When the meeting adjourned, Zhang Beihai called for Dongfang Yanxu to stay behind. Once everyone had left, he said, "Dongfang, I want to recover my position as acting captain of *Natural Selection*."

"Acting captain?" She eyed him in surprise.

"Yes. Give me operational permissions over the ship again."

"Sir, I can hand over the captain's chair of *Natural Selection* to you. I mean it. And the Authority Committee and the body of citizens certainly won't oppose it."

He shook his head with a smile. "No, you'll still be the captain,

with a captain's full power to command. Please trust me. I won't interfere with your work at all."

"Then why do you want an acting captain's privileges? Is there a need for them in your present position?"

"I just like the ship. It's been a dream of ours for two centuries. Do you know what I've done for this ship to be here for us today?"

When he looked at her, the stony hardness that had been in his eyes was gone, revealing a tired emptiness and a deep sorrow that made him look like a different person. He was no longer the calm, grim survivor who thought deeply and acted decisively, but rather a man bent with the weight of time. Looking at him, she felt a concern and compassion she had never felt before.

"Sir, don't think about those things. Historians have a fair evaluation of your actions in the twenty-first century: Choosing research in radiation propulsion was a key step in the right direction for humanity's space technology. Perhaps at the time, it . . . it was the only choice, just like escape was the only choice for *Natural Selection*. Besides, according to modern law, the statute of limitations ran out long ago."

"But I can't get rid of the cross I bear. You can't understand. . . . I have feelings for this ship, more feelings than you. I feel like it's a part of me. I can't leave it. Also, I've got to have something to do in the future. Having things to do puts my mind more at ease."

Then he turned and left, a tired figure floating away, turning into a small black dot within the huge white spherical space. Dongfang Yanxu watched until he disappeared into the whiteness, and a loneliness she had never felt before surged in from all sides and overcame her.

In future Citizens' Assembly meetings, the people of Starship Earth immersed themselves in the passion of creating a new world. They held lively debates on the constitution and social structure of the world, drafted various laws, and planned the first election. . . . There was a thorough exchange of views between officers and soldiers of different ranks, and among the different ships. People acknowledged their prospects and looked forward to Starship

Earth forming a core that would snowball into a future civilization, continually increasing in size as the fleet reached star system after star system. An increasing number of people began calling Starship Earth a "second Eden," a second point of origin for human civilization.

But this state of wonder did not last very long, because Starship Earth truly was a Garden of Eden.

As *Natural Selection*'s chief psychologist, Lieutenant Colonel Lan Xi headed the Second Civilian Service Department, an agency of military officers trained in psychology that was responsible for psychological health on the ship during long space voyages and in battle. When Spaceship Earth began its journey of no return, Lan Xi and his subordinates went on alert, like warriors facing an attack from a powerful enemy. The plans they had rehearsed on many previous occasions had prepared them for a wide range of possible psychological crises.

They agreed that the biggest enemy was none other than "Problem N": nostalgia, or homesickness. This was, after all, the first time that humankind had embarked on an endless voyage, so Problem N had the potential to cause a mass psychological disaster. Lan Xi commanded CSD2 to take every necessary precaution, including establishing dedicated channels for communicating with Earth and the three fleets. This enabled everyone on board to maintain constant contact with their family and friends on Earth and in the fleet, and allowed them to watch most of the news and other programming from the two Internationals. Although Starship Earth was seventy AU away from the sun, meaning that signals were delayed nine hours, the quality of communication with Earth and the fleets was excellent.

In addition to conducting active psychological counseling and adjustments when signs of Problem N cropped up, CSD2 psychological officers also prepared an extreme means of responding to a large-scale mass psychological disaster: quarantining an out-of-control crowd in hibernation.

Subsequent events demonstrated that these concerns were

superfluous. While Problem N was widespread on Starship Earth, it was far from out of control, and did not even reach the level of previous, ordinary long-range voyages. Lan Xi was confused by this at first, but he soon found a reason: After the destruction of humanity's main fleet, Earth had lost all hope. Even though the ultimate doomsday was still two centuries away (using the most optimistic estimate), the news from Earth informed them that the world, plunged into chaos by the heavy blow of the great defeat, was full of the stench of death. For Starship Earth, there was nothing on the Earth or in the Solar System to provide them with sustenance. Nostalgia for a home like that was limited.

However, an enemy nevertheless appeared, one that was more ominous than Problem N. By the time that Lan Xi and CSD2 realized it, their position had already been overcome.

Lan Xi knew from his experience that on long space voyages Problem N tended to crop up in soldiers and low-ranking officers first, because their jobs and responsibilities commanded less of their attention compared to high-ranking officers, and their mental conditioning was comparatively poor. So CSD2 turned its attention to the lower levels from the start, but the shadow first fell upon the upper levels.

Around that time, Lan Xi noticed something peculiar. The first election for Starship Earth's governing bodies was about to take place, an election that would be open to the entire population, meaning that most of the senior commanders were facing a transition from being military officers to being government officials. Their positions would be reshuffled, and many of them would be replaced by lower-ranking competitors. Lan Xi was surprised to learn that no one in *Natural Selection*'s senior command was overly concerned about the election that would determine the rest of their lives. He saw no senior officers engaging in even the least bit of campaigning, and when he mentioned the election, none of them was at all interested. He couldn't help but recall Zhang Beihai's absentmindedness during the second Citizens' Assembly meeting.

Then he began to see symptoms of psychological imbalance

among officers above the rank of lieutenant colonel. Most of them started to become increasingly introverted, spending long periods alone with their thoughts and sharply reducing their social interactions. They spoke less and less at meetings, sometimes choosing to become completely silent. Lan Xi noticed that the light had disappeared from their eyes, and their expressions had turned gloomy. They couldn't look anyone in the eye for fear that others would notice the fog in theirs. When they occasionally met someone's gaze, they would break away immediately like they had been shocked. . . . The higher the rank, the more serious the symptoms. And there were signs that it was spreading through the lower ranks, too.

There was no way for psychological counseling to proceed. Everyone stubbornly refused to talk to the psychological officers, so CSD2 was compelled to exercise its special power to conduct mandatory counseling. Still, most of their subjects remained silent.

Lan Xi decided that he needed to talk to the supreme commander, so he went to Dongfang Yanxu. Although Zhang Beihai had once held supreme prestige and status on *Natural Selection* and the whole of Starship Earth, he had rejected it all, withdrawing from the race and insisting he was an ordinary person. The only duties he had retained were those of acting captain: transmitting the captain's orders to the ship's control system. The remainder of his time he spent wandering *Natural Selection,* learning about the specifics of the ship from officers and soldiers at all ranks and showing a constant affection for the space ark. Apart from this, he remained calm and indifferent, practically unaffected by the ship's mass psychological shadow. He was no doubt trying to remain aloof, but Lan Xi knew of another important reason for his immunity: The ancients were not as sensitive as moderns, and in the present circumstances, numbness served an excellent self-protective function.

"Captain, you ought to give us some indication of what's happening," he said.

"Lieutenant Colonel, you ought to be the one giving us an indication."

"Do you mean that you don't know anything about your present state?"

An infinite sadness welled up in her dull eyes. "I only know that we're the first humans who have gone into space."

"What do you mean?"

"This is the first time humanity has really gone to space."

"Oh. I see what you mean. Before, no matter how far humans traveled into space, they were still just a kite sent aloft by Earth. They were connected to Earth by a spiritual line. Now that line has been severed."

"That's right. The line is severed. The essential change is not that the line has been let go, but that the hand has disappeared. The Earth is heading toward doomsday. In fact, she's already dead in our minds. Our five spacecraft are not connected to any world. There is nothing around us apart from the abyss of space."

"Indeed. Humanity has never faced a psychological environment like this before."

"Yes. In this environment, the human spirit will be fundamentally changed. People will become—" She suddenly broke off, and the sadness in her eyes vanished, leaving only gloom, like a cloud-covered sky after the rain has stopped.

"You mean that in this environment, people will become new people?"

"New people? No, Lieutenant Colonel. People will become . . . non-people."

At that last word, Lan Xi shuddered. He looked up at Dongfang Yanxu, and she met his gaze. In the blankness of her eyes, all he saw were tightly closed windows to her soul.

"What I mean is that we won't be people in the old sense. . . . Lieutenant Colonel, that's all I can say. Just do your best. And . . ." The words that followed seemed like she was talking in her sleep. "It'll be your turn soon."

The situation continued to deteriorate. The day after Lan Xi's talk with Dongfang Yanxu, there was a vicious injury on *Natural Selection*. A lieutenant colonel with the ship's navigational system

fired upon another officer bunking with him. According to the victim's recollection, the officer had awakened suddenly in the middle of the night and, noticing that the victim was also awake, had accused him of eavesdropping on him talking in his sleep. In the struggle, his emotions had gotten away from him and he had fired the gun.

Lan Xi went at once to see the detained lieutenant colonel. "What were you afraid of him hearing you say in your sleep?" he asked.

"You mean he really heard it?" the attacker asked in terror.

Lan Xi shook his head. "He said that you didn't say anything."

"So what if I did say something? You can't take sleep talk for the truth! My mind doesn't really think that. Surely I'm not going to go to hell for something I said in my sleep!"

In the end, Lan Xi was unable to draw out what the attacker imagined he said in his sleep, so he asked whether he minded going under hypnotherapy. Unexpectedly, the attacker once again blew up at this suggestion, lunging at Lan Xi and strangling him until the military police finally came in and pried him off. Leaving the brig, one MP who had overheard the conversation said to Lan Xi, "Lieutenant Colonel, don't mention hypnotherapy again unless CSD2 wants to become the most hated place on the ship. You wouldn't last very long."

So Lan Xi had to contact Colonel Scott, a psychologist aboard *Enterprise*. Scott also served as the ship's chaplain, a position most ships in the Asian Fleet did not have. *Enterprise* and the other three ships in the pursuing force were still two hundred thousand kilometers away.

"Why is it so dark over there?" Lan Xi asked as he looked at the video sent over from *Enterprise*. The curved walls of the cabin Scott was in had been adjusted to glow a faint yellow, and they displayed an image of the stars outside, making it look as if he was inside a fogged-over cosmos. His face was shrouded in shadow, but even so, Lan Xi could still sense Scott's eyes slipping quickly away from his gaze.

"The Garden of Eden is growing dark. Blackness will swallow everything," Scott said in a weary voice.

Lan Xi had consulted him because, as chaplain of *Enterprise*, he would likely have had people confide the truth in him during confession, and he might be able to pass on some advice. But at these words, and noticing how the colonel's eyes loomed in the shadows, Lan Xi knew that he would come up with nothing. So he suppressed the question he was about to ask and turned to another, one that surprised even him:

"Will what happened in the first Garden of Eden be repeated in the second?"

"I don't know. At any rate, the vipers have come out. The snakes of the second Garden of Eden are even now climbing up people's souls."

"You mean, you've eaten the fruit of knowledge?"

Scott slowly nodded. Then he bowed his head, but did not raise it again, as if he was trying to hide the eyes that would betray him. "You could say that."

"Who will be expelled from the Garden of Eden?" Lan Xi's voice quavered, and a cold sweat was on his palms.

"Many people. But unlike the first time, this time some people might remain."

"Who? Who will remain?"

Scott gave a long sigh. "Lieutenant Colonel Lan, I've said enough. Why don't you seek the fruit of knowledge for yourself? Everyone's got to take that step, after all. Isn't that right?"

"Where should I seek it?"

"Set down your work, and think about it. Feel more, and you'll find it."

After speaking with Scott, Lan Xi halted his busy work amid chaotic feelings, and stopped to think, as the colonel had advised. Faster than he had imagined, Eden's cold, slippery vipers crawled into his consciousness. He found the fruit of knowledge and ate it, and the last rays of sunshine in his soul disappeared forever as everything plunged into darkness.

On Starship Earth, an invisible, taut string was being pulled close to snapping.

Two days later, the captain of *Ultimate Law* committed suicide. He had been standing on the aft platform at the time, a platform enclosed in a transparent dome that made it seem exposed to space. The stern of the ship faced the Solar System, where the sun was by now no more than a yellow star just a bit brighter than the rest. The peripheral spiral arm of the Milky Way lay in this direction, its stars sparse. The depth and expanse of deep space exhibited an arrogance that left no support for the mind or the eyes.

"Dark. It's so fucking dark," the captain murmured, and then shot himself.

When Dongfang Yanxu learned that the captain of *Ultimate Law* had committed suicide, she had the premonition that time was up, so she convened an emergency meeting with the two vice-captains in the large spherical fighter hangar.

In the corridor on the way to the hangar, she heard someone behind her call her name. It was Zhang Beihai. In her gloomy state of mind, she had practically forgotten about him for the past couple of days. He looked her up and down, his eyes full of a fatherly concern that gave her an undreamed-of sense of comfort, for it was hard to find a pair of eyes without a shadow on Starship Earth these days.

"Dongfang, I don't think you've been right lately. I don't know the reason, but you seem to be hiding something. What's going on?"

She didn't answer his question, but instead asked, "Sir, how have you been lately?"

"Well. Very well. I've been touring all over the place and studying. I'm familiarizing myself with *Natural Selection*'s weapons system. Of course, I'm only scratching the surface, but it's fascinating. Imagine how Columbus would feel visiting an aircraft carrier. I'm the same way."

Seeing how calm and relaxed he was now, Dongfang Yanxu felt a little jealous. Yes, he had completed his great endeavor and had the right to enjoy tranquility. The history-making great man had turned back into an ignorant hibernator. All he needed now was protection.

With that in mind, she said, "Sir, don't ask anyone else about the question you just asked. Don't ask about any of this."

"Why? Why shouldn't I ask?"

"It's dangerous to ask. Besides, you really don't need to know. Believe me."

He nodded. "Very well. I won't ask. Thank you for treating me like an ordinary person. That's all I've been hoping for."

She said a hurried good-bye, but as she went her own way, she heard the voice of the founder of Starship Earth behind her: "Dongfang, no matter what happens, let things go as they will. Everything will be okay."

She saw the two vice-captains in the center of the spherical hall. She had chosen to meet them here because the size of the hall made it feel like they were in the wilderness. The three of them floated at the center of a world of pure white, as if the whole universe was empty except for them. It lent a sense of security to their conversation.

Each of them looked in a different direction.

"We have to make things clear," she said.

"Yes. Every second we delay is dangerous," Vice-Captain Levine said. Then he and Akira Inoue turned around to face Dongfang Yanxu. His meaning was clear: *You are the captain, you speak first.*

But she didn't have the courage.

Whatever happened now, at the second dawn of human civilization, might be the foundation of a new Homeric epic or a Bible. Judas became who he was because he was the first to kiss Jesus, and that made him fundamentally different from the second one to kiss him. It was the same now. The first to speak would mark a milestone in the history of the second civilization. Perhaps he or she would become Judas, or perhaps Jesus, but whatever the possibility, Dongfang Yanxu did not have that courage.

But she had to undertake her own mission, so she made a smart choice. She did not avoid the gaze of her vice-captains. Language was not necessary now. All communication could be accomplished through the eyes. As they stared at each other, their interlocking

484

gazes were like information conduits linking their three souls together and communicating everything at high speed.

Fuel.

Fuel.

Fuel.

The route is still unclear, but at least two clouds of interstellar dust have been found.

Drag.

Of course. After passing through them, the spaceships will drop to 0.03 percent of the speed of light due to drag from the dust.

We're still more than ten light-years away from NH558J2. We'll need sixty thousand years to get there.

Then we'll never arrive.

The ships may arrive, but the life on board won't. Even hibernation can't be sustained for that long.

Unless . . .

Unless speed is maintained through the dust clouds, or we accelerate afterward.

Fuel is insufficient.

Fusion fuel is the only source of energy aboard ship, and it needs to be used in other areas: environmental systems, possible course corrections. . . .

And for deceleration once the target system is reached. NH558J2 is much smaller than the sun. We can't achieve orbit relying solely on gravity for deceleration. We'll have to expend large quantities of fuel, or else we'll fly by the target star system.

All of the fuel on Starship Earth is basically enough for two spacecraft.

But, if we're careful, it's enough for just one.

Fuel.

Fuel.

Fuel.

"And then there's the issue of parts," Dongfang Yanxu said.

Parts.

Parts.

Parts.

Particularly parts for critical systems: fusion engines, information and control systems, environmental systems.

It may not be as urgent as fuel, but it's the foundation of long-term survival. NH55J82 doesn't have a hospitable planet for settlement or establishment of industry, or even the necessary resources to do so. It's just a place to refuel before heading to the next system, where industry can be established to produce parts.

Natural Selection *has only two levels of redundancy for key parts.*

Too few.

Too few.

Apart from the fusion engines, most of the key parts on Starship Earth are interoperable.

Engine parts can be used after modification.

"Can all personnel be gathered onto one or two ships?" Dongfang Yanxu said aloud, but her voice was only meant to guide the direction of their eye communication.

Impossible.

Impossible.

Impossible. There are too many people. Environmental and hibernation systems can't accommodate them all. If present capacity is boosted even a little, it will be disastrous.

"So, is it clear now?" Dongfang Yanxu's voice resounded in the empty white space like the mutterings of someone deeply asleep.

Clear.

Clear.

Some people must die, or everyone will die.

Then their eyes went silent. The three of them felt an intense desire to turn away, as if shaken by thunder from the depths of the universe that made their souls quake in terror. Dongfang Yanxu was the first to stabilize her own gaze.

"Stop it," she said.

Stop it.

Don't give up.

Don't give up?

Don't give up! Because no one else has given up. If we give up, then we'll be expelled from the Garden of Eden.

Why us?

Of course, it shouldn't be them, either.

But someone has to be expelled. The Garden of Eden has a limited capacity.

We don't want to leave the garden.

So we can't give up!

Three pairs of eyes, so close to breaking apart, locked together again.

Infrasonic H-bomb.

Infrasonic H-bomb.

Infrasonic H-bomb.

Every ship is equipped with them.

It's hard to defend against a stealth launch.

Their gazes separated temporarily as their minds were pushed to the brink of collapse. They needed rest. When the three pairs of eyes met once again, they were uncertain and erratic, like candles flickering in the wind.

Evil!

Evil!

Evil!

We'll become devils!

We'll become devils!

We'll become devils!

"But . . . what are *they* thinking?" Dongfang Yanxu asked softly. To the two vice-captains, her voice, while soft, seemed to linger uninterrupted in the white space, like the buzz of a mosquito.

Yes. We don't want to become devils, but who knows what they're thinking.

Then we're already devils, or how else could we think of them as devils unprovoked?

Very well, then we won't think of them as devils.

487

"That won't solve the problem," Dongfang Yanxu said with a gentle shake of her head.

Yes. Even if they aren't devils, the problem remains.

Because they don't know what we're thinking.

Suppose they know that we're not devils?

The problem still exists.

They don't know what we're thinking about them.

They don't know what we're thinking about what they're thinking about us.

That carries on in an endless chain of suspicion: They don't know what we're thinking about what they're thinking about what we're thinking about what they're thinking about what we're . . .

How can this chain of suspicion be broken?

Communication?

On Earth, perhaps. But not in space. Some people must die, or everyone will die. This is the unwinnable dead hand that space has dealt for the survival of Starship Earth. An insurmountable wall. In the face of it, communication has no meaning.

Only one choice is left. The question is who makes that choice.

Dark. It's so fucking dark.

"We can't delay any longer," Dongfang Yanxu said decisively.

No more delays. In this dark region of space, the duelists are holding their breath. The string is about to snap.

Every second, the danger grows exponentially.

Since it's all the same no matter who pulls it, why not pull it ourselves?

Then Akira Inoue suddenly broke the silence: "There's another choice!"

We sacrifice ourselves.

Why?

Why us?

The three of us could, but do we have the authority to make this choice on behalf of the two thousand people on Natural Selection?

The three of them were standing on a knife blade. Though its cuts

were painful, a jump off either side would be into a bottomless abyss. These were the labor pains for the birth of the new space humans.

"How about this?" Levine said. "First lock in the targets, and then think it over some more."

Dongfang Yanxu nodded. Levine called up a control interface for the weapons system in the air and opened up the window for the infrasonic H-bombs and carrier missiles. On a spherical coordinate system with *Natural Selection* at the origin, *Blue Space, Enterprise, Deep Space,* and *Ultimate Law* were displayed as four points of light two hundred thousand kilometers away. The distance masked the structure of the targets, for at the scale of space, everything was just a point.

But the four points of light were ringed with four red halos, four deathly nooses indicating that the weapons system had already locked on the targets.

Stunned, the three of them looked at each other and shook their heads to say that it wasn't their doing.

Apart from them, privileges to place a target lock in the weapons system were also held by the arms control and target screening officers, but their lock placement had to be authorized by the captain or vice-captain. That left just one other person with direct privileges to lock a target and launch an attack.

We're idiots. He's only someone who's changed history twice! He realized all of this first!

Who knows when he realized it? Maybe when Starship Earth was founded, or even earlier, when he learned that the combined fleet had been destroyed. He is the last to show worry. Like the parents of his era, always keeping their children in mind.

Dongfang Yanxu flew across the spherical hall as fast as she could, followed closely by the two vice-captains. They went out the door and down that long corridor until they arrived at the door to Zhang Beihai's cabin. Suspended in front of him was an interface identical to the one they had just seen. They rushed forward, but the scene from *Natural Selection*'s escape replayed itself: They crashed into the bulkhead. There was no door, just an

oval-shaped area where the bulkhead was transparent.

"What are you doing?" Levine shouted.

"Children," Zhang Beihai said, the first time he had addressed them this way. Even though his back was turned, they could imagine that his eyes were as calm as water. "Let me do this."

"You mean, 'If I don't go to hell, who will?'[24] Is that it?" Dongfang Yanxu said in a loud voice.

"From the moment I became a soldier, I was prepared to go there if necessary," he said, continuing with the weapons' prelaunch operations. From outside, the three of them saw that while he wasn't skilled at these operations, every step he took was correct.

Tears welled up in Dongfang Yanxu's eyes, and she cried, "Let's go together. Let me in. I'll go to hell with you!"

He made no answer, but continued his manipulations. He set the guided missiles for manual self-destruct so that they could be detonated by the mother ship while in flight. Only after finishing the last step did he say, "Dongfang, think. Could we have made this choice before? Absolutely not. But now we can make it, because space has turned us into new humans." He set the missiles' warheads to explode at a distance of fifty kilometers from each target. This would avoid causing the targets any internal damage, but an even greater distance would still be within the fatal range for any life aboard the targets. "The birth of a new civilization is the formation of a new morality." He removed the first safety lock on the H-bomb warheads. "When they look back in the future on everything we've done, it may seem entirely normal. So, we won't go to hell, children." The second safety lock was removed.

Suddenly, the alert sounded throughout the ship like the crying of ten thousand ghosts in the darkness of space. Display interfaces popped up in midair like snowflakes, showing a huge quantity of information that *Natural Selection*'s defense systems had received about the incoming missiles, but no one had time to read it.

24 *Translator's Note:* This popular quotation sums up the great vow of the bodhisattva Ksitigarbha (Dìzàng Púsà) not to achieve Buddhahood until all living beings are saved.

There was a space of just four seconds from the sounding of the alert to the detonation of the infrasonic H-bombs.

Images transmitted back to Earth from *Natural Selection* showed that Zhang Beihai may have understood all of this in just one second. He had imagined that his heart had grown as hard as iron through the arduous procession of more than two centuries, but he had overlooked something hidden in the deepest part of his soul, and had hesitated before making the final decision. He tried to restrain the trembling of his heart, and it was that last moment's softness that killed him and everyone on board *Natural Selection*. After the month-long face-off in the darkness, he was just a few seconds slower than the other ship was.

Three small suns lit up the blackness of space, forming an equilateral triangle with *Natural Selection* at the center, at an average distance of forty kilometers. The fusion fireball lasted for twenty seconds and sparkled with infrasonic frequencies that were invisible to the naked eye.

The returned images showed that in the three seconds that remained, Zhang Beihai turned to Dongfang Yanxu, flashed her a smile, and spoke: "It doesn't matter. It's all the same."

The exact words were only a guess, because he didn't have time to finish before a powerful electromagnetic pulse arrived from three directions, vibrating *Natural Selection*'s enormous hull like a cicada's wings. The energy in these vibrations was converted to infrasonic waves, which, in the image, looked like a fog of blood that enveloped everything.

The attack had come from *Ultimate Law*, which had fired twelve cloaked missiles armed with infrasonic H-bombs at the four other ships. The three missiles fired at *Natural Selection*, which was two hundred thousand kilometers away, had been launched before the others so that the ones fired at its three neighboring ships would reach their detonation points at the same time. A vice-captain had taken over after the suicide of *Ultimate Law*'s captain, but it was unknown who ultimately made the decision to launch the attack. And it would never be known.

Ultimate Law was not one of the lucky ones remaining in the Garden of Eden at the end.

Of the three other pursuing ships, *Blue Space* had been the best prepared against unexpected incidents. Before it was attacked, it had turned its interior into a vacuum and put all personnel in space suits. Because infrasonic waves were impossible in a vacuum, no personnel were injured, and the body of the ship suffered only minimal damage from the electromagnetic pulse.

Right after the nuclear fireballs exploded, *Blue Space* began its counterattack with lasers, the fastest response possible. It lit up *Ultimate Law* with five gamma-ray laser beams and burned five huge holes in its hull. Its insides quickly caught fire and there were minor explosions, causing the ship to lose all combat capability. Harsher attacks from *Blue Space* followed, and under continuous attack by nuclear missiles and a rain of railgun fire, *Ultimate Law* exploded violently, leaving no survivors.

At almost the same time as Starship Earth's Battle of Darkness was going on, a similar tragedy was taking place far on the other side of the Solar System. *Bronze Age* launched a sudden strike on *Quantum,* using the same infrasonic H-bombs to kill off all life inside its target, but preserving the target ship whole. Because the two ships had sent only minimal information back to Earth, no one knew exactly what had taken place between them. They had both gone into intense acceleration to escape from the probe attack, but they had not decelerated like *Natural Selection*'s pursuers had, so their remaining fuel ought to have been more than enough to return to Earth.

The boundlessness of space nurtured a dark new humanity in its dark embrace.

In the expanding metal cloud formed from the explosion of *Ultimate Law, Blue Space* rendezvoused with *Enterprise* and *Deep Space,* neither of which showed signs of life, and collected all of their fusion fuel. After stripping them of their hardware, *Blue Space* flew the two hundred thousand kilometers to *Natural Selection* and did the same to that ship. Starship Earth was like a

construction site in space now, the massive hulls of the three dead ships dotted with the sparks of laser welding. If Zhang Beihai had still been alive, the scene would certainly have reminded him of the aircraft carrier *Tang* two centuries before.

Blue Space took pieces of the three derelict warships and set them up in a Stonehenge formation, forming a tomb in outer space. There, they held a funeral for all the victims of the Battle of Darkness.

Wearing space suits, the 1,273 crew members of *Blue Space* assembled in a floating formation at the center of the tomb. These were the remaining citizens of Starship Earth. Around them, huge pieces of spaceships towered like a ring of mountains, the gashes cut into the wreckage like enormous mountain caves. The bodies of 4,247 victims remained within this debris, which cast its shadows over all of the living as if they were a mountain valley at midnight. The only light was the iciness of the Milky Way where it shone through the gaps between the wreckage.

Moods remained calm during the funeral. The new space humans had passed through their infancy.

A small votive lamp was lit. It was a fifty-watt bulb with a hundred spare bulbs next to it that would be automatically substituted in the lamp. Powered by a small nuclear battery, the votary lamp could remain continuously lit for tens of thousands of years. Its dim light was like a candle in the mountain valley, casting a small halo onto a high cliff of the wreckage and shining on a piece of titanium bulkhead engraved with the names of the victims. There was no epitaph.

One hour later, the space tomb was illuminated one final time by the light of *Blue Space*'s acceleration. The tomb was traveling at 1 percent of the speed of light. In several hundred years it would decelerate to 0.03 percent of light speed due to the drag from interstellar dust clouds. It would still reach NH558J2 in sixty thousand years, but *Blue Space* would already have headed off toward its next star system more than fifty thousand years before that.

Blue Space traveled deep into space carrying plenty of fusion fuel and an eight-fold redundant supply of critical parts. There was

so much material it was impossible to fit it all inside the craft, so several external storage compartments were attached to the hull, completely altering the ship's appearance and turning it into an enormous, ugly, irregular body. Indeed, it looked like a traveler on a long journey.

The previous year, on the opposite side of the Solar System, *Bronze Age* had accelerated away from the ruins of *Quantum* in the direction of Taurus.

Blue Space and *Quantum* had come from a world of light, but they had become two ships of darkness.

The universe had once been bright, too. For a short time after the big bang, all matter existed in the form of light, and only after the universe turned to burnt ash did heavier elements precipitate out of the darkness and form planets and life. Darkness was the mother of life and of civilization.

On Earth, an avalanche of curses and abuse rolled out into space toward *Blue Space* and *Bronze Age,* but the two ships made no reply. They cut off all contact with the Solar System, for to those two worlds, the Earth was already dead.

The two dark ships became one with the darkness, separated by the Solar System and drifting further apart. Carrying with them the entirety of human thoughts and memories, and embracing all of the Earth's glory and dreams, they quietly disappeared into the eternal night.

"I knew it!"

That was the first thing Luo Ji said upon learning about the Battle of Darkness that had taken place at the edges of the Solar System. Leaving behind a baffled Shi Qiang, he ran out of the room and raced through the neighborhood until he stood facing the northern China desert.

"I was right! I was right!" he shouted at the sky.

It was late at night, and, perhaps because of the rain that had just fallen, atmospheric visibility was excellent. The stars were visible,

although they weren't nearly as clear as in the twenty-first century, and they were far sparser than before, since only the brightest could be seen. Yet he still swelled with that feeling he had on that cold night on the frozen lake two centuries ago: Luo Ji the ordinary person had disappeared, and he became a Wallfacer once again.

"Da Shi, I have in my hands the key to human victory!" he said to Shi Qiang, who had followed after him.

Shi Qiang laughed. "Oh?"

Shi Qiang's slightly mocking laughter dashed Luo Ji's excitement. "I knew you wouldn't believe me."

"So what will you do now?" Shi Qiang asked.

Luo Ji sat down on the sand, and his mood crashed rapidly. "What should I do? It looks like there's nothing I *can* do."

"You could at least find a way to report it upstairs."

"I don't know if that would work, but I'll give it a try. Even if it's just to fulfill my responsibility."

"How high up will you go?"

"The highest. The UN secretary general. Or the chair of the SFJC."

"That won't be easy, I'm afraid. We're just ordinary people now. . . . Still, you've got to try. You can, uh, go to the city government first. Find the mayor."

"Very well. I'll go to the city, then." He stood up.

"I'll go with you."

"No, I'll go alone."

"Even at this rank, I'm still an official. I'll have an easier time meeting the mayor."

Luo Ji looked up at the sky and asked, "When does the droplet reach Earth?"

"The news said it'll arrive in ten or twenty hours."

"Do you know what it's coming to do? Its mission wasn't to destroy the combined fleet. Nor was it to attack the Earth. It's here to kill me. I don't want you to be with me when it does."

Shi Qiang laughed the same mocking laugh again. "There's still ten hours, right? By that time, I'll just stay farther away from you."

Luo Ji shook his head with a wry smile. "You're not taking me seriously at all. So why do you want to help me?"

"My boy, it's up to the top whether they believe you or not. I always play things safe. If you were selected from out of billions of people two centuries ago, there's got to be a reason, right? If I delay you here, then won't I be condemned by the ages? If the higher-ups don't take you seriously, I won't have lost anything. It's just a trip into the city. But there's one thing: You say that the thing that's flying toward Earth is coming to kill you. I don't believe that at all. I'm well acquainted with killing, and that's excessive, even for Trisolarans."

They reached the passage from the old city to the underground city in the early hours of morning and saw that the elevators going down were still functioning normally. Lots of people were coming out carrying large quantities of luggage. Few were going down, however, and on their elevator there were only two other people.

"Are you hibernators? They're all going up top. Why are you going down?"

"The city's in chaos," one of them, a young man, said. On his clothes, fireballs shone continually against a black background. A closer look revealed that it was an image of the destruction of the combined fleet.

"Then what are you going down for?" Shi Qiang asked.

"I've found a place to live on the surface, so I'm going down to get a few things," he said. Then he nodded at them. "You on the surface are going to get rich. We don't have any houses there, and the property rights to the surface houses are mostly in your hands. We'll have to buy them off you."

"If the underground city collapses and all those people rush to the surface, there's probably not going to be any actual buying or selling," Shi Qiang said.

A middle-aged man huddling in a corner of the elevator was listening to them, and he suddenly covered his face with his hands and let out a whine. "No. Oh . . ." Then he squatted down and started crying. His clothing showed a classical biblical scene: a naked Adam and Eve standing beneath a tree in the Garden of

Eden as a bewitching snake crawled between them. It may have been a symbol for the recent Battle of Darkness.

"There are lots of people like him," the young man said, pointing disdainfully at the weeping man. "Unsound of mind." His eyes lit up. "Actually, doomsday is a wonderful time. The most wonderful time, even. This is the only time in history where there's a chance for people to abandon all of their cares and burdens and belong entirely to themselves. It's stupid to be like him. The most responsible way of life right now is to enjoy ourselves while we can."

When the elevator reached the bottom, Luo Ji and Shi Qiang exited the hall and immediately smelled the strong, strange odor of something burning. The underground city was brighter than before, but it was an irritating white light. Looking around, what Luo Ji saw through the gaps in the huge trees wasn't the blue sky, but a total blank. The projection of the sky on the vault of the underground city had vanished. The blankness reminded him of spherical spaceship cabins he had seen on the news. The lawns were littered with a mess of debris that had fallen from the huge trees. Not far off was the wreckage of several crashed flying cars, one of which was in flames and surrounded by a crowd of people who were picking up other combustibles from the lawn and throwing them into the flames. Someone even threw in his own clothing while it was still flashing images. A ruptured underground pipe sprayed a high column of water, drenching a group of people who played around in it like children. From time to time they would scream excitedly in unison and scatter to avoid debris falling from the trees, then they would regroup and continue their revels. Luo Ji looked up again and saw fires in several places on the trees. The sirens of flying firefighting vehicles screamed as they flew through the air, dangling plucked tree leaves that had caught fire. . . .

He noticed that the people they met on the streets fell into two types, much like the two people they had encountered in the elevator. One type was depressed, walking with dull eyes or simply sitting on the lawns enduring the torment of despair, a despair whose cause had now shifted from humanity's defeat to the present

difficult living conditions. The other type was in a state of crazed excitement and grew intoxicated from indulgence.

Traffic in the city was in chaos. It took Luo Ji and Shi Qiang half an hour to hail a taxi, and when the driverless flying car that carried them passed through the huge trees, Luo Ji was reminded of his first horrific day in the city and felt the tension of riding a roller coaster. Fortunately, the car soon arrived at City Hall.

Shi Qiang had been here several times because of work, and was fairly familiar with the place. After a considerable number of steps, they finally received permission to meet the mayor, but they had to wait until the afternoon. Luo Ji had expected complications, so the mayor's acceptance of the meeting caught him by surprise, since this was an extraordinary time, and they were little people. At lunch, Shi Qiang told Luo Ji that the mayor had taken office the day before. He used to be the official in charge of hibernator affairs in the city government and was, in a way, Shi Qiang's superior, so he knew him fairly well.

"He's one of our countrymen," Shi Qiang said.

In this age, the meaning of the term "countryman" had shifted from geography to temporality. But it wasn't used between all hibernators. Only those who had entered hibernation at roughly the same time counted as countrymen. When they got together across the long years, temporally based countrymen shared an even closer affinity than geographically based countrymen used to.

They waited until half past four to see the mayor. High-ranking officials in this age typically possessed a star quality, with only the most attractive getting elected, but the current mayor was plain. He was about Shi Qiang's age, but far thinner, and he had one trait that made him identifiable as a hibernator at a glance: He wore glasses. They were definitely antiques from two centuries ago, because even contact lenses had long since disappeared. But people who used to wear glasses tended to feel that something was wrong with their appearance when they didn't wear them, so lots of hibernators wore them even after their vision was repaired.

The mayor looked utterly exhausted and seemed to have

difficulty rising from his chair. When Shi Qiang apologized for the interruption, and congratulated him on his promotion, he shook his head. "These are vulnerable times. Us rugged savages come in handy again."

"You're the highest-ranking hibernator on Earth, right?"

"Who knows? As the situation develops, we might have countrymen promoted to even higher positions."

"And the former mayor? Mental breakdown?"

"No, no. There are strong people in this age, too. He was very competent, but he was killed in a car crash in a riot area two days ago."

The mayor noticed Luo Ji behind Shi Qiang and immediately extended a hand. "Oh, Dr. Luo, hello. Of course I recognize you. I worshiped you two centuries ago, because out of those four people, you seemed most like a Wallfacer. I really couldn't figure out what you wanted to do." But their hearts sank at the next thing he said. "You're the fourth messiah I've received in the past two days. And there are dozens more waiting outside who I don't have the energy to see."

"Mayor, he's not like them. Two centuries ago—"

"Of course. Two centuries ago, he was selected from billions of people, and it's for that reason that I decided to see you." The mayor pointed at Shi Qiang. "There's something else I need you for, but we'll talk about that afterward. First, let's talk about what you've got. But I have a small request: Can you not talk about your plan to save the world? They're always so long. First just tell me what you need me to do."

After Luo Ji and Shi Qiang explained what they wanted, the mayor immediately shook his head. "Even if I wanted to help, I couldn't. I've got piles of stuff of my own I need to report to the senior leadership. But that level's lower than you imagine. It's just provincial and national leaders. It's hard for everyone. You ought to know that the senior leadership is handling even bigger problems right now."

Luo Ji and Shi Qiang had been paying attention to the news,

so naturally they knew about the bigger problems that the mayor referred to.

The annihilation of the combined fleet saw the swift resurrection of Escapism after two centuries of silence. The European Commonwealth had even drafted a plan to select one hundred thousand candidates for departure through a nationwide drawing, and the plan had been passed by a popular vote. But after the results of the drawing, the majority of those who had not been picked were furious, leading to widespread rioting. The public turned unanimously to Escapism as crime against humanity.

After the Battle of Darkness erupted between the surviving warships in outer space, accusations of Escapism gained new meaning: Recent events had proved that when the spiritual bonds with Earth were snapped, people in space suffered total spiritual alienation. So even if escape were successful, what survived would no longer be human civilization, but some other dark and evil thing. And like Trisolaris, that thing would be the antithesis of human civilization and an enemy of it. It had even been given a name: Negacivilization.

As the droplet came closer to Earth, the public's sensitivity to Escapism reached a peak. The media warned it was highly likely that someone would attempt to escape before the droplet's attack. Crowds flocked to the vicinity of the space ports and the base points of the space elevators with the intent of cutting off all channels into space. They did indeed possess that ability. In this age, the citizens of the world all had the freedom to own weapons, and most of them had small laser guns. Of course, a laser pistol posed no threat to the cabin of the space elevator or the launching spacecraft, but unlike a traditional gun, a large number of lasers could focus their light on a single point. If ten thousand laser pistols fired at one point at the same time, they were unstoppable. Crowds numbering in at least the tens of thousands, with up to a million people in places, gathered around the base points and launching sites, and at least a third were carrying weapons. When they saw a cabin ascend or a spacecraft launch, they would fire their weapons

simultaneously. The straight path of the laser beam made aiming incredibly precise, so most of the beams would focus on the target and destroy it. In this way, Earth's transport links with space were almost entirely severed.

The chaos grew worse. Over the past couple of days, the target of the attacks had shifted to space cities in synchronous orbit. Rumors flew thick online that certain cities had been converted into escape ships, so they too became subject to attack by the people of Earth. Owing to the vast distance, laser beams dissipated and were weakened by the time they reached targets in space, and given the additional factor of the space cities' rotation, no material injury was caused. But the activity became a kind of collective entertainment for humanity in those last days. That afternoon, the European Commonwealth's third space city, New Paris, had been subject to simultaneous irradiation by ten million laser beams from the northern hemisphere, causing the temperature in the city to rise sharply and prompting the evacuation of its residents. From the space city, the Earth had been brighter than the sun.

There was nothing more for Luo Ji and Shi Qiang to say.

"I was really impressed with your work at the Hibernation Immigration Bureau," the mayor said to Shi Qiang. "And Guo Zhengming. You know him, right? He was just promoted to director of the Public Security Bureau, and he recommended you to me. I hope you'll come work at the city government. We need people like you right now."

Shi Qiang thought for a moment, and then nodded. "Once I've settled things in my neighborhood. How's the situation in the city right now?"

"The situation is deteriorating, but it's still under control. Right now the focus is on maintaining the operation of the induction field power supply. Once that goes, the city will collapse completely."

"These riots are different from those in our day."

"Yeah, they are. First, their source is different. They're sparked by total despair for the future and are incredibly hard to handle. At the same time, we have fewer means at our disposal than in those

days." As the mayor was speaking, he pulled up an image on the wall. "This is the central plaza from a height of a hundred meters."

The central plaza was where Luo Ji and Shi Qiang had taken refuge from the flying car. From this vantage point, the Great Ravine Memorial and its surrounding patch of desert couldn't be seen. The entire plaza was white, with white dots crawling around like rice in a pot of porridge.

"Are those people?" Luo Ji asked in wonder.

"Naked people. It's a tremendous sex party, with more than a hundred thousand people, and it's still growing."

Acceptance of heterosexual and homosexual relations in this era was far beyond anything Luo Ji had imagined, and some things were no longer considered remarkable. Still, the sight before them came as a shock to both of them. Luo Ji was reminded of the dissolute scene in the Bible before humanity received the Ten Commandments. A classic doomsday scenario.

"Why doesn't the government put a stop to it?" Shi Qiang asked sharply.

"How would we stop it? They're completely within the law. If we take action, the government would be the one committing a crime."

Shi Qiang let out a long sigh. "Yes, I know. In this age, police and the military can't do much."

The mayor said, "We've been through the law, and we haven't found any provisions for coping with the present situation."

"With the city like this, it would be better if the droplet smashed it apart."

Shi Qiang's words jerked Luo Ji awake. He asked hurriedly, "How long until the droplet gets to Earth?"

The mayor replaced the image of spectacular promiscuity with a breaking news channel showing a simulation of the Solar System. The eye-catching red line that marked the path of the droplet looked like the orbit of a comet, except that it terminated close to the Earth. In the lower right was a countdown clock indicating that if the droplet didn't reduce speed, it would reach Earth in four

hours and fifty-four minutes. The news crawl was now displaying an expert analysis of the droplet. Despite the terror gripping the world, the scientific community had recovered its senses after the initial shock of defeat, so the analysis was calm and sober. Though humanity knew absolutely nothing about the droplet's energy source and drive mechanism, the analyst felt that it had run into a power consumption problem, because its acceleration toward the sun after destroying the combined fleet had been particularly sluggish. It had passed close by Jupiter but, ignoring the three warships at the base, used the planet's gravity to accelerate, a move that further demonstrated that the droplet's energy was limited to the point of exhaustion. Scientists believed that the notion that the droplet would crash into Earth was utter nonsense, but they had no idea what it had actually come to do.

Luo Ji said, "I have to leave, or else the city will really be destroyed."

"Why?" the mayor asked.

"Because he thinks the droplet wants to kill him," Shi Qiang said.

The mayor laughed, but his smile was stiff. Apparently he hadn't laughed in a long time. "Dr. Luo, you're the most self-absorbed person I've ever met."

Luo Ji and Shi Qiang drove off immediately after traveling back to the surface from the underground city. The city's inhabitants were pouring out in large numbers, which meant that ground traffic was so heavy that it took them half an hour to leave the old city and reach full speed on the highway to the west.

On the car's television, they saw that the droplet was approaching Earth at a speed of seventy-five kilometers per second and showed no sign of slowing. At that rate, it would arrive in three hours.

The weakening of the induction field power supply slowed the car, and Shi Qiang had to tap a storage battery to maintain speed. They reached the large hibernator residential area, but drove past New Life Village #5 and continued westward. They stayed silent along the way, speaking little and focusing their attention on the breaking news on the television.

The droplet passed lunar orbit without slowing. At this rate it

would reach Earth in just half an hour. No one knew how it would behave, so to avoid a panic, the news didn't predict a point of impact.

Luo Ji made a determined effort to welcome the moment he had long wanted to postpone, and said, "Da Shi, stop here."

Shi Qiang stopped the car and they got out. The sun, now nearing the horizon, cast long shadows of the two men on the desert. Luo Ji felt the earth beneath his feet turn as soft as his heart. He almost lacked the strength to stand.

He said, "I'll try my best to reach a sparsely populated area. There's a city ahead of us, so I'm going to turn this way. You find your own way back, and get as far as possible from the direction I'm going."

"My boy, I'll wait for you here. When it's over, we'll go back together." Shi Qiang took out a cigarette from his pocket and looked around for a lighter before remembering that the cigarette didn't need to be lit. Like the other things he had brought from that distant past, his personal habits had not changed at all.

Luo Ji smiled a little sadly. He hoped Shi Qiang actually believed that, because at least that would make their parting a little easier to take. "Wait if you'd like. When the time comes, you had better move to the other side of the embankment. I don't know how powerful the strike will be."

Shi Qiang smiled and shook his head. "You remind me of an intellectual I met two hundred years ago. He had the same hangdog look you've got. I remember him sitting out early in the morning in front of the Wangfujing church, crying. . . . But he got out okay. I checked after I woke up: He lived to be nearly a hundred."

"What about the first guy to touch the droplet, Ding Yi? I believe you knew each other, too."

"He had a death wish. Nothing you could do about that." Shi Qiang looked up at the sky clothed in sunset, as if reminding himself what the physicist looked like. "Still, he was a truly broad-minded man, the kind that could accept any situation. I never met anyone like him in my whole life. Seriously, a great mind. My boy, you ought to learn from him."

"And again I say to you: We're just ordinary people, you and I." He looked at his watch, knowing that there was no more time for delay. He extended a firm hand to Shi Qiang. "Da Shi, thank you for everything you've done for me the past two centuries. Good-bye. Maybe we'll meet again in some other place."

Shi Qiang did not take his hand, but gave him a wave. "Cut the crap! Believe me, my boy. Nothing's going to happen. Go, and when it's over, hurry back and get me. And don't blame me if I make fun of you tonight over drinks."

Luo Ji got into the car quickly, not wanting Shi Qiang to see the tears in his eyes. Sitting there, he strove to etch the rearview-mirror image of Shi Qiang onto his mind, then set off on his final journey.

Maybe they would meet again someplace. The last time it had taken two centuries, so what would the separation be this time? Like Zhang Beihai two centuries before, Luo Ji suddenly found himself hating that he was an atheist.

The sun had now entirely set, and the desert on either side of the road shone white in the twilight, like snow. It suddenly occurred to him that it was along this very stretch of road two centuries ago that he had driven in the Accord with his imaginary lover, when the northern China plain was covered with real snow. He felt her hair blowing in the wind, its strands teasing him with their strange tickles on his right cheek.

No, no. Don't say where we are! Once we know where we are, then the world becomes as narrow as a map. When we don't know, the world feels unlimited.

Okay. Then let's do our best to get lost.

Luo Ji had always had the feeling that Zhuang Yan and Xia Xia had been brought into the world by his imagination. He felt a stab in his heart when the thought entered his mind, because, at this moment, love and longing were the most excruciating things in the world. Tears blurred his vision as he strove to keep his mind blank. But Yan Yan's lovely eyes stubbornly surfaced through the blankness, accompanied by Xia Xia's intoxicating laughter. It was all he could do to focus his attention on the television news.

The droplet had passed the Lagrange point,[25] but it still sped toward Earth at constant speed.

Luo Ji parked the car at what he thought was the most fitting spot, the border between the plain and the mountains, where there were no people or buildings as far as he could see. The car stood in a valley surrounded by a U-shaped ring of mountains, which would dissipate some of the shock waves from the impact. He took the television from the car and carried it onto the open sand, where he sat down.

The droplet crossed the 34,000-kilometer geosynchronous orbit altitude and passed close by the space city New Shanghai, whose inhabitants all clearly saw the bright point of light pass rapidly across their sky. The news declared that the impact would occur in eight minutes.

The news finally predicted the latitude and longitude of impact: to the northwest of China's capital.

Luo Ji knew that already.

Twilight had fallen heavily now, and the colors of the sky had shrunk to a small space in the west, like a pupilless eyeball watching the world indifferently.

Perhaps as a way to pass the remaining time, Luo Ji began to look back on his life.

It had been divided into two entirely distinct parts. The part after he became a Wallfacer spanned two centuries, but it felt densely compacted. He passed quickly back through it as if it had been just yesterday. That part of his life didn't seem like his own, including the love that was engraved onto his bones. It all felt like a fleeting dream. He didn't dare think about his wife and child.

Contrary to his expectations, his memories of life before becoming a Wallfacer were a blank. All that he could fish out from the sea of memory were a few fragments, and the farther back he went, the fewer there were. Had he really been to high school? Had he really attended primary school? Had he really had a first love? Some of the fragments bore clear scratches, reminding him that those things had indeed

25 *Translator's Note:* Lagrange points are the five positions where a small object affected only by gravity can remain in equilibrium in relation to two larger bodies.

taken place. The details were vivid, but the feelings had vanished without a trace. The past was like a handful of sand you thought you were squeezing tightly, but which had already run out through the cracks between your fingers. Memory was a river that had run dry long ago, leaving only scattered gravel in a lifeless riverbed. He had lived life always looking out for the next thing, and whenever he had gained, he had also lost, leaving him with little in the end.

He looked around at the twilight mountains, recalling that one winter's night he spent here more than two hundred years ago, in the mountains that had grown tired of standing for hundreds of millions of years, and had lain down "like old villagers basking in the sun," as his imaginary lover had once said. The fields and cities of the northern China plain had long since turned to desert, but the mountains didn't seem to have changed. They were still plain and ordinary in shape, and withered grasses and vitex vines still grew stubbornly from the crevices in the gray rocks, no lusher and no sparser than two centuries ago. Two centuries was far too short for any visible change to come to these rocky mountains.

What was the human world like in the eyes of the mountains? Perhaps just something they saw on a leisurely afternoon. First, a few small living beings appeared on the plain. After a while, they multiplied, and after another while they erected structures like anthills that quickly filled the region. The structures shone from the inside, and some of them let off smoke. After another while, the lights and smoke disappeared, and the small things vanished as well, and then their structures toppled and were buried in the sand. That was all. Among the countless things the mountains had witnessed, these fleeting events were not necessarily the most interesting.

Finally, Luo Ji located his earliest memory. He was surprised to discover that the life he could remember also began on the sand. It was in his own prehistoric age, in a place he couldn't remember, and with people he couldn't recall, but he clearly remembered the sandy shore of a river. There was a round moon in the sky, and the river rippled under the moonlight. He was digging in the sand. When he had dug out a pit, water seeped through the bottom, and

in the water there was a small moon. He kept digging like that, digging lots of pits and bringing forth lots of small moons.

That was his earliest memory. Before that, everything was blank.

In the dark of night, only the light of the television illuminated the small patch of sand surrounding him.

As Luo Ji worked to maintain a blank state in his mind, his scalp tightened, and he felt like an enormous hand had covered the entire sky overhead and was pressing down on him.

But then the giant hand slowly withdrew.

At a distance of twenty thousand kilometers from the surface, the droplet changed direction and headed directly toward the sun.

The TV reporter shouted, "Attention northern hemisphere! Attention northern hemisphere! The droplet has grown brighter, and you can see it with the naked eye!"

Luo Ji looked up. He could actually see it: It wasn't too bright, but its high speed made it easily distinguishable as it crossed the sky like a meteor and vanished in the west.

At last the droplet reduced its velocity relative to the Earth to zero and rested at a point 1.5 million kilometers away. A Lagrange point. That meant that, in the days to come, it would remain motionless relative to both Earth and sun, squarely between the two.

Luo Ji had a hunch that something else might happen, so he sat on the sand and waited. The mountains, like old men beside and in back of him, waited quietly with him and gave him a sense of security. For the time being, there was no more important information in the news. A world uncertain whether or not it had escaped catastrophe waited nervously.

Ten minutes passed, but nothing happened. The monitoring system showed the droplet suspended motionless, the propulsion halo gone from its tail and its round head facing the sun. It reflected the bright sunlight, so that its front third appeared to be on fire. To Luo Ji, some sort of mysterious induction seemed to be taking place between the droplet and the sun.

The image on the television suddenly blurred, and the sound turned scratchy. Luo Ji sensed commotion in the surrounding

environment: A startled flock of birds took flight in the mountains, and a dog barked in the distance. It might have been a false impression, but he felt his skin begin to itch. The television's sound and picture jittered for a moment and then cleared up. Later it was learned that the interference was still present, but global telecommunications systems had quickly filtered out the sudden noise with their anti-interference capabilities. However, the news reacted slowly to this development because of the vast amounts of monitoring data that needed to be pooled and analyzed. It was another ten minutes or more before precise information became available.

The droplet was sending a continuous, powerful electromagnetic wave directly at the sun with an intensity far exceeding the sun's amplification threshold and a frequency that covered all the bands that the sun could amplify.

Luo Ji began to giggle, and then laughed until he choked. Yes, he really was self-absorbed. He should have thought of all of this long ago. Luo Ji wasn't important. The sun was important. From now on, humanity could no longer use the sun as a powerful antenna to transmit messages to the universe.

The droplet had sealed it off.

"Hah! My boy, nothing's happened! We really should have wagered on it." At some point, Shi Qiang had made his way over to Luo Ji. He had flagged down a car to get here.

Luo Ji felt like something had been drained out of him. He lay limply down on the sand, which was still warm from the sun. It was comfortable beneath him.

"Yes, Da Shi. We can go and live our lives now. Everything's finished."

"My boy, this is the last time I help you do Wallfacer stuff," Shi Qiang said on the road back. "That occupation must cause mental problems, and you've just had another episode."

"I hope that's the case," Luo Ji said. Outside, the stars that were visible yesterday had vanished, and the black desert and night

sky joined into one at the horizon. A section of road illuminated by the headlights stretched out ahead of them. The world was like the state of Luo Ji's mind: darkness everywhere, with one spot incredibly clear.

"You know, it'll be easy for you to get back to normal. It's time for Zhuang Yan and Xia Xia to reawaken. Although, with the recent chaos, I don't know if they've suspended reawakening. But even if they have, it won't be for very long. The situation will quickly stabilize, I think. After all, there's still time left for several generations. Didn't you say you can go and live your life?"

"I'll go inquire at the Hibernation Immigration Bureau tomorrow." Shi Qiang's words reminded Luo Ji of the bit of color that existed in his dull mind. Maybe a reunion with his wife and child was his only chance for redemption.

But humanity was beyond hope.

As they neared New Life Village #5, Shi Qiang suddenly slowed the car. "Something's not right," he said, looking ahead. Following his gaze, Luo Ji saw a glow in the sky cast by a light on the ground, but the high embankments on the roadway meant they couldn't see its source. The glow was in motion. It didn't seem like the lights of a residential area.

When the car turned off the highway, a strange and spectacular sight met them: The desert between New Life Village #2 and the highway had been turned into a shining blanket dense with lights, like an ocean of fireflies. It took Luo Ji a moment to realize that it was a crowd of people. All of them were from the city, and the light came from their clothes.

As the car slowly approached the crowd, everyone ahead of them raised their hands to block the glare of the headlights, so Shi Qiang turned them off, leaving them facing a bizarre, gaudy human wall.

"Looks like they're waiting for someone," Shi Qiang said, looking at Luo Ji, who tensed up at his expression. The car stopped, and Shi Qiang went on, "You stay here and don't move. I'll go have a look." He jumped out of the car and walked over to the crowd. Against the glowing human wall, Shi Qiang's stocky body stood

out as a black silhouette. Luo Ji watched him walk to the crowd, then exchange a few words with the people before turning and walking back.

"Turns out they're waiting for you. Go," he said, leaning on the door. Seeing Luo Ji's face, he reassured him, "Relax. It'll be okay."

Luo Ji got out of the car and went over to the crowd. He had grown familiar with the wired clothing of modern people, but in the desolate desert, he still had the feeling that he was walking toward the Other. But when he drew closer and could make out their expressions, his heart began to beat faster.

The first thing he had learned when he awakened from hibernation was that the crowds of every age have their own unique expression. The differences across time to this far-off age were remarkable—you could easily distinguish between moderns and hibernators who had only just reawakened. But the expressions Luo Ji saw now weren't modern, nor were they twenty-first century. He didn't know what era they belonged to. Fear nearly rooted him to the spot, but his trust in Shi Qiang propelled his steps mechanically forward.

When he had gotten closer to the crowd, he finally stopped, because he saw the images they had on their clothes.

Their clothing displayed pictures of Luo Ji—some still photographs, some videos.

Luo Ji had rarely appeared before the media since becoming a Wallfacer, so he hadn't left much of a visual record, but a fairly complete set of those videos and images was now on display on the people's clothing. On some people, he even saw photographs of his pre-Wallfacer self. The clothing took its images from the Internet, which meant that these images must be circulating worldwide. He also noticed that the images were in their original state and had not been subjected to the artistic deformation that the moderns liked to do, which meant that they had just appeared online.

When they saw him stop, the crowd moved toward him. When they got as close as two or three meters, the people in front held back the rest of the crowd, and then knelt down. Those behind

them knelt down successively in a wave of glowing people that receded along the sand.

"Lord, save us!" he heard someone say. The words buzzed in his ears.

"Oh god, save the world!"

"Great spokesman, uphold justice in the universe!"

"Angel of justice, save humankind!"

Two people came up to Luo Ji, and he recognized the one whose clothing wasn't glowing as Hines. The other man was a soldier with glowing badges and ribbons.

Hines said to him gravely, "Dr. Luo, I've just been appointed your liaison to the UN Wallfacer Project Commission. It is my duty to inform you that the Wallfacer Project has been revived, and you have been named the sole Wallfacer."

The soldier said, "I am special commissioner Ben Jonathan of the SFJC. We met when you had just been reawakened. I am also instructed to inform you that the Asian Fleet, the European Fleet, and the North American Fleet have agreed with the revalidation of the Wallfacer Act and have recognized your status as Wallfacer."

Hines pointed to the crowd kneeling on the sand, and said, "In the eyes of the public, you now have two identities. For theists, you are the angel of justice. To atheists, you are the spokesperson for a just, superior civilization in the Milky Way."

This was followed by silence, with all eyes focused on Luo Ji. He thought for a while, but came up with only one possibility: "The spell worked?" he ventured.

Hines and Jonathan nodded, and Hines said, "187J3X1 has been destroyed."

"When?"

"Fifty-one years ago. It was observed a year ago, but no one was paying much attention to that star, so the observations were only discovered this afternoon. A few desperate people in the SFJC wanted to find inspiration in history, and they remembered the Wallfacer Project and your spell. So they looked at 187J3X1 and found that it wasn't there anymore. In its place was a nebula of

debris. They scanned through all observational records of the star until its destruction a year ago, then pulled all of the observational data of 187J3X1 at the time it exploded."

"How do they know it was destroyed?"

"You're aware that 187J3X1 was in a stable period, like the sun, so it would be impossible for it to go nova. And its destruction was observed: A body traveling close to the speed of light struck 187J3X1. The tiny object—they're calling it a 'photoid'—was observed the instant it passed into the periphery of the stellar atmosphere by the tracks it made. Even though it was small in volume, its near-light velocity meant that its vastly amplified relativistic mass had reached one-eighth of 187J3X1's by the time it struck the target. It destroyed the star immediately. The star's four planets were also vaporized in the blast."

Luo Ji looked up at the night's dark sky, where the stars were practically invisible. He walked forward, and the people stood up and silently made a path for him, closing back together immediately behind him. They were all trying to push closer to him, as if yearning for sunlight amid the cold, but they respectfully left him a circle of space, a dark spot in a fluorescent ocean, like the eye of a storm. A man pushed forward and fell to the ground in front of Luo Ji, compelling him to stop, and then the man kissed his feet. A few others entered the ring to repeat that act. Just when the situation seemed about to go out of control, there were critical shouts from the crowd, prompting the people to scramble and retreat back into the group.

Luo Ji continued on ahead, but realized that he didn't know where he was going. He stopped, found Hines and Jonathan in the crowd, and walked over to them.

"So what should I do now?" he asked when he reached them.

"You're a Wallfacer, so of course you can do anything within the scope of the Wallfacer Act," Hines said to him with a bow. "Although the act still has restrictions, you can now mobilize practically all of the resources of Earth International."

"That includes the Fleet International's resources, too," Jonathan added.

Luo Ji thought for a moment, and said, "I don't need to tap any resources right now. But if I've really recovered the power granted by the Wallfacer Act . . ."

"There's no doubt about that," Hines said. Jonathan nodded.

"Then I'll make two requests. First, order will be restored in all cities, and normal life will resume. There's no mystery about this request. I'm sure you understand."

Everyone nodded. Someone said, "The world is listening, oh god."

"Yes, the world is listening," Hines said. "Restoring stability will require time, but because of you we have faith that it can be done." His words were echoed in the crowd.

"Second: Everyone, go home. Leave this place in peace. Thank you!"

The people were silent after hearing this, but soon began to buzz as his words were passed back through the crowd. The crowd began to disperse, slowly and unwillingly at first, but eventually the pace picked up and car after car headed off down the road in the direction of the city. The many people walking along the roadside looked like a long glowing colony of ants in the night.

Then the desert was empty once again. Only Luo Ji, Shi Qiang, Hines, and Jonathan were left on the sand littered with chaotic footprints.

"I am truly ashamed of my former self," Hines said. "Human civilization has a history of just five thousand years, yet we cherish life and freedom so highly. There must be civilizations in the universe with a history of billions of years. What sort of morality do they possess? Is there any point to that question?"

"I'm ashamed for myself, too. The past few days, I've even begun to doubt God," Jonathan said. When he saw Hines about to cut in, he raised his hand to stop him. "No, friend. We might be talking about the same thing."

They embraced, tears streaming down their faces.

"So, gentlemen," Luo Ji said as he patted them on the back. "You can go back. If I need you, I'll get in touch. Thank you."

He watched them go off, supporting each other like a happy

pair of lovers. Now he and Shi Qiang were the only ones left.

"Da Shi, anything you'd like to say now?" he said, turning to Shi Qiang with a smile.

Shi Qiang stood rooted to the spot, as stunned as if he had just witnessed a thrilling magic trick. "My boy, I'm damn confused."

"What? You don't believe I'm an angel of justice?"

"You'd have to beat me to death before I'd say that."

"And a spokesperson of a superior civilization?"

"A little better than an angel, but I don't believe that either, to tell you the truth. I've never thought that was the case."

"Don't you believe in fairness and justice in the universe?"

"I don't know."

"But you're in law enforcement."

"I said I don't know. I'm genuinely confused."

"Then you're the most sober one here."

"So can you tell me about the justice of the universe?"

"Very well. Come with me." Then Luo Ji walked straight out into the desert, with Shi Qiang following close behind him. They walked a long while in silence, then crossed the highway.

"Where are we going?" Shi Qiang asked.

"To the darkest place."

They crossed the highway to where the embankment blocked out the lights of the residential area. Groping about in the dark that surrounded them, Luo Ji and Shi Qiang sat down on the sandy ground.

"Let's begin," Luo Ji's voice sounded in the dark.

"Give me the easy version. At my level, I'm not going to understand anything complicated."

"Everyone can understand, Da Shi. The truth is simple. It's the kind of thing that, once you hear it, you'll wonder why you didn't come up with it yourself. Do you know about mathematical axioms?"

"I took geometry in high school. 'Only one straight line can be drawn between two points.' That kind of thing."

"Right. So now we're going to set out two axioms for cosmic civilization. First, survival is the primary need of civilization.

515

Second, civilization continuously grows and expands, but the total matter in the universe remains constant."

"And then?"

"That's it."

"What can you derive from those little things?"

"The same way you can figure out an entire case from a bullet or a drop of blood, cosmic sociology is able to describe a complete picture of galactic and cosmic civilization from those two axioms. That's what science is like, Da Shi. The cornerstone of every discipline is quite simple."

"So let's see you derive something."

"First, let's talk about the Battle of Darkness. Would you believe me if I said that Starship Earth was a microcosm of cosmic civilization?"

"No. Starship Earth lacked resources like parts and fuel, but the universe doesn't. It's too big."

"You're wrong. The universe is big, but life is bigger! That's what the second axiom means. The amount of matter in the universe remains constant, but life grows exponentially. Exponentials are the devils of mathematics. If there's a microscopic bacterium in the ocean that divides once every half hour, its descendants will fill the entire ocean in the space of a few days, so long as there are sufficient nutrients. Don't let humanity and Trisolaris give you a false impression. These two civilizations are tiny, but they are only in their infancy. Once a civilization passes a certain technological threshold, the expansion of life through the universe is frightening. For instance, take humanity's present navigation speed. In a million years, Earth civilization could fill the galaxy. And a million years is a short time measured against the universe."

"So you're saying that, taking the long view, the entire universe might have that kind of . . . what are they calling it, a 'dead hand'?"

"No need for the long view. Right now the entire universe has been dealt that dead hand. Like Hines said, civilization may have started in the universe billions of years ago. Looking at the signs, the universe might be packed full already. Who knows how much

empty space there is in the Milky Way or the universe, or how many resources are left?"

"But that's not right, is it? The universe looks empty. We haven't seen any other alien life apart from Trisolaris, right?"

"That's what we'll talk about next. Give me a cigarette." Luo Ji groped about in the dark for a while before taking the cigarette from Shi Qiang's hand. When Luo Ji next spoke, Shi Qiang realized he had moved to a spot three or four meters away. "We need to increase the distance to make it feel more like outer space," Luo Ji said. Then he lit the cigarette by twisting its filter, and Shi Qiang lit one of his own. In the dark, two tiny red planets stood in distant opposition.

"Okay. To illustrate the problem, we now need to establish the most elementary model of cosmic civilization. These two balls of flame represent two civilized planets. The universe is made up of only these two planets, and apart from them there's nothing else. Erase all of our surroundings. Can you locate that feeling?"

"Yeah. That's an easy feeling to find in a dark place like this."

"Let's call these two civilized worlds your civilization and my civilization. They're separated by a great distance, say, a hundred light-years. You can detect that I exist, but you don't know any details. However, I'm completely ignorant of your presence."

"Right."

"Now we need to define two concepts, 'benevolence' and 'malice' between civilizations. These words themselves aren't very rigorous in a scientific context, so we've got to restrict their meaning. 'Benevolence' means not taking the initiative to attack and eradicate other civilizations. 'Malice' is the opposite."

"That's a low bar for benevolence."

"Next, consider your options for dealing with me. Please remember that the axioms of cosmic civilization should be kept in mind throughout the process, as well as the distance scale and the environment of space."

"I could choose to communicate with you."

"If you do that, you should be aware of the price you'll pay: You'll have exposed your existence to me."

"Right. In the universe, that's no small thing."

"There are different degrees of exposure. The strongest form of exposure is when I know your precise interstellar coordinates. Next is when I know your general direction, and the weakest is when I only know of your existence. But even the weakest form of exposure makes it possible for me to search for you, because since you've detected my existence, I know that I'll be able to find you. It's only a matter of time, from the standpoint of technological development."

"But my boy, I could still take the risk to talk to you. If you're malicious, then it's my bad luck. But if you're benevolent, then we could have further exchanges and ultimately be united into a benevolent civilization."

"Okay, Da Shi. Now we've come to the crux of it. Let's return to the axioms of cosmic civilization: Even if I'm a benevolent civilization, can I determine at the start of our communication whether or not you are also benevolent?"

"Of course not. That would violate the first axiom."

"So once I've received your message, what should I do?"

"Naturally, you ought to determine whether I'm benevolent or malicious. Malicious, and you eradicate me. Benevolent, and we can continue communicating."

The flame on Luo Ji's side rose up and moved back and forth. Evidently he had gotten up and was pacing. "That's fine on Earth, but not out in the universe. So next we'll introduce an important new concept: the chain of suspicion."

"That's an odd term."

"The term is all I had at first. It wasn't explained to me. But, later, I was able to infer its meaning from the words themselves."

"Who didn't explain it?"

". . . I'll tell you later. Let's continue. If you think I'm benevolent, that's not a reason to feel safe, because according to the first axiom, a benevolent civilization can't predict that any other civilization is benevolent. You don't know whether I think you're benevolent or malicious. Next, even if you know that I think you're benevolent,

518

and I also know that you think *I'm* benevolent, I don't know what you think about what I think about what you're thinking about me. It's convoluted, isn't it? This is just the third level, but the logic goes on indefinitely."

"I get what you mean."

"That's the chain of suspicion. It's something that you don't see on Earth. Humanity's shared species, cultural similarities, interconnected ecosystem, and close distances means that, in this environment, the chain of suspicion will only extend a level or two before it's resolved through communication. But in space, the chain of suspicion can be very long. Something like the Battle of Darkness will already have taken place before communication can resolve it."

Shi Qiang took a drag on his cigarette, and his contemplative face emerged from the darkness for a moment. "It looks now like the Battle of Darkness has a lot to teach us."

"That's right. The five ships of Starship Earth formed a quasi-cosmic civilization, not a real one, because they consisted of a single species—humans—who were very close to each other. But even so, when they were dealt that dead hand, the chain of suspicion emerged. In actual cosmic civilization, the biological differences between different groups might be as high as the kingdom level, and cultural differences are even further beyond our imagining. Add to this the vast distances between them, and you have chains of suspicion that are practically indestructible."

"That means that the outcome is the same, regardless of whether we're benevolent civilizations or malicious civilizations?"

"That's right. That's the most important aspect of the chain of suspicion. It's unrelated to the civilization's own morality and social structure. It's enough to think of every civilization as the points at the end of a chain. Regardless of whether civilizations are internally benevolent or malicious, when they enter the web formed by chains of suspicion, they're all identical."

"But if you're much weaker than I am, you're not a threat to me. So I could always communicate with you, right?"

"That won't work, either. Here we need to introduce a second

important concept: the technological explosion. I didn't get a full explanation for this, either, but it was far easier to infer than the chain of suspicion. Human civilization has five thousand years of history, and life on Earth might be as much as a few billion years old. But modern technology was developed over the course of three hundred years. On the scale of the universe, that's not development. It's an explosion! The potential for technological leaps is the explosive buried within every civilization, and if it's lit by some internal or external factor, it goes off with a bang. On Earth it took three hundred years, but there's no reason why humanity should be the fastest of all cosmic civilizations. Maybe there are others whose technological explosions were even more sudden. I'm weaker than you, but once I've received your message and know of your existence, the chain of suspicion is established between us. If at any time I experience a technological explosion that suddenly puts me far ahead of you, then I'm stronger than you. On the scale of the universe, several hundred years is the snap of a finger. And it might be that my knowledge of your existence and the information I received from our communication was the perfect spark to set off that explosion. That means that even though I'm just a newborn or growing civilization, I'm still a big danger to you."

Shi Qiang watched Luo Ji's flame in the darkness as he thought for a few seconds, then looked at his own cigarette. "So I have to keep quiet."

"Do you think that will work?"

They smoked. The balls of flame brightened and their faces emerged from the darkness like the gods of this simple universe, deep in thought.

Shi Qiang said, "No, it won't. If you're stronger than me, then since I was able to find you, one day you'll be able to find me. And then there will be a chain of suspicion between us. If you're weaker than me, you could experience a technological explosion at any time, and that would take us back to the first case. To sum up: one, letting you know I exist, and two, letting you continue to exist, are both dangerous to me and violate the first axiom."

"Da Shi, you've really got a clear mind."

"My brain can keep up with yours so far, but we're only getting started."

Luo Ji was silent in the dark for a long time. His face emerged in the weak light of the ball of flame two or three times before he said, "Da Shi, this isn't a start. Our reasoning has already reached a conclusion."

"Conclusion? We haven't figured anything out! Where's the picture of cosmic civilization you promised?"

"If neither communication nor silence will work once you learn of my existence, you're left with just one option."

In the long silence that followed, the two flames went out. There was no wind, and the dark silence turned thick as asphalt, connecting sky and desert into a murky whole. At last Shi Qiang uttered one word in the darkness: "Fuck!"

"Extrapolate that option out to the billions upon billions of stars and hundreds of millions of civilizations, and there's your picture," Luo Ji said, nodding in the darkness.

"That's . . . that's really dark."

"The real universe is just that black." Luo Ji waved a hand, feeling the darkness as if stroking velvet. "The universe is a dark forest. Every civilization is an armed hunter stalking through the trees like a ghost, gently pushing aside branches that block the path and trying to tread without sound. Even breathing is done with care. The hunter has to be careful, because everywhere in the forest are stealthy hunters like him. If he finds other life—another hunter, an angel or a demon, a delicate infant or a tottering old man, a fairy or a demigod—there's only one thing he can do: open fire and eliminate them. In this forest, hell is other people. An eternal threat that any life that exposes its own existence will be swiftly wiped out. This is the picture of cosmic civilization. It's the explanation for the Fermi Paradox."

Shi Qiang lit another cigarette, if only to have a bit of light.

"But in this dark forest, there's a stupid child called humanity, who has built a bonfire and is standing beside it shouting, 'Here I

am! Here I am!'" Luo Ji said.

"Has anyone heard it?"

"That's guaranteed. But those shouts alone can't be used to determine the child's location. Humanity has not yet transmitted information about the exact position of Earth and the Solar System into the universe. From the information that has been sent out, all that can be learned is the distance between Earth and Trisolaris, and their general heading in the Milky Way. The precise location of the two worlds is still a mystery. Since we're located in the wilderness of the periphery of the galaxy, we're a little safer."

"So what's the deal with the spell?"

"Using the sun, I transmitted three images to the cosmos. Each one consisted of thirty points representing the planar projection of a three-dimensional coordinate system containing the position of thirty stars. Combining the three images into three-dimensional coordinates forms a cubic space populated by those thirty points. That represents the relative positions of 187J3X1 and its twenty-nine surrounding stars. There's also a label pointing out 187J3X1.

"Think about it carefully and you'll get it. A hunter in a dark forest, stalking with bated breath, suddenly notices that a piece of bark has been stripped from a tree in front of him. On the eye-catching bit of white wood that's been revealed is a position in the forest, written in characters all hunters can recognize. What will he think about that location? He's certainly not going to imagine that someone has laid out supplies for him there. Out of all the possibilities, the most likely one is that the blaze is informing everyone that there's live prey at that location that needs to be eliminated. It doesn't matter what motivated someone to leave the mark. What's important is that the dead hand has stretched the nerves of the dark forest to the breaking point, and it's the most sensitive nerve that's most liable to make a move. Suppose there are a million hunters in the forest—the number of civilizations on the billions upon billions of stars in the Milky Way could be thousands of times that. Perhaps nine hundred thousand of them will disregard the marking. Of the remaining one hundred thousand, maybe ninety thousand of them

will probe the location, and, after confirming that it has no life, disregard it. But one of the remaining ten thousand hunters will surely make a choice to fire on that position, because for civilizations at a certain level of technological development, attacking may be safer and less of a hassle than probing. If there's really nothing at that location, then it's no loss.

"Now," Luo Ji concluded, "that hunter has appeared."

"That spell of yours can't be sent anymore, right?"

"That's right, Da Shi. The spell needs to be broadcast to the entire galaxy, but the sun's been locked down, so it can't be sent anymore."

"Was humanity just a step late?" Shi Qiang flicked aside his cigarette end. The flame drew an arc through the darkness as it fell, momentarily illuminating a small circle of sandy ground.

"No, no. Think about it: If the sun hadn't been sealed off, and I had threatened Trisolaris with sending out a spell against them, what would have happened?"

"You would've been stoned to death like Rey Diaz. And then they would have enacted legislation to prohibit anyone else from thinking along those lines."

"That's right, Da Shi. Because we've already revealed the distance between the Solar System and Trisolaris as well as our general heading in the Milky Way, exposing the location of Trisolaris is tantamount to exposing the location of the Solar System. That's a death strategy. Maybe we're a step late, but it's a step that humanity would never be able to take."

"You should have threatened Trisolaris back then."

"Things were too weird. I wasn't certain about the idea at the time, so I needed to confirm it. After all, there was plenty of time. But the real reason was that, deep in my heart, I really didn't have the mental strength. I don't think anyone else would, either."

"Thinking about it now, we shouldn't have gone to see the mayor today. This situation—if the world learns about it, then it's even more hopeless. Think about how the first two Wallfacers ended up."

"You're right. The same thing would happen to me, so I hope

that neither of us says anything. But you still can, if you want. Like someone once told me: Either way, I've fulfilled my duty."

"Don't worry, my boy. I won't say anything."

"Regardless, there's no longer any hope."

They walked along the embankment and to the highway, where it was slightly less dark. The sparse lights of the residential area in the distance were enough to blind them.

"There's one more thing. That person you mentioned?"

Luo Ji hesitated. "Forget it. All you need to know is that the axioms of cosmic civilization and the theory of the dark forest were not my invention."

"Tomorrow I'm going into the city to work with the government. If you need any help in the future, just say the word."

"Da Shi, you've helped me more than enough. I'll head into the city tomorrow, too, to the Hibernation Immigration Bureau, to take care of waking up my family."

Contrary to Luo Ji's expectations, the Hibernation Immigration Bureau said that reawakening Zhuang Yan and Xia Xia was still blocked, and the bureau's director made it clear to him that his Wallfacer powers were ineffective in this regard. He consulted Hines and Jonathan, who were unacquainted with the details of the situation, but they told him that the revised Wallfacer Act contained a provision stating that the UN and Wallfacer Project Commission could take all necessary steps to ensure that the Wallfacer remained focused on his work. Which meant that, after two centuries, the UN was once again using Luo Ji's situation as a tool to coerce and control him.

Luo Ji requested that his hibernator settlement remain in its current state and be kept free of outside harassment. This request was faithfully executed. The news media and the masses of pilgrims were kept at a distance, and after calm was restored throughout New Life Village #5, it was like nothing at all had happened.

Two days later, Luo Ji attended the first hearing of the revived Wallfacer Project. He didn't go to the underground UN headquarters in North America, but attended by video link from his spartan

residence in New Life Village #5, where scenes from the assembly appeared on the ordinary television in his room.

"Wallfacer Luo Ji, we were prepared to face your anger," the commission chair said.

"My heart has been burnt to ash. It no longer has the capacity for anger," Luo Ji said, reclining lazily on the sofa.

The chair nodded. "That's a wonderful attitude. However, the commission feels you ought to leave your village. That little place isn't a worthy command center for the defense of the Solar System."

"Do you know about Xibaipo? It's an even smaller village not far from here. Over two centuries ago, that's where our nation's founders commanded one of the largest offensives in history."[26]

The chair shook his head. "Clearly you haven't changed at all. Very well. The commission respects your habits and choices. You should get to work. It's not going to be like back then, with you claiming that you're always at work, is it?"

"I can't work. The conditions for my work no longer exist. Can you harness stellar power to broadcast my spell into the universe?"

The representative of the Asian Fleet said, "You know that's impossible. The droplet's radio suppression of the sun is continuous. And we don't anticipate that it will stop for the next two or three years, by which time the nine other droplets will have reached the Solar System."

"Then there's nothing I can do."

The chair said, "No, Wallfacer Luo Ji. There's one important thing you haven't done. You haven't disclosed the secret of the spell to the UN and SFJC. How did you use it to destroy a star?"

"I can't tell you that."

"And if it were a condition for reawakening your wife and child?"

"That's a despicable thing to say at a time like this."

26 *Translator's Note:* Driven out of Yan'an by a Nationalist offensive in 1947, Communist forces established a base in Xibaipo, a village in the foothills of the Taihang Mountains in southwestern Hebei province. From there they directed the Liaoshen, Huaihai, and Pingjin campaigns, the decisive offensive in 1948 and 1949 that pushed the Nationalists out of northern China.

"This is a secret hearing. Besides, the Wallfacer Project doesn't have any place in modern society. The revival of the Wallfacer Project means that all decisions made by the UN's Wallfacer Project Commission two centuries ago are still in effect. And according to those resolutions, Zhuang Yan and your child would reawaken at the Doomsday Battle."

"Didn't we just fight the Doomsday Battle?"

"The two Internationals don't think so, since the main Trisolaran Fleet has yet to arrive."

"Keeping the secret of the spell is my responsibility as a Wallfacer. Otherwise, humanity will lose its last hope, though that hope may already be gone."

In the days following the hearing, Luo Ji stayed inside, drinking heavily, and spent most of his time in a state of intoxication. People occasionally saw him emerge with his clothes disheveled and his beard long. He looked like a tramp.

When the next Wallfacer Project hearing was convened, Luo Ji again attended from home.

"Wallfacer Luo Ji, your condition has us worried," the chair said when he saw Luo Ji's unkempt appearance in the video. He directed the camera around Luo Ji's room, and the assembly could see that it was littered with bottles.

"You ought to get to work, if only to restore yourself to a normal state of mind," the representative of the European Commonwealth said.

"You know what will return me to normal."

"The reawakening of your wife and child really isn't all that important," the chair said. "We don't want to use that to control you. We know that we can't control you. But it's a resolution made by the previous commission, so addressing the issue presents some difficulties. Bottom line: There must be a condition."

"I reject your condition."

"No, no, Dr. Luo. The condition has changed."

At the chair's words, Luo Ji's eyes lit up, and he sat up straight on the sofa. "And now the condition is . . ."

"It's simple. Couldn't be simpler. You just have to do *something*."

"If I can't send a spell out into the universe, there's nothing I can do."

"You have to think of something to do."

"You mean, it could be something meaningless?"

"So long as it looks significant to the public. In their eyes, you're either the spokesman of the force of cosmic justice or a heaven-sent angel of justice. At the very least, these identities can be used to stabilize the situation. But if you do nothing, you'll lose the faith of the public after a while."

"Achieving stability that way is dangerous. It'll lead to no end of trouble."

"But what we need right now is to stabilize the global situation. The nine droplets are coming to the Solar System in three years, and we have to be prepared to deal with that."

"I really don't want to waste resources."

"In that case, the commission will provide you with a task. One that won't waste resources. I'll ask the chairman of the SFJC to explain it to you," the chair said as he gestured to the SFJC chairman, who was also attending via video. The SFJC chairman was evidently in some space-based structure, because the stars were shifting slowly across the broad window behind him.

He said, "Our estimate of the arrival of the nine droplets in the Solar System is based entirely on speed and acceleration estimates obtained when they crossed the final interstellar dust cloud four years ago. They differ from the one that's already here in that their engines operate without emitting light. They don't emit any other high-frequency electromagnetic radiation that could provide a position. This is likely a self-adjustment made after humanity successfully tracked the first droplet. Locating and tracking such small, dark bodies in outer space is incredibly difficult, and now that we've lost their tracks, we don't know when they'll reach the Solar System. We don't even know how to detect that they've arrived."

"So what can I do?" Luo Ji asked.

"We hope that you can lead the Snow Project."

"What's that?"

"Using stellar hydrogen bombs and Neptune's oil film, we will manufacture clouds of space dust that the droplets will leave tracks in when they pass through."

"You've got to be joking. You do realize that I'm not entirely ignorant about space."

"You were an astronomer once. That makes you even more qualified to lead this project."

"Making a dust cloud was successful last time because the approximate path of the target was known. But now we know nothing. If the nine droplets accelerate or change course while dark, then they might even enter the Solar System from another side altogether! Where are you going to spread the dust cloud?"

"In every direction."

"You mean to say that you're going to manufacture a ball of dust to envelop the entire Solar System? If that's the case, then you're the one who's been sent by God."

"A ball of dust is impossible, but we can make a ring of dust on the ecliptic plane, between the asteroid belt and Jupiter."

"But what if the droplets enter outside the ecliptic plane?"

"That can't be helped. But from an astrodynamics perspective, if the droplet group wants to encounter every planet in the Solar System, then the greatest likelihood is entry on the ecliptic plane. That's what the first droplet did. That way, the dust cloud will be able to capture their tracks, and, once captured, the Solar System's optical tracking system will be able to lock onto them."

"But what's the point of that?"

"We'll at least know that the droplet group has entered the Solar System. They might strike civilian targets in space, so all ships will need to be recalled, or at least those in the droplets' path. And the inhabitants of space cities will have to be evacuated to Earth, because those are weak targets."

"There's another matter that's even more critical," the Wallfacer Project Commission chair said. "Identifying safe routes for the possible withdrawal of spacecraft into deep space."

"Withdrawal into deep space? We're not talking about Escapism, are we?"

"If you must use that name."

"Why not begin the escape now?"

"Present political conditions do not permit it. But when the droplet group approaches Earth, a limited-scale flight might become acceptable to the international community. Of course, it's only a possibility. But the UN and the fleets must make preparations for it."

"I understand. But the Snow Project doesn't really require me."

"It does. Even inside the orbit of Jupiter, creating a dust cloud is an enormous undertaking and will require the deployment of almost ten thousand stellar hydrogen bombs, more than ten million tons of oil film, and the formation of an enormous space fleet. To accomplish that within three years requires taking advantage of your current status and prestige to organize and coordinate the resources of the two Internationals."

"If I agree to undertake this mission, when will you wake them?"

"Once the project is started. Like I said, it won't be a problem."

But the Snow Project never got fully off the ground.

The two Internationals were not interested in the project. What the public wanted was a strategy for global salvation, not a plan that would merely inform them of the enemy's arrival so they could escape. Besides, they knew that this wasn't the Wallfacer's idea. It was just a plan implemented by the UN and SFJC that exploited his authority. A full launch of the Snow Project would bring the entire space economy to a standstill and lead to a general economic recession on Earth and in the fleet. In addition, contrary to the UN's prediction, as the droplets drew nearer, Escapism turned even more repugnant in the eyes of the public, so the two Internationals were unwilling to pay such a high price for an unpopular plan. As a result, both the construction of a fleet to gather the oil-film material on Neptune and the manufacture of sufficient stellar hydrogen bombs to supplement the fewer than one thousand from the Great Ravine that were still usable made very slow progress.

But Luo Ji poured himself entirely into the project. At first, the UN and the SFJC had only wanted to exploit his prestige to mobilize the resources needed, but Luo Ji immersed himself in every detail of the project, spending sleepless nights shoulder-to-shoulder with the scientists and engineers of the Technical Committee and proposing many of his own ideas. For example, he suggested that a small interstellar ion engine be installed onto each bomb to allow them a certain degree of mobility in orbit, enabling timely adjustments to the density of the stellar cloud in different regions. More importantly, the hydrogen bombs could act as attack weapons. He called them "space mines," and argued that even though stellar hydrogen bombs had proven incapable of destroying droplets, they might in the long run be useful against Trisolaran ships, because they had no evidence that the ships were also constructed out of strong-interaction material. He personally determined the orbit for every bomb's deployment. From a modern technological perspective, his ideas may have been full of a twenty-first-century ignorance and naiveté, but his prestige and Wallfacer status meant that most of his suggestions were adopted.

Luo Ji treated the Snow Project as a means of escape. He knew that he wanted to escape reality, and the best way to do that at present was to involve himself deeply in the project. But the more he devoted himself to it, the more disappointed in him the world became. Everyone knew he had only attached himself to the largely insignificant project so that he could see his wife and child as soon as possible. The world waited for a plan for salvation that never materialized. Luo Ji declared over and over in the media that without the capability to use stellar power to send out a spell, he was powerless to do anything.

The Snow Project ground to a halt after a year and a half, at which time only 1.5 million tons of oil film had been collected from Neptune. Even adding the 600,000 tons collected for the Fog Umbrella, the figure was still far from what the project required. Ultimately, 3,614 stellar hydrogen bombs packed in oil film were deployed in an orbit two AU from the sun. This wasn't even a fifth

of the intended number. When detonated, they would form a large number of independent dust clouds orbiting the sun, rather than a continuous dust cloud belt, greatly reducing their effectiveness as a warning.

It was an age in which hope came as quickly as disappointment, and after anxiously waiting for a year and a half, the public lost faith and patience in Luo Ji the Wallfacer.

At the general meeting of the International Astronomical Union, a body that last attracted worldwide attention in 2006 when it revoked Pluto's eligibility as a planet, a large number of astronomers and astrophysicists were of the opinion that the explosion of 187J3X1 was a chance occurrence. Being an astronomer, Luo Ji may have discovered certain signs that the star would explode. The theory was full of holes, but more and more people came to believe it, accelerating Luo Ji's decline in prestige. In the eyes of the public, his image gradually transitioned from messiah to commoner, and then to fraud. He still enjoyed the Wallfacer status granted by the UN, and the Wallfacer Act was still in effect, but he no longer had real power.

Year 208, Crisis Era

Distance of the Trisolaran Fleet from the Solar System: 2.07 light-years

On a cold, drizzly autumn afternoon, a meeting of the New Life Village #5 Residents' Council came to the following decision: Luo Ji would be expelled from the neighborhood on the grounds that he was affecting the normal life of the neighborhood's residents. While the Snow Project was in progress, Luo Ji had frequently gone out to attend meetings, but the majority of his time was still spent in the area, and he kept in contact with various Snow Project entities from home. Disruptions had only worsened as his position declined, since from time to time crowds of people would gather at the foot of his building to jeer at him or throw stones at his window. Media interest in the spectacle was enough to make reporters as numerous as protestors. But the real reason for Luo Ji's expulsion was that he was an utter disappointment to the hibernators.

When the meeting adjourned that evening, the neighborhood committee director went to Luo Ji's home to inform him of the council's decision. After pressing the doorbell repeatedly, she pushed open the unlatched door and practically choked on the mix of alcohol, smoke, and sweat that filled the room. She noticed that the walls had been converted into city-style information surfaces that allowed information screens to be called up anywhere with just a tap. A confusion of images filled the walls, most of them displaying complex data and curves, but the largest showing a sphere

suspended in space: a stellar hydrogen bomb packed in oil film. The transparent film with the bomb clearly visible within it reminded the director of a marble, the sort of thing children liked to play with back in Luo Ji's day. It rotated slowly. There was a small protrusion at one pole—the ion engine—and in the sphere's smooth surface was the reflection of a tiny sun. All of those dazzling screens turned the room into a huge gaudy box. Since the lights were off, they were the only source of illumination, dissolving everything into blurry color so that it was hard at first to distinguish what was a physical presence and what was just an image.

Once the director's eyes had adapted, she saw that the place looked like the basement of a drug addict, the floor littered with bottles and cigarette ends, the piles of clothes covered in ash like a garbage heap. She eventually managed to locate Luo Ji among the garbage. He was curled up in a corner, black against the backdrop of the images like a withered branch that had been cast aside. She thought he was asleep at first, but then noticed that his sightless gaze was fixed on the piles of garbage on the ground. His eyes were bloodshot, his face haggard, his body gaunt, and he seemed unable to support his own weight. When he heard the director he greeted her and turned toward her slowly, then just as slowly nodded at her, so that she knew he was still alive. But the two centuries of torment that had accumulated in his body had now completely overwhelmed him.

The director didn't show the slightest bit of mercy toward this man who had been totally used up. Like other people of their era, she had always felt that, regardless of how dark the world seemed, ultimate justice was still present in some unseen place. Luo Ji had first validated that belief and then mercilessly shattered it, and her disappointment with him had turned to shame and then anger. Coldly, she announced the results of the meeting.

Luo Ji nodded slowly a second time, then forced a voice through his swollen throat. "I'll leave tomorrow. I ought to be going. If I've done anything wrong, I ask for your forgiveness."

It was only two days later that the director learned the true meaning of his final words.

In fact, Luo Ji had been planning on leaving that night. After seeing the neighborhood committee director off, he rose unsteadily to his feet and went into the bedroom in search of a travel bag, which he packed with a few items, including a short-handled shovel he had found in the storage room. The shovel's triangular handle poked out of the travel bag. Then he retrieved a filthy jacket from the floor, put it on, slung the bag across his back, and went out. Behind him, the room's information walls continued to flash.

The hallway was empty, but at the foot of the stairs he ran into a kid, probably just home from school, who stared at Luo Ji with a strange and unreadable expression as he left the building. Outside, he found that it was still raining, but he didn't want to go back for an umbrella.

He didn't go to his own car because that would attract the attention of the guards. Walking along the street, he left the neighborhood without running into anyone. Then he walked through the protective forest belt outside the neighborhood and he was in the desert, the drizzle sprinkling on his face like the light caress of a pair of cold hands. Desert and sky were hazy in the dusk, like the blank space of a traditional painting. He imagined himself added to that blank space, like the painting that Zhuang Yan had left behind.

He reached the highway, and after a few minutes was able to flag down a car carrying a family of three, who warmly welcomed him aboard. They were hibernators on their way back to the old city. The child was small and the mother young, and they were squeezed next to the father in the front seat, whispering to each other. Occasionally the child would burrow his head into his mother's bosom, and whenever this happened the three of them burst out laughing. Luo Ji watched, spellbound, but he couldn't hear what they were saying because music was playing in the car, old songs from the twentieth century. He listened as he rode, and after five or six songs, including "*Katyusha*" and "*Kalinka*," he was filled with a longing to hear "*Tonkaya Ryabina*." He had sung that song to his imaginary lover on that village stage two centuries ago, and later with Zhuang Yan in the Garden of Eden on the shore of the lake that reflected the snowy peaks.

Then the headlights of an oncoming car illuminated the backseat as the child was glancing backwards. He turned entirely around to stare at Luo Ji, then shouted, "Hey, he looks like the Wallfacer!" The child's parents turned to look at him, and Luo Ji had to admit that he was.

Just then, *Tonkaya Ryabina* started playing.

The car stopped. "Get out," the child's father said coldly, as mother and child watched him with expressions as chilly as the autumn rain outside.

Luo Ji didn't move. He wanted to listen to the song.

"Please get out," the man said, and Luo Ji could read the words in their eyes: *Not being able to save the world isn't your fault, but giving the world hope only to shatter it again is an unforgivable sin.*

So he had to get out of the car. His travel bag was tossed out after him. As the car drove off, he ran after it for a few steps in the hopes of being able to listen to a little more of "*Tonkaya Ryabina,*" but the song disappeared into the cold, rainy night.

By now he was at the edge of the old city. The old high-rises of the past were visible in the distance, standing black in the rainy night, each building's few scattered lights looking like lonely eyes. He came across a bus stop and sat shielded from the rain for nearly an hour before a driverless public bus finally arrived that was headed in the direction he wanted to go. It was mostly empty, and the six or seven people who were seated there looked like hibernators from the old city. No one on the bus spoke, just sat silently in the gloom of this autumn night. The journey passed smoothly until a little over an hour later, when someone else recognized him, and then everyone on the bus unanimously asked him to leave. He argued that he had paid the credits to buy a ticket, so surely he had the right to a seat, but a gray-haired old man took out two cash coins—rarely seen these days—and tossed them at him. So in the end he was forced off the bus.

As the bus started up, someone stuck their head out the window to ask, "Wallfacer, what are you doing with that shovel?"

"I'm digging my own grave," Luo Ji said, to a burst of laughter from the bus.

No one knew that he was telling the truth.

The rain was still coming down. There wouldn't be any more cars now, but fortunately he wasn't too far from his destination. He shouldered his backpack and headed off. After walking for about half an hour, he turned off the highway and onto a path. It got much darker away from the road lamps, so he took a flashlight out of his bag to illuminate the ground under his feet. The path grew more difficult, and his sodden shoes squished on the ground. He slipped time and again into the mud, which covered his body, and he had to resort to using the shovel from his bag as a walking stick. All he could see ahead of him was fog and rain, but he knew that he was walking in the right general direction.

After walking another hour through the rainy night, he reached the cemetery. Half of it was buried beneath the sand, while the half on slightly higher ground was still exposed. He used the flashlight to search the rows of headstones, ignoring the imposing monuments and only looking at the inscriptions on the smaller stones. Rainwater on the stones reflected the light like flashing eyes. He noticed that all of the headstones had been erected in the late twentieth and early twenty-first centuries. Those people were fortunate—in their last moments, they must have believed that the world they lived in would exist forever.

He didn't have much hope that he would find the headstone he was looking for, but, as it turned out, he found it quickly. The odd thing was, despite the passage of two centuries, he recognized it without even looking at the inscription. Maybe it was the wash of the rain, but the headstone showed no traces of time. The inscription, GRAVE OF YANG DONG, seemed like it had been cut yesterday. Ye Wenjie's grave sat beside her daughter's, the two tombstones identical apart from the inscription. Ye Wenjie's bore only her name and the dates of her birth and death, reminding him of the small tablet at the ruins of Red Coast Base, a memorial for the forgotten. The two headstones stood silently in the night rain, as if they'd been waiting for Luo Ji's arrival.

He felt tired, so he sat down next to Ye Wenjie's grave, but he soon began to shiver from the rain's chill. Grasping the shovel, he stood up and, next to the graves of mother and daughter, began digging his own.

At first, digging into the wet ground required little effort, but as he got farther down, the earth turned hard and was littered with stones, which made him feel like he was digging into the mountain itself. He at once felt both the power and the powerlessness of time: Maybe only a thin layer of sand had been deposited over the course of two centuries, but the long geologic age when humans were not present had produced the mountain that now housed these graves. He dug with great effort, resting frequently, and the night slipped away unnoticed.

Sometime after midnight, the rain stopped, and then the clouds parted to reveal some of the starry sky. These were the brightest stars that Luo Ji had seen since arriving in this age. On that evening 210 years ago, he and Ye Wenjie had stood facing the same stars.

Now he saw only the stars and the headstones, the two greatest symbols of eternity.

Finally, he ran out of stamina and couldn't dig any more. Looking at the pit he had dug, he saw that it was a little shallow for a grave, but it would have to do. Doing this was nothing more than a reminder to others that he wished to be buried on this spot, anyway. His most likely resting place would be the crematorium, where he would be burnt to ashes and then discarded in some unknown place. But it didn't really matter. It was highly likely that shortly after his death, his remains would join the world in an even grander fire and be reduced to individual atoms.

Resting against Ye Wenjie's headstone, he quickly dropped off to sleep. Perhaps it was because of the cold, but he once again dreamed of the snowy field. On it he saw Zhuang Yan holding Xia Xia, her scarf like a flame. She and the child were calling soundlessly to him. He shouted back desperately for them to leave this place because the droplet would strike right here, but his vocal cords produced no sound. It was like the entire world had

gone mute, and everything stayed absolutely silent. But Zhuang Yan seemed to understand what he meant and walked far across the snowy field holding the child, leaving a string of footprints in the snow like a faint ink mark on a traditional painting. The snow was blank, and the ink mark was all that revealed the land, revealed the existence of the world. The impending destruction was all-encompassing, but it was a destruction that had nothing to do with the droplet. . . .

Once more, Luo Ji's heart tore painfully and his hands clutched at the air in vain, but in the blankness of the snowy field, there was only Zhuang Yan's distant form, now a small black dot. He looked about him, hoping to find anything else that was real in the blank world. As it turned out, he found it: two black tombstones standing side by side on the snowy ground. At first they were eye-catching in the snow, but then their surface began to change. They turned to mirrors that recalled the finish of the droplet, and their inscriptions disappeared. He bent down toward one of them, wanting to look at himself in the mirror, but what he saw in the mirror wasn't a reflection. The snowy field in the mirror did not have the figure of Zhuang Yan, just a line of faint footprints in the snow. He whipped his head around and saw that the snowy field outside the mirror was just a blank expanse—the footprints had disappeared. When he turned back to the mirrors, they reflected the blank world and were practically invisible themselves. But his hand could still feel their cold, smooth surface. . . .

He awoke when it was just daybreak. The graveyard was clearer in the first light of dawn, and from his prone vantage point, the surrounding headstones made him feel like he was in a prehistoric Stonehenge. He had a high fever, and his body's violent trembling sent his teeth chattering. His body seemed like a wick that had burnt dry and was consuming itself. He knew that the time had come.

Leaning against Ye Wenjie's headstone, he tried to stand up, but then a small, moving black dot caught his attention. Ants ought to be fairly rare during this season, but it was indeed an ant crawling on the stone. Like its fellow ant two centuries before, it was

attracted by the inscription and devoted itself to exploring the mysterious crisscrossing trenches. Luo Ji's heart experienced a last spasm of pain as he watched it, this time for all life on Earth.

"If I've done anything wrong, I'm sorry," he said to the ant.

He stood up with difficulty, trembling weakly. He had to support himself on the headstone to be able to stand. Reaching out a hand, he straightened his soaked, mud-covered clothing and wild hair, then groped in his jacket pocket for a metal tube: a fully charged pistol.

Then, facing the dawn in the east, he began a final showdown between the civilization of Earth and the civilization of Trisolaris.

"I am speaking to Trisolaris," Luo Ji said. His voice wasn't loud. He thought about repeating himself, but he knew that they could hear him.

Nothing changed. The headstones stood quietly in the stillness of the dawn. Puddles on the ground reflected the brightening sky like countless mirrors, giving the illusion that the Earth was a mirrored sphere with the ground and the world just a thin layer on top. The rain's erosion had exposed small pieces of the sphere's smooth surface.

It was a world that had not awakened yet, and didn't know that it was now a chip placed on a cosmic gambling table.

Luo Ji raised his left hand, revealing an object on his wrist the size of a watch. "This is a vital signs monitor linked through a transmitter to a cradle system. You remember Wallfacer Rey Diaz from two centuries ago, so you certainly know about cradle systems. The signal sent from this monitor travels the links of the cradle system to the Snow Project's 3,614 bombs deployed in solar orbit. The signal is sent once every second to maintain the bombs in a non-triggered state. If I die, the system's maintenance signal will vanish and all of the bombs will detonate, turning the oil film surrounding the bombs into 3,614 interstellar dust clouds ringing the sun. From a distance, the sun's visible light and other

high-frequency bands will appear to flicker through the dust cloud coverage. The position of every bomb has been precisely arranged in solar orbit so that this flickering will generate a signal transmitting three simple images of the sort I sent out two centuries ago: each image an arrangement of thirty points, with one labeled, for composition into a three-dimensional coordinate diagram. But, unlike last time, the position will contain the transmission of Trisolaris relative to its surrounding twenty-nine stars. The sun will be a galactic lighthouse casting that spell, in the process, of course, also exposing the position of the sun and Earth. To receive the entire transmission at any single point in the galaxy will take more than a year, but there ought to be more than a few civilizations that have the technology to observe the sun from multiple vantage points. If that's the case, they may only need a few days, or even a few hours, to obtain all the information they need."

As daylight brightened, the stars went out one by one like the gradual shutting of innumerable eyes, even as the morning sky slowly opened in the east like a single giant eye. The ant continued its climb, threading the maze of Ye Wenjie's name on her gravestone. Its species had been living on the Earth a hundred million years before the emergence of this gambler who now leaned on the stone. Even though it had no care for what was now happening, it held a stake in the world.

Luo Ji left the gravestones and stood beside the pit he had dug for himself. He placed the tip of the pistol to his heart and said, "Now, I'm going to stop the beating of my heart. By doing so, I will be committing the greatest crime in the history of our two worlds. I express my deepest apologies to our two civilizations for the crime that I commit, but I have no regrets, because this is the only option. I know the sophons are nearby, but you have ignored humanity's call. Silence is the greatest form of contempt, and we have put up with this contempt for two centuries. Now, if you wish, you can continue to remain silent. I will give you thirty seconds."

He marked time according to his pulse, counting two beats to a second since his heart was beating so rapidly, but in his

heightened anxiety he started off wrong and had to begin again. So he wasn't certain how much time had passed by the time the sophons appeared. Possibly less than ten seconds in objective time, but subjectively, it took a lifetime. He saw the world before his eyes split into four parts: one part made up of the real world that surrounded him; the other three, deformed images in three spheres that appeared suddenly overhead, whose mirror surfaces were exactly like the gravestones he had seen in his last dream. He didn't know which of the sophons' dimensional unfoldings this was, but the three spheres were big enough to cover half the sky above him, blocking out the brightening light in the east. In the spheres' reflection of the western sky, he could see a few lingering stars, and the bottom of the spheres reflected a deformed graveyard and his own image. What he most wanted to know was why there were three of them. His first thought was that they symbolized Trisolaris, just like the work of art that Ye Wenjie had seen at the final ETO gathering. But looking at what the spheres reflected—an uncommonly clear, albeit deformed, picture of reality—he had the sense that they were entrances to three parallel worlds, implying three possible choices.

But what he saw next negated this notion, because the three spheres flashed the same word:

Stop!

"Can I discuss terms?" Luo Ji asked, looking up at the three spheres.

First put down the gun, and then we can discuss terms.

The words displayed simultaneously on the spheres in letters that glowed a striking red. He saw no deformation in the line of text. It was straight, and seemed as if it was both on the surface of and within the spheres. He reminded himself that he was looking at a projection of higher-dimensional space into a three-dimensional world.

"This is not a negotiation. These are my demands, if I am to go on living. All I wish to know is whether or not you accept."

State your demands.

"Have the droplet, or rather the probe, cease its transmissions toward the sun."

It has been done as you ask.

The spheres' answer was faster than he anticipated. He had no way to verify it at the moment, but he sensed subtle changes in his surroundings, as if a background noise whose continued existence meant it had escaped notice, had disappeared. Of course, this could be an illusion, since humans don't sense electromagnetic radiation.

"Have the nine droplets en route to the Solar System change course immediately and fly away."

This time the answer from the three spheres was delayed by a few seconds.

It has been done as you ask.

"Please give humanity the means to verify this."

The nine probes will emit visible light. Your Ringier-Fitzroy Telescope will be able to detect them.

This was still impossible for him to verify, but he believed Trisolaris.

"The final condition: the Trisolaran Fleet may not cross the Oort Cloud."

The fleet is now under propulsion power for maximum deceleration. It is impossible for it to bring its speed relative to the sun to zero before reaching the Oort Cloud.

"Then, like the droplet group, set a course away from the Solar System."

Changing course in any direction is death. This will cause the fleet to fly by the Solar System and into the desolation of space. The fleet's life-support system will not last long enough to return to Trisolaris or search for another viable star system.

"Death isn't a certainty. Perhaps human or Trisolaran ships can catch up and rescue them."

This will require a command from the High Consul.

"If changing course is a lengthy process, get started on it now. That will give me and all the other lives a chance to live on."
The period of silence lasted for three minutes. Then:

The fleet will begin to change course in ten Earth minutes. Two years from now, human space observation systems will be able to observe the change of heading.

"Good," Luo Ji said, as he removed the pistol from his chest. With his other hand he leaned on the gravestone, trying not to fall. "Were you already aware that the universe is a dark forest?"

Yes. We knew about it long ago. What's strange is that you only realized it so late. . . . Your state of health concerns us. This won't unintentionally interrupt the cradle system's maintenance signal, will it?

"No. This device is far more advanced than Rey Diaz's. So long as I am alive, the signal won't be interrupted."

You really should sit down. That will help with your situation.

"Thank you," Luo Ji said, and he sat down against the head-stone. "Don't worry. I'm not going to die."

We are in contact with the highest levels of the two Internationals. Do you need us to call you an ambulance?

He smiled and shook his head. "No. I'm not a savior. I just want to leave here like an ordinary person and go home. I'll rest for a bit and then be on my way."

Two of the three spheres disappeared. The text on the one that remained, which no longer glowed, now seemed dim and dreary.

In the end, strategy was where we failed.

Luo Ji nodded. "Blocking the sun with dust clouds to send an interstellar message wasn't my invention. Twentieth-century astronomers had already proposed the idea. And you actually had multiple chances to see through me. During the duration of the Snow Project, for example, I was always concerned with the precise placement of the bombs in solar orbit."

You spent two whole months in the control room remotely controlling the ion engines to make fine adjustments to their positioning. We didn't care about that at the time because we thought you were just using the meaningless task as a way to escape reality. We never imagined what the distance between the bombs really meant.

"Another chance was when I consulted a group of physicists with questions about sophon unfoldings in space. If the ETO was still around, they would have already seen through me."

Yes. Abandoning them was a mistake.

"Also, I requested that the Snow Project build this peculiar cradle trigger system."

That did remind us of Rey Diaz, but we did not pursue those thoughts. Two centuries ago, Rey Diaz was not a threat to us, nor were the other two Wallfacers. We transferred our contempt for them onto you.

"Your contempt for them was unfair. Those three Wallfacers were great strategists. They saw clearly the inevitable fact of humanity's defeat in the Doomsday Battle."

Perhaps we can begin negotiations.

"That's not my affair," Luo Ji said, and let out a long sigh. He felt as relaxed and as comfortable as if he had just been born.

Yes, you've fulfilled the Wallfacer mission. But you've got to have some suggestions.

"Humanity's negotiators will no doubt first propose that you help us build a better signal transmission system, so that we'll have the ability to transmit a spell into space at any time. Even though the droplet has lifted its seal on the sun, the present system is too primitive."

We can help build a neutrino transmission system.

"They may, as far as I understand things, be more inclined toward gravitational waves. After the sophons arrived, this was the area in which human physics progressed furthest. Of course, they'll need a system whose principles they can understand."

The antennas for gravitational waves are immense.

"That's between you and them. It's strange. Right now I don't feel like a member of the human race. My greatest desire is to be rid of it all as soon as possible."

Next they'll ask us to lift the sophon block and teach science and technology across the board.

"This is important to you as well. The technology of Trisolaris has developed at a constant speed, and two centuries later, you still haven't sent a faster followup fleet. In order to rescue the diverted Trisolaran Fleet, you have to rely on the future of humanity."

I must go. Are you really able to go back on your own? The survival of two civilizations hinges on your life.

"No problem. I feel much better now. After I go back, I'll immediately hand over the cradle system, and then I'll have no more to do with all of this. Finally, I'd like to say thank you."

Why?

"Because you let me live. Or, if you think about it a different way: You let us both live."

The sphere vanished, returning to its eleven-dimensional microscopic state. A corner of the sun was peeking out in the east, casting gold across a world that had survived destruction.

Luo Ji slowly stood up. After taking a last look at the gravestones of Ye Wenjie and Yang Dong, he stumbled slowly back the way he came.

The ant had reached the summit of the headstone and proudly waved its feelers at the rising sun. Out of all life on Earth, it was the only witness to what had just taken place.

Five Years Later

Luo Ji and his family could see the gravitational-wave antenna in the distance, but it was still another half-hour drive away. Only when they arrived did they get a real sense of its enormous size. The antenna, a horizontal cylinder a kilometer and a half long and fifty meters in diameter, was entirely suspended about two meters off the ground. Its surface was mirror-smooth, half of it reflecting the sky and half the northern China plain. It reminded people of a few things: the giant pendulums of the *Three Body* world, the sophons' lower-dimensional unfoldings, and the droplet. The mirrored object reflected a Trisolaran concept that humanity was still trying to figure out. In the words of a well-known Trisolaran saying, "Hiding the self through a faithful mapping of the universe is the only path into eternity."

The antenna was surrounded by a big green meadow that formed a small oasis in the desert of northern China, but this meadow had not been specially planted. Once the gravitational-wave system had been completed, it began sending continuous, unmodulated emissions that were indistinguishable from the gravitational waves emitted from supernovae, neutron stars, or black holes. The density of the gravitational beam had a peculiar effect in the atmosphere: Water vapor collected above it, so that it frequently rained in the antenna's vicinity. At times, the rain only fell within a radius of three or four kilometers, and a small, circular raincloud would hang in the air above the antenna like a giant flying saucer, leaving the brilliant sunshine in the surrounding area visible through the

rain. And so this area grew lush with wild vegetation. But today, Luo Ji and his family did not witness that spectacle. Instead, they saw white clouds gather over the antenna, only to dissipate when the wind blew them away from the beam. Yet new clouds were continually forming, making the round patch of sky seem like a time wormhole to some other cloud universe. Xia Xia said that it looked like the white hair of a giant old man.

As the child ran about on the grass, Luo Ji and Zhuang Yan followed behind, until they reached the antenna. The first two gravitational-wave systems were built in Europe and North America, and employed magnetic levitation that suspended them a few centimeters from the base. But this antenna used antigravity, and could have been raised up into space if so desired. The three of them stood on the grass beneath the antenna, looking up at the huge cylinder curling up over their heads like the sky. Its large radius gave the bottom a low curvature, which meant there was no distortion in the reflected image. The setting sun now shone beneath the antenna, and, in the reflection, Luo Ji could see Zhuang Yan's long hair and white dress fluttering in the golden sunlight like an angel looking down from the sky.

He lifted up the child and she touched the antenna's smooth surface, pressing hard in one direction. "Can I make it turn?"

"If you push long enough, you can," Zhuang Yan said—then, looking at Luo Ji with a smile, asked, "Right?"

He nodded at her. "With enough time, she could move the Earth."

As had occurred so many times before, their eyes met and intertwined, a continuation of that gaze they had held in front of the *Mona Lisa*'s smile two centuries before. They had discovered that the language of the eyes that Zhuang Yan had dreamed up was now a reality, or maybe loving humans had always possessed this language. When they looked at each other, a richness of meaning poured from their eyes just as the clouds poured from the cloud well created by the gravitational beam, endless and unceasing. But it wasn't a language of this world. It constructed a world that gave it meaning, and only in that rosy world did the words of the language

find their corresponding referents. Everyone in that world was god; all had the ability to instantaneously count and remember every grain of sand in the desert; all were able to string together stars into a crystal necklace to hang around a lover's neck. . . .

Is this love?

The lines were displayed on a lower-dimensional unfolding of a sophon that appeared abruptly beside them. The mirrored sphere seemed like a droplet that had fallen off of some melted area on the cylinder above them. Luo Ji knew few Trisolarans and didn't know who it was who was speaking to them, or whether this one was on Trisolaris or on the fleet that was growing increasingly distant from the Solar System.

"Probably." Luo Ji nodded with a smile.

Dr. Luo, I have come in protest.

"Why?"

Because in last night's speech, you said that humanity had been so late to realize the dark forest nature of the universe not because your immature state of cultural evolution caused a lack of awareness of the universe, but because humanity has love.

"Isn't that correct?"

It's correct, though the word "love" is a little vague in the context of scientific discourse. But what you said next was incorrect. You said that humanity is probably the only species in the universe to have love, and it's this notion that supported you through the most difficult period of your Wallfacer mission.

"That's only an expression, of course. Just a nonrigorous . . . analogy."

I know that at least Trisolaris has love. But because it was not conducive to the civilization's overall survival, it was suppressed when it had only just germinated. Yet the seed possesses a stubborn vitality, and will still grow in certain individuals.

"May I ask who you are?"

We've never met. I was the operator who transmitted the warning to Earth two and a half centuries ago.

"My god, and you're still alive?" Zhuang Yan exclaimed.

I won't be for much longer. I've been in a dehydrated state, but over the long years, even a dehydrated body will age. However, I have seen the future I hoped to see, and for this I am happy.

"Please accept our respects," Luo Ji said.

I only wish to discuss with you one possibility: Perhaps seeds of love are present in other places in the universe. We ought to encourage them to sprout and grow.

"That's a goal worth taking risks for."

Yes, we can take risks.

"I have a dream that one day brilliant sunlight will illuminate the dark forest."

The sun was setting. Now only its tip was exposed beyond the distant mountains, as if the mountaintop was inset with a dazzling gemstone. Like the grass, the child running in the distance was bathed in the golden sunset.

The sun will set soon. Isn't your child afraid?

"Of course she's not afraid. She knows that the sun will rise again tomorrow."